She walked into the middle of a triangle of love.

Helene Loncourt, on the day of her wedding to Thomas Sturbridge, looked up and caught the expression on her groom's face as Sheila, the beautiful wife of his best friend Ian, stepped into the room. Now Helene knew why Tom treated her with such distant, polite kindness. He would be her husband, and she would love him all her life—but his love would belong forever to Sheila Ives.

Yet, in the circle of Helene's love, would develop the fateful intertwining of two families as the children of Tom Sturbridge and Ian Ives grew up together. Ravaged by the battles of England and Ireland, the hatred between Catholic and Protestant, the violence that would drive them across the seas to America THE STURBRIDGE DYNASTY would flourish and endure.

The Sturbridge Dynasty

Joan Bagnel

WARNER BOOKS

A Warner Communications Company

WARNER BOOKS EDITION

Cover design by Gene Light

Cover art by James Griffin

Warner Books, Inc., 75 Rockefeller Plaza, New York, N.Y. 10019

 A Warner Communications Company

Printed in the United States of America

First Printing: May, 1982

10 9 8 7 6 5 4 3 2 1

For my dear son and good friend, Tom Cipolla,
With my deepest love and gratitude,

Joan Bagnel.

TABLE OF CONTENTS

STURBRIDGE IVES CAMPION

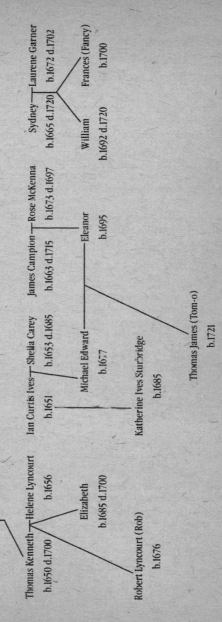

STURBRIDGE

Sir Thomas — Lady Anne
b.1605 d.1675 b.1629 d.1672

Thomas Kenneth — Helene Lyncourt
b.1650 d.1700 b.1656

Elizabeth
b.1685 d.1700

Robert Lyncourt (Rob)
b.1676

IVES

Ian Curtis Ives — Sheila Carey
b.1651 b.1653 d.1685

Michael Edward
b.1677

Katherine Ives Sturbridge
b.1685

CAMPION

James Campion — Rose McKenna
b.1663 d.1715 b.1673 d.1697

Eleanor
b.1695

Sydney — Laurene Garner
b.1665 d.1720 b.1672 d.1702

William
b.1692 d.1720

Frances (Fancy)
b.1700

Thomas James (Tom-o)
b.1721

BOOK ONE
A Ring of Steel

One

"Ring in the Valiant Man and Free"

1 Homecoming, 1660

It was the year of grace, 1660, and King Charles II of England, long exiled on the Continent, was restored to his throne and to his rejoicing people. The dour fourteen-year-long rule of Cromwell, self-appointed Lord Protector of the realm, was ended at last. Church bells rang, maidens tossed flowers and ribbons in the king's path as Charles made his triumphant way into London.

With Charles came scores of loyal friends and supporters who had fled England under Cromwell, given up homes and estates and fortunes to be with their true sovereign in exile. Many of them returned home now with children born and raised to love England who did not remember the sight of an English springtime or the feel of English soil beneath their feet. Yet to the children, no less than their fathers and mothers, this restoration was a most joyous and longed-for homecoming.

Among such loyal patriots was Sir Thomas Sturbridge, baronet of Spring Mount, Somerset, in the beautiful south country of England. Sir Thomas, together with his wife, Lady Anne, and their ten-year old son, Tom, did not linger long at the festivities in London. After paying homage to the King for whom they had sacrificed much, they withdrew into Somerset and prepared to live the quiet, peaceful life of the country without further involvement in the nation's politics.

Sir Thomas Sturbridge had spent the last twenty years of his busy life longing for such seclusion, a rest from court and military intrigues, a quietness about him in which he might work his still-limber body until it had a good, healthy ache to it of an evening.

13

He wanted time to watch his son grow into manhood, time for long rambling walks and uninterrupted talks with Lady Anne, time to read his books and think his thoughts without reference or concern for what was the politic thing to do. He had had enough of all that. Spring Mount and his own small family were enough for the Baronet.

However, and most unexpectedly, the King was soon to interfere with Sir Thomas' few, simple dreams once again. This time his interference came in the form of a reward. Sturbridge had supported his sovereign in many helpful ways, not the least of which was the loan of large amounts of money over the years. He trusted that one day that money might be returned. But he asked nothing of Charles. Perhaps because this state of affairs was so unusual, the King decided that Sir Thomas must have some recognition, some small tribute for his unflinching devotion. At the moment money was out of the question. The Crown was well-nigh bankrupt and debts were paid in other ways or not at all.

Thus, in the first bright flush of victory after regaining his throne, Charles II bestowed not one but two unlooked for gifts upon the master of Spring Mount. The first raised Sir Thomas to the lofty position of Viscount Sturbridge, Lord of the Realm. It was a title the old soldier dismissed with a laugh and promptly forgot all about. He was not able to dismiss the second of Charles's inspirations so easily. Being practically penniless did not prevent the King from dispensing property with a lavish hand and he gave to Sir Thomas a large estate in Ireland. Properly managed such an estate earned a fair income from rents and sale of farm goods. Charles might well have kept the land for himself. He could, of a certainty, have made good use of any monies gained from it, so it really was a generous gesture on his part.

Sir Thomas did not need or particularly want another estate to look after and he tried more than once to make this clear to the King. But Charles insisted, would not take no for an answer, and at length, most reluctantly, Sir Thomas accepted the unseen estate and, the following spring, after the crops had been planted at Spring Mount, he went to Ireland with many misgivings, to inspect his royal gift.

It was to be a very brief visit as far as he was concerned. He would simply look the place over, set whatever needed it to rights and restore it to its original owners. Since it was his to dispose of, he felt not the least compunction about this plan. He had no taste for the taking of other people's property and never for one moment did he consider this "gift" rightfully his own.

He planned to be away from Spring Mount no more than three or four months and he saw no earthly reason to uproot Lady Anne and young Tom once again just as they were happily settling into their own home again. So he went to Ireland alone, to County Waterford in the southeast. And what Sir Thomas found when he rounded a great, broad bend in the Blackwater River altered forever the course of his own life and the lives of his descendents.

Cromwell had passed this way, or some of Cromwell's men, it made little difference. All they had left behind them wherever they went in Ireland, was ruin and desolation. Sir Thomas rode his big grey stallion through a land of silence, eerie silence, a land in which no birds sang, it seemed, and the only faintly discernible sound carried by the rough sea winds that swept like lost souls back and forth across the ravaged land was the keening wail of the widow and the orphan, the outraged and the abandoned of the earth.

The tiny village of Kilbree watched with apathetic eyes as the English Lord rode through. There had been no crops planted, none harvested in more than a year. Most of the young men had been killed. The small, once-crowded cottages of Kilbree were rapidly emptying as the old people died and the young ran barefooted and wild-eyed, heedless of law or right. Starvation was their only fixed and constant and obsessive thought. The babies died and their hungry mothers thanked God for such a mercy. . . .

Sir Thomas passed through the village quickly, although he had intended to stop and rest his horse and himself. He had meant to talk with the people, to ask them questions. But once he saw them he had no more questions to ask. He already knew the answers. And the hatred he already bore towards Cromwell, the only real hatred Sir Thomas had ever indulged in himself, filled his heart and welled up into a few bitter tears in his fierce grey eyes as he rode straight through Kilbree Village, down the long, empty, dirt road to Kilbree House.

The great house, built during the early 16th century, still stood, enormous, dark and towering upon a steep hill above the surrounding countryside. When he first glimpsed it that soft spring day of 1661, Sir Thomas shuddered. It would have been far better, he thought, if Cromwell had simply razed it to the ground as he had razed so many other houses, great and small.

Kilbree looked like the mutilated body of some hapless prisoner who had been slowly tortured to death. Parts of the house had been put to the torch; other parts had been pillaged for wood and stone and iron and whatever else had been needed by the invader. Now it stood, blackened and silent, the few smashed and scattered pieces of its old glass window panes dully reflecting back a faint, ironic reminder of its former magnificence.

Kilbree House had belonged to a man named Ives, now dead. Ives had been a Catholic and he had had a son. Not one of the fearful lot of servants at Kilbree, who had no place else to go and so had moved back into the house when Cromwell departed, seemed able to tell Sir Thomas what had become of Ives' son. If the boy still lived at all, he would be about ten years of age, almost the same age as young Tom Sturbridge. The thought of his own son, carried off into exile, growing up without home or homeland, made Sir Thomas absolutely resolute in his determination to find that boy of Ives'.

The village priest, sensing in Sir Thomas a different kind of Englishman than he had encountered before, helped in the search and within a month, young Ian Curtis Ives was turned up. Too tall, too thin for his years, clad in filthy rags, half-starved, Ian was brought down out of the hills where he had been hiding. They had to carry him bodily, kicking, scratching, punching and biting every step of the way until they set him on his bare, calloused feet before Sir Thomas.

And there he stood, rage and hatred mixed upon his dirty face, but he stood straight and looked fearlessly upon the countenance of yet another Englishman.

At first Sir Thomas had looked at the boy calmly, but the sight of him was too much for a moment and he turned away abruptly, to gaze down into the blazing fire in the hearth. What in God's name could he say to this poor child, he wondered. How could he reassure the boy that from this day on he would be looked after, educated, and, if he would accept it, even cared for by a man whose own heart had been broken more than once by the stupidity and evil that dogged the footsteps of mankind through all its hard, sorrowful history?

Finally, taking a very deep breath, Sir Thomas turned again and contemplated the boy before him. His first instinct had been to see only the small child in that proud, thin face, to put his own strong arms around Ian for a shelter, for a "strong habitation" from the cruelty of the world.

But he quickly discarded that impulse. The child in Ian had gone, never to return. This boy was a man now and if he were to be reached at all, it would be on that basis and no other. *Later*, thought Sir Thomas, *perhaps later* he might learn to love someone, to trust someone again. . . .

He cleared his throat and spoke to the boy, directly, as one man speaks to another, praying that God would direct his tongue, his heart.

"You are Ian Curtis Ives?"

The boy's head lifted. The blue eyes blazed. "I am."

"Then . . . this is your house."

"Is it, now?" The contempt in his voice was unmistakable.

"Yes, it is. And you must live here now and learn to manage this great estate."

Ian's eyes darted about the scorched and blasted walls, the still-gaping holes in the roof where Cromwell's 42-pounders had smashed the great wooden beams to splinters. His lip curled derisively.

"This 'great estate'?" He mimicked Sir Thomas' pronunciation of the words to perfection. "Are ye daft, Englishman?"

Then, in spite of himself, in spite of the pity he felt for the boy and the enormous shame he felt for his own countrymen, something in the lilt of Ian's voice, something which seemed to say that for all his ignorance and suffering and hatred there was still that which was human and therefore Godly left alive in this lad . . . then Sir Thomas laughed heartily and his eyes twinkled as they often did.

"Maybe. Maybe I *am* daft," he nodded. "But there it is, Ian Curtis Ives. This house is yours. This land is yours, for all any King in England can say or do about it now. And whatever you may feel about me and about what was done here, I am offering you my protection . . ."

But that had been the wrong word, the worst word of all. Sir Thomas broke off, cursing himself silently. He watched Ian's fair eyebrow lift sardonically.

"No, you're right, my lad. That word, 'protection', it has come to have a different meaning, hasn't it? But damn it all, Ian Ives, don't hang a man for a mis-said word! I am offering you my . . . *help* then, does that suit you better? My help in rebuilding Kilbree House, putting the people back to work and the fields back to growing. I've got a great deal of money and more owing me. I've got a name *you'll* not know, but King Charles knows it and likes it well enough and that might come in handy from time to time. It is an honourable name, like your own, and I'm pledging it to you this day, if you'll have my help. Now . . .'' Sir Thomas spoke gruffly, not used to making long speeches, frustrated by the inability he felt to truly convey his feelings to a ten-year-old boy. "Now, what do you say to that, Ives? Come, come, the sooner you agree with me the sooner we can both sit down to a bite of supper!''

For years afterwards, Sir Thomas teased Ian about that moment and often repeated the notion that only the one word "supper" had turned the trick. For suddenly Ian's thin shoulders slumped and the rebellious look flickered uncertainly in his intense blue eyes. He nodded slowly and replied:

"Yes, I think I can do that, if you're speaking true. Could I have something to eat now?'' A fleeting shadow of the child within him hovered in his weary face as he looked around and saw the old table cleared of debris and spread with a white cloth, set with dishes and glasses and a serving woman just entering from the kitchen carrying a platter of steaming beef. Once again Sir Thomas had to fight back the urge to hug him. Instead, he led the boy to his seat and was careful to ignore the way Ian tore the thick slices of beef with his fingers and his teeth, paying no attention to the utensils by his plate. *Time enough for him to remember and to learn*, Sir Thomas told himself. And for the first time since he had come to Ireland, he attacked his own meal with a good appetite.

Much later that same night he wrote a long letter to Lady Anne.

"I had thought, my dearest wife, that no man could be happier than I, after ten lonely years of exile, to return to my own home at last and to be able to raise our son on English soil. But here in Ireland I have found a task barely begun, one which will take many years to complete. Perhaps only those who have been cast out themselves can understand the hurts inflicted by such cruelly enforced disinheritance. Through God's merciful love and care, we have been given back what is ours. Yet, in this unhappy land, such is not the case. I have pledged myself to undoing some small part of the mischief wrought upon this one family at least, and must leave it to the consciences of my fellow countrymen to do ' ₂ rest.

"I do not ask you to come here now, Anne, my love, but I shall need you in the months ahead, you and Tom both. This boy, Ian, needs a mother and a father, too, and a brother with whom he can begin to share his private woes and joys. He is a proud, good lad, I think, and with love and gentle discipline will grow into a fine man.

"Write to me, Anne dearest, and tell me your thoughts and if you believe I have done well in this matter."

He read his letter over and was about to sign it and send it off with the messenger already mounted and waiting outside. But then, with careful deliberation and because he must always be completely honest with those he cared for, he dipped his pen once again into the ink and added these lines:

"I have decided that the boy must be raised a Catholic. It is the faith of his fathers, the faith into which he was born. I can do no less, whatever the obstacles. . . ."

2 Spring Mount and Kilbree

For a long time, the obstacles were not great. Not far off there in Ireland, away from the court, away from a sadly divided Parliament which looked with great suspicion upon King Charles' indulgent attitude towards Catholics. Charles himself was a Protestant, but he had married a Catholic queen. If Catherine of Braganza had produced for England a Catholic heir the Civil War might well have begun all over again. However Charles was bored with his queen and she produced no heir whatever. Parliament worried about Charles' brother, James, who, it was darkly rumoured, was a Catholic himself. James would inherit the throne upon his brother's death. . . .

But with so much to be done and not enough hours in the day to do them all, these pressing national problems seemed very remote to the Sturbridge family. Sir Thomas was fully occupied in managing two vast estates, raising not one but two boys. Once in a great while he noticed that time was passing swiftly. Once in a great while they heard a piece of news from court, news about the wild romp of a reign King Charles was making of his restoration to power, but somehow it all seemed part of another world and nothing to do with them.

They soon settled their lives into a very comfortable routine.

Autumn and winter were spent at Spring Mount in England. There the boys were tutored from eight in the morning until three in the afternoon. Then they were free to ride and hunt, to seek out Sir Thomas in some distant field, seated on his favourite grey, overseeing the workmen at harvest or chopping down trees for the winter fires.

But as soon as the first warmth of spring settled over Britain, the household moved to Ireland. Ian and Tom gleefully shed shoes and hose, coats and collars, and ran about like young colts frolicking in the green fields. Here Tom soon learned to be a proper fisherman and Ian, sitting lazily beneath a favourite big tree by the river, studied his loathed Greek languidly, with much more of an eye to the tug on his line than the phrase on his tongue.

From their first meeting the boys got on famously. They had eyed one another suspiciously when Sir Thomas introduced them, then spent two hours fighting it out on the overgrown back lawn at Kilbree House. They discovered that neither one could beat the other. That bit of necessary business settled, they accepted each other and went on to become close friends.

Sir Thomas had made it quite clear from the outset that there was no reason why one should try to beat the other. Spring Mount and the lands in England and the title, these would belong to Tom one day. Kilbree House, its forests and meadows, its great shining length of the Blackwater River, these were Ian's birthright. Sir Thomas regarded Kilbree merely as a trust and it was not long before Ian came to know and love the man who seemed so different from all other Englishmen.

Very quickly Sir Thomas and Lady Anne realized that both of the boys were lacking in the usual book learning. Tom, growing up in Holland and, later, in France, had picked up a smattering of several languages, some Latin and Greek, a shaky comprehension of the way the world was put together, and absolutely no mathematics whatever. Ian long ago had begun to learn his numbers and Latin. And there it stood: two rather worldly-wise young gawks, as Sir Thomas dryly put it, with not a decent education between them. He wanted them both to attend University, but first they would have to be taught at home until they were prepared for more advanced studies.

Tom complained and groaned a great deal. Ian did likewise, for he had even more to study than Tom. True to his word, Sir Thomas arranged for the priest to come several times each week to teach Ian his religion. Tom, who had gotten used to quizzing Ian on his Greek, as Ian helped Tom with his geometry, now found himself acquiring a good knowledge of the Catholic faith as well, for the only way to get Ian to study his Catechism was to take the little question-and-answer book wherever they went and keep asking troublesome questions until Ian had it all straight in his head.

Tom could not make out much difference between his own religion and Ian's. Lady Anne had seen to it that her son grew up with a clear understanding of his duties to God and his fellow man. When Tom came to her with questions now, she sent him to his father and Sir Thomas would shake his grey head as he leafed through the Catholic book and mutter that it was only men, after all, who made such differences seem important. God, he was positive, did not give tuppence for rite and ritual, only for a good heart and a courageous, honourable life. He would then carefully explain to Tom the actual differences between the two faiths, but for a long time Tom was as likely to show up at Mass of a Sunday morning as he was to attend services in the family chapel. There were no real differences between the two young friends and rarely so much as a small quarrel. They did not even quarrel about Sheila Carey. . . .

3 Truest of Friends

Sheila was a part of their lives from the first. A tiny, thin bit of a girl, long wild red hair down her back and laughing grey eyes, Sheila could outrun either of the boys, outclimb them on any tree in Waterford County.

She and her mother lived in a big, empty house across the river from Kilbree. Her father had been killed the same day as Ian's father, and Sheila and her mother had fled during the night to Kerry where they had cousins. Not until Sir Thomas had the satisfaction of seeing the first harvesting of the wheat on Kilbree land did the Careys venture home again.

Ian barely remembered Sheila, but she knew him well enough. Girls it seems, always had such excellent memories. Hadn't she pushed him head-over-heels into the river long ago, so he might fetch her up a nice shiny gold carp to play with? Ian always swore it wasn't true, but Sheila would simply smile and nod and Tom knew it *was* true. Still, he could not blame Ian for denying it. What fellow wanted to remember a girl had got the best of him, and him too young to defend himself?

Sheila remembered the bad times, too. But unlike Ian, who had told Tom all the details of what happened when Cromwell's men came, Sheila Carey would not speak of such things. Sheila lived only in the present, whether from choice or because her fragile soul could not bear the black memories that had scorched it once, nobody ever knew.

Tom loved her the very day he first set eyes on her, but even then something in him recognized that it was not to be. There was always a kind of old, understood bond between Sheila and Ian, even if neither of them seemed to realize it just yet. Certainly they never mentioned anything about it the whole time the three of them were growing up together. But Tom, who had inherited a sensitivity about other people's feelings from both mother and father, knew that he and Sheila would never share the same total understanding that existed between her and Ian.

Tom kissed her once, after some holiday dance or other in the village, when he'd had a glass of wine too many and allowed himself to imagine what he knew, cold sober, was impossible. It was an awkward, amateurish kiss, almost missing her mouth altogether. And when he had done it and pulled back from her, his eyes watching her with mingled fear and love, Sheila did not move but stood and slowly touched first her own lips and then his with the tips of her fingers. Then she smiled a bit and said very softly:

"Now we are the truest of friends forever, are we not, Tom?"

He realized that she knew how he felt. The touch of her hand sent a warm wave of sheer delight coursing through his body, but Sheila had chosen the kindest way, the way most loving and most careful, to tell him the eternal limits of their relationship.

It was Tom, then, who turned away, so she would not see what he regarded as unmanly tears in his dark blue eyes. Tom blinked those tears away and turned back to her with a cheerful grin, the grin she would recognize as his familiar way of saying, "It's all right, I understand. Everything is fine now."

Sheila, quite anxious about him, saw the grin, not missing the last of those treacherous tears. She nodded very briskly and pressed his hand fiercely. And that was all that ever happened between the two of them. Much...no, all...was now understood for the rest of their lives.

And Ian appeared, laughing, from some gaming tent, carrying a ridiculous looking stuffed rabbit with glass eyes he had won for Sheila. Tom saw the light of love leap instantly into her eyes when Ian came. He understood. He only prayed that the pain of understanding would some day ease a little.

It was from that time on that Sir Thomas noticed the hint of sadness in his son's face. It did not take him long to realize the cause of it. He could not blame Sheila, nor Ian either. But Tom was seventeen. It was time for a change for both boys. How fast these seven happy years had flown! But now it was time for them to go away to school....

4 University Days

Sir Thomas wrote to the King, requesting royal permission for his Catholic ward, Ian Curtis Ives, to attend Oxford University along with his own son. Catholics were barred from the Universities, but the King had been known to make exceptions.

An exception was made in Ian's case. A place was found for him at Oxford and he and Tom spent the next few years studying, working, fighting mutual enemies at school. Their friendship flourished. And, despite the general feeling against Catholics, Ian was popular with the majority of the students.

Tom's future lay with the military, following his family's notable services in England's armies for generations. But he could easily understand Ian's occasional wistful, restless moods. Ian's future was far from settled, despite Sir Thomas' efforts. Kilbree was there, of course, ready for him when he came of age, but Ian did not trust the English government. And, although he never said as much to Tom or his father, somewhere deep in his heart, Ian Ives really believed that once Sir Thomas died, Kilbree would be taken away again.

All Ian ever said about the future was that, if such a thing were possible, he would not mind a "bit of sword and saddle" himself. He looked back in time and he saw what might lie ahead and he was anxious to be able to fight, if necessary, to preserve King Charles on the throne and, after Charles, his Catholic brother, James, who had more than once spoken out boldly about a new leniency towards Catholics in England and Ireland. Neither Sir Thomas nor the boys had much use for James otherwise. He was an arrogant, pompous, thoroughly overbearing rogue who continually caused his brother much embarrassment.

Sir Thomas dreamed on peacefully in his two miniature country kingdoms hardly noticing the passing of time until Lady Anne died suddenly one night, in her sleep. And Sir Thomas was shocked out of his tranquil thoughts to see with sudden, sharp clarity that, despite all he had done for both of his sons . . . for some time he had thought of them both as his sons . . . there was more yet to be accomplished.

Five years at Oxford had not changed that look of hidden sadness in Tom's eyes. Sir Thomas decided that what was needed was a wife for Tom. A wife who could be only half as wonderful as Lady Anne would soon make the boy forget Sheila Carey. Now because Sir Thomas was really a very worldly and experienced man, part of him knew that this was the sheerest nonsense. But he brushed aside what he knew to be the truth and set his mind to finding a wife worthy of his son.

Ian's future was another matter. As long as Sir Thomas lived . . . and as long as the King remembered . . . Ian's property was safe. Now Sir Thomas was forced to the same question which Ian had reached himself. How long, mused Sir Thomas uneasily. How long?

And so he wrote once more and for the last time, to the King at Whitehall. His ward, Ian Curtis Ives, having done quite well at Oxford, now required a post, a commission in the army, something commensurate with the Sturbridge position. Sir Thomas realized that the army had no Catholic officers at the time, yet once again, with the King's most generous permission Sir Thomas Sturbridge begged to remind His Majesty of the many services. . . .

Two commissions were forthcoming in the King's Dragoons. One for Ian, one for Tom. Captains, suddenly, one day, grand and tall, utterly splendid looking in their tight white breeches, the scarlet coats, the polished gold buttons, the new Italian swords which were Sir Thomas' special gift to them.

That much was done now, and the old man breathed a sigh of relief. Far easier, as the world had it, to steal a man's lands from him than to have him ousted from the King's own service. If Ian served with honour, they would probably leave him in peace. If he managed to serve with some *distinction*, they would likely forget he was a Catholic altogether.

The Royal Dragoons were sent on manouevers up along the

Scottish border. Things were never very calm up north. Manouevers in full sight of malcontented and brooding Scotsmen served as a convenient warning.

And Sheila Carey married Ian just after he received his commission. Tom stood up for his best friend, stood by Ian's side in the little stone church in Waterford City and watched Sheila become the wife of another man. Sir Thomas gave the bride away. All through the ceremony he gazed not so much at the happy faces of the bride and groom as at the face of his son. There was a lump of pride mixed with sadness in the old man's throat as he watched Tom clasping Ian's hand and smiling, then turning to Sheila, kissing her small hand very lightly, very properly. His father thought a man would have to be blind to miss the bleak look in Tom's eyes at that moment. A wife must be found for that boy. A wife for Tom, and soon.

5 A Betrothal

Tom went north with his regiment while Ian spent six weeks at home in Ireland with his new bride, and then joined the Dragoons. And those were six of the busiest weeks Sir Thomas had spent in a very long time. He had a multitude of friends, many close neighbors and old Army companions. One such neighbor and old comrade at arms was Ernest Lyncourt, Baron of Longdale, not three miles from Spring Mount. The Baron had one child, a daughter named Helene. Sir Thomas had never seen the girl, but reports of her through the years had it that she had grown into a great beauty. The Baron, a widower, had sent her off to school in Switzerland. And now, at seventeen, she was coming home.

After inspecting a miniature of herself which Helene had sent her father, Sir Thomas came to the conclusion that if the artist who had painted it had been but the veriest liar of the world and a damned lack-luster talent into the bargain, still the girl was marvelously lovely. A different type altogether from Sheila, Sir Thomas noted gratefully. Helene Lyncourt was dark, a cloud of soft black hair curled about her neck, large sparkling dark eyes set wide apart in a cream-coloured face, full pink lips upturned for a hint of humour in the corners, a straight, pert nose, firm chin, an intelligent brow. Quite a look of calm, perhaps even of strength about her. It was to be hoped that the lass' figure and carriage might prove equally attractive. . . .

* * *

Sir Thomas asked so many questions that the Baron laughingly reminded him, over a freshly opened bottle of Marsala, that he was looking for a *wife,* not buying a horse. . . .

"Although, damme, Sturbridge," the Baron added with a wink, "if twas myself doing the looking, I don't know but what I'd be a jot more particular about the horse!"

The two old friends drank a quiet toast to the match and by the time he rode home to Spring Mount late that night, Sir Thomas had arranged all the details of his son's forthcoming marriage save one: he had yet to mention the subject to the bridegroom.

Several times during the next few months, while the Dragoons were still up north, Sir Thomas wrote to Tom, fully intending to go into the subject openly. Each time he ended by writing a short, somewhat muddled bit of a note which succeeded only in alarming Tom about his father's health. Yet, to each anxious inquiry arriving from the north, Sir Thomas impatiently replied that he was in the best of health, never better, and would the younger generation please refrain from putting people in their graves prematurely? Tom was more puzzled than ever and would have gone straight home but there were only another few weeks left and he decided not to give his father cause to quarrel with him.

Too, Tom knew his father as well as any man alive and had managed to read somewhat between the lines of those cantankerous little letters. By the time the Dragoons went on leave and Ian was on his way swiftly back to Ireland and to Sheila, Tom had a pretty good idea what was on Sir Thomas' mind. And he had made up his own mind to be agreeable about it. Once Sheila had pledged herself to Ian, it had become a matter of indifference to Tom whom the girl would be. He would be kind to her. It was not in Tom's generous nature to be otherwise. But, love her? Never.

He waited patiently, day after day at Spring Mount, while his father worked up to the matter. And then, one night, they sat talking very late after dinner, sitting before a blazing fire in the drawing room. Tom was unusually somber. Sir Thomas fortified his courage with another drink of brandy. Then he insisted on filling Tom's glass again. And still the old man sat and watched the flames leaping and hesitated.

Unable to bear it any longer, Tom stood up with his back to the fire, setting his glass aside on the mantel. And he smiled.

"Well, Father, when are you going to tell me about my wedding?"

Sir Thomas blinked, then laughed. "So you knew, you scamp, did you?"

Because he knew how very much it mattered to his father, Tom tried valiantly to match that happy tone, to capture at least a faint echo of the laugh. He nodded cheerfully, swallowing hard before he answered.

"Oh, I knew you'd get around to it sooner or later. What *is* it in this world of ours that cannot abide a bachelor? Well, tell me, tell me, who is the lucky lady to be?"

Somewhat surprised, Sir Thomas raised a bushy eyebrow.

"Lucky is she? I don't know about that, sir! If you ask me, she'll be taking on a handful, the job of a lifetime! Tom, do you mind me talking now and again about my old friend, Lyncourt?"

Tom obligingly tried to recall the name. Something in his manner was beginning to bother his father very much. Sir Thomas had not expected enthusiasm, not at first, but he had instead assumed there would have to be a great job of persuading ahead of him. Tom's affable pose could not entirely cover the strain he was under. A certain grim tightness around his large, generous mouth made his father wince and speak much faster than he usually did.

"Oh, yes, yes, Tom, you remember the chap. He's Baron Lyncourt now, over at Longdale, *you* know Longdale. Well, he's got himself a pretty daughter of a marrying age, just home from school on the Continent. She's got thirty thousand dowry and another ten thousand a year from her mother's will when she marries..."

"I'm sure the young lady is suitable, father. I trust your judgement, naturally," said Tom quietly.

This almost laconic remark irritated Sir Thomas more than any argument could have done. When he spoke again his voice had an unusual sharpness to it which both surprised and confused his son.

"Yes, yes, of course, you may depend on it. She's quite suitable, as you say. It's a good match. And...it's already settled!"

Tom looked at him without saying anything for a moment, then, mildly, he replied, "Father, I've tried to make it clear, I have no

27

quarrel with you about this. I really have tried my best to be agreeable, but you . . ."

"Damn it, Tom, that's the point!" Sir Thomas' uneasiness boiled over at last. "Why should you be so damned agreeable? Don't you care what you do with your life?"

"My life is pretty well set I think Father. I have the army and . . ."

"Devil the *army'll* warm your feet of winter's night, lad! We're talking here of marriage, of children! Your children. Haven't you ever thought of that?"

Tom turned away quickly. "Not recently, Father," he said, his voice strained.

Sir Thomas exhaled sharply. "All right now, Tom, this once and never again I'll say straight out what I know is in your mind. Do you think I haven't realized how you felt about Sheila all these years? Do you think I haven't seen the hurt in you? Well, but you knew it as well as any of us, the thing simply wasn't to be. Now she's married and happy. You know she's happy with Ian. Would you change that? Would you have her anything less than the happiest she can be . . . and still claim that you love her? No, no . . ." Tom seemed about to interrupt, but his father raised a hand to stop him. "No, wait a little. Hear me out. I see now what you've decided to do. But, Tom, that's only the half of it. You'll marry, won't you, to please me, not yourself? You'll marry anyone I would have picked, sight unseen, because you believe you can never love another woman. And, you're right, Tom, you never will . . . because you'll never let go of Sheila in your heart and you'll never see that you *can* love again elsewhere, and happily! Tom, Tom, what kind of life is that for the lass you do wed? Won't you owe her anything at all?"

His voice breaking, he reached out and gripped his son's shoulder. Tom looked at him, his eyes bleak, and patted his hand awkwardly.

"I . . . I'll try, Father, I swear it. She will never know there was someone else. And . . . I'll take good care of her, I promise you. I'll try to make her as happy as you and Mother were. . . ."

Sir Thomas' eyes were misty. He cleared his throat loudly and embraced his son with a sudden ferocious strength that amazed Tom and left his father trembling. Tom insisted that he sit down again, then went and got them both a bit more of the brandy. Together they drank a toast to the future.

"Well now, Father," Tom smiled, "you haven't even told me the lady's name. What is she called? We can't go on just saying *her*, now, can we?"

Sir Thomas chuckled. "Helene. Helene Lyncourt. How do you like it, eh? Musical sound to it, don't you think? Your mother would have said that. Musical. Maybe she is, too. Musical, I mean. They teach the girls marvels of things these days at those fancy schools. Oh, she'll be a credit to the family, my boy, you'll see, you'll see!"

6 Helene Lyncourt

Just that agreeably, just that hopelessly, Helene came into the Sturbridge family. She was introduced to Tom a few weeks later. She saw a very tall young man, with serious deep blue eyes set in a handsome, rather craggy face, a large nose, broad mouth, a keen, wide smile, an easy, graceful yet thoroughly masculine way of moving and with it an impression of immensely virile strength which could not help but attract her. Unlike many other young men Helene had met, Tom Sturbridge did not seem to feel the need to strike a heroic pose when he talked to her, nor did he make any attempt to impress her with his broad shoulders and deep chest.

Obviously, Helene thought to herself, he was a man who knew exactly what he was and appeared not unsatisfied with it, on the whole. He was rather quiet-spoken and thoughtful, but not without a keen sense of humour. It was only the look in his eyes that bothered her somehow, that sad look which made him seem older than he really was. It was romantic, she told herself, it was intriguing. . . .

During all the long, boring, lonely years at boarding school, as her body grew and developed, Helene's ideas of what men were like and then, finally, of what the one man in her life would be like, had crystalized into someone very like Tom Sturbridge. And although she was but seventeen and quite innocent, she had not been in Tom's company ten minutes before she knew with absolute certainty that she would love him with all her heart for the rest of her life.

In that same short ten minutes she also realized that, in spite of great efforts he made to conceal the fact, he was deeply in love with someone else. Who the lady might have been, what had happened to separate them, Helene had not the least idea. It was quite possible she would never know.

To her it mattered little. She loved him. She made up her mind

29

that she would try to bring him happiness if that was at all possible. At the very least she might help lessen the pain of his loss.

She accepted his formal proposal of marriage with a quiet dignity that touched Tom to the heart. How many girls ever married the one man in all the world whom they truly loved? This was her reasoning, the single thought she concentrated upon. As for the rest of her youthful dreams, she packed them away as she packed away her short, somber-hued school dresses.

Meanwhile, as the wedding plans went forward briskly, there were long, quiet walks with Tom through the orchards and gardens of Spring Mount, dances at several of the great houses in the neighborhood, dinner parties given for them by friends of both families. Helene hoped that Tom was beginning to know her better, that he could see he was marrying neither a gossip nor a fool nor a woman who would try to rule his life from the bedroom with miserly measured doses of love. Helene knew very little of that side of marriage, just enough to realize that it was important to be generous, to be kind, to be honest. Only . . . it would have been so very nice if Tom were able to love her, just a little bit. . . .

7   For Love's Sweet Sake

Ian and Sheila, already expecting their first child, arrived at Spring Mount a few days before the wedding. Helene was to meet them both at the grand ball Sir Thomas was holding in honour of the bridal attendants. Baron Lyncourt insisted upon riding over from Longdale on horseback, while his daughter and her maid came by coach. When Helene hurried in a bit late and somewhat flustered because of it, she found the visitors from Ireland standing in the midst of a large group of people eager to meet her.

Tom had told her a great deal about Ian Ives, a bit about his wife Sheila. Helene was nervous. Knowing how very close Tom and Ian were made her wonder if Ian would accept her or resent her as a stranger, an outsider.

Before Tom was able to say a word, Ian came striding toward her, smiling broadly. He caught her white-gloved hand and pressed his lips to her fingertips.

"This is Helene," Ian said with great warmth. "Now I shall have a sister, too, just as Sheila has always been a sister to Tom," he said graciously.

"A sister! Oh, yes, how kind of you to say so!" murmured

Helene. Ian's easy, cheerful familiarity struck just the right chord and already she began to feel a real part of the family. She looked up at Ian and smiled shyly. So this was the man Tom thought of as a brother. How much alike they were, she thought. Ian was fully as tall as Tom, but he appeared just a bit shorter. His frame was that of a heavier man and if he had not always been so active and athletic he might have put the extra weight. But Ian was lithe and limber, with a head of curly golden hair set proudly atop broad, straight shoulders. His limbs were long, his hands and fingers thin and seeming delicate. But, like Tom, there was a subtle strength and virility about Ian, and a frank openness that won Helene's heart very quickly.

Ian released her hand and, with a laugh, embraced her with both arms and kissed her soundly on the cheek. He glanced over at Tom, who stood nearby, tall and handsome in his dress uniform, the candlelight sparkling on his gold lace and buttons.

"There's an Irish welcome, eh, Tom? You've found a real beauty for yourself, my friend, a real beauty!"

Helene saw that Tom smiled back at his friend, but suddenly she caught sight of the most beautiful woman she had ever seen in her life, standing across the grand hallway before a blaze of candles, her tiny figure quite perfect. She was dressed in a gown of flowing green silk, a cascade of emeralds at her throat, her flaming hair pulled back by gold combs and hanging long and shining from the crown of her head. There was a sweet smile on her lovely lips, but, Helene noted with dismay, there seemed to be a tiny frown between her delicate brows.

Ian followed her silent gaze and then laughed again. "That is Sheila, my wife," he said, his voice filled with pride.

In that instant Helene saw the look in Tom Sturbridge's eyes as he gazed at Sheila Ives. Helene felt herself turn cold as ice. Her heart began to pound violently. Sheila. Yes, of course. It was Sheila whom he loved!

Suddenly it seemed to her that everyone and everything but Sheila had somehow faded far away, swallowed up and shimmering out of shape, quite unreal in the flickering candle light. Suddenly she could not hear their voices, nor the distant sound of the quartet playing in the ballroom.

For years afterwards Helene dreamed about that moment. She could see herself walking slowly, so slowly, across the wide hall.

31

She could feel the thick, soft carpet under her thin dancing slippers. She could actually count the number of steps she was taking. As though she were in some sort of trance, she sensed rather than saw Sheila moving towards her. The frown on Sheila's beautiful face was more intent now. Sheila's red lips smiled, framing the beginning of a courteous phrase of greeting, but those large grey eyes were trying to read something, too. What was it? What was Sheila Ives *thinking?*

Helene faltered and stopped for a moment, feeling a rising hysteria inside of her. I must say something, I must! she told herself. But what does Sheila want to know? Why is she studying me this way? Why?

And Sheila always remembered watching the lovely dark-haired girl in the deep pink gown with a spray of garden roses artlessly tucked into the folds of silken tissue at her breast. Sheila saw the panic in those rich brown eyes and grasped the realization dawning in them as Helene looked at Tom Sturbridge and then at her, then back and forth again from one to the other. Imperceptibly, Sheila sighed. She knew. Helene knew that Tom loved her. Everything would have been so much easier if only Helene had not seen the truth. Sheila felt uneasy about Tom, although she had no reason to reproach herself. She had never led him on but she knew he still loved her, or thought he did. But if Helene were the right girl for him, if she really loved him, might she not help him to forget about that old, hopeless passion?

It was that thought that accounted for the anxious little frown on Sheila's brow as she approached Helene. "Dear God," Sheila prayed, "please let her love our Tom with all her heart, please!"

She studied Helene's flushed face gravely. Did this young girl, who did not know Tom at all, who could not possibly have begun to discover all of his endearing qualities, did she love him even a little? Sheila knew that this was an arranged marriage. Still, such marriages sometimes worked out better than those begun with romance and moonlight and airy, unrealistic dreams. . . .

When the two women met in the center of the Great Hall at Spring Mount, Sheila placed her hands on Helene's hot cheeks and looked very deep into her eyes, without speaking. Then, as though she were satisfied about something, she smiled again and kissed Helene, hugging her very tightly. And she glanced at Tom with a tear in her eye that nobody saw but Helene.

"Well, Tom Sturbridge," Sheila said softly, "Ian is quite right. You've found yourself a beautiful bride. I think you will never be sorry, neither one of you!"

Helene saw Tom flush darkly as he heard those few quiet words, spoken almost as a kind of blessing. And for one tiny moment she caught a glimpse of the raw, naked anguish in his dark blue eyes as he looked at Sheila. Seconds later his face once again wore its customary expression of composure. His smile was genuine, his entire manner calm and sunny again.

Sheila, too, had seen that look. She squeezed Helene's hand as their eyes met silently. No more passed between them then; no more was necessary only the entire understanding of two loving women and the complete acceptance by one of them of a role she must play, for love's sweet sake, her whole life long. . . .

8 Wedding Day, Wedding Night

How she had gotten through those last few days before the wedding Helene never really knew. She forced herself to face the inescapable fact that, if she went through with this marriage, she would never in all her life possess him completely and of a certainty he would never make the effort to completely possess her, to learn and to understand her most secret thoughts and needs, to develop that so rare instinct between lover and loved one which comprehends totally, leaping from earth to moon in one great loving step, no need for questions or answers, only *knowing*.

She thought she would give her life if once, only once, Tom would ever look at her the way he had looked at Sheila Ives. But he would not. Before, when she had not known who the woman was, somehow it had been easier. Now it was agonizing to know that she would live out the rest of her life in a one-sided intimacy with the man she adored. Yet she was committed to this step. She would not retreat now. . . .

The Wedding Day, a blur of candles, lilies in golden vases on the altar of the Sturbridge chapel, crowds of townspeople, servants, friends, relatives, well-wishers outside, promises repeated obediently as the minister spoke them, white gown of hand-made Brussels lace, veil reaching to the floor, her own face as white, surely as either gown or veil, her eyes filled with hot, burning tears as she saw the heavy, twisted-gold marriage ring upon her finger and she thought of all that ring should mean, did mean, to her. But not to him.

They would not begin their wedding journey until the next day. The night was long in coming and yet it arrived much too soon. Downstairs the musicians played on in the Great Hall, sitting high above the merry dancing guests in the Minstrels' Gallery with its fine wood carving and the bouquets of flowers banked all about them. Violins playing so gaily, so sweetly, Helene walking up the stairs, looking down, seeing lovely Sheila dancing in Ian's arms, a happy smile on her lips, her velvet gown of midnight blue picking up the light of the candles in subtle, sinuous highlights. . . .

We are being led to one another like stallion to mare, for servicing, Helene thought, bitter for one moment. But she knew it was not so. Everyone at Spring Mount treated her kindly, even affectionately. The maids undressed her, giggling a little, the older ones dabbing sentimentally at their eyes as they hurried about the bridal chamber. The youngest of them all, a girl no more than twelve, stood up on a footstool to brush out the bride's soft black hair, marveling at its silkiness as it curled and waved down Helene's back to her knees.

She stood patiently, her hands numb and cold, and let them do with her whatever they pleased, whatever they must. She prayed that they might find something more that tradition demanded be done on this great occasion. She prayed that they would stay with her a little longer and not leave her all alone to wait for him to come to her. She knew in her heart he would not really want to come; she knew that the vision of Sheila swirling about in blue velvet in the ballroom, happy, triumphant in her fulfilled womanhood, would be in his mind and in his heart even when he came to his bride tonight. He would be wishing that the child Sheila carried in her belly was *his* child, and that the joy of planting that child in its most sweet nest had been his, not Ian's. . . .

The maids left her then, the smallest and the youngest looking up at her, quickly pressing a tender little kiss upon one of her icy hands, then running out after the others, closing the heavy door, locking out the world. And Helene was alone. They had left a single tall white candle burning in a silver stand beside the bed. Helene stood very still, clad in her long, white linen nightrobe with its finely sewn tucks across the low-cut bosom, its innocent pale blue ribbons, its lacy edgings. She stood, slim and white and quiet as the candle across that silent room. Almost hypnotized, she watched its twisting little tongue of flame seek out the shadows by the bed.

She tried to think what she must do, what she must say to him when he came. She knew that he would do everything. He would not expect her to know exactly what was going to happen. But, if he did not love her, not even a little bit, would he be patient with her? Would he be gentle and kind?

On that night, Helene did not yet know enough of men and women together to yearn for a time when he would be *impatient*, eager, unrestrained and even, briefly, savage, with his love-making. On that night she could only think: *he does not love me, he does not want me . . .*

And then, because she was very strong although she did not yet even suspect it, she thought: *I will not cry tonight. I will never let him see me cry. If he does not love me, at least I will not make him despise me.*

Even as her lips silently formed the last of those determined words, the door opened slowly and Tom Sturbridge came in, and closed and bolted it behind him. He, too, was prepared for the ritual, dressed in a long, wine-red dressing gown, still wearing his breeches and boots, the white lace of his thin lawn shirt open at the throat.

Helene looked at him and thought her heart would burst with the love she felt for him. She did not realize that at that moment her pale face blushed deeply and her brown eyes seemed to leap out to him brightly across the dark room. Tom smiled sadly, thinking what a sorry bargain she had made in this marriage, almost hating himself that he did not, could not love this altogether lovely young girl.

"You are very beautiful, Helene," he told her quietly.

She said nothing, nor did she move. He realized that she was afraid. He did not know her secret, of course; he did not suspect that she was aware of his true feelings. Damn his soul, why shouldn't he love her? he asked himself, standing there, feeling like a fool, wishing he might have the whole day suddenly undone, and Helene gone free and free-hearted from his father's house!

Helene caught the troubled look in his eyes and heard the gentle note of regret in his voice. She realized that her fears about this night were unnecessary. She relaxed a little then, and even managed to smile at him. He walked across the room to her and touched her dark hair with his hand.

"Don't be afraid," he said. "You mustn't ever be afraid of me."

"I am not afraid," she said truthfully, looking up at him. And then, unable to keep herself from saying one thing more, she turned

35

her head away so she could not see his eyes, and she murmured, "I love you."

His hand, resting lightly on her hair, tightened suddenly.

"I'll take care of you," he said, as he might say to a child. "I want you to be happy, Helene. I will try to make you happy."

"Yes," she breathed, knowing that he meant what he said, knowing now what the extent of their life together would be. He would treat her wonderfully well and kindly, always. She had nothing to fear for her future. She was his wife.

"Yes, I know you will, Tom," she whispered and, feeling the rush of tears coming, she buried her face against his chest and clung to him with both arms, shaking from head to foot, feeling that she must die because he did not love her. But her heart was not quite broken yet. Not yet.

Like a fluttering young bird he held in his hand, feeling her quivering body against his, feeling . . . sensing . . . her vulnerability, he put his arms around her and held her close, to comfort her, he thought, and because it must, in any case, happen this way.

He held her against the length of his body and felt how cold she was through the thin linen nightrobe she was wearing. He felt her cheek against his and it was blazing hot. He glanced down at her. Her eyes were closed. The long sweep of black lashes were touched with a trace of tears she had forgotten were there. His heart went out to her; for a moment he forgot the terrible ache inside of him. For a moment he forgot the feeling of Sheila dancing in his arms after the wedding supper and the light kiss on the brow she had given him when the dance ended and she had wished him happiness. . . .

"It's all right," he whispered to his bride. "Hush, hush, Helene, it's all right."

He picked her up in his arms, cradling her head against him, and carried her over to the marriage bed, thinking only to comfort her, terribly aware that she must never know that comfort was all he had to offer her.

He placed her down amongst the pillows and sat beside her, holding both of her cold hands in his own, to warm them. Helene opened her eyes and saw his anxious face bending over her and felt the warm, clean breath of his mouth. His look was all concern for her now; his thoughts were all of her, she realized. But she could not forget the agony that had been so very apparent in his expressive eyes when he had looked at Sheila. And suddenly she thought, *poor, poor Tom, how dreadful it is for him, too!*

With a little cry of sympathy, she pulled her hands free and placed them on his face and pulled his head down to rest on her bosom, holding him there, patting and caressing him tenderly.

For a while he seemed content to remain there and gradually she could feel the tension leaving his arms and shoulders. *Why, if I can do that much for him,* she thought almost happily for an instant, *if I can be of some comfort to him, then I am of use after all!*

He felt the rapid beating of her heart, the warmth returning to her limbs, the gentle heat of her round young breasts against his face. He lifted his head and kissed her on the lips, tenderly, very softly. She sighed and put her arms around him. . . .

She is very sweet, he thought. His kiss became more urgent. Helene responded quickly to his slightest touch. He was very kind, very careful not to alarm her. But, a bit later, when he lay above her and possessed her innocent, loving body for the first time it was the face of Sheila Ives he saw looking up at him, smiling, smiling; it was Sheila's white arms he felt around his neck. . . .

He shuddered and cried out and tried desperately to forget Sheila, but the moment passed. There was nothing left but to finish it quickly, to get it over and done with, and then to hate himself because he could not dictate to his own heart. When the final release came to him, it did not even matter very much.

Long after he slept, tossing fitfully in the big bed, Helene walked about the bridal chamber in her bare feet, no longer feeling the chill night air. Sometime later she became aware that she was very tired. A great, drawing ache had taken hold of her muscles. She sat down in an armchair by the open window, looking out across the grounds of Spring Mount.

But her restless eye could not seem to look at anything for very long, until she noticed the gently rising hill off in the distance, standing out black and stolid against the horizon. Above it the moon moved in stately procession, followed by a train of little stars. Crickets were chirping down in the gardens. Signs of an orderly, regulated world. . . .

Helene leaned forward, folding her arms upon the windowsill resting her head on her arms. And now the tears flooded forth, unseen, unheeded by Tom. She thought, *now it is complete.* Now that she knew at last what love was all about, she realized what was irretrievably lost to her.

So, this was the thing between a man and a woman, the thing that drove them, possessed them, kept them together or tore them apart. She nodded, trying to blink the tears away. Beyond the apprehension and the first great pain, what wonder there was in it! What unspeakable possibilities this loving held in its secret, special power!

She knew how much she had wanted Tom to hold her, to come into her body and make her his own, to be hers in that unique way. He had been so sweet about it all, so gentle, so careful of her feelings. He had been all those things she had hoped he would be. But somewhere in the confusion of that first time of loving, a cloud had come over his face; she saw it in his eyes, she heard it in his voice when he cried out wordlessly. And, although he did not suspect it, he had gone away from her then. He had left her behind somewhere and lost and longing to catch up with him again, unable to find him or make him see her anymore.

"Oh, Tom! Tom!" she moaned, not daring to cry it aloud as she wished to do, to shout it, to scream it, to inform that remote stately moon, those orderly crickets in the grass that it had all been for nothing, for nothing!

A hunger she had never felt fully before took possession of her body, her heart, her senses, and for a wild moment or two she thought it would drive her mad. She jumped up from the chair and hastened back to the bed where he was sleeping. She crouched down by the side of the bed and looked at his face, and dared to stroke it with her fingers, pushing back a stray lock of hair that had wandered across his brow. *Will it always be like this?* she thought. Would she always feel such pain, real, physical pain, such unfulfilled, torturing longing for him, for that "something more" of which people spoke and always wistfully? *I want him,* she thought, realizing that the thought, even the words were childish.

But, I want him! insisted her anguished heart. "I want him!" She did not realize she had spoken the words aloud. Tom stirred, opened his eyes and saw her crouching there, felt her fingers upon his cheek.

"Come to bed, Helene," he said, his voice husky. "Come, you'll catch cold there."

He pulled the covers down and she crept into the warm spot he had made with his sleeping body. For a moment she lay stiffly beside him, not touching him, because she wanted so very much to touch him. In the darkness she heard him sigh. And she moved over against him and, of her own accord, she kissed him hard on the mouth and on the neck and chest. For an instant his body went rigid, as if in protest, and then he turned fully towards her and buried himself in her receptive arms, desperately wishing that he might find oblivion there. . . .

9 A Garden On The Hill

They traveled north through the lake country on their wedding trip, staying at quiet country inns, going for long, rambling strolls about the lakes. They learned much more about one another. They found that they both liked many of the same things. They both enjoyed reading and traveling. Tom was delighted when she told him she had studied Greek and Latin at school, and had more than a passing acquaintance with the classics. She amused him vastly with little anecdotes about her schooldays in Switzerland. He told her what he could remember of his childhood in Holland and France. Some day, they agreed with great enthusiasm, they would go back to the Continent and see everything there was to see.

Tom told her a great deal more about his family, and about Ian and himself. But he never mentioned Sheila unless Helene did, and then he changed the subject as soon as possible.

They became friends. They would have been better, faster friends were it not for the nights and the embarrassing, silent ritual they engaged in. Tom acted as though he were doing her some grave wrong whenever he touched her intimately. He was apologetic. He did what he did quickly, silently, and then turned away from her to sleep, leaving her wide awake, sick with yearning, silent too.

She thought a great deal about children during those six weeks. She knew nothing whatever about having babies, but she became convinced that she and Tom would never have a child and this troubled her deeply. She remembered Ian and Sheila, so terribly happy, so excited about the child they were expecting. But Ian and Sheila were in love with each other. Surely out of a lonliness and unfulfilled longing like her own, how could a child ever be conceived? Helene was still naive enough to believe that a woman knew the very instant a child had come to life within her body. She thought in that moment a feeling of overwhelming joy would fill the heart of such a woman. And in six weeks of marriage, Helene had never known such a moment of joy.

They returned to Spring Mount liking one another, each wishing to make the other happy, each, for different reasons, feeling it was impossible.

The day they came home, Tom left her for a little while to stay in the study and discuss some matters about the estate with his father. Helene left the two of them together and went wandering outside, away from the house which was now her home. She climbed to the top of the hill she had seen from the bedroom window on her wedding night. She walked briskly to the very crest of the hill, moving in long, strong strides, the full crimson skirts of her silk brocade traveling dress billowing out about her feet. When she reached the top, she took off her new, gay red-feathered bonnet and shook her hair loose, enjoying the feeling of the wind blowing it about her face and shoulders.

She sat down in a heap of skirts in the frail grass and thought there had never been so beautiful a place. A perfect place for children to romp and run . . .

I must make something I can love! she thought fiercely, *something that is my own!*

It was then that she began to plan her garden, on this bare, grassy hilltop dotted with a few scrubby bushes here and there. It seemed to her that this hill, "her" hill as she came to think of it, had significance only she could understand. No other bride at Spring Mount loved this special spot, only she. Looking down towards the house, one could see the gardens other brides had taken pride in, four or five of them in various places about the lower grounds. Tom's mother, Lady Anne, had been partial to ferns and delicate, small wildflowers. Her garden, just beneath the windows of the masterbedroom, was a little gem of low hedges, small brooks and tiny, fragrant clusters of pale colours amidst bushes of deepest green holly leaves. Some other Lady Sturbridge had planted an herb garden in intricate patterns of a dozen different greens.

But Helene made her garden upon the hill and often went to it when there seemed nowhere else to go. Early each morning she fled the questioning eyes of the servants and ran quickly through the tall, dark stand of trees out back, then across the stable path, past the springing fountains and slender marble columns which encircled a pool spangled with the flashing sprites of goldfish swimming about. She ran on until she reached the hilltop from which one could see the distant, frothy grey ocean.

She had planted roses, only roses, in four large circles within a square of trellises and climbing red blossoms. Each circle enclosed a small group of benches and white-painted iron garden chairs and tables. The roses in each circle were all of the same colour, pink, white, red, and every shade of yellow that would grow in England. The yellow garden was her favourite. It stood highest on the hill. Beyond it a few yards and one climbed away from the land and stood where it dropped suddenly into a green valley and, beyond that, the sea.

Much to the amusement of Tom and his father, as soon as the next spring thaw allowed she had insisted upon planting every rosebush with her own hands. She grudgingly allowed the servants to carry the heavy outdoor furniture up the hill for her, but it quickly became law at the house: nobody touched those precious roses except Lady Helene!

10   First Flowerings And Last

It was just after Christmas when word came from Ireland that Sheila's baby had come too soon and died. Tom promised that he and Helene would be there for the great occasion, but it was three months ahead of time. They visited later, of course, and found Sheila a trifle pale, a bit easily tired, but that was understandable.

Helene was quickly able to forget her qualms and doubts about the four of them together. They got on famously. On the morning the Sturbridges were to return to Spring Mount, Sheila put her arms around Helene and kissed her warmly and wished her joy in every thing . . . and a child of her own in her arms before next they would meet. It was the only reference Sheila ever made to that first, lost child of hers. Helene's eyes had filled with quick tears and her return embrace was every bit as warm. She came away from Kilbree thinking to herself, *who, indeed, could not love Sheila?*

Sir Thomas came quite often to the hilltop garden to watch Helene tending her plants, to sit and talk with her. When Tom was away with the Dragoons, she spent most of her time there. Sir Thomas never said a word about it, but when he watched her busy hands cultivating the flowers he could not help but wish it might be a grandchild of his upon whom she lavished such care.

The first roses at Spring Mount had bloomed and dropped away and budded anew when the old soldier died. And it was not until a full year after his death that Helene bore the grandchild he had always longed for. . . .

She was faintly puzzled when she found that she was carrying the child, for nothing had really changed between Tom and her. They were closer than ever, greater friends than either of them would have believed possible. Because it mattered so very much to her, she found that she was able to bear the odd, empty places in their relationship: the many times it would have been so natural for their hands to touch or to join, the special moments when the words she had never heard him say, "I love you," would have helped so much. . . .

And one morning she had felt quite weak and ill. The next day she felt even worse. When the doctor told her she was with child, she looked at him in amazement and he laughed in her face, boldly reminding her that she had been a married woman full three years now and ought not be so surprised.

How happy Tom was then and how delighted later, when his son, Robert, was born, looking the very image of old Sir Thomas, even in his long white Christening robe and little bonnet. A new kind of bond grew between Helene and Tom because of the baby. For the first time she began to see how much her husband depended on her, how he enjoyed her company and valued her opinions. She looked forward to the nights when she would go into the nursery to look at the baby for the twentieth "last time," and then she and Tom would sit together by the fireside and talk about the future. If it was not complete happiness, it was, at least, peace.

Away off in Ireland, Sheila had her own son, Michael, at last, about a year after Rob was born. Ian looked at the year-old Rob and the infant Michael together and clapped Tom on the back heartily, saying, "It's the two of us all over again, isn't it, Tom?" And that was all right with Helene, too.

But Sheila must never have another child. She told Helene this one morning, a secret she would never reveal to Ian. She and Helene were sitting together in the pretty little sewing room at Kilbree, the room Ian had fixed up as a surprise for her when she was still recovering from Michael's birth. He had had the walls lined with blue watered taffeta, with silver and blue drapes across the wide windows and wall shelves filled with delicate blue wedgewood pieces. A room for a Madonna, Ian had said . . .

But Michael's birth had been hard, too hard, a breach birth, and he was a big child. His toes had come out very pink and curled up at the tips, so crowded had he been inside of her . . . Sheila laughed and made a joke of it, but Helene heard the tremor in her soft Irish voice. And then Sheila told her. No more children, ever. Sheila would have no sympathy from Helene . . . she took her outstretched hand and gave it a quick, affectionate squeeze, but her grey eyes glowed and she tossed her head with defiance.

"Ah, the doctors! They don't know it all, do they? Mind Mrs. Grace, our cook? Well she stayed an old maid till she was fifty and when she was fifty-two and long past all that, you'd think . . ." Sheila's small, straight nose wrinkled with laughter . . . "why, didn't she up and give birth to a nine-pound girl with hair redder than my own and a tooth besides? The *doctors* all told her it couldn't be done, but they *don't* know everything!" Sheila's laugh was merry enough, but her eyes were far too bright.

Helene smiled at the tale, but then she said, "Sheila, don't put yourself in danger. Remember, you've got a husband and a son to think of now. Promise me you'll listen to the doctor. *Promise!*"

Sheila nodded almost carelessly and picked Michael up from his cradle. "Aye, don't worry about me, Helene. Don't worry about anything, will you? You should never have a care in all the world. Not *you*," she emphasized, her manner quite solemn.

"Oh? And why not me?" Helene laughed, puzzled, somehow embarrassed. And Sheila, nuzzling the baby against her, smiled.

"Oh, a hundred reasons I can think of," she answered lightly. "I like you. No, it's more than that now. I suppose we have gotten to be like sisters, you and I, just as Ian said. It's a good thing we have, too, with them so thick! And . . ." she paused, looking into Helene's eyes with serenity . . . "because you've made Tom so happy."

Helene flushed, dropping her eyes. "Have I?" she whispered.

"Yes, you have. Don't you know that?" demanded Sheila. "Don't you know he talks about you and about Rob all day long, and thinks of nothing but you two?"

"It's Rob," replied Helene, rising, moving restlessly across the small room. "That's what has made him happy. I see it, too. And, I'm grateful. I . . . I love him so very much, Sheila!" she blurted out suddenly, not meaning to say it at all.

"I know that," Sheila said promptly. "I knew it that very first night at Spring Mount. I could see it in your eyes. Sure, no one could miss that light! That's when I knew Tom would be all right. That's when I first knew that you and I would be friends."

Sheila seemed about to say something more, but changed her mind for the moment. There was always that one place, that one delicate, untouched area in their relationship which neither of them ever ventured into, one subject they never mentioned. It was as though an unspoken agreement existed between them. And Sheila yearned to break that silence for, just as she had perceived the light of Helene's love for Tom shining in her eyes that first night, now, too, she saw the hidden sorrow and the hunger in those same eyes. Sheila had her own thoughts about Helene and Tom Sturbridge and one day, she vowed, she would say something at last.

Two

"The Mighty Hopes That Make Us Men"

1 Sedgemoor Plain

A soft night wind was blowing steadily across the Channel from France, an easy, early July wind that picked up the faint sounds of singing from the soldiers of King James encamped on Sedgemoor Plain. Here and there throughout the muddy marshland, small camp-fires flickered in the darkness. Other fires marked out the perimeter of the camp, blazing up along the row of sixteen great, dull black iron cannon that sprawled like a pack of sullen, sleeping hounds.

A pale red sun had clung stubbornly to its narrowing piece of sky all through the hot afternoon. Finally, close to nine o'clock, the sun had departed, leaving the starless field of black to a bright half moon. But the moon seemed ill at ease this night, this particular night of July 6, 1685; the moon, indeed, seemed bent on hurrying from one small dark cloud to another, as though she would hide her face nervously on this, the night before the battle.

Captain Tom Sturbridge finished the last of a scant half-mug of rum and, still holding the battered tin mug in his hand, stared up at the sky, watching the moon. There was a faint smile on the Captain's good-looking face, a smile much belied by the unconscious, habitual touch of some inner sorrow in his deep blue eyes.

Graceful and silvery he thought the moon, like a lacing of crystals amidst black velvet, or silvery tissue of a silken gown clinging to Sheila's beautiful white shoulders. He lay back on the damp ground, with his heavy woolen cloak folded beneath his long, muscular body, and he looked at the moon and he thought of Sheila, Sheila as he remembered her from years ago, laughing down at him from the top of a marble staircase in Kilbree House, Sheila in a black velvet and silver gown, her long auburn hair curled into thin elegant ringlets, the devil of merriment and yet so much sweetness in her large, grey eyes. He thought of Sheila, whom he had loved since he was ten years old, Sheila Carey, the dearest lady who had ever graced the green hills of Ireland. Sheila Carey . . . Ives. Ives not Sturbridge, no, not Tom's wife after all. No one knew that he loved her, loved her even now after all these long years, would always love her. Sheila Carey Ives. Captain Sturbridge shivered slightly and looked away from the lovely moon. He gave the empty tin mug an absent-minded shake, then remembered with some regret that the rum was finished. He shifted his gaze to stare with distaste at the cold white ghostly mists floating aimlessly across the moorland.

Now where the devil had Ian got to, he wondered suddenly, his wandering thoughts drawn back to the present. He had no idea how long he'd been lying there dreaming like a schoolboy, wasting time and thought and feeling on hopes and illusions he had long ago put from him. Ian had gone to look after their horses, he remembered now. Their horses were perfectly all right in the capable hands of two stablemen from Spring Mount. But Ian worried and fretted about horses as if they were children. Tom knew very well what had become of all the sugar the two of them had left for tomorrow morning's tea. Ian would be standing feeding it to the horses, patting their great heads and stroking their warm noses, talking to them as though they were any two intelligent men-at-arms in the King's Dragoons. Ian and his horses! Tom chuckled and jumped up, stretching to ease the stiffness from his bones.

"Ah, I thought you'd gone to sleep on me," came Ian's deep voice just behind him. Tom turned around and saw Ian standing there, smiling broadly. He was holding something under his arm.

"What's that you've got? You've not been . . . foraging again, have you?'' grinned Tom. Ian Ives' well-known ability to discover unsuspected sources of food and drink, cartridges, tinder, blankets and anything else a soldier might run short of in the field was a great comfort to the men under him and to his brother officers, too, although sometimes a source of considerable contention from the original owners.

"Just a bit of whiskey,'' Ian replied. He set the small wooden keg down and threw some soggy branches on the fire where they smouldered pungently. Ian wrinkled his fine, straight-cut nose and waved the smoke away.

"I ran into some lads in the Irish Fusiliers, over there by the ditch." He indicated the far side of camp, where they had found a mucky ditch so wide and so deep that some of the veterans among them had immediately nicknamed it the Sussex Rhine.

"And how did you persuade them to part with the whiskey?'' drawled Tom, much amused, watching Ian pour two brimming mugs full of the fiery Irish drink they'd both grown up on.

"Drink up, me lad, and don't ask questions,'' laughed Ian. He sat down close to the sparse fire and Tom, pulling his cloak around his broad shoulders, sat across from him.

"I only meant,'' remarked Tom wryly, "is it likely that they'll come looking for the stuff?"

Ian's face clouded. "After tomorrow?'' he murmured. "I don't think so.''

"Then it will be tomorrow?''

Ian nodded. "Aye, tomorrow all right. Bristol's closed her gates against Monmouth. He's had no choice but to turn about and ride back to Bridgewater. He's there now, waiting. Like us. Until tomorrow.''

Tom caught a strange, somber note in Ian's voice and looked at him sharply. But Ian seemed at ease, except that his thoughtful blue eyes gazed a trifle restlessly about the camp.

It was after eleven now and the wind from France had begun to turn quite cold. The two men huddled quietly beside their slowly wasting fire drinking the whiskey, thinking their own thoughts. And then a sickly sighing of the weak blaze caught Ian's attention. He looked down at it in disgust and arranged the last few scraps of damp wood about it.

"Good God!'' he remarked. "What I'd give now for five minutes in front of the big hearth at Kilbree!''

Tom yawned, longing to pull off his tight leather boots and give his cold feet a good stretch.

"Shouldn't take long, I expect, and we'll all be home again," he replied. "This whole campaign is nothing but a tempest in a teapot anyway. Monmouth must know by now that they've taken Argyll and Rumbold and that whole rebel lot up in Scotland. Once his poor volunteers see our cannon they're likely to turn on their heels and leave him high and dry!"

"Aye, it'll be a slaughter," said Ian darkly. "Your 'good Protestant Duke' is finished before he starts, for all the good tomorrow's fight will do him!"

Tom snorted in protest. "He's not *my* bloody Duke!"

"Well, anyway, he's got nowhere to go now but through us, if he can . . . and he can't . . . or back into the sea, God grant him speed on his way!"

Tom grinned and leaned over to clink his tin mug against Ian's making a toast of that ironic little prayer. For a while they sat idly watching the men around them. No one slept yet, though many of them tried to rest. The snatches of singing they had heard earlier had died away now, as the scurrying moon climbed higher. The night was passing quickly, too quickly the moon pointing like a cold finger towards the dawn. Nearby a soldier busied himself cleaning a musket he had cleaned already. Talk was hushed, apprehensive. Everything had happened so quickly during the last two weeks. This was the first day most of them had had a chance to look about this flat countryside of the West and to wish themselves back home again. A number of the men were from Sussex and Kent—Kirke's two regiments of infantry not long back from Tangier, the Household Cavalry down from London, the Dragoons—all of them rousted out of barracks or back from home leave, fetched by urgent messages from Whitehall, summoning every man-at-arms to the support of King James II.

The cause of this extraordinary upheaval was the handsome bastard offspring of poor dead King Charlie and that enticing slut, Lucy Walter. This thirty-six-year-old royal gentleman, created Duke of Monmouth by his fond father, had played right into the hands of the exiled Puritan fanatic, Shaftesbury, and all those who urged that an end be made of King James, who was now happily in power and eagerly awaiting his coronation day.

Monmouth had set sail in three pitifully small ships, an armada truly worthy of a fool, and, after evading royal warships for nineteen agonizing days at sea, had landed at Lyme Regis, marched into the town of Taunton and, rallying that old stronghold of Cromwell supporters, had the temerity to crown himself King of England. Thousands of farmers and miners, fearful of a Catholic king in Protestant England, had thronged to Monmouth's side and marched north with him, expecting to rouse all of England to their cause. The Earl of Argyll and "Hannibal" Rumbold, who had been involved in the Rye House Plot to murder both King Charles and his brother, James, had sailed north in another three ships, determined to gain Scottish support, only to be captured as soon as they landed.

But there was, after all, no grand march from north to south, from south to north, meeting triumphantly in London. Now Monmouth, leading six or seven thousand poorly armed, thoroughly confused and inexperienced volunteers, found himself caught in a trap with nowhere to go. Tonight he was a young man with one last, most desperate, most hopeless hope. And tomorrow there was the battle. . . .

2 Time, Like a Garden Well

Tom couldn't put his finger on the exact moment when he began to realize that something was bothering Ian. He took advantage of the moonlight to study his friend's face, a face he knew as well as his own, the face of the man who had been more than a friend, more than a brother, since they were boys together.

"You're damned quiet tonight, I must say," commented Tom abruptly.

"I suppose I am," replied Ian, scowling a bit. "I promised Sheila that I'd be with her at home now, with the new baby coming almost any day, not away from home, stuck off in some mucky flat place nobody ever heard of!"

Tom's head shot up swiftly and when he spoke again there was a sharp edge to his tone.

"Sheila's well, isn't she? There isn't any difficulty about the baby?"

"No, no, none she'd tell me, anyway," said Ian hastily. "But when Michael was born, eight years back, it took her uncommon long to get well again. I asked the doctor myself and he swore to me, *swore*, mind you, that she'd be up and about in a couple of months, the lying old devil! You remember, Tom, Michaeleen was almost a year old and she was still not herself. Ah!'' Ian kicked a few wayward chips of wood into the fire with sudden, vicious energy. "You English and your bloody damned Monarchy."

Tom's dark eyebrows rose and he gave a long, low whistle. "I've as little use for 'brave Jimmy' as you do."

"Aye, I know," muttered Ian. "But here I sit and I wonder what it is I'm doing, getting ready to defend one man who wants to be King of England from another man who wants the same thing. What is it to *me* who sits on the English throne?"

"Still," said Tom mildly, "as long as there's a chance. . . ."

Ian laughed harshly. "A chance, is it? A chance for me to keep Kilbree so Michael can inherit it some day? A chance that a Catholic King might stop persecuting Catholics and Dissenters? Oh, yes, I suppose it's the *chance* that brought me here—it's sure to God I am it's not the *man*! But, Tom, I don't believe much in that little chance. Do you honestly believe Parliament will let him have his way? It's not been so damned long since your Parliament beheaded a King who defied them."

"You're in a rare bad mood, Ian," said Tom.

Ian laughed but, to Tom's ear, the laugh had a hollow ring to it.

"Since I seem to be such bad company I think I'll just go and have a look at the horses." Ian spoke a bit too loudly into the queer, strained silence. He jumped up. Tom shook his head.

"Will you forget those damned horses, just this once?" he snapped.

"All right, then, all right. Do you want to get a bit of sleep, maybe? They'll no doubt come at first light tomorrow." Ian settled down again, his shoulders hunched over beneath his heavy cloak, a bleak look on his face.

"Ian, what's really the matter? I've never seen you like this before, not in all the years we have known each other. Is it really Sheila?"

Ian threw back his blonde head and sighed, trying to summon up a reassuring smile, but he knew better than to try to fool Tom Sturbridge.

"I'll tell you, Tom," he began slowly. "I don't know what it is and that's God's truth. I don't know what's bothering me this night. I don't like this place, for one thing." He looked about, shaking his head slowly. "I don't like the . . . oh, the feeling in the air, or the way the horses are keeping so damned quiet. Not like horses to be

49

quiet like this. And I don't much care for that lovin' ditch over there." He gestured towards the far side of the encampment. "Who the devil picked this place, do you suppose? Not the Colonel, I'll wager. He's been the only one to get so much as a glimpse of Monmouth for a week now. Don't you think that Kirke or Feversham might have consulted him before spreading the whole lot of us out like this? Suppose, just suppose they don't come at us all honourable and proper from the north as we expect them to? Suppose they come on foot, filter in during the night and lay up all around us in that damned grass? Sure, by sunrise tomorrow we could be surrounded by them! And what bloody good would those sixteen big iron *blatherskites* be to us then, eh?"

Tom, listening, nodded slowly. Soldier's grumbling, he told himself. Battle eve nerves. But, was that all there was on Ian's mind? How many, many campaigns the two of them had been through together, and Ian had never talked this way before. Tom watched him uneasily now, seeing the way Ian's long fingers clasped and unclasped spasmodically. And an unexpected surge of apprehension gripped Tom. He turned away, trying to think of some way to distract Ian.

"... she's so very fond of Helene, you know that, Tom," Ian was saying something else. Tom had missed part of it but Ian hadn't seemed to notice. He went on talking quietly, never once meeting Tom's eyes as he spoke.

"Sheila's got a way of knowing people, knowing what's in their hearts. She loved Helene the first minute she set eyes on her. I'll never forget how happy she was that night when she came out of the bedroom holding your little Robert in her arms, do you recall, Tom? Do you remember that look on Sheila's face as she walked up to the two of us and put the lad into your lap? 'A son for you, Tom,' she said, and all the time she was looking at me with those big eyes of hers filled with tears. God, how she wanted a baby of our own!" Ian's voice broke for an instant but, before Tom could speak, he rushed on.

"It was good of Helene to come over to us when Michael was born, and her with those smiling dark eyes ... why is it always the eyes of a woman you remember first and best, I wonder? There I was, standing by the fire, my hands shaking so hard I was afraid I'd drop the child if she gave him to me. She must have realized how I felt, your Helene, for didn't she smile at me then and hold the baby up close so I could have a look at him and kiss his face, and then she said to me, 'Sheila's waiting to see you', and, Tom, wasn't I waiting to see *her*, my God! My little darling, after carrying that great tall son of ours all those hard long months? Now there won't be anyone with her except the servants this time, with you and me off here and Helene hardly able to travel yet herself. How is that new daughter of yours, Tom? Little Elizabeth. She's not two months old, is she? And I've not seen her yet. Imagine your having a daughter and neither Sheila nor myself seeing her!''

"Plenty of time for that, Ian," Tom interrupted him pointedly, more and more puzzled and disturbed at the strange torrent of words that poured from Ian's mouth, more and more troubled by the note of *regret* in his voice.

"Time?" Ian repeated the word. "Aye, time. We always think there's so much of it, don't we? Like a great well in the garden, always full, always ready to be dipped into. And then, one day, we're so surprised when we come for another dipperful and find it's empty. No more time. Time's all gone; the well's gone dry. I'll never forget how surprised I was when your father died. For years and years I'd been watching his hair turn from grey to white, I'd seen the wrinkles on his face grow deeper and deeper, but I guess I really believed he'd just go on living forever. I wanted him to go on, never grow old, never die.'' Ian looked down at the ring on the middle finger of his right hand. "Do you remember the day he had this ring made for me, Tom? How long ago was that? When I was twelve, I think. Yes, the summer I was twelve. . . .''

Tom's eyes were drawn to the massive steel band that Ian wore so proudly and felt anew the pangs of grief and yearning he had felt when Sir Thomas had died, before he had seen his grandson, before he had known that Kilbree and Spring Mount both had heirs. And Tom glanced very briefly at the ring he wore himself, the gold and emerald Sturbridge family ring, with its ancient crest still ornate and only faintly worn from long use. He remembered that someone had taken it from Sir Thomas' dead hand and placed it on his own. He had recoiled at the realization of what it meant: his father was dead, the ring, the title, the estates now belonged to him. One day this ring would be passed on to little Robert Sturbridge, his son, but that other ring, the ring which Ian wore, that would belong to Michael, Sheila's son, Ian's son. It was as much a symbol of love and family and tradition as the one made of precious gold. Ian's ring was steel, a satiny gleaming steel, carved all in one piece and thick all about but especially at the front where it had been shaped into a smooth flat square. It was carved large, to fit a man's finger, but it had been made for a boy. . . .

3   Kilbree, 1662, A Ring of Steel

"Will this ring truly be Tom's one day?" Ian had asked when he was twelve and Tom was not quite thirteen. They were in Sir Thomas' cool, book-lined study at Kilbree House in Ireland. The boys had been taking turns trying on the Sturbridge ring. Tom had played with it before and after enjoying the brilliant green light flashing from its emerald stone as he held it up to the morning sunlight, he had handed it to Ian and amused himself by spinning his father's globe of the world in its wooden stand near the desk.

Sir Thomas, never too busy to spend time with the boys, looked up with a smile from his account books, to catch sight of Tom twirling the globe with great concentration. He was about to say something when he noticed Ian wearing his ring, carefully holding up his small hand so that it would not slip off. Sir Thomas kept his silence, curious as the changing expressions in the boy's face. Ian's light blue eyes widened as he twisted his hand first this way, then that, watching the flashing light dart about the room. He had smiled at the beauty of the thing, but then the smile had faded fast and a look of sadness had appeared in its place. His young voice had been wistful when he had ventured to ask the question, would the ring truly belong to his friend, Tom, one day? Sir Tom pondered Ian's expression. Did he envy Tom such a handsome ring? Did he understand and envy all that possessing it would mean?

But there had not been the slightest touch of envy on Ian's face that day, nor even the realization of the probable value of the ring. Instead, there was a look of infinite loss, a terrible grasp of what was irreplacable and Sir Thomas understood it at once. It was not the ring itself, but rather the idea behind it, the notion of something handed down from father to son, a symbol of loving and solid continuity. This was what Ian understood of the ring. This was what he longed to possess of it. What had his own dead father been able to leave to him but a noble memory and an estate burned and lying in ruins after Cromwell and his assassins had finished their bloody-handed work in Ireland?

Suddenly Sir Thomas rose up from his desk. He went swiftly to the mantel across the room, reached up and took down his old sword that went wherever he went, the sword he had first carried into battle as a very young man. He seized the old sword with a frim grip, looked at it with a fierce eye, then thrust it into his belt. The startled boys would have questioned his actions but he swooped down on them the next moment, took them each by a hand and swept them out of doors without a word of explanation.

Down the stone walk behind Kilbree House the three of them went, the boys running in an effort to keep up with Sir Thomas' long-legged, military stride. Out through the garden, past the duck pond, across the wide green lawns they hurried, and they did not stop until they had come to the stables where the blacksmith's shed stood. Only then would Sir Thomas let them go as he called out:

"Freyne! Jack Freyne! Blacksmith, come at once and get your fire blazing good and hot!"

The startled blacksmith appeared in the doorway of his shed gazing in some alarm from the two boys to his master and back again.

"A fire, sir? Is it a fire yer wantin', Sir Thomas? Is there maybe a horse that wants shoein' or the like?"

"No horse, Jack," bellowed Sir Thomas with a hearty laugh. "Something more important. Hurry up, Jack, it won't take long."

Tom and Ian, red in the face and out of breath, stood and watched as the blacksmith piled new chunks of peat into his open fire until it blazed up, all glowing and ruddy, and Sir Thomas told him what was wanted.

"A ring," Sir Thomas said, "a good, plain ring, a big ring for a man, mind you, Jack. A soldier's ring."

"A ring, yer Honour?" Jack Freyne had scratched his red head and squinted his eyes and looked most perplexed. "And what am I to make this ring of, then?"

"Not gold nor silver," said Sir Thomas. "Nor precious jewels."

"Not gold nor silver nor jewels neither," echoed the blacksmith. "Then what, sir?"

Sir Thomas drew the fine old sword from his belt and handed it to Freyne.

"You'll make a ring of steel, Jack," he said, and there was a sort of thunder hiding somewhere in his deep, resonant voice. It awed the two boys and they looked at one another big-eyed, almost scared.

"Melt down this sword and forge me a signet ring, Jack, flat and square across the top, for the lettering."

The blacksmith took the sword into his hands and, looking it over, trying the razor edge of it with his thumb, he clucked his tongue in disapproval.

" 'Tis a shame, such a fine weapon as this! Couldn't yer Honour send for a bit of steel, if steel's what ye want, from over there in Sheffield, maybe? There'll be an awful waste, one ring only. Sure why don't we wait and see . . . ?"

"Freyne!" Sir Thomas rarely raised his voice but he had done so that day, and the hidden thunder of it seemed to roar out into the open at last. "Make me the ring. At once!"

The blacksmith said not another word but set about his business. The boys watched in fascination as the sword slowly heated white-hot and the steel began to melt like so much butter. Freyne caught every drop of the molten metal into a thick, heavy iron mold, then quickly poured off a small amount onto his anvil. He set the mold aside and began to apply his hammer, working the steel on the anvil into a rough, flat strip. In a few moments he picked up the strip with a pair of heavy tongs and twisted the end of it about until they touched. Then into the fire he thrust the small circlet of steel, out again, and, with a smaller, lighter hammer, he pounded the two ends together, forging them into one solid, continuous ring. Into the fire once more it went. The boys jumped back as the red sparks flew up before their eyes. Then out again and into a pail of cool water, hissing and steaming, the surface of the water all roiled and bubbling from the great heat.

It did not seem to have taken any great length of time for the ring to be made, yet a couple of hours had gone by when Freyne and Sir Thomas agreed at last that the thing was done. Freyne let his fire burn down low and unattended while he took the ring outside the shed, into the afternoon sunlight. He kept an assortment of files about him and now he carefully polished the ring smooth, holding it up to the light every few moments to inspect it.

And then Sir Thomas seemed to remember that Ian and Tom were there. They had been sitting patiently on the grass, their eyes fixed on every move Jack Freyne made and neither of them had said a word. Sir Thomas took the ring and held it close so they might look at it. They stared at it and at him, waiting for an explanation. But he merely handed the ring back to the blacksmith and instructed him still further.

"Now I want you to carve the date into it, Jack," he said. "The year only, mind. This year. Put the '16' on the left side, along the circle there, and the '62' in the same place on the right. And in the square on top, put three initials: I, C, and I again. Make them plain and large, Jack, nothing fancy."

" 'I, C, I' yer Honour?" repeated Freyne, setting to work once more. He attached the ring to the edge of his wooden work table with a small clamp and began to strike in the date with hammer and chisel.

"Yes, that's it," nodded Sir Thomas. "ICI. For 'Ian Curtis Ives'."

"*My* name? Is that ring to be mine, then?" Ian stared at his smiling guardian in astonishment.

"Indeed it is, my boy," said Sir Thomas. "It is a special kind of ring, Ian, just as special in its own way as that signet ring of mine you were looking at this morning. I want you to wear it always, just as I wear mine, just as my father wore it when he was alive and as Tom will wear it after me. And someday, when you are very, very old, years from now, then you must give your ring to someone else, someone whom you care for very much."

"To my son, do you mean, sir?" blinked Ian, quite overwhelmed with the whole notion.

Sir Thomas' face crinkled into a broad smile. "Well, yes, it might be your son. But it needn't be, you know. I am giving it to you and you are not my own son. I want you to have this ring because I am as proud of you, Ian, as I am of Tom, here. And I know that your poor father, if he were here with us now, would be just as proud of the man you are growing to be. Your father died defending his country and his home. He could not have left you any finer inheritance than the memory of his courage. In his memory, then, I ask you now, Ian, boy though you are, to keep this ring and to wear it with courage, and give it only to one who will bring it honour."

Ian's face was very bright, but suddenly he glanced at Tom and shook his head uncertainly.

"What is it, Ian?" demanded Sir Thomas.

"That sword, sir," stammered Ian, flushing. "It was very old. Wasn't it to be Tom's sword one day, too? Like the gold ring?"

Sir Thomas looked squarely at his son then, a question in his clear, wise eyes. Tom felt at that moment that he had never loved his father so much in all his short life. There was no doubt in Sir Thomas' gaze, no smallest fear that his son would fail to demonstrate the kind and generous heart he had displayed since early childhood.

"I shall have a sword of my own when I am a soldier, Ian," Tom had replied instantly. "And so shall you. I'm glad that you've got a ring now, too, just like mine."

"Just like!" muttered the blacksmith, tapping the letters carefully into the steel. "Steel, that's all it is! Only steel."

Tom had thought his father would be angry then, but Sir Thomas only laughed at the ignorant man's careless words.

"Yes, steel!" he cried. "Steel, indeed. The sword it was made from has been carried into battle for nearly three hundred years and every man who wore it and used it, I think, was an honourable man, a man who believed in high principles and tried his best to live up to those principles. The Great God Almighty tells us: '...they shall beat their swords into plowshares...' Well, Ian, I doubt the world is ready just yet to live entirely at peace with itself, but perhaps we have made some sort of beginning here, beating *our* sword into a ring, at least. Whatever you do when you wear it, promise me that you will try to be brave and bold, and honourable. Can you do that, Ian Ives?"

But Ian could only nod his head, unable to give voice to the strong feelings in his heart. Jack Freyne shrugged off all the rich talk he was hearing and handed Sir Thomas the finished ring.

"Yes, that's what I wanted, exactly, Jack. I.C.I. A fine signet, isn't it, Ian?"

And then Tom piped up. "ICI. That's a French word, isn't it, Father? It means 'here', I think. Yes, 'here, in this place', something like that."

Sir Thomas looked up with a light in his eyes, and ran his finger softly over the deeply chiseled letters. "You're right, Tom. I never thought of it. 'Ici', here, in this place...indeed, my lads, we've got more than a handsome set of initials. We've got ourselves as good a motto as any great house in Europe. Here, in this place...I stand and I will not be moved from it. Here I make my fight, here I live or die for what I believe in. Take it now, Ian Ives, from my hand, in your father's place...."

4 I Heard My Name In The Wind

" 'Be brave, and bold, and honourable'," Ian was saying now, as the wind from France scattered the ashes of their fire, as he sat twisting the steel ring around and around on his finger. The ring fitted him well now, fitted the hand of the man, the soldier, for whom it had been made. "He was a grand man, your father, Tom. I suppose he would be here himself tonight if he still lived. God, I remember what ideas he had about your country and about mine . . . what they might be, what they ought to be, what we lads must grow up and fight to *make* them be!"

"Ian . . ." Tom began, and then he stopped. Ian looked at him for a short moment, a sad half smile on his lips, and he shook his head slowly. . . .

"I want you to have this ring, Tom," he said softly. "No, don't say anything, hear me out. All this night I've been listening for something, a thing I know you can't hear and I'm glad you can't. I went and stood by the horses before and when they knew it was me coming to them, they tossed their heads and I could see their big eyes rolling and their flanks quivering when I touched them. With the wind's rising I thought I heard my name called out, as loud and clearly as though whoever was calling was just behind me and I could see them if I turned around. . . ."

"Ian, for God's sakes. . . ." cried Tom. But Ian only smiled a bit and continued speaking more loudly, his voice overriding Tom's words. . . .

"I didn't turn around to look, Tom. I knew what it was, then. And I know very well, when I do look it in the face it will be the end of me. The hours have crept along, Tom, and I can still hear my name tossing about in that cold wind. Take the ring, now, take it from my living hand, will you, for I swear to you on the graves of both our fathers . . . I will not live through this battle!"

Tom stared sickly at Ian's outstretched hand, his open palm holding the ring lightly, waiting. Tom shook his head violently, and deliberately looked away.

"You bloody Irish!" he gasped. "You're all mad, every damn one of you! Voices in the wind . . . put that ring back on and shut up, will you? Will you, Ian!"

But, just then, the moon crept behind a black mountain of a cloud and the wind blew a mournful wailing shrillness across Sedgemoor Plain. Tom shuddered. "God, Ian, stop this!" he looked at his friend pleadingly. But Ian's eyes were distant, his attention focused on something else. And the steel ring still remained in the palm of his hand.

"Ian, everyone feels he's going to die on a night like this," Tom tried to be reasonable now, but he saw at once it was no use. If only he might distract Ian, get his mind on something else. "Ian, think of Sheila. She needs you with her. Think of that baby you've got coming. You have to see that child, Ian . . . and there's Elizabeth . . . you said yourself both you and Sheila haven't even set eyes on my daughter . . . maybe you'll have a little girl this time, have you thought of that? A beautiful little girl with red hair, just like her mother. . . ." Tom's words trailed off miserably. His heart sank, he knew of nothing to say, nothing to do. He glanced over at Ian, expecting to find him still staring off across the moor. Instead, Ian was watching him, his eyes full of sympathy.

"You'll have to look after Sheila now, Tom. Sheila and the little ones. Take care of her, Tom, she's not strong. She's too little herself for bearing children. . . . I'm leaving them all to you, God help you. But you'll know the right things to do, just like your father. You're very like him, you know, Tom?"

Tom sighed heavily. There seemed no way to reach Ian now. He could only sit and listen and pray as he had never prayed before that Ian was wrong. He had to be wrong. Surely men died in battles, but this fight that was coming, hardly a real battle, merely a skirmish it would prove to be, a few rounds fired, rebels dropping their weapons and running away from the troops. . . .

"I know she will be in good hands, Tom," Ian went on. "You've always loved her, haven't you?"

Tom started, but Ian only smiled his gentle, distant smile.

"How could you not love her?" he said simply. "How could any man who saw her, who knew her, not love Sheila? It has been the wonder of my life that she chose me instead of you. . . ."

"She . . . she loves you," Tom's words were coming slow and hard. The realization that Ian knew of his love for Sheila shocked him, not only because he had tried unsuccessfully to keep the truth from his dearest friend, but more so because Tom realized that Ian would never have spoken of it to his dying day . . . and he spoke of it now. "She's always loved you, Ian," he stressed hurriedly. "Anyone could have seen that when we were still children."

58

"And you never begrudged me her love, I knew that too," Ian said. "'Twas a cruel hell you wandered into, Tom."

"You've made her happy," murmured Tom.

"Yes," said Ian. "We've been happy. Remind her of that, Tom. And now, will you take the ring? I want you to have it."

"It belongs to Michael, not me," Tom insisted. "Save it and give it to your son."

"My son," mused Ian, sighing a bit. "I hardly know my son. A man doesn't get to know his son these first few years, I think. A little red-faced bundle always being carried about in his nurse's arms, a mite of a puppy scampering underfoot—" he chuckled fondly—"He will not remember me, I think. I had so much I was saving to tell him, to teach him. You'll have to do that now, Tom. I hope your Robert and my Michael will be friends like we were. . . ."

"We *are*," stressed Tom. Ian nodded, leaning over and clapping a hand on Tom's shoulder.

"Aye, we are, are we not? From the beginning. And that's why the ring must go to you. Remember, your father said I should choose the one to wear it. *You* wear it, Tom, for the sake of our friendship. Someday you can give it away, if you like. Don't wait till you're dead and gone and someone takes it from your finger. Let it be a living gift, just as I give it to you now, tonight. Give it to your son . . . or mine, if you want. Give it to the one who needs it most, the one who will wear it best. When things have been hard with me, I've often looked at it on my finger there and thought of your father and of you and all those 'men of high principles,' he called them, who carried the steel in it with them through sore troubles and high times, too. I've thought of what he said and sometimes . . . maybe because I'm Irish, as you say . . . but sometimes I've felt a bit of all that old honour and courage . . . and pride, too . . . come to touch me when I needed it most, through this ring. Will you take it now, Tom?"

Silently Tom held out his hand and felt the heavy ring pass from Ian's fingers to his own and, perhaps it was only a fancy, but he thought he could feel the warmth of Ian's hand still on the steel. He put the ring on the middle finger of his right hand and looked at it.

"Here," he said, "in this place. . . ."

"Live or die, I make my fight," added Ian quietly. "I feel better now, my friend, thank you for doing what I asked."

Suddenly Tom jumped to his feet, unable to bear the strain between them any longer.

"I only took the ring to humour you, Ian, remember that!" he cried, forcing a lightness into his voice which he certainly did not feel. "I'll wear it, I'll keep it now, since you insist . . . and I'll have the pleasure of handing it back to you tomorrow night when we've chased Monmouth back to Taunton and we're toasting an easy victory over a bottle of Canary!"

Ian smiled up at him and stretched out on the ground, tucking the folds of his cloak underneath his head for a makeshift pillow against the dampness. He said nothing more, though Tom would have led the talk upon less ominous paths. Several times, pacing up and down quite restlessly now, Tom asked a question or remarked upon how cold the night was growing, but Ian seemed to have fallen asleep. And, finally, Tom stopped pacing and stood there, looking down at him as he lay there so quietly, the moonlight making a golden frame of the thick fair curls about his face, a look of peace upon his features for the first time that long, long night.

What nonsense, Tom was thinking as he watched Ian sleep, how many of us have these premonitions of death and live on to be ninety! I *will* give him back the ring tomorrow . . . and I'll never let him live it down. But, the thought struck home, what if Ian was right?

He threw his head back and drew in a long cold breath. Listen as hard as he could, he heard no words called in the wind blowing so lonely now across the plain at Sedgemoor. And, at length, Tom Sturbridge lay down across from his friend, wrapped his cloak about him and slept, as the moon fled towards day and the white mists hovered, hiding the black breast of the land.

The night awoke in a shout! The voices of six thousand terrified charging men carried across Sedgemoor like the scream of one monstrous war creature invented in some mad alchemist's dark cell. The tethered, nervous horses, so strangely silent all though the evening, now reared and bucked in their terror, their inarticulate voices mingling in answer to the varied battle cries filling the cold damp air.

Monmouth's rebels had not waited for dawn to start their attack. Few of them possessed horses, indeed, few of them even knew how to manage a horse at all. And, as Ian had speculated, their hastily assigned officers had directed them to gain as much of the field as they could under cover of darkness, then, upon a signal cry, to spring to their feet and attack the sleeping camp. Surprise and dark night would carry all, Monmouth had been advised. The sparseness of wood on the plain had seemed to aid his plans. The soldiers' fires had died out early and could not be replenished. The very mists of the marshland had offered cover and protection to the untrained volunteers creeping so slowly, so carefully, almost on their faces in the cold mud, close and closer still, while the gun crews chatted idly or gambled on the mucky ground or slept beside their great wheeled charges. . . .

But Monmouth's men, for all they knew the countryside to the south and west, the lands about Taunton and Bridgwater and further to the north, around Bath and Frome, did not know Sedgemoor Plain.

They did not know of the wide and treacherous, mud-filled, slippery-sided ditch, that little "Rhine" behind which Feversham had placed his field pieces. The few officers of experience who had accompanied Monmouth back to England, had no illusions as to the probably fate of that first wave of men they ordered into the Royalist midst. Some one thousand or fifteen hundred presented the initial attack: not one man in four was armed even with so much as a snaphance pistol or a fowling piece. Many of them carried home-made pikes, thirteen feet long with sharpened iron heads and some had only pitchforks and workaxes for weapons. They had no sergeants to keep an eye on them, nor were any officers among them, they did not know they were but the cheap kindling of the fire of battle, sent on to start up the blaze, no more.

Yet they did rise up, upon the signal for which they waited, and they shouted themselves hoarse as they ran upon the startled soldiers scrambling hastily to their feet, reaching about for their own weapons in great confusion. Those encamped along the outer lines were trapped where they were by the onrushing force; many were thrust through throat or breast even as they lay sleeping by their dead fires, and never knew the battle had begun and, for them, already ended.

Feversham had kept the Household Cavalry close by their horses and, although roundly cursed by the men and officers alike, had insisted that the horses be left fully saddled and harnessed, planning as he had for a first light of dawn attack. Upon hearing the first sounds of battle, the Cavalry mounted up in quick and orderly fashion. There was now no question of a direct frontal charge. Instead, they split apart into two units, each riding around the far sides of the ditch to attack the enemy's flanks.

The gun crews were at their posts in a moment, but they received no orders to fire yet, for the range was too close, the ranks of the attacking rabble too thinly spread out to make for an effective barrage.

Tom heard men's voices in the distance and the frantic sound of the horses and, even as he jumped to his feet, instantly wide awake, he saw the Cavalry ride by, shouting to the Dragoons that it had started.

Ian, too, was on his feet in a minute. All about them, their men fell quickly into formation, the long line three men deep, armed with flintlock muskets, their sergeants shouting orders and each man's eye watching the raised steel-headed halberds in the sergeants' hands. Where those long, deadly spear-ended axes went, the men would follow even when the din of battle prevented their hearing an order to attack or to fall back.

"You were right," Tom said briefly. Ian flashed him a quick grin and then was gone, far to the right somewhere, a tall broad figure striding before the line of troops, two fine screw-barrelled pistols in his belt and his sword already drawn. Ian seemed to disappear into the darkness for an instant, then a brilliant scarlet flash lit up the ground and Tom saw him, standing, talking to his men. A sound like a volcano erupting, smoke enough to choke the lungs, and the big guns began firing at last, volley after volley as the enemy had finally been spotted. Well trained gun crews, men apart and special, second only to the Engineers in self-esteem and general respect prided themselves on being able to do more than merely ram a cannon ball down the gaping throat of a twenty-four pounder and fire it out into the massed ranks of an approaching enemy. The trick was to load the gun with special shells, made in the shape of iron spheres and filled with a charge of powder. A tapered wooden fuse filled with a quick burning powder was driven into a hole in the shell just before firing. The flash of the powder charge firing the shell lit this fuse, and gunners tried for a ricochet shot, causing a shell to land, bounce and roll along through the line of attacking troops. As it rolled, the wooden fuse burned and then exploded, sometimes in the very midst of them, sometimes just before their front line. . . .

The rebels, surrounded by bursting shells, seeing their friends and brothers fall, screaming, all around them, broke and ran like the green, unseasoned troop they were. Cheering broke out along the line of guns and the firing stopped abruptly. No need to waste ammunition on scattering crows. The battle was not over yet. Monmouth still had the large part of his army in reserve and, among them, some few seasoned veterans who could look down the throat of roaring cannon and keep right on marching forward.

They had not long to wait for the second part of the attack. A few mounted cavalry, leading behind them a loosely formed but fairly cohesive line, was seen coming in from the north. Those men who had turned and run, seeing support on the way, turned round again and fell in with their fresh troops to join the attack. They were still two thousand yards away; up and down the artillery line, the officers held off the signal to begin firing again, waiting till the last possible moment.

Tom had lead his men forward until they passed their own guns and fanned out, still fairly close together. He stopped their advance then, thinking to wait until they had the cover of an artillery barrage. And at once he saw the difficulty: no foot soldiers could possibly get close enough together to engage in hand to hand fighting. The ditch served as a natural redoubt. He heard his name called, turned, and saw Kirke frantically waving him back. He turned the men about and they moved well behind the guns again, swearing in disgust. Kirke rode over to him, shaking his head with the same disgust.

"Mount up the Dragoons," Kirke told him. "The best you can do now is ride out after the Cavalry and route those fools. This is no battle . . . we'll all be executioners, that's all!"

Tom and thirty officers of the Dragoons mounted up and rode out after the Cavalry, their horses reluctantly slipping and sliding their way across the ditch and up its steep, treacherous sides. As they were at full gallop, then, the guns began their deadly chorus behind them and they could see Monmouth's army halt in the field and seem to look about uncertainly. Suddenly, several of them fell to the ground and the others looked to their flanks, as the household rode upon them hard and heavy, firing as they came. But this time the rebels did not turn and run, instead they stolidly closed ranks and began to move forward once again, into the ever more accurate range of those deadly cannon.

As Tom's men rode in to join the Cavalry, he saw that Monmouth had left his rear flanking forces behind to contain the Cavalry, hopefully while the main body moved on. These men had muskets and some of them pistols as well, but they were not used to working together and they were no match for a full cavalry charge. Once the first round of musket fire had done its work, the hideous triangular bayonets presented a terrifying wall of oncoming steel. In another moment, Tom was in the midst of the charge himself. Armed only with a sword he rode straight into the solid ranks of them and saw their upturned, frozen faces, their mouths open, screaming, as they were run down by the horses, trampled under those hard, chopping hoofs.

Tom had ridden through the line, wheeled his horse about and started back again. As he turned, he saw eight or nine of the rebels close on his heels. He pulled up sharply to avoid the spears they awkwardly thrust at him as they ran at him and looked about quickly, calling for fire support from the musketmen. But he was quite cut off from the others, Dragoons and Cavalry and even as he realized his situation, the horse he rode uttered a ghastly strangled shriek, lurched unsteadily and collapsed. Tom barely avoided being crushed under the beast's enormous body. He went down with it but managed to pull his leg over and across the saddle quickly, finding himself hard on the ground, sword somehow still miraculously in his hand, and the rebels fast closing in on him.

He tried to get up, slipped in the horse's hot fresh blood, grasped backwards at the pummel of his saddle to steady himself and tried again. Seven or eight men came lunging at him, thrusting bayonets as they came on. He thought to himself it was ridiculous, it was impossible odds, even while he parried the bayonets as best he could with his sword . . . and suddenly the sword broke clean in two, the end flying off somewhere out of sight. The rebels, their eyes gleaming whitely, sweat streaming down their frightened, hopeful faces, lunged forward. He felt the bayonets sliding along the sword hilt he still held, and felt their murderous sharp edges scaling his fingers to the bone. He stared down for a second, watching the blood pouring from his hand, and almost laughed, wondering why he still held the useless broken sword in his torn fingers. . . .

And then a bayonet pierced his right thigh and another, going deeper, struck him through to the hip bone. He fell down again, his legs sprawled helplessly in front of him, and watched as one of the rebel force ran up to his fellows waving a cavalry musket he had just taken from the body of a dead soldier. The fellow stopped when he saw them ringed about Tom, silently contemplating him, their bayonets and spears still poised, their faces puzzled now, as if they wondered what to do with him.

The man with the musket in his hand looked about at them as if he could not believe his eyes.

"Kill him!" he kept shouting at the others. A couple of them made a half-hearted start forward, spears pointed directly at Tom's chest and stomach. He lay back against the horse's body, his arms flung out at either side, and contemplated them, waiting to be killed. But, it seemed, they could not bring themselves to finish him there, like that, helpless and, to their minds, as good as dead already. The man with the musket spat angrily, then pointed the weapon at Tom's head. Tom watched with great interest as the man bit off a piece of the paper cartridge, then poured a bit of gunpowder from it into the frizzen pan of the musket and the rest of the powder down the barrel. He rammed home the musket ball and the wadded up cartridge paper, moving very precisely, very carefully, very smoothly. He was well trained, Tom judged. He was giddy now, his head swam, and he felt his hands and feet go quite cold. Yet he did keep on watching the movements of the man with the musket and, he noted calmly, it was now pointed directly at him once again. The flint was in place, the cock pulled back against the spring. . . . Tom closed his eyes and tried to think of a prayer. He thought, instead, of his father, and he heard the shot go off and braced himself to take the ball full on. . . .

He felt nothing, nothing whatever. Around him the rebels screamed . . . . he heard horses pounding the earth very close . . . he struggled against the longing to drift off into sleep and opened his eyes again. The man with the musket lay crumpled on the earth himself, a large uneven hole in his forehead. The musket had fallen from his hands and was still unfired. Five of his own Dragoons rode on past him, chasing the rest of the rebels. One of the young Dragoons quickly closed in behind a fleeing boy no more than fifteen, who carried a pike and seemed to have forgotten he had it at all. The Dragoon rode up alongside the boy and, leaning over out of his saddle, caught him across the back of the neck with a strong, steady swing of his sword.

The last thing Tom Sturbridge remembered of the Battle of Sedgemoor was the sight of that boy's body suddenly jerking upward, like a puppet with its strings first pulled crazily taut and then quickly released to fall in a limp heap. The hapless boy raised his arm as though he would try to pull the gaping wound closed with his hand, the forgotten, useless pike flying off to one side, and then, as he realized it was all over for him, he uttered a long, drawn-out wail of anguish and fell, letting Death have its inevitable way.

Tom fainted then, and did not see the end of the battle. He did not see the farmers and the miners stand their ground valiantly while the roaring, puffing, crouched and leaping cannon slaughtered them where they stood. Nor did Tom see the remnants of that pitiful army chased through the countryside and picked off two or three at a time, like so many flushed pheasants in a meadow. He did not know that Monmouth himself had fled the field.

5 After The Battle

When Tom regained his senses, it was evening. The air was still fetid and heavy with the stink of gunpowder and sulphur. He found himself lying underneath a broad shade tree on a gentle rise of grass. He could not be sure, but he thought someone had put something warm under his body, perhaps a blanket or his own cloak. He could not immediately recall whether he wore the cloak or not when he went into the battle.

No matter. He felt warm enough and very thirsty. He shifted restlessly, and was amazed to find that he could not feel his right hand or his right leg, either. He struggled up, leaning on the left elbow and suddenly felt a pain so frightful that he cried aloud from the sheer shock of it. Yet, at the same time, he was glad to feel it; he looked down the length of his body and saw that the leg was still there. He forced himself to see the pain through, to wait until he became accustomed to it. In fact he quite gave himself up to the pain, to gauge its full extent, what it would do to him, if he could remain conscious despite it, before he tried to move again. He stayed leaning on his elbow until his head had cleared a little. And then he looked around.

He was lying in a long row of wounded men. Down at the far end of the row he could see the surgeons and their assistants. Near them, moving down the line, a few volunteer orderlies were bringing water to those who were able to take it. Across from him there were more rows of soldiers. For a moment, he wondered why no one seemed to be paying any attention to them, until he noticed how still they lay. Many were covered over with blankets or cloaks and even those who had no such covering had their faces, at least, overspread with their jaunty scarlet coats. They were the dead, he realized. He saw several bodies with the brass helmets of the Light Dragoons placed upon their still, unmoving breasts. He turned away, his throat suddenly constricting, only to have his glance fall upon the wide green field beyond the trees. There were several people moving about the field, a few wagons picking up the rebel dead and wounded, women hurrying from one body to another, seeking out their own. Their distant cries of grief mingled with the low groans of the wounded all around him.

"Water, Captain?" inquired a youthful voice by his side. Tom looked up swiftly, then vowed to move his head more slowly next time, as his senses swam sickly. He nodded gratefully and the young fellow bent down to hold a tin of water to his dry lips.

"Yer a'goin' to be fine, sir," smiled the soldier. "I heard the Colonel a'talkin' to the doctor when they brought you in."

"What about . . . what about Monmouth?" Tom whispered, his voice barely croaking out the sounds.

The soldier stood up again, grinning, and nodded towards the green field.

"He run off, that's what they're a'sayin', anyways. We kept on shootin' at them and we killed a lot of 'em, but nobody's caught up with the Bastard yet. We'll get him, sir, don't fret yer eyes about *him*!"

Tom smiled shakily and lay back again, content to rest and think that it was all over now and he could go home again. He found that he was able to lift his right hand if he did not try to do it too quickly. They had bandaged up his torn fingers tightly. He stared at the bandages and promised himself that he would have them changed and the wound cleaned frequently. He must begin to move and exercise the fingers as soon as possible or the hand would become useless.

He lifted his left hand then and held it in front of him, placing it just beside his right. And the first thing he noticed was the Sturbridge ring, gleaming gold and flashing green. He had always worn it on his right hand. Someone had removed it and put it on the left. He was surprised and pleased to see it, knowing how thoroughly the wounded were stripped of all valuables by battlefield looters and scavengers.

And then his eye lit upon the ring next to his own, the ring upon the middle finger of his left hand. It pressed, massive and unfamiliar around his finger, a heavy band of dully glinting steel and the letters carved into it, "I.C.I."

Tom stared at the steel ring and laughed aloud, ignoring the fierce tide of pain that ripped through him. He looked at that ring, smiling, remembering that ridiculous conversation he had with Ian. When had it been? Only last night, he thought. Ian and his voices calling in the wind! Then, abruptly, Tom's little snort of amusement turned into a sharp gasp and the prayer he had been searching for hours earlier now came unbidden and quite naturally into his mind.

"God, grant that I live true and when it comes, that I face whatever death Thou shall send me with courage and with grace!"

But, he hadn't been killed out there! It was all over and he was still alive! Now he must see Ian, that great donkey, and give him back his ring!

He drifted off into sleep, still smiling to himself, and when he awoke again, it was dark. All around him he could hear the stifled sighs and moans of men in pain. Soldiers with lanterns passed along the lines of the wounded, carrying crude wooden staves and stones. Here and there they paused to hammer one of the staves into the soft earth and then they hung a lantern upon it, a flicker of light in the oppressive darkness.

Tom was feeling much worse now. He lay very still and stared up at the distant stars, wondering why Ian was not there. He flexed the fingers of his left hand. Both of the rings were still where they had been. So, Ian had not come by to see him as he slept. If he had, Tom was positive, he would have taken back his own ring himself. Where the devil was Ian, then?

A lantern moved slowly down the line, quiet voices talking as it swayed along, pausing briefly beside each wounded man. The surgeon was coming around to tell them that the wagons would be along soon and they would be taken into town, to warm rooms and soft beds.

"How are you feeling, Captain Sturbridge? Thought we'd lost you there for a bit!"

Tom looked up and saw that Colonel Kirke had accompanied the surgeon. Kirke smiled down at him. Tom noticed that his left arm was bandaged and bound up in a makeshift sling.

"Oh, I'll manage, sir," he said, his tongue thick and dry in his mouth. "But what's become of Ives? I thought he'd be here by now."

Kirke looked away, clearing his throat. "Ives? I haven't seen Captain Ives since the first charge this morning. Didn't he ride out with you, Sturbridge?"

Tom frowned, trying to remember. "No, I don't think so, sir. He may have gone out on the other flank, though, once we ordered back the infantry. Could you find out for me sir? I . . . I've got something of his that he'll be wanting back."

Kirke bent over and patted Tom's shoulder gently. "Don't worry, that Irishman can take care of himself. But I will inquire, I promise you, and as soon as we find him we'll send him to you." Then he moved on down the line quickly. The surgeon stopped to inspect the bandages on Tom's right leg, nodded to his assistants and followed Kirke. Evidently there was nothing to do now but wait for Ian. But hours passed and Ian did not come. A few wagons arrived. Tom insisted that they take some of the other wounded men before him. He would just as soon wait a bit longer.

He had developed a fever by this time and had to argue mightily to persuade them to leave him behind, but when he began to shout and thrash about, they calmed him as best they could and agreed he might stay, but only until they had unloaded in town and come back again. Tom quieted down at once. Surely Ian would have come back by then. Surely.

6 Here, In This Place

It was four o'clock in the morning and Ian had not come. Kirke had returned twice, each time reporting that no one had seen Ives all day. He sent a detachment of men out, finally, to search through the woods and fields, but the men were exhausted themselves and the search was slow, hampered by darkness and unfamiliar terrain. Kirke was still waiting for them to return and report to him. But now he had no smile, no sure, confident words to give Tom.

And Tom, whose fever soared, was killing angry with Ian by now. *When he does finally get his bloody arse here I'm going to beat his head in for him!* Tom kept saying it over and over to himself and sometimes aloud. When Kirke went away the last time, however, he realized that he must do something about Ian himself.

Maybe they'll never find him, Tom thought incoherently. He spent the better part of half an hour manoeuvering in the darkness, moving slowly, very slowly, until he had got his left knee under him, with his good left arm pushing on the ground for support. The entire right side of his body seemed made out of red-hot lead, burning with pain and heavy-dragging. But he kept at it gamely until at last he stood up on both feet, wavering about like a drunken man, his left arm flailing helplessly as he sought something to hold on to. As he stood there swaying, the young soldier who had given him the water hours ago, spotted him and came running.

"Oh, my God, sir! Oh, my God, yer can't do that! You'll kill yerself sure!"

"I've *done* it, soldier," murmured Tom dryly. "Now, shut up and find me a stick, something I can lean on. Hurry up. Anything will do."

The boy ran off again and for a moment Tom believed that he had only gone to fetch back the surgeon. But the lad returned, carrying a glowing lantern in one hand and a stout length of wood in the other. He had pulled up one of the light posts they had only recently set out. Tom grabbed the piece of wood from him and leaned his weight upon it. . . . good, it held. It was longer than a cane, more like a staff or shepherd's crook and would bear him up as long as he managed to stay pretty well balanced. He gritted his teeth and swung his good leg out before him, leaving the burden for some seconds upon the doubly wounded right side. Bile rose in his throat and there came a roaring sound into his ears but he did not lose consciousness. As quickly as he could, he dragged the right leg up and, exhausted by this one wretched step, he clung to the rude staff, perspiration streaming down his taut face.

"Good, I'll manage it," he murmured, annoyed that the boy simply watched and shook his head doubtfully.

"Listen to me, now," Tom whispered as forcefully as he could, "I want you to go and find my stableman, Jessup is his name. He's an old fellow, about fifty or so, no hair on top and a very round, red face. Jessup," he repeated. "Bring him here to me. He'll be with the horses, I expect. And bring back that lantern, do you understand?"

The boy went off on the run, holding his lantern before him so he could see in the moonless night. Tom lost sight of him almost at once. He had no idea how long the boy would take on his errand, or even whether Jessup himself was still alive. But enough time had been lost already. He steadied himself and took another step with the staff. He found quickly that he would do much better to lead off with the wounded leg instead of the other way around. It was almost useless, could not be bent an inch. . . . he cursed the slowness of his movement as he crept by inches along the ground but hurrying any faster rendered the pain powerful enough to overcome him completely. Still, he did not stop again as he dragged his way past four or five other men lying on the grass. Once he thought to call out Ian's name very loudly, with the notion that someone else might have seen him, might know what had become of him. But the shout he raised was barely audible, and no one answered him. A part of his mind hammered wildly at him to lie down again, before he bled to death. He could not tell whether the leg was bleeding or not; he had mercifully still been unconscious when they had pressed the white-hot searing iron against his wounds that afternoon, to cauterize them. But he refused to think about his leg, now. Stubbornly, madly, he moved forward, looking for Ian. He believed that if anything were to stop him now, even for an instant, he would fall and not get up again. He must not let that happen. Somewhere out there, Ian waited for him.

By now, Tom had admitted to himself it was likely Ian had been wounded, too. The total force was far from accounted for even now; he had known engagements when search parties continued bringing in the wounded for days afterwards. Yes, that was it, Ian had been wounded. He must have mounted up and ridden off along the left flank that morning, why he might be miles away right now, waiting. . . . the thought of such a distance plagued Tom as he struggled along. He did not think he could ride, even if he were to be lifted onto the horse and tied into the saddle. But, he could send Jessup . . . devil take the man, where was he?

"Captain Sturbridge? Where are you, Captain?"

Tom paused for a second. That was not Jessup's voice, it was only the boy back again. He was about to call out when the young fellow came quickly to his side, still carrying his lantern, and quite out of breath.

"I'm sorry to report, Sir," he panted, trying to keep his voice down at the same time, "Mr. Jessup can't join you, he says, he is alive and begs the Captain's pardon, but due to him havin' his arm sliced off above the elbow, they has him bound up to a board to hold him still and he is just at point of bein' loaded into the wagon, sir!"

Tom nodded, trying to think what to do now. Despair filled his heart as he scanned the broad expanse of fields and slopes around him and realized that he had come scarcely a dozen feet.

"Excuse me, sir," the boy's voice startled him. "But, if the

Captain don't lie down and rest pretty soon now, them cuts'll be like to open up again.''

"What's your name, soldier?" Tom demanded.

The boy sighed. "Willy, sir. Ain't yer a'goin' to listen to me, Captain?''

Tom shook his head. "No, Willy, I am not. It seems we must manage without poor Jessup. Very well. Out there somewhere, Willy," he said, lifting his chin to indicate the dark fields, "out there is my friend. I will not leave this place until I have found him. Understand me well, I will *not* leave without him. Now, if you will kindly walk in front of me and hold that lantern high so I can see the way, we will begin to look for him, Willy.''

"Yer killin' yerself, sir, excuse the liberty!" cried Willy in desperation, looking about for the surgeons or for some officer who might help him get Captain Sturbridge in hand. But there was no one. Tom Sturbridge pulled his crippled body a few inches further through the grass, his eyes fixed upon the flat black horizon ahead.

"Come on, Willy-boy!" he cried sharply. Willy swallowed hard and moved a few paces ahead of him, lifting his dim lantern. A faint ruddy circle of light touched the ground just in front of them. Willy moved obediently, deliberately, keeping out of Tom's way, trying to pick out the easiest, most level path to walk. Behind him the Captain was so silent that several times Willy turned his head, expecting to find that his companion had crumpled over. But the Captain was still following, his knuckles white as the fingers clutched the wooden staff, his face a deathly grey, his eyes narrowed and bloodshot. And Willy would look at him pleadingly, but the Captain had no strength in him for argument, only a supernatural will to keep on moving.

He'll faint soon, thought Willy to himself, and he prayed very hard that it would happen quickly. How he would drag the Captain's senseless body all the way back to where they had started he could not imagine for the life of him, but if it did not happen very soon now, the Captain would surely die.

Once they did stop, near a clump of bushes and Tom said Ian's name a few times. But he did not wait to hear any answer. He only moved on again. Willy had a bright thought then. Once he had heard that ghastly scratching voice, he did not want to hear it again if it could be helped.

"Captain, sir," Willy spoke up as they inched along. " 'Twill save yer throat if I was to yell out every now and again, like, and we can keep goin' and listenin' all the while. What do yer say to that? Only tell me the man's name we be seekin', plain and clear."

"Ives," came the awful, hollow croak behind him. "Captain Ives."

"Yes, sir. Captain Ives," repeated Willy. He called out the name into the dark air and marched along, calling out again every few yards. There came back no answer, however. And at length Willy spoke up again.

"Captain, sir, where be we a'goin'? Is there some place yer saw him early in the day, maybe? A spot yer think he'll still be?"

"No, none," whispered Captain Sturbridge. "Keep on. And call out, for God's sake! Call out!" Once more, for the hundredth time, Willy shouted as loudly as he could:

"Captain Ives! Captain Ives, can you hear us? Captain Ives!"

There was no answer. Willy knew there would be none. He walked on. The oil in the lantern was nearly gone when his silent companion groaned suddenly and Willy heard a slight thumping sound behind him. . . .

He's down, now, thought Willy, turning fast. But, no, Captain Sturbridge was still erect. He had stopped moving, half bent over he stood and struck the dark ground about him with the staff in his hand.

"What's this place?" he demanded, a touch of strength returning to his voice. "This ground, Willy, this ground! Tell me! It feels different from the rest, softer, muddier. . . . speak up, boy, tell me where we have come?"

Willy squinted and gazed around him. At first he saw nothing, but then he was able to make out a tiny, barely moving stream up ahead of them.

"Oh, 'tis only a bit of water, Sir, what y'might call a brook. . . ."

"That's why it feels different." Captain Sturbridge seemed to be talking more to himself than to Willy now, so Willy waited and said nothing. "Water. . . . I hadn't seen it from the Plain. Move on, Willy, and hold the lantern lower, shine the light alongside that brook if you can, go slowly now. . . ."

He stayed closer to the boy, now, and insisted that Willy call out Ian's name repeatedly, as they moved cautiously along the edge of the brook. Willy saw nothing unusual, but for some reason, the

Captain became greatly agitated, forcing himself to move faster, and shouting, "Ian! Ian Ives, answer me! Damn you, Ian, speak up if you hear me!"

It was Willy, with the lantern hanging almost to the ground, who spotted him first. Only an odd-seeming shadow lying there in the wisps of reedy grass at the brook's edge, at first just another dark form amongst the rounded rocks by the water.... Willy noticed something and swung the failing light far over to his left. A form, hard to make out, lying half in, half out of the water... he caught his breath harshly and, without saying a word to the Captain, ran ahead, scrambling and slipping on the mossy rocks and mud. A moment later he squatted down and looked. It was a man, all right, a soldier, Willy made him out to be, wearing the long tight white breeches and the black boots. He lay on his stomach, chest and shoulders and head in the water. He was dead.

"What is it?" Captain Sturbridge came up behind him, his voice urgent, trembling. "Is it...? Turn him over, Willy." His tone was suddenly cold-hard, almost imperious.

"Yes, sir." Willy, shaking himself, put the lantern carefully aside and, seizing the body by the legs, pulling and tugging with all his strength, managed to get it up onto the grass. Then he looked up at Captain Sturbridge, questioningly.

"Turn him over," again that cold voice spoke. Willy turned the dead man over on his back... and the hair on the back of his neck rose as a chill of horror ran through him....

"Oh, God!" said Willy, turning away. "Oh, my God!"

Tom Sturbridge, clinging to his crude wooden staff, looked down upon the face of the man who had been friend and brother to him almost all his life. "Ian," he whispered.

It was Ian Ives, late of His Majesty's Light Dragoons, dead. He had received the full thrust of an iron pike through the throat and lay now with the hard oak wood shaft of it broken off about six inches from the head, which was still embedded in his neck. He had fallen from his horse and cracked the wood as he fell, then evidently he had crawled along until he reached the brook and bled to death, or drowned.

"Is it him, sir? Your friend?" asked Willy, unable to bring himself to look at the still-wet, white face, at the staring blue eyes, at the awful thing sticking out of the throat.

74

"Yes, Willy," Tom replied evenly. And he lowered himself down on the ground next to Ian's body and threw away his wooden staff as if he would have no further need of its support. The wounds in his leg had opened again, and he had felt the warm blood pushing insistantly against the thick bandaging. He cared nothing at all for that now. He pushed the lantern closer to Ian's face and leaned over and kissed the cold brow. With his one good hand, he picked up Ian's hands, first one, then the other, and clumsily placed them on his friend's breast. . . . it was only when he felt those stiff fingers, then looked more closely at them, that Willy heard him groan aloud.

"Look, look here, Willy," Captain Sturbridge ordered, "see how he tried to get the iron out. . . ."

Willy looked as he was bidden, and then looked away hastily. The dead man's fingers were cut through to the white bone from tip to palm, split as he had attempted to grasp the pike-head and pull it from his throat.

"Go back and fetch some help, Willy," Captain Sturbridge said quietly, not even looking up at him now, only looking down at his dead friend. "Hurry as fast as you can. And take the lantern."

"But, what about you, sir? I can't be off leavin' you here all alone."

Captain Sturbridge looked up at him for an instant and Willy could have sworn he saw a smile on the Captain's face. . . . but the oil was burning very low in the lantern and he could not be sure of that. . . .

"I will be all right, son. Go along now. I shall just stay here and wait. Don't be long in coming, Willy. . . ."

"But, sir. . . ."

Captain Sturbridge looked away from him, turning his head, and placed his left hand over the dead officer's two clasped hands.

"Go on, Willy," he said.

Willy picked up the lantern, looked about and took note of his bearings. He noticed a faint dusky glow off to the east and realized it was dawn, at last. He looked down at the dead man and the man soon to be dead and wanted to say that they would not have to do without a light for very long, even with him taking away the lantern, soon the sun would be on its way. But he didn't say anything, after all. He began to run, to run back across that open field and all in this world he wanted then was to set eyes on a walking, breathing, talking man, any man still sound and whole. As he ran, skirting along the brook's edge, he heard a terrible sound, a sound that made him want to run all the faster. It was the Captain weeping.

"Well, Ian, you were right about everything," Tom said, looking down at Ian's uncomprehending face. "I thought to find you by me when I woke up, but you knew better, didn't you?"

He took hold of the splintered wood haft of the pike, careful to keep his fingers away from the deadly sharp iron head, and pulled the devilish thing out of Ian's throat. There was no blood left to come gushing out of the fearful wound. Still, he was glad he had waited until the boy was gone before he did it. He closed Ian's eyes with his fingertips and smoothed the matted blonde curls back from his brow. He did not know what else he might do for the dead man, now, except to wait with him and keep him such company as the living may ever keep the dead.

He was hardly aware of it but his own tormented body had grown quite cold, his muscles very stiff. If he had tried to stand up again, even with the wood to lean on, he could not have done it. He did realize that he was growing light-headed and that he no longer felt the pain so badly. He had wept, briefly, when first he settled down by Ian's side, but then the tears had passed. He did not believe that he would live to weep for Ian again and he was glad of that.

His left hand tightly pressed on Ian's hands, he looked at the two rings he wore, one his own, one Ian's. He hoped that he would still be alive when help came. If they came soon enough, he would direct that good young lad . . . what was his name? . . . . Willy. . . . direct Willy to take the two rings to Helene at Spring Mount. One must be sent across to Ireland, he thought. Michael must have his father's ring, and little Rob shall have mine. Too soon, came the faint voice of life left in him, too soon. Boys ought not to have to wear such rings nor bear such losses. But they would have to wear them now; they would have to grow up fast indeed and look after their mothers, look after Helene and Sheila. . . .

His head had dropped forward. Death, the final enemy, had struck down Ian without warning, wildly and brutally, a grinning hag riding the wooden shaft of a rebel's pike. And now Death, in another guise, came licking her lips after *him*, stealthily, subtly, offering the peace of painless sleep. . . .

Even as Tom looked at the steel ring on his finger and even as he realized how close he was to closing his eyes and letting go, the three letters, I.C.I., seemed to grow larger and brighter, until they had a positive diamond-light glitter. Ian Curtis Ives, he remembered, be brave and bold and honourable. . . .

"You were, Ian, you were all that!" He glanced toward the sky and for the first time noticed the grey soft dawn approaching. He saw his wooden staff lying by the brook, and drew it toward him. He could not use it to pull himself to his feet again, but it was not necessary anyway. Someone would be coming soon. Meanwhile, the feeling of the wood against his palm was reassuring.

"I'll just sit here with you, Ian, and wait for them," he said companionably. He decided he could not look at Ian's face and mutilated throat anymore, so he fixed his gaze on the spreading gold and rose clouds to the east.

"I'll tell Michael, when he's old enough to understand, Ian. I'll tell him how you died, and why. We won, you bloody old donkey, but I suppose you know that. I'll take care of them, don't you fear, Ian. Kilbree will be safe now, King James will see to that. I'll try to bring them up the way you'd want, and I'll tell Michael about the ring. And. . . . and Sheila. . . . she'll never lack for anything, Ian. . . ."

But his voice broke and he fell silent, thinking of Sheila hearing the news of Ian's death, Sheila so close to her confinement now, perhaps already delivered . . . Sheila, whom he loved. . . .

"So you always knew that, Ian?" he whispered. "You always knew how I felt about Sheila. But for her, there was never anyone, only you. She'll be lonely, now, won't she? Oh, Ian, Ian," his tired voice rose in sorrow, "Ian, did you have to go now?"

He knew the answer to that, of course. In the last few minutes he had gone through much and the effort spent in battling that final enemy, and winning . . . for awhile . . . was too much for him at last. Once again he felt the nausea and the cold come over him and, just before he lost consciousness, he began to long for the sunny bedroom at Spring Mount, and a very clear picture of Helene standing in the doorway and smiling at him, entered his mind for a moment. . . . Helene, dressed in a plain white morning gown, running in from that garden of hers . . . Helene smiling at him, holding a basket of fresh cut white roses. How surprising it seemed, when all the time he had been thinking of Sheila. . . .

Three

"I Think There Is No Unreturn'd Love"

1 The Sun's Bright Promise

The battle was over. They had fought at Sedgemoor. The news arrived at Spring Mount before noon the same day. The messenger, riding north to London with his tidings of victory, stopped on his way for a hot meal in the Sturbridge kitchens, a change of horses and he would be on his way again.

He had not come from Tom Sturbridge, as Helene had first assumed, but from Feversham, anxious to let King James know that Monmouth had been routed and his cause lost. Helene let the man tell what he knew without interruption, without asking the only question that really mattered to her: did Tom still live? Was Tom all right?

Only after the messenger had finished his meat and bread and wine and was ready to ride again, only then did she mention Sir Thomas Sturbridge, whose hospitality the fellow had just, all unknowing, enjoyed. Did he know anything of the light Dragoons, Helene asked, had he heard aught of an officer named Sturbridge?

The messenger whipped up his mount and rode off, shouting carelessly back to her that the last he had seen of Sir Tom Sturbridge he was "somethin' wounded but most like would live."

Wounded! Helene stood at the iron gatepost watching him ride away, one hand clutching her slender throat. Wounded. How? And how badly?

Rob, now nine years old and furious with everyone because he had not been allowed to ride away to Papa's war with the other men, came running down the path to his mother, angry all over again because he had wanted to watch the messenger ride away. He came to a halt at Helene's side, his round face red and scowling, his brown eyes, so much like her own, snapping bright little sparks of annoyance as he looked down the road and saw only a distant wisp of dust from the horse's hoofs.

"Oh, Mama," Rob cried mournfully, gazing up at her with reproach, "he's gone and you didn't tell me! Why did you . . . ?" Then the child fell silent as he noticed the strange, preoccupied expression on his mother's face. "Mama?" he whispered, the brown eyes suddenly widening with fear. "Papa isn't . . . ? That bloody Bastard, Monmouth, didn't go and kill my Papa, did he?"

In spite of herself, Helene smiled. She shook her head, running her fingers gently through the boy's thick, dark curls.

"Hush, Rob, no bad words, remember? Papa is alive, darling. He's all right. He has been hurt . . . I don't know how, but he will be home very soon now and we'll have him feeling just fine again in no time."

She spoke with a brisk cheerfulness that lacked real conviction. Rob sensed that she did not entirely believe what she was telling him and that, moreover, she wanted to believe it herself every bit as much as she wanted him to believe it. The boy took her hand, gripping her fingers tightly in his small, brown fist, and began to draw her back to the house.

"Don't you be afraid, Mama," he said reassuringly. "Uncle Ian will look after him. Papa said that he and Uncle Ian always look out for each other. Me and Michael shall do that, too, when we're in a war." He nodded confidently.

"Michael and *I*," said Helene softly. She bent her dark head very fast and kissed him. Rob suffered this patiently for a few seconds, then pulled her along with him again.

"Come, Rob, let's go upstairs and tell Elizabeth that Papa is coming home," proposed Helene as they entered the front door. Rob's affectionate smile changed into a quick, quizzical glance, his right eyebrow sharply upturned, looking so much like his grandfather that Helene's eyes instinctively sought out the large painting of old Sir Thomas which hung over the grand staircase directly facing the main entryway. How she had loved that wise, dear man, her father-in-law! How much she still missed his presence in the house since his death ten years ago!

"He's alive," she murmured under her breath, hoping that something of Sir Thomas lingered to hear it about those old walls, something that lived on loving them all.

"Elizabeth doesn't know anything about Papa and the battle," Rob was saying somewhat disdainfully. "She's only a baby, Mama . . ."

Helene fixed the boy with a significant look. Rob's mouth curled.

"Well . . . couldn't we wait and tell her later?"

Helene laughed and raced him all the rest of the way up the staircase to the second floor and down the hall to the nursery wing.

Two-month old Elizabeth was sleeping soundly in her curtained cradle. Her nurse sat nearby, nodding to herself as she dozed in the warm July air. Helene kissed her daughter's round pink cheek very gently and whispered, "Papa's coming home, love."

Only later did it occur to Helene that she ought to have inquired after Ian as well as Tom. It troubled her that she had not asked, but she reasoned, surely they would both have come through the fight together; surely the messenger would have mentioned it if Ian had been hurt, too.

Her thoughts centered entirely on Tom now. Round and round in her head ran terrible pictures of what injury he might have sustained. She had the servants make up a feather bed downstairs in the library and she kept the entire household up very late carrying furniture downstairs, rearranging everything to make a proper sickroom ready for Tom's return. She dispatched a note to Dr. Johnson in town, telling him what little she knew, asking him to be ready to come out to Spring Mount as soon as she would send for him. Rob thought the whole thing terribly exciting, as he raced upstairs and down, fetching all sorts of things he was positive his father would want close to hand the very moment he came home.

Next morning, before anyone else was stirring about the house, Helene was up, wide awake and waiting. She dressed herself quickly, not wishing to wake her maid, not wanting to talk to anyone else this so-special morning. She went downstairs quietly and let herself out through the French windows in the newly arranged library. As she walked past the stables she could hear the horses stamping and whinnying in their stalls. She quickened her steps, not wanting to meet the stablemen, and climbed the hill towards her rose garden. From there she would be able to see down past the house, straight into the village and along the main road. That was the way he would come; she would be the first to see him from far off and she would be waiting on the front steps by the time he reached the house.

But now her eyes turned toward the sea. She wondered suddenly what had happened to Monmouth. Perhaps he had been killed. Or, perhaps he had turned back to his ships and escaped out to sea again.

Oh, what did it matter anyway? she thought impatiently. Right now the only thing that mattered in all the world was Tom's homecoming!

She raised her head, sniffing deeply of the morning air. The scent of the roses just opening mingled with the sweetness of newly cut grass. The men had been out haying only yesterday and a faint, far-off, fresh tangy dash of the ocean wafted through the sweetness for a few seconds and then, with a shift of the wind, was gone again.

He is coming home to me, she thought, her heart lifting with buoyant gladness. To *me*. She prayed in her mind that God might look with mercy upon all the wives, all the mothers and sweethearts whose men would not be coming back from Sedgemoor. But Tom Sturbridge was coming home. "Thank you, dear Lord!" Helene whispered. "Thank you!"

Her eyes swept over the main road. It was still empty. She had not really expected him yesterday or last night. Tom would not leave until he had talked with his men and seen to it that they were being looked after properly. He would undoubtedly have rested the night at Taunton. She wished he had thought to send some word ahead. No matter. He would be there himself in a little while . . .

And maybe this time, this time when he comes back, she thought, I will see him stand in the doorway and he will look at me as I go to meet him . . . he will look at me in a different way, a new way.

She caught her breath, her heart beginning to pound wildly. Why not? she cried silently. Why not? It might happen. It could happen. . . .

Helene put her hand out and grasped the back of one of the garden chairs. She gripped the hard, cold iron strongly, her fingernails digging into the soft flesh of her palm as she tried to push away that old, tantalizing dream, that dream she could never quite forget despite all the years that had passed and the time had gone when the dream might have come true, if ever it were to come true. She rarely allowed herself to give in to it. It hurt too much; it was a little like dying each time it ended and she was forced to remember that it was only a dream after all. . . .

But today she surrendered herself to dreaming it anew, forcing away the pain and the knowledge that it could never, never be. Here, in this place which was so especially her own, she gave herself up to it. And suddenly Tom Sturbridge loved her with all his heart. Suddenly Sheila Ives simply did not exist, had never existed. There was no one else in the whole universe but herself and him. . . .

He stood close to her, so close that they almost touched, and he looked down at her face with eager, loving eyes, eyes languid with desire. Slowly he touched her chin with the tips of his fingers, tilting her head back, back, his mouth coming closer to hers . . . she could feel the strong pressure of his arm around her back, pulling her against him; she could hear his deep voice whispering her name, and, just before his lips closed over hers, he said the words that made the moment magic:

"I love you, Helene! I love you!"

A light breeze filled her nostrils with the intoxicating scent of the roses around her. And it seemed that she lay back upon a bed of softest, tumbled, fluttering petals, there, just there on the shoulder of this hill of hers, and Thomas lay with her. Their two bodies were joined, their arms clasping one another and still he looked at her, a poignant sadness underlying the look of joy in his hot face, and he strained her slender form to him and said, "I love you, Helene, only you, only you!"

Oh, God! She swayed unsteadily, clutching the hard iron chair convulsively, her eyes closed, tears running down her cheeks. *Fool!* she told herself furiously, fool of the world! It's all a lie and you know it. The little, hopeful scented breeze died a'borning amongst the heedless, useless roses.

Helene opened her eyes, felt their stinging and shook her head firmly. No, he did not love her. That was the truth of it, the only truth there was for her. He did not love her and he never would. She pulled her fingers from the chair and moved away resolutely, further up the hill, past the roses. He did not love her, not in the only way that mattered. He was fond of her . . . but he loved Sheila. She had known it from the beginning and she had accepted it . . . *remember that,* she reminded herself, *remember, you accepted it, you knew what it was going to be like. . . .*

But another voice inside of her cried out in protest: *no, no, I did not know! How could I? I did not know what loving him could be until I awoke, completely, body and soul, and realized too late what was missing!*

Once again anguish rose in her throat, choking her, and she walked the green hillside faster, faster, more determined than ever to put this desperate illusion behind her. She walked and she watched the road and she waited all that first full day after the battle. But he did not come.

She waited a second morning, for she was sure that when he came it would be in the morning. The light of morning would guide Tom back to her from Sedgemoor. She had infinite faith in the sun's bright promise; she distrusted the night and its sad, suspicious shadows. But he did not come on the second day either. The road was no longer empty by then: as far as her eye could make out it was filled with little groups of slow-moving men, on foot, in wagons, a few mounted on horses. They were heading home from Sedgemoor. But not Tom. . . .

She sent servants out to question them several times, but they were only passing through to more distant towns and villages. They did not know Tom Sturbridge or Ian Ives. They reconstructed the battle in bits and pieces, all differing vastly until it seemed like a great hodge-podge in her anxious mind.

Poor old Jessup. They had brought him home with his arm cut off, brought him home in a hay wagon and left him at the grooms' quarters for his wife to tend him. Nobody had told Helene, until Simpson appeared to serve dinner in Mrs. Jessup's place. Helene barely waited to hear Simpson's quiet remarks, then she ran from the table and sought out Jessup. But he was dead then, and his wife crying soundlessly, rocking back and forth with her arms folded about her, and the small room filled with the stench of the congealed hot oil the surgeons had used to cauterize the stump of the arm. . . .

Helene stood in the doorway, gasping, the question on her lips unasked. She turned away from the pitiful scene, unwilling to intrude, when Mrs. Jessup caught sight of her and called to her.

"Sir Tom must be all right, my Lady," said Mrs. Jessup kindly, so steady-voiced that Helen marveled at the woman.

"How . . . how do you know?" Helene whispered, her lips very dry.

"Because my man told me that Sir Tom sent for him the very night after the battle," Mrs. Jessup replied. "He wanted him to go on some kind of errand . . . I never did get the particulars of that, M'am, but Sir Tom was surely alive right then and there ain't none of us has heard any different since. . . ."

"Thank you, Mrs. Jessup," Helene replied and would have asked what she might do for the widow, but Mrs. Jessup turned away then, already forgetting she was there, and, picking up her husband's remaining hand, she held it against her face and began to weep again.

Helene walked swiftly back to the dining room and, after ordering the carriage sent round, she called young Alice, once the littlest of all the maids, now a fresh-faced, blooming young woman of eighteen, to go upstairs and fetch down her mistress' heavy cloak. While she waited Helene paced impatiently up and down the Great Hall. She must go herself and find Tom, find Ian, wherever they were. She must head straight for Taunton first. If they were not there, then surely they would be in one of the nearby towns. She must find out where the Dragoons were quartered, speak with the officers, keep on asking until she had her answer.

She admitted to herself now that they both might be wounded, that Tom's injuries might be much more severe than she had allowed herself to imagine. He might not be in any fit condition to be moved, even ten miles to Spring Mount. But, why had neither of them been brought here as Jessup had been. . . . ? The implications of *that* question she could simply could not face, not yet.

She threw her black cloak over her shoulders and stood by the front door, wondering what was delaying the carriage when Simpson came hurrying to her. Speaking in a trembling voice most unlike his usual even tone, he implored Helene not to leave the house.

"Monmouth has not yet been found, my lady! The countryside is full of rebels and our men out after them. Every coach, every wagon is being stopped and searched. The King has called for the lot of them been brought here as Jessup had been. . . . ? The implications of found and killed in town since this morning. It isn't safe for you to go. Why, they might take your carriage . . . they would do anything to escape. Oh, my lady, think of the children! Think of . . ."

In the end, Helene reluctantly gave in and sent only the two coachmen to search for Tom and Ian. As she headed upstairs to the nursery, dispiritedly untying the strings of her cloak, she heard the sound of carriage wheels moving around the courtyard to the front entrance. I *should* be going with them, she thought with great misgiving, and turned to go back down again, ignoring Rob's voice calling to her, even ignoring Elizabeth's faint, fretful crying.

Skirts flying, she raced across the front hall and flung open the heavy door, ready to call out to them to wait for her, wondering where on earth Simpson had disappeared to. . . .

Just as she reached the bottom step of the stone terrace outside the carriage came rolling by, gathering speed as it went, and she caught a glimpse of old Simpson himself, wrapped like a tall, thin wraith in his weathered black greatcoat, a flintlock blunderbuss laid across the crook of his arm, sitting up on top next to Jed, who was driving.

"Simpson!" she waved to him frantically, running out into the gravel driveway. The old retainer heard her voice and turned to look back as the carriage dashed down the long sweeping drive with its border of ancient oak trees.

"I'll find them, my lady!" Simpson shouted with all his might, and waved the short, fat-barreled brass weapon so that she would be sure to see it. Jed whipped up his four horses, grabbing the old man's shoulder and pulling him down on the seat lest he fall out.

Helene watched them out of sight, smiling wanly at Simpson's bold courage. Then, her cloak over her arm, she went upstairs, bracing herself for another argument with Rob, who was sure to be put out because *nobody* ever let *him* do anything. . . .

There was not much sleeping at Spring Mount that night. Several times musket fire could be heard in the countryside. Cook pointed out soldiers marching on the main road. The servants bolted all the doors and shuttered the enormous downstairs windows. They all felt beseiged by an invisible presence named Monmouth and an invisible army behind him.

5 Decisions

On the third morning, having no word yet from Simpson or anyone else, Helene told herself that if Tom did not come today, he would not come at all. If he did not come today, then he was dead. . . .

But late that afternoon, old Simpson returned, worn out with seeking and asking and searching. He came back in an empty carriage drawn by four weary, stumbling horses.

Helene stood stiffly in the Long Salon with its ceiling-high tapestries, holding on to the marble mantel for support as the old man presented himself to her. He had not found Sir Tom. He had not found Ian . . . then he stopped speaking and he cleared his throat several times, clasping and unclasping his thin, arthritic fingers. . . .

"Yes? What is it? Go on, Simpson!" Helene urged him, a cold shiver going through her. "You were saying? About Ian Ives. . . . ?"

"Master Ives is dead, my lady, killed by Monmouth's troops,"

Simpson replied, his voice pained. "I had it from Colonel Kirke himself. He was just leaving Taunton to go up to London. They have taken Monmouth, ma'am...."

"Oh, damn Monmouth! I don't want to hear about Monmouth!" cried Helene in distraction. Simpson stared at her. "I . . . I'm sorry, Simpson. But, you said . . . you *did* say, didn't you? Master Ives was *killed*?"

"Yes, my Lady. Twas Sir Tom who found his body . . ."

"Tom found him," echoed Helene vaguely, her thoughts overwhelmed by the utter unreality of Ian's being dead. Then she heard what she had just said. "Tom found him? Then . . . then Tom is alive! But, the wound, Simpson . . . he was hurt . . ."

Simpson nodded. "Hurt badly, but not fatal, that's what the Colonel told me, and sends his respects to you, ma'am. . . . and . . ."

Helene's fingers ached from gripping the mantel. She turned away from the old man, stretching her arms out along the ornately carved marble, resting her cheek for a moment upon its cool expanse. She could not seem to get her breath. Her grief for Ian was warring with the wild relief she felt for Tom. . . .

Alive! Tom was alive! The messenger had been right. But then she turned her head again, bewildered by a new thought.

"Well, then, Simpson, where *is* Sir Tom? Why hasn't he come home?"

"He's gone, my lady." Simpson spread his hands apart as though he had just watched a bird take flight from them.

"Gone? Gone? Gone where?" Helene's dark eyes were snapping and a sharp edge crept into her soft voice. Good God, would the old man never tell her?

"Gone to Ireland, ma'am. With the . . . with Master Ives. Sir Tom insisted upon escorting Master Ives home to be buried at Kilbree. He took some of his men with him and embarked from Lyme Regis . . ."

Helene was startled. "Did he not leave some word for me? Some message? Something?" she demanded.

Simpson looked tired and utterly blank for a moment, then smiled and began fishing around in the multitudinous pockets of the greatcoat. At length he produced a scrap of paper, somewhat creased and dirty, and handed it to her.

"Helene . . ." Tom had written and she barely recognized the choppy scrawl as his handwriting . . . "Ian is dead. I am all right. Please have no fears about me. But I must take him home. Sheila is unable to travel as you know. I will write you from Kilbree when it is done. Kiss the children for me. As ever . . . Tom.'' And then, at the very bottom, he had added, almost as an afterthought: ''You will be told that I am wounded. Rest assured, I will recover. It is only the right leg.''

She read every word of it twice, three times, treasuring each one, tracing out the letters of his signature with her fingertip. *Of course he would take Ian home, of course he must do that,* she told herself. And now, seeing it written down before her eyes, she remembered all over again that Ian was gone. And Sheila! Helene cried out, pressing the little note to her lips, the blood draining from her face. Sheila was to have the baby so soon, that forbidden baby, that baby she had written them about so happily! Helene had written back, not chiding her, it was too late for that, but promising to come to Kilbree and be with Sheila for the delivery . . .

Dimly she realized that Simpson was still standing there. She looked at him, seeing the sagging, aged shoulders and the exhaustion in his face. She forced herself to begin putting her thoughts in order.

''You say they have captured Monmouth? And what of his supporters?'' she inquired.

Simpson nodded. ''They've got about three hundred of them under guard in Taunton, my lady. Monmouth is being taken up to London. King James agreed to give him an audience, although God alone knows why His Majesty should bother . . .''

''Then the roads are safe to travel again,'' Helene cut him short, her thoughts racing.

''As safe as English roads ever are, ma'am,'' replied Simpson cautiously, watching her face, suspicion dawning in his faded eyes.

''They are a great deal safer now that Mul-sack's been hanged!'' snapped Helene. Instantly she regretted her quick tongue as she saw Simpson's hurt look. ''You must go and rest now, have something warm to eat. And send Alice to me, Simpson.''

''Yes, my lady,'' he nodded, still watching her. He started to leave the room, then hesitated.

''Is Your Ladyship planning to . . . to go somewhere, perhaps? Because if Your Ladyship *is* . . . planning to go somewhere, I mean . . . I should like to remind Your Ladyship that the roads are still full of deserters and there are other highwaymen than Mul-sack!''

"Simpson," sighed Helene, "I am going to Ireland. Tonight. We shall ride to Bristol in the carriage and take a ship from there."

His worst fears realized, Simpson opened his mouth to protest but Helene did not give him the opportunity.

"Simpson, Sir Tom is wounded. And, as I am sure you know, Mistress Ives is..." She blushed and Simpson drew a very great breath. "She is... not strong just now. I must go and help her. I will take Alice with me... and Jed, I think..."

"And myself, of course, ma'am," added Simpson, drawing himself up tall. Helene was dismayed. She had planned to leave him in charge at Spring Mount. But one look at his determined expression and she knew he would never consent to stay behind.

"Very well, Simpson. Thank you. Mrs. Jessup can look after things for a few weeks."

"And the children?" he reminded her. "They will remain behind with Nurse, of course?"

The children! There was so much to think of...

"No," Helene said. "I can't leave Elizabeth, of course. And I will not leave Rob. It will do him and his father good to see each other..."

Rob must be with Tom, she thought, trembling. They love each other so much, and if that wound proves worse than Tom is letting on... oh, dear God! She felt suddenly weak-kneed and dizzy. If that wound becomes infected, might it not prove fatal after all?

Suddenly she felt a strong, steady arm supporting her... surely not the arm of an old man... She looked up and saw Simpson at her side, his arm securely across her back. Did he know what she had been thinking? Did he guess that she wanted Rob to be with his father in case...

Impulsively she kissed the weathered cheek lightly, tears in her eyes.

"Thank you... for everything, Simpson," she said, swallowing hard. "I'm all right now."

At once Simpson bowed and withdrew his arm. "I shall send Alice to you, my lady."

The arrangements were made quickly enough. And it was only when Alice went off to pack and Nurse was feeding Rob and Simpson was down in the kitchen recounting his adventure to the rest of the household, only then did Helene allow herself some time to sit down, alone, and try to get a bit of rest before they set out.

She curled up in Tom's armchair in the library, sipping a cup of strong, hot tea. Her mind was teeming with plans and contingencies, lists of things she had forgotten to tell someone to pack. . . .

After a while, when the late evening shadows began to creep long-fingered through the tall window, Helene set the half-finished cup of cold tea aside and vowed that she would, indeed, close her eyes and nap.

The night was so warm that she had not ordered a fire lit. She sat in the big, yet somehow cozy room, unable to keep her eyes closed, unable to find any rest or relief from her troubling thoughts. She gazed around at the walls filled with hundreds of books and manuscripts which had been old Sir Thomas' chief joy. Scholars came to use that library sometimes. Visitors never failed to seek it out and marvel at its four Shakespeare folios, its Chaucer originals, its rare books from all over the world. She and Tom had spent so many contented hours there, reading, talking about the future, about the children. . . .

She moved her head back and forth against the chairback, wishing it would not ache so. She needed to keep a clear head from now on, she thought sternly. There would be plenty to occupy her at Kilbree. Her mind dwelt fitfully on Sheila's condition, then on Tom's wound, and the long, hard journey he had insisted on making in spite of it. She thought of Ian, dearest Ian, whom she had learned to know more from the stories Tom had told her than from the few real conversations she had ever had with Ian since her marriage. Ian had always been a bit shy with her, she believed, a bit quiet. Yet she knew that he liked her. There was never anything in his manner except a friendly, somehow hopeful encouragment. She knew he worried about Tom, that he hoped his friend would find happiness as he had. . . .

Did Ian know that Tom loved his wife? She had often wondered about that. They were so close, surely Ian must have known. . . . Ian, poor Ian. She shivered. Poor Ian, so happy with his wife and child, having to leave them. How desperately alone Sheila would feel. . . .

Helene looked down at her hands suddenly, and saw with amazement that they were shaking badly. His wife. Leaving his wife. Sheila was a widow now.

Helene clasped her hands together tightly so they would stop shaking, but she could not control the spasmodic pounding of her heart, and she could not still the evil little voice which rose up in her

89

mind to mock her now. Tom was on his way back to Kilbree, not to Spring Mount, back to Sheila, Sheila, whom he had always loved, Sheila whom he still loved.

She jumped to her feet, feeling that she must do something, anything, and at once or she would scream. It was all wrong, all wrong and she was mad to think it. Sheila would never, never. . . .

The words stabbed through her like sharp knives. *Sheila* would never? Sheila would never love Tom. Yes, that was probably true enough. But, she hadn't said to herself, *Tom* would never. Why? Tom's face came into her mind, his usual look of care and tenderness for her so clear in his eyes. But she could never forget that other look she had seen in his eyes on her wedding day, lost, full of sorrow and regret, his eyes . . . looking at Sheila. . . .

No. No, no, never! Helene felt sure she must have shouted it as she threw open the library doors and rushed into the hallway. But the footmen were calmly going about lighting the candles as they always did at this time of day. They bowed respectfully as they passed her standing there, staring about her blindly. She had not uttered a single sound, yet she ran swiftly up the enormous staircase with one hand pressed hard against her mouth, as though she had cried out . . . or as though she were afraid that she *might* cry out. . . .

She darted into her bedroom, forgetting that Alice would be there with some of the other maids, helping with the packing. There were three other girls hurrying about and Alice was just coming out of Helene's large wardrobe with two or three frocks over her arm. A small traveling trunk stood open beside the bed. When Helene entered, the maids looked up. They saw the ghastly expression on her face and became alarmed. Alice quickly put the dresses aside and shooed them all away, warning them to be quiet as they went. Then she shut the door after them and cast a worried glance at her mistress.

"Won't you have a nice lie-down, my lady?" Alice said calmly, as she moved the little trunk out of the way. Helene shook her head, distracted, her eyes roving in a strange, restless way about the room.

"No, no, there's no time. We must be leaving soon. Go on with the packing," she muttered.

Alice clucked her tongue in disapproval but resumed her task, looking anxiously over at Helene every so often. Helene sat down at her dressing table and stared with unseeing eyes at the flat leather jewelry cases that Alice had set out so that she might decide which pieces she wished to take. Without realizing what she was doing, Helene began to finger her wedding pearls with nervous, agitated motions of her hands. She prayed to herself, as she had not prayed before, not even when she had been in labour with the two children. She prayed for strength, for control of herself whatever would happen in Ireland. Those who are strong are always those who pray for strength, strength to accept and bear what they cannot change. The weak pray only to change what they cannot either accept or bear. Helene was stronger than she realized. She wondered now, *when will the moment come? When shall I begin to hate myself for simply being alive?* When would it happen that it would finally strike home to her with full, crushing force . . . the realization that she was all that now stood between Tom and the only woman he had ever really loved? Even if he never looked at Sheila again, even if he left Kilbree this time and never allowed himself to return, how could he not think of Sheila? How could he not think of what might be, for her, for himself, if only Helene . . . He would, he must grow to hate her after all!

A terrible sob escaped her lips. She grasped the strand of fine white pearls convulsively, her head bent, and began to weep bitterly.

Alice was at her side. "You wouldn't want to go gettin' them pretty pearls wetted too much, ma'am," she said gravely. Carefully she unwound the necklace from Helene's fingers and placed it back in its black velvet lined box. "Pearls're ever so much care, ma'am. Like children, pearls are. We can't go mistreatin' 'em now, can we?" She placed her hand very gently over Helene's still tightly clenched hands. The soft, thoughtful gesture touched Helene immeasurably. She looked up at the maid, her pale cheeks wet and streaked with tears.

"No. You're right, Alice. Thank you for . . . reminding me," Helene said and Alice could see that she was herself again. She glanced at her ravaged face in the looking glass and laughed a short, harsh little laugh. "Fetch me a handkerchief, will you, Alice? Fancy the sight of this face in a sickroom! I'd scare poor Sir Tom out of his wits!"

"Oh, and that wouldn't do, would it, ma'am?" Alice smiled, handing Helene a fine, lace-edged handkerchief, delicately turning away as her mistress dried her eyes. Helene sighed, wishing, as she so often wished, that she was not so inclined to weep in times of crisis.

"Crying is a waste of energy, Alice," she said decidedly. But Alice, who had been with her since her wedding day and had rarely seen her cry at all, became quite indignant at this.

"'No, Ma'am, it is not either! Cryin' is good for the eyes. My mother always said so. Cleans'em up and clears 'em out!" She looked at Helene with a worried little scowl, hesitated, then asked, "Beg pardon, Ma'am, but is it for Master Ives you be cryin'? It can't be over Sir Tom, now, and him almost as good as new . . . once we gets our hands on him! I mean . . . you ain't heard nothin' more about Sir Tom, have you? Nothin' worse?"

Helene gazed into the young girl's patient, concerned face.

"Of course not," she said evenly. "Why else would I be crying, except for Master Ives? We shall all miss him terribly," she added. And she stood up full of energy all of a sudden, and headed for the nursery. "I must see if the children are ready yet."

She sailed out of the bedroom, her head high, her cheeks very hot. But she had won control of herself again. Come what may, she vowed not to give way to blind panic another time. The awful fear that had taken hold of her ebbed away as reason gained the upper hand. Tom was a man of honour, a man to be trusted without reserve. And Sheila was her friend. They both needed her. She would not fail them. *Ian can rest easy in his grave,* she thought. Immediately his name brought back the sharp bite of grief again and she thought, *it is we who will not rest, all of us who loved him and depended on him . . . .*

3   A Talk with Rob

"Robert, I want to talk to you, dear," she said to her small son. Nurse looked over at her queerly, her lips pursed. But Helene had made up her mind what had to be done, whatever Nurse chose to think about it. At first she had intended to say nothing of Ian's death to Rob until they had reached Ireland.

But when she came into the Nursery, Nurse was dressing Elizabeth and Rob was kneeling up on the window seat, his round, grave face resting on his hands as he looked out at the night-covered countryside. Hearing his mother come in, he had turned to her with that unexpectedly adult look children sometimes find out of nowhere. At that instant, Rob had about him the look of his father, concern in his dark eyes, a sort of reassuring little smile, his lips parted as if he were about to ask a question to which he already had the answer.

Helene went to sit by him at the window. Nurse looked at them for a moment and sniffled loudly. Helene smiled, putting an arm around Rob, and the two of them leaned quite close to the glass and saw their faces reflected there together.

"Rob, did Nurse tell you where we are going?"

He nodded brightly. "Kilbree," he said. It was his favourite place in the world besides home. It was, in fact, another home to him.

"Yes, to Kilbree," his mother said. "Your papa has already gone there ahead of us."

The boy wriggled with excitement. "And we shall be there soon, with Papa and Aunt Sheila and Uncle Ian and . . ."

Helene pulled him suddenly, almost roughly, against her.

"No," she said, keeping her voice steady. "Rob, listen to me, darling. Try to understand. Uncle Ian is dead. He was killed in the battle. The same battle Papa was hurt in, you remember. Uncle Ian was very, very brave . . ."

But Rob said nothing and she knew better than to push him just yet. He stared out across the shadowy lawns and gardens, his eyes very wide and very bright, terribly bright. Helene waited. And at last he said:

"Is Papa dead, too?"

"No, Rob. Papa is alive. He was hurt; his leg was hurt, but he will be fine again very soon, I promise you."

"But, now Michael will have no Papa," Rob frowned, turning to her with a perplexed look that almost broke her heart.

"No, Rob, he will not."

His eyes filled with enormous tears and he clung to her. "That's not fair!" he shouted against her shoulder. "That's bad! Michael loves his Papa, he told me he does. Just the same as Papa and me!" he shuddered, sobbing.

"Yer hadn't oughter said nothin, M'am," scolded Nurse severely. "That there boy ain't goin' ter understand it. Yer jist upsettin' him for nothink! He'll 'ave the nightmare, see if he don't!"

"He understands more than we think," responded Helene as she held Rob and kissed his wet cheeks. She did not say that telling Rob about Ian after they reached Kilbree, a house in mourning with Sheila grief-stricken and about to undergo another ordeal Rob would *not* understand, finding his own father hurt, in pain, sorrowful . . . it would be too much for the child to take in all at once. Now he would have some little time, not much perhaps, but some, to accept the fact of Ian's death. Fleetingly she wondered how young Michael would manage. She wondered, indeed, how any of them would manage. . . .

4 Willy Duncan

In later years, Tom Sturbridge did not remember very much of his journey from the battlefield of Sedgemoor to Ireland, nor about the four long, terrible days until Ian's funeral. Tom almost died himself, then. No one who saw him tossing and moaning in feverish delirium after he reached Kilbree House would have given him four more days to live, not by half and half of that again. He was unconscious almost all the way from the quays in Waterford City, during the bone-crushing ride over the dirt back roads lying in the bed of a crude wagon which bumped and thumped along on heavy, solid wooden wheels. Tom had brought with him twenty men of the Light Dragoons. It was they, not he, who delivered Ian Ives' body to his widow. In fact, Tom did not see Sheila at all for the first three days, although she looked in on him very often and pressed the doctor with questions. But the doctor only shook his head and sent her away.

Despite dire medical predictions and despite the well-intentioned but sadly bungling attempts to treat his wounds, Tom did not die. When the wounds festered, the doctor used his lancets to bleed him even more. He saw the scorched flesh where the army surgeon had originally cauterized thigh and hip with hot irons and refused to even try closing the jagged edges together again. When his fever soared the doctor dosed him with laudanum and mulled wine and pontificated that the end was very near now. . . .

Helene arrived before they killed him with ignorance. She threw out the doctor and all of his assistants with their bags full of powders and potions and their glass jars black with live leeches. She herself, with hands as cool and steady as those of any man, cleaned away the dead tissue and cauterized afresh and then applied clean linen bandages over the wounds. It was Helene who went storming into the kitchen demanding fresh-killed beef and brewed up quarts of rich broth to give Tom back some of his lost strength. A bit later, when the fever had abated, she mixed quantities of egg-nog with double measures of Irish whiskey and new-skimmed cream.

Helene always remembered those few days as a continuing nightmare of traveling without rest, arriving at dawn with exhausted children and servants, of holding Sheila in her arms as they both wept over Ian, and then Sheila quickly leading her to Tom's old bedroom that he'd had as a boy at Kilbree. Helene thanked God fervently that Sheila was still on her feet, still moving about, in command of herself and her household, neither delivered of her child nor giving any sign of going into labour just yet.

In Tom's darkened, stifling room, with its windows tightly shut and draped, sat a huddled figure off in a corner, his glazed eyes watching the vain movements of the helpless maids intently. Only when Helene had sent them all away and went about the room throwing back the draperies and unlocking the windows to let in the fresh early morning breeze, did the silent figure stand up and address her at last.

"Be you his wife, Mistress?"

Startled, Helene whirled about to look at him. "I am," she replied. "Are you another one of those . . ."

He shook his head quickly, moving closer. "Not me," he said with great scorn in his youthful voice. "I'm Willy, my lady."

Helene regarded him with perplexity. Was he one of Sheila's servants or a friend of Tom's? And what was he doing here in Tom's room after she had just ordered everyone out?

"Willy?" she repeated.

"Aye, Willy Duncan, that's me," nodded the youth. "Private Willy Duncan, my lady, of the 23rd Regiment of Foot." He tried to snap to attention smartly and give her a brisk salute, but she could see that the boy . . . he could not be more than sixteen or seventeen years of age . . . was terribly pale and tired, his movements stiff and weary. She noticed that even as he spoke directly to her, his eyes roved continually back to Tom and when he addressed her again there was a note of great urgency in his husky young voice.

"Please, yer Ladyship, I been awaitin' and awaitin' for them doctors and sich like to do somethin' afore the man dies. You was right to pack 'em all off, you was. Every time I stood up and asked 'em to stop a'bleedin' of him, they tuk it real bad, comin' from the likes of me, y'know, and they tolt me to be still or I'd have to leave. I *knew* they wasn't doin' him no good, but nobody'd listen to me!"

Willy Duncan won Helene's heart on the spot. From then on, it was the two of them who remained with Tom, never leaving his side more than a few minutes at a time for two days and two nights. It was Willy who helped her bathe Tom, Willy who heated the irons when she cauterized the wounds again, Willy who helped her change the dressings.

At the end of those forty-eight hours, Helene knew as much about Willy's short life as he was ever likely to think important enough to tell anyone, and he had become her devoted admirer and firm friend forever. It was from Willy that she learned at last the details of the battle and the terrible night that followed it, and the long, arduous journey afterward. In turn, she told him a great deal about Ian and Tom and their life-long friendship. Their quiet voices had a soothing effect upon the injured man and very often he would lie there listening while they talked and nodding his head weakly.

Later in the second day, when Tom's fever had begun to go down and he was able to sleep fairly soundly, Helene sat, exhausted but no longer in fear for his life, upon one of Sheila's dainty, crewel-embroidered silk chairs and Willy sat on another while they ate supper from a tray. Helene looked over at her husband, dozing with his left hand across his chest and she noticed for the first time he was wearing Ian's ring as well as his own. And it came back to her all over again, the reality of Ian's death. That was when she told Willy the story of the two rings.

"I was a' wonderin' what kind of ring that be," Willy nodded, his loose, flaxen hair brushing over his eyes. He pushed the hair back, trying to tuck it behind his ears. "It belongs to Master Ives' boy now, don't it, ma'am?"

Helene replied that she imagined it did, although she did think that an eight-year-old boy was a bit young yet to wear a man's ring. Willy seemed somewhat thoughtful at that.

"He'll be takin' it all terrible hard, though he do be so young," said Willy gravely. "If you folks thinks he'll be like to forgit it, or not understand it, it'ud be dead wrong on yer, 'cause he'll never forgit. I know that for a true fact, ma'am, for I were but six when my dad died and I never forgot it, not for a minute."

"Well, Willy, Sir Tom must be a father to Michael now," said Helene slowly, her voice troubled. Willy said no more and she saw that he could barely keep his eyes open. She insisted that he go and get some sleep, promising faithfully to call him if Tom so much as stirred. Reluctantly the lad left, closing the door very softly behind him, and she was alone with her husband for the first time since she had arrived at Kilbree.

She stood up, surprised at the nagging ache in her back and shoulders, and tip-toed over to look at Tom. He slept very deeply now, and there was a light, healthy sweat on his forehead. Satisfied, Helene walked to one of the tall windows and pushed aside the richly lace-edged white curtain. Since leaving England she had not noticed the sun's rising nor its setting. Down below she saw the men leading the cows back from pastures in the distant fields. She looked across the river and wondered at the numbers of people walking about. No one had yet told her that Ian's body was resting there until the burial.

She drew a chair close to the bed and sat down again, taking Tom's limp hand in her own, holding it gently. Minutes passed without a sound in the peaceful room. Helene felt drowsiness stealing over her and soon she fell asleep, her head resting alongside Tom's on the pillow. . . .

5 Riding Away Towards The River

He had not imagined it. It *was* Helene there with him. Tom opened his eyes, his nostrils filled with the sweet scent of her hair, that familiar, lovely perfume she always had about her. He had thought he was dreaming at first. He seemed to remember Sheila's face far off in the darkness, Sheila's face very pale, looking down at him with tears in her grey eyes. He had wanted to say something to Sheila, to tell her   something, but what it was he must say entirely eluded him. After that there was nothing but the pain and voices buzzing around him . . . then silence. Once or twice he had thought he could hear Helene's deep, soft tones, but that was impossible. Helene could not be out here at Sedgemoor, out here on the battlefield, with all the dead men lying about. . . .

Now he turned his head slowly and he saw her, her face not three inches from his own. There were dark shadows under her eyes, and little lines of fatigue about her mouth. He felt her hand in his. Suddenly much of the past few days began to come back to him. He knew that he had reached Kilbree, he and twenty men and that boy, Willy. He strained to hear the sounds of the house; far off, on another floor, he heard children laughing. One of the voices sounded like Rob. He looked back at Helene. She must have brought the children with her. He wished that she had not made the difficult journey, nevertheless he was glad she was there. He remembered that she had promised to be with Sheila when the baby came . . .

Sheila! He thought her name and a physical shock went through his body. Was she all right? How long had he been there like this, out of his mind, useless when he had meant to take care of everything, everybody!

His sudden, agitated movements woke Helene at once. She sat up quickly, afraid that she had awakened him.

"Tom," she whispered, her whole heart in her voice and in her eyes. "How are you, my dear?"

His mouth felt very dry. He tried two or three times to get the words out but could only shake his head ruefully. She brought him cool water and let him drink a bit of it.

"There now, don't try to say much. You're getting better, do you understand me? The danger is past. Willy Duncan pronounces you on the mend and he seems to be right about everything!"

She smiled at him, a gaiety in her voice covering the wild relief she felt. Tom looked past her, toward the closed door and managed at last to whisper a word.

"Sheila?"

Suddenly all of the shock and fear and exhaustion of the past week took possession of Helene. Tom spoke one word . . . and her head reeled dizzily; she reached out and grabbed hold of the bedpost to keep herself from falling. She felt as though a knife had pierced her breast, cutting off breath, too sharp, too real . . . his first thought had been of Sheila! She closed her eyes and fought down the rising tide of blackness inside of her. Of course he must be anxious, she told herself, of course . . .

She forced herself to open her eyes and to answer him with composure.

"Sheila is fine, Tom. The baby has not yet come. You mustn't be concerned, now, Tom. Everything is all right."

His eyes followed the movements of her lips as she spoke.

"Ian? She knows?" he murmured.

"Yes, she knows. It's been four days . . . almost five, since you came to Kilbree. Sheila knows. And she is bearing it wonderfully well, Tom . . ."

His head moved from side to side, and his deep blue eyes flooded with remembered horror.

"They killed him, Helene! With a pike through the . . . through the throat, oh, my God! My God!" He went on repeating the two words over and over until she became alarmed.

98

"Tom!" she said distinctly, but he did not seem to hear her. "Tom, listen to me! You've got to think of Michael now, do you understand? Michael and the little one soon to come, think of them, dearest, they need you! Please, Tom, please, you must put everything else from your mind, you must get well . . ." She was crying, watching his wasted grey face against the white pillow, seeing his dry, fever-cracked lips mouthing despair and horror that had lived on in his mind as fresh as the moment he had first seen Ian dead. "Tom, listen! Listen to me!"

With great difficulty he focused his eyes and saw that she wept. He reached out a weak hand, touching her sleeve.

"Helene?" he said, in Rob's little boy voice. She swallowed, summoning a smile to her lips, and looked down at him resolutely.

"Tom, dear," she said. "God has chosen to take Ian from us, but you remain, my love. You and I, we'll take care of Sheila, won't we? And we'll see to Ian's children. God spared you so that you might give Ian's ring to his son one day." She took his hand and kissed the fingers, pressing them against her cheek. "Now, my dearest love, you must lie very still while I fetch you some strong broth . . ."

"You're going away?" Tom whispered plaintively.

"Only for a moment," she smiled back at him, opening the door to call one of the servants. But there was Willy, just outside, sitting crossways in a velvet chair, his long legs in their muddy black boots draped over the arm, sound asleep. She touched his shoulder softly.

"Willy," she said. "Willy, he's awake."

Instantly Willy was on his feet, smiling widely.

"Can I have a look at 'im?" he begged and she could not refuse. She led him back into the bedroom where he approached Tom's bed as if it were the royal throne of England, with enormous deference, a deference slightly offset by his broad grin.

"Well, sir, look at *you*!" Willy cried heartily. Tom studied his face, then smiled, too.

"You're Willy, are you not?" he asked. "You are the brave lad who helped me find . . ."

"I *am*!" interrupted Willy quickly. "Me and 'er Ladyship here, we threw them doctors and all out, didn't we, ma'am? And here you are, bright as tuppence in the mornin'!"

"Thank you, thank you for everything, Willy," said Tom. His

voice faded a bit, then, putting great effort into it, he went on. "Willy, have they . . . have they buried Ian?"

Glancing hesitantly at Helene, Willy shook his head. "No, sir, not yet. Tomorrow."

"Tomorrow," repeated Tom, his eyes fluttering closed again. Helene drew Willy away from the bed.

"Can you go down to the kitchen and bring up some hot beef tea Willy? And, on your way, perhaps you might stop and tell Mistress Ives that Sir Tom is awake and . . . and asks for her."

Willy went off. Tom seemed to be sleeping again. Helene sighed. After she had given him the broth, she must go and see about the children. She sat by the window to wait for Willy's light tap at the door. . . .

But Tom was not really sleeping. In another moment his eyes opened again and he peered about the room, which was rapidly growing darker as the sun went down. He caught sight of Helene gazing off across the river, a look of infinite sadness on her face. His eyes eagerly studied the long, silky hair she had tied back out of her way; his gaze roamed past her face to her hands, lying loose in her lap, soft, gentle, capable hands, he had always thought them the kind of hands a woman ought to have. Suddenly, for the first time since he and Ian had ridden off to join the regiment, he felt at ease. How many, many nights he and Helene had shared this very bedroom when they visited Kilbree. It was home to him, as much as Spring Mount was home. How natural it was, that he should open his eyes and see Helene sitting there . . . serenely, he thought . . . how very good it was just to be with her again.

He could not recall a time when he had not enjoyed the sight, the voice and the company of this woman whom he should not have married. He knew that she loved him. He tried very hard never to let her suspect that he could not love her in return. If it were not for Sheila, he would undoubtedly love Helene. There was a kind of vital strength in both of them, each so different looking, each so very lovely in her own way. But, more than anything else, it was that hidden source of strength they both possessed which he admired.

Yet at this moment, Helene looked somehow . . . defeated. He had never seen her looking so sad, so tired. But of course these last days had taken their toll of all of them.

Tom's restless eyes moved past Helene, toward the door, and he waited to see Sheila, dreading what he would see in *her* face, not knowing the right words to say that might give her comfort.

Sheila came in softly, quickly, just as she always moved, although she was heavy with the child. She opened the door and stood there so quietly that Helene did not hear her. Sheila's always pale face was not much changed. Tom did not know what he had expected to see. Her auburn curls were tied back into a severe bun at the nape of her neck and she was dressed all in black, with a wide Irish woolen shawl about her. The grey eyes were very dim, without a touch of light in their depths, but as she looked at him a sad ghost of a smile touched her lips.

"Tom!" she cried softly. "Thank God!"

She moved over to the bed, leaned down with some difficulty and kissed him on the brow. Helene heard her now. She stood up, hesitating, thinking that the two of them must have this small moment . . .

Sheila touched Tom's hand. But then she saw Ian's ring upon his finger and she pulled back with a sharp gasp. Helene hurried to her and put her arms around her.

"Oh, my dear, forgive me!" whispered Sheila, clinging to Helene. "Tom, do forgive me. It was just . . . you know . . . when I saw his ring . . . the last time I saw that ring was on his finger and Michaeleen was teasing him so, wanting him to leave it here with him when he went off to the battle . . ."

"Sheila, sit down," said Helene, gently pushing her into the chair by the bed. Tom still said nothing. He lay there staring at her white face and lusterless eyes and could not seem to speak. But apparently Sheila never noticed his silence. She leaned back, holding Helene's hand as if she would never let go, and she talked.

"Helene's a wonder, Tom, isn't she? But how would you know and you half out of your wits all these days? Helene and that young lad, Willy . . . he's down in the kitchen right now, terrifying Cook and all the maids. And . . ."

"Sheila!"

His voice struck her silent. Tom reached out to her and clutched her other hand.

"Sheila, I didn't see it happen. I didn't know. We became separated right at the beginning. They surprised us. We didn't expect them to attack until dawn, but they came in the darkness. I rode out with my men. I saw Ian near the cannon. He must have ridden around the other side . . . and then I was wounded . . . I tried to find him . . . they were all out looking for him, Sheila. But Willy and I, we found . . ."

Suddenly he stopped speaking and stared at her with horror.

"Sheila, did you . . . did you see his body?"

"No, I did not, Tom," Sheila replied. "Your men wouldn't let me look at him. You brought him here wrapped all in blankets but you wouldn't let them bring him into the house, don't you remember? No, I suppose you don't. Well, twas yourself gave them orders to carry him to the old chapel over the river . . . you were shouting and giving orders to everybody, sending people into town for the priest . . . it was all a confusion. And then, in the midst of it, you fainted dead away and Willy carried you up here."

Tom settled back, glancing with relief at Helene. The less that Sheila knew right now about the way Ian had been killed, the better for her . . . and for her unborn child.

"Willy told me they're burying him tomorrow. I shall be there, of course," he said, summoning up all of his small store of strength into his voice. Helene started to protest, but he would not listen to her.

"They can carry me in a sedan chair. Something can be arranged," he insisted. "But I will be at Ian's funeral."

"Sheila, how are the children? How is Michael? Did you tell him?" asked Helene, realizing that nothing would change Tom's mind.

"Oh, fine, they're all fine. They've kept pretty quiet, don't you think? I spoke to Michael. I don't know if he really understands. He didn't cry when I told him . . ."

Helene remembered what Willy had said. "Perhaps you're right. He is still so young," she murmured quickly. "I told Rob before we left home."

Sheila nodded, saying nothing. Tom struggled to lift his head from the pillow, alarming both women terribly, but he would have his way.

"Sheila, you know what Ian is . . . what Ian was to me," he began, stumbling over the words. "I want you to know, now and always, that you have no need to be anxious for your home or your children or yourself. I will hold Kilbree for Michael, just as his father died to keep it for him . . . and I'll try for the rest of my life to be like a father to him . . . to them both," he added.

Sheila stood up again, pulling the dark plaid shawl about her small shoulders, as though she were suddenly quite cold.

"I never thought otherwise, Tom," she said simply. "You and Helene, you're our family and we are yours. God bless you both for everything, my dears. Now I must go and see about supper." She moved toward the door, stopped, turned back once more.

"I might as well tell you now: I will not be there tomorrow. Do not expect to see me at the grave. You know it is not for any lack of love for Ian," she smiled briefly, brokenly. "But I will not see him put into the ground, nor covered up from me. My last memory of him is as I watched him riding away toward the river, the sun all shining on his hair as he went . . . that's the way I will remember him. I carry his child and I will not bring it into the world with the thought of its father dead and cold in my mind."

She turned and was gone, but the note of desperate determination in her voice seemed to linger after her. Helene looked helplessly at Tom. His head had fallen back upon the pillow, his eyes were closed again, and she could see a thin trickle of tears on his cheeks.

She thought of tomorrow with dread and she wondered about all the tomorrows after it . . . and then Willy came barging into the room, bearing a large tray with soup and bread and fresh milk on it, shushing all of Helene's protests, clumping heavily about the place till she wondered if it was the same catfooted young fellow who had been there all this time . . .

But, insisted Willy noisily, a man must eat a man's food and be done with broth and other such feminine delicacies if he wanted to get his strength up again pretty fast . . .

In five minutes' time he had a linen napkin tucked under Tom's chin and was spoon-feeding him, interspersing each bite with humorous remarks which eventually succeeded in bringing a smile to Tom's face. And later, when Tom slept again and Willy was about to take the tray away, he said to Helene at the door, "I run into Mistress Ives on my way up here. She be lookin' that poorly, my lady, I think it's well nigh her time."

Helene looked at the youth in astonishment and felt the blood rush to her cheeks. "How do you know so many things, Willy?" she asked, not entirely sure whether she should be pleased or embarrassed at his frankness.

"My mother had ten of us and I'm in the middle," he remarked with a grin. "Weren't much we didn't know, of plain things, I mean, livin' so cozylike in a three-room cottage!"

Shortly afterward, Simpson came and rapped quietly at the door, begging the opportunity to sit with Sir Tom. He had been barred from the sickroom along with everyone else, but now he would be put off no longer. Helene was very glad to see him. She left the old man sitting in her place by the bed, his Bible in his lap, a beatific smile of satisfaction on his face every time he gazed down at Tom. Helene stole away, intent upon finding Sheila.

But Sheila was sleeping. Alice, together with Sheila's maid, Meg, were chatting quietly outside the room. Helene decided not to disturb Sheila but wandered off to the nursery up on the third floor, expecting to find the boys sound asleep.

Only little Elizabeth slept. Rob and Michael were in their night-clothes, sitting up quietly side by side in their beds, and there was Willy Duncan, his uniform coat put aside, in his shirt sleeves, telling them a story and making shadow figures with his fingers on the wall.

Helene paused by Elizabeth's cradle, looking down at the baby for a moment, listening to the story Willy told. She marveled that somewhere in this house of sorrow a corner could be found where winged horses and presumptuous frogs could still bring bright smiles to the faces of children. She marveled that children could forget, for a while, their fears and unhappiness.

There sat Michael, a head full of shining blond curls exactly like his father's, big, blue eyes, his chin resting on his hands as he listened raptly to Willy. And Rob, her own Rob, whose reaction to Ian's death had been anger at the injustice of it . . . Rob was twisting a lock of dark hair around and around one finger, grinning with delight at the frog's hopping legs, the white horse's great wings on the wall.

Only when the tale was done and the boys had applauded enthusiastically, demanding more, did anyone notice Helene. Willy saw her and jumped up, reaching for his coat, putting it on inside out in his haste to appear properly attired before her.

"Mama!" cried Rob, joyfully throwing his arms around her. Right behind him came Michael, the two of them almost bowling her over with enthusiasm. Willy came to her rescue, threatening no more stories ever if they did not get underneath the covers at once. Snickering, not really believing him, they bounced into the two beds and lay there making frightful faces at one another while Helene kissed them good night.

"Willy Duncan," she smiled, emerging from the children's double embrace with her dark curls flying loose and her ribbon lost on the floor, "Willy, you are a godsend!"

Willy took this very seriously. Rubbing his chin thoughtfully, he replied, "That 'ere might jist be, Yer Ladyship. I believes the Lord does work in mysterious ways with His wonders . . . not that *I* am no wonder," he blushed to the roots of his fair, straight hair. "But I was brung up religious, ma'am. And I think the Lord sent me to Sir Tom that very night as he lay on the ground awaitin' for Master Ives that was. Maybe, ma'am, maybe!"

Helene smiled. "I do not know what we should have done without you, Willy," she said warmly. Willy's face brightened and then he stopped, for a second, his vain struggle with the coat to bring it right side round.

"Well, ma'am," he said, "yer aren't goin' to do without me, beggin' yer pardon. I'll not leave Sir Tom, not ever, ma'am, if he wants it that way and can find work for me to do about yer place. No, ma'am, you've gone and . . . and *acquired* me, please Yer Ladyship!"

Four

"All Are One Now, Roses And Lovers"

1   July 15, 1685, A Sunny Morning

It was a sunny day in Ireland, dry and bright and warm, July 15, in the morning, and they were burying Ian Curtis Ives. Far away in London Ian's enemy, the enemy he had never seen, the Duke of Monmouth, had just been beheaded. But no one at Kilbree would have cared that day. That day belonged to Ian and the whole town turned out to pay him honor.

Down past the long, meandering road from the house, out through the stone and black iron gates, across the clear, sweet Blackwater River, lay another, smaller piece of land belonging to the Ives estates. Back in the days of Queen Elizabeth's golden reign . . . not quite so golden but just as memorable for Ireland . . . a tiny stone church had been built on that spot, hemmed in all around by tall, thick-trunked trees that hid the sight of it from road or river.

Here priests had been hidden, in a bare loft above the wooden altar table, and here, when it was forbidden, came the country people to hear mass and to pray for peace and endurance and freedom. In Cromwell's time the little church was found, its priest killed inside it, its stone roof bombarded as though it had been a cathedral stronghold. In ruins and quite desolate, it remained a sad, aging, useless pile of stones until Sir Thomas Sturbridge happened across it one day and ordered it restored.

When the delighted people of Kilbree had finished the simple business of rebuilding it, Sir Thomas found that Mass still could not be said within its walls. Blood had been spilled there and only a Bishop had the power to resanctify it as a church. But there were only three Bishops left in all of Ireland at that time and none could be got to travel openly for such a dangerous purpose. So the little building remained empty and Mass was said, when it was fairly safe, about two hundred yards behind it, still on Ives property, up on a facing of stone against a hill, an outdoor "Mass-rock" like so many others in Ireland.

Tom Sturbridge had found a use for the old church, however. All these four days and nights, since he had brought Ian's body home, the little building had been used to house the coffin and an honor guard of Dragoons. The men were all Ian's old friends and they had taken turns guarding his remains while the people of the countryside came by to say farewell. . . .

2   Be Thou My Strong Habitation

"Be Thou my strong habitation, whereunto I may continually resort: Thou has given commandment to save me; for Thou art my rock and my fortress . . ."

The priest's voice rang out strong and clear on that bright day of Ian's funeral. There were above two hundred people gathered there on the grass, watching the simple wooden coffin with its honour guard, their blazing scarlet uniforms and polished brass helmets the only touches of color in that somber assembly. The priest stood and said words that were more for these people than for the man they had come to bury. Ian Ives had no further need of words, or of

106

deeds, either. His way was finished on this earth. It was they, with their sad, troubled faces, their grief, their anger, who needed words of hope now.

Thomas Sturbridge, true to his word, sat stiffly upright in a litter chair, carried from the house by four of his own men, his bad leg, strapped tightly to a wooden board attached to the chair, sticking almost straight out before him. Everyone in Kilbree knew young Sir Tom, had known him since he was a boy running barefoot and wild on summer holiday with Ian. Many of the people made their way to where he sat and shook his hand and spoke of their sorrow for Ian and his young widow. Through it all, Tom sat like a stone, unable to answer them, but they understood. The effect of getting there and sitting erect through the long mass was enormous, but he gave in neither to the pain nor the grief. He, too, wore the bright Dragoon uniform, the splendid helmet, the gold lace and engraved buttons, his sword strapped on at his side.

Helene sat beside Tom, watching him anxiously. She had not been to many Catholic services, and she tried very hard to follow what was going on, but her Latin was more basic Cicero than that of the Church of Rome. In the end, her thoughts dwelt constantly on those few words in English: "Be Thou my strong habitation . . ." They went around and around in her mind until they became a little prayer by themselves. Two houses and one master now, helpless children to raise. They would all need a "strong habitation," she thought, looking round at Robby and Michael. Helene's reflections were interrupted in the next moment, as the coffin was placed by the side of the open grave and the small company of Dragoons ranged themselves on either side of the grave.

On a signal from Tom, they raised their long flintlock pistols into the air and fired one last salute to the dead Captain. Even as the powder flashed bright pink against the sky and puffs of white smoke filled the air, workmen lowered the coffin into the ground on straining, taut-pulled ropes. There was a momentary pause as one of the ropes seemed caught on something . . . then suddenly it gave way, the coffin lurched frightfully on one side and went crashing noisily to the bottom. Until then, young Michael had been very still. He had watched the soldiers fire their guns with great interest, but when he heard the coffin crash he jumped to his feet and ran over to the grave, shouting at the top of his lungs. Helene ran to him and put her arms about him, the tears flowing unheeded down her own cheeks, mingling with the tears on Michael's, and she led him away still crying for his papa.

The women of Kilbree, somewhat awed by the presence of Thomas and his lady and the English Dragoons, could hide their feelings no longer. Hearing Michael's desolate voice, several of the older women, who surrounded the still, open grave, began to keen wildly.

Stony-faced, Thomas ordered his chair carried forward. Leaning far over, he picked up a clod of earth from the ground, and threw it into the grave. Everyone looked at Helene—it was the son's place to throw in the next handful of earth—she stood apart from them, still holding Michael by the hand. She couldn't, she could not bring the child back to that grave! No one moved. The wild keening went on and on; the priest looked at Helene questioningly, then at Tom. But Tom did not seem to notice anything.

Helene took a deep breath, but still did not make a move. The moment seemed frozen, doomed to last forever. She felt hysteria rise up in her, a force beyond her control. God, why didn't somebody do something?

Robby saw the awful look on his mother's face and he looked at Michael standing next to Helene, his fists doubled at his sides, a dark frown on his face. Robby slipped out of his seat and ran over to Michael. Taking him by the hand—Robby pulled his friend with him, hoping his mother would follow them, wondering why she simply stood there in front of all those people and did not take notice of Michael.

Robby drew Michael over to his father. He plucked at Tom's sleeve.

"Papa, what should we do?" asked Robby, now very scared, for even the weeping ladies were all looking at him. Tom looked down at the two little boys and a great sob tore from his throat. Michael suddenly spotted his own father's ring on Tom's left hand. He pulled away from Robby and flung himself at Tom furiously.

"That's my papa's ring, you can't have it, you can't have my papa's ring!" the boy shouted. Tom held him very close, and, when Michael stopped for lack of breath, he slowly drew the steel ring from his middle finger and placed it in Michael's palm.

"It is your ring, now, Michael," he said gravely. "I wore it only to bring it safely back to you. Dry your tears, and go and do what the priest tells you to." Michael, his eyes fixed on the ring, seemed reluctant to move. "Go on, now, go with Robby."

The two children walked slowly back to Ian's grave and the priest handed Michael a small spade with a bit of black earth upon it.

Michael seized the spade, tossed the dirt into the grave, and threw down the spade without looking at it. Robby picked it up, shoveled some more dirt into it and added his little offering to the rest.

Helene came forward and repeated the boy's action. Then she took them back to their seats. Other people took their turn, and some of the women threw flowers into the half-filled grave. Tom slumped forward in the chair, and Helene immediately called the soldiers to carry him back to the house. Then she turned to bring the boys away with her, but Michael brushed her hand away and ran off. She looked after him, worried, but Robby took her arm, as though he were suddenly a man grown, and led her toward the stone bridge.

"He's angry," Robby explained, meaning Michael. "I knew he would be angry. But you mustn't mind Michael, Mama. And . . . don't tell his mother what he did, will you?"

Helene looked down at her son in surprise. When had Robby become so wise and how was it she had never noticed it before? But she *did* mind Michael, she thought. There was a look in his eyes when he looked at Thomas—a look of resentment, was that it? But he had always loved Thomas, had followed him like a puppy when the families visited. Deeply troubled, more tired than she realized, Helene picked her way through the grass, hardly realizing as she walked along, that sometimes she was actually leaning on her son's sturdy little arm. And Rob trudged on, feeling very hollow inside, feeling the whole world had changed and would never be the same again. He felt the slight pressure of his mother's weight from time to time and it was the only thing that day that made him feel any better at all. He realized that his mother could be afraid and not know what to do. He had never realized this before. And he also realized that something could happen to his father, could hurt him, could make him disappear from them all into a big deep hole in the ground like Uncle Ian. . . .

3 Fly, Blackbird

All that warm, bright morning the blackbirds had been flying in from as far away as Tralee and Killarney, on their daily route through the countryside. They gathered to feed and roost in the Waterford trees and bushes and were as always very partial to the rooftop of the little stone church and the rock ledges about it. Today they had been disturbed by the crowds of people in their favorite spot, but only to the extent that they continually rose up into the air in large, cloudlike groups above the grave.

Sheila had watched the birds from her window since just after dawn. She could not imagine how she had slept at all last night, but she had, and did not awaken until the birds' morning voices beckoned her out of her bed. She had slept on a trundle bed next to the window. She could not bear to lie alone in the big bed that she had shared with Ian. She would never sleep in that bed again. She had vague plans, half thought out during the last few terrible days, of moving into one of the other bedrooms down the hall after the baby was born, of shutting up the master bedroom for good.

She had not heard the funeral, of course, but she had heard the gunfire and realized what it must be. Soon they would be coming back to the house, she thought, looking down at her bare feet, her loose linen nightdress, feeling that she must hurry to dress and greet the guests in the house. But, somehow, she did not want to move away from the window, she did not want to stop watching the blackbirds. Tonight they will fly back again, back to Killarney . . . she had been to see the lakes with Ian, and she remembered hearing the thousands of voices in the wind as the blackbirds flew in at dusk. They flew in regiments and battalions, Ian had said laughing, in ten different directions.

There was a slight sound at the door. Sheila turned, hoping it might be Helene.

"Who's there?"

"It's me, Michael, let me in!"

She hurried to open the door, sure she heard the boy crying.

"Michaeleen, what are you doing all by yourself, my darling?" She put her arm about him and led him into the room. He sat himself down on the trundle bed and rubbed his eyes ineffectually with one hand. The other he held queerly in his pocket. Sheila gave him a handkerchief.

"Here, now, dry your eyes, my darling, and tell Mama what has made you cry."

"Mama, is Uncle Thomas my father now?" He looked at her with big, tearful blue eyes, the corners of his mouth pulled down.

110

"Your father?" cried Sheila. "No, of course not, darling. You have your own father, you know that."

"But—but he's dead. I know he is. They put him down in the ground, and the soldiers shot their guns and everybody threw dirt on Papa, even me, they made me throw dirt on him, I didn't want to, but Uncle Thomas—and the priest, too—and Uncle Thomas had Papa's ring on his hand—look!" Michael pulled his hand out of his pocket, at last, and showed Sheila the steel ring. Her breath caught in her throat at the sight of it. Fighting back the desire to cry, she said very quietly,

"Well, Michael, Tom brought it all the way back from Sedgemoor Plain for you. There's no reason to be angry, is there?"

"He didn't bring it back for me! He had it on. *He* was wearing it! And Robby said Uncle Thomas was going to be my papa now! I don't want anybody else to be my papa! I don't like Uncle Thomas anymore!"

Aye, little boy, thought Sheila, her heart aching as she looked at her son's small, bent head and heaving shoulders, aye, you hate Tom right now because he's alive and your papa's dead. She sat down by him and cradled him against her and felt the baby move, a rapid fluttering motion that lasted quite awhile. We're all here, sorrowing together for you, Ian, she said to herself. God help me to know what to do and the right things to say.

"Michael, son, now listen to me. Can you hear Mama, can you listen well and not cry again, not right away?" He looked up at her solemnly, and nodded, a small shiver running through him.

"Very well, now," Sheila said, sitting up straight and leaning her aching back against the wall. "Long ago, your papa's father was killed, too, fighting in a battle. Your papa was only a little boy, like you, and he was left all alone . . . his mother was dead. . . ."

"How old was he?"

"Oh, a bit older than you."

"*How* old?" Michael insisted.

"About ten."

"That's a lot older than me!"

Sheila smiled and hugged him. "Listen, now, here's the thing of it: Tom Sturbridge was around the same age then, and he and his father came and found your papa and took care of him and loved him very much. They helped build Kilbree again and Tom's father and mother were like your papa's own family. That's how much they loved him. And, he and Tom were like two brothers together, the way you and Robby are now, do you see?''

''Y-yes,'' Michael murmured uncertainly.

''Well, just suppose for a minute that something bad happened to Robby. How would you feel about that?''

He did not reply, but his mouth fell open at the impossible suggestion that anything could ever happen to Robby!

''All right, and if something bad did happen to Robby, how would you feel about Skip and Bess? Wouldn't you feel sorry that they would never have Robby around to play with or ride again? Wouldn't you want to take good care of them for Robby, and try to help them not miss him so much?''

Skip was Robby's dog, Bess his pony, and when Michael came to Spring Mount he played with both of them, too. ''Yes,'' said Michael, a light dawning in his eyes.

''That is how Uncle Thomas feels about you and me and . . . and everybody here at Kilbree. He loves us. He loves you. He wants to take care of us because something bad has happened to Papa. Do you see, now, my darling?''

''I think so,'' said Michael. He looked at the ring in his hand. ''I wish I didn't make a fuss at Uncle Thomas,'' he sighed wistfully.

''Oh, I'm sure he didn't mind one bit,'' his mother replied. ''But, later on, after everyone's gone home, do go to him. Tell him you're not angry with him anymore.''

Michael looked surprised for a minute. ''Does he feel bad?''

''Mmmm . . . he might, you know, just a little. He loves you very much. And, Michael . . . he would have given you Papa's ring as soon as he thought of it, I'm sure.''

Michael stood up, smiling at her with Ian's wide, sensitive mouth, and Sheila felt her heart turn over. But she smiled right back at him, a radiant smile that suddenly turned into a shocked grimace, and then into a frozen stare of anguish. She caught her breath hard, clenching her teeth to keep from crying out, and turned her head away so he could not see. But Michael was looking at her in alarm. Sheila held up her hand to him to wait, to be patient, and in a few more seconds the smile was back.

She kissed him and hugged him and said, ''Darling, be a good boy and run down to the kitchen. See if Meg is there, will you? Or Cook or any of the maids, and tell them I would like them to come

112

up and . . . help me get dressed for the company.'' Obediently Michael ran to the door. But, just before he went out, he looked back at her, frowning.

"What is it, Michael?" Sheila's smile was strong and steady.

"I love you, Mama. Bad things can't happen to *you*, can they?"

"No, no, of course not, darling! Now, please, Michael, fetch Meg to me . . . quickly!" She strove to keep her voice normal.

He ran out the door and clattered down the polished wooden stairs in his heavy Sunday boots. When he was out of sight, Sheila's smile disappeared abruptly. She lay back on the trundle bed, her hands twisting the skirt of her nightdress tightly. She tried to remember to take in a deep breath of air before the next pain sundered through her like a shuddering, splintering crackle of lightning that seemed to go on until she felt she would be torn in two. But it did not come when she expected it, it came when she had sat up again and decided it might be a false alarm. It came, leaving her breathless, gasping, falling back among the pillows once more and finding no relief no matter how she twisted and turned and arched her back. Then, it was gone again, as if nothing had happened. Damn the girl, where was Meg? she thought frantically.

Ah, but darling, she directed the thought to the stirring baby inside her, you've picked the devil of a time to arrive! She thought longingly of Ian, and then the next pain took her over. It seemed never to end . . . she broke into a sweat, feeling the panic of fear coming on with the pain, and, although she never intended it, she screamed.

"Mama, Meg isn't . . ." Michael, running back into the room, stopped in the doorway and looked at her with horror. She was writhing around on the low bed, her face pale, strained, almost unrecognizable. Sheila barely heard him and she could not answer him right away. The little boy wanted to go to her, but he could not make his feet move. He stared and stared and, not even realizing it, he began to scream with terror.

"Michael, stop it!" Sheila raised herself clumsily on her elbows, reaching out a hand to him. "Go, darling, go and find Aunt Helene! Go quick, Michael, Mama needs help! Pl—ease, Michael . . ." her voice broke off breathless, her head fell back again and once more he saw the strange, awful twisting of his mother's suddenly monstrous-seeming body.

He ran from the room, the sound of her voice in his ears no matter how hard he ran or how far away he got. He ran out the back door of the house, past some of the maids just returning from the burial.

"Michael Ives, where do ye think you're going like that?" spluttered old Aggie, the parlourmaid, as he brushed by her, almost bowling her over into the kitchen garden. "That boy!" she snapped, pulling her shawl very straight about her shoulders to express her annoyance.

"Ah, sure, the poor lad," said her companion. " 'Tis a hard day for him, Aggie." But she was only a vegetable cook in the kitchen of the Ives house and her opinions hardly counted.

The two women lingered a bit in the garden before going in. There was a mountain of work ahead of them and they were not, either of them, eager to get to it. And so it was not until they climbed up the three shallow stone steps and opened the kitchen door that they first heard Sheila's voice from upstairs. Aggie's aggrieved feelings were forgotten in a trice, her old, aggravated bones responding with vigor to the cries of her mistress.

"Go back," she called over her shoulder. "Go and get Lady Helene and find Meg. Send someone into town for the doctor!"

The vegetable cook did not seem to understand for a minute, but Aggie's sharp voice crying, "Go on! Go on, for the love of God!" did at last get through to her. She was out the back door again fast enough, running with her skirts gathered away to one side, shouting as she ran, hoping someone, anyone, would hear her.

Just at the bridge she encountered Thomas, being carried by four soldiers, the others following behind. Helene walked next to the litter chair, hand in hand with Robby.

"Oh, my lady, come quick! It's Mistress Sheila!"

Willy, who had been walking on the other side of Thomas' chair, came round quickly.

"It's Sheila," Helene explained tersely. "Could you see that Sir Thomas is put to bed safely, and then look after Robby and Michael?"

Suddenly, the nervous little cook jumped. "Michael! Oh, but he's not at the house, my lady! He must have heard his ma yelling and got scared. Aggie and me, we saw him running as fast as his legs would take him."

"I'll find him, never fear," said Willy, swinging Robby up onto his shoulders. Helene said a few quick words to Thomas, then ran on into the house and up the stairs to Sheila.

4 The Tower

Kilbree House stood on a very gently swelling hill, its front entrance facing toward the river. Behind the house, beyond the stables, the smith's shed and the carpenter's shop all to one side and separated from the house by a stand of trees, lay the small lake where Sheila's two prized black swans paddled about and families of brown ducks paraded. On the other side of the lake stood a very old tall stone tower of the kind used by holy men and hermits sometime in the past. The tower was half in ruins. Its severe grey splendor, softened round about with moss and climbing ivy, was reflected in the lake's clear eye. Ian had liked the place. He and Tom had often played there when they were young. No one could find them once they had scrambled up the craggy interior and many an hour they had sat in the heat of the afternoon, talking, planning, wishing they were already men. It was a boy's kind of place.

It was to that tower that Michael took himself, running as though the devil were on his heels. He had not known where to go except someplace no one would ever find him. He had never been as far away from the house and he had never seen the tower up close. Once, when he had asked Ian about it, Ian had told him it made a wonderful hiding place. And hiding was just what Michael wanted to do now, hide from everyone and everything.

He climbed up as high as he could inside the tower, and when he sat down, rubbing his wet cheeks, he found that he was still clutching his father's ring in his hand. He looked at it, then slipped it over each of his fingers in turn. It did not fit any of them, not even the thumb. But he left it on his thumb, turning it round and round, faster and faster as he remembered what he was running away from.

Mama! he thought, looking up quickly, as if he expected to see her standing there. Michael's cheeks burned with remembered rage. She had lied to him! She had told him nothing bad would happen to her, only just a little while ago. But he had seen for himself, he had seen her lying on her funny little bed by the window, holding on to her clothes and crying and yelling like that. Something bad *was* happening to her, something awful. Michael made himself recall as much as he could of how she had looked, what she had done. She had been scared. He hadn't ever seen her scared like that before. Why, she had shouted at him when she saw him standing there. He had only come back to tell her that Meg was not home yet . . . and how she had looked at him! How she had yelled . . . he forgot what she was saying, he had, indeed, hardly heard the words at all. For, at the first sight of Sheila in her agony, Michael's mind refused to register anything else. He did not remember how he got out of the house, nor that he had run into the two servants on his way.

He sat in the shadows, sniffling, trying to figure it all out for himself. But everything was so mixed up, ever since Papa had gone away and died. Mama hurt, that was one sure thing. Nobody ever yelled like that unless they were hurting very badly. But what had hurt her? Bad things could happen to her, they *did* happen to her . . . and that meant . . . he gulped . . . that meant that even as bad a thing as *dying* could happen to her!

Michael sat and sobbed his heart out, all alone on a ledge in the gloom-haunted old tower, every question in his mind answered and all the answers wrong. He cried until he had no more crying in him, until his eyes burned and his throat felt scorched dry and swollen. And then he lay down on the little ledge of stone and fell asleep while the long day went on.

5 Michael And Willy

The hours had worn away, the sun was almost a memory of itself, and Robby was downstairs in the kitchen with Cook and the maids, cutting out cake men and boats and lop-eared dogs, happily chatting with whomever came rushing in and out of the big room. Willy had seen to it he had his supper. Both nurses were downstairs, too, and Elizabeth's cradle was being gently rocked by the fireplace. The sounds from the second floor were too frightening for the children to listen to and they could hear them quite distinctly up in the nursery. It was God's mercy, all agreed, that the kitchen got none of that sound, for it was in a different wing of the house, the old wing. The rest of Kilbree had been added on bit by bit by different members of the family, but the kitchen—a stolid, stone room with a wall-wide, ceiling-high hearth you could stand in—was part of the original house.

Willy had gone out again, by himself, taking only a quick mug of hot tea for his supper. As evening came on, the air grew cooler and damper. Even with his good woolen army coat he still felt uncomfortably chilly.

He and Robby had looked through the stables, the haylofts, the grooms' quarters, almost everywhere, he supposed, and Michael had not turned up. Sooner or later that blessed baby up there struggling so hard *would* be born, and Willy knew mothers well enough to predict that as soon as it *was* born, Michael's mother would be sure to look around and ask where her boy was.

Willy wandered slowly, carefully, out toward the lake, admiring the black swans until he saw them come out of the water and walk about a little bit. Now he saw very clearly, albeit a little short of proper respect for natural history as a science, what people meant when they talked about "a duck out of water." One of them things out of water is a queer sight indeed, thought Willy, wishing the big awkward birds would go back where they belonged and again be as graceful as God intended.

Ah, Michael, Michael Ives—he conjured Michael up in his mind's eye—where be you now, boy? And what made you run off the way you did?

He was terrified into it, Willy decided. No doubt about it. No one knew what happened back at the house. Maybe he had heard his mother crying out . . . the boy had had to take too much all at once, too much, Willy shook his head. That's the way they always comes, in fours and fives, never mind yer twos and threes, and who's ever prepared proper for misery in such big doses?

He was standing at the edge of the lake, looking in every direction. The only sound he could hear was the harrumphing of the old bullfrogs in the reeds.

He was just about to turn back when he noticed the tower, looming up out of the evening shadows like a vagrant Celtic god with narrow, nasty eyes.

"Great bloody awful things," shivered Willy at the sight of it. "Shouldn't want you in my backyard!"

He half turned, thought a second, and then started toward the tower, calling softly as he walked along . . .

"Michael! Michael Ives, answer me! Are you up there, Michael?"

Ah! he told himself, a bit wide in the eyes now that he was so close to the stone thing, first he had gone out looking for the father, and now the son. Michael, you'd best be alive when I find *you*, or

I'm keepin' clear of Iveses from this on! "Michael?" he said very loudly, pushing aside a pile of heaped stones and crawling inside the old ruin. His voice echoed back to him at once. Lor' what a place, Willy told himself . . . and then, as if from very far away, he heard a sob and Michael calling back to him.

"Is that you, Willy Duncan, down there?"

"It is, Michael, it's me!" shouted Willy, looking upward, trying to spot the boy.

"I'm not coming down, Willy," said Michael.

"Oh, you're not?" replied Willy. "Well, then, I'm coming up."

He scrambled and clawed his way up the walls until he reached the loophole ledge where Michael was sitting, his small arms wrapped about his knees, his teeth chattering from the cold. Willy wedged himself in next to the boy and wrapped his scarlet jacket around him.

"I just woke up, Willy," said Michael, not thinking it the least unnatural that Willy should be there with him, asking no questions, not prying, not scolding.

"Funny place to sleep," observed Willy.

Michael did not reply. Willy could barely see his face, but he seemed to be crying.

"You didn't go and hurt yerself, did you?"

"No. But I forgot . . . something. I had to do . . . something . . ." his voice trailed off.

"Oh, it'll come to you, sooner or later," Willy said. "Say, you had anythin' to eat?"

"No."

"Want anythin'?"

"No."

"All right, then. We'll just sit awhile, if that's agreeable to yerself."

They sat in silence for a moment or so and then, suddenly, the boy uttered a loud cry and moved so unexpectedly that he nearly tumbled down the length of the tower.

" 'Ere, now, can't go breakin' our necks, can we?" Willy grabbed him and pulled him back, but Michael struggled against him.

"Let me go! Let me go, Willy! I've got to find Meg . . . Meg and . . . and Aunt Helene!" he cried wildly, thrashing about until Willy feared they would both fall off.

"Wait a bit, Michael. Slow and steady wins the race!"

Willy got both his arms firmly about the boy and, with much difficulty, was finally able to hold him still. "Now, then, what's all this 'fetchin'' about?"

"Mama! She told me to run down and get Meg or Cook! I did run, I did! I ran as fast as I could, but there wasn't anybody there in the kitchen or the pantry, either. Then I went back up to tell Mama, and she . . . she was shouting at me! Something terrible was hurting her, I could tell . . . I could tell, Willy! And . . . and she said I was to get out and find Aunt Helene!" Michael stopped for breath.

"Yer Auntie is with her right this minute, young feller, so what's all the fadoodlin' about now?"

But Michael had remembered everything. In an odd little voice, he said, "Mama wanted me to help her, but I didn't, Willie, I didn't! I ran away to here and I was so angry at her. She lied to me," he added. "She told me nothing bad could ever happen to her, but it is, it is!"

Willy held him, considering what to do. Then he said, "We're a-goin' down now, boy. First me and then you right after me. You step where I step, hold on where I hold on. After we gets down, we're a-goin' right back to yer house and you can see for yerself that yer mama's just fine. Come on now, Michael Ives, I'm startin'. Follow me close, boy. . . ."

Willy climbed down very gingerly, trying not to look at the tumbled stones on the ground far below. He had to urge Michael along after him every step of the way. When the little boy hung on to a loose shelf of stones crumbling in his fingers, still seven or eight feet above Willy's head, he pressed his body tightly against the curved wall and refused to move any further.

"You'll have to jump it, Michael," called Willy, holding out his arms. "Come now, I'll catch you."

"No, no," gasped Michael, his eyes closed in terror. "I won't."

"Come, Michael!" ordered Willy, knowing there was no way he could carry the boy down safely.

Michael shook his head, making no sound. Willy stood just beneath, unble to reach him. The boy could not hang on much longer; in another few minutes he would lose his hold and he would fall. But Willy knew that Michael needed to make the decision to come down by himself.

"Michael," he called up to the boy, "I will catch you, I give you my word and, so far's I reckon it, I ain't gone back on my word yet...." There was no answer. Willy scratched his head and tried again.

"You got to trust somebody sometime," he said. "And besides, you h'ain't got no reason not to trust me, 'as you? Come on, Michael. Robby... he told me you was braver'n him, brave as your dad, *you* was, that's what your pal Rob told me only this afternoon. Me, *I* says to 'im, wot? No one's as brave as that 'ere Cap'n Ives! You can do it, Michael... Rob believes you could... your dad, watchin' right this minute from up there in 'eaven, 'e believes it... but me? *I* got to be showed!"

Michael opened his eyes, casting a panicky look down at Willy's confident, smiling face. Willy seemed so far away, his outstretched arms so small, so easy to miss....

"You can do it, Michael," repeated Willy. "Now... jump!"

Michael jumped, and landed in Willy's strong arms. The force of his weight almost knocked Willy to the ground. Willy tottered back and forth trying to get his balance, but he never let go of the child in his arms and, a moment later, the two of them were standing outside the tower walls, hand in hand.

Nothing is ever goin' to make that boy believe everything's all right until he sees 'is ma, Willy reasoned as they headed back to the house. Maybe the baby's come by now and Mistress Ives could speak to the lad for a moment, show him his new brother or sister. He'd soon forget thinkin' he'd failed her when she needed him then.... Yes, Willy decided to himself, the sooner that 'ere boy was set to rights about his ma, the better off he'd be. And, whistling loudly, Willy walked him toward the house with long, quick strides.

Five

"Remembrance Fallen From Heaven"

1 I Have Been A Shadow On Your Life

How long had Sheila been screaming like that, Helene wondered. She had lost all track of time since the moment she had entered

Sheila's bedroom. She and Meg and Mrs. Curley were there together through it all. Aggie had fled down to the kitchen in tears early in the afternoon. Helene recalled people coming in and out of the room, bringing things, taking things away again . . . how many times had she been asked if she wanted tea?

They had moved Sheila back to the big bed when the doctor came; it was easier for him to examine Sheila there. When Sheila realized that they were taking her from the trundle bed she tried to twist away from them, shaking her head pitiably from side to side, begging them not to. Helene alone had been able to calm her, persuade her it was for the baby's sake. At that moment another great pain overtook Sheila and Helene never knew whether it was her words or the pain that made Sheila stop protesting and let them do as they wanted with her.

Meg had brought several sets of fresh bed linens and set about taking down the heavy satin quilted curtains and hangings, so Sheila might have all the fresh air the warm afternoon allowed. The doctor wandered in and out at first, taking his tea downstairs, but later he did not leave the room at all.

Sheila lay on sheets soaked with perspiration. Helene had tried in the beginning to change the sheets, but moving Sheila proved so agonizing she let it go. They had gotten her into a light linen shift, which Helene, remembering her own experiences in childbed, ripped knee-high in length. And then, there was nothing to do but wait. How long it must seem to Sheila, Helene thought, sitting in a straight-back chair next to the huge oak bedstead. At first you count time between one pain and the next. But, after a while, there is nothing, no blessed island of painlessness at all, there is no "between," there is only pain that grows and grows and wrenches you apart until you wonder why your body is still in one piece, until you wish to God you would be torn in two and have done with it.

Helene herself was thoroughly worn out, and still there seemed no end in sight. She bathed Sheila's white face and neck, her arms and never-still legs with cool water and saw a fleeting recognition in the tortured grey eyes, a look of desperate gratitude. She sent Meg downstairs to fetch more water, to be sure to go out herself and draw it from the well, ice-cold, and be quick bringing it back. . . . Meg cast her a brief, injured glance as she quickly left the room carrying a tall stoneware pitcher with her. Helene sighed. She had never spoken so sharply to Meg before. They had been together with Sheila for Michael's birth, and that had been very hard, too. But she had not been afraid for Sheila then. And she was terribly afraid now.

"Lady Sturbridge, you must come away, even for a few minutes," insisted the doctor. "You are not so long out of childbed yourself, my lady. You will weaken yourself if you don't take nourishment. Come over by the window where it is cool and have a cup of tea with me."

Helene shook her head impatiently. She was holding on to Sheila's hands. Her own hands felt numb, her arms ached unbearably from the unchanging angle at which she held them so Sheila might have a hand to cling to. Sheila clutched both of her hands and squeezed them and pulled them. Once or twice, when Helene had been shot through with sharp pains, she had attempted to loosen Sheila's hold on her, and then had given up. The big grey eyes had rolled back toward her in sudden horror; Sheila had exerted strength she could not spare to hold her fast, and begged her not to let go.

"No," Helene said to the doctor now, "it seems to help her a little if she can hold on to me."

He shook his head disapprovingly, but then he disapproved of this entire business. He had warned Sheila Ives long ago and often, too, that she must never risk having another child. He thought, as the years had passed since Michael's birth, that she had heeded his warning. Now it was all for nothing. She was a tiny woman with narrow hips and pelvic bones, too small, too delicate for childbearing.

She cannot deliver it, he thought tiredly, looking back at the tiny, childlike figure on the bed . . . the huge mound of belly like an obscene malignant growth stealing the very life out of her. He looked at the magnificent dark red hair, now wet and stringy, spread out all over the pillows despite all Helene's efforts to keep it bound back and out of the way. He turned away again, wishing he might shut out the pleading in those soft gray eyes.

"Ah, God!" said the doctor aloud and quite safely, for no one else in that room could hear him, "God, take her fast, will you?"

"Doctor, how much longer do you think? . . ." Helene fairly shouted the words across to him.

He stared at her. What should he tell her? That there had been no bag of waters around the child? She knew that already and knew that the blessed, easing, quickening-up of the birth process that the breaking of that bag meant was not to be, not for Sheila. Should he tell her that at his last examination, not twenty minutes ago, the birth canal was not yet widened a full two fingers after all these hours and hours of strong, continual contractions. . . . and must be five, not two, for the child's head to come through freely? He considered his words carefully, but he did not realize that Sheila, too, was listening.

"It could be another twenty-four hours," he said flatly, looking straight at Helene, whose dark eyes opened wide with disbelief and horror.

"She will not last so long!" cried Helene. "Can't you do something? Can't you help her some way?"

He sighed. "I can give her opiates. You know that will not help. It will only slow it down."

"But she's not strong," Helene insisted, looking helplessly down at Sheila, whose eyes were, for the moment, mercifully closed. "She can't do it by herself! Can't you . . ."

"Lady Sturbridge," he interrupted quickly. "If she were further along, if we had a presentation of the head, then, perhaps . . . but even that would kill her."

"What are you saying?" cried Helene furiously. "You're telling me she's going to die, aren't you? You're doing nothing, nothing, and they're both dying!"

Meg returned at this moment, standing frozen in the doorway, the heavy, full pitcher of water held in both arms. She looked wildly from Helene to the doctor and then to her mistress, and swayed on her feet, going dead white in the face.

"Meg! Stop it," commanded Helene. "Get in here and close that door at once!"

"Ye won't let her die? Ye won't let her die, Doctor?" Meg was pleading, even as she obeyed and set the pitcher down on the shining waxed oak dresser.

"Helene." Sheila's voice seemed to come from somewhere far away.

"What is it, Sheila? What do you want, dear?" Helene bent over the girl on the bed, trying not to miss a word she might say.

"There is a way," she whispered, her breath coming short and harsh.

"A way . . . yes, yes, a way," repeated Helene, not understanding her. "A way to do what, Sheila?"

Sheila's gaze moved to the doctor's still figure by the window.

"He knows," she said slowly. "He knows what must be done."

Helene glanced at the doctor in confusion. "What is she talking about?"

He shook his head ever so slightly, but the movement was not lost upon his patient. Her grip on Helene's hands became frenzied . . . she placed one of her hands on Helene's shoulder, pulling her, tearing at the sleeve of her dress.

"Take the child!" Sheila told Helene, ignoring the doctor now. "He must . . . he must take it or . . . we will both die!"

"Mistress Ives," he said, coming to the bed, "Sheila, try to listen to me, will you?" He looked at Helene, however, as he spoke. "She doesn't understand, my lady. She is talking about a . . . procedure . . . by which I might surgically remove the child. Surgically, do you see?"

Helene looked puzzled, then realization came to her and she nodded, more afraid at this moment than she had been all day long.

"Oh, no, Mum!" cried Meg suddenly, clutching fearfully at the bedpost.

A ghastly onslaught of pains overwhelmed Sheila then and for some minutes to come. Her screaming, high-pitched, weak and thin, died away into a hideous gutteral growling low in the throat. But this time she opened her eyes and spoke to them.

"If I had the instrument in my hand now, I would cut this unmerciful flesh of mine and tear my child out into the world with my own hands!"

"Don't you see," cried the doctor frantically, yet his voice was never raised above a whisper . . . "Don't you understand? I can't make that choice!"

"Then you condemn us both to the grave!" groaned Sheila, turning her head away from him.

From that moment on, Sheila ignored the doctor's presence. She clung to Helene, would not take her eyes from hers, would hear no voice and no words said save the voice and the words of Helene. But Helene was ashamed to look at her. She had no comfort to offer Sheila now, no soothing promises to make her friend anymore.

"Helene!"

Sheila's eyes were open and clear. She tried to lick her dry, cracked lips. Helene reached for a glass of water, but Sheila shook her head violently.

"No, no! No time . . . Helene, listen to me!"

"I am listening, dear. But you must try to save your . . ."

Sheila's eyes rolled back in her head. She struggled for control, trying to raise her head up. "Helene, listen! Tom . . . Tom doesn't love me . . . please, listen!"

"Dearest Sheila," Helene said, kissing the soft cheek on the pillows. "Don't concern yourself with all that. It's in the past . . ."

Sheila stared at her, her head shaking slightly, and large teardrops gathered at the corners of her eyes. "I have been like a shadow on your life, I think," she spoke quite clearly. "I have thought so much about you and Tom and . . . all of us. Ever since Tom brought Ian back to me. I wanted to have the baby's birth over with and then find a little time with you, some quiet day we might be sewing, perhaps, or with the children . . . and I had it all planned, what I would say to you. But now . . . there isn't any time left . . . no time . . ." Her legs jerked wildly, her back arched and she shrieked . . .

Helene looked at her, thinking, I will never know what she was going to say. She sighed. What difference did it make anyway? She was trying to reassure me, she was being kind. It was typical of Sheila, who could never bear the slightest suggestion of sorrow in anyone around her, whose delicate, lovely spirit had known early suffering and loss—Sheila, who was always so aware of the hurts of others.

"Helene!" Sheila spoke to her again, so faintly, from so far away that Helene had to bend her head quite close to catch the breathy words.

"Helene . . . why didn't you see? It's you Tom loves . . . I knew it long ago. I thought everything was all right then, at last . . . but you went on thinking . . . wrong . . . all wrong. Tom loves you, Helene . . . you . . ."

Helene waited, but all she heard was Sheila's ragged breathing. Finally she lifted her head again and, in doing so, she caught Alice's eye upon her, full of understanding and sympathy. She could not bear it that they had all heard what Sheila said. She shifted slightly on the hard chair so that she could not see their faces staring at her. And she refused to allow herself to think of Sheila's words. Sheila Ives was a very loving woman, Helene told herself firmly, that was all.

After that, Sheila said no more, but simply gave herself up to the pain. Whatever they wanted to do with her, she seemed neither to notice nor to care. She no longer answered the doctor's questions. Only her tight grip on Helene's hands never weakened for an instant.

After another endless half hour had passed, Meg whispered in horror from her post at the end of the bed, "Her feet are ice-cold!"

The doctor went quickly and picked up one of Sheila's small feet in his hand, then let it go. The foot fell back on the mattress. Sheila said nothing.

He walked past Meg and Mrs. Curley, leaned down and carefully lifted Sheila's head a little bit. When he took his hands away, her head fell back heavily. Only the strength in her hands remained. She had seemingly willed those hands to cling to Helene. Now, whether that will still functioned or not, its effect had not abated.

"She's going!" cried Helene in terror. "Meg, rub her legs, her feet . . . get the warming pan . . . hot water . . ."

She did not see what the doctor was doing. He had gone to his medicine chest, placed open upon the armoire. She looked about for him impatiently. He should be here, doing something, thinking of something!

And then, he was back at the bed again, across from her on the other side, and he was pulling up Sheila's short, torn shift, up past her knees, over her thighs, roughly ripping the cloth so it would not obstruct his movements. And, in the bright light of candles and fire Helene did not remember being lighted, she saw the glint of steel in his fingers . . .

"Be ready for the child!" he ordered tersely. Meg came and stood behind him, miraculously calm and quiet now, a thickly folded length of fresh white cotton cloth in her hands.

"Hold her still, if you can, as quiet as possible!" He directed this at Helene. Sheila's body was still wildly thrashing about. Helene held her arms pinned down and Mrs. Curley, setting aside a steaming kettle of water, came to help her, her large strong hands holding Sheila's slim shaking legs wide apart. . . .

The doctor gave Helene one final, remorseful look, then turned his full attention to what he was doing. Sheila's eyes were open but unseeing, her gaze fixed blindly on the ceiling. Tears were gushing from them, spilling down her cheeks, but all Helene could see was the slender red line the Doctor seemed to be drawing, as if with a pen dipped in red ink, across Sheila's swollen abdomen, a line which instantly turned into a deep, curved gash that split apart the two halfs of her body.

In the midst of the flooding torrent of deep crimson blood, Helene saw faintly the child's form exposed, and then heard herself scream as the doctor flung away his dripping scalpel and inserted both of

126

his hands wrist-deep inside of Sheila's severed body. He took the baby from its mother, quickly placing it on the cotton cloth Meg held. He looked quickly at Sheila, placed his head gently upon her breast, felt her cold wrist for a pulse, but there was no sign of life left in her, only her two small hands still holding faithfully to Helene.

"She's gone," he said briefly, and turned to the baby.

Helene did not move, could not move. He's wrong, she said to herself. She felt like laughing at the poor young man with his sad, strained, guilty face. He was not really a very good doctor, she thought. Sheila was not "gone." How could Sheila be gone when Helene was still holding her hands and could still feel that awful grip? He is wrong, she said to herself, almost playfully. He is so very wrong.

She looked closely, with concern, at Sheila, wondering why nobody was beginning to clean up the ever-deepening pool of blood gathering under her body, soaking through the sheets and into the mattress and still pouring out of her, although now more slowly. All the pain will be over soon now, Sheila dear, Helene thought. We'll bandage you up and take such good care of you that. . . .

But then she realized that the strong grip she thought she still felt from Sheila's hands was only the gradual stiffening of the fingers. There was no real, living pressure from those slender white fingers, no returning squeeze, no answering warmth or feeling.

"She's dead," said Helene suddenly. The doctor glanced up hastily and there was enormous sympathy on his face.

"Yes," he said. "I think she was dead before her daughter was born."

Her daughter, mused Helene dreamily. She looked over at the tiny naked red form lying quite still on the white cotton cloth. He had cleaned the mucus from the nostrils and throat and ears and sponged the tiny, still-closed eyes. He had cut the umbilical cord and tied it off and was now massaging the small quiet body very gently.

"Is it . . . is *she* alive?" Helene swallowed hard.

"There is a heartbeat, but it's very weak. And she has not begun to breathe yet . . ."

Helene looked at him as if he were out of his wits. "She must breathe to live! Help her! Help her!"

He looked hurriedly about the room. "Bring me a basin of warm water," he ordered Mrs. Curley. In a moment it was by his side. He lifted the child's still body and gently lowered it into the water, holding it in both hands, and began to pour some of it over the child's head and shoulders with one cupped hand.

Mrs. Curley sniffed with disdain. "He'll go and lose that one, too!" she pronounced firmly. "A good wallop, that's what ye give a new baby. Gets 'em to breathing right off!"

"*This* new baby has been through hell, ma'am," murmured the doctor through his teeth, and he continued to move the child about in the warm bath. Helene turned away, suddenly losing interest. The child is dead, she thought, why does he trouble so? What a day of death for the little family Thomas loved so well.

She caught her breath very sharply as she remembered what Sheila had said to her, what Sheila had tried to do before she died. . . .

Oh, Sheila, she thought, at least you and Ian are together now. . . .

A sudden thin cry filled the room, and the doctor shouted, "Ha!" with all his might, lifting the now wiggling, squirming and very much breathing baby girl out of the water and into clean, fresh wrappings. Meg, weeping unashamedly, carried the baby over to the cradle that had been made just for her and placed her inside. And still Helene sat next to Sheila's cold bloody corpse, holding her hands, waiting.

Finally, it was the doctor who came to her and gently, very gently, loosened the living hands from the dead ones and spread a coverlet over Sheila.

"Come," he urged her, almost lifting Helene from the chair she had occupied so long. "Come over and see her little daughter." He led her by the hand across the room as though she were a child herself and did not let go of her until she was standing by the cradle. Meg was there, of course, and Alice, and Mrs. Curley, all leaning over, all smiling down at the child. Have they forgotten Sheila already? Helene wondered, mystified. Then she looked at the child.

She was going to be tall, just as Michael had been, Helene noted almost absently. Her fingers were long and shapely, her skin quite red, of course, and there were several strands of darkish hair on her head. She lay there comfortably, not shaking and quivering as newborn babies usually did, but smiling it seemed to Helene, yes, she thought with a shock running through her, definitely, the baby was smiling. A flash of resentment hit her at this child who lived because her mother had died. But when the baby moved her head about and began to wail, and her little chest to heave with crying and her small hands to flutter helplessly in the air, Helene felt her heart melt.

With a woeful cry, Helene leaned down and picked up the baby and held her very close against her, kissing her head and little hands feverishly, smiling and weeping at the same time, murmuring little loving words and sounds. The doctor looked at the two of them and smiled before he drew Mrs. Curley aside and told her what must be done now for Sheila Ives. The white coverlet over her body was already streaked with blood. Meg had opened the chest to find another when someone knocked at the door.

"It must be from Thomas," said Helene quickly, still cuddling the baby. "He's sent someone up to inquire . . ." And then it occurred to her that she must be the one to tell Thomas Sturbridge that Sheila Carey Ives was dead.

But she did not have time to anticipate the dreadful moment still ahead of her, because Meg had gone to open the door. She had opened it wide, not much thinking what she did, and there in the doorway stood Willy Duncan, a half-smile frozen on his instantly comprehending face. Willy Duncan, and with him—Michael!

"Meg, close it, quick!" cried Helene, her eyes flashing, but it was too late. Michael eluded Willy's hand trying to hold him back, and ran past the soldier, into the room, looking about for his mother.

At first he did not see Sheila on the bed. Mrs. Curley quickly stepped in front of the bed, her heavy, solid body squarely planted in the boy's way. Alice put on a brave little smile and held out her hand to him, walking back very fast to the doorway as she spoke.

"Come along, then, Master Michael, and we'll see what Cook's savin' up special just for you!"

Michael's face was filled with suspicion as he looked about him and, ignoring Alice altogether, he came closer to Helene.

"That's not Elizabeth," he said very loudly, pointing to the baby in her arms.

"Why, no, Michael. This is your very own baby sister," replied Helene softly, her voice begging him to understand, knowing he never would or could, not completely. "Michael, won't you come closer and look at her?"

"Where's Mama?" Michael demanded.

When they did not answer him immediately, the boy grew frightened. There was something going on in this room, this familiar room that he loved and associated with his mother and father. Why were they all just standing there, staring at him so strangely?

Willy moved into the room now, and headed for the boy, but Michael was too quick for him.

"No!" Michael shouted, running right past Alice and around Mrs. Curley's skirts to the bed. Before anyone could stop him, he saw the blood-soaked coverlet and began to pull it down, just enough so that he saw Sheila's pale, dead face, the tangled, lifeless auburn hair, the sparkling grey eyes he loved, now dull and staring at nothing . . .

With a shriek no one there ever forgot, the little boy threw himself upon Sheila's body, sobbing, brokenhearted, his hands twisted about in his mother's hair.

Willy reached him then and picked him up, screaming and kicking. He set Michael on his feet, but kept hold of his hand and looked questioningly at Helene.

She handed the baby to Meg and went to the terrified child. Kneeling down before him, she tried to gather him into her arms, to comfort him. But Michael thrust her away furiously.

"She's dead!" he kept repeating. "Just like Papa!" Then, a new thought occurred to him. He backed away a little, looking up at Willy, talking to Willy. "It's my fault!" he whispered in horror. "I was s'posed to get somebody to help her and I forgot! I was mean to her, I ran away!"

"What is he talking about?" asked Helene.

"He seen his Mum early on, like, when . . . it started, I guess," Willie explained. "She were all alone 'ere and she sent him to fetch you or someone to help. But Michael . . . well, he was mixed up just then, and he come away very mad, and spent all day up in that 'ere old tower."

Helene did not understand all of it, but she realized the boy was blaming himself. "Michael," she said, "it wasn't your fault. It wasn't anybody's fault. She . . . she just . . . died."

Michael listened to her for a moment. Then, his face dark and scowling, he pulled his father's steel ring off his thumb. He looked at it, his young face contorted with grief and misery, then he hurled the ring with all his might across the room at his mother's bed.

"I . . . don't want it anymore!" he sobbed fiercely. "I wasn't brave!" He glanced one more time at his mother's body and screamed like a soul in hell, then ran from the room, down the hall, down the back stairs . . .

Willy gulped. "I'll go to him, Yer Ladyship," he said, backing out of the doorway. He glanced toward Sheila and rubbed the back of his hand clumsily across his eyes. "I . . . I'm dreadful grieved for Mistress Sheila," he muttered, and went away quickly after Michael.

Helene looked at the opened doorway for a moment, then, sighing, she picked up the Ives ring and slipped it on her finger. She glanced at Alice.

"Go and find Sir Tom," she told the girl. "Tell him the child has been born. I will be there shortly . . . and Alice . . . say nothing more of Mistress Ives. I will tell him myself."

2   I Will Not Tell Him What Sheila Said

Tom Sturbridge had dozed, on and off, for several hours. He had been persuaded to take some tea, finally, and, two or three hours ago, Willy had brought Robby in to him, changed the dressings on his leg, and gone away again. Tom was still asleep there in the drawing room. He had stirred about restlessly, unable to really relax as long as Sheila's voice could still be heard. He did not know much about such things, but he thought it was taking a long time, too long . . . he wished he might see Helene. Helene would answer his questions truthfully, not like these scared servants, who, when he asked them what was going on, avoided his eyes and whispered evasively and got away from him as fast as they could. Helene never evaded anything, no matter what. Why didn't she come? Still, he was very tired and still quite weak, and he did sleep at last. He did not hear the sudden, dreadful silence when Sheila had ceased to cry out, and he did not hear the wailing of her baby as it began to breathe and to live, nor had he heard Michael screaming as he ran downstairs, away from newly born and newly dead.

Indeed he was not quite sure what had awakened him at last. He found himself still lying propped up on the gold damask sofa Ian had had sent over from France a year or two ago. He blinked and rubbed his eyes, and found that the fire was smoking a bit and his eyes were stinging.

He looked around. He was alone and the house was very quiet. The mantel clock rang ten. Where was Helene? He felt uneasy and cursed the wounds that kept him from jumping up and striding upstairs to find her.

That was it, of course, he realized it now. It was the silence of the place and Helene not being there with him. There was a bellpull within his reach. He decided to summon a maid. Surely by this time something must have happened . . . Sheila's screaming had stopped at last. His fingers fell back from the cord and he heaved a great sigh of relief. It was all over now, and everyone was admiring the new baby, taking care of the mother. Naturally things would be kept as quiet as possible, so Sheila might rest. Where the devil *was* Helene? She might have taken the trouble to inform him whether it was a boy or a girl, at least. Tom felt unaccountably irritable, and he rang the bell again, very hard. He found that he had developed an appetite. Good, he thought, with some satisfaction. Perhaps, a little later on, when all the excitement had died down, he and Helene might have a bite of supper before the fire together.

He became aware, gradually, of hurried footsteps and muffled voices outside in the hallway, passing up and down the stairs. Yet no one seemed to have heard him ringing. He gave another good tug on the bellpull and almost at once the drawing room door opened.

"Beg pardon, sir." It was Alice, standing timidly in the shadowy doorway.

"Yes, Alice . . . where is Lady Helene?" Tom squinted at her, wondering why on earth this least timid of maids seemed suddenly so shy.

Alice did not venture any further into the room. "My lady is still upstairs in Mistress Ives' room, but she sent me to tell you the child is born and she will be down directly. Thank you, sir!" She bobbed him a quick little curtsy and withdrew, closing the door again before he could detain her.

"Damned silly girl!" Tom muttered, shaking his head. He hadn't even had a chance to ask Alice if it were a boy or a girl.

The door opened again. His nerves were a bit frayed now and he fairly shouted, "Alice, have the kindness to come all the way in . . ."

"It's not Alice; it's me, Thomas," said Helene, her voice so low he could barely hear what she said.

Tom's eyes lit up when he heard her. "Well, then, come in, come in! Don't stand back there in the shadows like Alice, for heaven's sake . . . what's that you have there?"

Helene walked slowly towards him, holding the new baby tightly to her. And, when he saw what it was she carried, Tom's face broke into a glad smile, the first smile he had found within him in a long time.

"Sheila and Ian's daughter," Helene said, trying so hard to match his smile with one of her own. "Not an hour old, Thomas. Is she not beautiful?"

She held out the child so he might see the little face and curled-up pink fists. Tom Sturbridge looked closely at the child, a soft laugh in his throat, but then his face clouded over and he looked away somberly.

"Ian worried so about Sheila this time," he said, his voice husky. "He talked about the time when Michael was born, how you showed him his new son. And he talked about our little Elizabeth, how much he wanted to see her. . . ."

He fell silent, unable to go on. Helene waited, although all she wanted to do was to turn and run from the thing which must be said. But she did not run. She stood very still, waiting, remembering Ian, too. Helene would always stand still in the very eye of the hurricane, heart quaking, fingers trembling, the devil-voice of fear shrieking in her ears: "Be gone, run away, quickly, run!" But she would stand and wait. Now she was remembering the beautiful smile of victory and glory beyond pain that had been on Sheila's face on the day of Michael's birth, when they had placed him in her arms for the first time. They were both gone now, Ian and Sheila, both dead, and only two small, helpless children to show for what they had been, to mourn for them. And us, Helene reminded herself, we mourn for them. She looked at her husband with a heart overflowing with love and pity, wishing that she might ease the blow that had yet to be delivered. We shall always mourn for them, each of us in our own way, she thought, her throat constricting.

"What is her name?"

Helene started, looking at him. His eyes were on the child again. No one had thought about naming her. If Sheila had had her heart set on a particular name she had not told anyone.

"I . . . I don't know, Thomas," she faltered. At once his expression altered. The sound of her voice, something in the tone was wrong, he could feel it.

"And Sheila? What of Sheila?" he demanded, studying her face carefully, a cold finger brushing his heart.

Helene hesitated, searching for the right words, but there were no right words. She could not bear the look of alarm in his dark eyes.

"Sheila is . . . Sheila died, my love," she said quickly, and suddenly all of the strength went out of her and the terrible burdens of the past days overcame her. She sank down weakly into an armchair across from the sofa, cradling the baby in her lap. It was said, and she was afraid to look at his face. She stared into the crumbling embers in the fireplace, wondering hysterically for an instant if everything, everything in the world was even at this moment dying!

"How?" he whispered thickly. "Wasn't the doctor with her?"

Helene nodded tiredly. "He could do nothing, Thomas. She was not strong enough to deliver the child herself. She was almost gone when he—" She stopped abruptly, noticing the horror in his face. "He had to . . . *take* . . . the baby. For a while none of us expected the baby to live, either. But she did. She is healthy, I think. And now . . . oh, Thomas, all she has is us!"

The words had come tumbling out quickly. She wanted to talk, to keep talking, to say anything she could think of so she might not hear what Thomas would say now about Sheila. For now, in his immense grief, having lost her indeed forever, was he not likely to break the silence that had been between them all these years? Was he not likely to speak of his love for Sheila?

Thomas said nothing, however. He held out his arms to her . . . and understanding what he wanted at once, she gave him the little girl to hold. Thomas knew just how to hold babies, and he took this little one and held her head against his neck and supported her gently with his other hand, though it was still bandaged, rocking her a little bit as he held her to him.

Helene turned away from them and went to stand by the fire, one hand resting on the mantel, her head bent, the shining black waves of her hair tumbling loosely upon her slumped shoulders and down her back.

She thought: Sheila is dead but he will go on loving her in his heart the rest of his life, mourning her, remembering her beauty and the loveliness of her nature more vividly each passing year until, when he is old . . . and I am old . . . his thoughts will be filled with her, the springtime of his love, who died without ever growing old or faded or too familiar.

She had not forgotten what Sheila had said to her before she died. A last gift, she thought, so like Sheila. One last, dear thing she tried to do. Helene shook her head. It was wasted, Sheila, wherever you are, hear me. Your words were wasted because I know they were not true. Thomas does not love me. He loves you, Sheila. He will always love you. . . .

To Thomas, now, at this moment, the fact of Sheila's death was not yet real. His mind kept repeating over and over again to him, Sheila is dead! Sheila is dead! He was sitting in Sheila's front drawing room, holding Sheila's new baby in his arms, and Sheila was dead. He stared at Helene and he thought, it is over. He did not entirely know what he meant by those words, but no man is entirely responsible for the things his own mind tells him. And, in this moment, his mind seemed split in two, each half vying with the other for his feelings and he had, he found, feelings aplenty for both.

Sheila Carey . . . Ives . . . was dead. When he would come to accept that simple truth he knew he would mourn her as he had never mourned anyone else in all his life. Yet the pain of realization did not hit home just yet and he found himself looking intently at Helene. . . .

How straight she's trying to stand, tired as she is, he was thinking. She is worn out, full of sorrow like the rest of us. How beautiful she looks, nevertheless, in that simple black dress, without ribbon or jewel to ornament her own perfection.

Helene did not see it but Tom Sturbridge was smiling at her then in a way he was not aware of having smiled at her before. But Helene, struggling to keep back the tears, did not see it. And when, at last, she was able to stand quite erect once more and look at him with some composure, the smile had faded. He looked to her hopelessly and she remembered that with Sheila's death his last fond tie with family and boyhood was gone. He had his own two children to raise and now two others surely just as dear. He had Kilbree to hold in a world where his own home might be swept away from him at any time by the machinations of political men.

He needs me, she told herself. He respects me, he is fond of me, used to me . . . why must I torment myself by always wanting more? Maybe there wasn't any more, not for anyone. Ian and Sheila had had each other and a perfect love . . . but now they both were dead.

She smiled at her husband, a bit shakily, and saw that the terrible hurt in his eyes seemed momentarily to fade a little. I will not tell him what Sheila said, she decided. I will never tell him. . . .

In the midst of his sorrow, even as the truth clawed its slow, searing way into his heart, Tom watched Helene struggling to

135

reassure him with her smile, her small brave smile upon pale and trembling lips, and an astonishing wave of feeling flooded through him. His thoughts were in turmoil. His deepest feelings had been so carefully hidden away for so long, even from himself, for fear of hurting her inadvertently, that he had not had time for any new discoveries. Wild questions without proper words to them raced through his brain.

"Helene," he began to speak, trying to keep his voice from betraying the violent agitation he was undergoing. "Helene, I have to . . . I must . . ."

But at that moment she had remembered about Michael and the ring. She sat down and took the ring from her finger and showed it to Thomas. And the moment was past, the unasked questions returned, for the time at least, to their quiet unnoticed customary hiding place, like sad wraiths sinking back to their tombs at dawn after a quick forbidden midnight foray. . . .

He swallowed hard, tried to focus his attention on the ring, on what she was telling him about it.

"Where did you get it?" he managed to ask her.

She told him the whole story then and he looked very grave as he took the ring back and put it on his own finger again. He sat there, still holding the quiet baby, watching the ring glow like softest gray satin in the dying firelight and it seemed as if all of the various elements of tragedy of the last several days met, mingled and struck home only now. He felt in him a kind of giddy death of all feeling, briefly, and then the unwelcome return of feeling rushing through him like a fire through the blood.

"Where is Michael now?" he asked her.

"Willy went to find him. The child has been hiding from all of us for hours. I think he has not eaten anything since breakfast."

Thomas nodded thoughtfully. "It will not be easy for Michael, or for this one, either," he said, looking down at the baby. "What shall she be called? She must have a name."

"Sheila was asking for her mother. Could we not name the baby for Mrs. Carey?"

"Katherine?" Thomas looked down at the infant again. "Yes. Sheila would like that. Katherine it is then. My God, Helene . . ." he looked at her, suddenly stricken.

"Thomas, what is it?"

He handed her the baby and sat shaking his head, "It's just the same as my mother and father, and Ian . . . when we were small. I swore to him I would care for . . . for his family and hold Kilbree for Michael. But, Helene, am I the man my father was? Can I raise another man's children, teach them the things their own father and mother wanted them to know? Can I?''

Helene smiled at him. "Yes, you can. You can do all of those things, Thomas. You are more like your father than you know and, still especially, yourself. Never doubt yourself, my dear.''

"Michael will resent me," he murmured. "He does already.''

"Michael will remember that he loves you, in time," she said firmly. "For a while it will be hard for us all. But I will try to help all I can. We are good friends, you and I. Between us, we shall manage.''

" 'Friends'?'' Thomas looked at her, startled. "That's an odd choice of words, isn't it?''

Helene flushed. "Yes, I suppose it is. No matter, I spoke in haste, only to try to comfort you.'' She assumed a light, bantering manner and added, "We are friends, though, are we not?''

Thomas recalled for an instant the bright stab of feeling that had washed over him only moments before but her sweet patient eyes began to form a question, so, very quickly, he nodded. Yet he could not let it go entirely and he murmured, "I had rather thought we were something more. . . .''

The soft tapping on the door just then startled them both and he never heard her reply, "Did you, my dearest? I think not.''

The door opened and Willy presented himself, saluting Thomas smartly with his right hand as he held firmly on to Michael with his left.

"Evenin', Captain, Yer Ladyship. Beggin' yer pardon, but I thought you'd be somewhat relieved to see this 'ere lad. 'E didn't get so far this time as he did a'fore.'' Michael would have slipped away from him again but Willy drew him over and set him down on his feet between Thomas and Helene.

"Me and him 'as 'ad some'at of a talkin','' said Willy softly.

Michael glared up at the lanky soldier but he was not really angry with Willy. Willy now saluted once again and backed out of the room as if he were leaving the presence of royalty. And then they were left alone with Michael and his sister. Michael stared at the baby in Helene's lap, then pointed at her.

"Is that my sister?''

Helene glanced nervously at her husband. "Yes, she is. And, she has her own name now, Michael. Do you want to know what it is?"

But Michael had left off staring at the infant and looked instead at the steel ring back on Thomas' hand. Helene braced herself for another outburst but Michael was rather quiet.

"You got it back?"

"Yes," replied Thomas carefully. "I heard you didn't want it. Do you? You may have it right now. . . ."

"No!" exclaimed the boy, moving back a few inches until he was touching Helene. "I don't want that old ring anymore. You can keep it. You're brave, like my papa. It's just for brave fellows."

"But, you are brave too, Michael," said Thomas, his heart aching at the lost look on Michael's young face. Michael shook his head.

"Not me. I'm not brave." Then, suddenly trembling, he cried out, "My mama's dead, Uncle Thomas. I did love her, I did! But she doesn't know that!"

"She knows it, Michael, believe me, she knows you loved her," said Thomas, his voice breaking as he reached out to the boy.

Michael looked at him closely. "I did love her," he kept repeating, and all Thomas could do was answer him each and every time, "She knows you loved her, she knows."

The baby woke up and began fussing, trying to stuff her fingers into her mouth. Helene rang for someone to take the child upstairs to the wet nurse. Michael once again looked at his new sister, quite coolly, and it struck Helene suddenly that he must associate her birth with his mother's dying. Oh, no, she thought, they have only each other, he must not dislike her, he must not!

"She cries," he observed. "Loud, like Elizabeth."

"Yes," Helene smiled carefully. "She's hungry, just as Elizabeth usually is. And she's to have her own nurse, like Elizabeth."

Michael walked slowly back over to the baby and touched her face very gingerly, then her hand.

"Willy said she's mine. Willy said Mama had to . . . had to go away to Heaven but she left my sister for me. All for me," he emphasized, looking very hard at Helene.

"Why, of course, dear. She is your sister," stammered Helene, somewhat startled.

"And I'm to take care of her and look after her all her life, 'cause she's special," Michael went on, now holding the baby's hand in his own and the barest touch of a wistful smile hovered about his firm, wide mouth.

Helene laughed a little bit, so great was her relief at this most unexpected turn of events. He didn't hate the baby! Far from it, he accepted her as his own! In her enthusiasm she put out her hand to pat the shiny blond curls. But, with an angry cry, Michael slapped her fingers away and retreated a few steps back toward the fireplace.

"Michael!" Thomas stared at the boy, shocked. "Apologize to your Aunt Helene. At once!"

Michael shook his head stubbornly. "I will not!" He pointed to the baby girl Helene was holding. "You're not *her* mother, either."

Thomas' face was tense with anger at the child. He was about to speak when a warning look from Helene checked him.

"Thomas, wait," she said. "No, Michael, of course I am not your real mother. I am Robby and Elizabeth's mother. I know you have your own mother and your own father, dear—"

"You can't be them!" Michael's face was frantic as he searched for words to express himself. He looked at Thomas, pleading in his eyes. "Tell her to leave me and my sister alone!"

This time no look or words of Helene's could prevent her husband from speaking his mind. "Damn it, Helene, I *will* be heard!" he thundered furiously. "I won't have this from you, Michael, do you understand me? I know you are afraid and upset and nobody is blaming you for that, but your Aunt Helene has always loved you and been kind to you. You know that. You had better try to behave yourself, Michael. This very morning you were angry with me because I wore your father's ring, and now you've turned against Aunt Helene. . . ."

"You're a brave soldier, like my papa," piped up Michael, standing his ground bravely. "But *she* isn't any soldier. And she isn't my mama and she can't ever be!"

The stricken look on Helene's tired face hurt Thomas beyond belief. His impulse was to strike the boy, yet he understood Michael's feelings and could not bring himself to punish the child at such a time. He sighed, shaking his head slightly.

"We will speak of this another time, Michael," he said, finally, the full weight of the day's long list of sorrows overcoming him at last.

Helene stood up, placing the baby against her shoulder. Making an enormous effort, she managed to speak quite calmly.

"I will take Katherine upstairs now and find the nurse myself. I'll send Meg down to get Michael. . . ."

"Helene, this isn't settled," said Thomas, looking over at her with dark blue eyes hard as steel, still full of anger.

She sighed, shaking her head. "Isn't it, my dear? Well, never mind. Michael will learn to understand. Some day."

She walked from the room, her pale exhausted face stiff and expressionless, thinking with a kind of aching dread in her of the long years to come and the hard path she must tread.

She left behind her a vast silence, save for the steady ticking of the mantel clock and the sputtering-out of the unattended fire. Her husband sat looking unhappily at the little boy who was Sheila's son, who was Ian's son, thinking how he had loved those two now forever beyond his power to reach again, thinking, as he watched the unnaturally hard set of the child's soft, rounded features, *he* is just as unreachable as they are. Fearful, mistrustful, uncomprehending and filled with a great savage anger not yet realized . . . that was Michael Ives now, too badly hurt, too suddenly made aware of pain and loss.

Michael sat down by the fireside to wait. Someone must come and tell him what to do now. He sat hunched over, his legs stuck out awkwardly before him, his hands curled into fists on his lap. Suddenly he was very sleepy. The unreality of the day swept away from him into the rising smoke of the fire. He half wondered why he had been feeling so angry, so afraid. Drowsily he thought he would remember everything better later on. He was hardly aware of Thomas' still presence, not at all conscious of those hard blue eyes full of perplexity, full of troubled visions and doubts as they watched him.

Thus they remained for a long while, Sheila's son and the man who would have been her lover, and the blind minutes marched away building themselves into phalanxes of hours, regiments of years.

Six

"Flowers Fair In Vain"

1 Spring Mount, Fifteen Years Later

Elizabeth Sturbridge, astride the tall chestnut gelding she preferred above the other horses in the Spring Mount stables, rode quite sedately for the half hour it took to leave the boundaries of her father's estates.

The chestnut enjoyed the slow pace, trotting dreamily along an old lane seldom remembered even by the boys who drove the cows to pasture every day. Low crumbling stone fences on either side of the lane were overgrown with wild rambling English roses and stretching strawberry vines and moist mosses that glistened greenly now after the early morning rain. Elizabeth rode under an avenue of broad-trunked apple trees whose white-laden branches in springtime formed a sweetly scented canopy over her head. Fifteen-year-old Elizabeth delighted in the feel of the quick-flashing autumn sun as it beckoned to her unexpectedly through small openings in the gathered branches of the trees, bare and brown now in the mild late autumn of southern England.

Once beyond Spring Mount, she quickened her pace eagerly, ignoring the soft winnying protest of the horse, she flung back her head with a joyful little cry that her family would have been amazed to hear from quiet, shy little Elizabeth. She leaned forward, urging the horse on, and imagined that the flying hoofs were beating a rhythm excitingly close to that of the pounding of her heart.

Harry, she thought, and deliberately shouted his name into the languid soft air. "Harry! Harry Prescott!" And then, since only a shrewish old wren took alarm from the sound and bothered to reply, Elizabeth laughed from the sheer beauty of it and cried aloud in this strange exultation so new to her, "Harry loves me! Harry Prescott loves me!" And she laughed. Feeling her curled and pinned black hair fall about her shoulders, she tossed her head again. With her pale amber eyes glistening and excitement painting a bright pink glow on her usually lusterless cheeks, Elizabeth was almost pretty. . . .

The old lane ended in a tangle of wild trees and shrubs that edged the Prescott estate. A tiny stream meandered about as if lost and seeking its way through the woods. Elizabeth jumped down lightly and led the horse by a path barely discernable, picking her steps with care among the stones and brambles. She reached up automatically to straighten her hat and found she had lost it somewhere along the way. No matter, she felt more at ease without it, anyway. Harry was used to her just the way she way, no frills and furbelows for Elizabeth, no hat or gloves, either, if she could manage to get past her mother without them. Today she wore a decent enough old blue skirt and a white waist with little embroidered bluebells at the neck. She had had the outfit since she was twelve but it still fit well. Elizabeth had long since given up waiting and longing for her bosom to appear. She was as flat on top as a boy and resigned to it no matter how Helene and Cousin Katherine tried to reassure her. Once she married and had a child, Helene kept telling her, she would be amazed how her figure would blossom out. What nobody seemed to understand was that it mattered not at all to Elizabeth. Harry loved her. Harry, in fact, had once seen her stark naked, swimming all alone in the lake behind Spring Mount. She had been seven and Harry had been nine. She knew what boys looked like and Harry knew what he was getting.

She tethered the horse to a low tree branch and leaned back against the trunk, trying to imagine herself dressed in a white satin and lace wedding gown, her dark hair, the only part of Helene's exquisite beauty she had inherited, curled and rolled atop her small head, crowned with an orange blossom wreath and shimmering white veil. Elizabeth could imagine only a bit of such a picture, and then she laughed. Last year, when she was fourteen and deemed quite finished and turned out from Madame Blanchard's Academy for Gentle Females, her mother had ordered the dressmakers in and had a whole wardrobe made for her. For days and days she had stood patiently, arms outstretched, stomach pulled in, while they fitted her and measured her and clucked their tongues and snipped the gorgeous materials sent down from London and sewed tiny rows of ruching into the bodices and talked very loudly, very vehemently about bright ribbons on the sleeves, and deep lace collars. When it was all done, Elizabeth possessed a wardrobe befitting the daughter of Sir Thomas Sturbridge but the wardrobe did not do what she had thought it would. One long rainy afternoon, when the rest of the family were occupied elsewhere, she had locked herself into her room and, one by one, tried on the elaborate gowns, the tasteful velvets and brocades, the gauzy bright morning dresses and even the seductive black riding frock. She loved the soft feel of the different goods against her skin, but when she studied herself in her full-length mirror she knew she had been right about the new clothes. Nothing was changed. She stood looking at her reflection from head to toe, taking in every detail coolly.

She would never be a beauty, and all the lovely, well-made clothes in the world wouldn't help. She had cast aside the ball dresses quickly, telling herself after all she was not elegant, not tall, not distinguished enough to do them proper justice. Still she half hoped that something simple, unadorned, might make a difference, might turn pale, timid, thin little Elizabeth into at least a pretty young lady.

Instinctively she had chosen a delicate sprigged lawn frock, pale green picked out with little pink flowers, a long dark green velvet sash at the waist, matching ribbons at sleeves and neckline. It was the quietest dress of the lot and she loved it and crushed it to her flat chest when she saw it completed and cried girlishly, "Oh, the dear thing!" and all of the sewing women had smiled but a few of them had sniffed disdainfully.

But even the dearest of dresses hung about Elizabeth's short, thin, angular little body lankly. Even this simplest of gowns made her seem to disappear somewhere within the soft folds of cloth, and the dashing green ribbons attracted the eye far more than they framed her young form or provided a focal point to set off a too plain, too thoughtful young face.

Elizabeth had cried then, not so much because she was not beautiful and knew now that she never would be, but because she felt that somehow she had failed the lovely dress. She would wear it, of course, as she would wear all of the others at the proper times and on the proper occasions. What a dreadful waste of pretty things, Elizabeth had thought, the tears coursing down her cheeks.

But that was before she knew that she was to marry Harry Prescott and now everything was different. Of course they could not marry for another year, not until she was sixteen, and even that her father thought too soon. Yet Arthur Prescott, his near neighbor and old friend from the French war days, wanted young Harry married and settled as soon as possible. Of course they were young, but it was not as though they would be all alone in the world, Arthur had pointed out, clapping Thomas heartily on the shoulder as they had all stood to drink the toast when the terms of the betrothal had been settled. Once married, they could live on at Spring Mount if they chose, although Arthur made it clear he preferred his son to remain on his own estates.

What matter, what matter? Elizabeth's heart sang more sweetly loving than any lark in the meadows around her. What did it matter where they lived or how they lived, as long as they were together? She felt an unusual tightness inside her chest, as though she might burst apart, and her soul, flung free at last, might soar out and upward to the spinning clouds above, such was her great, open-secreted happiness that she was loved. She did not dismiss the love she had known all of her short life already: love of her mother and father, love of her tall, handsome, quiet brother, Rob, love of her cousins Michael and Katherine, more like brother and sister to her. But, she thought, as she reasoned it out, her thoughts leaping very lightly from plateau to plateau of amazing new happinesses, all of them rather *had* to love her, didn't they? Her family was close-knit, tender and open with each other, tending to bicker rather less than others of her friends she had observed. But, Harry did not have to love her. She supposed he did have to marry her, since his father and hers said so. But the day he arrived to pay her his formal respects on the occasion of their betrothal, he did not have to pause suddenly, right in the middle of bowing over her trembling hand and look up right into her face and smile the way he had. He even forgot the formal little speech he had been making and blurted out, "You're the only girl I ever met who seems to have a single idea in her head!"

What had she said to him that made him feel that? She couldn't remember a single word. Surely she had been only correct, certainly not witty or charming or brilliant. She did remember that her mother, standing at her side, had sighed just as suddenly, a great sigh of relief, and a quick bright smile had spread itself invitingly over her lovely face.

"You have done well, Elizabeth," Helene had murmured, stars twinkling in her rich brown eyes as she clasped young Harry's hand and reached her other arm around to embrace her daughter in a quick, fierce loving hug. Elizabeth had kissed her mother's soft cheek and felt tears start to her eyes. But why? What had happened there, all in the shortness of a breath and a breath and a single knowing glance?

It did not matter, for Harry loved her. Later he had told her how he remembered playing with her when they were both still children, how lonely he had been, his parents' only child on the vast Prescott estate, and how he had come to look forward to meeting her on those days when she would have stolen away from Rob and Katherine and Michael, feeling they would never notice she was not there with them, so very close were those three always and hardly room between them for her, although she knew they loved her. But she had felt alone nevertheless. Shy and quiet always, she did not shine so much as they and sometimes, it seemed to her when she had been very small, she could not bear the brightness of the glow about them and she had to run off to quiet, shadowy places like the woods, where she might shine a little by herself.

She and Harry had played in those days and, she supposed, trying to remember so far back as five or six years ago, they had talked about many things. Perhaps that was what Harry remembered about her, their long talks, their shared loneliness. It seemed so natural to him now that he should love her, but to her it was, each day, a surprise, a miracle she could hardly believe.

The chestnut nickered softly and Elizabeth jumped up, hearing swift footsteps approaching through the woods. In another minute Harry Prescott's broad-shouldered, sturdy form appeared, an anxious look Elizabeth did not recognize on his face, a look instantly replaced by a broad smile as soon as he caught sight of her.

"Elizabeth," he said in that softest of voices she loved to hear, "I'm late. Have you waited long?"

She shook her head gaily, throwing her slender body into his arms with abandon. Harry's arms encircled her tenderly for an instant and then, suddenly, tightened very hard, pulling her against him urgently. With a puzzled little laugh, Elizabeth squirmed around in his grasp and peered up at him. There, she determined, something was the matter. The smile was gone from his features and that strange anxious look had returned.

"Harry, you're crushing me, I think!" she cried, pushing him away a little, but only a little.

He tried to smile at her again, but he had never been able to hide anything from her and he could not do so now. Something had disturbed him, something he did not want to talk about. Elizabeth took him by the hand, drew him under the big tree by the stream and pulled him down with her. He lay with his head resting on her lap, staring silently up into the unapproachable world of the treetops overhead.

"What has happened, my love?" Elizabeth was afraid and could not let go of his hand. But he had no intention of letting go of her and held her fingers gently as he tried to gather his thoughts.

"Nothing has happened, Elizabeth," he began, hating so much to waste these lovely private times with her, hating to broach the subject they had always managed to avoid, so far. But he had just had a stormy session with his father and the subject, painful as it was all around, was quite fresh in his mind.

"Nothing has happened," he repeated a trifle too quickly, trying to get it all said without her becoming too upset. "Elizabeth, listen to me. You know I don't care about what goes on on your father's land or in your family, for all that. But people are talking. . . ."

"Oh, *that*," she dismissed his words scornfully. "People are talking . . . again!"

"Yes, my dearest one, and this time I'm afraid it's rather the wrong people. Father's just down from London. He met with the King's Council, twice."

"Just to talk about the Sturbridges?" her eyes twinkled merrily.

"No, on his own business. But your name came up in conversation, I mean yours and others, of course. King William is disturbed about the state of affairs here and in the north. They know all about the meetings your father and your brother and that wild Irish cousin of yours attend. Whitehall is determined to root out Jacobite support no matter how great the house or how highborn the men who are involved. Elizabeth, you might as well know this . . ." Harry sat up abruptly, looking at her very soberly, still holding her hand. "They are calling it treason now, openly, without any opposition from Parliament."

Treason! "What a dreadful word!" Elizabeth breathed, fear catching at her throat.

Harry nodded darkly. "Darling, we've got to have a talk with Sir Tom. We really must. My father can't . . . he says every time he's tried to bring it up, *your* father only laughs and asks him how the quail hunting is. You know about the bad feeling in town . . . it's worse every time I ride in, believe me!"

Elizabeth had no reason to doubt him. She nodded, remembering the black looks, the muttered insults, the coldness that had greeted her and her relatives on the few occasions they had gone into town recently. What had happened, she wondered? She remembered very well how she used to love riding in the great coach with Lady Helene and Katherine, stopping to look over new dress goods just arrived from France and Holland, sometimes taking tea in the quaint little village shop across from the inn. In those happy days, the people had smiled at them and bowed and murmured little pleasantries and inquired after Sir Tom's health. How long ago had that been? Elizabeth frowned . . . several years. But surely everyone had known even then that Papa and Rob and, of course, Michael, had never accepted the strange turn of events that had propelled King James and his wife and son into exile in France and turned over the throne of England to "those bloody usurpers, William of Orange and his wife, Mary," the only way she had ever heard her father or brother refer to the new king and queen.

". . . and then, of course, there's this business with the priest living right there at Spring Mount all these years," Harry was saying, but it seemed no longer Harry's own voice, certainly not Harry's words. She shivered, hearing the sonorous cold tone of Arthur Prescott unconsciously echoed in the voice of her beloved Harry.

"Oh, Harry," she sighed, "you know why he's there. It's just that Papa promised to bring up Michael and Katherine in their own faith. *We* don't have anything to do with Father McGuire. He *does* take supper with the family now and then, but he's so old, why, he hardly ever says a word to anyone and most of the time he just stays in his own chambers behind the chapel. Your father knows that . . . my goodness, he's met Father McGuire any number of times and he was always most gracious to him."

Harry shook his head. "Elizabeth, my father intends to have a talk with Reverend Drury next week."

Alarm spread swiftly through her. She flushed and caught his arm with cold fingers. "Why? Everything is arranged, everything! The betrothal ball is to be in two weeks; it's all planned."

"That's why we must speak to your father," he explained patiently. "Dearest, my father is very angry. He shouted and raved for an hour, he threatened to break the betrothal contract."

"No!" whispered Elizabeth, pressing her fingers against his lips. "Don't say it, Harry, don't say it! I couldn't bear it!"

Harry swept her into his arms, covering her face with kisses, trying to ignore the savage pounding of his heart with quick words of comfort and reassurances he knew rang hollow.

"I don't care what he says," Harry swore fervently against her sweet-scented shining hair. "When he calms down he'll remember his friendship with Sir Tom; he'll reconsider. It's just that he's fresh from court, up to his teeth in talk of conspiracies and plots. What have we to do with politics? We'll ask your father to assure Reverend Drury. . . ."

"Papa will never send Father McGuire away, Harry," said Elizabeth, her heart sinking. Sir Tom was genuinely fond of the old priest and often enjoyed long, philosophical talks with him. Besides, Father McGuire had known both Ian and Sheila Ives. Sometimes, after an evening's chat with the priest, Sir Tom would smile with a bit of a tear in his eye and murmur, "I didn't remember that day when Ian and I rode down into . . ." and it was almost as if those two quite legendary figures would spring to life for a little while as Sir Tom would retell the old tale while Katherine and Michael would hang on his words, their only link with parents they did not remember.

Harry ran his fingers nervously through the thick mop of brown curls that Elizabeth loved to twine about her own fingers. Hesitantly he said, "He may have to send the priest away, back to Ireland, just for the time being, love. But it isn't really whether old McGuire stays or goes that's bothering them—it's those secret meetings. And your Cousin Michael . . . Elizabeth, he has more enemies than he knows. He's too outspoken. Rob and Sir Tom, well at least they know to keep quiet in the right places. But Michael . . ." he shook his head.

"Michael is Michael," Elizabeth said simply. She knew how much Harry had wanted to be friends with her cousin, how often he had tried to draw Michael into the circle of young men who were his friends. Rob, whatever his political beliefs, had fitted easily into that easygoing, hard-riding, pleasure-seeking group . . . when he wanted to. They all liked Rob, they liked him so much that they simply chose to ignore his unusual preoccupation with political matters, to ignore it or pretend it didn't exist. Rob, always levelheaded, slow to anger, cool and fair in his judgments, was a favorite with everyone although intimate of none.

But Michael had always been a firebrand. Now in his twenty-fourth year he had about him the hard mouth and cynicism of a man twice his age. He had inherited the spectacular good looks of his father, the mane of brilliantly golden curly hair, the flashing light blue eyes that seemed to see everything there was...and to the heart of it at once. Michael was tall, even taller than Ian had been, broad in the shoulder, narrow in the hips, with heavily muscled arms and legs that had seen many a hard hour in the saddle. Like all the Irish, Michael had a way with horses and all other animals. And, save for the family itself, Michael had always been quite contented to confine his love and devotion to his horses and his dogs. There was about Michael, as there was *not* about Rob, a restlessness, constant motion and activity, unending and sometimes rather bewildering unhappiness. If Michael ever remembered the awful events of the day his mother died, his father was buried and his sister was born, he kept it to himself. He never so much as glanced at the steel ring Sir Tom wore and if he was aware that he might have back that ring at any time merely for the asking, Michael seemed not to care. Men said he was hard, and he was, although "tough," like the finest leather wrought in a battle saddle would be more to the point. Women, always fascinated by him at first, soon found he was impervious to their charms and dismissed him from their calculations either with disappointed sighs or with angry sniffs. Michael Ives was not to be had, not to be tamed or settled down, never to be domesticated. When he wanted what a woman could offer, he preferred the swift-bought affections of a tavern wench or local serving girl. He rarely saw the same woman twice.

Michael never let anyone forget that he was an Irishman and a Catholic. That, more than anything else about him, had alienated most of Sir Tom's friends and neighbors. The times were trying, nerves jittery. Everyone would have liked to forget poor old King James. But no one could quite forgive his hightailing it over to Louis of France and using French support to land himself in Ireland and be received as rightful king. Well, the hard-won Battle of the Boyne had settled that, of course. King William's Protestant forces had driven James out, never to return. Now his son lived and sulked in France and heard with tears in his eyes and a lump in his not-quite-royal throat that he was solemnly, lovingly toasted in secret at home as the "king over the water."

In the Sturbridge household, as in many others in both England and Ireland, at the end of the evening meal, the servants brought in silver bowls of water for each place. The wine glasses were refilled, everyone stood up, holding his or her glass directly above the water bowl and Sir Tom would call out very loudly, "Ladies and Gentlemen, the King!" No man could say he did not mean King William, no man could prove the silver water bowls were not set out so everyone might rinse his fingers after the meal. The little ceremony soon became popular . . . on board His Majesty's ships the traditional toast to the king had to be stopped altogether for the time being, as one wag laughingly reminded his fellow officers it looked "damned awkward" for loyal officers to raise their glasses and salute the king when they were all and always "over the water!"

Michael is Michael, Elizabeth had said. And after that, no more remained to be discussed. The two young lovers sat quietly together by the little stream, her dark head resting on Harry's strong shoulder, each lost in private thoughts and misgivings. Harry knew his father's implacable disposition. Once and for a long time, Arthur Prescott had deemed it most appropriate, honorable and gratifying that his only son be united with the family of his friend Tom Sturbridge. Lately Arthur had been taciturn about the match, now he seemed openly hostile. Harry would never tell Elizabeth the awful things his father had said . . . had shouted so half the household might hear him . . . about the way Tom Sturbridge was leading his family towards the brink of ruin. Nor was Arthur Prescott alone in his opinion. Nearly all the country gentlemen, backbone of the nation, despised the Jacobite supporters, despised even more the remnants of the Roman Catholic element who hung on and on, encouraged years ago by King James's damnable Papist sympathies, waiting their chance to gain a foothold once more in the professions, in the very Parliament itself. It was 1700 and much had happened in the fifteen years since Ian's and Sheila's deaths. Sir Tom struggled desperately to hold on to Kilbree House and its lands in Ireland, but the memory of his father's and his own services to England was fast fading in the harsh light of what men regarded as treasonous activities.

I shall never leave her, Harry was thinking as he enclosed Elizabeth in his arms, loving the feeling of her slight body against him. No matter what Father says, no matter what anyone tries to do to separate us, I shall never, never allow it. . . .

I must speak to Papa, thought Elizabeth. Papa will make it all right. She snuggled closer to Harry, wishing it were already two weeks hence and the night of their betrothal ball. Once that was over, once they had received the pledged good wishes of their families' friends and neighbors, everything would be all right again. No matter how people felt about kings and ministers and priests and all that business, surely their own personal feelings of friendship would matter much more in the end. Elizabeth closed her eyes and prayed very hard that Michael would go off on one of his frequent trips to Kilbree in the next day or two and perhaps stay away until the ball was over. But . . . a guilty feeling flooded through her . . . she loved Michael so much; ever since she was a little girl he had played games with her and with Katherine when he was not busy. It was not Michael's fault that she, Elizabeth, could not live up to the splendor of that tight-knit group of three, that she was sometimes quite in awe of them, of what they talked of and planned to do with their lives. It was not Michael's fault, surely, that she had found less and less to say to them as the years had passed, that, unlike Katherine, who dreamed very big dreams and fully expected them to come true, she dreamed only of a home of her own and a husband and children to care for. Now here she was, wishing that tall, dashing, wonderful Cousin Michael would go away, would stay away from what she knew would be the very happiest night of her whole life! If only . . . if only Michael would not speak out the way he did. . . . I shall talk to Papa about Michael, too, she thought suddenly and smiled to herself. Papa will arrange everything, just for that night, she was sure of it. Papa, who could never bear unhappiness in anyone around him, Papa who always knew when you were troubled or afraid and always knew how to fix things . . . yes, thought Elizabeth, daring to turn and kiss Harry's ear, thrilled to feel the sudden quickening of his warm breath against her face, Papa will know how to arrange everything for us. . . .

2 Bleak News From London

Sir Tom Sturbridge stood looking out the west windows of his small study at the back of the great house, awaiting impatiently the two swift horsemen who had just entered the courtyard.

Sir Tom's expression was grim. The news that Rob and Michael were bringing him was really no news at all, only a confirmation of facts they had all heard during the past weeks. Yet, before deciding what action to take, Sir Tom had insisted on finding out the exact state of affairs in London, as well as any additional details that might be picked up from reliable sources.

This much he was sure of: the young Duke of Gloucester, hardly more than a child, was dead. Last and longest lived of any of Princess Anne's numerous children, he was also, aside from his mother, the last Protestant heir to old King James's throne. Sir Tom had never wished the poor, sickly little boy any harm but, with his passing, the exiled Catholic son of King James now became second in line to inherit the throne. Anne's sister, Queen Mary, was dead. Mary's husband, William of Orange, was old, without heirs, close to his own deathbed. When he died, the crown would go to Anne, that foolish, clannish, easily manipulated woman. Unless one last enormous effort could be mounted and King James's son brought back from exile to claim his lawful inheritance.

Sir Tom sighed. What an odd position he found himself in, odd indeed for a Protestant Englishman—conniving and working to hand over the throne of his country to a Papist Pretender. Wasn't that the way Arthur Prescott had put it during one of his interminable harangues about patriotism and honor and duty to one's own proper God and station in life?

Tom Sturbridge felt the anger rise up in him again just thinking of the self-righteous, arrogant look on Prescott's round, fleshy face. Yet, what was it all about if not the absolutely rock-hard belief Sir Tom and his family lived by that they . . . and men like Prescott, too, had the God-given right to own their own opinions and express them freely? Wasn't that, more than any other single factor, what had guided them steadily throughout these increasingly difficult years?

Odd for a Protestant Englishman to support a Catholic king, odd to harbor a priest on his own property, odd, indeed, unless one understood the depth of the vision old Sir Thomas had imagined for his beloved England long ago. It was that vision so carefully, so sensitively inculcated upon his son's mind and heart which kept Tom Sturbridge still seeking, still believing in the reality of a homeland strong and united, with its people free to worship God however they pleased. Englishmen had always been a questioning, quarrelsome, independent-minded lot. Once freed from the fear men still found it possible to play upon to seek their own ends, there was no limit to what Englishmen might become, might do in this world. So believed old Sir Thomas, and he had lived his life accordingly. So believed

152

his son and his grandson. Yet, it was not happening. Tom Sturbridge worked and waited and tried to keep that faith alive in himself. But, of late, doubts had crept into his mind. Perhaps, after all, it could not be. Perhaps the old superstitions, the old terrors, had too strong a hold on the wills of Englishmen. What then? What other, brighter possibility existed?

I wish I knew, Sir Tom thought wistfully, and then his son opened the curtained glass doors and stepped in, followed closely by Michael Ives.

Rob embraced his father briefly, then threw himself wearily into a rust-colored velvet armchair, his long muscular legs stretched out before him, his usually animated face slack and expressionless. Sir Tom glanced at him and then at Michael, who, as always, was tense and nervous, standing with his arms folded tightly against his body. Michael's light blue eyes were glowering with inner rage he seemed unable, or unwilling, for the moment, to express. Silently Sir Tom poured three brandies. The younger men tossed theirs down at once and then Rob looked expectantly at Michael.

"Well, it's worse then we thought," Michael began, setting his glass down very hard. "Much, much worse."

Sir Tom's heart sank but he managed to speak in even, measured tones. "Tell me everything you've learned."

Rob's voice, husky with tiredness and disgust, picked up the thread of the tale . . . "They've settled on the succession. Princess Anne, of course, once King Billy is gone. And then . . . a German. A prince or some such from Hanover. . . ."

"A German?" Sir Tom was incredulous.

"Aye," drawled Michael sarcastically as he began pacing about the small room. "They've got it all figured out now. Seems the fellow is James I's great-grandson, something like that, eh, Rob? God, anything, anyone will do but the one man in the world the throne legally belongs to!"

"But that's hardly the worst of it, Papa," said Rob, and he glanced uncertainly at Michael. Michael uttered a short, ragged laugh and waved one hand a bit wildly.

"No, no, that's not the worst," he said, his lip curled. "Something a bit closer to home. Rob . . ." he suddenly broke off, looking very piercingly at Rob, obviously referring to a discussion they had had previously. Rob shook his head vehemently but Michael went on.

"Rob knows what I say is right, whether he likes it or not. What it comes down to, uncle, is that I've got to leave this place, my sister, too. We've got to go right away—today, if possible."

"Michael, I've told you before, it will never come to that. And we'll never let you go, you know that!" cried Rob with great heat.

"Boys, please," Sir Tom coughed lightly. The two of them turned to him, startled, as if they had forgotten his presence. "Tell me everything. What has brought you to this decision, Michael?"

Michael wheeled about, his eyes flashing fire. "It's happened," he said. "What we feared most of all. They've just passed some bloody law or other that says all Catholics eighteen years of age and over have to swear an oath of allegiance to the Crown . . ."

"That's nothing new," interposed Sir Tom, still hoping. Michael's fist pounded the table heavily.

"No, not that. But, hear what else: all Catholics must also forswear certain articles of faith. You know we cannot do that. We'd no longer be Catholics! We'd be excommunicated from the Church . . . and that's just what they're after, of course. There's pitiful few of us left here. They'll wipe that few up with a short spit to the cloth and then carry their hellish law right back to Ireland. It's the end of my people, I tell you, the end of Ireland as a nation!"

Sir Tom's voice was suddenly lacking in timbre as he looked away toward the windows again, murmuring, "You cannot swear such an oath, of course."

"Never!" cried Michael, his face working furiously.

Sir Tom nodded. "And the alternative, then?"

"He will lose the right to own property," said Rob.

"Kilbree . . ." whispered Sir Tom. Michael grimaced, his face contorted with pain and rage.

"All property owned by Catholics refusing to take the damned oath is to be turned over to their Protestant kin . . . Protestant kin, my God! How many Catholics have a nice handy parcel of respectable Protestant relatives, do you imagine?"

Sir Tom moved swiftly to his desk, his hands immediately busy searching through drawers and pigeonholes. "There's our answer," he said. "Kilbree can be signed over to us again. For the time being."

"Don't trouble to find the papers," replied Michael, his tone a trifle softer. "It's blood kin they mean. We're no real relations, you and us . . . ."

154

"By God we're a family and we always have been!" thundered Sir Tom, fingering a thick sheaf of legal-looking documents. "I'll send for the solicitors this very afternoon. They'll be able to work it out, Michael. I'll not lose you Kilbree, I swear it!"

"There's more, Papa," said Rob with a deep sigh. His father turned to him with a look Rob could not bear to see on that handsome, rugged face. Rob continued very quickly, staring at the rows and rows of books before him, unable to watch Sir Tom's stunned expression. "Any Catholic priest found officiating at a religious ceremony is to be imprisoned for life. And . . . anyone harboring a priest is subject to arrest, fine and loss of property."

Sir Tom gasped and could not speak for a moment. His gaze roved involuntarily back to the windows yet again and he found himself staring out at the gardens and stables, the wide clean white stones of the courtyard and the clustering trees beyond as if he were suddenly looking at it all for the last time, or as if he were a stranger in this most cherished home.

Finally Michael ceased his restless roaming about the small apartment and settled himself down on the sofa. He said nothing. His wide shoulders slumped, his head was bent low over hands tightly clasped together.

Rob watched his father with aching heart, wishing there was something he could say or do to help. But Rob had long been aware, although he had never said a word to anyone, that the dream of tolerance they had cherished was an impossibility. There would never be a Catholic king on the throne of England again and England itself would never, could never be any different. It was too small, too old, too wrapped up in grand ambitions ever to change. More than once, especially this last year, Rob had wanted very much to share these thoughts with his father. But he, too, was faced with the need for an alternative. And he, like his father, hardly dreamed what that alternative might be.

"We saw Arthur Prescott in London," mused Rob after a moment. "He's close to some of the council members. In fact he only returned home today himself, a few hours ago. No doubt he'll be coming over to talk with you."

"No doubt," echoed Sir Tom. "There's Elizabeth's wedding, of course . . ."

"Prescott may want to postpone it . . . or worse," said Rob bleakly.

Michael was staring at the two of them. "Why 'worse'?" he demanded. "Do you really want your sister married into that . . ." he caught himself up short, glancing apologetically at Sir Tom. "I'm sorry, sir. I know Prescott is your friend, but he's found other friends now, very powerful ones. I hate to see Elizabeth become part of Prescott's family . . ."

Sir Tom sighed. "You're aware she loves that boy of his deeply?"

Michael dismissed the idea impatiently. "She's very young. How can a girl like herself, barely out of school, not used to the world at all, know what love is about? Of course he's right enough looking, soft talking . . . why shouldn't she be taken in by him? But, you're her father. If you put an end to it and found her a husband elsewhere, in a couple of years she'd be thanking you for it!"

Rob frowned at the careless tone and shook his head. "Always the cynic, eh, Michael? Some people do fall in love once and forever, don't you believe that? I think Elizabeth is one of those."

Rob's dark eyes flashed briefly angry but Michael was not warned off. "Well then, love aside," he snapped a trifle brusquely, "Harry Prescott will never be allowed to marry her as things stand now. His father will insist on new terms and he'll be much happier if Katherine and I are away and out of it. I'll take old Father McGuire with me, too. Then as least the Catholic part of your problems will be settled."

Rob's face flushed. "While I live you'll not take Katherine from here!" he said, his teeth clenched. At this, Michael's eyebrow rose and his eyes narrowed. As if finally coming to himself from some strange, trancelike sleep, Sir Tom stepped between the two of them, resting a hand on each of their hard shoulders.

"We do not divide ourselves so the jackals may easily lick our blood," he spoke to them sternly. "*We* do not quarrel among ourselves, must I remind you of that?" Then, despite the edge in his voice, he betrayed a singular, unusual curiosity for a moment as he turned to Michael and asked, "Just where did you think you would go, boy, if you left us?"

"Somewhere far," Michael replied. "Yes, a far place. America, perhaps."

Rob's eyes narrowed in surprise but he said nothing. And his father slowly shook his head.

"No." Sir Tom's tone was adamant. "You'll not run away from this Michael . . . not for your own sake, not for Katherine's and, most assuredly, not for ours! We've a better chance now, right now, of creating some kind of order out of the chaos of the last hundred years than we've had before, don't you see that? Anne's claim to the throne can be challenged, strongly challenged. We've gained, not lost, in strength and numbers. We have solid support on the Continent. All that remains for us to do is use whatever time we have left us before the Usurper dies to join together and bring our rightful king home again. He will not forget those to whom he owes his power. King Charles did not forget what my father did for him. Then we will get the Test Act repealed . . . we'll change the laws against your people. But, we must fight for *time*. It is precious to us and we have no way of knowing whether it be long or short.''

"What shall we do, then?" Michael stared into those implacable dark blue eyes.

"Delay," breathed Sir Tom fervently. "Delay and delay again. Fight for time."

"Prescott and his new friends won't *give* you any time, Papa, can't you understand that?" Rob spoke up with a fierce strength that surprised his father. Sir Tom looked closely at him, marveling all at once that, much as he had known and loved the boy beside him all these years, he had still very much to learn of the man that boy was becoming.

"Papa," Rob said earnestly, "when Prescott comes to you . . . what will you tell him of Father McGuire? And Michael?" He glanced up briefly, "Michael must appear before the magistrate within thirty days to swear the oath of allegiance."

" 'Thirty days'?" His father's face was drained white. "Are you sure it's only thirty?"

Rob nodded miserably. "And they know damned well Michael will never go through with it. I wouldn't be surprised if they haven't already sent word to Dublin."

"I'll have to get to Kilbree!" cried Michael. "I've no doubt there's a regular list of would-be gentlemen waiting to get their hands on Kilbree." He pushed back the unruly blond curls with trembling fingers. "We've got to save what we can, get the servants out—God, my mother's things!"

Sir Tom would have tried to comfort him then, but Michael was not in the mood for comfort.

"I'll go with you, Michael," Rob was saying, and then his father shook his head in warning, motioning him to sit down again. Sir

Tom took his seat on the other side of the table. Color was fast returning to his cheeks and his customary brisk manner was again apparent.

"Sit down, both of you," he commanded, and they obeyed him. "Now," Sir Tom went on quickly, casting them a grateful smile, "there is much to be done. And, as you pointed out, Rob, not much time in which to do it all." He sat forward in his chair, his large, long-fingered hands clasped together under his chin. "Someone must be sent to Kilbree. But not you, Michael. It would be madness for you to set foot in Ireland now. Nor you, Rob. The Sturbridge name is too well known in that connection. But I am sending Michael away, for a few weeks. If he is not in the country, then the Magistrate will simply have to wait for him to return before administering the oath."

"You said I must not run away, sir," objected Michael, looking puzzled.

"And so you must not...and you will not. I am sending you with a message to...friends of ours...in France. You will leave from Bristol this very night on the turn of the tide. You will carry certain letters. They are written in a cipher and appear innocent enough to the ignorant eye, don't be concerned about that. What must be accomplished will take more than thirty days...hear me out, please," he said patiently as both of the young men before him looked startled and restive.

"The matter of succession must now be brought to a head. I have the sure instinct that if we do not accomplish our purpose now, we may very well never do so. I am prepared to go into exile if necessary. I lived my early boyhood on the Continent. We were in exile then..." he flashed a rare wide smile at them and they marveled at his composure, his amazingly rapid recovery from the shock of the news.

"Exile, at least in this century, would seem the only honorable way of life for an English...or an Irish...gentleman," he quipped, but there was a steel-hard ring to his words and neither of them smiled.

"If His Majesty in France can be brought to power soon, what I propose may never become necessary. However, Spring Mount will still be here, so will Kilbree....I do not think anyone would wantonly destroy two such fine estates. If we must temporarily uproot ourselves, well, the cause is much worth such a small sacrifice."

158

Rob heard what his father was saying and a small chilly voice inside his own heart began to scream that it was wrong, all wrong, it was only men repeating history's mistakes over and over again, that it would never work. And, kept on the insistant unpleasant voice, even if your father is right and the time of exile is short and you all come back in victory and triumph in the train of the true King, what then? Roman Catholics were not the only British subjects to suffer injustices no matter who wore the imperial crown.

Sir Tom was busy now, writing one special letter Michael was to take with him, and he did not see the look of doubt on Rob's face or, for that matter, the look of hopelessness on Michael's. His mind was racing even as he wrote the few hurried words which would introduce Michael Ives to the court in France, to the King in exile.

"I am sending Willy Duncan to Ireland," Sir Tom explained. "He, too, will leave from Bristol. While he is there, he will arrange for your passage to France, Michael. The *Rendezvous* is in port these ten days past. The Captain is an old friend." He took the massive gold Sturbridge ring from his finger and pressed it hard into the hot wax, then handed the paper to Michael. "After you have had something to eat and changed clothes, I will give you what else you must bring with you."

He was interrupted by a sharp knock at the door.

"Come in, Willy," he said without turning his head. At once the door was opened and Willy Duncan, these fifteen years as much a part of the household as any of the rest of them, came in on quick, silent feet and, when he stood before the table, a grin on his face for the two young men just come home.

"Yes, Willy, it was you and no other I wanted." Sir Tom proceeded to detail what he wanted Willy to do and Willy listened most attentively, all the time standing at rigid attention. Still, from the moment he entered the room, the terrible tension that had been building there seemed somewhat alleviated. Michael, for one, sat more easily back in his chair, the frown gone from his brow, allowing himself the pleasure of feeling that now, indeed, he had really come home again. Ever since that dreadful day long ago, when Sheila Ives had died giving birth to his sister, Katherine, Willy had never been far from earshot or really out of reach. He seemed to have an instinct about when Michael needed him, and he was always there to help.

Rob, too, was delighted to see Willy. He knew Willy as a kind of amiable, easy-going big brother, someone who always knew another game to play, another stream to fish, another story to tell.

As Sir Tom unfolded, as briefly as he could, the situation in which they now found themselves, Willy looked closely at this man whom he respected above all other men in this world and fought valiantly to keep his mouth shut, to keep from blurting out his indignation at a government he found utterly incomprehensible, whose disloyalties, shifting policies and black deeds against its own heroes he simply could not fathom. He looked at Tom Sturbridge now, remembering him as the tall young warrior wounded at Sedgemoor. The dark wavy hair was shot through with gray now and the handsome, craggy face with its strong, determined jaw was leaner, the wide, generous mouth thinner somehow and the lips tighter as if changed by repeated, unspoken-of suffering.

"I want you to be on your way this afternoon, Willy," Sir Tom was finishing his explanations, and orders. Willy blinked, glancing at Michael, and this time he had no grin for anyone.

"Will you be givin' me some sorta idea what I am to bring back to you from Kilbree, Master Michael?" he said reluctantly. Sir Tom looked at him strangely, his mouth open as if to say something but evidently he thought better of it and remained silent, waiting for Michael to answer.

Michael swallowed a couple of times. "My . . . my mother's jewels," he faltered. "Some of the small family pictures in the drawing room, if you can get them out. And, Willy," he added harshly, looking away from Willy's sympathetic eyes, "turn the dogs out, and give the horses to the neighbors. The cows, too, all the livestock. Let them find the place empty when they come to take it. . . . I would to God you'd burn it to the ground first!"

Willy murmured something softly but Michael did not hear him, so he spoke up a bit. "What about the servants, sir?"

Michael glanced at Sir Tom, not knowing what to tell Willy.

Sir Tom did not hesitate. "You tell every one of them that they will find a good home here with us if they wish to come back with you. Those who will not come you must send away with enough money to live on. Be sure no one is forgotten, Willy."

"How long will they be safe here?" Rob asked, and his father frowned at him as if he had gone too far.

"While I live, their lives are secure," said Sir Tom stiffly.

Willy, more concerned for the time being with the fate of Kilbree

House, looked puzzled at Rob's question but before he could ask its meaning, Sir Tom spoke again.

"Boys, go and get something to eat now. Michael, see your sister and your Aunt Helene, but say nothing of what we have discussed here. I will explain everything to them when I must. Now, leave me, all of you . . . and Willy, on your way out, send one of the footmen to me. Tell him to have a horse saddled, ready to ride."

Michael leaped out of his chair, throwing his arm about Willy's shoulder and the two of them went out of the room conversing in low, affectionate tones. Rob, close on their heels, paused to look back at his father and caught Sir Tom watching Willy and Michael with a touch of wistful sadness on his strong face. The next instant, Sir Tom noticed him standing there in the doorway. At once his expression altered; he smiled and waved his son away fondly.

Rob closed the study door quietly. Nothing ever really changes, he thought soberly as he climbed the great staircase to seek out his mother. Michael did love Sir Tom, of that Rob was quite sure, but that love was one born of respect and admiration rather than blind feeling. There was a *distance* to it, Rob decided, yet there had never been any distance between Michael and Willy Duncan. No, there had always been a closeness there, a trust between those two that had left little room for Sir Tom. Rob and Michael had understood each other well when they were little boys and even through the years of their adolescence. Rob used to understand most of the devils that hounded the younger boy's consciousness, had once been able to explain why Michael did what he did even when Sir Tom and Helene were hard pressed to comprehend the enormous reservoir of hidden anger and bitter bewilderment Michael still carried within him, feelings which flashed out with dazzling fury now and then. But, as the boys had emerged into young manhood, a strain—almost imperceptible at first—had developed between them. Now Rob was not quite so sure he understood Ian Ives' son anymore and, sometimes nowadays, he did not entirely care. . . .

3 Robert And His Mother

Rob stopped for a moment outside the door to his mother's sitting room, hesitating to knock just yet. She must not learn too much from him, she must not be frightened. Still, he had to tell her something. He and Michael had gone in haste to London ten days ago . . . surely she was aware of the rumors that were circulating then. He could not put her off, not Helene, who had always been able to look at his face and see at once if he was troubled about something. Troubled, he thought ironically, at last tapping on her door—we in England are more than troubled. We are coming to the end of something and we cannot slow it or prevent it, we can only be crushed by its passing or go on to the beginning of something new. But *what?* He strove once again to find the answer but the door opened to him and his mother threw her arms about him, laughing, crying just a bit, stretching up on her tiptoes to reach his cheek and kiss him.

"Rogue!" she cried softly, looking up at him with mock reproach as she drew him with her to the only chair in the room large and solid enough for a man to sit comfortably in. "I watched the two of you ride in almost an hour ago. Were you with your father all this time?"

Rob nodded, but his manner was guarded and, at once, Helene feared what he would have to tell her. More, she realized, she would have to pretend to be content with the little he would reveal and then try to discover for herself what he was leaving out. Undoubtedly his father had warned him not to alarm her.

Even as he spoke, picking and choosing his words so carefully, Rob knew he could not hide much from his mother. He informed her of the new arrangement of the succession. All that was of any surprise there was that Parliament should choose a foreigner, a German prince, over a native-born legitimate heir. Helene's delicate dark eyebrows rose when she heard this, but she made no comment. There was more, she knew it of a certainty now, when Rob jumped up and put a little distance between himself and her as he went on. He told her of the oath Michael would be called upon to take and he told her Kilbree would be forfeit to the crown as soon as Michael refused to take the oath. He did not mention Father McGuire or the harsh new punishments in store for those who harbored Catholic priests. He did not tell his mother that they were all in terrible danger, that they stood to lose Spring Mount, too, and that he and his father might be arrested at any time. Even now, knowing the facts as he did, he himself could hardly believe such things could happen to the Sturbridge family.

Helene sat very still and listened, thinking hard, trying to read the full story from what he was leaving out or skipping over briefly. If such repressive new measures were being taken against Catholics, she saw at once the danger her own family faced, for they were known Jacobite sympathizers who had antagonized neighbors and authorities for years by sheltering Catholics.

Helene realized suddenly that her son had fallen silent. She looked over at him. He waited for her to say something.

"It will be very hard," she said presently, not allowing herself the luxury of grieving over Kilbree, not quite yet.

Rob stared at his mother. "Hard," she said, her voice so quiet, "very hard," that was all. Would he ever truly understand her, he wondered? She was not given to weeping overmuch, yet he knew she felt things deeply and never forgot, never. He knew that, long ago, there had been some great trouble in her life. He knew it, not from her lips, but from little remarks, whispers, knowing looks and nods among the servants. They all adored Lady Helene; the remarks and whispers had not been snide but caring. As a child he had wondered about her, remembering from earliest days a certain secret sorrow she seemed to bear within her, something that showed in her eyes once in awhile and then was gone.

Helene was forty-four now. The once luxuriant raven-hued hair had turned to softest, shimmering grey, a pale, pearl grey like satin. To have grey hair was not unusual for a woman of her years, save that Helen's beautiful face had never seemed to age beyond young womanhood and was today as clear and firm and cleanly tinted as it had been when Rob was still a child. The dark brown eyes had never lost their luminosity; the soft pink lips, the strong sweeping line of the jaw . . . all were exactly the same. It was as if time had drifted gently, as in a dream, around Helene, refusing to rush in and work its minute changes, its vast destructions.

She was dressed in a favorite simple velvet gown the color of Spanish red wine, softly gleaming with highlights of her breasts and still-slim hips. The velvet fell to her feet in deep gathered folds from the high waist; fashion called for a wide white lace collar cut low over the bosom, matching lace cuffs on the long, full sleeves. The exquisite shining hair rose above her youthful face in a high coronet of the old Roman style she preferred, simple and unadorned by flower or feather ornament. Nor did she wear jewels, although she had many lovely ones and enjoyed displaying them sometimes, on some particularly joyful occasion. Just a while ago, before Rob and Michael had returned, she had been sitting at her dressing table with her jewel boxes about her, trying to decide what she would wear for

Elizabeth's betrothal ball and which jewels she would give her daughter for her wedding day.

But Helene possessed a quality that would have dimmed the brightest jewel she cared to wear, a quality of spirit which seemed to manifest itself physically in her appearance. It was this unique element of her personality that attracted people whenever she appeared anywhere. It had not always been a part of her. She knew whence it came and why, but she never explained it to anyone.

There was about Helene now a peculiar glow, a radiance that permeated her entire being, a shining in her eyes, a lightness in her step, a vivacious quickness in her every movement. Even now, as she sat contemplating the problems ahead, as her son watched her and waited to hear what she would say . . . and saw the tears gathering in her eyes as she thought about Michael and Katherine . . . there was still an aura of untouchable glory about her person that Rob found marvelous to behold.

She touched his hand lightly and said, "Bring them to me, Rob, I must speak with them both."

Rob stood up to do her bidding, but he hesitated, knowing well the mood Michael was in. He wished his father might come upstairs and see Helene first.

"Go on, dear," Helene prompted him.

Rob turned back to her and blurted out abruptly, "Michael wants to go away. He told Papa he wants to take Katherine and go to America."

Helene sighed, nodding. "He has spoken of it before. He does not believe we can hold Kilbree."

"Mother . . ." Rob stared at her very hard. "He's right. Kilbree is lost. And even . . ." He stopped suddenly, seeing the fear in her eyes. "I'll bring them here," he said very quickly and left her before he said too much. Helene stood quite still in the middle of the large room, her eyes fixed on the open doorway.

Kilbree is lost, she thought numbly. Rob said Kilbree is lost. What, then, will be Michael's inheritance? But, even as she thought of Michael, she remembered that Rob had been about to add something else and had stopped himself before he said it. There was a great deal more he was not telling her, she was quite sure of it now. Her instincts told her to seek out Thomas and ask him what had happened, but even as she moved toward the doorway, she heard the sharp clatter of horses' hoofs in the stone courtyard below.

Hurrying to the window she looked down and saw Willy Duncan riding off toward the Bristol road and, parting from him at the gate-keeper's lodge, one of the footmen rode swiftly in the opposite direction, toward town.

Helene found herself suddenly trembling violently. She sat down again at the dressing table. She knew that Thomas would find her and tell her everything in his own time. With an enormous effort of the will, she sat quite still, only her hands betraying the tension that was building within her. She toyed restlessly with the heaps of gold and silver necklaces before her, finally picking up a great topaz and amethyst brooch that had belonged to her mother. It was to be part of Elizabeth's betrothal gift, set aside long ago with the matching earrings, necklace and twin bracelets, when Helene saw that the infant blue eyes of her daughter were changing color.

A bit startled, she realized that she was holding the lovely piece clasped tightly in her palm, running her fingertips over and over the glittering gems. She remembered the intense look on Elizabeth's pale young face and the fierce new light sparkling in her amber eyes whenever she spoke of Harry Prescott. Fear like a quick hot touch of the Devil's passing shot through Helene . . . I wish the wedding were tomorrow, not a year away. So much can happen in a year, so many things can change. It was the first time she thought without one single touch of regret of her daughter's marriage. Always, before, she had felt Elizabeth's tender age a drawback, she had wanted them to wait.

And carefully she set the splendid brooch down and folded her hands to wait. . . .

4 Michael And Katherine Ives

"You sail for France tonight?" Katherine Ives whispered with a shudder. She turned to look at her brother, a hundred other questions on her lips but the sight of his face silenced them all so that, in the end, she had asked the most trivial.

"Tonight," he repeated. "But you know I hold no hope for this journey. It is as useless as anything I have done in my life. And God knows," he forced a thin smile, "I have accomplished nothing for all my good intentions and noble aspirations!"

"Don't!" she pleaded with him. "Please, Michael, not now—"

"Now?" he flung the word back at her heatedly. "Why 'not now'? You and I have both known this was coming! Nothing has changed for us and it will never change unless we *act*. Kilbree, freedom, our own lands—it was all only a dream, sister, an old man's dream. It pleased Sir Tom's father to use his influence at court to cadge favors for his down-and-out Irish dependents. But he's gone, and King Charlie's long gone and no one in all of England gives a tinker's damn what happens to the poor Ives family now!''

Katherine's head rose proudly. ''Some care, I think,'' she reminded him. ''Some whose house we stand in this minute. . . .''

Michael looked abashed, then tossed his head defiantly. ''You know I don't mean the family,'' he said. ''But, damn it, Katherine, you know I'm right. You and I should be going away from here, now, we should have gone long ago. The English will never accept a Catholic king . . . they've made that clear enough, God knows . . . there is no place for us here now. All the desperate missions to King Louis's court and all the secret meetings and plans and the grand rousing speeches of every damn-fool deluded Jacobite . . . myself with the rest . . . won't make any difference. King Billy wouldn't have dared countenance this new set of bloody-belly laws if he hadn't the whole country behind him. We've nothing left now, Katherine, can't you get that through your head? We're disinherited, homeless, landless . . . and *poor*, girl, dirt-under-your-fingernails poor! Whatever bits of valuables Willy Duncan might be able to bring back over with him won't dress you or put food in your stomach for six months.''

''We shan't go begging, I'm sure, Michael,'' she said with quiet dignity and a lift to her chin that infuriated him.

''I will not live vassal to Sir Tom Sturbridge all my days, no, nor to his son, either,'' he cried. ''I tell you I won't have my sister waiting on English charity!''

''Michael, stop it!'' Katherine's voice rose commandingly, the color coming and going in her cheeks. Michael saw the angry glint in her usually mild grey eyes. The tone of her voice brought him back to himself. He let out a big deep breath, trying to grin, as he leaned down to kiss her hot cheek.

''Always the great bear!'' he said, ashamed of himself at once. '' 'No manners, no style' . . . our tutor, old Brandy Mouth always said that, didn't he, all those years he spent working himself into fits trying to turn Rob and me out proper gentlemen. Well, he succeeded with Rob, at any rate . . .'' He saw the angry sparks come back into her eyes and silently cursed his foolish tongue. ''Katherine,'' he said slowly, "the truth of it is . . . I don't know what to do anymore. Sir Tom doesn't mind the prospect of honorable exile for the lot of us in France, but the mere mention of America seems to appall him."

"You spoke of America again?" she asked him eagerly. "Michael, is he really so much against it?"

Her brother nodded dispiritedly. "How can you expect otherwise? Whatever happens, Spring Mount—all the great houses of England— they'll always be here. Families like his survive, somehow. They fight when they have to, go off into exile when they must, until the wheel turns round again. It's not the same for them."

"Kilbree has been there for hundreds of years," she disagreed.

"Yes, but how many years did it belong to an Ives? *I* don't know, do you? No, no, we have nothing to wait for. Wherever we go we'll be in exile and nothing to go back to, even if we could. The only chance in life we have, sure you know it, is to leave it all behind us and start in a place like America, where you're born the day you land there."

Katherine nodded slightly. How many, many times they had talked of this same thing. Yet, always before there had been Kilbree waiting for them. Even Rob, years ago, had shared their enthusiasm for that strange new world across the sea. Her face clouded, thinking of Rob, of Rob and Michael and herself the way they used to be. What had gone wrong between those two, she wondered? Of late especially they quarreled often and bitterly, for no reason she could understand. Once we were all so close, she thought sadly, looking at this brother of hers whom she loved so dearly although she could not make him out.

At once her heart filled with love and pity for him and she went and sat on the floor beside him, tucking her skirts in about her feet and taking his hand in hers.

"How long will you be in France?" she asked him. He shook his head.

"I don't really know. Whatever happens there, we must be ready to leave here when I get back. And it will be to America, no matter what Sir Tom or Rob have to say about it."

" 'Rob'? What did he say?" She looked up at him, flushing a little.

"Why? What difference does that make?" Michael studied her face closely and Katherine avoided his eyes.

"Nothing. Nothing. What difference would it make? Why do you question me so, Michael?" But she knew why.

"And if I told you that Rob swore you'd never leave here, what then?" he persisted.

Her heart leaped gladly in her bosom. She tried to hide it, but the look was plain in her eyes. Michael put his hand on her shoulder—she felt the weight of it and the weight of his old anger like a stone pressing her down and helpless. She pulled herself away from him suddenly, hating with all her strong, proud heart that old familiar dread of him, her own brother. Why had he always acted as though he owned her, as if she belonged to him and him alone of all the world? Dear she was to him, she knew that and it made her glad . . . only, sometimes . . . even when she was a little girl she had seen the jealousy in his eyes, heard it in his voice, whenever he thought she loved someone else before him. For a long, long time his resentment had never been directed at Rob, for Rob had been devoted to Michael before she was ever born, and they had all played and talked happily together with no sign of jealousy in any of them. It was only after she had turned thirteen, two years ago, and the boys were already grown young men, that she had seen the old haunted look flash suddenly from time to time in Michael's eyes. Whenever she and Rob were laughing together over some silly thing, she would look up and see her brother staring at them from a distance with a darkness in his eyes that bothered her terribly. But she loved him so much . . . she loved Rob the same way. Despite Michael's refusal to feel a real part of the family, she knew they were all one and the same. She could not divide her loyalties. Yet, since Michael had begun to act so strangely, she had turned more and more to Rob. She felt more comfortable with him. He was easier to talk to, more open, less likely to flare up at the least little thing. Lately Rob had seemed somehow more wonderful to be with than anyone else in the world, for a reason Katherine had not yet figured out. Love had come very early to Elizabeth, but Katherine was not so ready to give her heart and her life into anyone else's keeping.

She sighed, her thoughts wandering from the enigma of her brother and Rob. And, without a word, she began to cry. Michael's hand moved from her shoulder, resting on her head as he drew her against him, trying to comfort her.

"We can never go back home again, can we?" she sobbed, her

entire body shaking. "But, oh, Michael, I love it so! I love it! What's to become of Kilbree, Michael? And us? What shall we do, tell me, Michael, tell me!"

Michael, his face bleak and weary, shook his head. He had no comfort to offer her, yet he was her brother, their mother had died and left this little sister in his keeping. Why could he not keep this from happening to her? When they were little, he remembered, he had held her tiny hand and never let her fall as she tottered along. She had trusted him then, looked up to him, knowing he would never let her down. And now all he could do was listen to her weep and see the fear and helplessness in her eyes and shake his fool head! He looked down at her...she still seemed so small, so much like the little girl with the tousled blond curls like his own, until she had begun to grow and comb the fine golden curls into two soft clusters framing her face, until she had begun to discover that there were stones in her pathway he could not sweep away before her feet.

Now she was almost a woman, he realized, wishing it were not so. Another year, two at the most, and she would not need him any more. He would not be her champion, her protector, as he had been for so long. Feeling the warmth of her next to him now, he looked down at her, studying her almost as if he had never really observed her before.

She was very tall for a girl of fifteen, tall the way he was, the way their father had been. Both of them had Ian's long, strong legs and the swift striding walk Michael just barely remembered. The only look of Sheila Katherine had about her was in the warm grey eyes and the quick, sweet smile. But she had the same liquid loving laughter in her voice that Sheila had had. She was thoughtful, too, given to dreaming such great dreams, yet no one could ever call her dreamy the way Elizabeth had always been dreamy and faraway, like a little elf living in a storybook world. No, Katherine's dreams were down-to-earth, plans for the future. Ever since she had learned to walk and talk, Katherine had been reasoning life out for herself step by step, graciously, lovingly . . . firmly.

But these days, Michael knew, he was no longer privy to her dreams. Did she now, like Elizabeth, long for a husband and a home of her own, and children of her own?

Michael resisted the thought, his fingers resting on her head, tightening, so that she moved away from him again. God, why did

169

she have to be a girl, to grow to be a woman, to suffer the careless embrace of some heedless man, to endure the agony and the awful danger of giving birth?

Michael stood up, turning away from her, fighting down the feelings of mad rage that filled him whenever he contemplated such a future for his sister. How short a time it had been since he had had great dreams of his own? Kilbree House was his, the greatest house in Ireland, he the master and his sister a fine lady dressed in silks and furs, The Lady of Kilbree and all its lands and waters from the mountains to the sea.

"Katherine," he began, his voice husky with emotion, "Katherine, I swear to you, I will . . ."

But whatever he was about to promise her . . . and it would have been half the world without regret . . . his words were lost in the startling sound of an ordinary knock at the door and Rob's voice outside in the hallway, calling them both.

Katherine rubbed the tears from her eyes and went to answer his knock. Michael noted that, despite her tears and her terrors, there was a look of dawning gladness about her, a swiftness to her movements that spoke more eloquently than words ever could. Rob was at her door. Rob had only to call her name and the world was transfigured for her. It was to be Rob, Michael knew it, had known it for years, and he hated that wild part of himself that forgot that he and Rob Sturbridge were almost brothers, that they had shared a bond between them from boyhood, which he was fast destroying. Michael prayed God to seek out and burn out that angry part of himself. Then he turned to greet Rob with something of the past in his vivid blue eyes, something of the old, shared camaraderie he had thrust away with both hands and missed so much all the while he did it.

One quick glance at Katherine's stricken face and Rob's heart ached all the more. All the way back from London, while he and Michael had spoken very little, Rob had thought what Katherine must face now would crush her. She must go with her brother. He knew she would never let Michael leave Spring Mount without her. Yet where had they to go? Rob knew Michael's heart better than did Tom Sturbridge.

No, nothing on earth could keep Michael Ives in Europe now, why, nothing had kept him in England, when he had been content to

170

stay with them at all, except his hopes and expectations of Kilbree and the life he planned for himself and Katherine.

Rob smiled at her as he came in. She had no answering smile, yet despite everything, a smile at his coming lurked somewhere there in the wide grey eyes. Her face was flushed and lovely. She reached out a slim hand to touch him very lightly, then seemed suddenly to become shy, the hand fell to her side again and she looked back at her brother for an instant.

I cannot be parted from her, Rob thought in anguish, I can never let her go from me.

"You've told Katherine?" he asked Michael unnecessarily. Michael nodded. "Everything?" Rob emphasized. Their eyes met in implicit understanding. Michael shook his head very slightly.

"Everything about Kilbree," he said carefully, and Rob understood. There was no point in alarming anyone about the ramifications of the new law.

"I have told my mother the same," said Rob, and Michael nodded again. "She would like to speak with you and Katherine."

The three of them went at once to Helene: Katherine eagerly, as a daughter to her much-loved mother, and Michael with some reluctance, the mask of reserve he had always worn with Helene slipping unconsciously over his features. In the beginning he might have become, to her, a second, cherished son but he would not have it so. Michael, orphaned, had deliberately chosen to remain so. Helene was not Sheila Ives and he would never let himself . . . or her . . . forget it. In time, slowly to be sure, he had learned not to be angry with Helene because she was not his mother and she still lived on and loved him and tried to help him. In time, Michael had learned to forgive the whole world for Sheila's dying. It was only himself he could not forgive.

5 A Practical Man

Arthur Prescott at fifty-five was the same man he had been at twenty-five, the man he would be, he often boasted, at seventy-five. As he was quite correct about the past, there was no reason to doubt his guarantee of the future. He regarded himself in the light of an institution, well-established, firmly rooted in principle and tradition, an on-going concern accustomed to succeeding in whatever careful enterprises seemed appropriate.

At twenty-five, he inherited a large and flourishing country estate from his father—who had died before his time but *high time*, to Arthur's way of thinking—and found himself as he had long expected to: rich, powerful, looked-up-to, depended upon. His ideas on all subjects had been formulated and frozen into place at a much younger age, so the inheritance had not caused him the inconvenience of having to rethink anything or make any changes in his attitudes or habits. Thus did his boast ring clearly true. Nothing changed or ever would; it was of immense comfort to Prescott to reflect upon this fact. Let kings come and go as they would, let parliaments and ministers flock in and out of office as regularly as the arrival of the English robin in spring, Arthur Prescott remained, country gentleman, man of devout and somber piety, not merely a *law* but, indeed, a fulsome Magna Carta unto himself.

Arthur Prescott needed very little to enhance his position or to add to his happiness. What little he did need he acquired as soon as he became aware it was wanting. When he had been master of the vast Prescott holdings for nearly ten years, it occurred to him one morning, precisely at eleven o'clock, that he was in need of an heir, that a rear balcony on the second floor where he might walk of an evening and enjoy the cool river breeze would be pleasant, and that three of his tenant farmers were holding back their rent payments. Being a practical man, Arthur Prescott at once put the carpenters to work erecting his balcony over the river, dispatched his overseer to evict the three farmers, and took himself a wife. In short order, there were three new tenants paying rents on the estate, there was a splendid shady balcony off the scond floor, and there was an infant son and heir in the nursery upstairs.

These three *items* on Prescott's agenda having been accomplished with relative ease, Arthur went on living his life as was his wont, and gradually lost interest in them. Save for a brief and most atypical stint in the military—during which uncomfortable but successful endeavor he had the chance to get to know Sir Tom Sturbridge, his neighbor, much better—Arthur Prescott stayed at home on his estates, bred a famous variation of hairless hound, avoided his wife and son like any gentleman of his class, and indulged his more than passing interest in clearing the countryside of Catholics, Baptists, Presbyterians, Quakers and other devilish dissenters. It was not so much from personal devotion to the Church of England that Arthur Prescott so zealously sought to annihilate these "scum," as he put it, but because he intended to thwart the winds of change in any form lest they blow the whirlwind *his* way and force him someday to rearrange his vast and moribund conceit of English destiny.

On this very day, after a damned rushed and unpleasant trip home from London, Arthur was taking the trouble to ride out again. He had made his thoughts quite clear to his son. There was no need to discuss anything with his wife. But, he must see Tom Sturbridge at once. It could not wait; although his spine was jolted entirely out of balance and he ached painfully through the hip area from spending fourteen hours in that damnable coach, he must now settle once and for all the disgraceful and dangerous state of affairs at Spring Mount.

Smacking his thick lips together, Arthur eased his horse back on to the grass by the roadside, slowing him down to a walk as he slid his rump painfully around in the saddle, seeking some more comfortable position. Tom Sturbridge, he was thinking, frowning mightily, Tom Sturbridge was a good man, basically, no one would deny that. Yet of recent years he seemed to care nothing what his friends and neighbors thought of him. Tom Sturbridge and he were friends, were they not? Had served together in the French war, shared common interests . . . surely Sturbridge would not jeopardize his own daughter's future.

Decidedly not, Arthur Prescott concluded as he rode in sight of Spring Mount . . . today he would explain it all very precisely to Sir Tom, everything he had heard while he was up in London, the not-so-careful whispers of "treason," the no-longer-veiled threats. After all, it was not as though Sir Tom had turned Papist himself, however much the rumors would have it so. Who were the Jacobite sympathizers anyway but Catholics and other cursed Dissenters and a few deluded sentimentalists harking back to the days of King Charlie? Gone forever, those days, Prescott reassured himself as he handed his reins to a stableboy who had run out to meet him.

Sir Tom, still working at his writing table, glanced outside to see who had arrived. It was far too soon to expect Hulme, his solicitor. He groaned when he saw it was Prescott even as he hurried to welcome him.

Arthur Prescott had determined to start out by being conciliatory and was prepared for the argument he knew would ensue. But Sir Tom was not fooled; he saw at once which way the wind was blowing. Prescott's full, fleshy face was very red, his thick brows knotted together querulously. He accepted the offer of a glass of port with a short "thank'ee," without paying his usual halfhearted compliments to the Sturbridge wine cellars.

Then he planted himself gingerly in one of the straight-backed chairs although it was obvious from his stiff movements that he would have vastly preferred a soft armchair by the fire.

Sir Tom surveyed his guest with resigned expectation. Time, he reminded himself, I must have more time. . . .

He sat down across from Prescott, flashing him a disarming smile that he hoped would hide the distaste he felt for the entire interview. Nevertheless, there was a purpose to be served.

"Ran into Robert up in London," began Arthur loudly.

"Yes, so he told us," said Sir Tom. "I believe you returned today, didn't you, just like the boys . . ."

"Yes, yes," said Arthur impatiently, setting down his empty glass.

"Enjoyed your trip, did you?"

"Damn, Sir Tom," exploded Arthur vehemently, "do you know you're in trouble, sir, great trouble?"

Sir Tom eyed his neighbor keenly. "I'm at a loss, Arthur, forgive me. What do you mean?"

"Treason, sir, treason's what I *mean*!" He watched Sir Tom's face closely, trying to calculate the effect of his words.

"Who accuses me of treason, Arthur?" inquired Tom Sturbridge quietly.

"Who? *Who*? Why, rather ask me, who does *not*?" sputtered Arthur. "I tell you, my friend, I have had it in the strictest confidence and from the highest authority . . ." he paused dramatically . . . "the King is no longer willing to overlook the organized efforts you people are making in behalf of the Pretender! You've been let alone so far because of your family's services to the nation . . . and your own, of course . . . but—"

"Oh, no, Arthur," interrupted Sir Tom blandly, but there was a slight edge to his tone now. "I've been let alone so far because no one has been able to bring any proof, any evidence that I have been involved in these 'efforts,' as you put it. And no one ever will," he added sharply.

Arthur was breathing very hard, cursing himself roundly that he had begun at the wrong end of his arguments.

"Be that as it may, for the moment, Sir Tom," he said quickly, "you and I are old friends, are we not? More than friends, surely, having been in the thick of battle together. Our lands adjoin, our purposes are much the same . . . we are about to become related through the marriage of my son and—''

''Get to the point, Arthur, I'm very busy today,'' Sir Tom cut him short. ''And I am well aware of the news from London.''

Arthur Prescott allowed himself a smile, although it nettled him that Sturbridge thought he could treat him in so cavalier a fashion.

''Very well, Sir Tom. I shall get to the point. And it is simply: Do you intend that the marriage will take place?''

Sir Tom's lip curled derisively. ''You already know I do. More to the point, do *you?* Tell me what it is you want from me, Arthur. I thought we had settled the details of the marriage contract weeks ago. But, obviously, you want to make some changes . . . or is it that you would like to withdraw altogether?''

Arthur got to his feet, an ugly glimmer in his small eyes now, and his voice was extremely cold as he spoke. ''You cannot continue to harbor the priest here.''

Sir Tom nodded, to Prescott's surprise. ''That is obvious,'' he replied just as coldly. ''Though why you should fear a dying old man is beyond me. But I shall not attempt to break the law, however unjust and stupid it is.''

Arthur glared at him. ''You should be careful what you say about the King's Laws, Sir Tom,'' he breathed.

Sir Tom's eyebrows rose. ''What I say in the privacy of my own home . . . to an old and trusted friend, Arthur?'' Sir Tom countered softly. Arthur coughed and walked past his host, helping himself to another glass of port.

''The priest will go?'' he asked again, his back to Sir Tom.

''I have already made the arrangements,'' replied Sturbridge easily. ''Do you think, after offering him my friendship and protection all these years, I would allow him to remain and endanger his life?''

Arthur turned around, a surprised look on his face. ''Why no, no, of course you would not,'' he said. ''Then that much is settled.''

''What else, Arthur?''

''Michael Ives,'' Prescott answered.

''No problem there. Michael is leaving England this very night.''

''Going back to Ireland, is he?'' Arthur's tone was bland but Sir Tom was on his guard.

''No, not this time. He is visiting friends on the Continent.''

Arthur sat down again, holding his brimming glass of port high. He looked thoughtful. "But he will return of course, in time to make his appearance before Magistrate Gladden? You know he cannot hope to hold his estates in Ireland unless he takes the oath."

Sir Tom felt like throttling him then, as he heard the smooth tone, the casual remark and realized he was treading on dangerous ground. He did not dare admit to this man that Michael had no intention of swearing the oath of allegiance or that they knew Kilbree House was already forfeit to the Crown. Michael could be arrested now or as he boarded his ship in Bristol harbor for illegal flight to evade the King's Law. His own word that he would not take the oath would be as good as his not taking it in reality . . .

"Michael will do what is right, never fear, Arthur," Sir Tom said presently.

"I shall hold you to that, Sturbridge," said Prescott, but he *was* relieved.

"I shall assume you do not object to Miss Ives' remaining with us temporarily, considering that she is still a minor and has no need at present to concern herself with the oath."

Arthur snorted contemptuously. "I suppose, with her brother out of the way, she can do no harm."

"I imagine not," rejoined Sir Tom, his voice heavy with sarcasm, which was entirely lost on Arthur Prescott.

"Well, Sturbridge, you see? There was no need of a quarrel between us after all, was there?" Prescott was almost stammering, his sense of relief growing every moment. He moved with effort to one of the soft cushiony chairs by the fireside, eased himself down with decided satisfaction. "Damned fine port, this," he remarked, draining the glass once more. He did not seem to notice that Sir Tom did not reply. And then he remembered that there was unfinished business between them and his momentary relief vanished. "But, now, it's all very well to settle these minor things so handily, however the King's Council feels very strongly about your other activities."

Sir Tom sighed. "We've made scant secret of our sympathies," he said. "The 'King,' as you are pleased to call that Dutchman, is *not* the true King of England."

Arthur's eyes bulged with horror and he threw up his pudgy hands.

"Please, please, every word you speak could send you to the scaffold!" he whispered throatily. "Even listening to such talk is dangerous!"

Sir Tom threw back his handsome head and laughed heartily. "Don't worry, Arthur, *I* will never tell!"

Prescott drew himself up coldly. "I want your word as a gentleman that you will stop supporting the Jacobite cause, that you will use neither your name or fortune to undermine His Majesty, King William's government, *and* that you will publicly announce your loyalty to the King—"

"Which king?" murmured Sir Tom, his dark blue eyes sparkling very brightly. Arthur rose majestically to his feet and waved his arm forcefully.

"King William, sir, God save him!" Then, lowering his voice, he added, "If you are not prepared to do as I request, there can be no question of a marriage between Harry and your daughter!"

Sir Tom clenched his fist, but managed to keep his voice under control. "Does it mean nothing to you, Arthur, that Harry and Elizabeth love each other?"

"What has love to do with marriage, Sturbridge?" spluttered Prescott indignantly. "I came here to you today as your friend, not to *ask* you for favors, sir, but to give you fair warning. You are on the verge of destroying your family, don't you realize it? I see that I cannot appeal to your patriotism . . . am I mistaken even in hoping to call upon your common sense? I tell you your name is linked with talk of *treason*," his voice actually trembled, "and you whine like a woman of *love!*"

The two men stared silently at one another for a long moment, then Sir Tom spoke, his voice very low.

"*Who* has linked my name with treason?"

"Rouncewell, Lord Blount, Staffordshire . . . the King himself has made inquiries," answered Prescott. "They have a list. Your name has been put on it. You are being investigated even now." He licked his lips nervously, just thinking of it.

Some of the leading members of the council, Sir Tom was thinking, how long do we have now? They will not have to look far to find their evidence . . . he turned back to Prescott and shrugged carelessly.

"Let them look as they will," he said.

Prescott was at his wit's end with the man. "All right, all right, Sturbridge," he declared, "perhaps you have been careful. Perhaps they will find nothing after all. But, whatever you do, do *nothing* now. They may forget about you. They may be satisfied and let it go. But any move on your part at this time and they'll be on to you."

"Why, Arthur, you sound a bit sympathetic," drawled Sir Tom.

Prescott shook his head solemnly. "Never," he said, and all the bluster was gone now, his voice and manner quite serious. "I have told you what I expect you to do. If you choose not to respect my wishes in this, you have only yourself to blame for what happens."

Sir Tom nodded, equally serious. "I understand, Prescott, believe me," he said.

Arthur walked to the glass door, opened it to let himself out. Then he called back over his shoulder, "The night of the betrothal ball will do very nicely, Sturbridge. Everyone will be there. When you make the announcement, follow it with your pledge of loyalty. I promise you the King will hear of it before dawn the next day." And he walked away without waiting to hear if there would be any answer.

Sir Tom, staring after him, sank into his chair slowly. What an odious man Prescott is, he thought, feeling suddenly very old and terribly tired. He wished he might rest and think of nothing whatever, yet Prescott's warning words resounded through his brain. *Do nothing now . . . any move on your part at this time . . .*

He straightened up suddenly. Michael was leaving for France tonight, carrying letters that could incriminate them all if they fell into the wrong hands! And yet what else was there to do? Rob is right, he thought, there really is no time left . . . but Michael must go just the same. If ever we are to restore the King it must be now. We have run out of resources, our hand is forced on every side.

So be it, he decided abruptly. Now where the devil were Hulme and his little army of pen-scratchers, law clerks and bookkeepers? There was so much to do, so quickly . . .

Almost without realizing it, Sir Tom left his study and headed upstairs to find Helene. It was an old, sure instinct that drew him to her, his flagging spirits gradually beginning to revive even as he reviewed the situation in his mind and faced the peril that lay ahead for all of them. He knew he could do no less than tell her everything. Above all, he needed to know what she thought, what Helene would say.

6 Forever And Ever, Today

Neither of them had spoken for a very long time . . . and that was the wonderful thing about being in love, Elizabeth knew. So few words are needed, really. A touch of his hand, or a look on his face and I understand what he means.

She shifted her head a bit, raising her chin from his shoulder where it had rested so peacefully all the while, and peered closely at Harry Prescott. She expected to see the same happy smile she knew was on her own face, but Harry, not realizing he was being scrutinized, looked far from happy. He was staring off at the swift-flowing stream nearby, his tanned, ruddy face plainly troubled.

"Why, Harry," she exclaimed, "what is it?"

Harry started, tried to laugh, but Elizabeth was not fooled. She sat up straight, ignoring the pull of his arm around her waist.

"Come, tell me at once or I shall be angry with you," she said, a bit piqued.

Now he did smile at her, fondly, his free hand reaching over to brush the fine tendrils of hair from her brow.

"If I said nothing, would you leave it at that?" he asked, knowing what she would say.

"No indeed, I would not. It isn't 'nothing' . . . and I wish I hadn't asked you, for I know what it is!"

"Do you, Elf?" he murmured, looking away with a small sigh.

"It's your father, what he said about us maybe not being married after all," she replied steadily, although the awful words made her lips tremble.

"And if we could not marry, Elizabeth?"

Her amber eyes grew big with terror. "You're saying we won't, that's it," she cried. "You've been thinking about it all the time we were here together and you were afraid to tell me!" She pushed him away from her and glared at him, her chest heaving.

Harry took her by the shoulders and shook her thoroughly until she burst into tears. At once he hated himself and drew her gently against him, holding her, trying to soothe her fears away. His own fears seemed to have vanished suddenly; he felt only a great anger, and the anger made him feel very strong and calm.

"I will marry you, Elizabeth, I swear it," he told her over and over. "If my father withdraws from the contract, you and I will go away. We can always find some little church where nobody knows us and get married . . ."

179

Finally she listened, because she wanted to believe him.

"Where would we go, Harry?" she asked him.

Harry stopped to think a moment. He pictured in his mind the vast estates of his father, the great manor house, the marble and carved mahogany staircases, the enormous reception hall alight with a thousand candles as it had been two years ago when the Duke and Duchess of Devonshire had paid them a visit . . . he saw the way life was supposed to be for Arthur Prescott's only son and that son's bride and he remembered in a great rush of separate visions crowding into his mind all together the vast emptiness, the coldness and loneliness of that house in which his father had such pride. He remembered growing up without anyone but busy, impatient servants to talk to, growing up hardly knowing his own parents, escaping as often as he could to the inviting cheerful presence of the trees and the meadows, of wandering about in bare feet and torn old breeches looking like any cotter's lad, glad for the chance to run free in the sunshine and grass, to tumble in rough play with the shepherd's dogs, to find a kindred little spirit one day by a brook, to discover he was not the only lonely person in the world, to be with and learn that he loved and would never part from her no matter what the world . . . or his father . . . intended.

Harry took her hot, pink face in his cupped hands and kissed her on the lips very softly and felt her grow quite still under his touch.

"I'll find us a cottage somewhere, with trees all about and a flower garden for you," he said with positive conviction that it was possible. "Dovecotes in the back, and one of those great fat sleepy cats you like so much dozing off on the windowsill. . . ."

"And dogs, Harry," she said, falling in with his idea at once. "Two dogs. A great big one to keep watch over us, and a little fluffy white one for company. Can we do it, Harry? Can we really?"

Gone from her mind in the instant was the elaborate and elegant ball she had been looking forward to. Gone, too, was the secret dream of her life that one day she would be exactly like her mother, a great lady. A cottage, he'd said, and she thought with delight of Harry and her sitting by their own small hearth of an evening, the floor pungent with fresh, sweet-smelling straw, and no one to tell them they must dress for dinner, no one to scold when they allowed the dogs to come in and dry their muddy paws by the fire, no silly kings and their problems, their comings and goings to worry about . . .

"Why not? Why couldn't we?" Harry was caught up in the

180

dream, his words rushing out very quickly. "I have money saved, a great lot of it, I think. We can buy our own house and a couple of horses for plowing . . . and a cow, too, for milk."

Elizabeth laughed, trying to picture herself milking a cow. She gazed at him with eyes brightly tender with love and she believed in him with all her heart. She felt much better now, forgetting how worried Harry had looked a while ago. If Harry said they would marry and live together forever and always, then it was true, it was true because he was Harry and her love.

She threw her arms around his neck, still laughing, her heart entirely free again. Harry felt the lithe pressure of her against him and thought, Why not? Why shouldn't we be as happy as we please? Nobody cares what we do anyway. But he did not believe in the dream himself, try as he might. He heard her voice laughing in his ear and felt the heat of her sweet breath as she laughed and suddenly he felt like crying. What was happening to him and Elizabeth? He was afraid, not entirely sure of what. He glanced at her uncertainly and saw that she looked beautiful again, beautiful as only he knew her and even then only once in a while. He was jealous of that special beauty and hoped no one in all the world would ever notice it save him. And all at once the fear and pride, the old loneliness and the new amazing love gathered themselves together in one great surge of emotion and he caught her and crushed her to him, burying his hot face in her neck.

"I love you so, Elizabeth!" he cried, pressing ardent kisses on her soft, throbbing throat. "I have always loved you!"

She laughed again, for the pure joy of it and because it was so strong, it made them strong, invincible against everything and everyone else. Let Katherine dream of shining deeds and adventures and glory streaming down out of the heavens, let her, indeed, exulted Elizabeth in that moment; yes, let everyone go their ways and leave us alone, my dream is here in my arms, real to my touch, alive a heartbeat from my heart, and he is all I want or need now or ever!

A year, a year, a year is so *long*, she was thinking as the hot insistent feeling of his mouth against her skin made her catch her breath strangely. How wonderful it will be then, every day all of our lives will be like this, every day and every night . . . and then the long year seemed as nothing, no time at all for Elizabeth to wait. She did not quite understand what was happening to her; innocently wanting to be the closest she might be to Harry, to touch him completely, to be enfolded, enveloped by him and he by her, she fell back upon the grassy bank of the stream, pulling him with her, holding him closely cradled in her arms. She had so many things she wanted to say to him; thoughts whirled wildly about in her mind but she couldn't seem to concentrate properly. So it was that she said nothing at all but only pressed herself hard against him as though she might melt and dissolve and in some inexplicable way become part of him.

A year, Harry was thinking in despair, knowing exactly how long a year of wanting her would be . . . will the world change so much in a year, he asked himself harshly? Will my father care any less in a year that he and *her* father pledge their loyalty and devotion to two different kings?

He shivered, feeling giddy and distraught and clung to her desperately while the answers to his questions pounded like thunder in his head. My God, my God, Harry realized somehow, we don't have a year and then a lifetime!

He pulled his head up and looked at her lying there with her eyes closed, the happiness of her smile, and for a moment it was as if he saw her dead before him. He gasped, his heart pounding. With cold, shaky fingers he touched her cheek, his fingers trailed along her throat and moved to brush softly against her girlish breast . . . was she alive, was she breathing, did her heart still beat? His mind did not form the questions anymore, only his heart inquired.

"Elizabeth!" he whispered, and the sound seemed to explode into the rapt silence of the trees' domain. A dozen quiet birds echoed his anxious tone, fluttering nervously from their dark perches as he bent over her.

She opened her eyes at once, startled to see the fear in him, and she said, "I am here, Harry; hold me, my love, hold me!"

He gathered her small body into his arms and rocked her against him, back and forth, back and forth while he spoke words of love and promises of forever to her and he said to himself all the while, we haven't even tomorrow, all we have is right now, it will never be like this for us again, never, never . . .

He was no longer afraid. He had passed beyond fear into a certainty that offered no particulars and held out no hope. And presently she sensed the truth he was feeling, though his words said so many other things. She lay against him and she knew there could never come another day when she would love him more than she did at that moment. Something would change it all, of that she felt quite sure now. Something... if only the passing of time... would begin to fashion another Elizabeth, another Harry, and even if those two specters loved each other then, it would not be the same.

Stay! Stay, stay with us a little while longer, she begged the swift-driving clouds above them, but the clouds went their way, and the sun stood far off from them, not caring at all, and the earth kept on turning beneath them, straining impatiently, blindly toward night...

This day must last, thought Elizabeth very clearly. I must make it like no other day we have ever known. And the memory of it must do me, whatever happens, until I die.

She sat up straight and took Harry's hands in her own, twining their fingers together gently. He looked at her in some surprise, for there was an unusual firmness to her soft mouth and a calm about her that reminded him instantly of her mother. She smiled at him, her amber eyes glowing.

"God," she said out loud, "God, be my witness: you are my husband, Harry Prescott, and I, Elizabeth Sturbridge, I am your wife. Forever and forever, I swear it."

She was right, he knew it at once. This was the only way it could be. "I swear it, too," he said, looking into her eyes. "Forever and ever, Elizabeth."

"Now it's done," she said. "Now we belong to each other and God knows it. And I don't care what happens, nobody can ever take you away from me!"

Gently she disengaged her fingers from his ... he felt the loss of touching her as though it were a physical shock, but he said nothing, only watched her as she stood up very slowly and began to unlace the blue ribbons of her bodice. Fascinated, he saw her undress before him, letting the garments slip one by one to the ground unheeded until she was completely naked, the heavy waves of glistening dark hair hanging loose to her barely rounded hips. She stood quite still and straight, her face flushed, her eyes closed so that the delicate fringe of black lashes seemed to be sweeping soft crescents across her cheeks.

Harry looked at her with a lump in his throat, remembering Elizabeth as he had seen her naked once before. Then she had been all gawky arms and legs, straight as a boy, lean and awkward, still wet from her swim. That Elizabeth of his boyhood memory was gone now. The shy, loving girl of even a few minutes ago was suddenly replaced by a quiet, waiting young woman who stood before him and offered him the love of her fragile, pliant body. She looked at once so patient and so wise, yet so totally vulnerable that Harry was almost afraid to touch her.

He had been very silent and he made no move toward her . . . she opened her eyes and looked at him with a little crooked uncertain smile. With a low cry, he jumped to his feet and folded his arms around her. He picked her up nestled against his body and, for a moment, held her there in his two strong arms and believed he might dare the devil to touch her or the world to take her from him. Then he set her down tenderly on the grass where the oblivious sun was pouring warm wavering rays across her body and he lay down with her to love her forever and forever, today.

Seven

"Dare To Be Strong For The Rest!"

1 What Honour Demands

"I cannot stay without Michael," Katherine was saying, but Rob shook his head, refusing to let her go on.

"You mean, you *will* not stay without him," he said, a bit too loudly, trying very hard to keep his voice matter-of-fact and not icily cold. But he felt cold now, deadly cold, and he was not sure whether he was glad or sorry that Michael was gone and they could not quarrel.

"Oh, Rob, will you not try to understand?" She pleaded with him but Katherine, too, was proud and her plea was edged with exasperation. "I am all he has in the world now."

"And is that your pleasure?" he asked, his tone stinging with reproach. "Is that enough for you? What will you do one day when your brother brings a wife home to take your place?"

" 'Home'?" she repeated the word scornfully. "We have no home now. And . . . Michael will never marry."

Rob laughed, a short bitter laugh. "I know that well enough. He's in love with a ghost and trying to fit you into her place!"

Katherine gasped, her bright eyes blazing up, and her hand moved involuntarily as if to strike him. Then, regaining her composure with great effort, she said, "This is an old argument, Rob. You have never cared that it hurt me. You do not care now. Yet, you want me to believe that you love me, that you say these cruel things in the name of Love . . ." She looked at him a long moment . . . "If that is what love means, keep it from me, I could not bear the pain it brings."

Rob meant to say more. Instead, he turned from her and bent to stir the logs blazing in the fireplace. Michael had left for France not two hours past and this was the first opportunity Rob had found to speak with Katherine alone. How had they come to quarrel so quickly, he wondered, poking about absently with the fire tongs. He had only meant to reassure her that everything would be all right. No, much more than that, he had needed to be with her tonight, to speak of the love he had for her, to offer her himself and his home for her own.

But Katherine had just come from saying good-bye to Father McGuire. After Michael had left, she and Helene had helped the aging priest pack his few belongings and leave the small rooms he had occupied at Spring Mount for nearly fifteen years. And then, when they had stood in the courtyard with the old man, waiting for them to bring the carriage around, Katherine had clung to his arm and wept and asked him over and over where he would go. Father McGuire had looked at her, a bit confused, the night wind stirring wisps of his thin white hair about his small pink old face, and blessed her, his hand describing the sign of the cross over her, but he would say nothing, nothing. Sir Tom had then ordered Katherine back to the house at once. He wouldn't even allow her to watch the priest ride off. How strange and how somber Sir Tom's face had looked, how sharp his voice when he sent her away. Then, by the time she had gotten upstairs to her own room, still crying, when she had run to her window to look out, the carriage had already gone. She could not even see the lantern that swung from the back of it as it headed down the driveway and on to the long flat winding road.

No matter, she sank weakly down on the window seat, her back turned against the night outside, and dried her tears. She would never have believed her uncle would send the old man away like that, never. And she would never understand it. Well, the world was turning upside down, anyway. Nothing was as it had been only this morning. What shall we do, Michael and I, now that Father is gone? How shall we receive the Sacraments? How can we attend Mass every Sunday? Sir Tom is afraid, she concluded incredulously. He sent Michael away, and then Father McGuire. Will I be next?

Helene had been no help, either. Katherine had rushed to her eagerly, full of faith in the aunt who had never failed her all her life. But Helene looked terribly tired and terribly sad and said very little. She explained, briefly, why it was necessary that Father McGuire must be gotten away, for his sake and for theirs. More than that she could not tell anyone. And, Katherine sensed, there was more on Helene's mind, there were things Sir Tom had told her . . . or maybe the boys had . . . and nobody wanted Katherine to find out. She resented being treated like a child, being protected from the truth as though she could not deal with it. When Helene went to kiss her, Katherine had pulled away and gone to stand looking out the windows, hating herself for treating Helene so. But Helene seemed to understand. She had merely said, "Good night, then, darling," and Katherine left, feeling alone, angry, puzzled and, although she refused to recognize it, afraid.

She knew it would be impossible to sleep now. She considered talking to Elizabeth, whose room was just next to her own. But again, Elizabeth was acting very strangely, making it clear in her quiet little way that she didn't want to talk to anybody tonight. Elizabeth had come in sometime late in the afternoon, had changed for dinner and hardly touched a bite. She had listened avidly to the talk at the dinner table, her big eyes watching them all so intently the whole time. But as soon as the table was cleared for dessert, Elizabeth had excused herself, kissed Michael very quickly on the brow, and gone back to her room, where she had been ever since. Helene, seated at the head of the table, had watched her daughter closely, a tiny worried frown between her eyes. Yet she had not followed Elizabeth upstairs, had asked her no questions, apparently content to wait until the girl came to her with whatever was on her mind.

I am not so patient, thought Katherine, wishing that she were. She hesitated, almost knocking at Elizabeth's door, then shrugged, and went downstairs to the library. It was her favorite room in the huge house, a place where she had found the world in books as a small child, a place where she might ask questions and get answers when no one else around her knew them. She went there now, relieved to find it empty, one small silver candelabra with three candles burning in it on a long table by the windows. She walked around the room, enjoying as always the rich sweet smell of the leather book bindings, enjoying the silence and the peace of a place where books were honored. How many times, after a bitter quarrel with Michael, had she escaped into this haven and, after a little while, found that the presence of the room and its contents had a calming effect on her agitated heart? Too many times to count, she thought, wandering to the shadowy corner by the windows where Sir Tom's great globe of the world stood in its wooden stand.

This was where so many of her questions had begun, she recalled. Standing on tiptoe as a little girl, twirling the globe around and around with her fingers, stopping it suddenly and pointing to one place, one name and asking what it was, why was it written in Latin, how could the sea keep from spilling over if the earth was really like this, round and spinning, forever on the move and restless? She studied that globe, finding a strange affinity between it and her own restless yearning heart. She, too, felt sometimes lost amid the maze of stars in the gigantic universe, pulled as was the little earth in all the myriad directions of their mighty powers. How does it know where to go, she had wondered? How does it have the strength to keep on its own way and never falter or fall, lost and tumbling without purpose through the emptiness of black, unknowing space? That was when Katherine began to understand God a little: the library, with its sweet leather smells, its hushed and waiting silence, its simple model of the earth she stood upon and identified herself with, came to mean much more to her in seeking out God than did the great old church she went to in Ireland or the little chapel at Spring Mount. If God could keep it all straight in His head, she knew, then He would have no difficulty keeping His eye on her, too. If only He would make Himself so clear to Michael, she had often wished fervently.

Rob found her there by herself, her back to the door as she stood twirling the polished globe with her fingertips, staring out at the night. He came here to be by himself for a while, to drink a solitary brandy and light a fire to drink it by, to rest, to think things through for himself.

He almost spoiled the moment by speaking to her when he

realized she was there. Some instinct bade him be still, so he entered the room very quietly, and leaned his tall body against the door-frame, simply watching her. He'd had little enough opportunity recently to look at Katherine as much as he liked. When her brother was there he made it plain enough he didn't want Rob looking at her at all. Then, too, all this past year, Katherine herself seemed unable to relax around him. She was always moving, talking, gesturing, walking away from him at the very moment he was about to reach out and touch her. She was there . . . yet she was not.

So now he stood in the shadows, studying every detail of her as though those details were not at all familiar to him, as though he had not really seen her clearly since they were children together.

She still wore the dress she had put on much earlier for dinner, white and simply cut, a heavy brocade figured with cream-colored designs shot through with threads of gold. The sleeves were French-cut, tight to the elbow, a graceful gathering of white lace and gold ribbons falling almost halfway down her slim arms. The glints of gold in her gown picked up the marvelous bright pure gold of her hair, dressed in three long curls at the back of her shapely head. She was unaware, as she stood that way, that the three candles by her cast a soft subdued radiance on her clear, fine skin so that it gleamed like pearl. Rob remained where he was with difficulty. All he wanted to do was cross the room quickly and take her in his arms. He must have moved or sighed then; whatever it was, she turned and saw him there. The troubled look on her lovely, heart-shaped face vanished for an instant as her remarkably iridescent grey eyes sparkled at the sight of him and a smile hovered about her full, expressive mouth. But the smile disappeared as he walked toward her. She turned her head away, striking the still-spinning globe a sharp rap with her ivory fan, and walked to the mantel . . . the stiff, erect lines of her body told him plainly she wanted to be left alone.

So they had talked of the priest's leaving and of Michael, and it seemed to Rob that she deliberately misunderstood everything he tried to say to her. He stood up, put the tongs back and stared at the striving flames, wishing that he might tell her everything that was in his heart. They remained like that, silent with each other, the only sound in the room the hissing and crackling of the fire, each of them wondering in bewilderment why it had become so difficult for them to talk to each other. He wished he might put her mind at ease about

188

the priest, but yet there was a sort of sullen resentment in him that she could willingly believe Sir Tom would ever abandon anyone.

Katherine felt wretched, knowing she had hurt him, but she was hurt, too, and had withdrawn to a distant place inside herself to sit out the storm she knew was about to break over her head. She moved away from the fire, from Rob's nearness, and sat down on a small sofa across the room.

"Will you go into exile, Rob?" she asked him. "To France, as your father wants?"

He looked over at her sharply. "I don't know," he admitted. "It may not become necessary."

"You can always wait it out," she said. "Spring Mount will be here. But I want to move on. I want to see what else there is in the world outside of our great houses and cities and all the old, old places and problems . . ."

"Michael has talked about America again, I see," remarked Rob coolly.

"I don't need Michael's talk to think for myself!" she snapped, tapping the folded fan nervously against her palm. "I want to go, Rob. I have always wanted it. While there was still Kilbree there was little point in thinking of it. But, now . . . it is the answer for us, Rob, surely you can see that. Michael . . ." she saw the hostile look in his dark eyes. "Well, leave Michael out of it," she amended quickly. "Aren't you ever tired of staying in the same place, living your whole life just as your father has lived his, and his father and all of them all the way back? Don't you want something new, something different, a chance to stretch yourself completely and find out what else there is in the world besides England?" There was a smoldering fire in her eyes, an excited note in her voice that dismayed him.

"Why does it mean so much to you?" he asked, feeling cruel. "Your life would be no different no matter where you live. You're a woman. You'll marry and have children and see no more of the world than your own spinning wheel."

"Why does it mean so much to *you*?" She threw his own words back at him, her voice low and tense with feeling. "Isn't that what you offer me yourself? I will *never* marry if what you say is the truth and that is all I may look forward to in this life. God made me a woman but he didn't make me a fool as well. I've seen enough of

189

what you men have made of this lovely world of ours to want to turn my back on the lot of you! Oh, I understand how my brother feels here, in this precious England of yours. Outside of these walls, this house . . ." she glanced with loving eyes about the room . . . "*we* are prisoners of war—one war or another. And you, Rob, you're just as much captive as we are. You are a prisoner of everything that has been in the past."

"What in God's name do you want, Katherine? Tell me that!" Rob demanded heatedly.

"I seek something . . . somewhere I may strike a new beginning," she answered him without an instant's hesitation.

"America," he murmured flatly. But there was an odd look in his eyes.

"Yes, America. Why not America?" She blazed at him, not angry now, but amazed to see that he was actually considering what she was saying. "Michael and I are Irish and we must live here, in England, to be safe from the English! Is that not ironic, Rob? And now we . . . and you who *are* English, face the necessity of living in yet another country, one so like this in all save language that the differences hardly matter . . . again, so we can all be safe . . . from the English! Oh, Rob, Michael is right about this . . ." She leaned forward, her whole body taut with urgency. "Why can't we be safe by going to live in a country from which we cannot be driven out, a country so vast that there must be room in it for people to forget their differences, for all of us to find what we dream of . . ."

"The alternative?" Rob mused, his words coming slowly. "We are to admit our cause is a hopeless one, escape what honor demands of us despite all hopelessness . . . is that the alternative?"

She realized he was talking much more to himself than to her. Indeed, he had almost forgotten she was there. She stood up quietly and went to him, her fingers clutching his arm impulsively. How strange it was, she wondered, she felt closer to Rob than she had in a long time.

"Speak to your father, Rob," she said. "Whatever happens here, we will not be the cause of the downfall of this house. We cannot stay, however dear to us you are . . . you and your family," she added very quickly, dropping her hand from him. "France is not the answer for us, nor Holland, nor any other land in Europe. We will not be driven out again, Rob, never, never again!"

He turned to look at her, marveling once again at the subdued passion in her proud face. What must it take for a man, any man, to reach that passion and claim it for his own? Her beautiful clear eyes shone with determination as she looked him directly in the eye. Vainly he sought one faint hint of womanly weakness. Of docility, she had none. Her manner was frank, her courage superb. Yes, he realized bitterly, she would go where Michael went, not because Michael wanted her to, but because she believed in what her own heart told her.

If only it were so clear, so simple for me, Rob thought. He stretched his hand out and traced with his fingers the soft, hot cheeks before him, trailing his fingers along the firm, rounded jaw. He could feel the tiny insistent throbbing of her pulse under his touch. His large expressive hand closed suddenly, and very carefully, about her slender throat.

She did not move, she did not seem the least bit stirred at the intimacy of his touch. Her intense gaze never wavered.

"You fear nothing?" He said it lightly, removing his hand at once, but he felt a stab of pain through him as the warmth of her skin vanished from his fingers. How close he had been to taking her into his arms in that moment. Only the fear that she would not be moved one jot had stopped him.

"I fear much," Katherine replied, barely whispering. "I fear *everything.*"

Rob moved from her restlessly. "Not you," he said. "You never cried when you were small, that day you wandered off behind the house and got lost in the trees . . . you didn't cry then. And when you tried to jump your pony over the stream once, do you remember? You fell and couldn't stand up for the pain . . . and you didn't cry. Next morning, with the bandage on your leg I saw you limping down to the stables to feed the pony carrots."

"I didn't know anyone was watching me," she smiled at him.

"I was," he said, without an answering smile for her. "I saw you go up to him and pat his nose and talk to him. Any other girl—and most boys your age—would have been afraid to do that."

"I was afraid, Rob. I remember it, too. I loved the pony and then all of a sudden I was afraid of him. I didn't know what to do. It made me so angry that I should be afraid of something I loved. I suppose it was my anger that made me go out there and have it out with him. We ended friends, though, and I was never afraid of him again."

He wheeled about, his own eyes flashing now, and said, "But that is the way of a *man*, to use his anger to overcome his fear!"

Katherine's soft, remembering smile disappeared abruptly. She nodded briskly and when she spoke again her voice was distant.

"That is the way of a human being," she said coolly. "It pleases men to believe it belongs exclusively to them. Good night, Rob."

She walked very quickly past him, her head held high, and when he called her name she did not turn or hesitate. A moment later he heard the swift tapping of her little wooden heels as she climbed the stairs. He stood there, quite alone, staring after her for a moment, then he turned to go back to his fire and his untouched glass of brandy.

But, although the fire was blazing mightily now and the candles were still lit, Rob Sturbridge felt that in leaving, Katherine had taken all light, all warmth from the room. He lay down on the sofa, his long legs stretched out, turning the brandy glass slowly around and around in his fingers.

For the first time, he began seriously to consider the possibility of leaving England behind forever. America... how often he and Michael had talked of it when they were only boys. He and Michael... and Katherine, he recalled. The three of them, always the three of them. The world they had known seemed even then too small, too confining to contain their exuberant young spirits. What adventure that far-off place conjured up in their minds, at an age when adventure was *all* in the mind. And now, would he not gladly leave everything behind, if he could follow her no matter where she went? A part of him would do that and never look back, certainly.

But he was committed to the cause of healing England's woes. He was a Sturbridge, he was his father's son. Both of them believed in the rightness of what they were trying to do. Tom Sturbridge would never turn his back on the past, would never cease to believe in his country's future and the part he must play in bringing it about.

Rob put the glass aside and threw his aching head back, sighing.

He, too, must stay, and he must let her go. You will lose her, a nagging voice inside of him said over and over, you will lose her...

For she would go, of that he had no doubt. He could not bear the thought that she would not remain simply because he wanted her, he needed her so much. No, she would go before he had ever had the chance to win the love she had not yet realized was waiting inside her untouched heart. And he would stay, whether in England or in

France, and fight until the cause was lost. He was convinced now that it could not be won. And it could not be abandoned.

He had drifted off into a restless sleep there in the library and the fire was almost dead an hour later when footsteps moved softly down the hall outside, a dark figure noticed the sputtering candles and stopped in the open doorway to look in.

"Rob?" Sir Tom called his son and came in slowly, untying the strings of his long black cloak as he moved. He stood over the sleeping youth, noting the unfinished brandy on the table next to him, and the tiny beads of perspiration that had gathered on Rob's tired face and brow. Sir Tom sighed, casting the cloak and his hat aside, and sat down near Rob to wait. He was quite exhausted himself and thought he might finish the drink Rob had left. Reaching over to pick it up, he inadvertently made a small noise. At once Rob sat up, his eyes heavy with sleep, his hand reaching instinctively for the sword he usually wore. Then he saw it was his father, a tired apologetic smile on his face.

"Just getting back?" asked Rob, running his fingers through the thick mop of dark wavy hair that fell to his shoulders.

"Yes," his father nodded. "I was not able to go until after ten. Hulme was here, in the study, and everything took much longer than I expected. It will be a ticklish business," he added, and Rob looked disturbed. "But Hulme is a good man," his father reassured him. "He will manage it all . . ."

"How soon? Does he know it must be done quickly?"

Sir Tom swallowed the rest of the brandy in one quick gulp and shivered as the fiery liquor raced through his cold, weary body.

"He knows," he said. "And his commission will be double, consequently."

Rob snorted, swinging his legs to the floor and stretching himself awake.

"He'd better be ready with a good story—or a valid passport when they question him," he said. His father laughed.

"Men like Hulme are never caught short."

"But men like ourselves . . ."

Sir Tom looked away from his son's eyes. "The old man is settled in now," he remarked, frowning. "I have left Ralph with him."

" 'Ralph'? He's almost as old as Father McGuire himself!" said Rob, surprised. "Why not one of the younger chaps?"

"Well, for one thing, Ralph has been with him for years, he's

193

comfortable with him. And Ralph claims he can cook. They will be isolated, Rob. We cannot have meals prepared in the kitchen here and carried over there every day. Someone is sure to suspect. No, Ralph will do very well. And it will not be for long.''

''I wish I had told Katherine,'' said Rob. ''She thinks we have abandoned the priest, she can't understand what's happening, and you can hardly blame her.''

Sir Tom's eyes flickered. It had pained him immeasurably to order Katherine away earlier tonight, to forbid her even to watch the old man she loved so dearly leaving Spring Mount. Tomorrow, he knew, she would insist upon being told where he had sent Father McGuire. Well, perhaps after all, he would tell her, tomorrow. But it would be better for her, for all of them, if nobody knew that the priest was still at Spring Mount. They had moved him and Ralph to an old abandoned cottage once used by shepherds, at the very edge of the forest, but still on Sturbridge land.

''Does Mother know?'' Rob asked him presently.

''Yes. She knows everything. What you did not tell her, she pieced together for herself. Perhaps *she* can make Katherine understand—''

''Katherine will not stay with us,'' Rob broke in. ''When Michael returns, they will go.''

''We will all go, if necessary,'' his father said, but Rob shook his head.

''No. Not to the Continent. To America. She will not reconsider.''

Sir Tom looked sad, but he spoke firmly. ''She will reconsider, believe me. And so will Michael. The letters he carries now will put into motion the final objectives we have been working for. I have informed His Majesty that within six weeks, two months at the outside, he will be landing in England. An army will be there to meet him and a large force will move down from Scotland as soon as James Peggie receives word he has arrived. It's all but done and over, Rob . . .''

Rob stared at his father. ''It's just beginning!''

''Keep your voice down!'' ordered Sir Tom sternly. ''If you mean the battle, yes, and the sooner begun, the sooner won. But all these years of waiting and hoping, planning, living like spies in our own country . . . that is at an end. We have more than sufficient funds. I am not the only man in England who has been carefully, secretly selling properties, taking the profits from merchant ventures, mortaging everything, even their own homes, to raise the sum required. And we have it, now, lad! We have victory within our grasp, please God!'' Sir Tom's weary face was alight with hope and faith and he did not notice the dismay in his son's eyes.

"Where? Where will it be?'' asked Rob dully.

"That is the word Michael will bring back with him. The King's advisors are the only ones who know. Once Michael returns, you and he and I will leave here at once and each of us will travel with a list of names and places. The men in those places await only our signal to join us. We will meet together again on the day the King's ship drops anchor in English waters. Michael should be back in a fortnight and we set out at once. So you see,'' Sir Tom stressed, as if to dispel any doubts his son might still have, "we shall move before our enemies suspect what is happening and we shall win a speedy victory. Once the King is here, I believe Englishmen will forget he is a Papist and remember instead that he is one of them and the legitimate son of the true King of England.''

"You are counting on support from the people?'' Rob asked him incredulously.

"I am,'' replied Sir Tom fervently. "Without the people, no king can rule for long. If we, the nobles, must lead them, must guide them to do what is right, then that is our responsibility. But in the end it is they who shall decide. And rightly so.''

No, Father, no, not here, Rob wanted to shout to Sir Tom, the people here, people everywhere, are sheep afraid to seek out a new pasture by themselves. The dogs must lead them, must drive them, the dogs and the shepherds. And what if the shepherds themselves are wrong and lead them only over the abyss. . . .

Rob swallowed very hard. He saw the concern on his father's face and a rush of love filled him with self-reproach. Impulsively, he seized Sir Tom's hand and pressed it hard.

"You are right, Papa, we will make a good fight of it,'' he said with a broad smile and a resolute nod of the head, and Sir Tom nodded too, laughing, and stood up. They went upstairs together, arm in arm, and everything seemed to be settled for both of them.

But Rob, watching his father go into his own rooms, was sick at heart. Why could he not believe any longer? Why *now* of all times, when what they had been working for all their lives was about to be realized, could he not have faith in what they did? Why did he feel sick with apprehension when his father . . . and his country . . . needed him the most?

Never had he loved his father more than tonight and never had he longed more desperately to be out and away and *finished with the cause his father loved.*

2 The End Of A Long Day

There was really nothing to do but wait now. Helene was already dressed for bed, in a long satin bedgown with loose flowing sleeves and, over it, a matching satin robe, sleeveless and trimmed round the wide-cut neck and down the front to the floor with white ermine fur. Above the gleaming white cloth, her face shone with its usual secret radiance, although tonight her cheeks were somewhat pale and there were shadows under her great dark eyes.

She walked around the room, poked the logs in the fire until they blazed up brightly, picked up her half-forgotten cup of tea only to set it down again when she found it had gone quite cold, fingered a book or two by the bedside and then decided she would not be able to concentrate on reading after all.

Now she went back once more and sat down on the deep cushioned velvet seat before her mirrored dressing table. She had cleared the table earlier herself, tossing all the combs and brushes and pins and bottles of perfume carelessly into drawers. Only the jewelboxes reamined. She inspected them now. There were six, fine gold and silver-tooled leather lined with velvet in deep blue and green. She picked up the largest of them and opened it again.

This contained all of the jewels she was planning to give to Elizabeth. Several of the pieces had once belonged to Lady Anne. Helene touched a gold and diamond necklace and earring set, thinking of her husband's lovely mother in the portrait downstairs, wearing this very necklace. And here were the rubies her own father had given her when she married. The topaz and amethyst set she had been looking at this afternoon, the pearls that had belonged to her mother whom she could not remember, they were all here. She carefully straightened the links of a delicate silver filagree chain, then closed the box and set it aside by itself.

She looked at the jewel boxes, not really wanting to open them again. Somewhere in one of them was the gorgeous sapphire and diamond set she had been saving for Katherine when she married. Of course, Katherine would have Sheila's emeralds, all of Sheila's lovely things. Helene reminded herself that she must find those sapphires and put them away safely, or better, as she remembered the determined look on Katherine's face when she had spoken to her and Michael earlier, she would give her the jewels very soon, perhaps as a birthday present.

Helene sighed softly, opening another box and finding her wedding pearls inside. She took the intricate necklace from its velvet nest and held it up against the candlelight. She would never give this to anyone, not this necklace. Her long, sensitive fingers stroked the satiny-feeling pearls as she marveled once more at the rosy glow of them. She wore them very often. Her portrait, painted at Sir Tom's insistence ten years ago, showed her with these pearls about her neck above a gown of deepest gold taffeta edged with beaver from America.

America. There it was again, that name, that place! Hastily she put the pearls away and shut the jewel case with a snap. Was it not hard enough to listen to Michael, pacing up and down this very room today, his face hard and set, his voice agitated as he told her of his decision? Why must America be his choice, she thought, knowing she was probably being unreasonable. But he would take Katherine from them, too . . . no, Helene shook her head a little. No, that was not right. Katherine's heart was set on leaving with him, and America . . . again, America! was her own goal.

Helene had not argued with them this afternoon, nor tried to talk them out of what they seemed bent on doing. She had only begged them to wait a little longer, just a little. But she had seen the fierce look in Michael's eye, the touch of scorn that had passed across his face and was gone the next instant. Yes, of course they would wait . . . a little, he had assured her. Katherine had wanted to say more but a look had passed between brother and sister then and she had closed her mouth and said nothing.

So they think I don't understand what is in their minds, mused Helene sadly. Do they, knowing me as they have, believe I cannot understand the implications of all that is happening around me? We have lost Kilbree House, we are about to embark on the most dangerous undertaking of our lives with our own home and estates tied up in mortgages that can ruin us if we should fail. Every shilling we have has gone to support the Jacobite cause, to pay for the training and equipping of men at arms, for ships, for guns . . . she jumped to her feet suddenly, her head throbbing, and threw open the windows. There was a storm moving in from the sea . . . she could watch the black clouds rushing over the hills, erasing the stars as it came its cold way. Looking down toward her garden she noticed the rose bushes already beginning to feel the fingers of the wind roughly tossing them about. A distant soundless spear of lightning lit up the blackness for an instant and was gone, only to reaffirm its presence in a wild cannonade of thunder. The wind blew the curtains billowing about Helene's small form but she did not move away. Their last storm had uprooted several of the older rose bushes. By the time she had gotten to them, they were finished, torn beyond salvaging, their dark slender roots rotted black and slimy.

We are like them, she thought. How we cling to our beloved hillside here and wait to face out any storm that comes. But we, too, can be uprooted by what is going to happen. . . .

She turned from the windows, finding no peace here either. She picked up a sheaf of papers on her nightstand, determined to keep busy and not to give in to her fears. She leafed through the papers, forcing herself to concentrate. Bills, invitations, replies to her invitations to Elizabeth's ball, more bills. The musicians she had originally intended to play that night were promised elsewhere, but their manager had taken it upon himself to employ another group, even more suitable for the occasion, he wrote to assure her . . . the thunder roared again and she quivered, tossing the papers aside. Poor little Elizabeth, the thought struck her as suddenly as had the sound of the thunder.

Poor Elizabeth? Why, she asked herself? In other days, watching her shy daughter wandering off by herself, apparently so alone, so unable or unwilling to let herself be a part of what the other three were doing . . . yes, then Helene had often thought "poor Elizabeth," wishing she could hold her daughter close forever and shield her from the trials a nature such as hers often found unendurable. Elizabeth, shut up inside of herself, sweet, obliging, sensitive . . . but unable to communicate her feelings and desires to anyone, how much life could hurt a child like that. But, ever since Harry Prescott had entered her life, Elizabeth had begun to blossom. Harry filled her life, Helene knew and rejoiced about it, and was content to watch her little daughter reach toward womanhood with quiet happiness.

But the wedding was still a year off. In a year Elizabeth might be in France with the rest of them, in exile that knew no time or year of ending and held out no promise for the future. If the King were not reestablished on his throne very soon, Spring Mount would no longer be theirs. Elizabeth's dowry would be gone, of course, and Arthur Prescott would not hesitate to break the marriage contract. Like her son, like her husband, Helene was beginning to feel pressured and constrained by time, and the thought went through her mind now, as it had through theirs today—there isn't any time left.

She envisioned Elizabeth's flushed face tonight at dinner and wondered once again if something unusual had happened to her today. There was quite a new look in her daughter's light eyes, a new depth to her voice and an assuredness in her movements that had amazed Helene.

That is the way I always wanted her to be, she thought tenderly. She is happy, no doubt of that. What could have brought about this change? She is loved. Helene smiled to herself. But then, Elizabeth had known for a long time how Harry cherished her. It was no secret, and Harry was so forthright, so openly proud and protective of her, anyone could see how much he cared. Yet, today has been different for my child, Helene could not let go of the notion. She closed her eyes, recalling what the girl had said . . . not much at all, and how she had hardly eaten anything, how her mind, no, her entire *being* had been so plainly elsewhere . . .

And then it hit her. So simple she had overlooked it. Or perhaps it was that she still kept Elizabeth too much the child in some secret part of her heart. She is not a child, she is a woman now, Helene knew all at once. She has been loved, she has given herself to him completely, that was it. Her hands began to tremble, thinking of Elizabeth and Harry Prescott together in the act of love.

Yet it would have been that way sooner or later, she told herself. As her mother, I should disapprove. But I do *not* . . . she caught her breath. There would never be another man for Elizabeth . . . she of all people understood that very well. No, I am not unhappy for her, Helene decided emphatically, no matter how things may be complicated for us all, I would not deny my daughter this special happiness.

And she refused to look ahead into Elizabeth's life tonight, she refused to follow the ramifications of that love-making. The day had brought enough to think about already. Let Elizabeth have her joyous secret . . . I will not even ask her about it, Helene vowed.

And then, just as the storm broke atop the hills nearby and the fitful rain began clamoring against the windows, Thomas came to her. She thought she heard low voices in the hall outside; she was right, as he opened the bedroom door she saw Rob for an instant, and it seemed to her from that brief impression that she had never seen her son's face so unhappy and so uncertain . . .

"Was Rob with you?" she asked her husband, puzzled. She knew that Rob had gone out as far as town with Michael much earlier, to see him on his way.

"No," Sir Tom replied, his voice husky with weariness. "I found him sound asleep downstairs in the library."

"And Father McGuire? Is he all right?" she was anxious about the old man, sick at heart that he should be pursued and hounded so in his last years. He had thought to find refuge and peace to end his days with them at Spring Mount . . . she had no illusions as to what his fate would be should he be found out.

Sir Tom nodded, sitting down in his special wingback chair by the fire.

He leaned over and spread his hands to warm them and Helene observed that he was more quiet than usual and seemed not inclined to talk. She sat quietly beside him, curled up on a low footstool, knees drawn up to her chin, her arms clasped about them, and watched the flames dance to the beat of the wind as it pushed its way through the curtains. Once she murmured something about forgetting to close the windows and started to get up, but Thomas rested his hand on her shoulder and said, "Let them be." He sat back in his chair and closed his eyes, his fingers still idly stroking the white satin sleeve of her gown for a while. Then he was motionless, his breathing light and even and she thought he had gone to sleep. She slipped carefully from his side, thinking to pull off his boots and throw a cover over him, for she was loathe to disturb him at rest. But he felt her move away and instantly his eyes opened, his hand reached out to her.

"Stay with me, my love," he murmured, smiling the special smile he saved for her, that smile no earthly trouble could dismiss, no tragedy, no intrusion of the world could alter. And so she sank down by his side again and lay her head back on his knees and studied for the ten thousandth time the face she loved beyond forgetting.

And Thomas, watching her, running his fingers slowly along the warm silky curve of her neck, felt in the instant that there existed no one else in all creation save the two of them. Inside this room, this was the fortress of the strength they made together, with which they had faced their lives together, always. . . .

Had it, indeed, been always? Thomas frowned fleetingly, and smiled again to see the momentary anxiety on her lovely face. When did I start to love her, he wondered? Odd, he could not remember *not* loving her. It must have been from the beginning . . . yet he knew it was not so. Once, long ago, there had been Sheila Ives. He tried to think of Sheila now and it was as if a curtain parted in his mind and, across the stage of his memory, a dozen Sheilas sprang to life and smiled and went their way one by one, till none remained, but always hovering in the background and slowly lighting up the darkness was Helene, approaching closer and closer until the sight of her filled every particle of his consciousness.

He bent down and kissed her now, the tiredness of the long day miraculously fleeing away at the touch of her mouth on his, at the quivering quick response of her warm seeking lips. He felt her arms slide up around his neck, she twisted her body lithely so that she knelt upright against him and pressed herself to him with a strange little moan in her throat. His right arm held her tight as, with his left, he caressed her face and neck and breasts and felt the heat of her cheeks spread like a fire over her silky white skin.

"I love you," he whispered against her ear and, she thought, why, anyone would smile to hear those simple words spoken after fifteen years as if for the first time. "I love you, Helene, my love, my only love!" he said, and his voice was throbbing and urgent.

Helene closed her eyes and felt his lips move in little light kisses from her ears to her cheeks and brows and then touching each eyelid so gently she could feel his breath stirring her lashes.

He rose to his feet, drawing her up with him, never relinquishing his hold on her. He led her to their bed and pushed her down on the pillows with a gentle, tender thrust and, for a moment, he stood over her, his fingers reaching out to extinguish the candles nearby, and his striking, indigo blue eyes gazed down at her exactly as though he had never known love with her before.

Helene, her glowing, radiant face and body framed round about in the silvery strands of her long flowing hair, watched him pinch out the candles; she closed her eyes tightly and listened as he removed his clothing quickly and came to her with all the eagerness and need of a lover finding his first embrace.

And when he strained her against him, whispering her name over and over again as he buried his hot face in her breast, Helene felt the miracle of her life happening all over again, always new, always a beginning, and she gave herself up to the totality of love unreserved, remembering, remembering. . . .

3 A Winter's Day, Fifteen Years Ago

They had returned to Spring Mount the week after Sheila's death. She had been laid to rest beside Ian, next to the swift-flowing curve of the Blackwater River near Kilbree and there was no more to be done. The townspeople had turned out to mourn Sheila's passing as they had Ian's, their wild outpouring of unrestrained grief having left them all a bit stunned, and awfully quiet. No one in the family ever quite remembered the details of those few days after Sheila died, or how the funeral was arranged, or, even, quite how they had all gotten packed up and moved out and back to England.

It was Willy, of course, Willy and dear old Simpson, who managed it all. The four children and two nurses, Alice and the luggage, Tom and his Dragoons, and Helene were all somehow transported by wagon and boat, by ship and by coach, without much mishap and with relatively good speed.

And then they were home, the children settled into a busy regime with nurses and tutors and, in a few weeks, the house was running as usual, with a bit of additional turmoil. The Dragoons remained long enough to see that Sir Tom was on the mend, then they rode off to rejoin their regiment while Mrs. Jessup praised heaven they were gone from her kitchen and larder, and Robby and Michaeleen waved their arms numb from the walkway atop the east wing of the house.

And, it was over: the war, the battle, the deaths and the grieving. They heard almost daily news from Taunton, where the trials of Monmouth supporters were held, those grim frightful mockeries of justice soon called the Bloody Assizes, and over three hundred people were executed within the month. And even that was past. Serenity descended upon Somerset with the first frost of autumn, and July seemed a century away.

Thomas recovered steadily from his wounds, Helene could see that for herself. She did not need the doctor's encouraging, then glowing reports to know that her husband's body, grievously damaged though it had been, was healing itself.

While the last days of summer remained pleasantly warm and there was always a mild sea breeze stirring through the gardens, Thomas lay resting and reading, sometimes napping, outside the house around back, in Lady Anne's charming garden spot amid the holly hedges. They set up a couch for him there, and a little table and chairs. Helene served him his meals with her own hands and often brought her food too, so they might share as much of the day as possible. Thomas grew tanned and even put on a little weight, though his face remained thin and haggard-looking. But the haggard look, Helene knew, was really all in his eyes. He looked haunted, his eyes never met the direct gaze of anyone speaking to him and often his attention simply wandered from the conversation, to stare out vacantly over the hills. Not that he engaged in anything that could remotely be called a conversation anyway . . . he rarely spoke a word and she could tell it cost him great effort and annoyed him to even answer a simple question in what had come to be his usual monosyllabic yes or no.

She tried to draw his attention to the children, but this proved unsuccessful as had everything else she thought of to bring him back to them. Michael did not wish to see his Uncle Thomas and withdrew into a sullen silence whenever she insisted he must. The baby, Katherine, did not seem to exist for Thomas after that first night. He would look at her tiny form for an instant and then his eyes would go quite blank and he would look away. Robby seemed to understand that something terrible was happening inside his father and often came unobserved to sit on a patch of grass near Thomas but out of his line of vision, and simply, gravely, watch him. Helene herself put a stop to this. It wasn't good for the boy. His own appetite was suffering and he was beginning to wake up with hideous nightmares during the night, dreams he could neither remember nor describe to his mother.

She never spoke of Ian or of Sheila, sensing that Thomas could not bear it if his silent pain were to be revealed and let loose into the light of day. For weeks, until the wind blew chill from France, she sat and watched him wish himself into the grave with Ian and with Sheila. She ached to touch him, to put her arms about that rugged, suffering face and draw it tenderly against her bosom and stroke away the torment and loss he was enduring. But, somehow, she could not so much as lay a finger on him, she could not try to force him to remember her. She was, she felt hopelessly, beyond his consideration now, not even a nominal part of his life anymore. It frightened her to feel this way and her fear soon gave way to a sort of bleak, boundless despair.

Weeks passed. Thomas limped about, at first with the aid of a crutch Willy Duncan had carved and put together with amazing skill; later a cane sufficed. And, before Christmas that year, he was able to stand and walk alone, with a limp that would never leave him but that seemed slight enough except when the weather turned damp and wet.

He began to take an interest in the business of the estate, often spending long hours in the morning in his study. She found out from Alice, who knew it from Willy, that Thomas had sent detailed instructions for the management of Kilbree to Mrs. Curley and, a few weeks later, had arranged for Ian's regular overseer to remain on in Ireland and keep everything going there.

Helene heard this piece of information with a thrill of renewed hope. If he could bear to think of Kilbree and its business, surely that must mean he was beginning to adjust to the way things were now.

One evening, over dinner, she ventured to inquire casually about a possible trip to Kilbree in the springtime. Thomas heard her; his eyes seemed to pin her to her chair with their intensity and coldness. He had abruptly set down his glass, thrown off his napkin, pulled himself to his feet, and stood there glaring down at her as if he had not heard her right.

"Leave me alone, can't you?" was all he managed to say before he moved quickly from the room, but his voice had been edged with suppressed fury such as she had never heard from him before. She sat there at the table, all conversation suddenly stilled, stunned, listening to the painful drag of his wounded leg across the polished floor. Then the strain, the horror of the months past rushed in on her. She stood up, her fingertips pressed tremblingly against the table edge for support, looking around her in confusion while the tears streamed unchecked down her pale cheeks. She tried to speak, but ran from all the shocked, sympathetic, uncomprehending eyes that were turned to her, seeking explanation.

That was the worst of his anger, that one night. The next day and long afterward he seemed ashamed of his outburst and his manner grew milder, but never less remote.

He took to walking far from the house alone, refusing with a silent shake of his head all offers to accompany him and even Willy's companionship.

Helene, watching him set off alone, day after day, wondered what would happen if the hurt leg gave out and he were to fall somewhere far from help. She reckoned with his anger and disregarded it, sending his favorite hound out after him. If anything went wrong the intelligent creature would know enough to come back and fetch someone from the house.

Nights were the worst times of all. It had been only natural when he first came home and was so ill that she should sleep in the adjoining bedroom, close enough to hear him call if he needed something, enough removed so her comings and goings would not disturb him when he did doze off. But when he was better, he said nothing about her sleeping apart from him and she did not know what to do. Night after night she lay wide awake listening to his silent, even breathing only a few feet away, waiting for him to wake and miss her and call her name. But he never did.

He might as well have died when Sheila died, Helene thought many times throughout those endless weeks. She remembered that she had become content with what she and Thomas had together. They had been good friends at least. They had talked, they had shared so much, they had enjoyed their children, their home. She might have gone on like that all her life, even knowing she did not possess what mattered most, his love.

But now, how she missed those precious evening hours of talk. Now they sat in silence across the hearth from each other, and they might have been a thousand miles apart. As the days flew by she saw he was much recovered and, to all appearances, settling back into his life as it had been before. He began to see a few friends. He went into town two or three times. He took up his correspondence once more, devoting a couple of hours a day to it. The servants began to breathe more easily about him; the doctors visited infrequently. The cold damp dreariness of autumn died away into a brisk blue-skyed windy winter and still there was a silence between the two of them that Helene could find no way to bridge.

It was the year before her father died. He rode over to see them very often. Thomas was cordial to the old man but, aside from talking of the children, he had nothing to say. Baron Lyncourt, grown stout and querulous, red in the face and often short of breath, did not like what he found at Spring Mount. He usually arrived while the family was still at breakfast . . . everyone could hear him at the front door when Simpson let him in, stomping the fresh snow from his boots and shouting mightily for his pot of coffee and his brandy and kippers.

The children adored him, even Michael, and ran to greet him, dragging him back into the morning room with them, talking and laughing excitedly. Nothing would do but that the two babies be produced at once, and he would sit at the table, bouncing an infant on each knee while two nervous, disapproving nurses stood aside waiting for him to drop one of their precious charges.

The Baron was a man who seemed oblivious of everything but never missed much. He observed that his son-in-law seemed well and recovered but that he excused himself from the family as soon as he had eaten. He also observed that his daughter grew more pale from week to week, that the faint shadows under her eyes were darker, the tightness at the corners of her mouth more pronounced, and that she was losing weight at an alarming rate. None of this sat well with the Baron. Each time he came he resolved he would speak to Helene about it. Each time, when he handed the infants back to their jumpy nurses and sent the two little boys off to feed sugar to his horse, he would clear his throat with alarming force, fold his arms across his bulging middle, and begin to address himself to the situation . . . Helene would raise her huge dark eyes to him and plead in dumb misery that he say nothing.

And so he said nothing. And his misgivings gave way to grave concern. His doubts went far beyond irritation with Thomas. He did not know the cause of the growing rift between Helene and her husband, but he did know that it was like to kill his daughter. When his notions on the subject reached that point, he spoke up, suddenly, startling himself almost as much as he startled Helene.

It was another early morning visit, like all the rest. But Robby was sick in bed with a heavy cold and Michael was moping around upstairs. Helene had been up all the night before with Robby. She sat at the nearly empty table with an untouched plate of cold food before her, her fingers pulling a piece of bread into crumbs. Thomas across the table from her, seemed not to know she was there. He looked up briefly when the Baron came in, invited him to take a seat, and said not another word. For once Lyncourt was quiet, missing the distracting chatter of the boys. He spoke several times to Helene and each time she would start uneasily and give some perfunctory answer, then lapse into silence again. The Baron drank his coffee thoughtfully, resolved to keep his opinions to himself, until Thomas pushed his chair away from the table and stood up. At once Helene, her face flushing vividly, leaned across and caught hold of his hand.

"Will you not stay at home today, Thomas?" she asked him in a tone of such fervent passion that the Baron, his cup halfway to his mouth, stared at her incredulously.

"I . . . no, I cannot," Thomas answered her hastily, glancing at Lyncourt and then quickly away.

"Please!" She began to rise to her feet, still clutching his hand. Thomas looked at her very hard, opened his mouth to speak and then shook his head, turning away.

"No," was all he said, pulling his hand from hers, and Baron Lyncourt shuddered at the dead flat finality in his voice. Thomas left the room without looking back and for a moment father and daughter remained frozen into place while she stood staring after her husband, all color instantly drained from her face, and he slammed the delicate china cup indignantly back on its saucer.

"No more of this, daughter!" cried the Baron, going to Helene and embracing her tenderly. But she was unmoved; she stood like a stone with his arms about her. The Baron kissed her cold cheek and gave her a little push back into her chair.

"I have been silent long enough, Helene," he declared wrathfully, wishing at the same time he might speak more softly, more gently. But that was not his way; bluster had always been his way and Helene and everyone who knew him understood it. He would have to trust to that understanding now. "Damn it all, Helene, what has happened between you and your husband?"

Slowly her gaze fell on him and she shook her head, her lovely eyes imploring him to be still. "Nothing, Father," she breathed.

"It is not like you to lie to me!" cried the Baron. "Helene, I knew from the first this was no love match. But I knew Tom Sturbridge, I knew his father, and I damn well knew the lad would treat you right. And he has, I'm the first to admit it . . . I'd have cut his ears off long ago if he hadn't!"

Helene smiled faintly, fondly, and patted her father's hand. But he would not be wooed away from his theme.

"You've been happy, girl. You've got the children, everything a woman could need or want. I know the lad was hurt bad in that bloody business at Sedgemoor, but, name of God, Helene, why has it changed him? And he *is* changed. As you are, my pet...." His loud tone and bluff manner dropped away. He took her hand and kissed her cold fingertips with affectionate gallantry. "Helene, I cannot bear to see what's happening to you. You'll fret yourself into a fever, you will, it happens all the time. You're not strong, you're thin and pinchy-looking, I can see it all right, like a high-stepping horse off its feed and edging into the strangles...ahem..." he cleared his throat violently, pressing her hand very tightly... "Pardon the...er...er...expression, my dear, but..." he stopped altogether, looking distressed and at a loss. Helene kissed him impulsively, then sat back with a brisk air that did not deceive him for a minute, and told him the whole story from first to last. He said not a word throughout, asked no questions, did not interrupt once, but his heart sank as he began to understand.

Helene was on her feet as she finished, pacing back and forth before the tall sun-filled windows. "I understand the agony that he endures, I understand it completely," she said. "But, Father, I cannot see what will happen to us now. I cannot go on living this way any longer. He has shut me out of his life...his life!" she repeated with a half-mocking ghost of a laugh. "He has no life anymore, only the appearance of it. I cannot reach him, I cannot help him...my God, I cannot even help myself!"

When she had remained silent for a moment, her back turned to him so he could not see the tears in her eyes, the Baron spoke, his voice very gentle, very surprised.

"You love him, my dear. Strange," he mused. "Strange, I never knew you loved him. One expects so much of a wife, one often overlooks love."

"'Love'!" Helene's quiet weeping changed into a harsh desperate laugh. "I have been content without love...almost," she added truthfully. "But now, there is nothing. Nothing at all. And, Father," she whirled about to face him, "it is killing me, *killing* me!"

Baron Lyncourt found his own eyes suspiciously moist, but he was above all else a pragmatic man. What is to be done, he thought at once, what is to be done? He martialed every scrap of logic he could think of, glanced once more at his daughter's taut face and promptly threw logic to the winds.

"Go to him," the Baron said strongly. "Wherever he is, wherever he goes, be there with him."

"But, he doesn't want—" began Helene, and he cut her short.

"I don't give a flying fig what the devil he wants!" snapped the Baron. "If he gets what he wants we'll have a whole baker's dozen of funerals on our hands. Blast it, Helene, the man doesn't know what he wants anymore. *He's* not thinking straight...he's not thinking tuppence a damn! So you've got to set him straight. Don't let the chap out of your sight and don't let him forget you're there. If he shouts and orders you away, well, damme, girl, shout right back at him, stir him up, *wake* him up, keep after him till he remembers you're alive. You're not wasting away in your grave...and don't look at me so reproachfully...I'm as much a Christian as you are and I know it's a bleeding shame poor Mistress Ives is gone from us...but what's that to you and him? D'you want him noodlin' the rest of his life away like he is?"

"Father," Helene couldn't help smiling at the old man as he sat there rapping his spoon sharply against the table emphasizing the beat of his words with its clanking. "Don't you see how that would make him hate me?"

"Bah!" replied the Baron noisily. "Nonsense! Hate you? Hate *you*? How could any man hate a lovely lass like you, eh? Tell me that, how could he?"

Helene shrugged a little. "You make it sound so simple, Father," she said wistfully.

"Hmph!" he snorted, and fixed her with a very stern look. "Look here, girl, not to make mincing matters of it, I've never known you stand a coward before anybody—man, woman or child. I've never known you to snivel or whine and I've never, never known you to *give up* without a good fight. You wanted the fellow. You love him...well, go out and fetch him, then. He needs you, Helene. He's a strong man all right, all the Sturbridges are strong men. But in a thing like this, a man's kind of strength counts for nothing. Women...women like yourself, my lass, have got a kind of strength all their own, like a tree that grows by the shores, whipped round about by every gale and tempest the sea can conjure up against the land, but that tree will bend and sway and seem to give, then lie back and never fight the wind but let it blow its worst...its roots go down to the earth's middle and beyond, I think, and it will never snap or break in any storm. *That's* a woman's strength. It's different from ours, it needs to be different. And it's that strength of yours you must use now, Helene. If you really love the man.''

Helene stared at her father, her eyes very wide, a wild fire of new hope taking hold at her heart.

''I may lose him,'' she temporized, and all the while the blood was coursing madly through her veins so that she felt her entire body more alive in that moment than it had been in weeks.

''Do you *have* him now?'' asked the Baron pointedly. He picked up the coffee pot and poured himself another cup. He was astonished to see that his hands were trembling and he coughed a great deal and very loudly so she would not notice.

''No, I do not,'' she admitted.

There seemed no more to be said, then. Each of them, father and daughter, sat at the long, damask-covered table, drinking their coffee quietly. When he was finished, the Baron went upstairs to visit with his sick-abed grandson, pausing on his way to lean over and plant a light kiss on Helene's brow. She remained in the dining room for a while more, half listening to the hushed voices of the servants as they went about their morning tasks.

And then she ran upstairs, looked in on Robby for a moment, and hurried down the hall to her dressing room. She pulled on her fur boots, dressed herself in a heavy warm wool frock and threw a full-length hooded cloak of white fox skins about her shoulders.

She would find Thomas, stay with him, make him talk to her. Somehow, she would reach him inside the remote little hell he was living in these days. Father is right, she thought, her heart lifting dizzily as she rushed past an astonished Alice downstairs in the Great Hall. Alice, just on her way up with an armful of Helene's freshly laundered clothes, turned and called after her.

''M'lady! Are you going out in the snow by yourself? Wait and I'll fetch Jed 'round with the trap!''

''Never mind, Alice!'' Helene called over her shoulder. She stood at the top of the front steps, looking around. Thomas was nowhere in sight.

Now, a few weeks from Christmas, the ground was all covered in white snow as far as the dark hills behind it. Here and there a single naked tree stood up jagged and black against the whiteness, like a pointing finger drawing her attention to the busy-minded sky with its trails of vivid blue reaching out through fast-moving grey-and-white cloud chargers. There was a faint, distant line of green just before the rise of the hills. Those would be the trees, looking dull and sleepy now amid the stark freshness of the bright white meadows's breast. Helene walked with her head bent against the wind. The force of it, heading inland from the sea, was stirring up the light-lying snow almost as though it were falling anew. She could barely see around her and not well enough to notice if anyone had come this way before her. She was discouraged and wondered if she ought not turn back before she grew tired. Surely Thomas, with his hurt leg, could not have come so far. Thomas must have simply walked through the rose gardens on the hill. If she turned around right now she could still find him there . . . .

But, she did not turn around. Something inside her kept pushing her on, one tired foot after another. Sometimes she would stop to get her breath, leaning against a crooked tree trunk for a minute, then going on once more.

She kept her eye steadily on the nearing stand of trees and realized she was covering a great deal of distance without strain. She felt encouraged when she began to make out the individual spikes of the tall firs' branches, and even the hills, she could see now, were nearer, not so dark and forbidding-looking but bare and brown and somewhere tender-looking without their summertime grass.

A few times she was positive she could hear the loud barking of a deep-voiced dog, a big dog, she thought, stopping each time to listen carefully. But it must be just the prankish wind, she decided, trying out some new trick of sound as it whooshed gleefully through the trees. Once she turned to look back and was surprised at how far away the house seemed now, only a little toy, a dollhouse in the distance with the sun gleaming from its west windows like chunks of gold embedded in the stone. We shall have to get the girls a dollhouse just like that when they are old enough, she thought. And, remembering the children, she shivered suddenly, not from the icy wind. Where was Thomas? Well, he is not lost, surely, she laughed at herself, rubbing her cold gloved hands together. Coming out this way, coming here, it had been insane. She might have waited until Thomas returned this afternoon, she did not have to go out looking for him . . . and, she realized with cold dismay, when you do find him . . . what will you say to him? She had not thought of that. You have not thought your way through *any* of this, she told herself with chagrin. Doubt, colder ever than any trick of the wind, blew its moribund chill breath through her and she stopped, irresolute, measuring the distance she had come against the distance she had yet to go and all of it, perhaps, for nothing. He wanted to be alone, he had made it so very clear. She felt she lived on at Spring Mount through his sufferance only now. A woman's home is just where the man she loves still loves her, nowhere else. Oh, Thomas! she cried silently, am I so *very* hard to love?

She plunged into the dark world of the trees, grateful to feel the wind drop down. All around her the great green firs rose into the watchful sky and she, at their base, felt held secure in the palm of their thin-fingered brown hands, like any wild-hearted fox or homebound deer. But feeling cared for, somehow, by the eternal impersonal scan of nature, brought home to her lonely soul how much she longed to feel safe within the loving arms of the man who knew her best.

She moved more and more slowly, touching, then grasping the lower branches of the fir trees as though she were pulling herself from one to the other with no strength of her own left to sustain her through to the end. She realized there were tears trickling down her cheeks, and anger at this rank betrayal by her own body gave her a few moments' additional energy. But the disdained tears dried and were forgotten, her spirit wearied, and at length she stood still, knowing she could go no farther. It was no use, was her only thought now, she would rest awhile and then find her way home. She sat down beneath one of the trees, in a spot where the snow had not drifted, and folded her arms about her underneath the cloak. She leaned her back against the trunk, pillowed by her thick furs from the gnarls and bumps of the wood. It did not seem so cold anymore. She felt grateful for that much. Five minutes, she told herself, five minutes and she would jump up and be on her way back, only five minutes . . .

Ten or fifteen yards to the left of where she rested stood a tiny woodsman's cottage, a hut merely, long unused. But presently, from its small tilted chimney there emerged a pungent curl of gray smoke from a fir fire. The hound sniffed it and whined in his throat, but found his way to the warm fireside where his master stood breaking small branches with his hands and feeding them into the blaze. The dog, who had been sleeping while the man gathered up the wood outside and started the fire, felt uneasy. He looked up and whined again. The man smiled and patted his great head, which pleased him but it did not allay his uneasiness. Still, he quieted down and stretched out by the fire, watching his master. A moment later, the dog was up on his feet again, walking to the wooden door, which stood a few inches ajar. He whined deep in his throat and scratched at the door. The man seemed startled at the sound he made, then walked over and opened the door wide to let him out. But, once outside, the dog was at a loss as to what had brought him there. He hated the cold wetness of the snow on his paws. He circled around and then came back to the doorway, and, for no reason whatever, he began to bark.

His master shook his head, then sighed a bit and laughed, and followed the hound outside, pulling his cloak about him.

"Just when I've got the fire going, you want to romp!" his master said, throwing a stick into the air. The hound sprang after it ... it was still his favorite game and the puppy in him had never died after all. But just as he had the flying stick within his reach, the dog turned his back on it and ran off through the trees. His master picked the stick up himself and followed slowly, whistling the dog to him several times. He heard the beast barking again and thought he had flushed some sleepy, indignant badger from its winter bed. He followed the sound of the barking and saw the hound leaping around and growling mightily. And then the man noticed what the dog had found and his heart jumped within him.

"Helene!" he cried, hurrying to her. She was lying in a little heap in the snow, her back against a tree, asleep. He bent down and touched her cold face, wondering how long she had been out there. Not very long, he judged. He had been this far when gathering up the wood for the fire, half an hour or less, he reckoned. But when he touched her she did not stir and the muscles of her face were stiff and icy under his warm hands. "Helene, can you hear me? Open your eyes!" he cried, pulling her up against him. Her head rolled, her eyelids fluttered, she looked up blankly and moaned, and then was still again.

Somehow he got her back through the trees and into the cottage, lifting her light form in his arms as though she weighed nothing. He could not move as fast as he wished and all over again he cursed the man who had driven the bayonet into his leg. But, at last, she was inside. He laid her down on the bare floor next to the fire and removed her boots immediately. Her feet were soaked and felt like ice to the touch. The long heavy brown skirt of her dress was rigid and half-frozen from being dragged through the snow. He pulled the fur cloak from her shoulders and, after shaking it free of snow, spread it out on the floor. He fumbled with the myriad tiny buttons of her dress and finally, impatiently, ripped the bodice open from neck to waist and pulled the ruined cloth from her body. The skirt was next, and the wet petticoats, one by one he stripped them away from her, meanwhile calling her name frantically as he worked. The dog, at peace now, lay quietly watching, nuzzling Helene's cold fingers now and then. Once she opened her eyes a bit and murmured, "Thomas?" and her husband's eyes lit up as he held her face between his two hands and answered eagerly, "Yes, yes, it is Thomas, Helene! You are safe now, do you hear me? Do you understand me?" But then he realized she did not really hear him, she had not really seen him with her . . . she spoke to a phantom in her half-conscious mind, she saw an image of him in her heart only. The realization that she wanted him and no one else stabbed him through with remorse. He worked over her faster, until all of the sodden clothing lay in a discarded heap behind him, and he had stretched her pale form on the fur cloak. He removed his own thick woolen cape and spread it over her, then began to rub her arms and legs, her hands and feet, gently, methodically, in long rhythmic strokes, to stir up her blood and bring some warmth and feeling back into her. And, eventually, the pain of feeling returning under his hard fingers restored her to consciousness. She tossed her head, groaning, and her teeth began to chatter uncontrollably.

"Thomas?" she whispered. "Thomas, is it you?" She struggled to sit up, but he held her down firmly.

"Don't try to move," he cautioned her. "Everything is all right now."

"I was trying to find you," she said faintly, her eyes wandering in confusion about the unfamiliar room.

"Never mind," he said. "Just rest. Don't talk yet, get warm."

She smiled a bit vaguely. He noted with relief that the color was beginning to return to her cheeks. He touched her forehead, wondering if fever would set in. Her skin was pleasantly warm and, although her brown eyes were very bright it was a reflection of the firelight, not the false brilliant glitter of fever. He pulled down a corner of his cloak, revealing one rounded white shoulder and laid his hand there, too. She was still cold, so cold, he thought, frowning in his concern. Helene saw the frown, touched his face with a shaky finger.

214

"Don't be angry with me," she breathed. "I wanted to be with you no matter what you said. Oh, Thomas, don't go away from us like this anymore!" She sighed a deep, shuddering sigh and her whole body began to shiver again.

He could not bear to see her suffer this way. Her few words had touched him to the heart, filling him with the full force of overwhelming sorrow and guilt he had spent all these weeks trying to elude. Looking down at her, his courage returned to him and he allowed the grief and pain to flood through him. He had been like a shipwrecked man clinging blindly with numb fingers and no hope to a scrap of wreckage. If he had let go and turned only a bit, he might have seen the shore and let the ocean tides bring him to dry land. Instead, he clung on to numbness and despair, afraid he would be taken up bodily and washed away if he faced the full impact of his torment.

Now he did face it and was amazed at the strength of it, at the physical shock that overtook him. All the events, all the tragedy since Sedgemoor came back to him in every frightful detail and all of it laced through with his own fear that he could not handle it. In fearing that he would break and fail those who now looked wholly to him he forgot what kind of man he was . . . and almost broke in the forgetting.

He lay down next to Helene and took her trembling body into his arms, pressing himself against the length of her, trying desperately to infuse the heat from his own body into hers. She buried her face against his chest, her two small hands creeping up to close about his shoulders.

"You are so warm," she murmured gratefully, and he wondered if she could hear or feel the giddy thumping of his heart. He did not know what to say to her; he had so much to say, so much to explain. He realized now how much he had thrust upon her all this time, how totally he had relied on her understanding, her good sense. How had he been able to forget she also loved him? Their life together had been wrought most fragilely; they had lived in a stately minuet of carefully restrained words and actions, of purposefully strung together civilities and determined goodwill. But now the dance was over. The measures he had heard in his heart and moved to with some grace were finished; Sheila's death, Ian's death, these had broken forever the old, familiar patterns. The realization that had struck him the night of Sheila's death—that he was free at last from that old, hopeless love and longing—he had pushed that to the back of his mind, despised himself for ever thinking it at such a time, in such a place. Now he allowed himself to think it again . . . he pressed his lips fervently on Helene's soft cheek and found to his amazement that, the first great flood of unrestricted pain having struck with all its strength, it had subsided and *not returned*. Instead, his heart was filled with a great rage of tenderness for the woman in his arms. He looked at her as though he had never really seen her before . . . and he had not, of course, not through eyes so clear and unclouded by past sorrows and regrets.

"Helene?" he said gently. Her eyes were closed, her breath coming in easy, even measures. For a few seconds he thought she had fallen asleep. And then, without opening her eyes, she replied.

"Don't wake me, my love, let me stay with you a while more!"

His lips brushed her face, her eyes, her hair. "Always, Helene," he said. "I never want you further from me than the length of my arms away."

She stirred, and looked at him as if she had not heard him aright. He, moving very carefully, slipped his arm beneath her, cushioning her head and shoulders. "Sleep, Helene, sleep as long as you want, I will not leave you."

But now sleep fled away as she looked at him smiling at her, and noticed that the old, habitual soft veil of sorrow that had always been in his penetrating blue eyes was gone. She pulled away, startled and unsure of herself. He whom she loved so completely, he seemed a stranger now. He had never, never looked at her this way, so openly, so directly, all walls between them miraculously dissolved in the instant. She mistrusted it, uneasy and afraid.

"I love you, Helene." He spoke simply and from the heart so newly unfettered that he was like a boy with his first love.

She stared at him, hardly believing that it was his lips, his voice that said the words she had dreamed he would say to her one day and dreaming all the while knew bitterly he never would. One day had come at last; he said the only words that she had ever needed from him, and she cried silently to herself: speak to him, answer him, hurry! And she was speechless, hating herself as she felt the precious seconds speeding by . . . speak now or lose him forever, a voice inside tormented her.

And still she did not know him completely. He expected no answer, he was not waiting for her to say something. He watched in fascination the changing expressions of her face and long before her own mind found words for her to speak, he saw in her eyes, clearly and for all time, the unchanging, proud staunch light of love.

Thomas Sturbridge smiled, flinging aside the cloak that separated her body from his and caught her in his arms once more. "I love you, I love you!" he repeated over and over, then his lips found her mouth and he kissed her as he had never kissed her before, hungrily, urgently, while his hands caressed her breast, then moved on down over her smooth warm belly and thighs. Never had he wanted any woman so before . . . he marveled that he had known this lovely body for years, had fathered two children by her and now could find every part of her so new, so desirable.

At last Helene responded; gladly discarding the need for words, she found the words she needed at once. It was real, it was no dream, it was not only another tormented fantasy like the rest she had conjured up on all those nights she had lain awake beside him in their marriage bed, wondering if she were going quite mad, wondering what he would do if she suddenly threw herself upon him, woke him from slumber, and pressed her longing lips upon his hard-muscled chest.

It was no fantasy, she knew, her entire being pulsating with joy. She reached out for him and, without another word, he turned and wrapped his strong arms about her. She felt the tingling heat of his quick breath in her ear, then the seeking touch of his lips and tongue. Her mind lost its ability to differentiate between the sensations she was feeling . . . she sprang, abandoned to their mutual passion, wholly out of herself, and, as she gave herself over to the ferocious gladness of release, she could only think he loves me! He loves me and no other!

Later she would remember Sheila's dying words and whisper to her lovely shade somewhere her thanks and her true farewell. But now no shadow of Sheila Ives hovered in that small room, not in his heart, not in hers. There was only the sleeping hound, the playful wind outside, the snapping fire, and their love exchanging, blending, becoming something new and perfect.

4 And Always England, Just Over The Horizon

I have been loved! Helene cried the triumphant words in her heart now, fifteen years later, as still holding her close, he lay back on his side.

"I have been loved," she said the magic words again, this time aloud and Thomas kissed her hot face, smiling at the odd choice of phrase. Yes, he loved her, he thought with a touch of tender amusement. But he had always loved her, had he not?

Toward dawn, for they had not slept this night, they talked together quietly, watching the disappearing stars and moon, the gray mist covering all, like nature rolling down a curtain between the pageantry of night and the splendid masque of day.

"I thought of that old cottage a while ago, Thomas," she said. "And of the first time we were there together."

He wound her gleaming hair about his wrist and fancied himself for a moment a Viking raider such as Somerset had seen long ago, with his wrists and arms encircled by bold pagan silver bracelets like this.

"It's in your mind now, because of the priest," he murmured, and then chuckled, "do you suppose we've left a little of our love abiding there? Maybe it will haunt the good man and bring him ungodly dreams!"

"Thomas!" she chided him, but she could not resist laughing. "I think there must be a good deal of ourselves about the place, but at his age I doubt . . ." and they both laughed aloud. Yet, remembering Father McGuire brought everything else back vividly and their laughter soon died away into silence.

"Will it be France, if we must leave here?" she asked him.

"Yes, France," he said soberly. "I pray God we shall not be put to it. But if we must go, rest assured, there is plenty of money set aside to live on in comfort . . . until we return."

"I was not thinking of the money," she said slowly. "It's the children. My dear, Michael and Katherine will not go with us, I am sure of it. And Elizabeth . . ."

He sighed, nodding. "Elizabeth will not easily be parted from Harry Prescott . . ."

"Must she be?" asked Helene. "Thomas, could you not give her leave to marry the boy now? Once wed, she will be safe with his family."

"My darling, if we are forced into exile, there will be no wedding. Arthur Prescott made himself very clear on that score today. No matter which way the wind blows, Elizabeth will have to give him up . . ."

"No!" Helene said very quickly, sitting bolt upright beside him.

"If they are already married, Arthur will have no choice but to take his daughter-in-law in . . . and, Thomas, she will never give Harry up!"

Sir Tom looked at her without speaking. He wanted to tell her that even if Arthur Prescott was inclined to offer Elizabeth his protection . . . which he was not . . . she would not be safe anywhere in England after her family was gone. He started to explain, then thought better of it. Helene had enough to worry about now; let them handle the problem of Elizabeth when they came to it. There was little enough time left now, anyway. He forced a smile to his lips and kissed her lightly.

"You're probably right, my love. We'll find a way, never fear," he said. And, because she wanted to believe that, she let it go for the moment.

"Thomas, could we not go to America instead of France?"

Sir Tom's eyebrow rose sharply and he looked at her in great surprise.

"You, too, Helene? This is the first time you have ever mentioned such an idea to me."

"I know, dearest," she said, a bit uncomfortably. "But I have wondered much about France. In America we would be among our own kind, at least. We might go to the Virginia Colony. We wouldn't have to give up Katherine and Michael . . . Katherine is too young to go off alone to a strange land . . ."

"She would have her brother," said Sir Tom, his voice a bit flat.

"Oh, *Michael!*" scoffed Helene. "How could he care for a fifteen-year-old girl by himself? Besides," she added, recalling the look of misery on Rob's face earlier that night, "Rob loves her very much. He wants to marry Katherine. You know that, Thomas. America might be the answer for us all. If Arthur Prescott refuses to let his son marry Elizabeth, why then, we could take them with us."

"You cannot bear to let your chicks wander out from under your wings," he said wryly, and she fell silent. "Helene, England is our home. It's where we belong, where our children belong after us. Some day Spring Mount will belong to Rob. Elizabeth and Harry will have Longdale. The storm will rage around us for a little while, yes, and it would not be unwise for us to take temporary shelter out of the wind. France is that shelter, far enough away to be safe for the time being, but still near enough that it will be easy to come back from when the air has cleared. France is familiar, another part of Europe and the way of life we know. If I go to France, my love, I know I will come home again. . . .

"But, America? It *is* another world, as far from my imaginings as the moon. I remember, Ian and I used to talk about it long ago. To us it was all adventure, red savages, great forests and cataracts, a place for me to *play* in. We never thought of towns and cities there. I still cannot imagine buildings and stone streets on the edge of a wilderness!

"Helene, I know this well . . . if I were to take our family there, we would never return, I believe that with my whole heart. We would be done with England, we would be turning our backs on what is rightfully our own. I do not think one can go halfheartedly into a new world, looking back over one's shoulder for a glimpse of home. I cannot abandon my own country and its people. If we are defeated here, I can go to France to work and plan for the day things will be changed. I shall never become a Frenchman, I should always be alien, a visitor, waiting only for a fair breeze from home to leave . . . but America, I think, would ask for much more from me. Never to look back, never to remember, to give myself up entirely to a new life. And this I cannot do."

Helene smiled and took his crippled hand in hers, running her fingertips around the engraved letters on the steel ring he always wore.

"Here, in this place," she murmured, nodding. "I understand, Thomas. It shall be France, then, as you say, and always England just over the horizon. . . ."

"With God's help we shall never have to go at all," he said, and kissed her, then gestured toward the light beginning to pour in at the windows. "Tomorrow . . . *today*, we shall get up and see what's to be done. But now, my dearest love, put your arms around me and sleep with me. Trust to God to guard our lives a few more peaceful hours."

She nodded, closing her eyes against the intrusive light and snuggled down against him, warm, safe, loved and secure within the powerful circle of his arms.

Eight

"The Power Of Love And Honour"

1 Preparations

Nothing was to appear any different, no plans were to be changed. Those were Sir Tom's orders. So the arrangements went forward apace for the betrothal ball. Since it was just to be two weeks before Christmas, Helene had decided to have the decorations done with a holiday motif, the colors red and green, white, silver and gold. Two thousand tall white candles, enough to fill every sconce and candelabrum at Spring Mount, enough to light the great house all night long, these had already been delivered and lay in long boxes in the cool kitchen storerooms. Dressmakers had come and gone, Sir Tom himself had spent an afternoon in the wine cellars picking out dozens of bottles of his best vintages, Mrs. Jessup supervised the preparation of enough food to carry an army for a week—which was just as well, as the army would be there in full force. A score or more of Sir Tom's old officer friends from the Dragoons had been invited, along with their ladies.

Every room in the house was turned out, polished up, linen changed, windows washed, floors waxed. The Great Hall was lined with mirrors and every day for a week three maids with buckets of water and fine linen cloths went at those mirrors with a vengeance until they shone like diamonds. The carpeting on the grand staircase was taken up and beaten, piece by piece, and then set down again and the railings and banisters polished. The flowers began to arrive a week before the ball, as Helene had planned. Every step of the staircase was transformed into a little garden with huge vases filled with holly and tall fir branches, tied round about with wide red velvet ribbons. Roses arrived by ship from the Canaries, ordered eight months before, hundreds and hundreds of them, all deep red and creamy white, to be set into Irish crystal vases in the ballroom and dining room. Helene wished the season were different and her own English roses from the garden on the hill might grace her daughter's betrothal, but when the flowers were in place she had to admit they looked properly splendid.

The mistletoe was Rob's idea. He and Katherine went out one afternoon and were gone for several hours. Helene could have used six extra hands to help and was ready to scold the two of them, until they came in laughing from the brisk December air, their arms filled with fresh-cut pale mistletoe branches. She and Katherine and Elizabeth spent the evening tying them up with gold and silver ribbon and hanging them over all the doorways downstairs.

There was a great deal of laughter, many merry jokes. Everyone worked with a will and nobody talked about what was really uppermost in their minds. No word from Willy, no sign from Michael. Amidst the happy preparations, there was an undercurrent of tension, of waiting for something to happen. Elizabeth seemed blissfully unaware that anything might be wrong. Every day she bloomed more bright-eyed and rosy-cheeked, running on light feet from one task to another about the house. Helene could hardly bear to look at her happy face. More than once, when Elizabeth was rattling on gaily about some wonderful thing Harry had said or some lovely gift she had just received, she saw a look of such tender agony on her mother's face that she broke off in the middle of a sentence and ran to kiss Helene and coax a smile from her.

Arthur Prescott sent over two wagonloads of fresh-killed pheasants, ten small sacks of precious brown sugar from Jamaica, two dozen hams and a wooden crate packed with rare golden rum, also from the West Indies. Evidently Arthur was satisfied with things; he had laid down the "law" to Sturbridge and, sensible fellow that he was, Sir Tom had knuckled under for his daughter's sake. In fact, Arthur had gone so far as to make a special trip into town, to confer with Magistrate Gladden, to reassure that stern Puritan judiciary official that Sir Tom Sturbridge would offer no further concern to His Majesty's wishes, that Sir Tom would, in fact, render them all publicly a splendid speech proclaiming his undying loyalty and devotion to King William's government and to the laws of Parliament.

Magistrate Gladden had listened to all of this with interest, wondering just how big a fool Prescott really was or if, on the other hand, Sturbridge had indeed decided to cease his treasonous activities and think of his family's welfare. Magistrate Gladden waited patiently for the thirty days allowed Michael Ives to come forth and swear the Oath of Allegiance and Supremacy. Ives would not swear such an oath, Gladden knew very well. Ives believed, or was supposed to believe as a Catholic, that the bread and wine at Holy Communion were changed into the flesh and blood of the Savior—the doctrine of Transubstantiation. The oath called for a complete renunciation of that doctrine. Ives would not willingly consent to burn in Hell for eternity, and that he would do, said the cursed Papist heretics, should he deny any article of his faith. Thus, Gladden thought, we have him. If only Sir Thomas Sturbridge were such a simple matter. Yet, he reminded himself patiently—patience, the single most valuable virtue a Puritan must possess, the single virtue poor foolish Cromwell never had—patiently, Gladden moved, and slowly, gathering together evidences he needed before he could dare touch Sir Thomas. There was, for instance, the solicitor, Hulme.

Soon Magistrate Gladden and Master Hulme would sit down together and amicably discuss the state of Sir Thomas' business affairs. Hulme would sign an affidavit. Gladden would inquire as to the disposal of Sir Thomas' vast fortune, flowing like a small river of gold away from the estate for the last four years . . . where? and to what purpose? Why was a nobleman of England, master of a mighty house, signing away, bit by bit, the very substance of that house, nay, the very house itself and all that went with it? He would have the answers to those questions soon, Gladden knew. And he would have the answers from Sir Thomas Sturbridge himself.

2   All That Is Left of Kilbree

Willy was back four days before the ball, looking much the same as ever, although his face was even paler and he was hard put to find a smile for anyone. He had come down from Bristol by coach, sitting up on top with a bundle tied in black cloth on his lap. He had hired the coach outright, all for his own use, and paid the driver double without argument. No other passengers, Willy insisted, and the coachman shrugged. Gold in the hand answered all questions. If the lout wished to ride in luxury all by himself, why, let him!

But Willy did not come alone. He brought the silent, somber people of Kilbree House with him and the coach was for their use. He brought Mrs. Curley and the ancient cook, Mrs. Grace with her daughter, Nellie and the faithful Meg along with a few others who had no place else to go.

Helene, with Katherine at her side, entered the room then and the little group of refugees clustered around them, hugging and kissing and curtsying and Mrs. Grace wept with abandon on Helene's breast.

"I am so very glad to see all of you!" smiled Helene, her arms around the stooped old woman. "You are safe now, you'll stay with us always, I hope Willy told you that."

"He did, ma'am, he did," murmured Mrs. Grace loftily.

"Where's Father McGuire, then?" asked Meg suddenly. The rest of them looked expectantly at Helene. Katherine's lips tightened as she replied very quickly.

"Not here," said Katherine. "But safe away. I thought Willy told you about the new law—"

"Gor', Miss Katherine, I've 'ad enough explainin' to do just gettin' ourselves here in one piece," protested Willy. He picked up the black bundle he had been carrying and handed it to her. "This is all I could take out, miss. And you'll find one or two trinkets missin' when you tote them all up. We was stopped and searched more'n once and yer mama's fancies helped buy our way on again."

Katherine held the small bundle in her hands. She looked down at it and swallowed, then spoke to him again, her voice quite choked.

"This is all that's left of Kilbree, Willy?" she asked. "What of the furnishings, the linens and silver and crystal and . . . and all the paintings and my father's guns? What happened to all that?"

"Oh, it's all there right enough," said Willy glumly, "did anybody want to get a ball through 'is 'ead tryin' to cart it off! Miss Katherine, I did what yer brother told me. All the beasts is gone, to the neighbors, and I took the liberty of givin' them servants what wouldn't come away with us the chickens and geese and the cows. They'll be needin' somethin' between them and the winter now they've no place to work . . ."

"But they could all have come with you!" cried Katherine. "Didn't you tell them? Why did you only bring these few?"

Willy shifted his weight from one foot to the other and replied patiently, "These was all would come, miss. The rest had someplace to go, cousins and relatives and such. We was in much of a hurry, y'see, not knowin' exactly how long 'twould be before the soldiers showed up to take the place over. I think we done pretty well, considerin'."

"Of course you did, Willy, forgive me, please?" Katherine's voice softened at once. She ran over to Willy and kissed his cheek impetuously. "No one but you could have taken care of it all and come through safely. I'm upset, just upset, you see . . . with Michael still gone and . . . and it's so hard to think of Kilbree empty and alone and none of us there now or . . . or ever again . . ." her voice failed her altogether and she broke down, crying piteously.

"Darlin', darlin'!" cried Mrs. Grace, trying to comfort her, but it was Meg who reached Katherine and drew the bright curly head onto her stout shoulder and put a protective arm about her. She and Helene got the sobbing girl to sit down then and Katherine stayed with her head resting against Meg, clutching the unopened bundle to her breast.

The rest of them all started talking at once, telling Helene the whole story of Willy's arrival in Ireland, how he'd taken care of everything in a snap and carried them all off afraid for their lives . . . but nothing ever scared Willy. They heaped their praises on him until his pale face was scarlet with embarrassment. Then Helene had Alice show them to their rooms so they might rest and catch their breath before dinner. She kept Willy with her, however, moving away from Meg and Katherine at the fireside. Katherine had opened the bundle and looked down at what was left to remind her of her parents. Helene saw with a sad smile that Sheila's emeralds were there, and the two little miniatures of Ian and Sheila painted long ago before Michael's birth. Katherine's and Michael's silver christening cups were there, a half-dozen rings, bracelets she couldn't even remember, diamond shoe buckles. Ian's gold and enamel buttons, a few brooches, a jade and ivory fan from China, a bit of fine Limerick lace Helene recognized as part of Sheila's wedding veil, the same bell and shamrock pattern as her own.

Helene turned away from the pitiful little pile, all that was left of a great house and its people, and saw that Willy was looking at her with great sympathy. She smiled at him.

"Was it very bad, Willy? Was anyone hurt?"

"Not so bad, my lady," he shook his head. "We got off before they might of started hurtin' people. Poor Miss Katherine," he added, nodding toward the two by the fire. "I wish I could ha' done more about her things, but we was lucky to get away with that much."

"Did anyone make mention of Michael? Any of the officials?" she asked him anxiously.

"Once or twice," he replied, his voice grim and angry. "Sir Tom

225

was right . . . if Master Michael had gone instead of me, they would ha' took 'im on sight. He cannot go home again, my lady, not never.''

Helene nodded. "We are very worried about Michael, Willy. He should have sent back some word from France by this time. Sir Tom has sent a man to Bristol, hoping to find a ship that has been in a French port recently, to inquire for any messages. He ought to be back tonight.''

"Beg pardon, my lady," said Willy, in some distress. "But . . . what will Master Michael do when he does get here? He can't show himself in public or they'll be after 'im to swear that bloody oath. Wouldn't he be better off just stayin' away till . . . till everything's ready?''

"Yes, perhaps that is what he has decided to do," said Helene, her voice lifting a little. "He could send back whatever information is needed and simply remain with His Majesty until he lands in England. Yes, yes . . . Michael would be in no danger, then. That *must* be what the King has commanded him to do!''

"Still . . .'' reflected Willy reluctantly, "I recall to mind Sir Tom was expectin' *himself* back and not no message without him. . . .''

Then he saw the fear in her face and hastily went on, "But the best of us . . . Sir Tom, too, has got to h'obey whatever the King says, do we not, my lady? So, turnin' the matter h'over in me mind, *I* says *you* are in the right on it and that be just what Master Michael is doin' right this blessed minute!''

Helene looked only slightly less doubtful but she held out her hand to him with a smile.

"What a good friend you are, Willy!'' she whispered. "I'll let you go to Sir Tom now and tell him everything yourself. And . . . thank you, Willy. Again!''

Willy went off with an easy-going grin that vanished as soon as he was away from her. Well he knew what Sir Tom's orders to Michael had been and they had *not* included waiting around in France!

Helene sat together with Meg and Katherine by the fire, looking through the things from Kilbree. She picked up the two little portraits of Ian and Sheila and struggled to keep from weeping.

"You're like the two of them," she said to Katherine. "I have not seen these pictures in such a long time, since you were just a little girl. You're a perfect blend of your dear mother and father, darling. They would be so very, very proud of you today!''

226

Katherine tried to smile. "I wish I had known them, even for a little while, like Michael. You know, Aunt Helene, Michael remembers Father sometimes. When we were young he used to tell me how he looked so tall and handsome in his gold helmet and scarlet coat."

"Michael must remember your mother, too, dear," said Helene carelessly, turning over the emeralds in her hand. "How he loved her! They were very, very close, Sheila and her son. You would have been close to her, too, Katherine . . . Sheila was like that. Sheila had love enough for all of us. Hasn't Michael told you what your mother was like? Surely—"

"No," said Katherine, an odd catch in her voice. "Only you and Uncle Thomas have talked about her . . . and Willy, of course . . ."

"Now, Miss Katherine, be fair. All of us at Kilbree have a thousand stories about your blessed mother and you've been listening to the lot of them since you were no taller than a grasshopper!" protested Meg, looking reproachfully at her young mistress.

Katherine kissed her swiftly. "Of course, Meg darling," she said. "But I meant, here. In England. My brother has never said a single word about Mother, not once, not in all this time. I would have remembered if *Michael* spoke of her. How strange . . ."

Not strange at all, thought Helene. But she merely smiled and said, "How like a boy . . . to remember the helmets and the uniforms best! Michael and Robby . . . *Rob*," she amended, laughing a bit, "that's all they talked about, the only game they liked to play . . . battles and wars and . . . what d'you call it? . . . *Maneuvers!*" She was pleased to see that Katherine laughed and even Meg allowed a smile to escape her dour countenance. She stood up to go back upstairs and rescue Elizabeth from the clutches of the overzealous seamstresses who were insisting on remaking the ballgown sleeves for the fourth time.

"Come on, dear, bring your lovely things upstairs to your room and then, for Heaven's sake, come help me with Elizabeth and that gown. The poor child, they're driving her mad trying to cut the neckline past absolute *scandal* and she won't hear of it!"

3 Waiting, Four Days Before The Ball

There was no message from Michael. The man arrived back close to midnight at Spring Mount and reported that there had been three merchant ships in Bristol harbor that had touched port in France before reaching England. He had hung around for hours until he got the chance to speak to the Captain of each of the ships, asking for letters for Sir Thomas Sturbridge. There had been nothing. And there were no more ships due in from the Continent for another week or more.

"Captain Sir Tom, sir," said Willy ponderously, trying to keep from yawning, as he had not slept in forty-eight hours, "it strikes me we are headin' into some heavy weather, sir."

"You're beginning to talk like a sailor, Willy!" smiled Rob.

"It were the crossin' of St. George's Channel twice't so close together, like," said Willy solemnly. "I pick things up and they stick with me. It's a natural gift, my mother told me."

Sir Tom ignored their banter, thinking over everything his messenger had told him. It might be just as well Michael was not home now . . . they would only have to hide him as they were hiding the priest. Michael must have realized this and was delaying his return on purpose. Yet, he frowned, all was depending on what word Michael would bring back with him. Further delay only put off the action they would take, and give them that much less time to warn the others to be ready. . . .

"I don't like the feel of things," he admitted. "Yet, the boy must be safe. If he had been taken we would have heard by now, surely. And his greatest danger was at the start, while he carried those letters with him. Coming home, the only message will be the King's own words, a single sentence, nothing more is needed. Only that he agrees to the time and place we have settled upon among us here at home. A word, just yes or no—Michael surely stands in no danger when he lands at Bristol."

"Ah!" Willy exhaled loudly. "Wait up, now, see, is that right, no offense, Captain, sir . . ."

"What is it, Willy?"

Willy scratched his chin thoughtfully. "Leavin' aside h'entirely the subject of 'is Majesty what ain't amongst us *yet*, why Master Michael has still the oath to take. If anyone was to entertain some doubts about 'im takin' that 'ere oath, then maybe there'd be a watch set, like, and when 'e steps off 'is ship they'd like to grab him and put it to 'im on the spot, will 'e nor won't 'e swear and so on and so on, d'ye see? And Master Michael bein' the pious Catholic gentleman that 'e *be* . . . well . . ." and he spread his hands out, palms up, the rest of his meaning all too clear.

228

"But who would set such a watch, Willy? They would come here first, asking for him. They still must wait the thirty days."

"Mmmm," said Willy scornfully, "like they was waitin' those same thirty days before they could take Kilbree, eh? It 'as been my h'experience, Captain, sir, that *they* ain't too careful nor h'exact when it comes to enforcin' the law that's on their side!"

"Willy's right, Papa," declared Rob. "We shall have to find out what has happened to Michael. They'll put him to the torture and they won't stop till they get the evidence they want against *you*."

"Michael would die on the rack before betraying those who trust in him," said Sir Tom rather stiffly. "No, Rob. We may be quite wrong in this. There is still a chance that he has merely been delayed . . . a broken carriage wheel, a lame horse, he could have missed his ship back. We will wait until after Elizabeth's ball and if we have heard nothing by then, I'll send someone after him."

"You're wrong, Papa!" cried Rob urgently, then stopped suddenly, shocked at his own words.

"That's all right, son," smiled Sir Tom quietly. "I've been dead wrong a number of times. . . ."

"But this time it's Michael's life," said Rob stoutly. "Let *me* go. I could be in Bristol by tonight, in France tomorrow afternoon. I'll find Michael wherever he is and bring him home with me!"

Sir Tom hesitated, glancing at Willy. Willy was nodding his head, in complete agreement with Rob.

"And suppose we lose you both?" His father sighed.

"*I* shall h'accompany Rob 'ere, Captain, sir," Willy spoke up eagerly. "We can 'op it to froggy-land and back within the week and none the wiser. I do think it's best, sir, don't you?"

"*We* won't be carrying any messages, Papa, so we'll be safe enough," added Rob.

"Except, as Willy pointed out, on the way back. Alone, the two of you would be safe enough, as far as I know now. But if you find Michael—my God, you've *got* to find him!—what will you do if they *are* waiting to arrest him when he lands?"

"Simple," said Rob. "We won't land. We won't stay with the ship till it reaches port. I'll pay the Captain and arrange a boat to row us ashore off Gravesend. You have Jed send a man with some horses to wait for us there. We'll land on the beach somewhere quiet and ride home while they—whoever *they* are—are still waiting for us at Bristol or Dover.''

"Yes," nodded his father slowly. "It is possible. But, Rob, once the ship does arrive, they will know you were on it soon enough . . ."

"By that time, will it really matter? Things will be out in the open at last, just as we've always hoped and planned. Can we go, Papa?"

"Your mother will never forgive you for missing Elizabeth's ball," said Sir Tom with a sad little smile, and he nodded, to Rob's great delight.

"I'll bring Elizabeth and Harry back something marvelous from Paris for a wedding gift . . . one of those monstrous ormolu gilt clocks with the painted birds and flowers," grinned Rob, his excitement almost overwhelming. It was something to *do*, something besides sit and wait and wait some more till a fellow went crazy!

"If Michael gets home before we do, leave word with Mother where you'll both be and we'll join you immediately."

Sir Tom hugged his son very hard. "You will remember to be careful every minute?"

"Don't worry nor fret about 'im, Master Michael neither, Captain, sir," Willy reassured him heartily. "Keepin' in mind we 'as precious serious work on 'and once we gets back 'ere, and a bloomin' King to set square on 'is throne at last!"

"God bless you, Willy!" laughed Sir Tom. "God bless you both. Come back safe, come back soon. And . . . come back with Michael."

They were about to leave him then, when he called them back to him, the expression on his face a strange mixture of pride and sorrow.

"Rob," he said, "take this now." And he pulled Ian's steel ring from his crippled hand and held it out to his son.

"Papa!" cried Rob, his gaze fixed on the little band of steel, "why?" he demanded, his face very pale. Sir Tom shook his head, smiling, and placed the ring in Rob's palm.

"Because I want you to have it," he said very simply. "It is like taking my blessing with you wherever you go. It would have been yours soon enough—"

"It's Michael's," protested Rob. "It was his father's, it belongs to him!"

"Michael Ives will never wear this ring, believe me, Rob," said his father gravely.

"Why? Why haven't you given it to him all these years? I've never understood that."

"Put it on, Rob," ordered Sir Tom, and when Rob reluctantly slipped the heavy band on his own finger, he said, "I gave it to Michael once. I offered it to him a second time. And I told him it was his whenever he wanted it. All he had to do was say so."

"And he never has?"

"He never has," repeated Sir Tom, his voice constrained. "Michael is a strange person in many ways. I have loved him since the day he was born, we all have, but ever since his parents died, he cannot seem to accept love from anyone, except perhaps Katherine. And you, Willy, you've been very close to him."

"I understand him and he knows it, that's all, sir," observed Willy, his face troubled. "Michael keeps everyone at arm's length from him, don't you know? It ain't only yerself, all of you, it's the whole world I'm thinkin'. And, sir, yer right about that . . . he'll never put that ring on his finger, so do as yer father says, Rob, and don't fret on it. Michael don't believe he *deserves* that ring, am I right, Captain, sir?" His shrewd eyes met Sir Tom's and found assent there.

"One thing, Rob," his father said. "I must be honest with you now as I have always tried to be all your life. I would have given the ring to you anyway. It's not, as you know, the usual sort of ring, not like this one . . ." he glanced at the Sturbridge signet ring on his left hand. "It was given to me to be mine by my dearest friend. He told me to give it away when it was needed most, to give it to whomever I chose. If we fail in our endeavors for the King, it may be all I ever have to give you. You know the state of our affairs. I want you to wear it—first, because I believe in some peculiar way it possesses a kind of power, perhaps the power of love and honor, and it can help you when you need help. It helped save my life once, in a way so strange and so personal I doubt I could even explain it now. And, too, you are my only son, the 'best-loved,'" He smiled and embraced Rob again. "You know its story, you know what it means to wear it, like a talisman, perhaps. You will never dishonor that ring or this house, Rob. It is yours by right."

Rob stared uneasily at his father. "Then give it to me when I return," he said slowly, studying his father's face. His meaning was quite clear. Sir Tom began to smile at Rob's sober expression, but he could not evade the penetrating scrutiny of those grave, loving eyes.

"Rob," he began, and then stopped. Willy wandered discreetly to the bookshelves at the other end of the room and began to peruse the titles before him as if his life depended on it. Sir Tom threw a wry little look at Willy's back. No help there, he thought, and Rob must be answered.

"Rob," he began again, "you know the history of this little bit of steel. And the history of our own family ring. I received my father's ring after he had died and for some time to come, I swear to you, the feel of it was heavy on my hand. I'd so much rather have seen it still where it belonged, on his living finger. I have a bad feeling about it . . . you have heard me speak of this before. The steel ring has been passed, in its short history, from living hand to living hand, from your grandfather to Ian Ives and from Ian to me. And that is the way I want it to go on. God grant you and I meet safe again," he cried suddenly, fervently. "And grant, too, that this little family of ours shall live on and prosper for years to come. I have no thought of dying, Rob. I don't hear my name being called in the wind as Ian swore he did. But *I* will do my part and wait for your return home with a better grace if I know you have the ring. I will never take it back again, Rob. The time has come, don't you see? for me to pass it on, that's all. If I live to be an old man, as my father did, I hope to see the day when you will give it to someone else. When you do, it will be only because something inside of you tells you it is the right time to do it. As it is the right time, now, for me to give it to you." He fell silent then, after the rush of so many words, and hoped his son understood and accepted.

Rob nodded and embraced him closely. "I shall bring it back again, Papa," he said, "I swear it!"

After a moment, Sir Tom clapped him on the shoulder, laughing, and sent him and Willy away. Willy had to sleep the night through, despite his protestations that he could go another three days as he was, and Rob therefore was to make all the arrangements. Whatever question lingered further in Rob Sturbridge's mind at that moment, he did not ask it and he felt it in his bones . . . as Willy often said . . . that if he had pursued the matter further, his father would not have been inclined to answer him.

4 Cooperate With The Crown

"An excellent Madeira, sir," pronounced the little man sitting just across from Magistrate Gladden. He raised the plain, heavy glass to his thin lips once again and this time drained it. It *did* help moisten his dry mouth and throat a little bit. But the moment it was gone, he could feel the dryness return and he wished the Magistrate would offer to refill the glass.

"I am told it is very fine wine," said the Magistrate, and to the little man's dismay, he returned the glass stopper to the decanter without noticing the empty glass. "I myself do not indulge, of course. But I see no reason to deny to other men what my own religion declares unfit for *me*."

The little man licked his lips quickly, his tongue darting out like the testing tongue of a serpent, but he did not answer and for a moment the two sat facing each other without a word. Master Hulme, for it was he, Sir Thomas Sturbridge's trusted solicitor and business adviser, had gotten over the initial panic he had felt when the Magistrate had asked him to drop by for a chat. Master Hulme and the Magistrate had had, it is true, little to discuss in the past... all the more reason, suggested the Magistrate smoothly, for the two of them to become better acquainted. Magistrate Gladden, for all his austere and even fearsome reputation, was pleasant and unhurried in his manner. Master Hulme, upon careful if hasty reflection, had decided he had nothing to hide from the law... or rather, nothing he would not be *able* to hide from the law... and, feeling more confident, pretended to be quite as unhurried as his host.

The Magistrate was a very tall man and carried himself proudly. He was the leading Puritan judiciary official in Somerset and was consulted on points of law and religion from as far away as London. At fifty-three his face was still handsome, although the lifelong habit of frowning when he thought had induced the folds of skin about his brows and under his eyes to deepen prematurely. His mouth was a trifle too long in the underlip, which he constantly thrust out and then pressed in upon the upper lip with a severity that bespoke continual self-repression. His hair, like his eyes, was gray, and close-cropped to a large intelligent head. An unfortunately frivolous tendency of his hair to curl softly around his face was, like all else about the man, controlled rigidly by the simple expedient of wearing it cut so.

He had survived the ups and downs of political changes by always keeping in the background of his work, by never developing a public personality, by never depending upon other men and certainly never trusting them. He performed his often tedious tasks very efficiently, very quietly. He spoke out against no one and carefully wove a sturdy reputation for *seeming* fair and impartial even though he was neither. But, again, no one had ever been able to say just why the Magistrate was the most feared man in the county. No one paid much attention to his single-minded persecution of dissenters . . . they had very few of those fellows down in Somerset, anyway. His equally single-minded determination to cut to the very heart of the ungodly Jacobite conspiracy was actually known only to a few, among them Arthur Prescott. Gladden was from the old Puritan stronghold and county seat of Taunton. He had early and wisely kept himself aloof from the Duke of Monmouth's foredoomed invasion and therefore was not remembered as a part of it. Of course, being a prudent man, the Magistrate had been ready to jump whichever way the Fates pointed. Monmouth had failed and was no more. Gladden merely watched and waited and counted his success in small progressive steps rather than in one wild fling for glory. Thus Monmouth perished and Gladden prospered.

The meeting with Master Hulme today was another small step in the Magistrate's master plan. Most of what he would ask the little man he already knew, the information slowly and painstakingly gathered and written out by Gladden's numerous agents. He glanced down at the neatly piled stack of paper before him. They held Sir Thomas Sturbridge's life story, in a manner of speaking: military records, accounts of his political activities thoroughly documented, financial reports—some of them secretly copied from Master Hulme's own most secret documents—lists of dates, places, names in England, in Scotland, even in France; copies of orders for arms and munitions arranged for, paid for, by Sir Thomas Sturbridge to support the overthrow of King William and the installation of a Papist usurper on the lion throne of England. The Magistrate placed his open hand, palm down, across the damning pile of evidence on his desk.

The gesture was not lost on Master Hulme. The little solicitor, who had built his career on the careful avoidance of personal involvement in any cause, worldly or heavenly, now experienced a quick touch of scorn for the man he faced. Hulme's guiding star was pounds sterling. If he could be said to have a religion at all, then his religion was money, the making of it, the saving of it, the taking of it. And in this he was not much removed from the realm of other men's devotions. Thus, with the true contempt of the man of business for the man of zeal, Hulme relaxed suddenly and completely, sat back in his chair and smiled expectantly at Gladden.

"It is time for you to look about for other clients, Master Hulme," said the Magistrate. Hulme's manner remained calm, barely interested.

"You have gained all you will from your arrangement with Sir Thomas Sturbridge," Gladden went on, purposely looking away from the solicitor. "Your commissions have paid you a handsome profit . . ." he pretended to be scanning a page of his report, though he knew the facts by heart. "And now those commissions—and the business upon which they were earned—will cease."

"Are you ordering me to withdraw from my client's affairs?" asked Hulme boldly.

"I order no man," Gladden said. "I merely inform you that it is at an end. Sir Thomas Sturbridge is at an end," he emphasized slowly and allowed Hulme time to realize fully the implications of his words.

"This happens," Hulme murmured with a small shrug. But at once his guard was up. He weighed quickly the extent of damaging testimony he might reveal about Sir Thomas without revealing anything about his own involvement.

Magistrate Gladden despised the man. But then, he despised all men, with a certain weary loathing for these weakest of God's vessels, the whole species, male and female; he could not pretend to understand the workings of the Almighty's mind when He created mankind. In this, as in certain other things, the Magistrate was annoyed with God and longed sometimes to have it out with Him. Meanwhile, however, Hulme was to be used.

Gladden's mild almost benign smile, disappeared. He leaned across the desk and pointed his finger at Hulme.

"I will destroy you," he said icily. Hulme started, his eyes staring wildly. "Yes, I will do so," repeated Gladden. "I have enough proofs against you to send you to the scaffold tomorrow morning. . . ."

"Against *me*?" stammered Hulme, a tiny flame of anger mingled with his understandable terror. "Not me, sir! If you intend to bring evidence against one of my clients—one of my *many* clients—pray do so and I shall endeavor to assist you. It is the Law, sir, and I respect the Law! But, as for *me*—"

" 'The Law'!" cried Gladden passionately. "The Law you speak of is what men make it today and change tomorrow and forget the day after! I care nothing for the Law. Unless the *Law* be useful in furthering the Divine Will of God! Sir Thomas Sturbridge breaks that Law you claim to respect, Master Hulme, and in carrying out his commissions *you* do the Devil's work in helping restore that Papist usurper to the English throne! Your fortune—your very *large* fortune, Master Hulme—has been built upon the expediency of treason. It is *you* who wickedly disregard the only Law that *is* the Law—the Law of God!''

Hulme, whose face had turned a sickly yellow-white, struggled hard to compose himself. ''What do you want of me, Magistrate?''

The Magistrate sniffed with disgust, eased himself back in his chair and began to place certain of the papers in front of Master Hulme for his perusal.

''I want your signed testimony that these figures are accurate, Master Hulme.''

Hulme glanced at the pages, trying to hide his terror as he saw the records of his most private and indiscreet transactions spread out before him.

''Is that all?'' he breathed, without looking up.

''No, it is not,'' returned the Magistrate. ''I shall also require your signature to evidence that your client, Sir Thomas Sturbridge, attempted to entice you into joining his conspiracy, promising you double fees upon occasion and, further, greater considerations once King William was deposed.''

There was no way in the world that Magistrate Gladden or any of his agents could have found out that Hulme had already accepted double fees on several occasions and, in fact, had demanded the same for any future work he undertook for Sturbridge. ''Promised double fees'' however was very different.

''Yes?'' came the voice of the Magistrate from far-off icy places.

''Sir Thomas did—make mention—of the—er . . . expression 'double fees,' I recall that he did indeed, sir,'' said Hulme. What Sir Tom had said, in fact, was that Hulme was a damned bloody knave and a thorough-going scoundrel demanding double fees for the same services he had been happy to render only a year ago for half as much!

''You, of course, ignored such promises and reported what was said and what was done to the authorities immediately?'' said Gladden, his heavy voice inexplicably lighter, almost friendly. Hulme clasped his hands together to keep them from trembling. He hung his head and shook it mutely.

"You did *not*?" asked Gladden, apparently surprised. Hulme cursed the man in his heart for the horrible game he was playing.

"I did not know what to do, sir," he muttered. "Sir Thomas is master of one of the largest estates in England, a very powerful man. I did not want to . . . upset him. . . ."

"No," agreed Gladden, "naturally. But now, unfortunately, you are going to have to upset him. In fact, Master Hulme, you are going to cooperate with the Crown to such a degree that it will be made very clear that Sturbridge is guilty of treason. Upon your word, corroborrated by other witnesses of course, the man will be arrested—"

"And imprisoned?" asked Hulme hopefully.

"And imprisoned until he confesses his grave errors."

Torture! Hulme felt his head swimming and he forced himself to ask, "And then? . . ."

"He will be executed. Upon *your* evidence." The Magistrate stressed that point again.

"If he is, for some reason I find difficult to conceive at this time, *not* found guilty, not executed . . ." Gladden paused delicately, then fixed Hulme with his penetrating gaze. "We still have you . . ."

"Me?"

"We still have you and your double-dealings, your illegal sales, your unregistered transactions, and your altogether ill-gotten profits. We have no wish to persecute an honorable solicitor, Master Hulme. Your services are too valuable to the community for us to *lose* you to the machinations of fanatical revolutionaries. Therefore, I believe . . . that you will make a remarkably impressive witness. Am I correct in my assumption, Master Hulme? If I am not correct, now is certainly the time to disabuse me of my utter confidence in you."

"No, no!" cried Hulme in desperation. "You are correct, correct in all details, Magistrate. Do I have your word that no harm will come to me . . . afterward?"

"My word? Nay, master, my *oath* on it!" smiled the Magistrate, rising to show the thoroughly shaken little man out. Hulme scurried away still carrying his hat in his hand, having forgotten to put it back on his head.

Yet it was not all Magistrate Gladden's day and not everything came easily his way. For instance, he had been informed about Willy

Duncan's return from Ireland. And he knew within six hours, when Michael Ives had landed back in Bristol. The young man had been allowed to pass through unmolested, according to orders issued previously: Watch him, follow him where he goes but do not stop him. Michael was a homing pigeon . . . where would he go but back to Spring Mount to report the news from France?

But Gladden had not expected Sir Tom to risk sending his only son after Michael. No one had been told to follow Rob, and those who had followed Willy had long since quit the trail. So Rob and Willy were on board ship bound for Le Havre before the Magistrate knew of it. He mulled over the unfortunate news. Everything was arranged; the time and place determined for the downfall of Sir Thomas. Before that haughty gentleman would die, he would reveal the full extent of the linked chain of the conspiracy that stretched from Scotland to Ireland to England to France. There were many names on the Magistrate's long list, but there were many he only suspected. Sir Thomas would fill in the blanks. Yet now there was great likelihood that when they took Sir Thomas, his son and fellow conspirator would be beyond their reach.

The Magistrate forced his tall body into a semblance of humility by kneeling on the hard floor of his chamber. And he cried to Heaven for assistance in carrying out the mission he had told himself many times was the work of God asked of him to do. But God, as usual, seemed occupied in other places, and, as usual, in the end, the Magistrate rose to his feet unanswered, and set about solving the dilemma himself.

Nine

"As The Bold Should Greet The Brave"

1 The Morning Of The Ball

The morning of Elizabeth's betrothal ball everything was beautiful at Spring Mount. But the family was abstracted and went about the last-minute preparations very quietly indeed.

There was an air of waiting all about the place. Spring Mount was preparing for a grand and gala event, but the mood was not one of holiday anticipation but rather dread apprehension.

Rob and Willy had been gone three days and it was too soon to expect any word from them. Michael seemed to have disappeared from the face of the earth. There would be men at the ball as anxious to hear Michael's news as was Sir Tom, men who would toast the bride and dance and drink and eat and congratulate the bridegroom, then ride off in the dawn hours to begin spreading the news of the uprising. Yet, so far, there was no news for them to take away.

Sir Tom went about his usual duties and the extra duties being host of such a ball entailed, hardly saying a word to anyone. Each time he saw a rider turn off the main road and head toward the house he waited stonily, sure it would be some warning that the plans had been found out and all of them betrayed. A dozen times a day he had talked himself out of the wild notion that he must send Helene and the girls and the servants away at once. The ball drove him to distraction and yet, for Elizabeth's sake—and because there was nothing he could do now but wait—he strove valiantly to seem happy, even merry, and all the while his waking-sleeping tortured dreams depicted Michael being slowly torn apart on the rack, in his agony, and Michael's face would melt into Ian's features and then it was Ian he was watching helplessly in the hands of King William's executioners.

Helene was sick at heart over the absence of the boys. Although she never said so, she did believe in her heart that something terrible had happened to Michael, and that same something terrible now lay in wait for Rob.

She moved, walked, talked, gave orders to the rushing servants, gave advice to the girls, gave comfort to the folks from Kilbree, all in a state of unhappy trance. The slightest untoward happening, a small delay, a bit of trouble in the kitchen and she found herself longing to run away from them all, to lock herself in her bedroom like a terrified child and wait for the bad time to pass. Instead, she wandered through the big house, speaking calmly when she felt like shouting, smiling when she was positive she must weep in another moment.

Elizabeth sat quite forlornly in the tiny reception room off the main drawing room at Spring Mount. No one noticed her; no one even missed her. She had awakened this wonderful morning and thought immediately of Harry and then of what day it was, the day of her ball come at last! She had run downstairs eagerly, wanting to help, wanting to talk and laugh and share her joy with everyone. But Sir Tom was already in his study, having taken no breakfast. Helene was on her way into the kitchen with a vexed frown on her brow, her voice a trifle testy as she spoke to Alice. Her own mother, thought Elizabeth indignantly, her own mother on *this* day of all days, hadn't even bade her good morning. I don't think she saw me at all, Elizabeth told herself as she slipped into her place at the table and waited for Katherine, sipping her tea, to smile and tease and say something wonderful.

But Katherine's eyes, she had noticed a moment later, were quite red and there were shadows under them Elizabeth had never seen before. Well, of course, she was worrying about Michael. That was only natural, reasoned Elizabeth, and at once she made up her mind to be extra nice to Katherine today. Why should she not be kind and loving to everyone, indeed, she smiled to herself and her breath came in excited little gasps. She loved them all so very much! She loved the whole wide world, which tonight would gather round and be happy for her and Harry!

She must have laughed a little or made some slight sound, for Katherine started and almost dropped the cup in her hand, then looked at her reprovingly.

I am older than she is, thought Elizabeth, but sometimes she seems to be a hundred.

"Did I bother you?" she inquired a bit crossly and instantly regretted her tone of voice—where was her resolution to be very kind and loving to Katherine today?

"Of course I did, I must have startled you. I'm sorry. I seem to be in everybody's way this morning..." she rattled on, flushing hotly. Katherine tried to smile but it didn't work. Then she reached across the table and touched Elizabeth's hand gently.

"This is your day, dear," she said, but there was no gladness in her voice. "It's we who are the nuisances—nobody should trouble you the day of your betrothal. Forgive me. I...I am preoccupied...." her voice trailed off as though she had forgotten she was speaking. Elizabeth jumped up impulsively and ran around the other side of the table to hug her.

"I am so happy I think everyone must be, too," she cried. "But I have not forgotten Michael, Katherine. I pray for him every day. I know he will come back safe."

"And Rob, too," murmured Katherine. Elizabeth pulled away from her and stared at her in surprise.

"Rob? What is the matter with Rob?" she demanded. "He's only been gone three days. Why do you speak of him as you do of Michael?"

Katherine pushed her chair back and stood up. "Because I am foolish," she said with a peculiar little laugh. "When I worry so much about one person, I have a way of making it seem as if everyone is a problem. It's the Irish in me, Willy's always telling me that . . ." but when she mentioned Willy's name, Katherine suddenly pressed her fingers against her lips and her eyes brimmed with unshed tears. She shook her head violently when Elizabeth tried to comfort her, and rushed out of the dining room.

Elizabeth sat alone at the table, mechanically chewing her food without tasting it, wondering what was happening to everybody and why today was on the way to being ruined. When the maid took away her dishes, she wandered from room to room, admiring the flowers, the greens, the high polish on the fine oak parquet floor in the ballroom. And somehow she found herself sitting all alone in this tiny room where guests sometimes waited to see her mother and father. She sat very primly, imagining she was a visitor to Spring Mount and seeing it for the first time. She loved this old house and everything in it. One day it would belong just to Rob. She would miss it so, she thought sadly . . . and then spoke most severely to herself: Not today, nothing is going to make me unhappy for a single minute today.

She began, thus, to feel much better, not quite so ignored or rejected. She decided to go up to Katherine, to sit down and talk to her very *logically* . . . and explain many things to her. She knew Katherine well enough to realize she must not directly offer comfort when she was afraid. Fear made Cousin Katherine angry, angry with herself Elizabeth supposed, somewhat in awe, as usual, of Katherine's ways. If one were to let on one knew she was afraid of something, that, too, would anger her. No, the best thing would be to talk quietly and sensibly and distract Katherine's mind from her troubles.

I *am* rather special today, Elizabeth thought with delight. I seem to be understanding so many things about other people and about myself. That was another marvelous thing loving Harry was doing for her, she observed.

She bounced up from the green satin-skirted armchair she had been drooping in for almost an hour, and was about to go running up to find Katherine and confide all of her amazing new thoughts, when a small movement outside the windows caught her attention. She stopped and went to look more closely. Then she sighed with annoyance. It was another messenger or somebody, some man on horseback riding very fast indeed, for the horse's flanks were covered with foamy sweat. What kind of gentleman or the servant of a gentleman, she thought with disdain, would treat a fine horse that way?

And then she looked more closely and gasped and cried out in great excitement although no one was about to hear her.

"It's Michael! Michael! He's safe and he's back and . . . Michael!"

By now she had run out into the main entranceway and startled the busy servants by rushing past them, tugging open the great carved oak door by herself and dashing outside, down the steps, waving her arms and shouting deliriously.

"Michael! Oh, Michael, it's me, it's me, Michael, and you haven't missed my ball after all!"

Michael Ives reined in his exhausted horse and allowed the animal to walk the short distance from the bend of the driveway heading around back to the sweeping curve of fine gray gravel that circled the front of the house. As he slumped forward in his saddle, he talked to the horse and patted its head and shortly he came up to Elizabeth.

"Michael . . . !" She started to babble away happily when she finally noticed the greyish pallor of his unshaven face and the look in his eyes, and her words of greeting died away. She stepped back from him a little and watched him climb down from the horse, swaying slightly on his feet.

Michael rubbed his neck and face and eyes, blinking rapidly as though he were in a daze, and then focused his gaze on her.

"Elizabeth!" he cried, his voice lifting. "I didn't know it was you, love! I'm so tired I'm not—"

"Come inside, Michael," she interrupted him gently and slipped her thin arm under his and around his back. "You look terrible . . . but you look wonderful to me!" He started to laugh at her and at the idea of her tiny frame lending him strength and support, but as they walked into the house it was she who guided them both.

"Everyone will be so glad to see you, Michael." She kept talking as she spotted one of the maids running to tell the others he had come. "Papa has been very worried and Mama has been snapping everyone's head off and they hardly ever talk to us except about you—and Rob and Willy, of course. Here we are, now, sit down and I'll fetch you a good strong brandy. You do drink brandy, don't you? Harry says brandy is good for you sometimes."

She guided him back to the little room she had just left and pushed him down into a chair. She had pulled a footstool toward him and was lifting his muddy-booted feet one by one onto it when he grabbed her forearm and stopped her, a bewildered frown on his face.

"Elizabeth, wait, dear. What's that you said about Rob and Willy? That your parents are worried about them? Why? Why, tell me, Elizabeth!"

Elizabeth, kneeling by his feet, looked up at him anxiously.

"I forgot. Of course, you don't know. Papa sent Rob to Paris to find out what happened to *you*. He's not returned yet and Papa's had no word. You've *all* had the whole house turned upside down with nerves and alarm." This last she said rather primly, thinking for an instant of the ball, but Michael's reaction terrified her. He dropped his hand from her arm and sighed very deeply, his head falling back hard against the chair.

Elizabeth jumped to her feet. "Michael! You aren't sick, are you? You aren't *fainted* . . . oh, Michael, I'm sorry . . ."

At this moment Mrs. Jessup came hurrying into the room, carrying steaming tea and scones and a decanter of Irish whiskey. Mrs. Jessup poured out a hefty glass of the liquor and, taking Michael's head in her crooked arm, bent over him and got him to swallow a good bit of it. He coughed and sputtered and at length she took the glass from his lips and surveyed him with grim satisfaction.

Elizabeth felt in the way and embarrassed, but he caught sight of her anxious little face and smiled at her.

"Darling, I'm sorry I gave you such a fright. I'm all right now. Really all right. I've been traveling for days without much in the way of sleep. All I need is a wash and a shave and some clean clothes and I'll be myself entirely!" Without his realizing it, a soft touch of the Irish lilt invaded his usual crisp quick tones and Elizabeth felt like crying herself.

But she did not. She smiled the brightest, bravest, most womanly smile he'd ever seen on her plain little face and nodded quite cheerfully.

"I'll see to it," she said. "And I'll send Katherine to you."

"All my thanks, Princess," he said, "but, not Katherine. Not yet. Find your father, sweetheart, and tell him I've something to say to him right away."

Elizabeth left him in the care of Mrs. Jessup and went to find Sir Tom.

"Michael's in the reception room, Papa," called out Elizabeth. "And he's got something to say to you..."

"I should hope so!" answered Sir Tom with a jubilant note in his voice and a bright gleam in his eye. "Is he well?"

But he did not wait for her to reply. Elizabeth watched him hurrying as fast as his bad leg would allow him to get to Michael. There seemed nothing more she could do to help so she went off to find her mother and Katherine and tell them Michael was back safe.

2 A Frank Talk

"Weeks? More like months! It seemed like a damned *year* in the waiting!" Michael growled.

Sir Tom nodded. "I can imagine, Michael. Well, it seems our information was wrong there, at least. I was under the impression His Majesty would be in Paris until the Christmas holidays were over."

"He was partridge shooting in the south of France," Michael snorted. "They kept me cooling my heels for a week thinking I was waiting for an audience, and *then* they told me he wasn't even in the city!"

"So you rode south?"

Michael downed his third cup of hot tea in one swallow. "Aye, I went to meet him. And meet him I did. And Dunley. And Forbes, and that great crashing bore, Lord Brentwood Hadly—"

Sir Tom leaned forward eagerly. "All that after, Michael. Tell me, what did the King say?"

Michael hesitated; then, his face quite grim, he replied. "No."

Sir Tom stared at him. "No? My God, boy, do I understand you to tell me His Majesty refused to—"

"'His Majesty'?" snapped Michael sarcastically. "It seemed to me His *Majesty* had precious little to say about the whole thing! The rest of them . . . they all had a lot to say."

"They spoke against the plan? Michael, they *did* read the messages in cipher? They understood what we were offering? They comprehend the true situation here at home?"

"They comprehend everything," retorted Michael flatly. "I was puzzled at first at their reaction. It didn't seem to take them any time at all to have their minds made up and their answers ready, sure it was all the same answer anyway, 'no,' to a man, 'no' and the King, when he finally got around to saying *his* piece, Jesus Christ but the man sounded like a piss-poor echo of the rest of them!"

"You say you were puzzled at *first*? Explain your meaning."

"Aye, at first. I mean, it's a big issue, isn't it? Wouldn't any man, nay, any group of royal advisers, want to be taking a bit of time and mulling over before they came to a conclusion one way or another? But, not these fine fellows. I thought to myself, they knew ahead of time what I was going to bring them and what it would say. They've *had* their mulling-over time already—and they've had their orders—"

" 'Orders'? From the king?" puzzled Sir Tom.

Michael laughed shortly. "Aye, from the King. Not *yours*. Louis, the French King. Why else do you suppose they had me twiddling my thumbs two whole weeks in Paris? I forgot to mention, when I met His Majesty, there was someone else with him."

"Someone else?"

"A French someone else. Monsieur de Forêt. I couldn't place him at first. But after awhile I remembered he had been in conference with the man I first presented myself to in Paris, and he stayed in the room throughout our whole talk. I never laid eyes on him again until I saw him at the hunting lodge with Hadly and the others."

"And you believe that he went there secretly before you, to discuss the whole thing with them?"

" 'Discuss,' Sir Tom?" Michael shook his head. "Nay, but to tell them what their decision must be. And, when I pieced the whole little game together, I faced de Forêt with it and asked him straight out for an explanation. And I got it, right enough."

Sir Tom's face was apprehensive as he listened. "Well? Go on!"

"It's simply this: King Louis does not believe the time is right to launch the invasion of England he has promised all along. He promised men and ships and weapons to back up His Majesty's *coup*. But not *now*, not yet. Louis rather enjoys playing host to a possible King of England, holding him over William's head, threatening what

245

he might do. He cares nothing for the right or wrong of it—what King ever did? It keeps his country in a rather cozy position.''

"God damn him to Hell!" cursed Sir Tom bitterly. "But, what of it, after all? We don't need Louis and his army *or* his navy. We don't *want* a French invasion of England, we'd only have to fight them off all over again. Surely you were able to make His Majesty see that? He must understand, from the information you gave him, that we are sufficiently prepared here right now to bring about his restoration without France lifting one finger in the doing!"

"And that is the core of it," replied Michael slowly. "He does not see or understand any of what you say. He is hesitant, afraid to jump the Channel all by himself, without the French fleet all around him to protect his soft arse. He told me himself, Sir Tom, now he has bad dreams of poor old Charles I and his head being lopped off like that. And the way they threw his own father out bag and baggage . . . England is not *kind* to her kings. Life in France, for the time being, is safe and pleasant. And, one thing more: he does not quite trust his supporters here at home."

"Doesn't *trust* us?" cried Sir Tom indignantly. "Why not? In what way have we ever deceived him or given him cause to doubt our loyalty?"

"Perhaps 'trust' was not the right word. I meant, rather, that he lacks confidence in the extent of sympathy his cause enjoys in England, and he doubts that even the support of loyal men like yourself can do much to change the sentiments of the people."

"Oh, stop it, Michael, for God's sake, stop it! The man's afraid to make a move, that's obvious enough. He doesn't dare anger Louis by taking the plunge himself—if he failed where would he go then? Louis would hardly invite him back to France again. That damned, devious hypocrite!"

"His Majesty, Sir Tom?" Michael raised an eyebrow.

"Louis," snapped Sir Tom. "Never trust the French, Michael, never. My God, I thought the King would be delighted with our news!"

"He fears another Battle of the Boyne, sir, a bloodbath rather than a victory. He does not want to take the chance."

"God, but it's not he and his advisers who are taking the chances! Everything was arranged, everything! If it is not done as we planned—I tell you, Michael—it will never be done at all. To think that the King himself . . ." his voice faltered. "Oh, I would have believed anything of his 'advisers.' Certainly 'tis safer for those gentlemen to stay on in France than to risk their fat behinds in battle. And it would be only the one battle, mark me, Michael, just one quick decisive victory in the field and the whole country would see we are in earnest, we have the means, the men, the *heart* to do it. And then it would be all over . . ." but the sudden explosive volley of words petered out to a strained silence.

"It *is* all over, isn't it, Michael? It's all over, all for nothing and nothing to show for it. Stillborn."

Michael's heart went out to Sir Tom in that moment. He sounded so finally, utterly defeated.

"I don't know," Michael temporized. "Perhaps it's just the time is wrong."

"No!" cried Sir Tom. "If the King is afraid to place his future in the hands of those who have sacrificed everything to help him, then, Michael, the time will never arrive!"

"What will you do?"

Sir Tom rubbed his forehead as if his brain were racked and pounding against the bones of his skull. "What will I do?" he repeated, almost in a daze. "There is nothing we can do here now, nothing at all. I had thought to fall back to *France* . . ." he all but spat the word out with contempt. "I thought of it all as a kind of long battle and the possibility of exile as merely a temporary retreat . . . those words are cherished by army men like me, Michael!" he laughed darkly. "I counted on victory and a change, a voice in England's affairs in years to come. As it is, even this house will be lost to the bankers and the moneylenders in a very short time. And once word gets out of His Majesty's decision, those who have been waiting, poised ready to jump one way or the other, well, they know where to land now! None of us is safe in England any longer."

"Will you go to France, then?"

For a moment he thought Sir Tom had not heard his question. There was no answer. Then Sir Tom pulled himself erect, threw his shoulders back and seemed to cast off the heaviness of shock and betrayal.

"I will not crawl my way to Louis's court like a whipped cur!" he said. "It is over. Perhaps you have been right all along, Michael. Perhaps it is time for us to make a new beginning."

Michael looked incredulous. "You mean America?"

"Yes, America. I do not know what else we can do," he admitted frankly, and Michael admired him the more for it. "Others have gone there and found a home. I have said and said it more than once that I could not leave England without a backward glance, I could not give my heart and my hopes unreservedly to any other land. But we must live, we must go on, somehow. Doors are closing on all sides . . . you have been right."

"Rob, too," remarked Michael gently.

Sir Tom's head shot up defensively. "My son shares my dreams for England."

"No, he does not," Michael said firmly. "Rob loves *you* and honors what you honor, wants what you want. In that he's like you when you were young and thought the way old Sir Thomas thought. Rob has had no faith of his own in this cause . . . no, wait, hear it all! Rob has no faith in the future of this country. She will not change, and that has always bothered him. I have heard him say that more than once."

"But not to me," muttered Sir Tom.

"No. Not to you," agreed Michael, wishing his words were not so hurtful. "But to me, yes. And to Katherine. He would never say such things to you, but they have been in his heart for a long time now."

Sir Tom stared at him and Michael saw the anger rise, then fade from his eyes, and he nodded very gravely. "I begin to understand," he said at last.

"Everything his grandfather believed in . . . and taught to you and my father, Rob believes in, too. The only difference is, he believes such grand dreams need fresh soil for tilling and Europe is old, worn out from too many failed crops, too many wars, too much betrayal. He believes . . . *I* believe . . . all those dreams can be begun anew and realized. In America."

" 'In America,' " repeated Sir Tom slowly. "I have heard it is already full of dissatisfied people, restless people from everywhere."

"Aye," said Michael urgently. "Restless people. Men and women who are seeking something and will not be content until they find it or make it themselves."

Sir Tom rubbed his eyes and suddenly startled Michael by crying out, "But he is my *King*! How can I abandon him now?"

"He has abandoned *you*," said Michael coldly. "Turn about, Sir Tom."

The sudden burst of anguish died away, futile its coming, and he knew it even as he had said the words. He nodded.

"There's more yet," Michael said then. "I think I was followed."

" 'Followed'! In England?"

"In France and at sea. And, I know for a fact I was followed back from Bristol. That's why I was so long in coming. I thought once or twice I would have to make a fight of it. I doubled back several times, rode far out of my way. Once I deliberately waited at the side of the road until whoever it was would ride up, but directly I stopped I heard them no more."

"But you were not stopped? No one asked your business or attempted to see the papers you carried?"

"I was not detained in any way. Some of the time I thought it was my imagination, but it wasn't. Once I saw de Forêt and realized who he was, I knew. I can't imagine why they let me be. Now that I'm back on English soil, they can demand I swear that damned infamous oath of theirs. They could have arrested me on the spot for that alone."

"Yes. We shall have to make our plans quickly. You must keep out of the way a few days, a week, no longer. By then we shall be ready to go and Rob will surely be home . . . my God, *Rob*!" he cried. "They must be following him, too. We have no way of knowing that they will not apprehend him simply because they let you slip by them."

"Elizabeth told me you sent him to find me," said Michael. "It's only been three days. He could hardly be back yet. But what possible excuse could they use to hold him? They would have to have evidence, a case already prepared. You've had no hint of any such activity?"

"No, no," said Sir Tom. "Nothing. Yet. Except Arthur Prescott, of course. He was over here full of alarms and warnings and threats, begging me to do nothing. Tonight when I make the betrothal announcement I am supposed to give a great speech that will allay any suspicions of my loyalty and devotion to the Dutchman. . . ."

"You cannot make such a speech, surely?"

"No more than you can swear that oath. No, no, never fear. I'll say something glorious about England and tradition and the brother-hood that binds all England together—you know the kind of thing, rousing and sentimental. Everyone will cheer and forget all about it with their next glass of rum. And even Arthur will believe I said what he expected."

"Where shall I stay now?" asked Michael without comment.

"We've got Father McGuire over in the little cottage in the woods. You can go there. There's room enough, though snug. No, wait a bit! If Rob and Willy get clear of France, they will not sail as far as Bristol. They will put ashore in a boat off Gravesend. I do not know when . . . but I promised to send a man with horses to wait for them. He's there now."

" 'Gravesend'?"

"Go to Gravesend, Michael," Sir Tom said, speaking in swift, decisive tones. "Wait there for Rob and Willy. Tell them everything. I will send Jed along with a wagon. He will be carrying the money I have put aside for us to live on, some clothing, nothing more. When Rob arrives, send the man who's there now back to us with word. We will be ready to come ourselves. In the meantime, use part of the money to arrange our passage to America. If there is no ship bound for the Colonies, book passage for us to the Canaries. We can make connections from there."

"Passage for how many?"

Sir Tom paused to consider. "I'm not sure. We must take the priest with us, some of the servants who wish to come. Ten, twelve, I don't know. Do the best you can."

"And how long will you wait here?" Michael asked, looking a bit troubled. "If something has gone wrong with Rob, it could take weeks before we'd hear."

Sir Tom's mouth tightened painfully. "One week," he said. "No more. If Rob has not returned in that time I will send the others to you and you will leave with them immediately. Immediately, you understand that?"

" 'The others'? You will not come?"

"I will not leave without my son or some word of him," said Sir Tom soberly. "I will keep safe, never fear. There are friends I can stay with and I will simply sail to join you a bit later."

Michael frowned. "Aunt Helene will never consent."

"Helene will do as I ask," replied Sir Tom. "One thing more, Michael. Once you have reached your destination safely, do not return to Spring Mount. And do not allow Rob to return, either. No matter what he says, how he tries to persuade you, keep him there with you. There are one or two little taverns on the shore road out there, quite out of the way. They let rooms, and at this season they'd be bound to be empty. We shall manage everything at our end, you do the same at yours. Are we agreed?"

"We are," said Michael heartily. "When shall I go?"

"Sleep first. Then, tonight, when the house is full of guests and the ball is at its height, ride out. Stay clear of town, go parallel to, but not on, the shore road."

"And Jed? The wagon will take much longer than a single horse . . ."

"I shall have him load it with firewood, seasoned and ready for sale. His story will be that he is taking it to trade for limestone to build a new smokehouse. I think he will be all right."

Michael stood up. "So, we do not separate after all," he said. "Rob will be glad." There was a touch of resentment in his tone for a moment, then it passed. "I am glad, too. I have wanted to find something for myself, something that is my own. New. Different. I don't know. A thing not touched by any . . . past regrets . . ."

"Michael," began Sir Tom, groping for the right words, aware of never having found them all through these years, afraid he would not find them now. "Michael, how is it that you and I have always . . . *missed* each other? I've loved you and your sister all your lives but, somehow—"

"But," said Michael quietly, "you loved our parents more. We are not them and you keep looking for parts of them in us. That's where we've *missed*, as you say. We needed to be loved because we were ouselves, not merely because we were their children."

"But, God knows," cried Sir Tom hotly, "that is surely a common enough thing!"

"I expect it is," agreed Michael. "If they had lived and raised Katherine and me, we would have learned bit by bit to see ourselves through their eyes *as* ourselves, separate, individual people. But all we saw was *them* through your eyes." He tried to smile as he said it, to soften the harsh words but, of course, there was no softening of words like that and he knew it.

"I'll go, then," Michael murmured, and yet he did not want to leave things as they were. "Poor little Elizabeth," he said. "What will she do without Harry Prescott?"

"I shall ask Harry to accompany us if he will," said Sir Tom a bit stiffly. "But nothing of this will be told her until tomorrow morning. She must have this one night for her happiness."

Michael said, "Of course." He turned to go and happened to glance down at Sir Tom's hand. "Where is the steel ring?" he asked suddenly.

Sir Tom considered a moment, then said simply, "I gave it to Rob before he went." And he wondered how Michael would react.

It was a while in coming, but then Michael smiled broadly.

"You were right to do so," he said. "It should belong to him."

Sir Tom's answer was swift and biting in spite of himself. "It *should* belong to *you!*"

Michael's smile grew wider. "Not so," he said mildly. "I never wanted it, not since..." He closed his mouth abruptly, afraid of saying too much.

"We will not have much chance to talk again, not for a long time," said Sir Tom sadly. "I hardly think we have talked *now*."

Michael walked to the doorway, paused to look back. "What would we say? I am not my father's son. It's *he* you wish to talk to—"

"Oh, but you *are!* You are his son," cried Sir Tom. "Can't you see it? Can't you let yourself admit it once? Just once?"

Michael considered his father's friend carefully, feeling once again, as he so often did, the unforgotten guilt rise up into his lonely heart. When he spoke his voice was hushed, his tone final, "It's too late for me, Uncle—"

"'Too late'? At twenty-four?" broke in Sir Tom.

"Yes," said Michael sorrowfully. "Let it rest there." And he went away to find Katherine, leaving Sir Tom alone with his thoughts.

He has not called me "uncle" in all these fifteen years! The fact, so small and insignificant, served best to point up how far off seemed Sedgemoor Plain just now, how futile seemed a life's work failed and waiting to be done over, how wrong it seemed that a father be taken from his son so soon to leave a wound that never healed.

3 I Drink The Health of My Motherland, England

"Bless me, Sir Tom, but they do make a charming couple!" bellowed Arthur Prescott, already somewhat in his cups and trying desperately to feel mellow. He stood with a glass of punch in his hand, attempting to smile benignly at the same time he was surreptitiously studying his host's face, voice, manner... anything about him that might reveal a clue as to how things would go later on when it came time for the announcement.

Sir Tom nodded absently, his eyes following Elizabeth and Harry Prescott as they moved together at the head of a line of dancers in the spritely *gigue*. He had never seen his daughter look so pretty or so happy. Her small hand held securely in his large one, Harry handed her about from one intricate pattern of the dance to another as though she were made of porcelain infinitely precious. When they swung in close together for a bow and turnabout, he caught her tiny waist and held her for a second, kissing her shining up-tilted little face. Elizabeth, in delicate yellow taffeta overlaid with snowy Brussels rose-point lace, looked like a windblown daffodil. Her glistening black tresses were simply dressed in soft curls descending from the back of her head and reaching past her shoulders. Tonight Elizabeth was resplendent in the amethyst and topaz jewels that were her betrothal gift and the excitement of the occasion had brought a fine color to her usually pale face and a sparkle to her amber eyes.

Arthur tossed down the remainder of his sherry and said to Sir Tom anxiously, "Wouldn't do to have anything spoil this for that little girl of yours, would it?"

His meaning was transparent, and Sir Tom looked at him with silent contempt, then hurriedly left his side to join a group of Dragoons around the punch bowl.

Arthur felt the perspiration soaking through his best lawn shirt and wished himself home in his bed and the thing done and over with. Left to his own devices for a moment, he looked about the huge room, noting ten or eleven faces he would wager would be wearing vastly different expressions in another hour or so. Ten or eleven of Sturbridge's Jacobite friends, Arthur wondered that they'd had the temerity to show up tonight. Every one of them had been mentioned to him in London, along with Sir Tom. He surveyed them with distaste, yet relishing the thought of what they'd say, what they'd think in a little while when Sir Thomas Sturbridge, their fellow conspirator, spoke his little piece. Yes, Arthur nodded to reassure himself, they could all go home then and count their friend lost to the cause forever. Maybe *then* we can all relax, he hoped. A raucous burst of laughter from the Dragoons startled him and he moved away, positive they had been saying something unpleasant about *him*.

He meandered through the crowded hall, avoiding little clusters of chattering ladies, of maids and footmen hurrying back and forth, and suddenly found himself face to face with Helene. She had been talking with a tall, heavy, red-faced maid who kept nodding and saying, "Yes, ma'am, yes, ma'am." Then the maid spotted Arthur, and had flushed a deep red and, touching Helene's arm to draw her attention to him, had run away upstairs.

Arthur stared after her, bemused. "Peculiar creature," he remarked, a bit put out. Helene looked at him rather coldly, he thought. What was the matter with these fool women?

"Not dancing, Lady Helene?" he muttered, trying to think how he might sound her out about what Sir Tom would say later.

"Not yet, Arthur," she said, and again her voice was quite cool. "Are you enjoying the evening?" Her eyes were watching something over his shoulder down the hall, her question was perfunctory—she cared not a whit if he was enjoying himself or not.

"Tolerably, ma'am," he drawled. "I anticipate an improvement a bit later on, I expect."

Now she looked straight at him, struggling to conceal her dislike and distrust. "Oh, the announcement, you mean? That's just a formality, isn't it? The children are betrothed, the contract signed; even the wedding date has been agreed upon, Elizabeth tells me."

Does she think I'm a fool? Arthur raged inwardly and covered his irritation with what he thought was a disarming smile.

"Nay, Lady Helene, you know I meant something else entirely. Twas the condition of this betrothal, you recall?"

His words struck home and for the first time since he had known her, Arthur enjoyed seeing Helene's perfect poise shaken. He could have sworn she trembled and her lips tightened, her whole face assuming a look of fear. For an instant only. And then, without a word, she brushed by him quickly and walked away down the hall.

Arthur watched her go, a feeling of satisfaction in his heart. He was aware she had never liked him, had never encouraged the match until she realized that Harry and Elizabeth had fallen in love. Romantic drivel, thought Arthur, and he turned to work his way into the crowded dining room. At that moment, a quick movement on the stairs above caught his eye. He looked up in time to see the red-faced maid emerging from one of the bedrooms. She was carrying a heavy tray laden with dishes. Someone held the door open for her. Arthur narrowed his eyes and watched. The girl bumped clumsily against the doorframe, the tray slipped from her hands and fell clattering to the floor.

The door opened completely then, and a man appeared, dressed in black, wearing riding boots and gloves, a black cloak thrown back over his shoulders. He stooped to help her pick up the tray, to retrieve the scattered dishes. As he saw the man's face clearly for the first time, Arthur swore under his breath.

It was Michael Ives. So, Michael had come back to Spring Mount. . . .

The maid hurried downstairs with her dishes and Arthur turned away from her quickly and lost himself in the crowd before she could notice him again.

Interesting, he reflected. No one in the county really expected Ives to return, not after the news had gotten round about the oath of allegiance and supremacy. Had Ives decided to take the oath after all? Perhaps to try to save that place of his in Ireland?

Gad, thought Arthur brightly, perhaps we shall have a clean sweep of the lot! Priest out of the way, Sir Tom about to dance to a different tune and toast King William this very night—and now Michael Ives himself maybe on the brink of redemption.

He began to feel fairly marvelous despite his earlier apprehension and loaded his plate with heaping servings of everything he could cram onto it, his appetite suddenly enormous. It was not until he sat down and picked up his knife and fork to begin the feast that he remembered how Michael had been dressed and also that he showed no sign of coming downstairs and openly joining the family celebration. And why was that ridiculous maid acting so nervous, so secretive?

Slowly Arthur set down his silver utensils. Michael Ives was in hiding! And, Arthur realized with mounting fury, obviously the Sturbridges were helping him.

He thrust the plate from him and got to his feet, shaking with rage. His intention was to find Sir Tom at once and confront him with what he knew about Michael Ives but as he began heading out of the dining room he found himself blocked by the crowds of guests on their way in to sit down for the supper. Arthur stood aside next to the doorway, waiting to let the others pass. A moment later he encountered Sir Tom and Lady Helene, leading Elizabeth, Katherine and Harry into the huge room. Sir Tom was smiling, saying something to Harry, and Harry, Arthur noted coldly, was smiling, too. Then Sir Tom looked up and saw him.

"Well, Arthur, I might have guessed you'd not be far from the supper table, eh? Come along now, we're just sitting down."

He threw an arm about Arthur's unwilling shoulder, drawing him along with the rest of them. Arthur glared at him, shrugging off the arm, but apparently Sir Tom did not notice his change of manner. He gestured the young people into their seats, held a chair for Helene to sit down and, when Arthur made a move toward a more distant seat, Sir Tom actually grasped his arm very firmly and insisted that his old friend take the seat right next to him.

Arthur was now diagonally across from Helene. No sooner had he pulled in his chair but he noticed that she was staring at him very hard. He sat back at ease and returned the stare coolly. He picked up his wine glass and tilted it in her direction, smiling in mocking salute, then drank a few drops. Helene attempted a matching smile but, then turned away, clearly discomfited.

Several times Sir Tom tried to get Helene's attention to ask her what was the matter, but she engaged herself in conversation with the gentleman on her right.

She has never looked lovelier, Sir Tom was thinking. Yet, he reflected, she had not seemed so nervous earlier in the evening but had been quite in command of herself despite everything he had told her. Earlier, as she greeted the guests, danced, talked to the children, there had been a rosy color in her cheeks that perfectly set off the cloth-of-silver gown she wore, a youthful flush that picked up the deep rich glow of the ruby necklace and the splendid crescent tiara of rubies set in the elegant high curls of her shimmering silver hair. But *now*... what had happened to upset her so? Her face had become white and drawn; her dark eyes held a haunted expression. Again he tried to get Helene's attention, to smile and reassure her that everything would be all right. But she did not turn around. Sir Tom glanced up at the clock on the mantel. It was just past midnight. Michael would be safely away by now, he judged. God speed, Michael, he thought.

"A pity the boys aren't here tonight," remarked Arthur suddenly. "Odd that Elizabeth's brother couldn't manage to put in an appearance for his sister's betrothal."

Sir Tom cast him an appraising look. "Don't be concerned,

Arthur," he said lightly enough, but there was a bit of an edge to his voice. "Rob would be with us if he could."

"Oh, indeed, indeed," replied Arthur testily. "But one wonders all the same. And young Ives . . . you did say he was traveling? On the Continent, wasn't it?"

"That's what I said, Arthur."

"Mmm," mumbled Arthur. "Yes, that's what I thought you said. But, y'know, Sir Tom, the eye plays strange tricks on a man. Now, speaking of young Ives—"

"We weren't, Arthur. Not really," said Sir Tom airily. "Have you tried some of the liver pâté? Helene tells me that—"

"I saw him not an hour ago!" Arthur blustered, "in this very house." He watched Sir Tom closely, trying to gauge the effect of his words. But he was soon disappointed.

"Him? Michael, you mean?" countered Sir Tom very smoothly, a small amused smile playing about his wide, good-humored mouth.

"Yes! Yes, of course!" snapped Arthur, losing patience quite soon with his game of cat and mouse. "I saw him upstairs in this house. I want you to tell me when he came back here, Sturbridge . . . and what is he going to do about the oath?" He realized that his voice was getting louder and louder, the overtones carrying a distance and several people seated around them glanced curiously at him and Sir Tom. He quickly lowered his tone.

"Damn it, Sturbridge," he continued tersely. "You promised me he'd be out of the way! Now you're keeping him here in secret . . . how long d'you think it will be before someone finds out? Then where will you be?"

Sir Tom looked at him with an easy, assured smile and only Arthur was close enough to see the implacable expression in those deep blue eyes.

"Arthur, you're on the verge of making a damned ass of yourself," he said. "Michael Ives is nowhere in this house. I assure you of that, on my word of honor. And, furthermore, I assure you he will not *be* in this house ever again."

The effort it cost Arthur Prescott to keep his voice down nearly choked him as he stared, eyes bulging, at the composed face of his host. "'ds blood, Sturbridge, but you push me too far!"

Sir Tom shook his head slowly. "No, Arthur," he murmured, "I simply tell you you are mistaken."

"You deny that Ives is here?" demanded Arthur hoarsely. "And do you also deny that he refuses to obey the law and take the oath required of him?''

Sir Tom paused, appearing to consider the question gravely. ''No. I think it's pretty clear to us all that Michael has consulted his conscience and concluded that, as a Roman Catholic, he cannot and ought not have any part of the thing. In consequence, he has removed himself from Spring Mount to avoid causing the family any embarrassment.''

'' 'Embarrassment'!'' Arthur ground his teeth in barely suppressed rage. ''Danger, you mean! Did you think we would not hear what has become of his Irish properties? The young fool's abandoned his family estates and done himself out of his inheritance all for the lack of a few words! What's a few words spoken before a magistrate and forgotten five minutes later? It was the *form* of the thing, Sturbridge, merely the form. *I* know—even Magistrate Gladden knows—there's no changing spots with Papists. Once a leopard, always a leopard, but the law must be satisfied.''

''I believe you've mixed your metaphors,'' remarked Sir Tom, quite unruffled. ''But now, Arthur, surely we can dismiss this subject? You asked me a question. I answered you, on my *honor*.'' A warning note came into his voice as he added, ''Any more would be . . . unfortunate.''

''You dare to threaten me, Sturbridge?'' breathed Arthur very hard. ''I saw what I saw. Nevertheless, it is not necessary for gentlemen to quarrel provided—'' he leaned very close and his own voice was full of menace—''provided there is basic agreement on the important issues.''

''Naturally, Arthur,'' said Sir Tom blithely. ''Now do finish your supper so we can proceed with the formalities. You *do* wish me to proceed?''

Arthur opened his mouth to say more, then changed his mind and nodded without another word. Time enough to say plenty later on, he promised himself, should the occasion arise. He said nothing else throughout the rest of the meal but sat in remote silence, waiting.

Farther along the table, Katherine Ives, too, was silent and sat staring down at her plate, unable to touch a bite of food. Indeed, only Elizabeth and Harry seemed oblivious to the atmosphere of growing tension around them. They held hands now and then as they sat side by side, and they both ate as if they had not seen food in a week.

At last the meal was over, and footmen cleared away the dessert plates while the maids set out dainty crystal dishes of rosewater, and fresh linen napkins. After the guests had rinsed their fingers, these too were removed and new wine goblets were brought to the table. Made of heavy silver, the goblets were engraved with the Sturbridge coat of arms on one side and the date and names of the betrothed couple on the other. The betrothal toast would be drunk from them and later the guests would take them home as memorial gifts of the evening.

Sir Tom got to his feet and was greeted by loud cheers and applause. One of the officers shouted a Dragoon battle cry and they all laughed, including their host. Then Sir Tom held up his hand for silence, waiting before he started to speak as the footmen hurried about filling the goblets with a rare, delicate Bavarian wine.

Helene clasped her cold hands together on her lap under the table, hoping no one would see how she was trembling. She looked up at her husband, her eyes glittering strangely, as though bedazzled by candlelight, and she could not see quite clearly for the painful throbbing in her head. She risked one quick glance at Prescott, noting gratefully that for once this evening he seemed to have forgotten all about her.

She saw at once that he was very angry. She shivered. What could Thomas have said to make him angry *now*, when it was imperative that his suspicions be set at rest?

"Dear friends," began Sir Tom, looking around at the faces smiling up at him. "One year from now, my daughter, Elizabeth, will become the wife of Harry Prescott. Tonight, as you know, marks the beginning of their betrothal. I ask you all now to stand with me, lift your glasses and toast the happiness and long life of these two dear children."

There was the noise of chairs scraping on the wood floor as they were pushed back and the guests stood up facing a blushing Elizabeth, a proud and somewhat embarrassed Harry. They all held up the gleaming goblets.

"To Elizabeth Sturbridge and to Harry Prescott, God bless them both and keep them always in His hand—Elizabeth and Harry, ladies and gentlemen!" And Sir Tom smiled at his daughter and drank her health, knowing as he did so it was all quite possibly a dream about to be shattered.

"Elizabeth and Harry, God bless them!" shouted dozens of glad voices, and the toast was done. There were more loud cheers and cries of "Good for you, Harry!" from some of the young men and then great applause as the betrothed couple stood up together and drank the health of all present and Harry said very quickly, with a shy smile, "You're all invited to the wedding!" and sat down again.

"And to the Christening a year later!" cried someone at the end of the room. More laughter and another burst of applause covered Harry's confusion, while Elizabeth blushed scarlet and lowered her eyes. But she, too, wore a broad smile all the same.

The great room began to rustle once more with renewed conversation until the guests realized that Sir Tom was still standing. They looked at him a bit puzzled, wondering what else he had to say to them. The talk died away quickly as everyone watched him expectantly, and Arthur Prescott leaned forward in his chair, alert and eager for every word that was to come.

"My friends, before we part tonight there are a few things I should very much like to say to you." His keen, penetrating gaze rested briefly, fondly on each face. The room was very still now. Even the footmen and the maids stopped their ceaseless motions about the table and stood quietly off to one side, listening to their master.

"We have been friends and neighbors all our lives, and our families for generations past. Each of you has, in your own way, demonstrated time and again those qualities of loyalty and friendship that make for good friends and good neighbors. I hope that I have done the same. You and I are not unique in this. We simply share a basic regard for one another, for one another's needs and rights. I have always believed . . . I *still* believe it is those qualities that have made England great among the nations of the world. Tonight, seeing these two young people so happy, seems an especially appropriate time to think about the good and happy things we share. God knows, my friends, our poor country has seen her share of unhappiness in modern times. Division, suspicion, hatred have managed to flourish too long among a people who, *left to their own devices*, are by nature generous and tolerant of each other—"

As they listened avidly to every word he said, Sir Tom's guests glanced uneasily at each other. There were a few hasty whispers here and there along the table. Jacobite friends sought each other's eyes, wondering where he was leading them, wishing he would bring it to an end. The Loyalists...and he had many friends among them...saw nothing whatever wrong in his remarks, yet they, too, began to feel uncomfortable and wished he had never started. "—so tonight I ask you to forget our differences, great or small though they may be, as I pray Englishmen everywhere must forget what divides them and remember, instead, what unites them into a great and powerful nation. We shall not long enjoy the world's respect or continue to command its admiration if we cannot show ourselves strong enough, wise enough to set our own house in order."

Get *to* it, thought Arthur in exasperation, get to your bloody damned point!

Here and there a low murmur of apprehension arose. The Jacobites sat on the edges of their chairs, beginning to wish they had never come.

"You who know me well know that I bear no ill will toward any man, for all men are, like myself, children of the same Father. But *no* man, however highly placed, has any claim upon the sovereign powers of the English people. No parliament, no church, no *King* may usurp or corrupt those sacred powers, and he who would seek to do so loses his right to rule. A king who consults with his people to discover *their* will and then does his best to carry it out is truly fulfilling the 'divine' right to rule. This my father taught me and this do I faithfully believe with my whole heart and have taught my own son."

He had said the dread word "King." There were muttered exclamations in the dining room, a few men jumped up only to be plucked on the sleeves by their wives and embarrassed into sitting down again. Helene prayed it would be over soon, soon. . . .

"But any ruler needs the trust and support of his subjects." Sir Tom glanced down at Arthur with a tiny, enigmatic smile. "I believe that it is time for Englishmen everywhere to put aside their differences and heal the wounds that divide them. Above and beyond what fealty we owe to our sovereign lord, the King, we owe our full loyalty and allegience to England. Kings, like ourselves, are children of the hour. They—and we—come and stay a short time and are gone. But the nation, England, remains, our mother, our inspiration and our chiefest purpose in life. Such is the obligation of our honor and the glory of our existence. . . ."

Arthur Prescott stood up. "High-blown words, Sturbridge! Say your piece, man, and say it clear!"

Everyone stared at him as if he had gone mad. Harry stood up, too, his mouth working but nothing came out. Sir Tom paused to look Arthur full in the face and then he nodded briskly, as if nothing untoward had happened, as if he were somehow grateful to Arthur for reminding him of something he had overlooked.

"Arthur is quite right, my friends," he said very mildly. "There is a point to all this and I have come to it. I am going to offer one more toast this evening. I would ask that you do not join me, it is a private matter and, I am informed, a thing urgently required of me. Therefore, remain in your seats, offer what toasts you will when I have done."

He motioned one of the footmen to him and had the man pour more wine into his goblet. Then he picked it up and said, "I drink the health of my motherland, England, which unhappy nation possesses no more loving and loyal son than myself—"

"The King, Sturbridge, the *King*, damn it!" hissed Arthur through gritted teeth. He ignored the frantic look on Harry's face and he cared nothing that little Elizabeth looked about to faint.

"Yes. The King," repeated Sir Tom gravely. "Ladies and gentlemen, His Majesty, the King, God bless him. God help him!" And he drank deeply from the silver goblet while they all watched him, stunned.

"Which king, Sir Tom?" shouted one of the Jacobites furiously.

"Shame, sir, shame!" came a dozen outraged voices. They were all on their feet now, looking uncertainly at Sir Tom.

"Yes, Sturbridge, tell us," demanded Arthur. "Which king, by God?"

"Do you not know your own king?" asked Sir Tom coldly. He looked out at the panicky crowd about him and, with a disarming smile, he asked, "Does any man here not know who is the King of England? I drank the health of His Majesty, the King. But if you, Arthur, say that is the health of any *other* man on earth, why then, I believe you come dangerously close to speaking *treason!*"

The guests looked at each other, confused, and then someone laughed a trifle hysterically. The laughter spread. Their sense of relief was enormous and, privately, his Jacobite friends thought Sir Tom had brought it off quite cleverly—whatever it was he had brought off. They enjoyed seeing Arthur Prescott shown up as the ponderous ass he was. Many of the gentlemen there were still not quite sure what had just happened but skilled hands that had flown swiftly to sword hilts in those few tense moments now reached out to encircle more innocent metal as the silver goblets were filled again.

But Arthur remained where he stood, eye to eye with Sir Tom, who gazed on him with an openly sardonic smile. Arthur could not meet that steady gaze for long. He dropped his eyes, struggling to find the right words to convey his disgust and disappointment. And, as he looked down at the table, at the place where Sir Tom had set down his empty goblet, Arthur noticed that the heavy white linen napkin belonging to his host had been crumpled carelessly and thrown down over a forgotten dish. Arthur's hand reached out, his fingers touched the linen cloth and he snatched it away, clear of the table.

There, underneath the napkin, was Sir Tom's crystal finger bowl, still half-full of scented rosewater. Sir Tom had stood up to drink the health of England's King—over the water! Arthur threw the napkin down, his little eyes darting furiously from Sir Tom over to Helene and then to his son, Harry.

"There is nothing so stupid, Sturbridge, as a man who tries too hard to be clever," he sneered, pointing down at the rosewater bowl.

"And if I told you that dish had merely been forgotten?" asked Sir Tom, his smile fading into an expression of contempt.

"'Forgotten'?" countered Arthur. "On your honor?"

Sir Tom's eyes blazed with fury. He lifted his left hand and slapped Arthur Prescott across the face in front of everyone. Helene screamed, then pressed the back of her hand against her mouth, staring at the two of them, horrified. Harry hastened to his father's side, picking up the same inoffensive linen napkin Arthur had just thrown down and tried to wipe away the trickle of blood that was oozing from the corner of his mouth. But Arthur pushed him away, cursing, then held on to him tightly at arm's length by his side.

"There is no more to be said," declared Arthur heatedly. "Any business between you and me is finished here, Sturbridge. . . ."

"No!" screamed Elizabeth. Helene went to her and put her arms around the stunned girl. Harry looked at his father and Sir Tom as if they had both lost their minds.

"Father!" he began pleadingly but got no further. Arthur glowered at him and Sir Tom looked at him very sadly.

"I apologize to *you*, Harry," he said. "I am truly sorry to have spoiled this happy time for you."

"Enough! Enough, Sturbridge," blustered Arthur. I trust your much employed 'honor' will stretch itself so far as my satisfaction!"

Sir Tom turned back to him with disgust. "Oh, Arthur, Arthur, you do try me so! Very well. I will have my representative call upon you tomorrow afternoon. Please arrange the time and place entirely at your convenience."

"Thomas, this has gone far enough!" cried Helene, pale with anger and fright. "Do you forget, we have guests?"

The dining room was in a state of confusion. The ladies were hurrying out to find their wraps and their maids; the gentlemen came crowding up around the two angry men, trying to persuade them to settle their grievances without bloodshed.

"Blood has already been shed," said Arthur stiffly. "*My* blood."

"Father, for God's sake, can't you—?" begged Harry helplessly.

"You and I are leaving this house now. At once. Come with me," commanded his father, pulling him by the arm like a child. Harry broke free of him and went to Elizabeth.

"Harry, do as he says now," whispered Helene. "I'm sure there will be no duel. Tomorrow they will both have cooled their tempers. Just go now, will you, my dear?"

"Harry!" cried Elizabeth, trying to seize his hand. But Arthur rushed him right past her and out through the mass of scattering guests before he could touch her or say a single word. Elizabeth buried her face in Helene's breast, weeping.

Sir Tom watched the Prescotts leave, without saying a word, then turned to his friends.

"It had to be," was all he said.

"The man's a fool, Sir Tom, not worth your trouble," said one of the young officers.

"Tom, what good will you do our cause now if Prescott should wound you?" One of the Jacobites, an elderly, worried-looking gentleman, came very close and spoke in low, urgent tones.

Sir Tom shook his head. "There is no cause now, Percy. I'd meant to ask a few of you to wait after the ball. I have had news from France. He will not—" but, still loyal, he changed it quickly— "he cannot come."

His friend looked stricken. "Then we are finished," he said.

Sir Tom's face remained impassive. There were too many about to say much more.

"Percy, tell the others for me. And, under the circumstances, I believe it's best you leave at once."

"What about you?"

Sir Tom embraced the elderly gentleman gently, murmuring, "We will survive. See you do the same, my friend!"

Percy hurried away and spoke to their other friends, who left quickly, with no farewells. Most of the other guests had sent for their coaches and waited outside on the front steps or just inside the doorway. Several of Helene's friends tried to comfort her and her daughter but, with Katherine's help she led the weeping girl away quickly.

Sir Tom watched them go, knowing he must soon speak to Elizabeth and tell her what the others already knew . . . and more than that, something he alone knew now.

"Helene," he called after her, "I will come to you in a little while."

Helene turned back to look at him from the doorway and it stabbed him to the heart to see the only angry look she had ever had for him.

"Thomas," she said coolly, "was this necessary? You did not have to let it go so far! You did not need to anger Arthur Prescott, not now, not with what we have ahead of us!"

"It was necessary, Helene," he replied. "Later I will tell—" but she had turned on her heel and left him.

Sir Tom stayed another half hour downstairs, seeing his startled and bewildered guests out, then he stood watching the last of their clattering carriages drive away into the darkness. The Dragoons offered to a man to stay with him if they could be of any service but he sent them away, too. They rode off together, wondering aloud what it had all been about, fully determined to come back tomorrow and stand by their commander.

When everyone was gone at last and the musicians paid and packed off unceremoniously in two wagons, Sir Tom went to speak to Mrs. Jessup and Mrs. Curley for a while. The two women heard him out without interruption, but when he had finished and turned away to go upstairs, they were both clinging to each other and crying.

Sir Tom headed for his own rooms to find Helene, but he heard voices farther down the hall, from Elizabeth's room, and went there instead, knocking lightly at the closed door. He could still hear his daughter weeping, Helene crooning to her, Katherine trying to reassure her.

Katherine opened the door to him, her great grey eyes wide with grief and apprehension. Across the room, Helene was sitting on Elizabeth's bed, beginning to unbutton the lovely betrothal gown. She looked up when he came in, her dark eyes accusing and, like Katherine's, filled with grief.

"No, don't undress her," Sir Tom said in a voice so peculiar that Helene's hands fell to her lap and Elizabeth turned around, curiosity momentarily overcoming her distraction.

"Why not?" asked Helene. "The poor child is exhausted, Thomas, she needs to rest. It has been a sorry night indeed. . . ."

"Indeed," he answered her very shortly. "Forgive me, but I must speak with all of you at once."

"Oh, Thomas, could it not wait until the morning? Explain it to us then, but we are all—"

"Helene," his voice rose sharply. "Enough, please. We must leave here now, tonight. By tomorrow morning we must be far away from Spring Mount. There is no time to pack or to change your clothing. Take your jewel cases and a warm cloak, each of you, and come downstairs as soon as you can. I have spoken to the servants. Mrs. Jessup is sending a boy to get Father McGuire and Ralph. The others will be waiting for us down in the hall."

"Now?" faltered Helene, her lips white. "Thomas, tell me, is it because of Arthur Prescott and the duel?"

A ghost of a smile flitted across his face. "The duel is a farce, my love. It will never happen, that's what I wanted to tell you."

The anger and accusation disappeared from her ashen face as she went to him and hugged him very hard. "Forgive me, Thomas. It was just that I could not understand why you would go out of your way to antagonize Arthur *now*, with all that there is at stake."

"Nor would I have done it, dearest, but I have tried to gain us a bit more time. Katherine, won't you go to your room now and prepare to leave, please?"

Katherine, who had been listening intently to every word he said, started suddenly, then nodded her head and left them together.

266

Elizabeth did not move but sat upright on the bed, her face set and stony.

"Elizabeth, do as your father bids you. Take your jewel case, find your warmest wrap and meet us downstairs," Helene commanded her daughter, then she and Sir Tom hastened back to their own rooms.

Sir Tom was still examining the barrel of one of the pistols when Helene sat down to wait for him, her jewel case on her lap.

"Now tell me, Thomas," she said calmly. "Why can we not wait as you said this afternoon? What happened downstairs between you and Arthur?"

"He saw Michael," Sir Tom answered, pulling the plug from his powder cask to check the amount inside. "It was an accident, I suppose. Arthur was furious, guessed right off that we were hiding Michael here. The more I thought about it, the more uneasy I felt. It wouldn't have taken Arthur very long to realize he was placing himself in a damned compromising position if anyone found out he knew Michael was here and didn't say anything."

"But still, he waited," said Helene, puzzled. "He sat there and waited for you to make that speech. If you *had* gone along with him on that, wouldn't he have kept quiet, wouldn't that have satisfied him?"

"No," Sir Tom shook his head. "Knowing Arthur, it would not. I thought at first he would leave the house right away, to get the authorities to come back with him and search until they found Michael. I suppose the only thing that kept him here then was waiting for what I would say. I delayed as long as I could, until I was sure Michael was on his way to Gravesend. If I had pledged Dutch Billy in my own blood, believe me, my dear, Arthur would still have left the ball and gone straight to Magistrate Gladden with his information about Michael. I didn't know what to do, I had to find some way to keep him away from Gladden just another few hours, just until tomorrow evening. So, I deliberately provoked this fraud of a duel."

"And Arthur will sit and wait to hear from you tomorrow afternoon," said Helene, at last understanding him fully.

He threw her fur cloak over her shoulders. "I believe so. When he does not hear anything, he will send someone to inquire. They will find we have gone. *Then* Arthur will hurry to the Magistrate

267

with his tale of woe. By that time, with God's help, we shall be far from here indeed.''

They left the room without looking back and walked quickly along the deep carpeted hallway to the staircase, still arrayed in twining ropes of holly and tall jars of pine and fir and roses. Only a single sputtering candle burned in a wall sconce near the stairs; the rest of the house seemed wrapped about in darkness and whispering silence. The scent of the flowers and greens was overpowering now, cloying to the nostrils. They hurried past the decorations that had lasted past need for lasting, past even remembrance in the face of what was happening now. Once Helene stopped, put her hand out and touched his arm to steady herself and she asked him, ''What shall we do if there is no ship?''

''We shall take whatever comes our way,'' he assured her. ''There are boats passing Gravesend every day, bound all around the world.''

Bound all around the world, she thought numbly, and suddenly she leaned against him in the darkness, trembling uncontrollably. But *this* is my world, she felt like screaming, I am bound about by this world I love, how can I leave it? And then she was acutely aware of his tall, solid presence next to her. Why, *he* is my world, she realized, almost laughing aloud. He and my children, wherever they are, that is the boundary of my world and all I ever need of the world. She leaned her head against his shoulder another moment, and then continued down the stairs into the dark hall below.

Just as they reached the hall and sensed the movement of other people about them, they heard the nervous whinnying of a horse outside and then the unmistakable sound of hoofbeats driving down the gravel road, heading away from the house.

''Strike a light here, somebody,'' called out Sir Tom impatiently. A second later another candle was lit and they could see it held in Meg's hands, lighting up her plump, scared face.

''Who was on that horse?'' Sir Tom demanded, looking around at the little group assembled there. There were whispers, people looking at each other, squinting in the dim light as they tried to see. And then, from the shadows, came Katherine's voice like a hollow echoing in the emptiness.

''Where is Elizabeth?'' she asked.

''Thomas! Oh my God, where *is* she?'' cried Helene frantically.

''I seen her just a minute ago, my lady,'' said Alice faintly. ''I come in with my cloak and she were standin' here already. Then I went back to fetch Nellie—she *would* lose her heavy shoes and have to look about for 'em—and when I come back just now, Miss Elizabeth was gone. I . . . I thought she was with you!"

"It's Harry!" said Helene. "She's gone to him! She'll never leave without him, I told you that, Thomas!"

"I'm sure he would gladly come with her," said Sir Tom slowly, but he sounded worried.

"Well, then, send someone after her and tell her that!"

"If she reaches the Prescott's Arthur will surely see her. He'll find out what we are doing," said Katherine.

"I'll go, sir," said old Ralph, who had been standing quietly next to Father McGuire all the while.

"Yes, do, Ralph," said Sir Tom. "Try to catch her before she gets to Prescott's house."

"And then should I bring herself and Master Harry back together?"

"Well, of course, Ralph," said Helene.

"No, just Miss Elizabeth," said Sir Tom, with a sigh. Helene turned to him indignantly. "My dear, *think*. Arthur cannot have any warning of what we plan to do."

"But, Thomas, it will break her heart!"

"She can write to him, Helene, once we are safe away, and you know Harry—he's the kind of young man who'll follow her and find her, even in America. Hurry, Ralph, she can't have gone too far in this loose snow."

Ralph left then and a few minutes later they heard the sound of his horse galloping down the drive.

"Father, are you all right?" asked Sir Tom, going to greet the old priest. Father McGuire had been awakened out of a sound sleep not half an hour before and sat, fully dressed and completely awake, calmly saying his Rosary.

"Right and ready," he replied lightly.

"It will be a hard journey, Father," said Sir Tom dubiously. "Can you ride a horse?"

He was startled to hear the old man's high-pitched laugh in that dark room. "Can I ride a horse? Young man, how can you be askin' an Irishman a question like that? I rode without saddle nor bridle before I could read or write. I may ache something considerable tomorrow this time, but I'll make it there, never fear!"

". . . awful and sinful, houndin' holy priests of God like they was animals!" came Meg's wavering tones, full of suppressed fury.

"What shall we do now, Thomas?" asked Helene in a low voice. "It may take some time before Elizabeth comes back. Are we ready to go?"

"The horses are saddled out back in the courtyard, my lady," said Mrs. Jessup. "Once't you are gone, the rest of us plan to leave before mornin'. From what Sir Tom says, it won't be safe to be found here. Oh, Mum," she broke down suddenly, sobbing softly. "To think on it! No more Sturbridges at Spring Mount that alwuz was here since anyone remembers! What's to become on us all?"

Several of the other women began to weep then and Helene looked around her, heartbroken. Ever since she was a young bride these people had surrounded her with kindness and service, had nursed her and her children and shared their lives. She tried to speak to them, but the words would not come.

"Now, now, now," said the priest suddenly, standing up. "None of that, ladies. We'll all meet again someday in a place we can't be taken from and all the runnin' and the tears will be forgotten. I'll tell you what, I'm going to say a little prayer for all of us right now . . . and you Protestants, you, too, Sir Tom, Lady Helene, feel free to join in if you will, because I'm only speakin' to the one Savior and twasn't Himself divided Christians up into parcels!"

Father McGuire stood in the midst of them there in the dark hall, and Meg held the candle very steady indeed at his side. Mrs. Curley and old Mrs. Grace got down on their knees and Mrs. Curley, glancing up at her daughter, clucked her tongue and pulled red-haired Nellie down beside her as the old man began to pray.

And Helene, with Katherine at her side, fell to her knees and clasped her hands together, the old soft Irish voice spoke sweetly in the shadows of Spring Mount and Helene begged God to bring her daughter safely back, and soon.

Outside, across the crisp fine snow, the shadow of the Christmas moon moved slowly on, shepherding the lingering stars along their way, leaving the sky blank and empty, neither dark nor bright, like a clear clean path for the riding in of the morning star.

TEN

"Raven Days"

1 Spring Mount Beseiged

The brooding blankness of the night's face presented itself to the Magistrate no different than it ever was. If any man could be said not to have noticed that there was a moon, that there were stars in all existence, surely that man was he. His nights, like his days, were mere expanses of time and space in which to carry out his various carefully measured allowances for life: so much time for books, so much for sitting in his courtroom, so much for the single meal he ate each evening, so much for prayer, his barren prayers never heard, never heeded, yet he prayed on, "religiously," as one would say, but long ago he had stopped waiting for an answer.

The Magistrate allowed some time for sleeping, too, yet he was a man who rarely slept. He drew his frantic energies from some source deep within himself rather than from food or sleep as other men did, he consumed himself in his own complicated entrails and would one day die of being himself and for no other cause anyone could determine. Of course no physician would dare publish abroad such opinions for fear of being called a witch. Yet, even now, if a physician were to have studied the Magistrate only a short time—and the Magistrate allowed no time for such frivolity—he would conclude that Gladden burned with a fever that was not earthly nor physical, a fever of the spirit which made him sick indeed and full of pain and for which he himself had lost the cure.

Tonight, as the beautiful moon sped away, Magistrate Gladden sat in his hard wood chair by a low fire and pondered the cases he would hear in the morning. He was surprised to hear an urgent knocking downstairs at his front door, but he ignored it. There was a man below whose business it was to answer that door.

Eventually, the knocking ceased but there was a commotion down below, voices, then footsteps on the stairs. The Magistrate put aside his notes and stood up. In another moment his own private door was assailed. He called out "Enter," and his man appeared, in his nightshirt, followed closely by Arthur Prescott, out of breath and out of patience.

"Damn it, Gladden, I have business with you! Kindly inform this cretin of yours—"

"Go to bed, Samuel," said the Magistrate quietly, and the man left at once, shutting the door behind him. "What is it, Prescott?"

Arthur sat down heavily, reached out to warm his hands at the fireplace, then looked away, disgusted. "I thought I would wait until tomorrow, but I changed my mind," he said rather incoherently.

The Magistrate sat down again upon his wooden chair and waited.

"It's Sturbridge," Arthur went on, now rubbing his hands for want of a fire. The Magistrate did not offer to kindle one.

"Sturbridge. Yes?"

"He's got Ives—Michael Ives, hidden away in that house, no intention in the world of getting him into town to appear before you. I saw him myself, tonight, at the ball."

"The betrothal ball," said the Magistrate, who liked to have all the facts laid out precisely.

"'Betrothal'! That's a good one, sir! There's no betrothal now. My Harry'll never marry that stick of a Sturbridge girl! I was going to come here at once, as soon as I saw Ives there."

"But you did not."

"No, no, I waited. Don't you remember, Sturbridge had promised me he would publicly pledge his loyalty to King William, drink a toast to him before all his damned Jacobite friends?"

"He did not do so?"

"He drank a toast all right," thundered Arthur, "but not to King William! He had a bowl of water hidden under his wineglass."

"Not that again," sighed the Magistrate, somewhat bored. "That sounds little like Sir Thomas Sturbridge."

"You are mistaken, sir. That sounds exactly like Sir Thomas Sturbridge! Anyway, I accused him. He insulted me. There was nothing to do but to settle it honorably."

"'Honorably'?" repeated the Magistrate faintly, wishing Arthur would get to the point.

"Yes, and then I took Harry and went home. But when I got there, I began to think—"

"At last!" murmured Gladden, but Arthur did not hear him.

"The more I thought about it, the more certain I was that I ought to come here and tell you about Michael Ives being back at Spring Mount.''

"I know," said Gladden. "I could have detained him in Bristol, but I did not."

"You let him go?"

"So far as he wished to go, no farther. Tell me, did Sturbridge deny that his ward was there?"

"Indeed he did! Swore to me the boy was not in the house—went so far as to say that Ives would never be in that house again! Liar!"

Gladden looked at him, suddenly very alert. "*Did* he? And did he swear it on his honor, I wonder?"

Arthur barked a choppy little laugh. "Oh, of course, on his honor! The damned hypocrite!"

"But if Ives were *not* there anymore?" mused Gladden to himself.

"Damme, sir, he *is* there, I told you I saw him with my own eyes!"

"Be quiet! Now . . . he returned only this afternoon. You saw him tonight, during the ball. When did you mention it to Sir Thomas?"

"When? Why—why when we were at supper, I suppose."

"Some time later, I would presume," said Gladden, his voice a trifle more eager than usual. "Tell me, when you saw the young man, did you get a good look at him? What was he doing? How was he dressed?"

"By God, Gladden, I don't know!" protested Arthur, but one look from those icy grey eyes and he began to think very hard. "Well, he was upstairs, in one of the bedrooms, just opening the door to let a maid out with a food tray. She dropped the tray and he came out into the hall to help her pick it up. That's all. Then he went back into the room."

"He was attired for sleeping?"

"No, he was dressed, completely dressed, even wore boots, come to think of it . . . and, gad, I remember he had on a riding cloak, I thought perhaps he'd only just come!"

"Or perhaps was only just leaving?"

"What, off again? Where to?"

Gladden rose to his feet and rang a little bell to summon his servant. "That is what I would very much like to know, Master Prescott. To let the spider run about in a web of my own making is one thing and he is easily pulled in on my thread when I want him.

But, if my spider has decided to slip loose of the web, I must have him at once. I did not think he would leave again so soon. My mistake. I shall not make another. I see I must go after him now and pull him in. Good night to you, Master Prescott, and sleep well, I do not think you will have to fight a duel tomorrow. Or any time.''

"B—but, what will you do? What about Sir Thomas?''

Gladden opened the door and motioned Arthur to leave.

"Sir Thomas Sturbridge will go to the scaffold. Eventually. He knows now his cause is lost, the Pretender will not come to England. He will have spread word of this to his Jacobite friends by now, they will all be running for cover. I want them, all of them. And I risk nothing now in taking them. King William's position is firm, he is in no danger of toppling from his throne. I act the necessary part of the vulture, only following behind to pick off what remains. Good night, Master Prescott. I shall not forget what you told me.''

Arthur soon found himself back on his horse with the whole wearying trip home ahead of him and not even so much as a thank you for all his trouble. And he dreaded what he would meet at home. Harry, for all he was a quiet, unobtrusive boy, possessed a remarkable streak of stubbornness. Arthur sighed and picked up the reins. Harry would be there, wide awake, with a hundred arguments, a thousand reproaches. And he would insist upon marrying Elizabeth, come what may.

Although Arthur did not know it then, Harry was not at home waiting for him. Harry had gone straight to his own chambers, packed a few warm clothes, gotten his secret horde of money together and come down again. He thought of leaving a letter for his father, then decided against it and, taking a fresh horse from the stables, he rode the long way round, over the hills and through the little forest, past the stream where he had spent such happy hours with Elizabeth, through the deserted fields and along the forgotten, neglected lane with its crumbling stone fences . . . he rode the long way round to Spring Mount, to find Elizabeth and take her away with him. There was no hope of a marriage as they had planned it now, he knew that quite well. Their only chance to be together lay in getting away, finding a little church where they were not known and, once they were wed, going as far from home as they could, maybe even up north into Scotland.

When he found the entrance to the lane, Harry dismounted and walked the horse quietly another twenty yards, then tethered him to a stout tree and continued on foot alone, moving stealthily toward the house.

He saw the great house looming up against the pale snow, blending into the vague black face of the sky. There were no lights showing. He moved cautiously around the outside of the house, looking hopefully at the tall ground-floor windows. None of them was open. He would have to circle around the front and go through the courtyard to the back door. He walked carefully onto the gravel drive and started to pass by the front entranceway when he noticed a tiny, flickering light in one of the front windows.

Harry stopped and looked again. Yes, there was a light, a small one . . . someone was still up inside. He stooped down and worked his way to a window, then raised his head quickly and peered inside. What he saw, as his eyes gradually picked out objects in the faint glow of the candle, was a small group of people dressed for the outdoors, all apparently gathered around one man with white hair. Some of them were kneeling down, he realized, and in the same instant that he was able to recognize the white-haired man as Father McGuire, he saw Sir Tom standing next to Lady Helene, both of them wearing heavy fur wraps. Harry looked closer, seeing Katherine Ives by the priest, picking out the familiar faces of the servants. But Elizabeth, he wondered, where was Elizabeth?

He stood up straight, prepared to present himself at the front door. Whatever was happening, his romantic plan to steal away secretly with Elizabeth was clearly impossible now. Suddenly Meg spotted him through the glass. The candle wavered frantically in her hand as she stared and shrieked at the top of her lungs. The others all turned to look in alarm, then Sir Tom realized it was Harry and opened the front door to let him come in.

"Harry, I'm glad you are here!" he said, quite relieved. Then, looking over Harry's shoulder as if he expected to see someone else, he said, "Then Elizabeth must have—"

"Elizabeth!" cried Harry, quite distressed. "Where is she?"

Sir Tom stared at him in dismay. "I thought you had come with her," he said, his voice flat. "She rode out a while ago; we assumed she went to you."

"No, no, she's not with me, I haven't seen her," said Harry. "I came the back way, through the woods. But, tell me—"

"Then she will go straight to your house," reflected Sir Tom slowly. "She will see Arthur. Harry, your father *is* at home, isn't he?"

Harry looked surprised. "Well, I expect so. We returned together. I was in a hurry and I didn't want to argue with him and I knew the minute we got back into the house we'd both be at it hot and heavy. So I left him down at the stables."

"Did you see him after that? Inside the house? Did you hear him come in after you?"

"N—no, come to think of it, I didn't see him. And I wouldn't have heard him. I was upstairs, in the other wing, getting some things together. I just took it for granted he'd gone off to bed. But, why do you ask? What difference does it make if Elizabeth sees him tonight?"

Sir Tom looked at the young man with deep sympathy. "Harry, you know what happened in this house this evening. You know, that is, what you *saw*. But there is much more to it. Forgive me for speaking ill of your father, but I believe he intends to have me arrested. It's a complicated situation and for all our sakes, I am taking my family away from Spring Mount. I had hoped we would be safely gone before he discovered our absence."

"You were going to take Elizabeth away? Without a single word to me? Why? Did you think *I* would betray you?" Harry looked at him in bitter reproach. "Sir Tom, wherever Elizabeth goes, I will be with her. We belong to each other. That's why I was coming here to get her. We just want to be together and out of all this political trouble."

"You're a good lad, Harry," Sir Tom smiled. "We sent one of the servants after her. If he can catch up with her before she gets to your father's house everything will be all right. But, if she reaches Arthur first—"

"Let me go after her, Sir Tom! I can make it look as though we had just planned to elope tonight. He need not find out about the rest of you."

"I am loath to let you go again, Harry. I expect Ralph will reach her before she sees your father. If you go off and miss her, we cannot wait much longer, my boy. We have made arrangements for a ship—"

"A *ship*?"

"Yes, a ship. We are leaving England, Harry."

"For France? Elizabeth told me you might—"

"No. Not France." Sir Tom's face twisted unpleasantly. "America. Harry, wait here with us for a little while. I'm sure it will not be long. In the meantime, I will go and have a final word with the men. I am sending them away from here tonight." He turned to look at the others. "Those of you who are not going with us, please say your good-byes now and slip away as quietly as you can. I do not think it will be wise to wait even until morning. Mrs. Jessup, are you ready?"

The housekeeper nodded. "Me and Mrs. Grace 'ere is goin' to my sister's. Let us take one of the wagons, it's a fair distance, Sir Tom."

"Of course," he nodded, but he looked at old Mrs. Grace in surprise. "I thought everyone from Kilbree would be going with us."

Mrs. Grace wheezed with emotion, shaking her head as she clutched at her daughter's hand. "Nay, Sir Tom, but I'd not live to see dry land again... I'm too old to be tossin' about on the big sea with all of you! But I want my Nell to go and she don't want to leave me. *You* talk to her, Sir Tom. You tell Nellie 'tis the best thing and she must go to serve Master Michael and Miss Katherine. Talk to the girl, Lady Helene, for 'tis disrespectful thick-headed she is and don't listen to nothin' *I* say nor never did!"

Sir Tom looked at Helene, who came forward and spoke to red-headed Nellie quite gravely.

"Nellie, for once in your life, will you do as your mother asks?" said Helene, and, for once in her life, Nellie had the good sense to keep her mouth shut, lower her eyes and nod agreeably. Helene squeezed her hand affectionately. Mrs. Grace smiled through her tears and rested her old head on tall Nellie's ample bosom.

Sir Tom left them there, heading out to the back of the house to make sure the horses were quite ready and to say a few words to the footmen and grooms, the gardeners and the stableboys who had been told earlier to pack up and clear out.

Harry looked at Helene, a worried little smile playing about his mouth, then went back to the window and looked outside, praying for the sight of Elizabeth riding homeward. He stood there restlessly, terribly conscious of the minutes passing faster and faster while he, all of them, could do nothing but wait.

There was a hazy light outside now, the beginning of the long grey before-dawn time of night. The only truly clear object in the heavens was the morning star staring down unblinking from a point over the black hills. Behind him, in the dark room, Harry felt the silence of the others as a presence weighing heavily on his consciousness. Only the rapid, barely audible praying of the old Catholic priest, the occasional muffled sobs of Meg broke into that oppressive stillness.

Elizabeth, his heart cried out in mute pleading, Elizabeth, my love, come back soon!

And then he saw something his eye had missed only a moment before. He had been scanning the grounds for sight of her, but had not thought to look so far away as the main road that stretched out far below the house. Now, just where the road passed by the cutoff into the Spring Mount driveway, down by the gates, Harry noticed a large black mass of something, something remaining fairly stationary at the gates. At first he could not make out any details of the thing, but, squinting narrowly through the windowpane, he gradually observed that the thing seemed to have parts to it, it had movement . . . and, in a few shattering seconds more, he saw very clearly that what he was looking at was a group of horses, horses without riders. Apparently they had been tethered at the gates and now stood, well trained and patient, silhouetted black against the sky. But where were the men who rode them?

Not realizing he had allowed a startled sound to escape his lips, Harry dropped down automatically and squatted by the window, his gaze searching frantically along the sides of the winding drive, trying to spot those missing riders.

But Helene had heard him and hurried to the window, looking down at him fearfully. Harry reached out and gave her a little push, which moved her away from the glass, against the wall next to it so she could not be seen from outside. Just as he started to explain about the horses, he saw what he had been looking for: a score or more of cavalry troops just beyond the front entrance, moving quickly out from the dense cover of the trees and thickets on either side of the drive.

"Harry! What is it?" breathed Helene.

Trying not to alarm the others, he nodded wordlessly. Helene dropped to her knees next to him and peered out, keeping her head down.

"Oh, God!" she moaned. "Too late! Too late!"

"What do they want?" asked Harry, somewhat bewildered.

Behind him came Katherine's voice. "They want my brother," she said. "I think they will tear the house apart to find him." She looked out with a steady gaze, watching the soldiers as they approached the entrance.

"Sweet Lord Jesus!" cried Meg softly. "They'll find Father McGuire here! Oh, they'll kill you, Father! They'll kill us all!"

"Meg, be quiet!"

Katherine's voice was hard, shockingly icy. The terrified maid whimpered.

"Aunt Helene, we shall have to get out to the horses," said Katherine.

"We cannot hope to outride them," answered Helene. "And they would only follow us straight to Michael . . . and to Rob. Somehow we shall have to make a fight of it—"

"Well spoken, my love!" It was Sir Tom and with him came eight or nine of the Spring Mount men. "Into the study, Bailey, you'll find the guns on the wall there." One of the men hurried away down the hall while the others, moving cautiously, spread themselves out from window to window. Sir Tom handed one of his pistols to Harry, then he spoke to the women.

"Now listen to me carefully," he said, his voice calm and unhurried. "Remain quiet, whatever happens. No tears . . . Meg, no screaming. Mrs. Jessup, be ready when I tell you. Go out through the back, don't stop for anything, don't even look back. Get to the horses. We will force them back from here and come after you. Helene knows where to go. . . ."

Suddenly there was a great booming thud at the front door, the careless shout of men's voices, the stomping of heavy-booted feet on the stairs.

"Thomas!" Helene ran to him and threw her arms about him.

Sir Tom clasped her tightly to him and kissed her, whispering, "Courage, my darling. And remember, whatever happens here, you must follow through with what we have planned, all of it, do you understand? Don't fail, Helene! Promise me!"

Dazed, her heart pounding at a wild pace, Helene nodded, but in truth she had hardly heard his words and the meaning of them quite escaped her. She felt him push her away from him. Alice reached out and took her hand, and together all of them listened as the pounding at the door grew louder, two, possibly three of the soldiers using the wooden stocks of their muskets to break through the latch.

Bailey reappeared from the direction of the study, his arms full of Sir Tom's fine flintlock fowling pieces and three or four long-barreled pistols. Silently he distributed the weapons to the other men at the windows. Sir Tom tossed a small brass powder flask to Harry.

"I've more when you need it," he said. Harry nodded, turning to face the door. And suddenly Helene screamed.

"Elizabeth! She'll come back, right into the midst of this!" She looked at Harry, her eyes full of horror, and he shuddered.

"I've got to get her, got to warn her away!" he cried. Sir Tom considered briefly, then nodded.

"All right. We'll force them to fall back and look for cover outside. When the others go, you go with them, take one of the horses and find her. But don't come back, whatever you do. Ride to Gravesend, Harry. We'll meet you there, please God!"

The heavy oak door shuddered under the pressure of repeated smashing blows. Sir Tom placed himself at a window facing out toward the front steps. "Be ready," he told the men. They crouched down, taking aim at the soldiers. Very deliberately he raised his pistol, holding it steady with his crippled hand . . . "Now," he said. "Fire!"

At once a volley of gunfire burst from every window in the front hall of Spring Mount. Two soldiers were hit and lay where they had fallen. The others shouted furiously and fell back, heading for the trees. The pounding at the door ceased abruptly. Sir Tom turned swiftly to Helene.

"Now, go. Go quickly! Harry, God-speed, my boy!"

Helene picked up her small black case and moved on soundless feet into the dining room, calling behind her, "Katherine, hurry!" But as she went, she heard the sound of answering gunfire from outside the house; someone screamed, there was a sound of glass smashing, more shots from the men in the next room. Helene stopped and turned back, thinking she was mad to leave Thomas, mad even to think of it. As she hurriedly retraced her steps, she encountered Alice coming after her. Alice took one look at her face and grabbed her hand, pulling her back into the dining room, ignoring her protests. They ran through the darkened ruins of the betrothal feast whose tables had not even been cleared away yet . . . Helene moved mechanically, one foot swiftly after another, without will or purpose, dragged along by Alice, passing now into the serving pantry, through another door, a dozen doors, she lost

280

count and all sense of direction, moving faster and faster. Behind her she was dimly aware of footsteps, harsh and hurried breathing, someone bumping into something in the shadows . . . she could not look back to see who it was.

Finally they reached the kitchen. She stumbled, almost falling as Alice raced for the back door, letting go of her hand for the moment. Again they heard the sound of guns and the awful insistent renewal of the pounding at the door. Helene stood still in the darkness, trying to catch her breath, then she turned as footsteps came nearby.

"Katherine!" she gasped, trying to see clearly.

"No, ma'am, it's me," said Mrs. Jessup. Helene cried out incoherently and rushed past the housekeeper.

"No, my lady, you cannot go back there!" said Mrs. Jessup, seizing her by the shoulders and holding her where she was.

"But . . . Katherine . . ." whispered Helene.

Harry Prescott entered the room, his pistol thrust into his belt. "Open the door!" he said harshly to Alice who struggled to throw back the stubborn bolt that held the door locked. Nellie Grace ran ahead to the door and pushed Alice, who was in tears, and fumbling blindly with the latch. The red-haired girl pushed the bolt with all her might. For a second it remained firm, then Harry added his strength to the effort and, with a long-drawn-out screech, the bolt began to move. In another moment, the door was open. Harry looked back at them and it seemed to Helene he would say something, but instead he slipped out into the darkness without another word.

"Wait!" hissed Nellie when Alice would have followed behind him. Nellie held the door open a crack and watched. "There's the horses, all right," she whispered to them. "He's got one . . . there he goes!" She shut the door and leaned against it heavily, her eyes closed tight.

As they listened, they could hear the soft, slow, infinitely slow, hoofbeats of a single horse moving through the stone courtyard . . . to Helene it seemed like the sound of thunder . . . surely the soldiers would have heard it by now, surely they would see him . . . every second that passed seemed a year to her, and the sound of Harry's horse grew more faint as he left the stone yard behind and rode out into the open, and then he gave the animal its head as they raced down through the back lawns, leaping the bushes and shrubs, swinging in a wide parallel to the side of the main driveway.

Helene prayed as she stood there in the darkness, striving desperately to hear the sounds coming from the front of the house . . . no more gunfire, now, only the unceasing pounding of the door . . . hysterically she almost wished it would give way, anything, anything to stop that awful sound . . . she looked about her, startled, as the sound did stop . . . she heard shouts and men running outside . . . they had spotted Harry! There came to her ears then the sharp, long-drawn-out cracking noise of a shot fired, then another, then several at once. Nellie, pressed against the door, quivered. "Jesus!" she said, "oh, Jesus, they've got him!"

"Look, girl!" cried Helene fiercely. "Look outside! They might not have hit him . . . he was riding a long time before they saw him."

Nellie looked at her cursorily, then, without a word, opened the door a tiny bit and looked out.

"Well?" demanded Helene, feeling that any moment now she must surely scream. Nellie shrugged.

"I dunno, ma'am," she said. "I can't see nothin' in that direction."

"We've got to get out of here ourselves, ma'am," Mrs. Jessup spoke up. Helene shook her head and once again turned to go back the way they'd come. Mrs. Jessup and Alice between them pulled her to the door. Nellie peeked outside, then ran down the steps.

"Come on!" she cried. Just across the courtyard stood a dozen horses, saddled, ready to go. Nellie rushed past the little kitchen garden by the back steps and headed across toward the horses. Then suddenly she stopped dead as she heard loud male voices approaching around the side of the house. Nellie stared wildly back toward the kitchen, made a few hesitant steps farther to the waiting horses, then, cursing under her breath, fled back to the other women.

"They're comin' round here!" she panted. "We got to go some other way!"

"Which way, my lady?" pleaded Mrs. Jessup, turning helpless eyes on Helene. But Helene hardly heard her and only shook her head.

"Where is Katherine?" she insisted. *"Where is she?"*

"I dunno, ma'am," groaned Mrs. Jessup, "we all just run. What will we do, ma'am?"

Before Helene could answer her, three of the soldiers turned the corner of the house, sauntering into the courtyard. They stopped when they came upon the horses, then walked about the nervous animals, laughing, admiring them.

"Gettin' ready to run, they was!" snickered one of them and the others thought he was quite a wag. Finally, after looking about in a very perfunctory manner, they headed for the stables.

"They won't be long in there, ma'am, once they see Master Michael ain't there," said Nellie, keeping her eye on the three men. "We got to get ourselves out right now, before they come back. 'Cause they'll plant theirselves right outside this door to keep anyone from gettin' away, or else they'll march theirselves straight back into the house through here."

"The garden, Lady Helene," Alice spoke up suddenly. "We could go through the hedges here and then up the hill . . . maybe they won't bother to look up there!"

"The rose garden?" asked Helene dimly, her entire attention riveted on the distant, persistent pounding of that door. A few more shots were fired; they hardly seemed to matter now, they were so insignificant compared to that frightful smashing. Her head and heart pounded so that she could not be sure whether the throbbing thudding was still real or only coming from inside of her.

"Come on, my lady," urged Alice. Nellie held up her hand a moment until she saw the backs of the three soldiers disappear into the stables. Then she nodded sharply and threw the door open wide.

Helene moved forward as in a dream . . . and just as she stepped through the doorway, she heard the distant shouts of men, the screaming of women . . . and the awful pounding stopped at last, as the massive thick oak door was sent crashing crazily half off its hinges.

"They're in!" she said, but Alice dragged her out and down the steps, over to the side lawn where the hedges grew six feet tall. Quickly the women pushed their way through the thick, thorny brambles and ran toward the hill. There was an open patch of ground they had to cover before they reached the sheltering stand of young trees.

They sprang across the open place, and then, their breath coming in harsh, rasping bursts, they found the trees. But they could not stop to rest yet, for they would not be out of sight until they had reached the hedgerows Helene had so lovingly planted almost at the top of the hill to shelter her roses from the sea winds. They ran on blindly, stumbling, falling, picking themselves up again, always moving ahead. They heard shooting somewhere behind them... whether they were being fired at or not they did not know and would not stop to look, but pushed on still...

And Helene ran with them, her mind hardly functioning at all save with the primitive instinct to escape, to survive somehow. She found herself with unsuspected strength, almost picking Mrs. Jessup up bodily and dragging her along. And when, at last, they found themselves surrounded by the thick hedges, Helene sank down, exhausted, on a garden bench and dully wondered how long they would have to wait till Thomas came to take them away to America.

2 Something On the Ground

Elizabeth urged her chestnut forward as quickly as she dared, feeling terribly guilty at the awful pace she had forced upon him for the whole four miles to Arthur Prescott's house. She did not slow down until they reached the entryway, then she jumped from the animal's wet, quivering back and knocked at the door until she thought her knuckles were bleeding. Where *were* they all, she wondered impatiently. I don't care one bit if Mr. Prescott turns me out, she told herself firmly, ignoring the quaking feeling she got whenever Arthur Prescott looked at her. But, after what he did to Papa tonight! Resolutely, Elizabeth summoned up all her courage and went right on knocking.

Finally someone came to open the door... the Prescott butler, Jasper, barefoot, in a long nightshirt and a woolen comforter wrapped round about him, a lantern in his hand, a decidedly unpleasant look on his face.

"No one's home, miss," Jasper informed her and did not invite her to come in.

" 'No one'?" she repeated, surprised. "Where is Mr. Prescott, pray?"

"In town, miss," yawned Jasper.

"How peculiar!" thought Elizabeth, but she was glad Arthur was not there. "Please inform Master Harry—" but she got no further.

"Not here neither, miss, I told you before," said Jasper, beginning to close the door in her face. "Come home, went upstairs, come down again, took his horse, went off somewheres. Good night to you, miss." And, before she could say another word, he had slammed and bolted the door.

Where could Harry have gone? She walked slowly back to the horse, patting him absentmindedly as she tried to think what to do now. Arthur gone to town ... in the middle of the night? After all that had happened at the ball? And Harry missing, too. Elizabeth climbed back up on the chestnut and turned away. She felt suddenly frightened, more frightened than at any time tonight, even when Papa had told them they must leave Spring Mount. When he had said that, all she had been able to think of was Harry. She had to get to Harry, he would know what to do, he would take care of her. But now ... she let the horse choose his own meandering way along, hardly paying attention to where they were going. After a while, she thought she heard someone riding very quickly behind her. She pulled the horse up short, turning around in her saddle to see who it was. It must be Harry, she thought, and once again all the fear and uncertainty drained out of her. The other rider waved to her, shouted something ... Elizabeth frowned. That was not Harry's voice. ...

"Wait. Miss Elizabeth, wait!"

"Ralph?" She watched him come up to her and noticed at once that he had been driving his own horse at least as fast as she had, the poor beast was covered with sweat and seemed to be limping.

"Oh, Miss Elizabeth, you give us all such a scare!" cried Ralph, maneuvering alongside her. "Your father wants you home right away, I'm to bring you back and no arguments!"

Without waiting for her reply, he took the reins from her hands and began leading her back toward Spring Mount. Elizabeth, furious, clung to the pommel of her saddle to keep from losing her balance.

"I won't go with them!" she said defiantly to Ralph's back. "They can't force me to go! I've got to find Harry!"

But, feeling defeated, not knowing what she could do now, Elizabeth wept silently. If only they would let her stay with some friends of the family. It wasn't that she didn't love them all, she *did* love them, but she belonged to Harry.

Ralph took the shortest way back to Spring Mount that he knew, a little-used, overgrown footpath that crossed the main road full half a mile before the main gates. He rode along carefully, watching so he would not miss the right turning. Once on that path, they would come out just west of the house, through a small stand of trees and a small fallow field, then they would be right at the beginning of the lawns. They made the correct turn and, sure of his way now, Ralph urged the weary horses faster. He heard Elizabeth crying every step of the way and it nearly broke his heart, but he steeled himself to the sound and went on.

"Ralph, what's that?" she called out to him a moment later. He had been watching the winding of the narrow trail and was not looking more than a few feet ahead. Now he looked up, reining the horses in sharply. Elizabeth pointed toward the trees just ahead of them.

There stood a single, riderless horse, his front foot pawing at something on the ground. As they watched, the horse trotted away, then whinnied anxiously, turned and came back to the same spot.

"An accident, most like, miss," said Ralph as they approached. They moved slowly, not to frighten the strange horse into running off.

"Look, there's someone lying on the ground," said Elizabeth, and before Ralph could stop her she had slipped easily from the chestnut's tall back and ran to the still form in the grass. "It's a man," she called back. "Ralph, hurry up and . . ." she had managed to turn the man over . . . Ralph heard her scream as though she had been stabbed through the heart. He ran to her, leaving the horses to fend for themselves, and found her huddled on the ground, moaning, rocking back and forth as she cradled the head of Harry Prescott in her lap. She looked up, her face expressionless, as Ralph stood over her.

"He's dead, Ralph," she said, almost strangling on the words. "Someone's shot Harry! My God, my God, my God!" she repeated, looking down at the dead white face of her love.

Elizabeth clutched Harry's body against her, getting his blood all over the front of her bright yellow gown, and she screamed and screamed till Ralph thought she'd lost her mind. Gentle, in his rough way, he got up and pulled her to her feet. She stood with blank face and wide, uncomprehending eyes as he picked Harry's body up and laid it across the saddle of his own horse.

"Come on, Miss Elizabeth," he said, "we'll take him home with us." She did not seem to hear him, and finally he had to pick her up, too, and put her on her horse. He jumped up behind her, knowing the big chestnut could bear their double weight the rest of the way back, and, leading his horse behind them, he went on through the woods. As he rode along he tried to puzzle out what had happened.

"Might a' been highwaymen," he mused aloud. "Him out alone

and late like, yes, might a' been . . . except I never knew no high-wayman to use no army musket!''

Elizabeth slumped over in front of him, unable to hold the reins or keep her seat without his sturdy arms holding her where she was. They made it through the woods all right, Ralph glancing back every moment or so to make sure Harry's body had not slipped off the horse. He was worried about Elizabeth, half afraid they would encounter the same assassin who had murdered Harry Prescott . . . and then he felt Elizabeth stirring in front of him. She sat up very straight, every muscle in her body stiff and tense.

"Shooting," she murmured. "Listen, Ralph, do you hear it? There's shooting at Spring Mount!"

Ralph stopped the horse and listened. Yes, she was right. He heard sounds of both musket fire and pistols and loud shouting. He looked at her anxiously. Whatever was going on, he could not let her go riding into it. He jumped down, pulling her off the horse next to him. Then he tied the reins of the other horse to a tree.

"You stay right here, Miss Elizabeth," he told her, jumping back on the chestnut. "I'll go and find out what's happening. Just you stay still, keep a watch over Mr. Harry . . ." and while she stood staring after him with vacant eyes, he whipped up the chestnut and disappeared into the darkness.

Elizabeth did not move for several minutes. The sound of the shooting that had startled her earlier seemed forgotten now. The night was very peaceful. She looked at Harry's body lying across the horse's back and she thought she must take him home. Papa would know what to do for Harry, she thought. She had all but forgotten what Ralph had said to her. Her only thought now was of home, got to get home, home . . . at Spring Mount . . . where problems were solved, broken toys mended, sick people made better . . .

She did not mind at all that Harry's body was strapped onto the horse. She slipped her foot into the stirrup and swung her body up expertly, landing forward of the horse's middle. Then she picked up the reins and headed out of the trees, down through the fallow field, home to Spring Mount with her broken toy for Papa to mend. . . .

3 And None of Them Looked Back

The great massive oak door crashed crazily on its hinges . . . another mighty shove from the soldiers outside and it fell away. They came into the hall in a rush and behind them came their sergeant. They held their muskets poised to fire but their orders were not to shoot now unless the other side shot first.

Inside the hall, most of the men of Spring Mount lay dead or dying by the windows. Backed up against an inside wall stood an old man in black, bending over an elderly stout woman who had collapsed. A buxom wench was holding the elderly stout woman in her arms, crying, and the most beautiful girl anyone there had ever laid eyes on stood in front of the others glaring at them.

The sergeant looked around, ordering candles to be lit at once, barely glancing at the group of people by the wall. As he stepped around the bodies on the floor, kicking one or two guns away from their outstretched dead hands, a dark figure staggered out to him from a little alcove by the staircase . . . reaching for his pistol . . .

The figure, almost tottering as it moved, nevertheless tried to pull itself erect. It stopped briefly by the group of women and the old man, then, without a word, moved toward the soldiers. As the candles were lit hastily, they could see it was a man badly wounded, a flintlock pistol still gripped between his fingers but hanging uselessly at his side. He limped, almost fell; they saw the blood coursing down his arm and there was a great gash in the side of his neck. He tried desperately to raise the pistol, to fire it at the sergeant, but it fell from his hand to the floor. His eyes followed its downward path and he heaved a great shuddering, sobbing sigh.

"Be you Sir Thomas Sturbridge?" inquired the sergeant at last and the bleeding man before him stared at him in wonder, and then shook his head, yes.

"Yes," he said aloud. "I am."

"I have here a warrant for your arrest," said the sergeant. "And also one for the arrest of one Michael Ives, Roman Catholic. Where is Ives, sir?"

"Where you'll never find him, Sergeant," said Sir Tom thickly.

The sergeant looked at him a moment, then gestured several of his men to search the house. They divided into groups of two, four of them heading upstairs to the bedrooms.

"He's not here," said Sir Tom patiently. "He's gone."

"Be that so for a truth?" said the sergeant. "We'll see now, won't we?" He walked over to the little group by the wall. "Who in hell are they?" He leered openly at Katherine, who turned her back on him, and then he laughed. "Yer daughter, Sturbridge? I didn't know you Jacobite devils made such pretty chickens!"

Sir Tom said nothing. The sergeant took his pistol from his belt and used it to point with. He touched Father McGuire lightly on the shoulder with the barrel. The priest brushed the weapon away as though it were as harmless as a fly and once again the sergeant only laughed. He pushed the priest up against the wall and, when he saw the Roman collar underneath his black cloak, his eyes lit up.

"A priest!" he exclaimed. "Oh, this is too good! Sturbridge, you've a lot to answer for, you have! Hey, priest, give us a prayer! Say something in Latin for the boys!"

Mrs. Curley muttered something angrily and, looking down at her, the sergeant did not laugh. Reaching out almost casually with his pistol, he dealt her a smashing blow on the head. Katherine screamed and reached over to catch her as she fell, but the sergeant stepped quickly between them.

"Nobody down here, Sergeant," said one of his men, just returning from searching the kitchen and dining room.

"All right," replied the sergeant good-naturedly, "stand by."

"Let me help her," said Father McGuire, his eyes on Mrs. Curley's unconscious form.

"Don't lay a finger on her!" snapped the sergeant. Katherine drew herself up and walked quickly to a small table where there was a bottle of brandy someone had thought to take on their long journey.

"Katherine!" said Sir Tom, and the sergeant watched her, his smile back and broader than ever. She ignored him, took the brandy and knelt down by Mrs. Curley, trying to pour some of it between her lips. And then, very slowly, she set the bottle down on the floor and looked up at the sergeant with hate in her eyes.

"She's dead," Katherine said. Meg moaned, burying her face in the folds of the priest's cloak. The smile faded from the sergeant's face and his easy-going manner changed abruptly.

"I asked you before and I ask you now," he barked at Sir Tom, "who is that girl?"

"None of your business," replied Sir Tom, swaying slightly on his feet.

The sergeant jerked a finger at two of his men. They came up behind Sir Tom and one of them struck him from the back with the butt of his musket. Without a sound, he crumpled and fell to the floor.

"Uncle Tom, oh God!" shrieked Katherine, springing forward. The sergeant seized her roughly.

"Where is Michael Ives?" he demanded, but Katherine hardly understood him, struggling in his grasp to break free and go to Sir Tom.

"Oh, you know, missy," said the sergeant. "I think we'd better take you back with us." Several more of the soldiers came down the stairs and he glanced up inquiringly.

"Nothing, Sergeant," they called out. "Not a soul anywhere."

The sergeant was very annoyed. This was to have been a short and simple night's work. Instead, he and his men had had to lay siege to the bloody place and fight for their lives! And now, one of the men they'd been sent for lay in a heap on the damned floor and who knew if he'd wake up long enough to answer any questions . . . Gladden would not like that at all, the sergeant knew very well . . . and the other one was nowhere to be found!

He looked at Katherine very thoughtfully. As if she read his mind, she shrank away from him. He let go of her for a moment, watching to see what she would do. She ran back to the priest's side and flung herself at his feet weeping, the elegant blond curls tumbling loose and unbound in a white gold wave down her quivering back. The old priest stood very still with the weeping, terrified women gathered about him, and his dark, sunken old eyes met the sergeant's gaze unflinchingly.

The sergeant was not entirely an ignorant man, for his time and his upbringing. He had been to France, he had seen a bit of Germany, something of Holland and luscious Spain, too. And he thought to himself now, this is a rare ridiculous sight! There is nothing businesslike about this, none of it, he thought, growing angry for the first time. What a bloody hero the papist bastard looks, don't he, with them all hanging on to him like he can work some miracle and me and the men will likely turn to stone or some such!

He turned away from the little tableau, utterly disgusted, and Father McGuire began to pray aloud, his quavering old voice gathering strength as he went.

" . . . dread not, neither be afraid of them.

"The Lord your God which goeth before you, He shall fight for you, according to all that He did for you in Egypt before your eyes . . ."

The sergeant turned back, somehow surprised to hear the old man praying in words he could understand, instead of some foreign gibberish.

"... And in the wilderness, where thou hast seen how that the Lord thy God bare thee, as a man doth bear his son, in all the way that ye went, until ye came into this place. ..."

A single shot, that was all it took at such close range. A single shot from the sergeant's pistol and it silenced the priest forever. He uttered a sad little sigh and touched Katherine's golden head for a moment, and then he fell down. The sergeant had never enjoyed killing a man so much in his entire military career. He stood over the small body and tucked the pistol away again, then he grabbed a thick handful of that silky shimmering hair and pulled hard suddenly, wrenching the girl's head back painfully, and dragged her up to her feet that way.

"Now all your 'eroes are gone," he said. "Yer in a bad way, it seems, missy!" He laughed, and, as he laughed his other hand snaked out quickly and tore the soft blue satin of her gown, ripping the delicate cloth from her shoulders and breast, and all the while he held her immobile, bent back, by her hair. The men around him snickered when they saw what he was about. Some of them wandered off to pick up odds and ends of valuables, a few headed for the dining room to find the silver, and several looked about for liquor. The magistrate was waiting back in town, they knew, but they were the sergeant's men and the sergeant seemed in no particular hurry. Two of them watched every move the sergeant made, with hungry, burning eyes ... he glanced over at them and snarled like a dog, to keep the rest of the pack at bay.

Katherine felt his wet mouth moving on her neck and screamed again and kept on screaming until he slapped the breath out of her.

He tossed her to the floor and tore the skirt of her gown in half, then swore furiously at the sight of the petticoats underneath it. He glanced over at one of the men.

"Give us that bayonet here," he ordered.

The man handed it to him reluctantly, "Say, you ain't goin' to cut her up yet, are you?"

The sergeant grinned at him and poised the bayonet over her abdomen. The man reached out to grab the wicked blade from him. The sergeant moved without seeming to move at all. He lunged forward with the weapon and sliced the man's hand almost to the bone. The fellow screamed and backed away, and the sergeant proceeded to hack the bothersome petticoats to pieces.

Katherine lay very still and watched him without seeming to. She believed with her whole heart that if he caught her looking at him he would kill her. She was filled with a terror the like of which she had never imagined could exist and, with that terror, came an anger that oppressed her being so entirely she felt she must explode from it. Her eyes watched the movement of the thin, triangular blade in fascination . . . she longed for just one moment to feel it in her hand, to turn it against him . . . she would not hesitate to kill him, she knew, and she could not find it in herself to feel ashamed.

At last he flung the blade aside, using his hands to pull the last of the cloth from her body. He moved her more conveniently, pulling her about the floor like a rag doll, and suddenly one of the men ran in shouting.

"Rider coming!"

The sergeant looked up at him in disgust. "Who?"

"I don't know."

"Shoot him down and get out of here!"

"Yes, sir!" snapped the man smartly, eyeing Katherine appreciatively. "G'wan!" shouted the sergeant and the man left.

"Sergeant, maybe you ought to see who it is," ventured one of the others timidly. The sergeant glared at him but got to his feet nevertheless.

"Watch her," he grunted, heading for the door. "And . . ." he added, "if you touch her I'll kill you."

He went outside then and the two remaining stood where they were, enjoying the sight of her lying there. She turned her head very slowly, there was Meg, all but forgotten, slumped by the priest's body, staring at her. "Help me, Meg," she whispered, but it was no use. Meg could not help anybody.

There were a few shots from outside, the sound of a horse galloping down the drive, and the sergeant's voice raised in a ferocious string of curses and shouts. The two men in the hall looked at each other in consternation, then ran out.

At once Katherine jumped up and picked up the discarded bayonet.

"Meg, get up!" she whispered loudly, running over to the girl's side. She pulled and tugged at Meg and at last got her on her feet and moving. "Come on, Meg, we can try to get out the back! Oh, hurry up, Meg, do hurry! They'll be back any minute!"

She shoved Meg with all her might into the dining room and was about to follow after her when she turned back to look at Sir Tom. "Go on, Meg, go on!" she called, kneeling down at his side. If he still lived, she thought, and then wondered how she could possibly get him out of there.

But, a moment later, when the sergeant came back inside, she was still kneeling by Sir Tom, crying tears of grief and rage. He was dead, the only father she had ever known and loved was dead. And, in a few more minutes she would be dead, too. She paid no attention to the sergeant now, but stared dully around this lovely room filled with blood and death.

He watched the expression on her face with satisfaction and came toward her unwarily, the momentary distraction almost gone from his mind now. Some old man, a farmer, maybe one of the people who had worked at Spring Mount, had come riding straight in across the front lawn as bold as you please. The boys had fired at him, fired and missed and kept missing and the old fellow had turned himself right around and was about to get clean away when they had thought to put a ball into his horse . . . down went the horse, legs flailing in agony, another shot or two finished the fellow off and that was the end of the thing. Now all he could think of was the girl. Ever a man to admire the right setting, he glanced around him with his usual smile and thought of the intriguing smell of blood that always stirred him on the battlefield. Peculiar, it was, come to think of it, but he liked it. He went into the third, the fourth, even the fifth advance over the bodies of wounded and dead, ankle-deep and slipping along in their blood, and had always found himself more powerful, bigger than life, full of a strange, exhilarating new energy that pushed him forward with glazed eyes and thumping heart, exactly as if he were thrusting himself to the belly into a woman's body—strange the things that make a man come to life—death and its accoutrements strongest, most thrilling of all!

The girl knelt upright by a dead man, her hands at her sides, naked save for a few rags of her clothing clinging to her here and there. Her eyes looked straight at him, blazing like fire in ice, and there was blood on her fingers where she had touched the dead man.

He stood above her and grabbed her blond head viciously.

Katherine raised her right hand very slowly, very carefully, the hand that held the forgotten bayonet. She stopped resisting the pressure of his cruel hands, suddenly going limp against him . . . and at once he eased the pressure, thinking she was surrendering. He dropped his hand from her neck . . . and, quick as a snake's tongue, she jabbed the bayonet outward and up, one thrust, putting the whole of her strength into it, and felt the blade sink deep into his groin! He fell back from her, grasping his body, screaming and she jumped up and ran as fast as she could. Behind her she heard him shrieking insanely . . . she never stopped, never paused but raced on the same way Helene and the others had taken earlier, out through the kitchen, down the steps . . . she saw as in a dream the patient waiting horses just in front of her . . . behind her came heavy footsteps . . . she gathered the last bit of strength she possessed to make it to one of those horses . . . and stopped in her tracks, appalled, as she saw Elizabeth Sturbridge, mounted on a dark horse, with a man's body lying behind her, come riding slowly, calmly into the courtyard!

Forgetting herself entirely, Katherine stepped in front of the horse and took hold of the bridle. "Elizabeth," she cried, her voice choked at the sight of Elizabeth's pale, staring face and then she saw that it was Harry Prescott whose body was strapped on the tired animal. "Elizabeth, turn around, quick! Ride away, dear, ride away!"

Elizabeth looked down at her, moving her head very, very slowly, and, apparently not noticing Katherine's condition, said in a sad sweet little voice, "Where's Papa? I have to talk to him about Harry."

"There she is, get her!" Soldiers appeared at the back door, ran out toward the two girls. Katherine glanced at them, then struck the horse's flanks with all her mights. The startled beast reared up on his hind legs, then burst into a gallop and began racing away as fast as he could go. Elizabeth screamed and threw her arms about his neck. The soldiers were at Katherine's side in an instant. One of them took careful aim with his musket . . .

"Oh, no!" cried Katherine. "No, no, no!" She flung herself at the man bodily, but too late. Even as the others pulled her from him, the weapon had been fired. A few seconds later, little Elizabeth fell forward on the horse's neck and slipped to the ground, dead.

The men turned on her, outraged at what she had done to the

sergeant, tired, sick of the night's work, not sure what they ought to do next, what they ought to be doing right now. Katherine stood where she was, the fight quite gone out of her, watching as the bewildered horse, with Harry still on his back, walked nervously back and forth and put his nose down to nudge Elizabeth's body.

They grabbed Katherine then and threw her on the ground and, one by one, very quickly, they took her. They were angry at her. Having looked forward with relish to what was left of her after the sergeant had finished, they now found no enjoyment in it whatever. There were no kisses, however rough, no caressing of her white, smooth body the like of which none of them had ever touched before, no, they were enraged with her; if they could have killed her they would have felt it justice, no more.

There was no part of her they did not violate, their hasty fingers were like claws scratching and tearing at her flesh until the blood ran down into the melting snow beneath her. This was not the usual soldier's rape, drunken and careless and sloppily stupid. This was, rather, a soldier's *combat* with his enemy face to face—to hurt, degrade, befoul in every way a man's rage and resentment at his own fear can suggest to him.

At last another one came to the back door and called to them: "We're leavin'! Got to get the Sergeant to a doctor before his guts spills out! Pike's bringin' the 'orses up from below . . . *will* you jacks pull it out and get inside 'ere; give me a 'and with Serg."

The three of them stood up and turned away from her. "Wait up," one said to the man in the doorway. "What's to be done with this one?"

The other man looked at her critically. "She looks 'arf dead to me. She'd *be* dead, too, if the Sergeant got 'is hands on 'er. Oh, come on, we got to move! Sun's almost up . . . and I tell you, the Magistrate will not be 'appy about all this." He left them, going back inside. The three of them looked at each other and shrugged, then cast a last glance at Katherine.

"*Come* on, then!" snapped one, the others smirked a little and they walked away, leaving her lying there. "Fancy that wench cuttin' up the Sergeant like that!" And, finally, they were gone.

Katherine lay fully conscious on the ground, engulfed in searing, surging pain. She heard the horses trotting up the driveway from the gates. She heard them mount up—the sergeant, cursing and swearing, moaning and groaning pitifully, was evidently strapped tight around the gut with pieces of torn clothing and placed on his horse by his sympathetic troop. Then, moving very slowly, they rode away down the gravel drive, and the voice of the wounded sergeant could still be heard in the still, dawn air all the way down to the main road.

Katherine knew that they were gone and still she did not move. She did not want to move, ever again. She lay on the cold ground, knowing that Elizabeth's body was only a few yards away, she lay there grieving somewhere inside of her for Elizabeth . . . and envying Elizabeth because she was dead, dead quickly and still clean, still herself. And she? She was filth now, corrupted and unclean. She had known all the things that men could do to women, except love them.

A long time later, or so it seemed to her, it might have been ten minutes or an hour, something moved cautiously close to her. She knew it was not one of the soldiers . . . what reason had they to be cautious near her? Is some one of us left alive, she thought, a dreadful croaking sound of laughter emerging from her aching throat . . . weren't we all accounted for, one by one? Is there someone besides me? But she did not bother to move.

"Miss Katherine! Oh, Jesus Lord, Miss Katherine! Are ye alive at all?"

It was Meg. Carefully, her small grey-green eyes looking wildly about in all directions, Meg crept out from behind the stone archway of the stable entrance. She crawled until she was next to Katherine Ives. She pulled off her heavy woolen skirt and ripped its seam from waist to hem, then as gently as she could, she placed it over Katherine's bruised and bloody body. And all the while, she talked and talked and talked in her soft Irish way, and half the talk was prayers and the rest was the best of Meg, always, the talk she saved for the private ears of children, hurt children, broken children. . . .

"There, there, *acushla*," Meg crooned, smoothing Katherine's blond hair back from her welted face. "Och, little girl, little girl, thank the Lord your poor Ma cannot see you this day! Miss Katherine, are you awake, darlin'? Say something to me, please! Say just one little word to Meg, *mavourneen!*"

Katherine tried to form words but she could not think of any that would matter anymore. She opened her mouth, gasping great breaths of the fresh clean morning air into her lungs.

"Elizabeth . . ." she said. Meg nodded, smiling that she could still speak at all. She took Katherine's hand in hers and held it to her cheeks and kissed her fingers.

"Yes, yes," she said softly. "Elizabeth. I hear you, darlin'. Elizabeth is . . ." she broke off hurriedly, unable to bring herself to look over at Elizabeth's body. "Miss Katherine, please try to get up—I'll help you, come on, now, there's a darlin'. We got to get away from this place before they come back . . . come on, now, please, just try to sit up and lean on me," coaxed Meg. She did not know whether there was anyone else left alive; she did not know whether Katherine would be able to travel, or where they could go if she *was*. But Meg's only concern right now was getting Sheila's daughter inside, finding some warm clothes for her, taking care of her. . . .

Katherine began to listen to Meg's patient entreaties and at last she staggered to her feet. The world turned suddenly black and clammy cold, she felt like vomiting and leaned heavily on Meg's stout arms until the feeling passed. Meg tied the makeshift garment around Katherine's body with a clumsy knot and slowly half led, half carried her back inside the house. Once in the kitchen, however, and Meg would let her go no further. She would not go back into the hall herself, and she refused to let Katherine return to the reminders of hell itself in there. She shut the kitchen door and ran into the maids' rooms, rummaging about in dresser drawers and chests until she found a pair of linen drawers, a chemise, a couple of heavy petticoats and finally a plain, worn blue woolen dress and an old knitted shawl. She hurried back to Katherine with the clothes, and, taking a pan of water and some clean rags, began to wash her clean again. Everywhere she touched was bruised or cut, the blood dry now and encrusted with dirt.

"I'll not make much of a job of it, I'm afraid, Miss Katherine," she apologized, trying to be gentle. "But we've got to get you into them clothes. I don't know where we'll go. Mrs. Jessup has a sister somewhere hereabouts, but I don't know her name or where she is, do you, miss? Please, Miss Katherine, try to think. We got to go right away!"

Katherine stared at her very hard, trying for Meg's sake to remember. "Gravesend," she whispered at last. "They're waiting for us at Gravesend."

Meg looked at her in dismay. "There by the shore, miss? But that's miles and miles from here. We'd never make it!"

Katherine attempted a smile and a deep cut in her lip opened and began to bleed anew. "No," she croaked hoarsely, touching Meg's hand. "Not *we*...you. I can't...can't..." she floundered about for words, unable to keep her mind clearly on anything.

"I won't leave you here, Miss Katherine," said Meg very firmly. She set the pan of water aside and began to dress the girl. Katherine tried to help but it took a very long time. Meg kept glancing uneasily out the window, down the drive, half expecting the soldiers to come back any minute. Finally she had Katherine dressed and the shawl knotted about her shivering shoulders.

"I'm going to go outside now, Miss Katherine, and see if I can't hitch up one of them horses to a wagon. You can't hardly ride noways and I'm not much good on a horse, myself. Can you stay here by yourself, miss, until I come back for you?"

"No!" whispered Katherine desperately, grabbing Meg's hand. "Don't leave me here alone, please, Meg!"

"All right, then, just come along with me out to the stables," said Meg, helping Katherine to her feet. She turned the two of them toward the door. There was someone standing there looking at them...Meg screamed at the top of her voice...Katherine lifted her head painfully and her eyes met the eyes of Helene. Katherine took a step toward her, staggered, would have fallen, but Helene caught her and held her up.

"Thank God you're alive!" whispered Helene, embracing her, tears running down her face as she saw how Katherine winced at the slightest touch.

"Ma'am, where did you come from?" cried Meg, overjoyed to see her.

"The rose garden. We've been hiding there for hours, waiting for them to leave. Nellie and Alice and Mrs. Jessup are with me. We must take the horses and ride quickly...."

"Ma'am," said Meg, her eyes cast down, "Miss Elizabeth... she's..."

"I have seen Elizabeth," replied Helene quickly. "The others are removing Harry's body from the horse. We shall not have time to bury them..." her eyes moved to the closed door, then back to Meg, a question in them that Meg could not bear to answer. Helene walked to the door, opened it....

"My lady, don't go in there!" implored Meg, but Helene shook her head.

"It's all right, Meg. I will be back immediately. Please help Miss Katherine outside...."

"She can't ride, ma'am," protested Meg. "We'll have to take a wagon."

"She must ride, Meg," said Helene. "We'll never make it any other way." She turned and went out into the hall, where lay the bodies of the dead and the wreckage of all that had been Spring Mount.

Helene found him lying where they had left him. Swiftly she knelt at his side and put her arms around him . . . how cold he was, she thought, how far away his spirit is from mine already! She kissed his cheeks, she kissed his mouth and, lifting each of his hands in turn, she kissed them, too. She looked for a long moment at the massive gold Sturbridge ring, then slipped it from his finger to take with her. Then she stood up again, and went to look down at the dead priest and the poor women by his side. For one frightful moment and because she was exhausted, Helene allowed it all to reach her, to touch her, the reality that was nightmare. She put her two hands up to her head, pressed her fingers against her skull and thought that if she screamed long enough, loud enough, the nightmare would go away. But then she remembered Katherine's battered face and beaten body. Katherine lived the nightmare and would go on living it for a long time. She remembered Rob and Michael and she remembered her promise to her husband. She lowered her hands and turned away from the sight of the dead, walking quickly back the way she had come. But, at the doorway she stopped and looked down at the great signet ring in her palm. With a cry of rage and despair she flung it with all her strength across the Great Hall of Spring Mount and turned her back forever on England.

Before midday they rode within sight of the crashing sea off Gravesend; Helene and Katherine, Meg and Alice and Nellie and Mrs. Jessup. They found Michael and Rob and Willy Duncan and a tall clean-limbed ship slipping away into the gray Atlantic. They sailed that same evening toward the unknown that was America, each of them locked into his own silent, unforgettable pain and none of them looked back.

Interlude

Massachusetts Bay Colony, Boston: 1720

The little oak saplings stood row upon row on the crest of a gentle New England hill, with a fair sea breeze blowing the half of their tender young growth on one side and a softer, more subtle breeze smelling of pine and cool forest earth ruffling their leaves on the other side. The saplings were a pretty sight with the close-lying, grey-blue sky over them but Willy Duncan disapproved of them and pitied them.

"Oh, they look well enough, Mistress Katherine," Willy admitted, "but I don't like ter see it done. Never have, never will. Seems t'me everythin' in this land grows straight and tall but these 'ere little trees o'yours. *I* think 'tis some'at against Natur', a'twistin' up of 'er 'andiwork to go a 'suitin' of our own purposes!"

Katherine Ives Sturbridge smiled at her ten-year-old son, Elliot.

"Nevertheless, Willy, our shipyards would hardly remain in business another six months unless we were sure of a continuing supply of timber like this. Where would our catheads come from? Or the futtocks, for that matter?"

Avoiding the knowing expression in Elliot's dark young eyes, Willy declared firmly, "For *that* matter, Mistress, *I* don't know th' one o'them things from th' other, though it be twenty year now us folk been a'studyin' on it! Seems t'me we might a'found enough a'them twisty, knotted trees in the woods hereabouts without a'plantin' of 'em ourselves. But, a'course," Willy hastened to add lest she be really annoyed with him or her son dismayed at his ingorance, "*I* be no sure hand at the buildin' of ships sich as yerself and Mister Michael. And Mister Rob."

Willy said Rob's name in a softer voice, watching her. Rob Sturbridge was dead these seven months now, brought home mortally wounded from one of the forays north into French Canada the men of Boston were forced to make in their endless fight against the raids of French freebooters out of Port Royal.

But after Rob's death Katherine had insisted that they all go on talking about him in a natural, every-day manner. Katherine was not one for tip-toeing around about the dead, nor about anything else, for that matter. So, although the mere sound of Rob's beloved name cut her to the heart each time she heard it, Katherine spoke of him very often herself and insisted they all do the same. Rob Sturbridge's only son was never going to forget his father, not if she had anything to say about it!

Now, as she heard that special note of tenderness in Willy's voice Katherine smiled and turned back to her inspection of the young oaks. They were eight and nine years old now and grew, as planned, bent close to the earth in strange, angular shapes, held tautly into their unnatural positions by heavy wire wound around their slender trunks. The wire was attached to short, thick wooden stakes pounded into the surrounding sod. In time the oaks would be cut to serve for the necessary curved sections of new ships. Meanwhile they had to make do with whatever could still be found in the woods. Each year it became more difficult to locate enough wild trees with naturally formed crooks to supply the enormous demands of the large Sturbridge-Ives Shipyards in Boston. There was already a ship being held up on the stocks waiting suitably shaped timbers.

Rob had been just about to set off on another trip into the countryside northwest of Boston, hoping to bring home enough hedgerow oak to finish that particular job. His untimely death had meant a long, costly delay in the finding of the right wood. The men they employed were very fearful of those dangerous journeys into forests inhabited by the hostile Abenaki Indians as well as the invaders from Canada who were likely to turn up almost anywhere. The men had willingly followed Rob Sturbridge on such trips. But now. . . .

Katherine stifled a sigh. *Now* was always the problem. Yesterday was over and tomorrow was in God's hands. But now there were a thousand worries and cares, problems to be solved, decisions to be made. And never in her entire life had she felt so dreadfully alone. If it were not for this child of hers and Rob's, this miracle child, this quiet, rather grave and serious-spoken boy at her side, she would simply have given up long, long ago. Elliot was her reason for going on with life when Rob died. Now she was both mother and father, she was everything to the child as he was everythig to her.

She had married Rob Sturbridge twenty years ago, just after coming to America. She had married in a daze, because then it had seemed so much easier just to give in, to stop seeking, stop questioning, just to accept. Whatever Helene and Rob thought right, then that had been enough for her.

She had not even known whether she still loved Rob when she married him. Was she still able to love? to give of herself in all ways after what had been done to her? She did not know the answer to that. Rob had treated her delicately, protected her, cherished her in every possible way. And, of course, there had been the work, the precious, spirit-redeeming work.

In those first hard years, when they were all slaving away sixteen and eighteen hours a day to get the business established, she had gladly buried herself, her energies, her thoughts and feelings in that business. And, gradually, she had begun to come away out of that terrible, lost place in her memory where she dwelt so much of the time.

For many years there had been no child born of her marriage to Rob and she knew in her heart that she was glad of it. She was afraid of a stranger, an intruder, who would take possession of her body and drain her strength and the little bit of confidence she had been able to build up. She knew just enough of childbirth to dread the tearing agony it would mean, not enough to know the joy that would make all the pain worthwhile. She associated the notion of birth with the old terror of the tearing, groping, hurting hands and bodies of the soldiers who had assaulted her that long ago, unforgettable night in England.

She knew all along how much Rob longed for a son, although he never spoke of it. And then, when it happened, when she knew that she was carrying his child after nearly ten years, when she saw the look in his loving eyes and the happiness in his face, the nameless fears left her and she became strangely content. When the boy was born at last and lay in her arms looking up at her with Rob's eyes and a thin patch of dark hair so very like Rob's hair, her contentment was complete and the past was forever behind her.

Katherine turned away from the little oak trees and headed back to the wagon below the hillside. Elliot ran on ahead of her. Willy hurried to keep her company. Katherine pulled her heavy woolen shawl close about her shoulders against the chilly Massachusetts air and strode down the hill with long, purposeful steps. Willy observed, not for the first time, that she never looked down to see if her path through the grass and tumbled rocks were clear. Knowing Mistress Katherine these past twenty years, he thought wryly, her path had *better* be clear! Mistress Katherine brooked no interference nor delay in her dealings with anything, animate or inanimate.

Willy studied the back of her head with mingled admiration and affection, noting the set of the straight, slim neck, the erect stiff back, the squared shoulders beneath the shawl of dark blue. Her silky, white-blonde hair was always worn back in a plain knot these days. Willy remembered the old days at Spring Mount, when a young, vivacious Katherine Ives had fussed over her looks and spent long hours before the looking-glass combing her waist-long tresses into a variety of fashionable styles from Paris and London. Those first years in America, how she had seemed to fade and turn hard, turn in upon herself, suffering in silence what anyone who loved her would have been glad to help her bear if she had only allowed it. . . .

But, Willy mused, that bad time was passed. The hardness did not disappear entirely but Katherine learned to keep it in reserve for her shrewd business dealings. A certain different, softer loveliness had settled upon her features, especially in these last ten years since the boy was born, a calm beauty that reminded Willy of no one so much as Lady Helene herself, God Rest Her Soul!

Willy sighed, thinking of the old days, thinking of Rob. Then he hurried ahead of Katherine to jump up into the wagon and take the reins into his own gnarled hands. Katherine was quite capable of handling a team. Woe to the horse who balked or reared under her firm hand! Yet it was a scandal to Willy that she appeared about town looking like any common farmer's wife, her hands calloused and hard and creased across the palms from holding the thick leather reins. Whenever he could Willy insisted upon driving her himself.

Now he sat up on the backless wooden wagon seat and looked down at her with the assured defiance of an old, trusted family friend. Katherine ignored his expression, refused to take his outstretched hand or Elliot's hand, either, and swung herself up next to them in one marvelously graceful motion.

"We'll go on to the yards now, Willy," she said, looking straight ahead of her. But she did put her arm around Elliot's shoulders and leaned just a bit against the little boy. Elliot held himself proudly and smiled up at her. Willy nodded, clucked his tongue to the horses and drove off.

Katherine had a great deal on her mind these days and little enough to say. Hours together might pass and she in the same room with a person, yet she did not speak. She was always busy, always scribbling away in her ledgers or figuring long columns of numbers: loads of timber, fifty cubic feet, 3,700 loads to a ship, 1,890 loads compass timber, 410 loads of *thick stuff* for planking. . . . How in the world did she ever keep it all straight in her head? But she did. And for close to twenty years she had been able to give Rob and Michael a precise picture of their financial situation down to the last shilling and farthing and penny, all at a moment's notice.

Aye, she's a wonder, nodded Willy, glancing at her out of the corner of his eye as they came in sight of the sprawling, bustling town of Boston just ahead. He urged the horses on a bit faster, knowing without having to look down at the boy that Elliot's eyes would be shining with boyish pleasure the faster they went. Aye, she was a wonder, no doubt of it, Willy's thoughts returned to the theme. She had lived through griefs and horrors without number and she survived it all. He recalled Katherine the child and the girl and thought proudly of the strong, capable woman she had become.

The girl was all gone now, that pretty, graceful young thing she had once been. She was thinner now, too thin to Willy's mind. Since Rob's death her face was too pale and dark shadows around the eyes and in the hollows of her cheeks made her look drawn and older than she really was. But those lovely, luminous grey eyes, the eyes of her mother, Sheila Carey, were still beautiful. They could be cool and piercing and look at a man straight on. But they had learned how to smile again at last.

She walked on thin leather shoes with little, tapping wooden heels, quickly, impatiently, always in a hurry. Perhaps that was still some last lingering touch of the child she had once been. Her melodious voice could speak crisply and even with an edge to it. But as the years had passed she had remembered the gift of laughter and even Rob's death had not stolen it away from her again.

She seemed older than her thirty-five years. Usually she dressed in plain, dark colours, in gowns of sensible wool and linsey-woolsey, sometimes even in frocks of dyed homespun when she was very busy at the yards or in the offices, the long sleeves rolled up above her elbows like any working man, her shapely arms sunburned and freckled. Yet Rob had lived to delight in seeing her arrayed once more in silks and satins from abroad. He had decked her in Helene's silver filagree necklaces and brought her dainty silver and diamond earrings from Paris to compliment her eyes. Rob had watched with joy and a heart full of gratitude as his steady, strong, complete love had helped her out of the Hell she had endured and into a new life of accomplishment and happiness.

"Stop, Willy. Please," she said to him suddenly, without turning her head to look at him. He started to rein in the horses obediently but she placed a gentle hand over his. "No, Willy. I mean, stop *remembering*. I always know when you're remembering things. Let it go now, dearest Willy. We've time yet to look ahead of us. Surely if Rob taught us anything at all it's that. Stop grieving, Willy. It cannot bring him back. It cannot bring any of them back to us or change today, can it?"

"I knows 'at," replied Willy, staring down at her slender fingers with a lump in his throat. "But it be damned hard, forgettin', all the same. I knew 'em all. *All* on'em. I feel so awful damn *old*, like I been a'grievin' for a hundred year and not like to stop now!"

"I know, Willy," Katherine said. "But you can spend your time sorrowing and before you know it today is gone, too, along with all those yesterdays. And whatever happiness there might have been today, you'll have missed it. Let's look to the future, Willy, for God's sakes! Let's look ahead to what's coming, not back at what's been and over!"

She spoke with a sudden passion, all the while patting his hand. Willy knew she was right, but he also knew that he could not stop looking back. But he'd have to try and see to it that she didn't catch him at it again. He set the reins down between his knees and took his thin clay churchwarden pipe from his pocket, stuck it between his teeth where it felt most comfortable and comforting and drove on without lighting it, saying no more.

"Why is Willy sad, Mother?" whispered Elliot into her ear, his high, boyish voice filled with curiosity and sympathy.

"Oh, because of Papa, I think, dearest," Katherine replied steadily, giving his shoulder a warm squeeze.

And Elliot nodded silently. His own small world, the world inside of him wherein he was most alive, had changed so terribly when his father died. And he had not yet the words with which he might understand that loss or deal with it. He was a well-educated lad. Katherine and Rob dreamed of his going to college and his tutors had started him off learning Greek and Latin when he was just five. But there was a vast difference between that kind of learning and the experiences of life. Elliot had no way of finding comfort for himself. He heard the adults talk about Rob. He saw that they were able to reach out to each other and to help each other, but Elliot found no help in talk. He had never voiced his own inner agony, not since the first moments when Katherine had told him the sad truth. One sharp, terrible cry had escaped his lips. And that was all. From then on Elliot fought a daily battle with loneliness and grief, alone, all by himself, and no one, not even his mother, ever suspected the depth of his sorrow. No one guessed at his anger.

Katherine folded her hands in her lap, holding on the ends of the blue shawl. She was glad for its heavy warmth against the wind which had picked up greatly as they approached the Bay. She looked out towards the sea, beyond the white sails sheltering at anchor in the harbour. From here she could not make out the masts and spars of the *Sheila Deare*, Michael's ship, but she was there with the others, preparing to up-anchor and cast off within the hour.

Thinking of Michael now, her fingers touched the little present she was carrying to him, along with a last letter from Rob, down in the deep pocket of her heavy skirt. There was no more time for changing her mind again, back and forth, as she had during those last precious months when Michael had stayed with her in Boston after Rob died. There was only one hour left for seeing him off again, only one hour in which she would simply hand him the letter and the gift and no more to be done about it.

And hadn't she planned it to be this way, when she told her brother that she would meet him at the shipyards before the tide turned? Yes, she had deliberately decided to make her inspection of the oak trees today, so there would be little time for talk.

A small frown creased her smooth brow. Michael had never spent so long in home-port before. It was a rare treat. Indeed it had almost spoiled her, the sight of him there every day and wonderful long hours for them to talk as they pleased without worrying about when he must be off again. He had promised he would stay through the winter and he had kept his word. She knew he would stay even longer, if she asked it, but Katherine saw how the days ashore heaped upon him like an ever-heavier burden. He did not speak of it but when she had insisted at last that he go, and he realized that she was in earnest, his eyes had brightened as he took her hand and kissed it impulsively. And then he saw that she had noticed how glad he was to go again . . . and he had looked away from her, ashamed.

Her frown deepened now as she felt the old fear tugging at her heart.

It was not fear for herself when he would be far away from her, although that had once been part of it. No, now it was just her fears for Michael himself. She no longer tried to understand why he still insisted upon sailing around the world year in and year out, no sooner home in Boston for a month or six weeks than he must be up and off again. There was no need for him to go anymore. They owned close to a dozen ships and had masters aplenty to captain them. But Michael was as restless as ever, never content in any one place for very long. At forty-four Michael Ives was as much on the move as he had been since his boyhood, wild and wandering without ever having found peace.

That last voyage, before he'd come home to find Rob close to death, Michael had been gone over five months, down to the Indies, over to England, then a quick, unnoticed dash to Amsterdam and back again, coasting warily along the Carolina coasts with a sharp eye out for pirates.

Pirates! thought Katherine darkly. They'd been troubled by pirates often in years past. No proper seaman counted himself free of those devils just because he had passed Albemarle Sound and Norfolk without spotting any ships belonging to that infamous Brotherhood. Rob had made many business trips down to New York Town and reported pirates all over the northern waters and whole shiploads of cheap goods to be had, no questions asked, along the wharves and piers of New York. Pirates and French privateers, if they didn't put you out of business one way they'd surely do it another. Pirate goods selling in the very same markets they themselves competed for cut heavily into the firm's profits and had already put many another honest mercantile establishment into bankruptcy.

But not *us*, Katherine told herself. We'll build the ships, more and more of them, better ships than England herself can produce, and then we'll drop the trading company altogether. Why take unnecessary risks when we can count on steady income from the yards and from those two woolen mills Rob had built only a few years ago? She had not wanted to put the money into those mills, not when the 1699 law expressly forbade it. But Rob . . . and Michael, too . . . had believed that the small risk was worth the profits they would ultimately reap.

Why should England demand that all wool produced in her colonies be shipped back home for manufacture and then the finished goods be sent to America and sold at double and treble the prices the colonists would have to pay if they were allowed to process the wool themselves? It did not make sense to Americans. It was just another one of those damnable laws England kept passing to enrich herself at the expense of her colonies.

Katherine had heard Rob speak of those laws often enough and at the top of his lungs. So Sturbridge-Ives had built their mills and other people did the same. To hell with England! So far they'd had no great difficulty about it. The authorities seemed content to look the other way more often than not. Even the Governor himself had been heard to remark that he'd damn well buy his breeches at home sooner than wait bare-shanked for a shipment to arrive over the ocean.

They had come far in America, far indeed, Katherine reflected. They had turned their hands to whatever promised to bring in a good, honest living. They had bought into Elliot Landon's old shipyards, standing idle at the time, with one aging, barnacle-laden, worm-ridden scow anchored nearby. Not much of a beginning, perhaps, but Elliot Landon had been honest with them. And when he had realized with astonishment that none of them knew the first thing about ships or ship-building or commerce, he had put off his own plans to settle down on his new farm until he had taught them what he could about the business.

That had been nearly twenty years ago and Elliot Landon still divided his time between the farm and the yards. There was no more he could teach them now, but Landon had become part of the family.

And, too, he could never bring himself to remain very long away from Helene.

The soft-spoken, forty-five-year-old bachelor who had left his small shipyard to help put down Indian raids on the frontier had come home to Boston with one arm missing and found his business bankrupt. But Elliot Landon had had no time to grieve about it, for he had taken one look at Lady Helene Sturbridge and lost his heart for all time. He had soon heard, although not from her lips, the story of their last terrible days in England and he had been wise enough... or foolish enough . . . to realize that his cause was hopeless and to love on anyway. Helene had loved but one man in all her life and it was enough. She would never love again.

Elliot Landon had accepted this fact with equanimity and became her close and trusted friend, a friend to the entire family. Without him they could scarcely have managed in the beginning. He was their advisor, their confidante, their friend, another father, uncle, elder brother, for years and years their most cherished guest at every holiday dinner and family gathering. It was Elliot Landon who had given Katherine away at her wedding, Elliot who had smoothed their way in this strange, new country, Elliot who had taught them, cheered their efforts, corrected their first, bungling mistakes, applauded their growing success. And when the miracle had finally happened, when a son was born to Katherine and Rob, both of them had thought at once to name the boy Elliot Landon Sturbridge. It was not a gesture of thanks but a symbol of love and of new beginnings. When some of their friends wondered why the boy was not christened with his father's name, Katherine had told them:

"There is only *one* Rob Sturbridge. This son of ours has not come into the world to take his father's place but to make his own place. Elliot Sturbridge—it's a good name. Whatever pride and honour my son will possess when he's grown he must earn for himself and he could have no better teacher than Rob and Master Landon. And our friend has no child of his own, you know."

Five years ago, when Helene had died, it was more Elliot Landon's quiet strength and wisdom than anything else that had enabled them all to bear her loss. Now he and Katherine ran the shipyards together and it had become impossible to imagine themselves as either a family or a business without him.

Both Rob and Michael had had so much to learn back in the beginning, and they had had to learn it all so quickly! Sailing had appealed to Michael. He had taken to it at once, learning every inch of the old ship from bow to stern, every bit of rigging, every yard of canvas. Although they employed experienced navigators and seamen aboard, Michael had not been satisfied until he mastered the ways of wind and tide, reef and current for himself.

Elliot Landon had sent him out with an old friend, a sea captain who had finally retired to please a wife who had missed him from home during forty years of voyaging. But six months after the Captain had settled down to his rocking chair by the fireside, his wife had died. She had died happy, with him at her side, Captain Jim always boasted, but what was he to do then, with neither wife nor ship to comfort him? Elliot wisely sent him back to sea again, Captain of the leaky old scow, with Michael Ives at his side every minute to watch and listen and learn. Before Captain Jim died Michael had become captain of a fine new ship and the old one finally sank to its well-deserved rest outside Boston Harbour.

Rob, too, had found his work and his pleasure, not at sea but in the shipyards. Elliot Landon worked with him until there was no part of the business Rob had not mastered. There had been problems, of course, some bad times, some testy moments. When they had lost the old ship half-a-dozen of their clients took their business elsewhere. But they had stuck it out and built the *Sheila Deare*, then won the same clients back and found twice as many new ones. The money that came in from trade went to refurbishing and enlarging the yards, as well as setting up their own blast furnaces and iron forges and starting the mills.

Next year Rob had planned to begin a small fishing fleet. It was a sound notion but now Katherine was not so sure they ought to take on still another venture. But whenever she was overwhelmed with anxiety for the future, all she had to do was think of her son and her imagination soared beyond a woman's ancient dream of safety and security and began to encompass the dream that had been hers and Rob's, the dream that must be passed on to young Elliot when he was old enough to understand it.

How Rob had loved this new land! He had found hope and reason to begin again here. He had taken his energy from its stern beauty and the daily challenge of its own new, changing, growing life. To Rob, this was the world. England, France, all of those old dying places seemed no longer to exist except as names on contracts and bills of lading. Rob had seemed to grow younger with the passing years, filled up with satisfying work and growth. He had dreamed dreams as large and magnificent as the great new land itself. He had dreamed of building an empire on this side of the Atlantic, a vigorous, unassailable, proud empire that could thumb its nose at Europe.

Only Helene had wondered at it all. Only Helene had looked at the three of them during those busy years and thought about the old times and that none of them had ever known a thing about trade or business, profit or loss not so long ago. She had been very proud of them, Katherine knew that. The boys knew it, too. Still, it had never failed to amaze Helene when they would come home to the big, comfortable brick house at the end of a long, busy day, tanned and hard-muscled, with callouses on their hands, with shirt-sleeves rolled up and their quick, sprightly conversation full of figures, per centages, cargo manifests.

At the dinner table, with Elliot Landon there more often than not, Helene's soft brown eyes had studied each of them carefully, noting with pleasure the enthusiasm and confidence in Rob's voice, noting with a touch of sorrow the restlessness and hard-driving determination so apparent in Michael. Helene was never deceived by his success as a sea captain. Michael did not love the sea. It merely provided an outlet for his ever-troubled spirit. Helene had said to Katherine once that Michael tackled the sea almost as though it were his enemy and she feared that the sea would respond in kind one day.

Willy guided the wagon skillfully through the crowded streets of town and turned in towards the yards. Katherine smelled the salt freshness of the sea full in her nostrils and felt her heart lift for a moment as it always did when she was close to the water. The sight, smell, sound of it soothed her soul as nothing else had ever done. To the sea she owed her sanity, she believed this implicitly. The long voyage over from England had been the best cure she might have found then. On the sea she felt part of the world of nature as God had first made it. Lulled and rocked by its endless motion, caressed by its winds, carried along by its innate purposefulness, she had learned to stop wishing for death, to cease brooding over what had been done to her. She had begun to live again, at first from moment to moment, then from one day to the next.

And when they had used the money Sir Tom had so carefully put aside and invested it in the old shipyard, Katherine was glad that their new life would keep them ever near the sea, a part of something on earth that was clean and wild and unspoiled. The sea could never be an enemy to her as it might be to her brother, but then Michael's deadliest enemy lived on inside of himself and, land or sea, he had never found any escape from it.

As the wagon turned in towards the Bay Road, she looked with pride at the great sheds, the mold-lofts, where the wooden hulls of their new ships were laid down. All around stood other sheds, storage buildings filled with seasoned timber and naval stores, tools . . . great two-handled saws and adzes, augers and broad-axes. The recently rebuilt rope works, four hundred yards long and only just roofed over a month back, stood behind the mold-lofts. Bending her head just a bit she could see the lads at work along the walk, hackling the hempen fibers through steel prongs. Others were taking the combed fibers and spinning them into yarn strands while still others were carefully laying the strands into rope. Huge barrels of tar mixed with whiskey, lamp-black and hot salt water stood close by for the soaking of the standing rigging, while a dozen young boys patiently rolled up the fresh, new rope into gigantic coils to be stored away for the running rigging. Miles and miles of rope for every ship and never quite enough, it seemed. But they were taking orders for rope from one or two other, smaller shipping concerns as well as manufacturing what they needed for themselves.

The horses moved slowly past the saw pits. Willy shook his grey-streaked head at the din of the men working in pairs as they cut planking which would be stored away until the great hulls were ready. A bit further on the rasping sounds of the huge saws blended with the noisy, even-measured clamour of the augerers as they skillfully bored three-foot holes through planks and rib frames, preparing them for the driving in of the "trunnels," the big wooden pegs which would hold the planking in place. Cheerful shouts from the boys running nimbly back and forth along the rope walk greeted Katherine as the wagon drew to a stop outside of the neat little one-room office. Elliot hopped down at once and begged to be allowed to join the boys at their work. With a laugh and an approving nod his mother let him go, calling after him:

"Be sure to come back in time to say goodbye to Uncle Michael!"

She looked around. There was no sight of Michael yet. The door was open and the office was empty. She glanced out across the water wondering if a boat from the *Sheila Deare* had begun to put in towards the dock to pick Michael up and take him back to begin the outward voyage. She saw no boat yet, however. There was still time enough for what she had to say to him today. There was still time enough for her to give him Rob's gift.

Her fingers closed once more over the small package in her pocket and she sighed, not caring whether Willy heard her or not. Let us not part today with a quarrel, she prayed silently. She did fear that Michael would be angry with her. Then she tossed her head stubbornly. Let him be angry with Rob, not with me, she thought. After all, it had been Rob's idea, not hers. And yet, she admitted, now that I've thought it over this way and that all these months, I believe that Rob was right.

Turning to Willy she said, "You've already said your goodbyes, have you not, Willy? Then go on to the forge. They will give you their accounts today. You may take your dinner there before you drive back for Elliot and me. We shall not leave until Michael has sailed."

Willy nodded, barely able to hear what she was saying above the varied sounds of the yards. Once again she refused his helping hand and let herself down from the wagon seat quickly. He made sure that she was clear of the rig, clenched his pipe even more tightly between his teeth, and drove off sighing as much as he pleased knowing that she could not hear him now.

Wistfully he, too, looked out at the *Sheila Deare* riding at anchor and wished he might have another word or two with Michael before he sailed. Willy adored them all but he was only really happy when Michael was home. The two of them went hunting together, and fishing and, once in a while, drinking and wenching. When Michael was in a mood to talk, other than about business, it was generally to Willy he talked. The bond that had grown between them years ago had never weakened, whereas Michael's bonds with the family sometimes seemed quite tenuous.

This time, when Michael had stayed with them so long, Willy had secretly begun to hope he would leave the sea for good. But he knew it was no more than a vain hope. Katherine did not really need her brother home with her. She was quite wealthy now, comfortable, with a fine home and servants, many powerful friends in the colony.

Elliot Landon helped her run the business...Willy doubted that Katherine would have any difficulty running things even when the day came that Elliot, too, passed on. No, Katherine had found her own way to survive and to live, to put down strong roots and look to the future. She had her son, her bond with tomorrow, and Michael could be easy in his heart about her. Ah well, sighed Willy, loudly and luxuriously, maybe some day. . . .

Katherine smiled absently, watching Willy drive away. Then, as she turned to go and wait in the office she caught sight of Michael down at the far end of the yards by the mast pond. With him stood Elliot Landon, now at sixty-five gone quite grey and more than a bit plump, squinting earnestly up into Michael's lean, tanned face. Michael had one arm thrown affectionately across the older man's shoulders and he was smiling as the two of them turned and began to walk towards the little office.

Twenty years of wandering the earth in all seas and all climes had matured Michael's boyish good looks. His face was stern when he was not smiling. A long, hard-jawed, angularly handsome face it was still but softened one step short of severity by the thick cluster of sun-bleached golden curls carelessly falling over his wide brow. He walked lightly on the balls of his feet, moving with a quiet economy of effort unusual in a man so tall and muscularly built. There was confidence in his stride and an unconscious air of authority in his demeanour. The bright sunlight reflected off the water was mirrored in the startlingly luminous blue eyes, making his skin look like bronze in contrast. It was Michael's habit to carefully conceal his true feelings from the rest of the world by assuming an ironic expression. Yet, to those who knew him best and loved him most, there could be no masking that old, haunted look of pain and hidden anger which had been a part of him since early childhood.

Katherine waved as he and Elliot finally caught sight of her and hurried to meet her. She watched her brother's face anxiously, hoping that Landon had not once more tried to persuade Michael to leave the sea and stay home to look after her and her son. She had done arguing with Landon on that score and if he did not entirely understand why she was so willing to let Michael go now, he had promised, in a half-hearted sort of way, that he would not press Michael about it.

She could see that Elliot Landon looked just a trifle downcast and that Michael was laughing. No wonder. How like Landon to drag him down to the mast pond not an hour before he was to sail and try to lecture him about those great pine and fir masts and spars that were kept there soaking under water! Those woods were resinous and could not be allowed to dry out lest they lose their soundness and resiliency in the open air. No doubt Landon had been telling Michael how short they were of necessary timbers, pointing out to him that the mast pond was far from filled. Katherine was pleased to see that Michael was laughing and that there was no sign of any strain between the two men. She allowed herself to relax just a bit. Michael must not go off feeling guilty. Oh, be honest, she told herself impatiently. It's *you* who is feeling uneasy because of what you've got to say to him now and you're just hoping nothing has happened to put him into one of his moods!

"I see Master Landon has been predicting imminent disaster again," she said playfully as they came up to her. "That mast pond of ours positively consumes him with gloom."

Landon looked at her reproachfully. "I am only trying to point out the woeful situation, my dear," he said in his mild voice.

"Aye," grinned Michael, kissing his sister. "Master Landon has been trying to educate me in the ship-building line again, Kate! He's been at it these twenty years past and my answer to him is the same as ever: you build them and I'll sail them. As for the rest, I could stand staring down into that great mucky pond forever and it would do none of us any good. I think he's ready to give up on me now, though. I do believe I've worn him down at last!"

Landon started to protest, but Katherine had no intention of wasting Michael's last moments ashore with a discussion of company business.

"It's the oak timber that is delaying us," she said quickly. "Rob was concerned about oak, not pine. We could be soaking down a pond full of pine and what good would it be if we didn't have the oak we need for the keels? But it's nothing for you to concern yourself with, Michael."

"If I may say so, my dear," interposed Landon, flushing, "it is something we must *all* concern ourselves with. Rob was looking for *pine* on that last unfortunate foray north, not merely pursuing the Frenchmen."

Katherine was becoming provoked. "Please," she said a bit shortly. "Surely you and I may discuss this another time?"

But Landon shook his head. "My dear Katherine," he persisted, "one half of this enterprise belongs to your brother. It seems to me he ought to know the problems we face, whatever they may be. Rob and I had planned an extensive journey into the Hampshire grants before his . . . his death. And it was to be *pine* we were after. All I have been suggesting to Michael is that he delay his voyage a short while more and take the men out himself as Rob was about to do, to look for another dependable source of timber."

Katherine's chin tilted dangerously. "And is there no pine to be found in all of Connecticut? Or New York? Or the Jerseys or anywhere at all an Englishman might go without standing in mortal danger? Why must we always look only to the north?"

"Because the only other kind of pine any good for making masts is yellow pine. Long-leaf pine," explained Landon patiently, ignoring her momentary pique. "And the pine we need grows very particularly scarce, only within a twenty-mile wide strip and that strip so far south—when you can find it at all—that it would be easier to look closer to home for another sort of pine perhaps not quite so perfect but useable anyway."

"Easier!" exclaimed Katherine. "Easier? With the French and the savage Indians growing bolder every day?"

"Even so," declared Landon. "We do not know very much about southern woods yet. Carolina, that is where the pine might be. Perhaps. No, no, don't be put out with me, my dear girl. Michael understands the problem."

Katherine stared incredulously at her brother. "You do not mean to say that you'll change your mind now, at the last moment? You'll not sail today after all?"

Michael saw the ill-concealed hope in her grey eyes. "I will sail today, Kate," he said quietly. "I must. You know I must."

She ignored Landon's disappointed sigh. "Yes," she said evenly, meeting Michael's pleading gaze with a determined smile. "I know you must. I do not know why Master Landon bothers you with these things. We shall manage as we always do. We shall find our pine and the oak, too."

Michael said no more but relief flooded his blue eyes and the small tension that had been building in him disappeared. But he watched his sister very closely, observing that she was more than usually impatient today. She had something on her mind and she had purposely let it wait until now, until almost the last minute, before she would speak of it. Whatever it is, thought Michael, it is obviously much more important to her than any business problem bothering Elliot Landon.

"Well, then, Master Landon, we'd best say our goodbyes now," he spoke up suddenly, very heartily indeed, embracing the anxious little man with great fondness. "My boat will be alongside in another few moments. I know I leave my sister and my nephew in good hands, old friend. When next we meet, please God, you and I shall toast the new ships in the best Canary vidonia I can find!"

Elliot Landon forgot all about his argument with Katherine as he put his one arm about Michael and thumped him enthusiastically on the back. His eyes misted as he cleared his throat and cried:

"God bless you, my lad, we'll miss you! We'll miss you as we always do, don't we, Katherine?"

He thumped Michael a bit more, then took out his pocket handkerchief and blew his nose loudly, mumbling something about "having some ledgers to look over, can't imagine where those bills of lading have got to" and he finally left the two of them standing there alone as he went off into the little office and slammed the door behind him as a final expression of his high emotional state.

Katherine looked out across the bay at the *Sheila Deare*. She could see the crew rushing about hoisting the shrouds and the capstan crew standing by to raise the anchor. A small boat pulled away from the port side even as she looked and began heading in towards the docks.

"So soon," she murmured. And then, louder, "You're always going away, Michael mine. Ever since I can remember, you've been going somewhere else."

Michael followed her gaze, saw the boat, too. "I'm tired of it too, love, would you believe that?"

"I'd believe it," she nodded. "I know it. Oh, Michael, Michael, won't you ever stay put anywhere?"

He did not reply and she regretted having said it at once. How could he answer that? She knew as well as he knew it himself, he did not have any answer.

As they watched the little boat seemed to move faster and faster over the choppy water. Katherine realized that he would be gone in another little while, gone, and if she did not speak up now he'd be gone without the thing said and done and she would have failed Rob's dying wish. For just a few seconds more she remained silent next to her brother, gazing at the boat. Then she folded her arms resolutely and turned to face him.

"Will you tell me now, do you think?" he asked her lightly.

"You knew there was something!" Her quick frown immediately gave way and her eyes sparkled. There was no resisting Michael, ever. She looked at his smiling lips, at his grave, waiting eyes and she swallowed very hard.

"Well, then," she began, speaking quickly now that it could not be put off any longer. "I have something to give you. A . . . a gift, of sorts. It is not from me, although my heart is in it as much as ever Rob's heart was. . . ."

"Rob?"

"Yes, it's from him. It was his last wish that you have it, Michael. He wrote out a bit of a note for you to read along with it, in case he did not live to tell you himself. You . . . you will not go against his dying wish, Michael? You could not do that, could you? Promise me!"

"Why have you waited all this time, Kate-mine?" he asked her softly.

She shook her head. "It does not matter."

"It might," he said, gently insistent. "Why, Kate?"

She thrust her hand into the deep pocket and took out the small box, handing it to him quickly. "The note he wrote you is inside. Go on, open it. Open it, why don't you?"

But Michael was staring at the little box. "You said that your own heart was in it, too. Why did you wait so long before you gave it to me, Katherine? What have you been afraid of?"

She turned away from his searching eyes. "I . . . I thought it would make you angry. Furious. With me . . . and with Rob, too. I could not bear it, that you would be angry with him and he in his grave. It . . . it has always made you so angry before. Oh, for the love of God, go on, open it before the boat gets here, will you?"

Michael opened the box. She watched him out of the corner of her eye. But his face remained oddly expressionless as he stood there looking down at the old steel ring with the initials "I.C.I." . . . for Ian Curtis Ives, their father. Katherine held her breath against the expected outburst.

"Read what Rob wrote," she urged him.

He picked up a small piece of paper folded once in half. He opened it with one hand, glancing at his sister.

"I know what it says," she told him hastily. "He had me read it back to him when he'd finished it."

Michael's voice was low, his carefully controlled emotions betraying themselves in the slight shake of the hand as he read aloud:

" 'For Michael Edward Ives, my friend and my brother. How I wish I might put this old token of our two families into your own hands myself, but it is better this way, I believe. I am entrusting this letter and this ring to Katherine. She will give them to you when the time is right, before you shall leave home on the next voyage. You know that the ring has always been yours by rights. My father and I have only kept it for you all these years. It has meant much to me, the wearing of it, the memory of our two fathers and what kind of men they were. But now I believe the time has come for you to take back the Sturbridge remembrance, Michael. Wear it with pride, as it has always been worn. Try to forget that anger and bitterness which has kept you from taking it long ago. Wear it for me and for all of us, Sturbridges and Ives, I beg of you. You will know when to pass it on to the next one . . . Rob.' "

Michael folded the little note again and put it back into the box with the ring. For a moment he said nothing. He only stared down at the ring. And Katherine waited, her heart beating very fast.

Finally he did speak, very, very softly. "Why did he do this? God, I'd all but forgotten the ring!"

"He always meant you to have it," she told him. "It troubled him very much. He used to speak of it to me sometimes. But neither of us wanted to cause you any unhappiness."

"It is not really mine, you know," her brother said, shaking his head. "It ought to go to your son, Rob's own son. I do not understand. . . ."

"No!" she shook her head. "It belongs to *you*. It wouldn't have made any difference if we'd had a dozen children. It is your ring, Michael. Rob wanted you to have it. *I* want you to have it. Please, will you accept it? And wear it? You will not refuse it now, surely?"

He saw that she was very close to tears. "You know it has never had the same meaning for me," he said slowly. "It has been as though something was always telling me that I wasn't good enough to wear the ring, or brave enough . . . worthy of it. Oh, I cannot really put it into the right words. I know it's all childish but I have felt better all this time with Sir Tom and then Rob wearing the thing. And now. . . ."

The little boat knocked up against the wooden pier a few yards away from them and one of the sailors called out to Michael.

"Right away!" he shouted back, keeping his eyes fixed on her.

"What will you do, Michael?" she asked, whispering.

He saw the pain in her face. He looked straight into her clear grey eyes and then he nodded sharply. He took the ring from its box and slipped it onto the third finger of his left hand. Odd, how it fitted there so perfectly. He put Rob's letter into his waistcoat pocket.

"I shall hold it in trust for my nephew," he smiled down at her. "An old bachelor like myself, I'll not be likely to have one of my own after all this time. If it will please you, Kate, of course I'll wear it. Just for the time being, just until that boy of yours is old enough to know all about it. But it *is* young Elliot's ring, my love, never forget that. Now, kiss me goodbye and I'll be off. I'll bring you back something wonderful this time, Kate, something grand!" And suddenly he threw his arms about her and hugged her to him fiercely.

Katherine's son came running to them from the lofts, out of breath and panting, waving frantically. Michael saw him and waited with a smile until the boy reached them. Then he picked Elliot up and held him tightly for a moment. Elliot squirmed, then slid agilely to the ground.

"And what shall I bring you next time, Elliot? A parrot, maybe? Or a monkey from Brazil?"

Elliot's dark blue eyes shone at the thought. He was about to answer his uncle when suddenly he caught sight of the familiar old ring, the ring he had always seen on his father's hand. He looked up, first at his mother, then at Michael, and he stepped back away from them, a look of anguish on his young face.

"What is it, darling?" cried Katherine in alarm.

"That is my father's ring!" said the boy coldly. Michael flushed and quickly began to slip the steel ring from his finger, casting his sister a dark look. But Katherine shook her head and pushed Michael's hand back as he held out the ring to Elliot.

"No, Elliot," she said firmly. "It is Michael's ring. It has always been his. Your father was only keeping it for him."

"Katherine, for God's sakes, let the boy have it!" said Michael harshly.

"It is time to go now, Michael," she replied stonily. "Elliot, bid your Uncle goodbye."

His young face frozen into a hard, unyielding expression, Elliot did obey his mother nevertheless and said a very terse farewell. Then he ran off towards the yards again, not looking back to wave. Michael watched him go with troubled eyes but Katherine stood her ground. Then she took his face between her two hands and kissed him, whispering:

"Do not think me hard, Michael. He must learn what is right. The sooner he learns that, the easier his life will be. The ring is yours. Go now, my dear, they are waiting for you. I'll pray for you, Michael, every single day. But you will be all right now. You've got Father's ring on your finger. At last. How glad he would be to know that! Goodbye, Michael, my dearest brother. Goodbye!"

An hour later she stood beside Elliot Landon and his young namesake at the end of the pier, watching the *Sheila Deare* gracefully manouvering her way past the anchored ships about the harbour, moving on out to the open sea. A hearty wind filled up the sails fore and aft, driving her smoothly across the shimmering golden path which the beckoning sun spread out upon the water. Soon only the wide-winged, snowy top-royals were still clearly visible from land, like briskly flapping sea birds' soaring bodies against the heart-blue Atlantic sky.

Katherine had looked anxious at her son's face, hoping to see his astonishing anger gone. And, to her relief, there remained no slightest trace of that brief show of resentment over the old ring. Elliot's young face was calm and slightly smiling as he watched the ship with rapt attention. His mother looked away again, forgetting the incident. But she had not thought to look into Elliot's dark blue eyes. If she had done so she would have realized that the anger, like so many of his deepest felt emotions, had been pushed far, far down deep inside of the boy and that *he* was far from forgetting.

But Katherine did not see any of that. She clung to the sight of those high, white sails long after the ship itself was out of the bay.

"God bless, Michael," she murmured. "God bless!" Now he belonged to the sea again, to the sea and the wind, the sun and the stars. But he has the ring, she thought, he has the ring now.

And finally she turned away, facing into the whipping wind that was carrying her brother's ship along. She walked the length of the pier with the wind whirling about her skirts, catching at the ends of her shawl, teasing colour into her cheeks and stinging her eyes with tears she refused to shed. Michael would go, as he always did, wherever the wind would have him go.

God's breath, she thought, bring him back safe from wherever it is you bear him now!

Book Two:
Belleterre

One

"Belleterre Plantation, Near Charles Town, South Carolina, Mid-August, 1720."

A dazzling white blur of a sun stood fixed in mid-sky, casting a shimmering haze over the wide acres of delicate yellow flowers. It was August, time to harvest the precious indigo plants of Belleterre. The long, straight rows of five- and six-foot-tall stalks quivered ever so slightly as a humid breeze touched them in its passage from the nearby ocean, on its way inland from the low-lying coastal plains of the Carolinas toward the distant, cool blue mountains.

The fleeting breeze stirred a few stray damp tendrils of glistening, Titian-red hair about Eleanor Campion's neck. Annoyed, Eleanor pushed the straggling hairs impatiently back into the thick abundant chignon from which they had escaped. The hair, the back of her fine, slim white neck, the collar of her white linen waist were all soaking wet with perspiration. The linen cloth clung to her body and she longed to go back to the house, strip herself naked and soak her tired body in a cool tub. Her mouth felt dry, although she had paused in her work not five minutes before to take a long drink of water from the covered wooden bucket she always carried slung from her horse's pommel. She decided not to take the time for another drink just yet. The day, begun before six in the morning, would be a very long one and all of it must be spent here in the fields or supervising at the vat sheds. No time to go back to the house or to send someone back to fetch more fresh water. She licked her lips to moisten them and spoke in a soft, low voice to her horse. He responded immediately, falling once again into the slow, steady walk she required of him, careful to keep his feet in the narrow dirt track that ran around the outside of the indigo field.

All around her moved the gangs of harvesters with their razor-sharp machetes, quickly chopping the thin green stems and the yellow flowers and the small, tender top leaves from the plants. Behind the harvesters followed young boys and girls gathering up the cuttings into big cloth sacks. The indigo must be harvested quickly, in no more than four days, and processed at once, within hours of cutting. The next weeks would be the busiest time of the year at Belleterre. Only a few of the workers could be spared to burn and bury the stubble of the plants; the rest of them would be occupied from morning to late night turning stalks, flowers and leaves into the precious blue dye.

As Eleanor rode around one corner of a field nearly picked clean, she came upon her overseer, Dogon, standing watching as the boys carried off the last few sacks and the harvesting gang moved on to another, more distant area.

"It goes well, Mistress," Dogon remarked, smiling, with more of an eye for the golden harvest than for anything or anyone else. "The vats are almost ready, too."

Eleanor reined in her horse, a small, worried frown puckering her brow. "Are you *sure* we've enough firewood to keep the vats going all day?" she asked anxiously, trying in vain to pat some of the perspiration from her face with an already saturated handkerchief.

"Please, Mistress Eleanor, do not be concerned. There is wood to keep them boiling all night long and Dan and his men will be out cutting more before dawn tomorrow," Dogon replied quietly, knowing his words were appreciated although they would be largely ignored. She would worry, he knew. She would go right on worrying about every small detail of the work. She would worry most of all when it was finished and the little thick squares of muslin-wrapped dye were shipped off to England. Last year's harvest, the best and most abundant in all the five years since they'd begun to grow indigo here on the mainland, the harvest that Eleanor had counted on to finish paying the many outstanding debts she had incurred putting Belleterre back on its feet, that harvest full of promise had been lost to them not five days out at sea. Seized by pirates less than fifty miles from Charles Town harbor, sold within the month, no doubt, in the wide open markets of New York for a vast profit . . . a whole year's work and hoping lost.

Eleanor tried to return Dogon's reassuring smile, but instead pressed her lips tightly together and nodded briskly, riding on. They both knew what was at stake now. This harvest, safely shipped and sold in London, would ensure Belleterre's future. If anything were to go wrong this year . . . Eleanor shook her head, refusing to finish the dark thought. *Nothing* would happen to the indigo this year, she vowed, a pang of sheer desperation cutting through her like a physical pain. No, she would keep Belleterre somehow . . . God knows there were enough people against her to discourage anyone but a fool and a "hysterical dreamer of a female" . . . those had been Uncle Sydney's own words on the subject, a "fool and a dreamer." Eleanor sighed slightly, not realizing she did so, and the horse, sensing her mood, nickered gently and turned his head around to look at her for a moment.

Uncle Sydney. Now, why had she had to go and think about him today? Nothing would suit him better than that she fail with Belleterre. Everything she had tried to build here her uncle despised. And she knew it was not only her uncle. Every neighbor around her secretly disapproved of her, of everything about her: her work, her life, the way she insisted upon running her estates, the foolhardy manner in which she lived here, right on the plantation instead of leaving it all in the hands of a competent overseer and moving into an elegant mansion in Charles Town. That was the way everyone else lived. Why couldn't she?

Of course Eleanor knew that none of those things really mattered so much to the aristocratic planters of the Carolina coast. What did matter to them, what bothered them, angered them, even, she guessed, *frightened* them, was that all of their estates were worked by black slaves, a vast, ever-increasing army of black slaves who already outnumbered their masters three to one and whose numbers grew in staggering proportions from year to year. Yet . . . Eleanor Campion did not use slave labor at Belleterre. Eleanor Campion refused to hear of owning such a thing as a slave, not white transported convict slaves from the Indies, not the useless, quick-to-die Indians, not the sturdy durable blacks so easily and, still, so cheaply available from the auction blocks in Charles Town. Eleanor Campion was a scandal, in effect, and Uncle Sydney did not hesitate to tell her so.

"*Dogon!*" Uncle Sydney had exclaimed. "Really, my dear! It's not a Christian name; it's not even a man's name, did you know that?"

"It was the name of his father's tribe, uncle," Eleanor had hardly

331

bothered to explain. "I do not know whether or not he *is* a Christian. Father told me his people came of the Dogon tribe in Africa . . . I do not even know *where* in Africa. I don't suppose he knows, either. But whatever he is called, he has served us well. I could hardly have dreamed of remaking this ruin of a place without his help."

"His *help!*" Sydney Campion had mimicked her tone nastily. "Why must you make everything you do an affront to your neighbors? I tell you, Eleanor, I've known these gentlemen all my life. Most of them were friends of your father's, too, before he abandoned his responsibilities and followed a will-o'-the-wisp down to Antigua . . . and I tell you, they will not put up with your notions very long!"

These remarks, spoken in Sydney Campion's usual dry, nasal drawl, the tone deliberately insulting, had aroused fury in Eleanor, who despised him anyway.

"I care nothing what my 'neighbors' think, uncle," she had answered him icily, trying to ignore the sneer on his face, that face that so little resembled her dead father's handsome, thoughtful countenance. "I mind my own business. Why cannot they return the compliment? God knows we live far enough apart! I manage my lands as I see fit. I haven't the time to meddle in other people's affairs. I will not be intimidated by these 'Christian gentlemen' you say are your friends!"

Sydney Campion's sneer had changed very quickly into a sinister frown of distaste and disgust.

"Island ways," he had sputtered. "Island ways! Being born there on Antigua has ill prepared you for the way we do things here in Carolina, my girl!"

"On the contrary," Eleanor's deep, musical voice had been tinged with contempt. "Antigua was a very model of perfection in the ways of slaves and masters. All I have ever had to do *here* was remember Antigua . . . and do precisely the opposite! That is why I own no slave and never will. If Belleterre and the other two estates Father left me must succeed because of slave labor, then I'll gladly see them fail and fall into worse ruin than your twenty years of neglect has left them. It was my father's teaching . . . your own brother . . . that showed me how wrong those 'island ways' really are! I learned my lessons well because of him. He was the strongest man I have ever known . . . and the gentlest of heart. Odd, how very different from him you are, *uncle. . . .*''

That had been five years ago, a couple of months after she had come to the place her father had spoken of so fondly as "home." Carolina, a land she had never seen, a place in which she now owned three vast and widely separated plantations.

She had nursed her father, governor of Antigua, through the yellow fever only to watch him die from it exactly as her mother had died twenty years earlier, a mother Eleanor did not remember. And when James Campion was gone Antigua suddenly seemed a place of strangers. She wanted very much to be gone from there. A new governor was soon appointed. Eleanor settled her father's few simple, well-arranged affairs quickly and decided that she would not, after all, go to live in England, even if everyone did advise her that that would be the proper thing for a young lady of her station. No, she looked instead to Carolina, curious about those half-forgotten plantations. Europeans had not been long in Carolina, merely a few short decades. The Campions had barely begun to lay claim to the new land; the plantations James had left behind had never produced a crop or showed a penny profit. But suddenly, to Eleanor, they seemed an answer.

It had taken little time for her to pack her belongings. She took only her clothing, her books, her guns . . . for Eleanor had early been taught to ride and shoot and take care of herself. Her character was the product of James Campion's labor of love, the desire to raise his only child to be an independent, self-sufficient useful human being.

Not much escaped Eleanor. Her mind was quick and analytical, her senses naturally sharp, honed even finer and more accurate by years of contact with a man who respected her ideas and encouraged her to respond with respect to others.

At the same time, no woman in the world was more completely a woman than Eleanor. Five feet four inches tall. Slenderly built with long, strong legs, shoulders a trifle broad for such a slim body, yet necessarily wide-spaced to frame and support the full high breasts that had so irritated then intrigued her when they had appeared shortly after her twelfth birthday. A bosom made accurate shooting a bit difficult at first but the problem was soon solved by a slight change of technique. Relieved, Eleanor had begun to enjoy her newly developing womanliness. It did not seriously interfere with

333

the activities she enjoyed most...and there was something remarkably enjoyable, too, about the admiring looks in young men's eyes whenever she entered a room.

Eleanor's own eyes were large and slightly almond-shaped at the corners. Their color, changeable as her many moods, was usually a lovely luminescent sea green, sometimes light and turquoise-cool. By moonlight and candlelight and when she felt very deeply, her eyes often took on the subtle depths of the richest emerald. Her hair, bronze and mahogany blended into shining hues, possessed a rippling natural wave. Her skin was faintly, warmly golden, unfreckled, unaffected by exposure to the sun. She bore a striking resemblance to her father, her features delicately refined from his broadly sketched, generous proportions. She had the same intelligent, discerning expression and the disconcerting habit of speaking directly and frankly to anyone, without guile or playfulness, looking straight into the eyes of the other person as she spoke and as she listened.

Her unusual upbringing had stood Eleanor in good stead when she had arrived alone and without much money in Charles Town, with neither father nor husband to guide or protect her. All she possessed was packed into two large trunks...but in her hands she carried most carefully a leather bag filled with the tiny, hard seeds of the indigo plant that grew so fitfully throughout the islands, that positively refused to grow at all the very moment someone attempted to cultivate it. Indigo, worth many times its small weight in gold anywhere in the civilized world, might make her fortune in Carolina— *if* she could make it grow in sufficient quantity, *if* she could process and pack and ship it properly, *if* indigo could be made to catch on at all in this place to which it was not native.

Of course, the moment Eleanor's plans were known, she became a laughingstock. Nobody bothered trying to raise indigo anymore, she was assured. It had been attempted several times on the mainland, every attempt meeting with abject failure. Now the plantation owners in Carolina were turning their attention to wheat and tobacco, hoping desperately to find a profitable staple crop that would bring them the cash return that tobacco had in Virginia. Yet these crops were failing, too. Carolina was too hot, too humid.

A few years earlier a ship passing through Charles Town had left behind a small bag containing Madagascar rice. The rice, it was found, did very well in Carolina. In fact, Eleanor had planned to try growing a large rice crop on all three estates, with only a small

334

experimental field to be set aside for the indigo. But after seeing the condition of the three places she changed her mind. Clearing neglected land for a rice crop would require more work, more hands and far more money than she could afford as an initial investment. Recklessly she had gambled everything on one cash crop of indigo, deciding to let the other two plantations wait a bit.

And in five short, hard years she rode knee-high along the yellow flowering fields, preparing to harvest the finest, biggest crop so far. *This* harvest must do well, she told herself again and again. She had barely enough money to keep the place going through this last year. She thought again of Sydney Campion. She knew better than to admit that she was having trouble at Belleterre. That information would only whet Sydney's appetite even more for the land he still maintained belonged by rights to him. Sydney, with his son, William, and daughter, Fancy, had been occupying the sprawling, tumbledown farmhouse out on the second, slightly smaller estate, named whimsically enough, although to the point, Eleanor often thought—Rogue's Fall. Her father had called it that long ago in his youth and the name had stuck. At Rogue's Fall Sydney and his family had raised some tobacco and vegetables in a halfhearted way. There had been money, not much, but enough to sustain Sydney in the notion that he was, after all, a gentleman farmer. Entrusted with looking after his brother's properties, Sydney had neglected them shamefully for twenty years and then, roused from his semitropical torpor by Eleanor's unexpected arrival, he had set up a positive howl of indignation when he heard she intended to take control of lands he had considered to all intents and purposes *his*.

Eleanor had said nothing about her uncle's continued residence at Rogue's Fall. At first Sydney and William had attempted to persuade her to make a new division of the estates, including them in the ownership. When she had refused, offering to sell them Rogue's Fall at a reasonable price, Sydney had begun his campaign to take what he claimed was his any way he could. Eleanor had been too busy and too worried to pay much attention to what he was up to. If she could not make a fair profit from this year's crop she would not have to concern herself with Sydney's machinations anyway—she would lose the lands for back debts.

Now she nudged the horse gently with her knee and turned him from the fields, heading a quarter mile beyond to an open, flat space near a thick stand of cottonwood trees. Here they had built the long, open vat sheds, roofed over against a sudden rain, and as far away from the house as possible. There was no odor in the world, Eleanor supposed wryly as she rode along, no smell quite so dreadful as that of the indigo blue pots. Careful as they all were during the "setting" of the blue pots and vats, the stink seemed to stick to their hair and clothing for weeks afterward.

As she approached, several of the women saw her and turned to call out and wave to her. They were stirring the cut plants into huge iron vats as tall as a twelve-year-old boy. Beneath the vats raged roaring wood fires, each with its own two lads close by to keep the fire fed from the piles of cut logs behind them. As the women poured straw and the sumac they used for tannin into the vats, a tremendous, many-fingered swirl of dark smoke puffed up into the already stifling air, coloring the clean, clear sky grey and murky. But everyone was very cheerful. Everyone had a smile for Eleanor, who tried so hard to summon up an encouraging, answering smile for them when she saw the hope in their tired, sweating black faces. They had stayed with her for nothing, for a roof over their heads, for coarse food . . . and not much of that. They had stayed and worked themselves into exhaustion fourteen, sixteen hours a day at Belleterre and she had not had the money to pay them a farthing in wages for ten months! She noted sadly their worn, patched clothing, like her own, but it was not the same thing. She was responsible for all of this; she was responsible to them and felt she should have been able to manage things better, somehow. Still, they had stayed with her, over one hundred fifty of them, and they worked and hoped with her now, for success and for just a little bit of money. . . .

"Well, and where would they go anyway, dear niece?" Uncle Sydney had laughed at what he considered her naïveté on one of his increasingly unwelcome visits. "One foot off of your Utopian Paradise here and they'd all be clapped in chains and parceled out to the farms and plantations in the neighborhood. Of course they've stayed. Where would they go? And, Eleanor, they *are* eating, aren't they now?"

His arrogant smile had widened then and an oily tone crept into his voice as he had added, "Just think, my dear, if you owned those hardy bucks and wenches of yours, you could sell a few of them in town. Enough to pay off some of those annoying bills of yours, eh?"

Eleanor shook off the memory of Sydney's unctuous, insinuating manner, walking slowly from vat to vat, chatting with the women, watching as more of the children appeared from the fields lugging their big sacks of fresh cuttings behind them. The sheds grew noisier and more sociable; the wood flared up in busy flames around the sides of the boiling vats and she allowed herself to believe for a minute that it might all work out this time.

She went to rest for a little while, sitting down on the grass beneath the shady cottonwoods with some of the women who'd been on their feet, like herself, since dawn. She sat still and upright, her arms wrapped about her knees, listening to their soft sweet voices, laughing now and again at the gossip.

She could see it all from here, almost the entire plantation, from sheds and fields to the sloping back lawn and the wilted brown grass behind the house. The house itself had been built up on the highest, coolest point of the property. She enjoyed looking at it like this, three stories high, pale sand-colored walls, white roof, dark green shutters and doors, surrounded by tall trees. It, like the land around it, had been nothing but ruins when she had first come there. The house had been no more than a shell, no roof left on it, only a crumbling stone chimney at one end, a habitation for wandering black bears, raccoons, squirrels, snakes and weasels. The land had been overgrown with swift-rising, tough palmetto, scrub oak and thorny, resistant ground-cover weeds and grass patches. No one could tell by looking just where the ever-watchful forest left off and the once-cleared fields had begun. The forest encroached a bit more each year, trying to take more of its own back. It had been twenty years, after all, since young, wealthy, ambitious James Campion had left to follow the woman he loved all the way back to where she was living on Antigua, to marry her, to share the love of a daughter with her . . . to bury her and, then, caught up in his many political activities in the islands, to stay on and on until finally he was appointed Governor, the best governor Antigua had ever had, they said. James had talked so many times about going "home" again. And then it was too late.

Eleanor had seen to it that the forest was forced back again and told it stolidly not to begrudge her a few sparse acres out of all its vast rich array. Now that forest stood, green black and pungent, at the edges of the well-tended fields. The house had been rebuilt, the land reworked. Indigo, valuable as diamonds, grew and flourished here for her, where she chose to live and call the land "Belleterre" —beautiful earth. And it was, because of her, very beautiful indeed. She and indigo had brought life back to these fields. Next year, if all went well, there would be indigo planted at Rogue's Fall, despite Sydney's protests. But even he could see the money in it, couldn't he? She would put rice in at the third place, Stag Run, when she could spare the labor and the money to clear it, too. Eventually there would be three thriving indigo plantations in Carolina. That was Eleanor's dream, three profitable plantations worked entirely by free labor, three strange little islands, she supposed, in a veritable sea of slavery and false ambitions for empire without compassion, rule without wisdom, profit without participation. If she could succeed, even in a small way, then surely the others would see what might be done in an atmosphere of freedom. Was there a chance for such a dream to come true? It *can*, she thought fiercely, it *can* . . . in spite of Uncle Sydney and the whole lot of them there in Charles Town!

She knew most of her neighbors hated her and her strange ways, yet they had grown to grant a sort of grudging respect to what she seemed to be accomplishing. Not one of them but half hoped she would still fail. Not one, however, who did not keep a close eye on her indigo gamble, ready to try their hand at growing the stuff themselves the very moment they saw she was really making money from it. They all knew very well what power the wealth of indigo could bring with it in the years ahead and it was as a kind of careful insurance now, she guessed, that they took care to greet her so courteously on her rare journeys into Charles Town, that they made sure to include her name on their guest lists for every ball and party. Privately they ridiculed her for refusing to use slaves. Who among them had not sworn that some day Eleanor Campion would be raped and murdered in her bed by some of her insolent free nigras? And, privately, they deplored the way she insisted upon living alone the year round in that huge house with not even the company of a respectable female relative to shield her name from scandal. Why, everyone wondered, did she not invite her uncle's daughter, Frances Campion, to come and stay there with her? Frances, or Fancy, as she had been called from childhood, was not much younger than Eleanor after all and, despite those sly tales one heard whispered about her now and then, still, Fancy was of a respectable family, a suitable companion. Of course, when one looked at the whole situation, it seemed very strange that Eleanor had not simply placed herself under her uncle's protection in the first place and been content to allow him, as her oldest male relative, to conduct the business affairs of the family.

There were dozens of stories going around about Eleanor Campion. She had heard them all, all neatly embellished, and she sometimes wondered how so many people found so much spare time to gossip when she could gladly have used another twelve hours to every busy day.

"Someone's coming from the house," one of the women nudged her, pointing. Eleanor squinted in the sunlight, trying to make out who it was.

"It's your boy, Ada," she said finally. "Maybe bringing some water." There were many small streams down at this end of the property but at this time of year they ran sluggish and muddy. The well they had dug two years past was very deep and supplied abundant fresh, cold water, but the well was up by the house.

"No, he isn't carrying anything," declared Ada positively. "Likely the boys have been fightin', y'know, and Matty's sendin' for you to settle things." She grinned as Eleanor sighed aloud and stood up.

"Miss, come quick!" It was Ezra, Ada's own son, who came running, ostentatiously holding two fingers pinched over his small nose as he approached the smoking, bubbling vats.

"What's wrong, Ezra?" demanded Eleanor. The boy seized her hand and began pulling her back toward the house. Eleanor shook her head, standing where she was. Ezra looked up at her anxiously.

"Ezra, leave off pullin' that way!" snapped his mother. "What's got into you, boy?"

"Nothin' wrong, miss," he said. "A man's here, Matty says. He wants to talk to Miss Eleanor. Come on, miss, it's too hot down here." Once again he attempted to drag her along with him, ignoring his outraged mother's admonitions. Eleanor strode over to her waiting horse and jumped up onto his back.

"Climb up, Ezra, you can ride with me," she ordered, reaching out her hand. The little boy looked dubiously at the huge animal, then leaped up behind her nimbly and clung to her, his small arms barely reaching around her slim waist.

She rode quickly across the fields, up the slope of the lawn. By the time they had reached the house the knot of hair she had so neatly tied up out of the way hours earlier had loosened entirely and her shoulders and back were covered with rivulets of tawny, damp waves.

339

Matty, who generally came to the house and cooked meals for Eleanor when she was working all day in the fields, now stood by the back door shaking her head. As Ezra skidded past her, full of vainglorious pride at having carried out his mission successfully and quickly, Matty swatted him with the back of her hand.

"I didn't tell that boy there was any hurryin' up to be done," she said, her expression clearly disapproving of the state of Eleanor's appearance. "What did he *say* to you?"

"He told me there was a man here to see me," replied Eleanor, trying in vain to smooth down her crumpled white skirt. "I thought . . . it isn't my uncle, is it, Matty?"

Matty's lively dark eyes narrowed. "I would not send the boy running for you if it was your uncle!" she spat the word, her voice sharp with contempt. "You go up the back stairs and wash yourself, change your dress. Then go to the parlor. I'm making some tea . . ."

"*Matty*, who *is* he?" demanded Eleanor in exasperation.

Matty turned back to the stove, shrugging, but there was a small, mischievous smile playing about her mouth.

"I don't know, I'm sure, girl," she whispered with a beautifully musical inflection in her voice. "Maybe some kind of sailing man from a fine, big ship in the bay. That's what he *says*. Very handsome, he is, for a woman who grows old without a man of her own, without children of her own . . . a woman who combs her hair and washes her face. Eleanor, I can smell the blue pots on you, I swear to God 'tis so!"

"Oh, nonsense, Matty!" snapped Eleanor impatiently, deciding to ignore once again Matty's pointed reference to her single state. Who had time for husbands and all that bother? She marched past the small, slender black woman without a backward glance, her head high. Straight into the front parlor she went without bothering to go and pin her hair up again. Some sailor, that's all he was, she told herself. Perhaps he brought news of that shipment of iron tools she had ordered from England fully six months ago.

"Mistress Campion? Mistress Eleanor Campion?" inquired a deep, strong baritone voice. Eleanor stopped short, her eyes traveling up and up toward the face of the man who spoke, who had jumped quickly to his feet as she entered the room and now stood towering over her. He seemed to be all legs, long straight legs clad in black boots and tight white breeches, narrow-hipped and flat in the stomach, with a wide, muscular chest and broad shoulders clad in a plain, heavy blue short coat. The very size of him standing there looking down at her with a puzzled expression, together with a certain aura of great energy that seemed to exude from him, filled up even this spacious room as no presence in it had ever done before.

Eleanor's cheeks flamed as she realized how she must look to him.

Nonsense! she told herself again, very sharply, trying to shake off the inexplicable effect this young man was having upon her.

"Yes, I am Eleanor Campion," she managed to answer him at last. "You have some business with me, sir?"

"I do, ma'am," he replied coolly. "My name is Ives, Michael Ives. My ship is the *Sheila Deare,* docked this morning in Charles Town harbor."

" 'This morning'? And you have come directly here to Belleterre? It must be urgent indeed, Mr. Ives."

"Captain, ma'am. Captain Ives. As to whether my errand be urgent or not is for you to decide. I promised to deliver a letter to you by my own hand and as soon as I could. Here it is, from a lady on Antigua who seemed most distressed when she gave it to me."

He took a small, fairly thick packet of pale blue paper, folded double across and sealed closed with red wax, from inside his coat and handed it to her.

Eleanor seized it eagerly, glanced at the thin, fine handwriting and uttered a small, glad, involuntary cry. He stood watching her, his piercing blue eyes studying her face with some interest, his head tilted at a slight angle as though he were looking at some strange species of creature, trying to figure it out. Eleanor glanced back at him, smiling in some confusion.

"Do please forgive my bad manners, Captain," she said. "Pray sit down and take some refreshment. You find me in the midst of harvesting. I've only just come in from the fields. I had no idea . . . I was not expecting callers. . . ."

Captain Ives did not smile, but he nodded somewhat gravely and seated himself on the edge of a fragile-looking blue satin chair by the hearth, his long legs appearing even longer now. Eleanor rang for Matty and sat down across from him, still clutching her letter tightly. She looked at it longingly, wondering if he would think her impossibly rude if she were to open it and read it at once. As if he read her thoughts, Captain Ives leaned back in his chair a bit gingerly and motioned to her.

"Please go ahead and read it, ma'am, never mind me," he said. "I know the lady who wrote it, Mistress Fletcher; she said she was an old friend of yours. She seemed to think it most urgent." And there was a carefully restrained curiosity in his manner as he sat there calmly. Eleanor cast him a grateful smile and opened the letter carefully, thinking aloud as she pressed the folded pages open in her lap.

"Yes, Ellen Fletcher is a very dear old friend indeed. She was married to my father's assistant years ago. Her husband died in a storm at sea on his way to England on business. I have not heard from Ellen in three or four years. She seemed distressed, you say?" She frowned a bit.

"Most distressed, ma'am. She insisted on paying me in Spanish gold for my trouble. I told her it was not necessary, that I would be glad to have one of my men bring you her letter. I intended to put in at Charles Town anyway, you see. But when I said that, Mistress Fletcher looked very upset. I thought she was going to cry, in fact. She took me by the hand and begged me not to entrust the letter to anyone else. She actually made me swear I would not let it out of my possession until I had placed it into your hands myself. She seemed almost afraid of anyone other than you knowing about it."

"How strange!" murmured Eleanor, quite puzzled. She did not remember Ellen Fletcher as a hasty or overly dramatic woman. She excused herself hurriedly and began to read:

My dearest Eleanor,

I shall omit the many questions I would ordinarily ask after so long a silence. What I have to tell you is of the utmost importance to you, although I do not know what you may be able to do about it. God knows, dear child, you have had much to contend with all by yourself and this new trouble may prove worse than all that has gone before. But at least you will have this bit of forewarning. Now and hastily, to the matter: your father's brother, Sydney Campion, has been exchanging letters over the past few months with Governor Able as well as with an attorney named Richards, a relative newcomer to Antigua. Sydney Campion has inquired most particularly about your poor, deceased mother. He has asked for information about your birth here, details of every kind concerning *you*, much that would seem none of his business in light of what you wrote me about him three years ago. I know he is no true friend to you even if he is your uncle. I do not yet know the extent of his hostility or what he hopes to accomplish with all of his prying. I only learned of this a few days ago and then only because of my friendship with the Governor's wife. She mentioned that Master Richards had spoken to her husband about an *inheritance* claim against someone who had once lived here. She spoke the name "Campion" and she is, of course, aware that your father once held the same post as her husband. Naturally I pursued the subject with great care. I do not yet know how your uncle hopes to substantiate his claims to your property, only that he has engaged Master Richards to act on his behalf in the matter. Please be on your guard insofar as your uncle is concerned and write to me as soon as possible to let me know you have received this safely. Pray God I shall discover more about it very soon. Your old friend,

Ellen Fletcher.

Eleanor's fingers trembled as she folded the letter once more. She had forgotten there was anyone else in the room with her and she sat with her head bowed in thought, feeling deathly cold, actually numb with dread. What did it all mean, she wondered dimly. What was her uncle up to now?

"Mistress Campion? Are you quite well?"

She looked up, startled, to see Captain Ives standing over her, genuine concern on his fine-featured face. A bit of a polite smile hovered on her lips, and then she dropped all pretense, shuddering.

"I . . . I don't really know," she said, her voice strained.

"It was bad news, then?" He sounded sympathetic and, as he spoke, his glance moved quickly around the big room, looking for some brandy or other restorative to give her.

"'Bad news'?" she whispered wearily. "Yes, I think so. Or, rather, a warning . . ."

Matty entered the room bearing a heavy silver tray laden with tea things and a plate of thin-sliced carrot cake. She looked over at Eleanor, then set the tray down very quickly and went to her, glaring at Captain Ives.

"What has he said to you?" she demanded loudly, taking Eleanor's small chin in her hand and studying the pale face intently. "What's happened, girl?"

343

Eleanor looked at her, shaking her head slightly, her glance moving to the Captain, who appeared genuinely alarmed. She tried to laugh a little and forced herself to speak calmly.

"What must the Captain think of us, Matty? Truly! Do serve the tea. I have had a most . . . unusual . . . letter, that is all. We can discuss it later. *Later*, you understand, Matty? Please, please pour the tea. I feel so stupid, my hands are not quite steady just yet. Captain Ives, do forgive me for all of this. Sit down and have your tea, or perhaps a bit of whiskey? I believe we have a bottle about here somewhere . . ."

Captain Ives opened his mouth as if he would say something but the imploring look on Eleanor's white face, the harsh, disapproving stare of the elegantly graceful black woman by her side, made him change his mind. Abruptly he straightened up, crossed the room and took his seat again. Matty said no more but quickly served the tea. He noticed that when she handed Eleanor her cup she clasped her hands about Eleanor's shaking hands and held them quite steady for a moment, until Eleanor had a firm grip of the saucer. It was a small gesture, full of unspoken but deeply felt affection, for all the apparent stiffness in the older woman's manner.

And when she took the empty tray and was about to leave the room, he noticed, too, that Eleanor Campion wordlessly placed the letter into her hand with a look of understanding between them that told him Matty would read it herself as soon as she was alone.

When Matty had closed the door behind her he spoke. "Will there be an answer, Mistress Campion? If there is I will be glad to carry it to the captain of a sloop at anchor in Charles Town. He sails for the Indies in three days' time. I would be happy to deliver it myself, of course, but I am heading home from Carolina now."

"'Home'? Then you are not from this part of the country, Captain Ives?" She tried to hide her disappointment. She did not want to trust any letter she would write to Ellen to anyone but this man; she had taken it for granted he would be sailing south again from Charles Town.

"No, ma'am. We're bound for Boston, in the Massachusetts Bay Colony. We've been at sea five months, nearly six now. I had some cargo to drop off at Charles Town this time but I've never touched port in these waters before."

Eleanor studied him with new interest. "Boston? I wouldn't have said so. You have the sound of . . . I was going to say a native-born

Englishman but, no, there's something else . . . I can't make it out. . . ."

"Irish, ma'am," he smiled briefly but the smile only served to reinforce the grave, almost somber aspect of his quiet face.

"'Irish'?" exclaimed Eleanor, determined to keep up the conversation despite her growing nervousness over Ellen's letter. "Were you born in Ireland, then? My mother's people were Irish."

He nodded, almost as if he'd known she was going to tell him that. He was watching her closely, realizing the effort it cost her to go on being polite, being the good hostess. His expression showed her very plainly that it was all right for her to drop the amenities and talk about what was really on her mind.

But Eleanor was too used to keeping her own counsel and far too prudent to confide in a stranger. She made one or two more stabs at light talk and then fell silent, finishing her tea, setting the delicate bone china cup and saucer down carefully on the table beside her.

"I . . . I would like you to stay and have supper with us, Captain Ives," she heard herself saying suddenly. Good Heavens, *why* had she said that now, today of all impossible days? Even if the damnable letter had not arrived there was to be no real supper served at Belleterre tonight or for the next several nights, not until the harvesting was finished. Matty usually left something for her on the back of the stove, something she could eat quickly whenever she came back to the house. She was vaguely annoyed with herself. She had to talk with Matty about Ellen's letter . . . why didn't she just thank this young man and send him on his way at once?

Yet, as she looked at him, her gaze sweeping the intense, unreadable blue eyes, the wide firm mouth, the longish square jaw, she felt an irresistible urge to trust in him, to rely upon him. Why? Did she instinctively sense the same aura of strength and dependability about him that had appealed to Ellen Fletcher? There is something . . . something very *fine* in him, she thought, at the same time laughing at herself for thinking it. Why, the man might be a cutthroat rogue for all she knew! Look, she commanded herself . . . not realizing that he was quite aware of her close, frank scrutiny . . . look at that unexpected, almost hidden little light in those very perceptive eyes, those eyes that both attracted her and troubled her, eyes that seemed to see right through her into her very brain and heart. What did that light mean? A stray, restless, darting glint of something unsaid, perhaps unsayable, in the handsome, tautly disciplined face? What did that strange light tell about this man? And, even as she looked and wondered and felt momentarily uneasy with him again, still, when she repeated her invitation she knew she very much *wanted* him to stay.

"Yes, I'll stay," he replied, unsmiling, but his expression softened as he looked straight and steadily back into her lustrous green eyes. "I should be delighted to take supper with you, ma'am, if it is no bother? You did mention a harvest?..." He paused delicately, watching her. He offered her a way out and wondered if she'd take it. But she shook her head firmly and, for the first time since he'd laid eyes on her, her smile was genuine and meant for him.

"It is the least we can do to repay your kindness in coming so far out of your way," she murmured.

But Michael caught the unconscious undertones beneath the well-mannered little speech and saw that she had just realized she did not want him to leave. The alert, disciplined hardness so habitual in his face disappeared for an instant, briefly, but long enough so that Eleanor caught a glimpse of the man inside the captain's suit of clothes. That glimpse revealed to her a person so alone, so withdrawn from others, so totally vulnerable even in the midst of all of his marvelous strength, that she involuntarily stepped back a bit from him, feeling a slight shock at the depth of his unexpected revelatory trust in *her*. Is this how it happens? she asked herself in amazement. Is this . . . this looking and really, really seeing inside of someone what it is like to know *love?* The thought, fleeting as it was, caught her entirely off guard. She made a helpless little motion with her hand, a gesture hitherto unknown to her. She amazed herself and had no explanation. She turned from him, not knowing what to say. She fought for composure and not until she thought the fight won was she able to look at him again, and even then hesitantly, wondering what she would see in those remarkable eyes.

And then she sighed with relief. His apparently habitual expression of grave, quiet aloofness had returned. He looked at her with polite interest now and nowhere could she discover that elusive light or the naked hunger of loneliness she had seen in him but a moment before. You wear your mask very well, Captain Ives, she thought with wry respect . . . would that *I* might learn to do so, too!

"Good, it's settled then," she said briskly. "I shall have to leave you to your own devices for the afternoon, I'm afraid. Perhaps you

346

would care to rest. Or, you might prefer to take one of the horses and look about the estate? I'm afraid I cannot spare someone to keep you company."

He looked amused. His fair eyebrows raised, a touch of irony appeared in his glance. "Please don't concern yourself about me, Mistress Campion. I'm sure I'll find some pleasant way to occupy the time."

"Then I'll ask Matty to have supper ready by seven. Will that be all right?"

He nodded, reaching for another slice of Matty's carrot cake. She looked at him for a few seconds, then went off, leaving him quite alone in the big, cool room with the slightly green-tinted sunlight filtering in through half-closed jalousies. He could hear her voice in a distant room and then the voice of her cook or maid or whoever "Matty" was, he was not sure. Then he heard the slam of the back door.

The place was quite still now. He felt comfortably alone here, rather peaceful and relaxed. He stood up to return his teacup and cake plate to the table. Passing by a window he looked out idly and saw the two women together walking very slowly back and forth on the scorched patch of green behind the house. The black one, Matty, was holding the letter he had delivered, waving it rather angrily, he thought, and Eleanor Campion was nodding her head. Her shoulders were slumped, the whole attitude of her body was one of dejection, defeat . . . and he felt an unexpected surge of hostility toward the distracted, middle-aged little woman in Antigua who had sent a letter that could so affect this magnificent creature.

Michael turned swiftly from the window, a scowl on his face. He eyed the delicate china clock on the mantel across from him. He shouldn't have agreed to stay, he told himself. It was none of his business, none of his concern. He wished he had never agreed to take the letter. He wished now simply to pick up his hat and go without seeing her again, without being drawn into whatever her troubles were.

He even walked into the dark hallway, and then he remembered that the man who had driven him out here in the mule-cart was long gone and he had no way of getting back to Charles Town unless he wanted to walk the whole fourteen miles in the heat of the day.

Then he shook his head and laughed, and knew himself three times a fool. But he turned back into the parlor, determined to ease

347

off his boots, stretch out upon that most inviting-looking sofa and get some sleep while he waited for whatever the evening would bring.

The sofa was even softer than he'd imagined. He draped his coat carefully over the back of it, tucked his boots alongside it and lay back to sleep. But, the moment he did so, his mind was flooded with a hundred questions. Resigned, knowing full well he would get no rest so long as his curiosity was unsatisfied, he folded his arms behind his head and gazed dreamily at the late summer sunbeams that poured in tilted and tenuous through the windows. . . .

I'll ask Matty to have supper ready, he remembered Eleanor Campion had said. I'll *ask*. Did these haughty Carolina plantation owners ever *ask* a slave to do something? He doubted it. He had seen enough of slavery, in the Indies, in England and France and Spain, as well as along the American coast. Slaves were *told* what to do, never asked. Strange, he mused. But it was only one of many things he found strange here. Perhaps it was only that the mistress of Belleterre was very fond of this particular black woman.

Other thoughts came pushing in. What kind of crop would be ready for harvest in the middle of August? Michael knew farming as well if not better than he knew the sea and he knew that every warm, sunny day in August and most of September, too, was desperately important to the final ripening of anything—grain, fruit or vegetable. Another mystery . . . and, even as the word flashed across his consciousness, he discarded the notion with irritation. Things remained mysteries only as long as they remained unexplained, no longer.

Once again his thoughts shifted and in his mind's eye he recalled the vision of Eleanor Campion smoothing the small pages of her letter with shaking fingers even as she struggled with her obvious emotion for control. Why should he care what news had been in that letter? He would have his supper; they would undoubtedly chat about farming and seafaring, the newest fashions in London, probably she would bring the conversation around to the subject of Ireland again, she would wonder if he might have come across her mother's family. Funny how people always thought everyone in Ireland knew everyone else. But, when the evening came to an early close, he would bid Eleanor Campion good night, take his leave of her and never see her again. And what of that? Nobody liked to be the bearer of bad tidings, he told himself a bit ruefully, then found himself grinning the next instant, an ironic, telling grin utterly bereft of merriment. Admit it, he told himself, there is something about this woman . . . this *girl*, for she was yet quite young . . . something about Eleanor Campion. . . .

For the life of him he could not fathom exactly what that *something* was, but he did not want to part from her so soon. He shook his head in chagrin and then yawned widely, his eyes closing, and drifted off to sleep with the disturbing memory of tumbling red gold hair and sweet, loving eyes and a soft caressing laugh. But, a dreamlike voice seemed to be telling him, Eleanor Campion had not laughed at all, not once. . . .

Two

"Indigo and Emerald"

1 Eleanor and Matty

"I have never been afraid of him before, Matty. *You* know I have always thought him nothing more than selfish and pretentious. But now . . ."

Matty folded her arms, frowning, and turned to Eleanor, her firm mouth twisted into a bitter, knowing grimace.

"I know that kind of man, I have told you more than once. He is no jest. He wants what he wants very, very badly and he will take it away from you if you allow it. He is not like your father. Why have you not seen this? Do not put so much trust in blood; it flows its separate rivers in us all and it does not remember the place from which it rises."

Eleanor had no answer for her. It was true, Matty had warned her from the start to get Sydney Campion and his family to leave her property. Matty had said more than once that she must protect herself from these people. But no matter how much she despised the man, he was her father's brother! She had allowed him to stay on at Rogue's Fall year after year . . . was she to shame her father's memory by casting his only living relatives out of the only home left to them? She had hoped Sydney would interest himself in what she was trying to accomplish, that he would help her and that, as a family, they might all profit from the development of the land. But Sydney had soon proved himself an ever-present thorn in her side, free to ride over to Belleterre anytime he wished, to criticize her and belittle her efforts. She knew she had only herself to blame that the man was still around to plague her. She looked at Matty, nodding thoughtfully. Matty had little patience with anyone who deliberately turned their back upon a dangerous enemy. But, that was the very thing. She had never before considered that Sydney was dangerous. She had, it seemed, sadly underestimated him.

"If only Ellen had been able to discover what his scheme really is," she remarked slowly, fingering the letter in her skirt pocket. "I don't know how to fight him. I don't know how he expects to win."

"You have waited too long," insisted Matty tersely. "You allowed him to choose the weapons he will fight you with . . . and he has chosen. Now you will be forced to defend yourself while he has had the advantage of the attack."

"I know," breathed Eleanor heavily. "But, Matty, why has he tried to find out things about me, and about Mother? Surely that has nothing to do with his claims. It is my father's will he must attempt to set aside and that will was examined by Governor Able himself and declared valid on every point. I sent a copy of it to a firm of solicitors in London, the firm Father dealt with himself, and they assured me I had no need for concern. I don't understand what my uncle is doing!"

Matty glanced at her shrewdly. "Perhaps he hopes to find some way to say the marriage between your parents was not just right. If he can do this, then can he not claim you are not the . . . legal . . . heir?"

Eleanor's head whipped around, her eyes pale and wide with sudden anger. "That's madness! They were married in Church. There were witnesses, friends of theirs. There was a certificate!"

Matty placed a hand on her shoulder. "It is only that we must try to think, for once, as he thinks. Your mother, she was a Catholic, no? How, then, was the marriage performed? By a priest?"

Eleanor shook her head in confusion. "I don't know! Father never spoke very much about her; it was too painful for him. She died a year after I was born and there wasn't anybody I could ask about her. She went to the islands as the governess of a wealthy family. She traveled up here with them to Charles Town—that is where Father met her—and after she went back to Antigua with them, he followed her there and married her."

350

"Perhaps that family remembers her," offered Matty hopefully. "You might write and inquire of them where your mother came from, if she still has relatives somewhere."

Eleanor shook her head. "No," she declared hopelessly. "The husband died and his wife took the children back to England. I don't even remember their name. Oh, Matty, you were with us so many years . . . don't you remember Father ever saying anything? Did he ever get a letter from Mother's family when I was little?"

"No, he did not," said Matty a bit stiffly. There was a hint of pain in her voice. Eleanor bit her lip, looking into Matty's eyes with infinite regret.

"I'm sorry," she whispered. "It all seems so long ago, so far away from us here. Sometimes I forget you loved him."

Matty's expression was hard, defensive for an instant, but then she smiled. "Sometimes I, too, am able to forget. It is better that I do. I am always very lonely for him, despite the years that are passing. But I do not forget, ever, that I love you, too. And he did not speak to me of your mother. As far as I know he never heard a word from her people."

Eleanor hugged the older woman, feeling once again as she had since she was six years old a sense of comfort and caring whenever Matty was with her. Matty had been so beautiful then, so proud and graceful in the simple cool clothes she wore, laughing at the frills and furbelows of white women's fashions in the tropics, choosing instead light cotton robes in the style of her own people, without sleeves, hanging straight in soft gathered folds to her ankles. Matty had never been a slave. She had married a French army officer on duty in Egypt, an aristocrat who laughed in the face of convention and loved where he pleased, who found her a beautiful child of Libyan nomads and wooed her as carefully and devotedly as he would have wooed any princess of any court in Europe. He had, at length, won her love for himself and married her once in her father's camel hair tent and again in his own Church. He had taken her with him to Antigua and left her for a distant battlefield, for war was, of course, his profession and his first passion. He had died on that battlefield, leaving Matty well provided for. His death, his leaving a black widow with a comfortable fortune alone in a land of black slaves had caused some consternation in Antigua. Matty was suspect, and stood in danger of losing her inheritance and her freedom. For a while she did not much care for either. She wished she herself might die of the loneliness and heartache. And then she had met the Governor of Antigua, a widower with a little girl to raise. After a time, she and James Campion knew they loved one another. He wanted her to marry him, he had begged her, tried every means of persuasion he could think of, but Matty realized the Governor of Antigua could not wed a black woman, not in that place where all others of her color lived enslaved and an Englishman might bed any wench he fancied so long as he did not dignify his lust with a marriage contract.

Matty moved into the governor's mansion, quietly, taking charge of the house, raising Eleanor, and if there were people who whispered about the Governor's black mistress they never dared say anything to his face. When James had died and Eleanor came to Carolina, Matty remained on the island. It was her home after all those years. She still had a little land of her own, a bit of money put aside. She thought she was safe enough. She had forgotten too much. . . .

She had not been safe. Eleanor was not gone three months when, under some legal pretext, Matty had been seized and her land and monies confiscated. Negroes were not allowed to own property. Negro women were not to live freely without the "protection" of a white master. Matty had been put up for sale along with the latest sorry survivors of a shipload of West Africans. The only thing that had saved her was the chance miracle of one of James Campion's old friends happening to stop by the auction square that particular afternoon. To his utter horror and astonishment he realized that the tattered, half-naked woman in chains before his eyes was the same person who had often graced the dinner table with her beauty and nimble conversation, the same woman whom James had thought so highly of and whatever her complexion, was known to have made him and his daughter happy.

The old friend paid fifty pounds in gold for Matty, but when the auctioneer's assistant had dragged her before him and forced her to her knees, the man could not look her in the eyes for shame. It had been Matty herself who stood up then and, almost smiling, thanked him quietly and begged him not to be troubled on her account. He had taken her home with him and put her in his wife's care, meanwhile writing to Eleanor of the whole disgraceful situation. Eleanor wrote back at once, asking if she might pay back the fifty pounds and send for Matty to come to her. And, when the next ship from Antigua dropped anchor in Charles Town harbor, there was

Matty, free once again, a gift from James Campion's old friend, a gift from Heaven. Eleanor had often had occasion to thank God for Matty's strong, reassuring presence these last five trying years in America.

Now Matty lived in her own small cottage not very far from the main house, never too far from Eleanor's voice and Eleanor's needs. She cooked for the other workers on the place; she trained several younger women to cook and keep house and, except during planting and harvest times, she taught reading and writing to any who wanted to learn. She knew very well, as did Eleanor, that the blacks were not supposed to learn such things, but everything else at Belleterre was different and extraordinary and condemned by the neighbors, too. Neither of them ever talked about Matty's little schoolroom in the cozy parlor of her cottage. Neither of them thought there was anything in particular to talk *about*. Matty was the only mother Eleanor had ever known and, now that her father was gone, Matty was the only human being on the face of the earth who could, with a quiet word or a meaningful look, influence Eleanor's tempestuous, headlong hurl through life.

2 There Is Also Desire

"I shall write to Ellen at once," Eleanor said with sudden decision. "Captain Ives promised to give my answer to someone who is going back to Antigua in a few days."

"Will you ask your uncle about this?" queried Matty sharply.

Eleanor shook her head. "No! Not until I have all the facts. But . . . perhaps William knows something. I might be able to—"

Matty's lips tightened disapprovingly. "He will tell you nothing," she said flatly. "I have said to you, watch out for that one, too. He is his father's son. Perhaps he is even more dangerous because he wants *you*, as well as the land. Sharpen your claws, little one, but know where to use them. William will be of no help."

"Oh, God, Matty!" cried Eleanor. "I'm so tired of all this! Why can't they all just leave us alone?"

Matty's stern face softened in sympathy. Still, she shrugged, nodding as if Eleanor had just said something telling.

"How do you like that one?" she inquired suddenly. "A most interesting man, I think."

"Who? You mean Captain Ives?" Eleanor's eyes widened in surprise. "I haven't given him a second thought. . . ."

Matty laughed shortly. "Think, then, child of my heart! You must take a man sooner or later. It would be just as well for us all if you picked the right one quickly."

Eleanor stared at the older woman for a moment, caught between amusement and dismay. Then she kissed Matty very lightly on the cheek.

"We can do very well without men," she smiled a bit wryly. "Oh, he's staying to supper, Matty. Could you have something ready at seven?"

" 'Something,' " Matty nodded. "You *do* like him, then, or he would be gone by now."

"Matty!"

"Go along back to the harvest," Matty was laughing at her and gave her a little push. Eleanor strode over to the patient horse and jumped up on his back. "We do *not* do so *very* well without them!" Matty called after her, but Eleanor sat up very straight in the saddle and did not look back. "Never mind, little one, you will find out for yourself one of these days," the black woman murmured to herself as she turned back to the house.

She heard nothing from the parlor and peered in before going to the kitchen. Michael Ives, his long, white-stockinged feet sticking up over the end of the sofa, lay fast asleep in the afternoon sun. A light trace of perspiration on his high, straight forehead dampened the blond hair, separating it into small, boyish curls.

Matty tiptoed past him and quietly drew the curtains against the bright sunlight. Then, with a small smile, she stared down at him for a few seconds, liking what she saw. As she stood there she could hear faint, far-off sounds of singing from the fields.

Little enough they have to sing about, she thought, if they cannot succeed with this crop. Yet she enjoyed the sound anyway. It was strong and quick, with no trace of melancholy to it. It reminded her sometimes of the singing of the herdsmen in the desert as they tended their flocks of goats, so long ago she barely remembered it, so long since she had been only a girl herself.

The man on the sofa murmured something in his sleep. His arm moved restlessly. Matty inspected him more closely. He was not much past forty, she thought. He looked much younger relaxed in sleep, almost like a child. Had he children of his own? she wondered suddenly. She had not thought before, but he was probably married. The idea irritated her and she wrinkled her small nose, annoyed that

354

it had occurred to her now. And, yes, now she noticed the dull gleam of metal on his hand . . . a ring. Some lover's keepsake, wife and sweetheart never any farther from his mind than a quick glance at her ring. . . .

Matty bent down low to examine the ring. She had never seen one quite like it before, massive and grey, quite plain, with neither gemstone nor plaited lady's hair-knot for adornment. It was a man's ring, she decided. Surely no woman would choose such a gift for one she loved. Matty noticed the well-worn initials, *I.C.I.* His name was Ives, she recalled. So it was only a family heirloom, probably his father's before him. I.C.I. She muttered the word it spelled in French, "ici." "Here," she translated, intrigued. Quite a compelling motto for any man to live up to . . . if it had ever been thought of as a motto.

She straightened up and bestowed another secret smile on him. Then she left him there to rest, closing the sliding double door from the hallway behind her.

Back in the kitchen she set her great stewpot on the stove, cut up a scant bit of beef and a great deal of potatoes and carrots and greens and left them simmering away together. Then she left the house to go and look for some early-ripening blueberries. If she found enough she might make a few sweet tarts for the supper. She refused to admit why it was, that as she walked along through the trees in her quick way, she felt elated for the first time in many years. Yet it was so and, in the close shade of the green-laden branches, her lips began to echo the words of the song she could still hear from the fields. And for no reason at all she thought of Eleanor's dead father and of the honorable French officer before him. Putting Sydney Campion resolutely out of her mind, she allowed herself the luxury of remembering the touch of a man's body against her, the feeling of love shared together, the exquisite languor of sleeping cradled in a man's strong arms. Eleanor must not be cheated out of that. Strength and resolution are not the only sources of joy. *There is also desire.*

3 Fancy Campion

Three fields were stripped that day and the long row of vats bubbled and steamed as more wood was piled beneath them and more pale yellow flowers stirred into them. The singing stopped a while later as a few of the men set to work burning the shorn stalks still standing and everyone else was busy in the sheds.

The afternoon eased by gently up at the house, the sun moving on at last, leaving the parlor cool and shadowy. Matty had returned and inspected her stew, baked her tarts and gone away again to her own house. And Captain Michael Ives slept on in the silent room, hardly moving at all.

Four days before, while still at sea, there had been one of those sudden, terrible Caribbean storms just as the *Sheila Deare* had sighted the tip of Florida to the west. A hurricane it had been, blowing its damned foul winds and strangling rain without letup while captain and crew struggled to keep the ship afloat, picking their way carefully back and forth along the slippery, wildly thrashing planks, riding out the storm's tormented rage. And since then there'd been precious little time for sleep. Michael had thought to deliver the letter and be back aboard ship before noon today, ready for a long nap. There was no work being done on the *Sheila Deare* this day. He'd given strict orders for every man to rest after their long, grueling ordeal.

It was not much past four when the sound of a horse's hooves might have been heard coming up the front drive, if anybody at the house had been listening. The horse stopped. Small, light footsteps came swiftly up the steps. There was a knock at the door, a pause, then a much louder, longer, more determined knocking. And, after another short pause, the door was slowly opened and a pretty voice called out,

"Eleanor? Eleanor? Anybody here? Matty, are you out there in the kitchen?"

There was no answer. The door was opened wider, then closed again and the footsteps proceeded straight down the hallway.

"Eleanor—you upstairs? Oh, where *is* she? Eleanor?"

Michael stirred on his sofa, his eyes opened briefly, then closed again. He'd thought he'd heard someone call. Must be mistaken. He stretched himself and began to turn around on his side when the hall door was opened and a small head poked inside.

"Eleanor, is that you, honey? Nappin' in the middle of the afternoon? How positively un—un*productive* of you, darlin'!"

Suddenly, in a state of utter confusion, Michael sat bolt upright, rubbing his eyes as he tried to see in the dim afternoon light.

"Why, *you're* not my Cousin Eleanor!"

Now the bright, cheery voice was much closer, quite inside the room with him. He squinted and stared very hard. Standing about six feet away, looking over at him with an expression of alarm and delight, was a tiny, dainty young lady attired in a dazzling scarlet riding frock, the long train of the garment draped gracefully over one arm. Michael had not the least idea in the world who she was or what she was doing there. He rose hastily, clearing his throat several times while he reached blindly about him for his coat.

The young lady opposite him regained her composure with admirable speed, now staring up at the full height of him, her eyes wide with surprise . . . and interest.

"You're very tall, sir," she observed boldly.

"I . . . er . . . um . . . where the devil is Mistress Campion?" Michael was horrified to discover there was a decided frog in his throat and his words came out harsh and scratchy. This evidently did not disturb his unexpected visitor one bit.

"Well, I'm sure I don't know, sir," she replied with a giggle. "Who the *devil* are *you?*" Her tone was roguishly merry as she repeated his own uncivil expression and she brushed past him as she went to the windows and began opening the curtains again, letting the late afternoon sun stream into the room.

"Captain Michael Ives, miss," he replied gruffly. "I'm Mistress Campion's guest." Gratefully he discovered his coat and put it on as quickly as he could, remembering then that he had also removed his boots and must present a sorry spectacle indeed, standing there rumpled and wrinkled and bleary-eyed in his stocking feet.

The lady turned back to look at him, charmingly flinging down the train of her gown behind her. With the sun at her back she seemed to be standing in a golden glow, framed about in light, and at last he was able to make out her features distinctly. Her hair, piled elegantly in little curls and rolls atop her head, was honey blond and soft about a face delicately oval, a tiny uptilted nose, two big violet blue eyes, a rather full, perhaps sometimes petulant mouth, a dimpled chin. She wore a most absurd little velvet and feather hat perched precariously aloft on the blond curls, scarlet, too, like her gown, and on her hands were slim, soft black kid gloves.

She was enjoying the long look he gave her. He rather imagined she was used to being stared at by men and that she usually enjoyed it. She was, all in all, quite a contrast with his absent hostess, Eleanor Campion. This one . . . what had she said? A cousin? Well, this cousin was most assuredly a high-flying, bright bird of fashion!

"How are you, Captain Ives?" she drawled in amusement.

"Since there is no one here to introduce us, I shall have to assume you are a gentleman and just introduce myself. I'm Fancy Campion, Eleanor's cousin. *Younger* cousin," she added, her violet eyes sparkling gaily, and she came forward with her little gloved hand extended.

Michael nodded very briskly, ignoring the hand, and sat down to put his boots back on. Fancy Campion withdrew her hand as if he'd bitten it, but continued to smile as she watched him.

"Speakin' of my cousin, do you know where she is, Captain? I know she wasn't expectin' me today, but she never comes into town, so I thought I'd just ride over and invite myself to supper."

"She's working, I think," said Michael. "Something about a harvest? . . ."

Fancy's gay laugh trilled out through the big room. "Oh, yes, of course! The blessed *indigo!* How could I have forgotten? And Eleanor is right out there in the fields with all those charmin' blackamoors of hers, workin' side by side and up to her . . . her shoulderblades in the blue pots! Eleanor is so . . . so virtuous about all that, you know."

"A rather admirable trait I'd say, to be hard working. Wouldn't you agree, Miss Campion?" He cast her a long, hard look of ironic amusement that entirely escaped Fancy.

"Heavens, yes, Captain! No one admires Eleanor more than I do, I'm sure. Except my brother, William, of course," she smiled with a certain calculation in her expression. "William is going to marry our cousin one of these days."

"Is he, now?"

"Oh, yes. Poor Eleanor's had to struggle with all this by herself far too long, Papa says. Papa's my Cousin Eleanor's uncle. I mean, *her* Papa and my Papa were brothers, before her Papa died, do you see?"

"I see," he answered her dryly. Fancy blushed, laughing again, and then went on talking blithely as she swept about the room, openly looking into chests and drawers, poking her exquisite nose into places Michael was positive she had no business, even picking up and riffling through a pile of correspondence lying on a writing table by the windows. Michael did not know quite what to do with her. He had the feeling that Eleanor would not approve if she were there but he was a stranger; he could hardly say anything to her own cousin. Finally Fancy seemed finished with her inspection. She turned her attention to him once again, seating herself grandly with her scarlet train spread out around her small, booted feet, motioning him to sit next to her. But Michael was wary of her. He took a chair across from her and wished someone else would come in.

"Now, Captain *Ives?* It is Ives, is it not? Captain Ives, do tell me all about yourself. You look so awfully young to be a ship's captain, I must say. Any sea captains I've ever seen were awful, walrusy old coots with whiskers down their tubby chests and tobacco juice streamin' from their mouths every time they said a word! And, my dear *sir,* the things they do say! Enough to make a lady blush just thinkin' about it! You certainly are an improvement! A decided improvement. . . ." Fancy rattled on, looking at him with frank interest, a little smile continually coming and going on her pouting red lips.

Michael saw very soon that he would not get a chance to say much of anything to her. She liked to hear herself talk far more than she cared to hear about anyone else. Beyond mentioning the name of his ship and the fact that he came from Boston, he told her nothing of himself. But he did seize the opportunity of finding out more about Belleterre and its owner. Fancy seemed delighted to answer his questions and terribly amused by everything she told him.

"I did not know indigo could be grown on the continent," he remarked. "It's a marvelous valuable commodity."

Fancy dimpled becomingly. "Indeed, Captain. Cousin Eleanor's just bound to be rich again one of these days, if the pirates don't grab on to her cargo again like they did last year. Oh . . ." she cast him a suddenly searching glance. "I suppose that's why you're here. She's planning to ship the indigo with you this time?"

Michael started to correct her, then remembered the secrecy surrounding the letter that had brought him to Belleterre.

"That might well be, miss," he told her solemnly. "Your cousin and I have had little opportunity to talk yet. I came here unexpected—unexpectedly *early,*" he amended quickly, fascinated by that cool, calculating expression he kept seeing in Fancy's bright eyes while all the rest of her pretty face kept right on registering girlish, buoyant charm for all she was worth.

"Well, we all—the family, I mean—we wish Eleanor every good thing in this world," she said earnestly, her long, dark lashes fluttering bewitchingly. "Of course, we . . . Papa and William especially, we do worry so about her!"

"She strikes me an uncommon sensible lady," said Michael innocently.

"Oh, yes, in many ways she's just positively *brilliant*. But, sir, Eleanor has some *notions* that lots of people hereabouts consider nothin' less than *bizarre!*" She leaned forward confidingly, the honey-hued curls bouncing around her face. "She keeps almost two hundred of those Africans here with her."

"That's not unusual in this part of the country, is it, Miss Campion?" His tone was suddenly severe.

Fancy's big eyes widened. "But, Captain Ives . . . they are *not* slaves, not a one of them!" Her voice sank to a whisper. "They belonged to our family. Most of them used to be slaves, you see. Our Grandfather Campion, he was the one who settled these three plantations and the niggers were his property. And then, of course, they belonged to Eleanor's papa, before he went off to the Indies. My papa tried, tried real *hard,* to keep things goin', but it was more than twenty years before Cousin Eleanor came to Carolina. She wasn't even born here but it all belongs to her now. And by the time she did come, why, things had gotten so run down, a lot of these blackamoors just up and run off and we never could get them back."

"You say they're not slaves now? Then how is it they're still here?" Michael was sure she was explaining things all wrong.

Fancy sniffed disapprovingly. "I *told* you Eleanor has some mighty strange notions. When she came here, just after her poor papa died of the yellow jack? . . . she just gathered all those black folks together and she told them they were all free, poof, just like that! I believe they thought she was a mite touched in the head. I mean, what did they know about bein' free and shiftin' for themselves anyway, poor ignorant lambs!" Her voice was heavy with sincere indignation. Michael shifted in his chair, trying desperately to keep his amusement from showing.

"Well, *any*way, Eleanor spoke her piece and then she said she was going to start up the place again and she'd need hands to work the fields. She said anyone who wanted to stay on was welcome as long as they liked and they'd be paid *wages* like any freedman or freedwoman! And anyone that wanted to go could go . . . she gave them money, too, and a paper sayin' they were free. She wouldn't try to hold anyone who didn't want to be here. The idea! But, do you know, only a couple of them decided to leave? And she let 'em, just like she promised. We tried to tell her . . . we really tried, but she wouldn't listen . . . my papa warned her she wasn't doin' anybody any good because the very minute they left Belleterre they'd be picked up—"

"But you said she'd freed them legally," put in Michael, puzzled.

Fancy clucked her tongue disdainfully. " 'Legally' doesn't mean much here, sir. We all have to look after ourselves the best we can. Not so long ago all this country hereabouts was wild, full of Indians and . . . and massacres and Lord knows what-all. No, sir, those Africans she let go off weren't two days gone when they were rounded up and taken off to Charles Town."

"And what became of them then?" asked Michael, again that peculiar hardness in his voice.

"Why, they were bought by some tobacco farmer and Eleanor was sent their purchase price . . . less the sellin' commission, of course. And, oh my, you should have heard her carry on! She fretted and fussed for weeks and weeks about those precious blacks of hers . . . she even tried to buy them back but the man wouldn't sell. Not that he didn't want her money, she offered him twice more than he'd paid for them. But he agreed with everyone else around here, he said Eleanor was settin' a bad example and he wasn't goin' to encourage some damn silly woman to go givin' those people ideas in their heads!"

And Fancy sat back, breathless, nodding significantly at Michael. The more she told him about Eleanor, the more fascinated he was becoming. He decided that, after all, he was glad he'd accepted the invitation to stay for supper. He remembered how he had almost bolted for it earlier and found that he was angry with himself because of it.

Now he sat there without saying a word, looking at Fancy and remembering Eleanor. He could not help but compare the two cousins in his mind. He found it difficult to believe that Eleanor Campion was really close friends with this frivolous bit of fluff and he wondered what William Campion might be like. Surely not much like the sister, he told himself, or a woman like Eleanor could not possibly care for him.

A tiny fleeting wave of warning crossed his mind, as it had before. None of this was his concern. Interesting, but it did not, it could not, touch his life. He told himself it was just that Eleanor reminded him vaguely of someone, he couldn't for the world think who it might be. Perhaps when she came back for supper and they talked again, perhaps then he might recall.

4 An Evening With The Campions

As it turned out, Michael did not have the two cousins to himself at supper that evening. Matty had returned, looked into the parlor to see if he were awake yet, and found Fancy there. Fancy greeted her with exaggerated cordiality, informing her that she had come to stay for the evening. Matty's expression was a study in self-control, but she merely nodded curtly and withdrew. A few minutes later, Michael could hear her moving about the kitchen, banging pots, slamming cupboard doors closed very loudly. Fancy shook her head, nodding in the direction of the noise.

"Matty doesn't like me very much, Captain Ives. I expect you noticed that. She's Eleanor's pet, so of course nobody can say a *word* against her. But you should *hear* the stories they tell about that wench when she was workin' for Eleanor's papa on Antigua! Shockin'! My brother William just despises that woman. William says once he marries Eleanor and becomes master here, that black slut will be the first to find out her place!"

Michael did not bother to reply. He was becoming exceedingly weary of Fancy's little confidences. He longed to discover what time it was, hoping Eleanor would return soon. However, a few minutes later, Fancy jumped up and ran over to the windows. Two men on horseback were just riding up. Fancy turned back to him, looking terribly pleased.

"I don't *believe* it! Captain Ives, you are goin' to meet Papa and my brother William after all! I had no *idea* they were comin' over, too! My, won't Eleanor be surprised!"

She appeared to be amazed at the coincidence but there was a false note in her tone, something in her eyes, her manner. Michael doubted that she was really surprised at the appearance of her father and brother. Instantly he was on guard. He had been the bearer of an important letter, sent secretly, in confidence . . . and he had seen enough of Eleanor's reaction to that letter, had heard enough of what Fancy had to say about her family to suspect they might have heard in town about Eleanor's strange, new visitor . . . and they might have come to find out what they could about him, about the purpose of his call.

362

"Oh, I'm sure she'll be astonished," he muttered, suppressing a sigh. Even if his suspicions were entirely unwarranted, it promised to be a long evening and an unpleasant one. He wondered that Eleanor's relatives could be so bloody inconsiderate. Surely they were aware how inopportune their arrival was, right in the middle of Belleterre's busy harvest time. He had little opportunity for further reflection, however, as Fancy ran to open the door for her father and brother.

Michael caught a glimpse of Matty in the hallway, hurrying to answer their impatient pounding. They did not wait to be let in but came tramping in as Fancy brushed Matty aside to greet them effusively. Michael pulled himself to his feet reluctantly and resigned himself to meeting two male counterparts of Fancy.

"Papa, you never said one word to me about comin' to Belleterre this evenin'!" Fancy was laughingly chiding the older of the two men, pulling him by the hand along down the hall and into the parlor. "I have just been entertainin' the most *attractive* gentleman. Come see what Cousin Eleanor's found!"

A fairly tall man with greying hair and a portly middle entered the room, trying to disengage himself from Fancy's grasp. Behind him, very obviously his son, a younger edition, somewhat taller, much leaner about the middle. Both of these gentlemen inspected Michael from beneath identical bushy eyebrows; both of them had the same look of ill-concealed mistrust even as they shook Michael's hand in turn and listened as Fancy did her best to explain who he was and why he was there. Fancy prattled on in her careless way. All of the usual polite things were said, but Michael realized at once that he was being mentally picked apart, examined and pigeonholed by two experts at the business.

"Well, sir, 'twill be a most pleasant table tonight with you here to tell us all the latest news from home!" said Sydney Campion expansively. "We do not get to town as much as we would like these days and we're sadly out of touch with the outside world. Are you just back from England, Captain?" He sat down in a chair by the fireside, glancing about the room with a quick, proprietary air. His son remained standing, lounging against the mantel, watching Michael's face with an expression of speculative contempt that made Michael itch to slap him soundly across his smooth-shaven, plump cheeks. Yes, *slap* him, thought Michael derisively. The fellow, good-looking enough in his sallow way, would never inspire another man with the desire to *punch* him about honestly. There was just enough surly effeminacy about William Campion's loose, full lips set in what seemed a perpetual sneer, to call up a sense of revulsion in most other men. He bore a passing resemblance to his sister, to the extent that one might see they were related, but the brother was the more intelligent of the two and far more subtle. He was in every apparent way his father's son and even his present youthful lack of flesh showed promise of heavying up in years to come. There was already a soft sag beneath the chin and his hands were damply flaccid and thick-fingered.

Michael started to say something trifling about his voyage to England when William Campion broke in.

"Damn that black wench, haven't we been here often enough for her to remember the brandy? I told her the last time to serve it up as soon as I had my foot inside the door. How Eleanor tolerates—"

He was cut off abruptly by Matty's entrance, carrying a tray with several glasses and a bottle of brandy on it. She ignored them all, set the tray down on a table, then turned on her heel and crossed the room again. But William stopped her, catching her by one arm, half-spinning her about.

"Pour it, Matty," he commanded, pointing toward the unopened brandy bottle. "I see my cousin has not yet taught you to be civil."

The look of quiet rage on the black woman's proud, quiet face was unmistakable. She pulled her arm free of him, walked back very quickly to the table and began to pour the liquor. Fancy gave a nervous little giggle, her eyes anxious as she watched her brother.

"Oh, William," she cried, "Eleanor's sure to hear you've been mean to Matty again. She'll *never* marry you if you don't behave yourself!"

"Shut up, Frances!" Sydney Campion barked. Fancy wilted under his harsh gaze. "William, sit down and mind your fool tongue!"

William, unlike his sister, did not come near to wilting. Anger flashed in his dark eyes and his lips seemed to mouth a reply, but he held his tongue as he was told nevertheless. Sydney turned back to Michael with a false, hearty laugh.

"Here on business are you, Captain Ives? I cannot say I've heard your name before, or the name of your ship—the *Sheila Deare*, my daughter said? Have you met my niece yet?"

"Briefly," replied Michael, accepting a glass of brandy from

364

Matty. "Thank you," he murmured, smiling at her sympathetically. She gave him a quick little nod, not quite a smile of her own, before her face resumed its remote, impassive expression. Michael realized in that instant that she had not reacted so much with gratitude for his small civility as with a certain measure of approval he had not felt forthcoming from her earlier in the day.

"I arrived at Belleterre in the middle of the day, sir. Mistress Campion was extremely busy. She invited me to stay for supper . . . I presumed so we might have the opportunity of talking this evening. It is a very pressing time for her just now, I understand." He said this deliberately and had the immense satisfaction of watching Sydney Campion bristle. Good God, thought Michael grimly as he tossed down the brandy very fast, are *all* of her relatives such horrors?

Matty left the room again but not before she and William had exchanged looks of pure, open hatred. William growled something to himself and once again his father cut him off very sharply.

"Papa, guess what? Captain Ives is going to carry the indigo to London for Eleanor this year. Isn't that just wonderful?" chattered Fancy, quite recovered from her short sulk. Sydney's eyes narrowed and he looked intensely interested.

Michael laughed shortly, shaking his head. "That is not yet settled, Miss Campion," he said, hoping devoutly that his surprise did not show on his face.

"My poor niece has had great misfortune shippin' her goods, Captain," Sydney informed him, allowing a lachrymose little sigh to escape his lips. "Pirates, sir. These southern waters abound with the devils, as no doubt you've had occasion to discover. If you have spent any time at all in the Indies, of course, especially recently, you must have heard talk of them?" His efforts to discover exactly where Michael had sailed from were quite transparent. Michael pursed his lips.

"Oh, we've had no real trouble with pirates. We did sight one or two of them around Jamaica and once we had to outrun them halfway up the Maryland coast . . . that would be about two years ago as I recall. But I did hear that your niece's cargo was stolen last year." And back to you, sir, he thought as he smiled at Sydney.

Sydney could bide his time, however. "A damnable shame," he said without blinking. His scratchy voice rose with indignation. "Lost her a fortune, a fortune! We wonder how she is managing things here now. She's a very proud young woman, Eleanor is, never complains, never tells her family anything that troubles her.''

William snorted over his brandy. A cast-iron look from his father subdued him somewhat but a shadowy ironic sneer hovered about his heavy mouth.

''The thing of it is, sir,'' Sydney went on in the same vein, ''you can find anything from indigo and fine laces to iron pots and ships' cannon, anything you like . . . for a price . . . right here in Charles Town. 'Tis said it's the first place the buccaneers make for as soon as they've a full hold of stolen merchandise. And nobody in town will do a damn thing to stop it. Why, the stuff's sold out in the open for anyone to see. I daresay a man might find and buy back his own goods along the docks, *if* he had the price of them twice over and then some! It's a foul disgrace, Captain, but of course it only shows the kind of corruption a royal governor winks his eye at.''

''A governor?'' inquired Michael, his brow raised. ''Do you mean to say that the pirates operate with the approval of the officials here?''

Sydney rolled his eyes in exasperation with a system he obviously found intolerable generally and particularly to himself as a well-born gentleman.

''Aye, the *approval!* The connivance, if you like, sir! Damme, Captain Ives, you're a man of the world with a ship of your own; you cannot be such an innocent you haven't heard all this before. Oh, there are many in high places this side of the water that do as they please and make their fortunes with none the wiser home in England!''

Michael thought his tone smacked more of envy than righteous anger.

''You seem mighty well informed about the affairs of Charles Town, Master Campion. I was under the impression that you did not get into town very often,'' he observed lightly. Sydney started and looked at him suspiciously but could not quite manage to make an insult out of Michael's remark.

''But, blast it, sir,'' sputtered Sydney, ''a man must keep informed, don't y'know?''

Weak, thought Michael, very weak. He gazed with exaggerated interest into the depths of his brandy glass.

''Of course you're not against turning an *honest* profit, I trust, Master Campion?'' he said quietly.

"Nay, not I, sir!" Sydney chuckled and looked relieved. "So long as my profit is 'turned,' as you say, by somebody else! A gentleman is above all that wretched commercial haggling, after all! No offense to yourself, Captain, of course!"

"Of course," echoed Michael, loathing the man more every passing moment.

"You see, Captain Ives?" broke in Fancy pointedly. "That is why Papa is so concerned about dear Cousin Eleanor! She *is* a lady but with her insistin' on carryin' on in business as she does, she gives other people a terrible impression of herself—and her family."

Michael fixed a steely blue eye on her. "She impressed me as every inch the lady," he said. Fancy had the grace to blush.

"Well, of course, dear sir," she floundered, embarrassed. "I did say it was merely the *impression* people get. No one respects Eleanor more than *I*, I'm sure!"

"We are quite aware of your feelings toward Eleanor, Frances," said her brother coldly. "Don't bore the good Captain." He stared insolently at Michael for a minute, a dark, insistent glint of curiosity in his eye and, when he spoke, a hard, insistent determination to satisfy that curiosity was in his voice. "Tell me, sir, how is it you came here to Belleterre?" Fancy gasped and her father let out a long, wheezing breath between his teeth. William ignored them both. "Did my Cousin Eleanor send for you?"

"No, she did not," Michael replied, icily returning William's hostile look. "But since I happened to find myself in Charles Town anyway and heard some talk of Mistress Campion's indigo cargo, I thought I might inquire about it."

"Oh, but that's not what—" cried Fancy, her violet eyes wide with sudden consternation. Then she bit her lip and fell silent, staring down with flaming cheeks at the faded pattern of the carpet. Michael realized at once how he'd blundered and cursed himself for a dolt. Of course, why hadn't he remembered in time? Fancy knew very well that he'd had no idea at all *what* crop Eleanor grew when he came there today. It had been Fancy herself who had told him. He cast her a long, speculative look and waited for her to go on and show him up for the liar he was. You're getting in deeper and deeper every minute, he thought, disgusted with himself, deeper and deeper all the time . . . and this morning you'd never laid eyes on the lady!

Neither Fancy's father nor her brother paid the least attention to her abortive little outburst. Evidently they were used to ignoring

Fancy. Michael found himself feeling a little sorry for her, despite her flighty ways and shallow, self-centered character.

But the moment for her to expose him was gone and she had said nothing more. Why? It was so obvious to him that Fancy had been part of her father's plan to discover something to his advantage about Eleanor's affairs. Fancy had done her best to learn what she could. So had Sydney. So had William. Michael found himself becoming uneasy, remembering the stricken look on Eleanor's face as she'd read the letter from her friend, a friend who had been desperately afraid that someone, the wrong someone, would get hold of it and read it.

Evidently Matty had sent warning to Eleanor that her relatives had arrived unexpectedly at the house. A horse rode up to the back and, a moment later, Eleanor herself could be heard coming in through the kitchen door. She climbed the stairs to the second floor without seeing anyone and then Matty looked in to say that the Mistress was dressing for dinner and would be down presently. Sydney and his son exchanged looks of some significance, which Michael did not entirely grasp. The conversation in the parlor dwindled away into halting pleasantries. All three men helped themselves rather liberally to the remaining brandy and Fancy tried to engage Michael's attention without much success, for he was too busy studying her father and brother and waiting with growing impatience for Eleanor to join them. Fancy pressed upon him half a dozen inquiries as to how the London ladies were wearing their hair these days, were the new hats really the size of meat platters and only held on the head with the aid of foot-long pins, and was there the least possibility of some Alençon lace being imported into the colonies again?

Michael offered her some perfunctory answers, all the while keeping his eye fixed on Sydney and William. Sydney had pulled himself out of his chair with some effort and begun pacing heavy-footed about the room. William sat cracking his large knuckles, glaring over at Michael every so often when he thought he was not observed. Michael did not even bother to hide the fact that he *did* observe it and the thought went annoyingly round and round in his brain... how in God's good name could Eleanor Campion bring herself to think of marrying him? If Fancy had not mentioned it, Michael knew that he would probably have found William merely a ghastly boor, a repulsive and easily dismissable young puff of a fellow. But as he tried to picture him as Eleanor's future husband... her *bed partner,* the manager of her estates and, indeed, her very life, the prospect sickened Michael and caused him to see William Campion as the very loathsome toad he was. And, too, every instinct in him cried out to Michael that William could be genuinely *dangerous.*

It was not until Matty called them into the candlelit dining room that Eleanor appeared at last. She stood quite still in the doorway, watching them as they took their places at the gleaming dark wood table. It was Fancy who noticed her first and was preparing to run over to greet her when Eleanor shook her head very slightly.

"Pray keep your seat, Fancy," she said. "Good evening, gentlemen."

She sat down at the head of the table, smiling politely at them all, and signaled Matty to bring in the food. Michael, diagonally across from her, studied her with undisguised interest. She looked somehow different tonight, he decided at once. Taller, much paler than she had seemed earlier and her eyes puzzled him.

He remembered the sparkle of emerald, but tonight her eyes were the cool grey green of the North Atlantic before a storm. She wore the glorious auburn hair pinned up into a great swirl of gleaming waves at the crown of her proud, erect head. Her gown was simply cut, a deep, teal green hue in dully glowing satin with long, tight sleeves to the wrist and a plain, unadorned bodice cut very low across her full bosom. Michael, who paid little attention to women's fashions, knew enough to realize it was a style of dress he had not seen in several years. Looking more closely he noticed that the seams were worn and frayed and there was evidence of careful, skilled mending. She had no jewel or bit of fine lace, yet he thought she had the look of a queen. He found, to his disgust, that there was a peculiar lump in his throat. She was a woman whose greatest ornament was her own beauty, yet the sight of her would make any man long to lavish fine silks and precious gems upon her.

"I had not thought to see you all tonight," she was saying to her uncle, and her voice was strained and cold. She avoided looking in William's direction and the narrow gaze with which she surveyed Sydney was bitter and angry. "What is it brings you to Belleterre at harvest-time, uncle?"

With a quick glance at Michael . . . who seemed not to notice it . . . Sydney replied, "Does a family need any particular reason to get together, my dear? We've not seen you in several weeks. William was concerned—"

369

"Indeed?" Eleanor asked mildly, still not looking William's way. "William was concerned? But I have told you before, all of you, there is no need for you to be concerned about me. We manage quite well here without your interference."

Sydney looked pained. "Eleanor, please! What will Captain Ives think of us?"

Eleanor turned to Michael, a slow half smile forming on her generous mouth. "Why, I am certain the Captain knows how it is with families, do you not, Captain Ives? There is always bound to be a bit of harmless bickering between the most loving of relations."

Michael grinned openly at the ironic emphasis of her words.

" 'Tis not unknown, ma'am. My sister, for instance, has a most . . . *lively* temperament, when the mood strikes her."

Eleanor's smile widened. "Do you have but the one sister, then, Captain? Is she married?"

"She was, ma'am, almost twenty years. Her husband's only dead these seven months."

"I'm sorry, Captain," breathed Eleanor delicately. "Has your sister quite recovered from such a sad loss?"

Michael nodded. "Yes, I think she has. She is not the kind to go all to pieces, whatever happens to her. And, thank God, she is not entirely alone. She has a son to raise."

"A son? How old is he?"

"Just over ten years, ma'am," smiled Michael, "and tall for his age. The image of his father, too."

"How lucky she is, then," exclaimed Eleanor softly, "that she will have such a precious part of her husband with her always! He must keep her quite busy."

Michael's eyes sparkled and he smiled broadly.

"Busy enough, but Katherine would find time hanging heavy on her hands if she did not have her work as well."

" 'Work'?" Eleanor looked intrigued. "What does she do?"

"What does she do?" laughed Michael easily. "My sister Katherine—well, my sister owns half of the largest, fastest-growing shipyards in Massachusetts Bay Colony, and an iron foundry and two woolen mills besides, as well as a very busy shipping company. And she runs them all, by herself, now that Rob is gone, with a bit of help from an old friend of the family. *That* is what my sister does!"

"She sounds wonderful. Very strong," murmured Eleanor appreciatively. "You must miss her, sir. I can tell just by the way you speak of her how close the two of you must be. When you return to Boston this time, will you be giving up the sea, do you think, so you can stay with her and help her raise your nephew?''

Fancy could stand it no longer. Both Eleanor and Michael had been oblivious to everyone else around them during this conversation. Now, very coyly, Fancy spoke up.

"Oh, Eleanor, have you no tact at *all?* Surely Captain Ives has a home and a wife and family himself. You *are* married, aren't you, Captain?''

Michael threw up his hands, laughing. "Good God, no! I am not! I am a contented bachelor and a very happy uncle . . . and that's the way I'm willing to leave it at my age!''

Eleanor's fine, silky eyebrow rose a trifle.

"At your age, sir? Why, you can hardly be more than . . . oh, I should imagine, thirty-five?''

"You flatter me, Mistress Campion,'' said Michael, much amused. "Forty-four. So you see what I mean. It is far too late for me to think about changing my 'wandering ways,' as Katherine calls them . . . my sister disapproves of me from time to time, but she understands me.''

"Ah!'' smiled Eleanor. "And that is everything, is it not?'' She raised her wineglass. "To you, Captain Ives, and to your sister and her son, good health and happiness to you all!'' She sipped from the glass, glaring around the table at her relatives until even William grudgingly followed the toast.

After this they ate the simple supper in silence for a few minutes. Fancy kept staring over at Michael, to his amusement. She had found out what she had been trying to discover all day. He was not married and was quite clearly fair game, although he had the distinct impression that even married men would strike Fancy Campion as game fair enough—if they were attractive or rich.

"Eleanor, dear, how is the harvest going?'' inquired Fancy, valiantly trying to keep up a good front before Michael. Her father and William seemed to be impressed with something Michael had said and their manner right now was even more intolerable than it had been all along.

Eleanor's cool manner toward her relatives appeared to warm up a trifle as she looked at Fancy with genuine affection.

"Quite well, Fancy, thank you. I expect, if the rains hold off, we shall be finished in a few days.''

"Frances tells us the Captain here may carry your indigo to market this year," said Sydney. Eleanor betrayed no surprise, but glanced at Michael inquiringly.

"I did say we might speak of it, ma'am," he said quickly. "Since that was the business that brought me to Belleterre today."

Eleanor flushed faintly pink. Her smile revealed her gratitude for his lie and she said, "And we shall speak of it, Captain Ives, after supper. Of course it will be another couple of weeks before we will be ready to ship, but if you cannot transport it yourself, perhaps you might recommend another vessel. I believe you did mention that you were on your way back to Boston now?"

Michael nodded. "Aye, ma'am, and cannot delay very long. We carry a cargo of some fifteen thousand fruit trees awaiting planting before the first frost and that comes pretty early in the north."

" 'Fruit trees'?" blinked Fancy. "Is that all?"

Michael grinned. "No, Miss Campion. We've rum aboard as well, and Malmsey, though 'tis not so well liked in Boston as the Canary vidonia and Madeira. And, of course, we never go home without as much coffee, tea, cocoa beans and lemons as we can pack in."

"Oh." Fancy pouted prettily. "Nothin' interestin'. Don't the ladies of Boston Town like beautiful clothes? *I* do, I'm sure."

"Indeed they do, miss. I warrant I've a list as long as your arm from Boston ladies for Holland lawn and Barcelona silk handkerchiefs and Osnaburg linen and Flanders thread . . . Boston ladies are mighty particular about their finery." As he spoke, Michael had an idea. He wanted to present Eleanor with a few dress lengths of fine goods in return for her hospitality but he had not known how to go about it so she would not be embarrassed and refuse. But Fancy was obviously used to being spoiled and had few scruples about accepting gifts.

"It would please me very much, Miss Campion, if your father does not object, I'd like to send you a few trifles we're carrying . . . nothing grand, mind you, but maybe a bit of flowered damask and some plain blue lutestring all the London *belles* seem to want this year. . . ." He turned to Eleanor as if it were an afterthought . . . "And you, too, ma'am. A seafaring man has little opportunity of returning such kind hospitality as yours. Perhaps you would accept a few odds and ends of cloth to convey my thanks?"

372

Eleanor's back was very stiff as she listened. Fancy saw the look on her cousin's face and uttered a little cry of sheer anguish.

"Oh, Eleanor, don't say no, please! If you do not accept the Captain's kind offer, then I shan't be able to, either. Eleanor, be a darlin', won't you? I've wanted a blue lutestring coat for years and you know how hard it is to get here! And you could have a lovely new gown yourself instead of that old satin of yours—my Heavens, you've had it for best since you *came* here!" And then she held her breath, watching her proud cousin's reaction. Michael shot Fancy a look of silent pleading to hold her tongue but Fancy simply did not comprehend subtlety. He feared that her words would only anger Eleanor, but his hostess was no vain bird of paradise. She shook her head in dismay at Fancy's outburst but smiled very graciously all the same.

"I shall not be the cause of your disappointment, Fancy," she said softly. "And 'tis very true I have had little time or cash for frills these five years past. Every time I wear this dress I pray 'twill not fall apart at the seams just one more evening. I would be very grateful to you, Captain Ives, and I thank you for the generous thought."

Sydney reddened and cleared his throat several times. His niece's frank talk about money matters disturbed him but Eleanor's candor only endeared her the more to Michael, who was accustomed to open, unpretentious and honest women like Helene and Katherine. He despised females who considered it bad form to be straightforward.

Fancy was looking anxiously at her father and Michael saw at once that he would have to appease Sydney's touchy family feelings or neither of the ladies would enjoy his presents. The damned old hypocrite, thought Michael, smiling through his teeth.

"Pray do allow your daughter to accept, Master Campion. Young ladies set much store by pretty trifles . . . and Miss Fancy already seems done up in the height of fashion. I'm sure you must be very proud of her."

Eleanor glanced at him quizzically and covered her smile with a delicate touch of her napkin to the lips but Fancy was altogether charmed and Sydney had no choice but to grunt his consent. Fancy clapped her hands delightedly until a dark look from her brother caused her to be silent once more.

"I warrant you'll have no further concern about money matters

373

once your indigo is sold," Michael said bluntly, directing his conversation only to Eleanor. "The market price rises higher each year. I am told the East African dye is not so fine as that from this part of the world. There is a great demand for it all over Europe. You might even think about selling some of yours in Boston and Philadelphia. Not everyone pays much attention to the Wool Act and a great many people are defying it altogether and manufacturing woolen goods here in America instead of shipping the raw wool all the way to England."

"That is gratifying to hear, Captain Ives," Eleanor replied thoughtfully. "I have over four hundred acres under cultivation at Belleterre alone. Next year, if all goes well, I plan to put in more indigo at Rogue's Fall . . . that is a somewhat smaller property my father left. My . . . the family lives there at present."

As she talked the coldness had crept back into her voice and she stared across the table defiantly at her uncle as though, Michael would have sworn, she were *defying* him in some way.

"It is never wise to limit yourself to one kind of crop, Eleanor," William spoke up suddenly in his infuriatingly soft, slurred voice. "Rogue's Fall does well enough with tobacco and vegetables."

Eleanor's look was very hard. "This is an old disagreement, William," she declared. "Surely of little interest to Captain Ives. I have made my decision about the property and my decision will stand."

William pushed his dinner plate away from him, sneering at the thin, watery stew he had barely touched.

"Well, my dear Eleanor—to hell with Captain Ives!" he asserted. Fancy gasped, staring at Michael, but William shot her a menacing look. "I did not come here this evening to entertain some Yankee sailor, Eleanor, and I will not sit about mouthing inane pleasantries when there is so much to be settled between us. Your pardon, I'm sure, Captain," he drawled insolently, hardly bothering to glance Michael's way, "but you see, you've thrust yourself upon us at a most inconvenient time!"

"William!"

Eleanor's voice rang out sharp and staccato. Her eyes were blazing now, her soft rounded breasts heaving with motion beneath the straining satin bodice. "Your conduct is inexcusible! I remind you, cousin, that Captain Ives is the only *invited* guest at my table tonight. I don't know what brought the rest of you to Belleterre—I don't want to know—but I warn you, William—"

"Take care, *cousin!*" William broke in, placing a restraining arm upon his father's shoulder when Sydney would have interrupted him. "No, Papa, I will deal with this. Once and for all time, Eleanor, learn that you cannot make *any* decisions regarding these three properties until your legal right to do so has been determined. And *that* is far, very far, from an accomplished fact. We have been very patient with you, cousin, but we will not go on being patient forever. I told you there is a way of settling this thing amicably, without the unnecessary and, I assure you, *unfortunate* consequences of a battle in open court!"

"I think it would be best if I were to withdraw, Mistress Campion," murmured Michael, tight-mouthed. But Eleanor shook her head without turning to look at him, her eyes fixed on William Campion's angry face.

"I pray you, sir, remain where you are," she responded in a low tone. And then, her voice much louder, she answered William, every word that came from her mouth edged with contempt and sarcasm.

"You are embarassing my guest, William, but I ask him to bear with us with as good a grace as he can. *I* have nothing to hide from him or from anyone." Now she did glance at Michael, a grim little smile on her lips. "You see, Captain Ives, it is my cousin's . . . and my uncle's . . . contention that all of our quarrels would be set to rights if only I were to marry him, thereby handing over to him legal control, nay, unquestioned ownership of all my holdings. Lacking a marriage contract, he and my uncle feel that they have no other recourse than to seize control."

"These lands belong to me by right, Captain," broke in Sydney Campion, his voice infuriatingly slow and pedantic. "The plantations, everything and everyone on them were my brother's property before he died. My brother James was somewhat eccentric, you might say. He left it all in my care and he was gone for the rest of his life. Why, we did not even know James *had* a daughter until Eleanor appeared shortly after his death. Naturally we wished to do everything in our power to help and comfort our niece, not only for her sake but for James's memory. Now you know very well, a young, unattached female, all alone, strugglin' to manage a business

375

both untried and risky . . . well, sir, we Campions are not business-men. The properties produced enough for a modest living and we have been content with that—''

"The properties were let go to hell and then some!" cried Eleanor hotly. "When I got here this place was in ruins. So was Stag Run and so it remains to this day. You only kept up Rogue's Fall for yourself and you know if it were properly managed it could produce ten times what it does now! I have told you before, I tell you now, uncle, I don't care what your opinions are, either of me or the way I run my affairs. I am James Campion's daughter and his only lawful heir. You saw his will. You saw the sworn affirmation signed by the attorneys in London. What more is there to be said?''

"That will is still open to investigation, Captain," said Sydney, ignoring his niece completely. Michael found the situation intolerable. Fighting to hold back his own temper, his blue eyes burning with anger, he riveted his attention on William.

"Pray, both of you, do not argue through me, *gentlemen;* the lady deserves your courtesy at least, since she obviously does not command your affection!"

Sydney glowered at him, his long nose pinched and white with resentful rage. And William stood up, moving so suddenly, with such force, that his chair toppled over. Fancy, looking from one to the other of them helplessly, began to cry.

"Have you appointed yourself my cousin's champion, Captain Ives?" demanded William. "Rest assured, sir, 'tis an unnecessary gesture. I daresay you might find any number of black bucks about the place more than eager to fight for her favors!"

For a moment there was not a sound in the room. Matty, who had been standing in the doorway to the kitchen with a silver coffeepot in her hand, set it down very deliberately on the sideboard and moved swiftly to Eleanor's side. Eleanor, stunned, began to tremble violently. She uttered a soft groan, reaching out blindly to clasp Matty's hand. And, surprisingly, Sydney spoke urgently to his son,

"You go too far, William! Will you never learn to command that temper of yours?" Sydney seemed very troubled at the turn of events, less for the slur on his niece's honor than because of some unspoken personal concern. But William seemed not to hear him.

"You will withdraw your last remark, Campion. At once," said Michael, his voice low, controlled, dangerous. William's eyes were

376

riveted upon Eleanor and the black woman who now bent over her with a protective arm about her shoulders.

"Nay, Captain, I'll withdraw nothing!" cried William wildly. "Papa, let me be, I tell you!" Gesturing contemptuously, he shouted, "Touching, is it not? My island-born cousin and her father's nigger mistress!" He sensed rather than saw a quick movement from Michael's direction. "I warn you, sir, don't involve yourself in this. You don't understand what you're getting into!"

"Enough, William!" roared Sydney in a terrible voice, a certain thrill of alarm in his tone. "You young fool, you'll spoil everything!"

But Michael had had enough of it. There was a hot throbbing in his ears, a great searing burst of fury clutched at his chest and he jumped to his feet facing William Campion even as Sydney attempted to pull his son away. William's arrogant, sallow features were twisted into a maddening leer, as if he'd finally triumphed in something he'd been after.

"Did you think we really believed that cock-and-bull story you told us, Captain?" demanded William thickly. "You've just come from the Indies. You admitted you'd been to Santo Domingo recently. And now, suddenly, you appear out of nowhere, here at Belleterre . . . a captain we've never heard of in Charles Town, from a ship we've never heard of! If you've business with Eleanor, why didn't someone in town know about it before this? If she intended to arrange with you to carry her indigo why has she contacted every other trading company in Charles Town about it? Just why *are* you here, Ives? What are you, some sort of spy? . . ."

He's been spoiling for a fight ever since he came in and found me here, thought Michael. Michael had no intention of answering William's questions, so he would have it; he would have his fight and be damned to him!

He covered the few feet between himself and William quickly and grasped the young man by his upper arm.

"Outside, Campion!" he ordered, pushing William toward the door.

"Call off your dog, Eleanor!" said Sydney, eyeing Eleanor intently. "At once, I say!"

Eleanor met his gaze, shivering at the quiet menace in his face. Matty's fingers tightened on her shoulder. She took a deep breath, then got to her feet, a wan smile on her white face.

"Captain Ives," she breathed, "please. Let it go."

Michael stopped where he was. "Cousin or no cousin, ma'am, it is not my habit to hear a lady insulted with impunity!"

Eleanor's strained smile was ghastly. Her great green eyes pleaded with him to understand what she could not explain.

"I appreciate your great kindness, sir, but, believe me, you would be doing me the worse disservice if you go on with this."

Michael, of course, did *not* understand. With a show of indifference he was far from feeling he shrugged, dropping his hand from William Campion's arm. He nodded stiffly to Eleanor.

"You know best, I'm sure, Ma'am," he said icily. Eleanor's eyes shone with unshed tears but he turned away deliberately.

William, however, was not so inclined to drop the matter. He reached into his breast pocket before anyone realized what he was doing and pulled out a small, ornate dagger, the kind many gentlemen wore in their riding boots, good for little except picking the occasional stone out of a horse's foot. It was Fancy's shrill scream that caused Michael to whirl about in time to catch sight of William raising the small weapon. With a furious snarl, Michael knocked the threatening arm aside and the knife skidded harmlessly to the floor. And then Michael did what he had longed to do all evening. He slapped that supercilious face with all his strength, an openhanded blow with the palm of his hand that left a bright crimson impression on the slack, fleshy cheek. By morning it would turn into a swollen, purple welt.

William fell back a few steps, his hand pressed against his cheek, but it was not at Michael he looked; it was at his father. Sydney's expression as he studied his son that moment was filled with scorn and he muttered something almost inaudible to William in the tone of voice a man might use to reprimand his dog or his slave. And then Sydney's hard gaze shifted to Michael again.

"You have interfered in something you do not understand here, Captain. For your own sake I advise you to leave Belleterre to itself and be on your way back to Boston as soon as possible."

"I need no advice from you, Master Campion," snapped Michael. "But I'll tell you what, I'll give *you* some of my own: Put your son on a short leash. I shall stay or leave as I wish, thank you very much, so keep that whelp of yours out of my way. No man has ever raised a weapon to me and lived to do it again!"

"Irish scum!" blustered William heatedly. Michael moved toward him once more, his fists clenched. Sydney turned his head toward Eleanor, his bushy eyebrow raised questioningly. And very, very quickly, Eleanor spoke up.

"Captain Ives, *please!*"

Michael hardly glancd at her. " 'Tis not yourself I'm defending now, ma'am. This fop has insulted *me!*"

Eleanor swallowed hard. "Captain," she whispered falteringly, "I must ask you to leave Belleterre. Now."

Matty mumbled something to her but Eleanor shook her head and the black woman stepped back, her arms folded, a look of infinite distaste on her proud, beautiful face. And Sydney Campion's expression relaxed in satisfied triumph.

Michael felt numb. He stared at Eleanor in bewilderment, knowing he was not able to conceal the hurt he was feeling. Once again, as she had earlier that day, she lifted her arm in that helpless little gesture he had found so touching and he could have sworn on oath she was acting against her own will. But he was angry, confused.

"If you will kindly make me the loan of one of your horses to get back to town, I'll gladly take my leave, Mistress Campion. I have no other means of transport," he said, rigid with humiliation.

Eleanor nodded, motioning to Matty. "Matty will show you to the stables, Captain. Please feel free to make use of the beast as long as you are in Charles Town. I shall send one of the men into town to fetch it back later."

"No need, ma'am. I shall have it returned in the morning."

And without so much as another word or look, Michael turned on his heel and strode out with Matty just behind him. He caught sight of Fancy as he left, her pretty oval face white with dread. He nodded to her curtly.

When the door closed behind him, Michael paused outside, throwing back his head with relief, taking in a great gulp of the cool evening air. What madness, he thought to himself! The entire day, utter folly and waste of time! He was thoroughly disgusted with himself and he allowed his annoyance to pervade his being in a way he ordinarily would not have tolerated. Beyond that, he was quite unwilling to face the feelings of hurt and disappointment he knew very well were in his heart. He had looked forward to spending some few hours with Eleanor Campion, a few quiet hours of getting to know her, perhaps discovering what trouble he had brought her when he'd delivered Ellen Fletcher's letter. That wretched letter, he thought! And them accusing me of being a—what was it?—a *spy*, for the love of God! They're a devious crew, that's sure enough, and they sounded as though they suspected I was in cahoots with Eleanor against *them!* Madness, that's what it was and it served him right for going against his better judgment in the first place, listening to that distraught woman on Antigua. For all he knew, Ellen Fletcher was as mad as the rest of them! Bah, and there's an end to it, he resolved firmly—too bad, though. Eleanor Campion was the first woman he had ever met who had caught his interest so instantly, so deeply. . . .

He walked along swiftly beside the silent black woman as she led him away from the main house. As his eyes became accustomed to the peculiar darkness of the countryside, so different from the phosphorescent glow of the night seas, he noticed that there was much more to Belleterre than he had realized. They passed by a large brick kitchen and washhouse and then a big barn, a cooper's shed, a smithy, an orchard over to the right of these with apple and peach trees in abundance. He saw several brick buildings of various sizes whose purpose he could only guess to be storage, a carpenter's shed and large, well-tended vegetable gardens all around a twisting gravel pathway leading to the stables and coach house.

Down a gentle incline were several brick cottages, their windows lit up invitingly, smoke curling out of the chimneys. He could hear dogs barking and a sleepy, die-hard cock crowing off in the barn. The entire plantation had about it a peaceful, comfortable feeling that stood in sharp contrast to the atmosphere of tension and hatred he had just witnessed at the house.

What hold do these people have over her, he mused? What is she afraid of? That they will find a way to take the land from her after all? But she allows herself to be badly used and yet will permit no one to lift a finger to help her. And, too, the question came maddeningly back again and again and would not be put down: How could she treat me so? How *could* she?

"You should have killed that one, Captain," Matty's rich, lilting voice broke the silence so suddenly that Michael was startled. "He is the Devil's own spawn."

"Indeed?" said Michael, feigning indifference. "A thoroughly detestable fellow, I agree. But evidently Mistress Campion finds him tolerable enough in spite of his . . . foibles."

"I had thought perhaps you were not a fool, Captain." Matty's tone matched his own for dryness. "Eleanor hates the man, hates the father, too."

"*But*, you see, 'tis *I* am heading for the stables, not either of them!" And this time he did not even attempt to hide his hurt.

Matty stopped and turned to him, seizing his arm urgently.

"Listen to me! You do not understand what is happening. There is no reason that you should. But this I swear to you. She did not wish for you to go. Had it been otherwise—" and then she closed her mouth abruptly.

"What was in that letter, Matty?"

She hesitated, shaking her head slowly. "I cannot tell you. But, look—" she gestured about her. "All of this will be lost to her, to *us*, if her uncle gets his own way. She is trying to keep it from happening but she does not know what he plans to do. That is why she allows him to come and go as he will now, to the end that she may discover something. And . . . she was once fond of the girl, Fancy. So you see, she had to send you away tonight. But, do not go away, Captain. Do not leave her to fight them all alone!"

"Why say these things to me, woman?" cried Michael angrily. "You never saw me before today, nor did she. Tell me, what have I to do with any of this?"

Her gaze was so clear, so strong and steady he could not endure it. He turned away, something in his very soul protesting, and he felt wrenched apart even as she answered him, saying exactly what he had known she would have to say,

"You love her," Matty told him simply. "You are the man for her. You know it. She knows it, inside, in the heart. So," she faced him as they reached the stable doors, "go now. Take the horse and ride to Charles Town to your ship. But you will come back again, Captain Ives. You will come back to her always, now that you have found her."

"My God!" Michael swore swiftly as she slipped past him into the stables. "No! I am not the one!"

"You are," she said a few minutes later as she handed him the reins of a tall, black gelding. He leaped up into the saddle and pressed his knees hard against the animal's flanks. It reared up with a wild wicked whinny of joy and turned as he wished it, riding off without another word down the long, tree-lined road to Charles Town. Matty, a bit of a smile lingering on her lips, stood to watch him gallop away as the reluctant moon at last began to touch the treetops with silver. He would come back, she knew. Sooner or later he would come back.

Then, with a quick glance at the main house, she set off to find Dogon, to tell him what had happened. Later tonight, she knew, Eleanor would want both of them with her and they would talk of the letter and of whatever Sydney and William had to say tonight. But she would not tell Dogon about Captain Ives, she decided. Dogon would hold that they already had enough to worry about.

5 Empty Moments, Restless Years

For several days, Michael resolutely put Eleanor Campion and her troubles out of his thoughts. The *Sheila Deare* took on six hundred gallons of peach brandy and traded off five hundred packs of playing cards out of a shipment three times that amount bound for Boston. A very neat profit was turned on both transactions. They did some minor repairs to spars and sails and purchased enough fresh meat and greens to last the short homeward voyage. They were ready to sail out of Charles Town harbor in five days' time, yet they did not sail but tarried a week, then ten days, then two weeks, and Michael was in a rare ripping mood and paced the decks roaring at his crew so hard that folks passing along the quays looked up in some alarm.

Mister Rainey, the first mate, complained very often and wanted to know what the devil was keeping them so long in this bug-infested place, and did Michael know or care to know that the forward quarters had been invaded by things the native people called palmetto bugs, which were the size of healthy rats and kept the men up nights tracking them down and killing them . . . and much, much more of the same until Michael outswore and outshouted him and then promised faithfully they would set sail on next morning's tide. Michael was angrier with himself than the mate could possibly have been. Two weeks, she'd said. Two weeks more and the indigo would be ready for shipping. But he had not heard a word from her. Tomorrow they would sail, let her do as she pleased with her bloody indigo. . . .

But Mister Rainey was not much mollified by promises. What were they waiting for, anyway? And even if the Captain was a bachelor, there was not a man of the crew who didn't have a wife or sweetheart back home . . . and besides all that, if they didn't leave pretty soon they'd have "fifteen thousand goddamn rotting fruit trees" on their hands and, unless Mister Rainey was much mistaken, Mistress Katherine Sturbridge would have something to say about unnecessary delays and Mister Rainey, for one, did not look forward to hearing a piece of Mistress Sturbridge's mind. . . .

Michael made his way to the peaceful seclusion of his small cabin. He flung his too-warm coat over the back of his chair and sat in his shirt sleeves, thumbing absently through charts he wouldn't need to consult again for another six months. And instantly the face and form of Eleanor Campion appeared before his eyes. Wearily he put away the charts. He had not slept well since he'd met the woman. At odd times during the days, even when he'd been busy supervising the loading of supplies, he'd look up for an instant and imagine he'd seen her just before him. Once more he reminded himself that he was well out of it, whatever it was, any sensible man could see that in a moment. He'd even toyed with the notion of riding out to Belleterre to see if she was all right and for the hundredth time since he'd considered it, he discarded the idea in disgust.

Now, alone in his sweltering cabin, he decided that what he ought to do this evening was leave the ship, go for a walk about Charles Town, perhaps have supper and a pint or two at Hatheway's Tavern, highly recommended to him for its superior brandy punch and fine billiard tables. Why not while away this last night in Carolina in an agreeable manner? Then at dawn, up anchor and home to Boston without a backward glance? He had just about made up his mind when he heard a rapid, light tapping on his door.

"Enter," he called out, not turning his head. He was finishing up the ship's log and signed the bottom of the page with a flourish. The door opened slowly. "Well, well? What is it?" he demanded crisply, still not looking around.

"It's me, Captain," purred a soft voice. "Now don't go and tell me you've forgotten all about me so soon!"

Michael whirled about, an irritated oath on his lips, but the words died away and he simply stared. It was Fancy Campion, her luscious red mouth upturned in a delighted smile, her wide, violet blue eyes innocent enough, to be sure. She pushed the door shut and stood leaning against it, letting him take his time looking at her.

And she was indeed a fetching sight, attired in pale lavender silk, with deep violet bows at the shoulders of the tight sleeves and down the front of the gown from the point of the deep *décolletage* to the hem of the wide, sweeping skirt.

"Fancy!" he murmured in dismay, wondering as he had before, what on earth he was to do with her.

"Delighted, sir!" she laughed, bending low in a deep curtsy that exposed even more of her full white bosom. Then she bobbed up again, strolling at her ease across the tiny space until she was almost touching him. "You do not keep your promises, sir," she chided him teasingly, her eyes darting all about the cabin in that curious, childish way she had. Her lace-gloved fingers ran carelessly over the charts and the logbook on his writing table. "Oh, now I see I was right! You've not only forgotten me, you've even forgotten the presents you promised Cousin Eleanor . . . and me."

Michael was stunned. He started to stammer something he hoped was polite, but Fancy only stamped her small foot impatiently.

"Tut, sir! Confess you were about to sail away without sending us some of those yard goods you offered . . . the lutestring, for instance? Well, *I'm* not too proud to come fetch them myself! You're not really angry with me, are you, Captain?" She came to a stop just in front of him and stood there deliberately enticing him, the scent of her perfume tangy and sweet in his nostrils.

"I seem to remember now," he said very coolly. "Believe me, Miss Campion, I had no intention of neglecting any promise I made to you *or* your cousin—no matter what happened."

Fancy smiled enchantingly, like a cat. "You really mean it, Captain? You *are* a man of honor, aren't you? Will you let me see the things now? Where are they? Down in the hold?"

"No," he said. "If you'll excuse me for a few moments I'll see to it they're brought here so you can pick what you like." He started to pass by her when she reached out her hand and leaned it on the table behind him, blocking his movement.

"Not one word about the other evenin', sir?" she drawled, her eyes taking on a sparkle. "Not one word about my dreadful brother and my papa? My, you're a real Christian, Captain Ives! You know, I really came all this way into town just to apologize to you. Why, you and I were gettin' along just fine until they had to come and spoil everything! But you wouldn't hold that against *me*, would you, Captain? I mean, you wouldn't think any the less of me because of my family?"

"Not at all," Michael muttered, smiling in spite of himself. He picked up her hand and, holding it, moved himself past her deftly, then he placed her hand back on the table edge, precisely where she had put it herself. Fancy made a little pouting mouth but her eyes were still full of devilment.

"Try to amuse yourself while I'm gone," he told her from the doorway. "Oh, by the way, there's nothing of any great interest in the drawers and the clothespress. Why don't you just have a seat, pour yourself a glass of Madeira if you like. I'll see what I can find."

"Don't be too long, Captain. I have a hundred things to do in town," she said.

"I thought you came in only to apologize to me," his keen glance brought color to her face.

"I have already done that, haven't I?"

Michael went off, determined to put together a few things that would appeal to her and get her off his ship as fast as possible. He'd had many a pretty woman look at him with that particular sparkle in their eyes, he knew it well, and he also knew that Fancy Campion was a pretty piece of troublesome baggage for any man who allowed himself to fall under the spell of her bewitching eyes. Was she only pretty, spoiled and headstrong? Or was she something more? Was she there to find out for her father whether he intended to see Eleanor again, if he would carry the indigo grown at Belleterre, if he knew more about the Campion family situation than he had let on? Had they sent her to enchant him just enough to discover something that might hurt Eleanor's chances of keeping her inheritance? Best steer clear of Fancy, no matter which way the wind blows, he decided.

He had no idea how long it took him to locate the lutestring and various other bales of goods he had in mind. He had to stop and check the invoices first and then he had to call one of the men to carry the stuff aft to his cabin. Let Fancy choose what she liked, he couldn't give up the notion of sending something out for Eleanor, too. He seemed to remember some green-striped shalloon and a pale pink damask that would suit her vivid coloring very well. . . .

He held open the door to the cabin as he said, "All right, then, Bailey, just set it all there on my table. I'll send for you later to clear away."

Bailey backed himself into the cabin, his arms loaded down with heavy bundles of cloth and many smaller, paper-wrapped packages.

Michael stood aside in the companionway to let the seaman out again when suddenly he heard Bailey utter a loud exclamation. This was followed closely by the sound of bundles and parcels being dropped noisily and a very red-faced Bailey came out again hastily.

"Bailey, what the devil—" thundered Michael, astonished at the man's strange behavior. Bailey, looking thoroughly miserable, kept his eyes on the toes of his boots as he touched his hand to his cap and went right on in full retreat.

"Beggin' the Captain's pardon, but, sir, hadn't yer oughter of tole a man you was entertainin' that there woman in yer bunk?" And then he turned tail and fled, leaving Michael still holding the door open.

"Fancy, where are you?" he called out as he entered the cabin. Bailey had left his bundles wherever he'd dropped them, the small area of free space on the floor was covered with brightly colored goods come undone and spilling out of their paper wrappings. Michael bent down to retrieve some of the stuff, and then he heard Fancy's amused little laugh. He straightened up... and then he understood why Bailey had behaved so peculiarly.

Fancy was curled up quite comfortably on his narrow bunk, her arms folded behind her head, a gay smile on her poppy-colored lips. She was naked, save for a bit of the violet ribbon tied to keep her waist-long blond hair back from her face. Her clothes were scattered carelessly across the back of the only chair in the room.

"What do you think you're doing, girl?" Michael asked sternly.

"I should think *that* would be fairly obvious," she replied coyly. "I'm waitin' for *you*. I hate waitin' and you've been gone ever so long. Come on over here, *Captain Michael Edward Ives*—my, what a manly name you've got. I don't think anyone's goin' to come knockin' at that door again all afternoon!" She laughed and held out her arms, beckoning to him.

But he did not move a step. He looked around, noticed almost at once that the middle drawer of his writing table was half open and a few sheets of paper carelessly left sticking out. Ignoring her, he opened the drawer fully and saw she had found his Master's papers. His logbook had been turned back several pages... evidently she had had time to read the entries he had made in the Indies, including the notation that he'd gone ashore on Antigua. Thank God he'd not written a word about Ellen Fletcher or her letter....

"I see you've been snooping again," he remarked, returning the papers to where they belonged, closing the logbook with an emphatic slam. "You've got some very bad habits, Fancy."

For a moment she was taken aback by his manner. Then she slipped from the bunk and walked slowly toward him. Michael surveyed her calmly, then deliberately turned away and picked up a length of yellow silk goods.

"Do you care for this one? It's from Florence, Italy," he asked her very casually.

Fancy was very annoyed with him. She snatched the yellow silk out of his hands and draped it seductively around her body.

"Who cares where it came from?" she sulked. "What's the matter with you, sugar? Do I scare you?" She shot him a look of challenge as she let the clinging silk slide to her feet.

"Why don't you look at the rest of them? Take your time," he replied. He eyed her nude body with cynical amusement mixed with some anger. And the anger disturbed him. She was like a pretty child, he thought, a pretty, spoiled, willful child. The appeal of her lovely body was undeniable . . . and now he understood the reason for his anger. . . .

"I don't need anything in this room except you, Michael Edward Ives!" Fancy whispered deep in her throat. "Wrap it all up again and send it out to my virtuous Cousin Eleanor, she could use a new dress." This time her smile was spoiled with spitefulness and a hardness he had not seen in her before.

He had not thought the sound of Eleanor Campion's name could affect him as it did in that instant. A strange thing happened to him even as he felt the anger and resentment ripple through him. But his eyes lingered on Fancy's bare limbs, her red mouth . . . an image of Eleanor standing naked there before him flashed through his mind, tantalizing him with its unreality. It seemed that the room reeled about him. He struggled to keep a grip on his senses . . . Fancy was watching him closely, fascinated at the play of emotions on his handsome face.

"Why are you doing this, Fancy?" he asked at last, his voice harsh and husky. There was a mute pleading in his eyes but Fancy did not see it. She closed the small space between them in one swift liquid motion and her arms were about his neck, her full, up-tilted breasts pressed hard against his thin white lawn shirt.

"I want you," she said, her violet eyes languorous and heavy-lidded. "I've wanted you since the minute I saw you there on the sofa at Belleterre." She gave a quick little shake of her head and the violet ribbon flew off, her loosened honey hair tumbling thick and warm about his face and neck.

Michael looked down at her bleakly, feeling suddenly exhausted, drained of wish or will. What did it matter, his mind told him carelessly? What did it matter, after all? He'd kissed hundreds of pretty women, why not this one as well?

Almost automatically he took her into his arms, not caring now, not ever really having cared. His body responded quickly to the feeling of her soft, hot flesh beneath his hard fingers. He covered her mouth with his and shivered in spite of his indifference as her small darting tongue licked his dry lips moist slowly, provocatively. What did it matter? This was what it always came to. This was what was waiting all along between any man, any woman, sooner or later. It was a quick, meaningless madness. It was pleasurable. It filled up the empty moments of his restless life.

Fancy clasped him tightly, began to pull him back toward the hard, narrow bunk by the porthole and he did not resist her. He sighed and, recognizing the sigh, grew angry. He had not sought this woman; he did not want her beyond the moment. A distant coolness always present in his brain reminded him that he did not really want her at all. But his body felt drugged with the heat of her, the overwhelming magnetism of her own desires. Yet, resentment swept over him. He thought suddenly of Eleanor Campion's sweet mouth, the firm strength of its generous lines. There had been something so strong and at the same time so *vulnerable* about Eleanor . . . in her presence he had felt alive as never before. And now, here in her cousin's heedless arms he felt entrapped, not enticed.

Fancy caught only the surface fire of his deep-seated, despairing anger, sensed the passion in the hard tightness of his arms, in the pressure of his taut body as she drew him down on top of her. The triumph of it filled her eyes. She laughed low in her throat as her fingers reached up under his loose shirt and playfully clawed his broad chest with her fingernails trailing across his skin, digging into him possessively. But in that brief second of time Michael opened his eyes to look at her again . . . and he saw the victory, the pride on her face. Like a lash across his bare flesh he felt the innate scorn of the woman who takes and takes from a man and gives nothing in the end but bitterness. It turned him cold in the instant.

He pulled back, thrusting her white, entwining arms from him, and stood up. Without a word he walked quickly to his cabinet and poured himself a glass of brandy, drinking it down all at one time.

"What is it, sugar?" she demanded, her voice still full of throbbing, promising caress.

"Put your clothes on, Fancy," he said bleakly.

"B-but *why?* What's the matter?" she stammered. She had been so sure of herself, so sure of him. "It's simple, Captain. Why are you makin' it complicated?"

He turned to look at her, his gaze measured and cool. "I don't want you," he said quietly. "Is that simple enough for you?"

"It *is* because of Papa and William!" she cried furiously as she jumped up and began dressing again as quickly as she could. "It's always the same, always! I can't help it if they're hateful! You *would* have wanted me, you would have taken me—you *know* you would—if you hadn't started thinkin' about the other night and Eleanor tellin' you to get out of her house. *I'm* the only one there who was *nice* to you!"

He listened to her talking, overcome once more by a feeling of weariness he knew well. He could not make her understand, he did not really care enough to try.

"I'm sorry," he muttered.

"You are the only man, the *only* man ever to refuse me! Why, you're the only man I've ever had to come lookin' for!"

"It's not you, Fancy," he lied with effort, wishing she'd be gone from him. "You're very lovely, believe me. But you see, I—"

"Oh, please, do not bother to explain," she snapped. "Come here and do me up in the back. You can manage *that*, can't you?"

He laced her gown with practiced fingers and tied an expert bow beneath the ruffled collar. "There, that's right, I think."

She inspected herself carefully in his small shaving mirror, twisting and turning it in every direction as she tried to see his handiwork.

"It's fine," she admitted. And then her eye fell on the forgotten dress goods. "Oh, dear!" she cried dejectedly.

In spite of everything, Michael could not resist a smile for the child in her. "Please do choose whatever you like. I'll have one of the men take them out to your carriage."

"I didn't come by carriage," she said uncertainly. "I'm staying in town for a week with some friends of Papa's." She looked at him with a little puzzled frown. "Do you really mean I can still have my presents? Anything I pick out? You're not teasing me?"

She was all little girl again, the charming petulant smile back on her lips, her eyes wide, her small hands fluttering with excitement. Looking at her now, Michael felt a strange mixture of pity and revulsion come over him. He picked up an armful of the material from his chair and placed it before her on the table with exaggerated assiduity, then planted himself in the chair and bade her enjoy herself.

Once she was sure he meant what he said, Fancy forgot all about what had nearly happened between them but a few moments before. Indeed, she as good as forgot he was even there. One by one she examined the bundles of cloth, unfolding them impatiently, holding them up before her as she tried to gauge the effect of the different colors against her face in the mirror. She overlooked nothing, uttering delighted little cries as she found twelve yards of wide Spanish lace, tossing the lace aside to seize the blue lutestring he had promised her. Then nothing would do but he find her a pair of scissors and, while he sat watching silently, she quickly cut and folded and wrapped her selections expertly. There was a very large pile when she had finished.

"Well, you are certainly the strangest man I have ever met," she pronounced archly. "Now, be a darlin' and have your man take all this to the Blake house. He can't miss it, it's just two streets over from Captain Rhett's place. Anyone in town can tell him where *that* is. . . ."

"Nothing for your cousin?" Michael glanced at the large parcel.

For a moment Fancy seemed flustered, then she dimpled very becomingly, clucking her tongue at him. "Oh, let Eleanor get her own clothes!" she blurted out when she realized he was quite serious. "She'll have enough money pretty soon to buy everything in Charles Town if she wants. Or, she *would* have, if she'd just be sensible about things."

"But she's not 'sensible,' is she?"

Fancy shrugged as she opened the door to let herself out. "Not where it counts. You heard her the other night. She could be the richest lady in Carolina if she'd forget all that stuff and nonsense about her precious Nigrahs. But she's promised them all pay for their work when the money comes in. When she's gone and paid them all and paid everyone the money she owes all over town, she won't have a shillin' left to call her own. That's why Papa gets so exasperated with Eleanor, don't you see? But I don't guess you want to hear another word about *her,* not after the way she's treated you.'' She swept out past him in a perfumed rustling of lavender silk petticoats and skirts, calling back very gaily and completely undaunted, ''I'll be seein' you, sugar—you can *count* on it!''

To his annoyance, after he'd had the cabin set to rights again, doing his best to ignore the knowing winks and sly leering of Bailey, Michael looked about him and felt it a lonelier place than ever. He had lived with himself long enough to know that the lonely place was *inside* of him, that it went with him, land or sea, wherever he went. But when his treacherous memory confronted him again and again with that sweet, tantalizing fantasy image of Eleanor Campion naked in his arms, he rose up with a curse on his lips and left the ship to go into Charles Town and spend the evening as he had originally planned. And tomorrow, without fail, he resolved grimly, the *Sheila Deare* would lift anchor and leave the Campions and their problems far behind!

Three

"A Flame-Haired Girl Sat Waiting"

1 Hatheway's Tavern In Charles Town

With this resolution fixed squarely in his mind, Michael felt almost relieved. He walked along the docks with his customary quick, long-legged stride, enjoying the sight of the late afternoon sun lazing over the pale, pearl shimmer of the Cooper River.

He found Charles Town a pretty place, not so large as Boston but possessing an air of genteel, old-world graciousness about it that Boston had not yet acquired. Charles Town was situated on a long thumb of land between the Ashley and Cooper rivers, this *new* Charles Town, he reminded himself. They had moved the place to this location a few years back. *Old* Charles Town had been across the Ashley, a plaguey spot where malaria and yellow jack abounded.

The new town was laid out in wide, pleasant grassy streets,

crossed by neat regular roadways. As Michael roamed about in leisurely fashion he passed a great number of large handsome homes enclosed by shady walled gardens. Yeoman's Creek ran around the lower part of the town and there were several drawbridges and footbridges, making it an easy matter to cross over into the beautiful, tree-lined park known as Button's Commons. Michael stopped just at the edge of the Commons, and saw that his perambulations had taken him far from the center of town, almost, indeed, into the countryside. He shook his head, chagrined, as he realized where his apparently aimless meanderings were leading: westward lay the beginning of plantation country. Fourteen miles upriver was Belleterre, and its lovely mistress, Eleanor Campion. Eleanor Campion, she of the luminous green eyes, with hair the color of sunrise, a mouth firm and generous in proportion, soft firm lips that made a man burn to crush them with his own.

Good God, was he never to get her out of his mind! Michael turned impatiently and retraced his steps back through Charles Town toward the Cooper River wharves and Hatheway's Tavern. A soft, lilac-misted dusk permeated the cooling streets now. The sounds of raucous laughter and lively music throbbed from the low-built building ablaze with lights that glowed invitingly in the early evening shadows.

As he approached the doorway several sailors emerged, talking noisily, carrying bottles under one arm, drawing along some of the waterfront doxies with the other. Michael had been in places like this over half the waterfronts of the world. He was hungry now and not particular about the company who would share his supper table. He went in, expecting nothing more than the usual noisome, dirty, crowded taproom. He found that Hatheway's was all of that and a bit more.

The usual assortment of seamen and land-dwelling wharf rats were there; the customary gathering of buxom, painted whores circulated among the crowded tables. But Hatheway's was much larger than it appeared from outside. Through a doorway into the rear there was another room. Michael pushed his way slowly, good-naturedly, through the mob out front, spotting two or three men from his own ship and giving them a nod in passing.

He then found himself in a wood-paneled chamber of good size with another, smaller bar along one wall, a huge stone hearth with a fire blazing away offering almost the only light in the room. Here the tables were set against the walls and partially curtained off from one another for privacy.

Down at the other end of the room opposite the bar there were three large billiard tables superior to any he'd yet seen in America, and in a corner a quiet card game was played while attractive, very young barmaids moved about silently clearing away glasses, serving food and drinks, occasionally stopping to look on at the billiard tables or the card game. It was so dark Michael could not tell at first whether there were a great many customers there or only a few.

He sat down at a small table, enjoying the quiet atmosphere of the place. One of the young barmaids detached herself from a group standing at the bar and came quickly to serve him. In very short order a steaming platter of beef and potatoes was set before him. He ordered a brandy but the girl shook her head in protest.

"Oh, sir, you wouldn't care for the brandy. 'Tis not a Carolina drink. None of our gentlemen can stomach the stuff!"

Michael smiled, amused at her audacious behavior. "Indeed, is it not? This is the first I've heard of it. I'm carrying enough Carolina peach brandy aboard my ship to keep half of Boston warm through the winter!"

The girl giggled. "Oh, we ships it out, right enough, sir. But here only old ladies and sick folk takes brandy!"

"Well, then, what would you suggest instead?"

She winked at him. "I'll surprise you, sir, if you like."

A moment later she was back again, and placed a very large silver tankard on his table. He started to lift it to his lips . . .

"Oh, no, sir, do wait!" She grabbed the tankard out of his hand with another little giggle and a shake of her head. He watched curiously as she went to the great roaring fire a few feet away and took a poker from the flames. She came back with it red hot at the tip and thrust it into the tankard and out again swiftly. There was a swooshing, smoky sizzle, the liquid bubbled wildly, and the odor of burning brown sugar assailed his nostrils.

"*Now* you may drink it, sir. Good health to Your Honor!" She bobbed him a neat little curtsy and hovered there watching him.

With a game shrug, Michael picked up the tankard again and took a very large swallow. He felt as though his throat had been ripped open. For an instant he gasped and choked violently, and then an enticing sweetly tart taste filled his mouth delightfully.

The girl nodded approvingly. " 'Tis flip, sir. I knowed you'd like it. We makes it with rum and pumpkin beer and brown sugar. Tell 'em to try *that* in Boston Town. That'll warm their toes for 'em!"

"*Warm* bedamned! That would *curl* their toes!" chuckled Michael as he took another long swallow.

The girl grinned. "Just you call out whenever you wants another one, sir. I'm Delia." She minced her way fetchingly across the room to another table, where they were calling for her, but not before she'd managed to bend over Michael to give a quick energetic swipe to the tabletop with a rag, just long enough to be sure he had gotten a good look at her cushiony little breasts half exposed under the white dimity waist she was wearing. And, for good measure, she brushed her hip against his arm before she left him.

A sweet-smelling tart, thought Michael, knowing she was his for the price if he wanted her. And suddenly he was depressed. The girl reminded him of Fancy Campion. Nay, he reflected bleakly, this *Delia* was likely a better-hearted wench than the conniving, vixenish little Fancy. He stared moodily at the remains of the drink in his hand. They were all the same, weren't they? A world full of Fancys and Delias . . .

He stretched his legs, leaning back in the hard wooden chair. He yawned and wondered why he'd come at all. Now, in this place like so very many other, similar places in which he'd spent his time, the weariness and boredom returned. The awful sense he always had of time wasted and nothing accomplished bore down on him unusually hard tonight. He picked away without appetite at the food growing cold on his plate, and made up his mind to drink down the rest of the flip and be on his way back to the ship.

But when he'd finished and was fumbling about in his pocket for the money to pay for it, Delia appeared once more, all smiles and small giggles, and set another steaming tankard down beside the first.

"I knew you'd be wanting another, sir, can't none of our gentlemen leave off with just one flip," she breathed into his ear. Before he could protest, she ran her fingers lightly through his thick blond curls, allowing her nails to scrape softly down behind his ear along the side of his throat. She leaned over him, her breasts touching his cheek coolly. "Come upstairs with me, darlin', I know how to make a fellow like you happy, don't I, though!" Her lips brushed his earlobe, and boldly she bit into the flesh. A sudden flash of pure

394

animal urgency shook Michael for an instant, and then he pulled away from her and slammed a handful of coins down on the table.

"Clear out!" he said in a low, sharp voice. "Take this and leave me alone!"

Delia, aggrieved and sorely put out with him, scooped the coins into her palm and, tossing her head airily, flounced away to the bar, where she stood whispering with some of the other girls, looking his way every few moments. But as soon as she had left him, Michael forgot she existed. He downed the second flip quickly, hoping the additional stimulant might lighten his depression. He could not go through the rest of his life comparing every woman he met with Eleanor Campion.

Utterly disgusted with himself he realized she was as much in his thoughts as ever. If he wasn't very careful, he thought, he'd find himself leaving Hatheway's Tavern and going back out to Belleterre, hat in hand like a penitent, to apologize . . . for what? He brushed the question aside impatiently. What difference did it make what excuse he made to her, even to himself, so long as he could see her again, be with her again? In the morning he would sail away from her . . . and that was just as well, he told himself forcefully. Just as well. And in the meantime, why was he sitting here alone, brooding, unable to concentrate on anything or anyone else? He glanced toward the bar, remembering Delia. Any other time in his life and he'd have been up the stairs and in her bed long before this, a few drinks, a laugh or two at some soon-forgotten, meaningless jest, a quick fumbling of hands and breasts, a few moments of forgetfulness and no harm done and nothing to regret or to remember afterward.

No! he thought savagely, getting to his feet. That was not what he wanted. He could not have what he wanted; very well, what was there to do but go back to the ship and try to sleep? One last night in Charles Town harbor and then away. Forever. He'd not come back this way again, he vowed. He'd put an ocean between himself and the lady of Belleterre.

Michael found himself somewhat light-headed suddenly. He had misjudged the effect of the flip. He looked toward the doorway, and then wandered over to the billiard tables to watch the play in progress for a few minutes, until his head cleared. At the bar the tavern keeper, a fat, lugubrious fellow with a perpetual tear in the corner of his eye, was working hard at filling his glass bottles from a huge oaken cask behind him. As he worked he sang at the top of a tremulous Scottish tenor voice, a dirgelike tune to which no one in the room paid the slightest attention.

Then suddenly one of the gentlemen at the card table threw down the cards in his hand and cried, "God's blood! Master Jennings, your caterwauling comes between me and my luck tonight! I haven't a card here worth wagering a farthing on!"

The others around the table laughed, but their companion jumped up and stalked angrily from the room, brushing against Michael as he went. Michael started to call after him but one of the other players noticed him standing there and beckoned to him.

"We've an empty chair here, sir, if you're inclined to play. Whist, sir, not every man's taste but we're quite mad about it in Charles Town. Shilling a hand, what do you say?"

Michael began to decline the offer politely when the other men seated about the table looked at him in a peculiarly intense manner. One leaned over and spoke quickly to the first. He folded his cards precisely and put them down in front of him.

"One moment, though, sir," he said, his tone of voice altered. "Will you be so kind as to introduce yourself? My friends object to playing with strangers."

"I'll not be playing, thanks anyway, but if it's any concern of yours or your friends I'm Captain Michael Ives of the *Sheila Deare*, out of Boston," retorted Michael stiffly, not liking either the question or the tone in which it had been asked.

"He *is* the man!" remarked another man across the table.

"Which man is that, sir?" inquired Michael coldly. He noticed that once again they exchanged hasty glances.

"Why, sir, the man who was over to Belleterre a fortnight ago, that's all," said the first too quickly.

"You have the advantage of me, sir," snapped Michael, feeling suddenly overwarm. The man he addressed nodded curtly.

"Matthews, Captain. Maurice Matthews. My plantation is quite close to Belleterre... but even closer to Rogue's Fall," he added with a certain emphasis.

"Then you'd be neighbor to Sydney Campion, I expect," said Michael very deliberately.

Matthews nodded, never taking his narrowed gaze from Michael's face. "Neighbor these five-and-thirty years, ever since old Campion came to Carolina when his sons were only boys. Neighbor, sir... and friend." There was no mistaking the open antagonism in his voice and manner.

"Come, come, gentlemen, too much talk spoils the game," put in someone else, but the others quickly hushed him with warning looks.

"You *are* the man who insulted William Campion and forced his cousin to turn you out of her house, isn't that the fact of the matter, Captain Ives?" demanded Matthews. Michael looked at him hard, his blue eyes lazy and dangerous now.

"It is not my habit to discuss a lady in a place like this, Master Matthews," he said very quietly.

But Matthews would not let it go. "Do you deny you are the man?" he persisted, an ugly smile tugging at the corners of his small, pursed mouth.

Michael glanced around him and sighed. "Mistress Campion *was* insulted that night, sir," he replied tersely. "But not by me. By her own cousin. As a matter of fact, I called him out because of it. You really ought to get your facts straight, Master Matthews. But I cannot blame you, in all truth. Anything that toad or his father would tell you is bound to be a damnable lie!"

A sudden silence came over the busy room. The landlord's singing continued for a few seconds, then faltered to a halt. Matthews smashed his fist on the table, scattering cards and coins all over the floor, his thin yellowish face contorted with anger.

"I'll not sit at a table with this rogue! I gamble only with gentlemen . . . and you, *Captain* Ives, hardly qualify! By God, no wonder poor Sydney was so distraught when I saw him. Well, my friends, Mistress Campion continues to amaze her neighbors, does she not? But who would have thought she'd tire so soon of that black buck of hers and turn to common sailors to pleasure her bed of a night?"

There were muffled guffaws at the table, laughter and hurried talk all around the room. Matthews's words had carried clearly to the men at the billiard tables, who stood lounging about, hanging about, heartily amused at every vicious syllable he uttered. The crackle of the great fire seemed terribly loud.

Michael put his face very close to the face of this friend of Sydney Campion's and said quite distinctly, "Master Matthews, your remarks are intolerable. I care nothing for your opinion of me . . . you are an ignorant, arrogant little man not worth bothering about. But the lady you insult is another matter, not so easily dismissed. I ask you to withdraw your insults. *Now.*"

But Matthews was surrounded by friends and not to be intimidated. He pushed Michael away from him with a disdainful hand. "I withdraw nothing. Leave us, Captain, before you come to mischief."

Michael caught at the offending hand of the planter, gripping his wrist and swiftly pulling Matthews to his feet. Behind him his chair crashed to the floor. The men standing about moved back very fast.

"Take your hand away, you dog!" snarled Matthews in a rage. Michael obliged, releasing him instantly with a twist and a pushing motion that nearly threw him down. Matthews swore volubly, grabbing at the table edge to right himself. And suddenly he pulled from a sheath at his belt a large Scottish dirk, its long tapering thin blade glinting brightly silver satin in the firelight.

"Maurice, don't be a fool! Put the knife away!" cried one of his friends, laying a restraining hand on Matthews's shoulder. But the hand was shaken off with a resentful oath. One of the girls screamed. Michael's hand had moved instinctively to his breast pocket, where he always carried a blade of his own. Matthews saw the gesture. For the first time his bravado seemed a bit uncertain. His eyes flickered as Michael calmly took the dagger from his pocket and, eyeing his antagonist warily, began to unbutton his coat for the purpose of wrapping it about his other hand during the fight that now seemed inevitable.

"Please, gentlemen, please!" quavered Jennings, the landlord. "No fighting here! Put up your weapons, I implore you!" He moved quickly enough for a fat man, interposing his broad body between the two of them. And Michael saw with contemptuous amusement that Matthews was relieved. Despite his belligerent façade he had no real stomach for the fight. He did not hesitate a moment but quickly replaced the dirk in its sheath. Master Jennings turned to Michael with a woeful, beseeching expression on his plump, sweating face.

"Captain, if you please?"

Michael put away his dagger without another word. As he buttoned up his coat once more he looked around the tight knot of men with Matthews, shaking his head slowly.

"Master Matthews talks of 'gentlemen'! Bah! You all heard what he said about that fine, lovely lady, a lady whom you all know, and not one of you so much as spoke up on her behalf. Is this Carolina courtesy, gentlemen? By Heaven, we may not be so grand as you in Boston Town, but we'd not leave it to a stranger to defend the good name of one of our women! You disgust me, *gentlemen*. I shall sail from Charles Town harbor with greater pleasure than I felt in leaving the slimy waterfronts of Hong Kong and Marseilles!''

"So long as you *do* sail, Captain, the sooner the better!" retorted Matthews. Master Jennings groaned.

Michael nodded briskly. "Tomorrow morning, sir, and bedamned to the lot of you *and* to Carolina!"

He started to turn away, only to hear Matthews remark, "There *will* be killing one day, because of her! Mark my words."

Michael turned back, his eyes blazing. Matthews's friends were anxious to avoid a brawl and urged him to come away with them, but something perverse in the man would not let the matter rest. He stared insolently at Michael as though daring him to reply. When Michael still said nothing, Matthews thrust himself free of the crowd about him and leaned across the card table until his face was only a scant few inches away.

"The uncle will win, Captain, make no mistake about that. He'll prove his case. The attorney's got all the evidence, Campion told me so himself. Daughter or no daughter, that woman will never inherit from James, nay, not so much as a farthing! You won't be so quick to defend . . . what is it you called her? A 'fine, lovely lady'?'' His gutteral voice sank to a hoarse, obscene laugh. "A lady! Not so, not when 'tis proved against her, not when Sydney proves she's naught but a—''

"Be silent, you drunken ass!" cried a deep, harsh voice unexpectedly.

Matthews flushed very red, his head jerking up angrily and they all turned to stare at a tall, broad-shouldered man wearing a long heavy mantle over an elaborately ornate suit of claret-colored velvet. His heavily muscled legs were clad in black riding boots and the point of a sword protruded from beneath the rich golden cloth of the cloak.

Michael realized that most of the people in the room recognized the newcomer. He saw awe in their faces, and fear as well. He was puzzled and wondered how long the man had been there listening to his quarrel with Maurice Matthews. He could not recall having seen the fellow in the tavern earlier. He glanced around, his gaze traveling swiftly toward the rear of the room, to the curtained alcove tables hidden in shadows. He must have been sitting back there,

Michael thought, and now he noticed for the first time at one of those tables there sat a very still figure, muffled to the chin in a heavy mantle, his face further concealed by the deep folds of a large hood.

His attention was quickly drawn back to the richly dressed stranger upon whom all eyes were turned. Matthews, Michael noted with interest, was actually trembling, his mouth opening and closing soundlessly like a netted fish.

"Your friends would like you to leave with them," said the stranger, stranger to Michael, at least. "They offer good counsel, Matthews. Follow it. Go home." One hand impatiently slapped against his velvet-clad thigh as he spoke.

Matthews swallowed very hard. "Yes," he whispered, licking his dry lips. "Yes, of course, Captain Keane. I will do that, at once."

Michael observed this interchange with a lifted eyebrow and a smile that had turned sardonic. Matthews saw his face.

"You'll see, Ives," he muttered. "Soon enough, you'll see!" Then, with a glance at the sword beneath Keane's cloak, he laughed nervously and hurried out accompanied by his friends.

The room remained deadly quiet even after the door had closed behind them. Michael was intrigued by the obvious power this man, Keane, wielded over the people around him. And now Keane was looking at him.

"What was he about to say, I wonder?" Michael said softly, almost as though he were talking to himself. "Tell me, do you know, sir?"

Keane's dark, hawkish face seemed never to have known a smile. What passed for one now appeared briefly in a twisted grimace of his thin, well-formed lips.

"The man's a fool," he replied. "But even a fool can do harm if he's allowed. Good evening, sir." He had the manner of one dismissing a servant. Michael found it insufferable.

"You didn't answer me, Captain—it *is* Captain Keane, I think?"

Keane's pose of hauteur disappeared. "It is," he said coldly. "As for your question, sir, I would advise you to mind your own affairs and let other people do the same . . . whatever your opinion of *Carolina courtesy!*"

"I fail to see what this has to do with you!" cried Michael, thoroughly exasperated.

"Captain Ives," drawled Keane in a bored tone, "I have no

quarrel with you. But I might observe that you seem to choose your friends recklessly—ignorantly, even—and you alienate gentlemen with whom you as a sea captain might wish to do business one day."

Michael threw back his head and laughed. "Matthews?" he said, "I hardly imagine—"

"Yes, Matthews for one," interrupted Keane. "But Sydney Campion is more to the point. You antagonize Campion. You attempt to thwart his purposes."

Michael looked at him incredulously. "Do I, indeed?" he scoffed. "Just how am I thwarting Sydney Campion's purposes, Keane? I am assuming now that you are well acquainted with his purposes. You are, aren't you?"

Keane's mouth tightened. "You're becoming tiresome, Captain!"

"No doubt," said Michael, "I am not so easily dismissed as your friend Matthews. I am astonished, sir, how many of you Charles Town gentlemen seem to resent the arrival of a simple sailing man from Boston. One would think you all had something to hide. I grow more intrigued every moment. Even if I had never laid eyes on . . . a certain lady . . . I would be inclined to offer her whatever services I could merely on the strength of the hostility I have found directed against her on every side by all of you southern champions of chivalry."

The steely expression in his eyes belied the bantering tone of his voice. For the first time Keane looked at him with something approaching respect. And Keane responded by throwing back his right arm casually, flinging one side of the gaudy mantle over his shoulder. His hand settled upon the hilt of his sword. The landlord, who had been watching the two men uneasily, moved forward, wringing his hands. He wavered into Keane's line of vision.

"Stay clear, Master Jennings!" snapped Keane, not bothering to glance at the fat timid man. His attention was now entirely focused upon Michael. "The lady in question is no concern of yours, Captain. She does not require your services, however extraordinary they might be. Just do what you said you were going to do. Leave Charles Town tomorrow. Leave the Campions to their own devices."

Michael took a deep breath. "Don't trouble yourself to warn me, Keane. The more I listen to you, the more I see what my course must be. Aye, I'll sail from Charles Town, happily and soon. But if I am still needed to ship Belleterre indigo, then by Heaven, I will! I'll see the lady herself tomorrow and arrange what I can to help her.

Thank you for making up my mind for me, Captain. I am in your debt!"

Master Jennings let slip a small moan of anguished apprehension as the two men stood facing each other, the anger hanging in the air between them like an invisible dagger.

Suddenly a small, discreet cough came from the table in the alcove shadows. Keane looked back and seemed about to say something, but the expression on his face changed. He shrugged carelessly and strode past Michael without another word. Michael wheeled about and saw Keane continue on his way out the door, where he paused for only an instant and looked back, his eyes meeting Michael's directly . . . and there was in those eyes an expression of hostility all the more shocking because it was so complete, so deadly, and Michael knew of a certainty that he had made an implacable enemy of this man whom he had never set eyes on before tonight. Then Keane was gone. A great conglomerate sigh seemed to pass through the room with his leaving and only then did the men at the billiard tables resume their game and the barmaids begin to move about again, making a great deal of noise as if to fill up the silent void as fast as possible.

Amidst the renewed talk and sounds of glasses and dishes no one paid any attention to the person who had been sitting in the alcove table. Now he stood up and threw some coins into the midst of the empty tankards before him and moved quickly to the door after Keane. But, just as Keane had himself, this other man also turned for an instant to look at Michael, who had not moved. For a few seconds the man's face was clearly visible, and then he was gone.

"William Campion!" gasped Michael under his breath.

"Excuse me, Captain, will you be wanting anything further?"

Michael jumped. Master Jennings was at his elbow, his smile no more than obligatory, his dark eyes plainly suffering.

"What? What is it, man?" demanded Michael, his thoughts whirling. William Campion had been there through it all, William, who wanted so badly to marry his fair cousin. William had sat there in the corner hidden from all eyes and listened to her vilified and almost made the cause of a crude public brawl!

"I said, sir, would you be wanting anything more to eat or dr—?"

"Who is Keane?" Michael cut him off abruptly.

Jennings blinked. "I—I could send Delia for more flip, sir, that's what you were drinking, wasn't it? Or, you know, Captain, maybe it would be better if you just went on your way now..."

Michael ignored his pleading, sheepdog eyes. "I want to know about Keane—Captain Keane," he reiterated.

"Have you never heard of Keane, then? Not in the islands? Not up along Albemarle Sound and Hampton Bay? Keane is... he's a pirate, sir, with a fondness for Charles Town that brings him back to plague us when it suits his fancy." Jennings confided this information in a low whisper full of dread, all the while staring anxiously about him as though he expected to see Keane come running at him sword in hand.

Michael frowned, bemused. "And what has William Campion to do with a man like Keane?"

Jennings took a few steps backward, his swarthy face utterly miserable. " 'William,' sir?" His voice shook dreadfully. "I'm sure I don't know what you mean!"

Michael smiled unpleasantly. "Don't you, though? That was William Campion sitting back there. He was here with his friend Keane, and he left directly Keane closed the door behind him. But you didn't see him, did you, Master Jennings?"

"No, sir, I did not!" asserted Jennings, and then he bolted for the relative safety of the bar.

Michael left Hatheway's Tavern at once and headed back along the dark wharves toward the *Sheila Deare*. It was not an especially long walk but, long or short, he was not in a mood to care. His anger over the night's business had grown into a steady rage, and the earlier depression he had known had long since given way before this overwhelming sense of resentment and injustice.

He stalked along the deserted wooden piers, relishing the sharp salt smell of the sea breeze blowing in from the Atlantic. Fog enveloped the ships lying at anchor and the tall warehouses that loomed crookedly out over the brackish water. Fog soon obliterated Hatheway's and even its glowing lantern lights seemed no more than dull splotches of color in the swirling gray night. He tripped once or twice on warped bits of rotten planking that had thrust up jaggedly from the old wooden causeway built over the muddy riverbank from one pier to the next. Michael noticed neither the fog nor the night nor the way before him, so busy was he with the fury that engulfed his thoughts and feelings.

Not until he had actually said the words aloud, back there face to face with Keane, had he known what he meant to do all along. For two long wasted weeks he had dawdled in this place with Eleanor Campion on his mind, unable to forget the events of that strange, unsettling evening, unable to leave Charles Town, unable—or afraid, he admitted now—to go back and face her again. What had made him afraid, when the raging North Atlantic and its hurricane winds and the scores of battles large and small he had fought around the world and even death itself had never had that singular power?

Yes, he faced it now: he *had* been afraid to see Eleanor Campion again. Perhaps it was because he had instinctively realized that she represented the end of searching, the final place from which he would not be moved further in this world, the last chance he would ever find to lay claim to whatever he thought worth fighting for, worth keeping if he could, worth dying for if he could not. And, to some small, stubborn blind part of him, that was frightening.

But, God's Blood! he swore to himself alone there in the Charles Town fog, he had seen this kind of thing before, hated it before, had been powerless to stop it before. Not this time! No, this time, somehow, justice must win out or there was nothing, after all, worth living for. It was very clear to him: they were conspiring to take her land away from her and they didn't much care how they did it. He thought, I'm sick to the heart of people being forced off the land; it's been done to me and mine and those dearest to me. Someone's got to help that girl, someone.

Aye, then, it's decided, we'll not sail in the morning. At sunrise I'll ride out to Belleterre and have this thing out between her and me. I'll tell her exactly what was said, not the insults of course, although she's undoubtedly heard them before and worse, but everything else that mattered . . . and he tried to think what *had* been said. But, there was really just Maurice Matthews's unfinished threat: Campion had an attorney working against her, Campion claimed to have some sort of proof. Proof of what?

But Eleanor would know that, he realized. She must tell him everything. She must let him see that mystifying letter he had brought her from her friend on Antigua. He was positive the letter had a great deal to do with it. And then he would arrange with her to take the indigo shipment and work out a way to help her hold her father's land.

A small, niggling doubt as to whether or not he would be

welcome at Belleterre was dismissed without further thought. What else could she have done that night but ask him to leave? The uncle had put her in an impossible position. And, as for what the black woman, Matty, had said later—why, that was all nonsense. One did not fall in love so easily. Or, one fell in love, whatever that meant, very easily and very often. As often as it took to rouse a wench and have her and forget her.

He fought down the stab of guilt that assailed him as Eleanor's face came into his mind. His business with her had nothing to do with love or desire. Tomorrow she'd see him, he vowed, no matter what he had to do or say to persuade her; she'd damn well have to let him in and she'd damn well have to listen to what he'd say!

He caught sight of the ruby glimmer of the ship's portside lanterns as he approached along the silent piers. Mister Rainey, his first mate, was up on the bridge. Michael could just make out the tiny ruddy glow of his pipe moving back and forth as he walked about the small area. Good, thought Michael, I can change the sailing orders right now, have it out with Rainey and over with tonight, then a good, long sleep and—

He turned toward the waterside, brightly illuminated suddenly as the full moon appeared through mist and fog almost directly overhead. He started to hail the ship's watch; he had his arm raised, and at the same instant, from somewhere in the shadows behind him, he heard the whip-crack of a pistol shot ring out!

Michael threw himself flat; then, crouching very low, he moved behind a pile of wooden crates and waited. For a moment there was nothing more. Then he heard a smothered curse, followed by the tiny clicking turn of a flintlock pistol cock from full to half and, finally, the snap and flash of the ignited charge going off in a second shot. The ball ripped into the crates that shielded him, splintering the flimsy wood not two feet above his head. If he'd still been standing upright it would have struck him through the heart. He himself was unarmed save for the dagger but even if he had had a pistol of his own with him, he could not see his assailant. As it was he offered a perfect target should he make a move to reach the ship.

"Ahoy the dock!"

It was the most welcome voice of the officer of the night watch shouting down from the ship's stern. "Who's there? Speak up, d'you hear? Speak up at once!"

Footsteps running about the companionways and decks, more

shouts, lanterns fetched quickly portside for a better look into the darkness . . . and Michael heard an angry voice muttering behind him, then the swift footsteps of a man running away.

Instantly he stood up and hailed the ship, ordering the men on watch to join him in giving chase.

But it was no use. Whoever had tried to shoot him had disappeared somewhere into the back alleyways and narrow dark passages around the mazelike warehouses and storage sheds. Not another soul was about, not one person could be found who might have seen a man running by. After an hour or so of futile searching, Michael led his men back to the *Sheila Deare*.

"Cutthroats, every one of 'em, Cap'n," pronounced Mister Rainey darkly. "Good thing for us we're sailing out of this damned pesthole come mornin' tide!"

"But we're not, Mister Rainey," Michael told him. "Hold her ready for further orders and keep a loading crew standing by. I'll let you know during the day when to cast off."

He left Mister Rainey shouting Massachusetts obscenities into the night wind on deck as he went aft to his cabin and closed the door behind him, suddenly feeling a trifle weak in the knees. He poured three full fingers of Irish whiskey into a glass and drank it down in one gulp.

Someone had just tried to kill him. In twenty years at sea he had faced plenty of waterfront toughs, the scum of every port whose business it was to prey upon seamen fresh off their ship with a few coins jingling in their pockets. But never before had he been set upon from behind with no chance of defending himself. This had been no common dockside pickpocket or strangle-thief who had singled him out purely by chance. Whoever it was had known him, known where he was headed, and waited for him.

He refilled the whiskey glass, settling back tiredly in his chair to think the thing through. It might have been that fool, Matthews, lurking about there in the dark, still brooding on their interrupted quarrel, still spoiling for a fight. No, Michael decided at once, the man who had shot at him hadn't wanted a fight, only a killing. Matthews might be many unsavory things but he probably didn't have the stomach for murder.

That left William Campion. It was the only answer that made any sense. Oh, William probably hadn't done the job himself. More than likely he'd gotten one of his pirate friends, possibly even Keane, to handle it. The important question was *why?* They had ignored him until tonight . . . and tonight he had goaded Maurice Matthews into saying too much. Michael shook his head. What had Matthews been about to blurt out that they didn't want him to hear? Keane had been quick enough to silence Matthews. Nothing had been revealed, nothing that Michael understood, at any rate.

He set the glass down on his writing table and absently twirled it around with his fingers. How had he suddenly become no longer a mere annoyance to them but a threat, a threat evidently so potent that they wanted him dead?

Something that had happened there at Hatheway's tonight had catalyzed them into taking action they had not anticipated. Very well, then, what? Michael went over the details of his argument with Matthews, his confrontation with Keane.

"That must be it!" he said aloud. Of course. He had told Keane that he intended to go back to Eleanor, to offer to ship her indigo cargo to market, to help her in whatever way he could! And he had seen William Campion there with Keane. If he were allowed to see Eleanor once more, if he told her what he'd seen, what he'd heard, she would be alerted to what they were up to. And it was obvious they were not yet ready to play out the hand; Sydney's little game was still incomplete. Keane had remarked about Michael's thwarting Sydney's plans. Michael found his head was aching abominably; wearily he rubbed the back of his neck, his thoughts going in circles. Sydney's plans . . . everyone knew what those plans were . . . it would suit Sydney that Eleanor remain short of money, owing large sums all over Charles Town, unable to purchase what she needed to keep Belleterre going—yes, and it would suit Sydney even better if her indigo never reached market at all, just like the shipment that disappeared last year.

Pirates had seized that shipment. Michael jumped to his feet, sending the papers and books piled on his writing table scattering all over the floor. Pirates! My God, he thought, that's where Keane fits into the picture, Keane, instigated and abetted by William and his father! They'd stop at nothing to cut the ground out from under her—and she knew nothing of what was going on! No wonder they had tried to stop him from reaching her!

Well, then, by God, they would *not* stop him! He would not delay until tomorrow, he decided suddenly. He would ride out and see her this very night. Murder had almost been done. Tonight it must be.

The attack on his life had failed. Could they lose their heads completely and go after her, could they dream of attacking her alone and unprotected as she was? It would be easy enough to blame whatever happened on some innocent black or some hapless passerby.

Michael opened his sea chest and took out two Spanish miquelet flintlock pistols. He thrust them into his belt along with a copper powder flask and a larger, leather flask filled with lead shot. He strapped on his sword, threw a heavy blue serge cloak about his shoulders and went up on deck. He informed Mister Rainey that he was going upriver at once and did not know exactly when he would be back. Mister Rainey thought he'd gone mad and said so, but Michael was already ashore and out of earshot.

He walked along swiftly but cautiously through the quiet streets of the town, heading for the livery stable. Fourteen miles at night through strange countryside where, it was said, over thirty thousand black slaves labored in doleful restraint. Fourteen miles at night upriver on a dirt road frequented by footpads, highway men and buccaneers like Keane come secretly—and not so secretly—ashore. Aye, Michael told himself grimly, best be prepared for anything. They might not risk coming after him again tonight, thinking he was safe aboard ship . . . unless someone was watching every move he made. He did not think he was being followed, but there was still the journey back, and that would be much later, when the moon was down.

The little brass clock under the brass dome by his bunk had read just on nine o'clock when he'd left the ship. A barbaric time to go calling, and it would be closer to eleven by the time he reached Belleterre. She might set the dogs on him this time!

Twenty minutes later, as the moon broke free once more and rode high out of the clouds above an avenue of graceful cypress trees, he was galloping swiftly upon a hired horse, heading up the silent, soft track road along the Ashley. In a very short time he had left far behind him the cheerful yellow window lights of Charles Town's stately mansions. And it seemed to him somehow that the moon beckoned and showed him the way to where a flame-haired girl sat waiting and watching the long, dark road.

2 Night Ride To Belleterre

It was nearly midnight before Michael rode across the broad meadow that fronted Belleterre. He was moving at a very slow pace now, both he and the horse dead tired. Half a dozen times on the long journey he had lost the road or turned off at the wrong place. He must have awakened half the hounds in Carolina as he went by this night. He had seen several large brick houses as he passed on his way, but nary a light in a window of any of them. There had not been a sound all the way other than the frantic barking of dogs and his own hard breathing, and the steady clip-clop of the horse's feet. He'd gone by rice fields and pineland and pasture and even passed an immense stretch of swampland without so much as a glimpse of another human being. He'd had no use, so far, for the two pistols beneath his coat, although there was an eerie feeling of danger in the very air about him as he rode on through the swelling white mists floating in from the river, and he felt better having the weapons with him.

At last he had sighted Belleterre, only because it was built on the rise of a hill and stood out clearly among the treetops. Otherwise he might have gone on and on until the road simply ended in forest and the tangled brush of the small hills leading into the mountains.

There were lights downstairs in the front windows of the house. Casting aside a momentary feeling of uncertainty, he guided the horse into the front drive. If Eleanor thought he acted rashly, it was up to him to make her see the danger that was fast closing in on her, the trap about to be sprung—

Suddenly, soundlessly, a tall, heavyset man moved out from behind a stand of thick-trunked tulip trees bordering the narrow drive leading to the house. Michael's horse whinnied fearfully, tossing its head. The man seized the bridle very quickly and held the frantic animal's head firm and steady until it quieted. Michael thought sickly, my God, I was right, they have come after her tonight!

He reached cautiously for one of his pistols, knowing it was probably a futile gesture, hoping he might yet bluff the rogue. Where were the rest of them, he wondered, all the while saying not a word, just moving his arm slowly, so slowly. Had they reached the house yet? Had they hurt her? A killing rage more sure and dangerous than he had felt hours ago took possession of him.

"Get the devil out of my way!" he ordered harshly, imperiously.

"What you want here, sir?" returned an equally harsh demand spoken in a rich dark bass voice.

Now Michael saw in the fragmentary moonlight that his assailant was a black man. Silently he cursed himself for a fool. What help had he expected to be coming out here all alone as he had? It did not occur to him to fear for his own life. His entire emotion was one of utter fury, at himself, at the black man blocking his way, at the thought of what might even now be happening to Eleanor.

"Take your hands off my horse or I'll blow your goddamn head off!" he thundered, having finally gotten hold of one of the pistols. He held it so the man could see it, praying the fellow did not understand how the thing worked.

It happened so swiftly he never could remember exactly how it was done, but the pistol was whisked from his grasp and sent flying through the air ten feet away from him. And the tall black man was now holding him by the arm.

"Best you gets down now, sir," said he. Michael did not bother to reply but dug his boot heels hard against the horse's tender flanks. His movement had the desired effect: the animal reared up, terrified, and Michael was sure the black man would be forced to relinquish his grip. Instead, however, he found himself unceremoniously yanked out of the saddle and thrown flat on his back, while the horse turned tail and raced back toward Charles Town.

"You wants mo' trouble, sir? We don't *need* no mo' trouble, but you gots it if you wants it," said the black man softly, standing directly over him. And now Michael noticed with great chagrin that his captor was holding a very large, gleaming machete.

"No, no. No more trouble," he said, struggling to get his breath. "Do you mind if I stand up?"

The black searched him quickly, found the other pistol and sent it fleeting after its companion in the grass. Then he nodded and gently assisted Michael to his feet again, even brushing off his back and shoulders for him.

"Who are you, sir?"

Michael might have been amused any other time by the black's quiet air of politeness. Now it only added to his anger.

"I'm Captain Michael Ives and it's none of your damned bloody business!" he blustered. The black man looked dubious.

"You not no plantin' man from Charles Town?" he inquired after a moment's hesitation.

"I am not! I'm a sea captain. From Boston. I've come to call on Mistress Campion. Where the devil is she? If you or your friends have harmed her, you dog, I'll—"

"It mighty late to come callin' on Mistress Eleanor this time o' night. I don't know what I'm goin' to do with you, sir, and that's a fact," replied the black slowly, ignoring Michael's questions and threats.

"What's all that racket out there, Dogon?" It was a woman's voice coming from the direction of the house. "You like to raise the dead! Who've you got there with you?"

Michael thought he recognized Matty's voice, yes, Matty, he remembered, Eleanor's friend, and no friend to William or Sydney Campion. He breathed a little easier, realizing that Eleanor was not in any imminent danger, not this night at any rate.

"Come on, sir," said the black man, giving Michael a small push with the point of the machete. "I'm goin' to show you to Matty. She'll know what to do with you. And don't you try nothin' like gettin' away from me now, sir."

He held his machete crosswise against his shoulder like a soldier with his longarms and marched Michael quick-trot up to the house. The front door opened, spilling bright yellow light out on to the veranda. Matty herself stepped outside, half closing the door behind her. She frowned and stared, and then she began to laugh.

"Well, I see you came back to us, Captain Ives. I told you you would!"

"You know this gentleman, Matty?" inquired Dogon, his voice filling with relief.

"Oh, yes, Dogon. I know him. Mistress Eleanor threw him out of the house not long back!" She smiled wickedly.

In a trice Dogon had a stranglehold on Michael. "What you want to come back for, sir?"

Matty shook her head. "Let him go, Dogon, it's all right. He's not going to hurt anybody, are you, Captain?" Once again the wicked, beautiful smile touched her features.

"On my honor, ma'am," replied Michael with restraint. Dogon released him and apologized for the "inconvenience," as he put it.

"I'm gonna go now and find them pistols of yours, sir. Have 'em back to you before you leave," he promised, turning away with a very polite nod.

"Wait just a minute!" Michael called after him. "What were you doing skulking around out there at this time of night?"

Dogon looked back, his gaze level, his face grave. "We watches out for Mistress Eleanor,'' he answered pointedly. "Ain't nobody gonna get by *us* and hurt her. This is her place. Her and us. And we takes care of ourselves. Evenin', sir!''

Michael stared after him, admiring the quiet pride in his manner.

"What's the matter, Captain? Never seen a black man stand up for himself before?'' Matty's voice was hard and testing, her gaze sharp.

Michael shook his head. "I have not seen very many free black men, ma'am,'' he said simply.

Matty's eyes flashed. "Man's not a slave unless he believes he is,'' she said, as if she challenged him to disagree.

"Aye, ma'am,'' nodded Michael. "*I* know that well enough. No matter who tells him he is or how often they tell him, or how much they're inclined to beat him to prove it. I know a good deal about slavery, ma'am. I come from a country other people have been trying to make a slave kind of place for a long, long time. And do you know what? There's nary a slave in my country, for all their trying! Sure, they're all madmen. You cannot convince them they're slaves were you to horsewhip them sunup to sundown!''

Matty's face softened. She smiled, pushing the door wide open for him.

"Come on in, Captain Ives. We're all mad here. You'll feel right at home!''

3 A Bend In The Road

Eleanor Campion sat on a low cushioned stool by the fire in the front parlor, her arms curled comfortingly about her drawn-up knees, her head dreamily to one side, looking into the leaping, lashing flames before her. The glorious red hair was all unbound and fell in heavy waves, tumbling over her arms and shoulders.

She was dressed for bed in a flowing white cotton nightdress underneath her favorite robe, a comfortable, threadbare old emerald green velvet. The robe, like so many of Eleanor's clothes, had seen better days. Yet it still sat on her shoulders and clung to the soft curves of her tall body like a queen's mantle might sit on the shoulders of majesty itself. On her feet were thin little heelless house slippers, hand embroidered in green and blue and faded gold threads.

She had not eaten much supper tonight and Matty had stayed and stayed, trying to coax her to swallow down a bit of the fried hominy cakes and some tea. But Eleanor was so tired she had no real appetite. She drank cups and cups of hot jasmine tea with Matty, the two of them sitting on the sofa before the hearth, not talking much, just thinking and dreaming the long evening away.

Neither of them had the heart to bring out into the open what was uppermost in both their minds. Eleanor had written an answer to Ellen Fletcher's letter. She had also penned an apology to Captain Ives, trying to explain in a roundabout way, without really explaining at all, why she had been so rude to him that night. And Daniel, whom she trusted second only to Matty and Dogon, had been sent into town with both letters sealed and hidden inside his shirt. His instructions were to deliver the letters to Captain Michael Ives of the bark *Sheila Deare*.

Daniel had returned promptly and reported to her that Captain Ives had been in town but a ship's officer identifying himself as Mister Rainey had taken the letters and sworn solemnly he would place them with his own hands upon the Captain's writing table.

Eleanor had gone very queer in the stomach when she learned that Daniel had not actually seen Michael himself, but she was somewhat reassured when Daniel explained that Mister Rainey had fire in his eyes and thunder in his voice when he swore, and that he had said: "By Almighty God . . . and I'm a Christian man and a churchgoing man, you tell your mistress to set her heart at rest about her letters!" Daniel had always been a quick and accurate judge of people. Eleanor thanked him and said no more about it. Daniel had also mentioned that the ship's crew was very busy and seemed to be getting ready to sail very soon.

That had been two days after Michael had been to her house. She believed that the *Sheila Deare* had left Charles Town immediately. She wished with all her heart that she had had the courage to go into town herself, to see Michael Ives and apologize to him in person. Oh, why had she let Sydney and William maneuver her so cleverly that night! She had been afraid, it was true, afraid that Michael and William would carry their quarrel to its logical, deadly conclusion. She cared nothing what happened to William, cousin or no cousin. It was for Michael's own sake she had told him to leave. And it was not just Belleterre he must leave, but Charles Town, too. She could never breathe easily until she knew he was safely gone. Sydney would have had little compunction about rousing some of his friends against Captain Ives. Those men were all plantation owners, the gentlemen who ruled in Charles Town, who ruled the entire tidewater region as far as seventy miles inland to the fall line of hills and high mountains. And Sydney, for all the rest of them knew very well he hadn't a great fortune behind him anymore, still, he was one of them, one of the original settlers and Sydney was treated with deference and respect in town, particularly since he had made it very clear that he did not accept her or the way she tried to run Belleterre.

So Michael Ives was safely away at sea. She could hardly hold it against him that he had not seen fit to acknowledge her note. The man had come to do her a favor and had been insulted by her entire family. She would never see him again, of course. If *only* she knew what he would do with her letter to Ellen! He had promised to carry the reply back to Antigua . . . he had probably ripped both letters to pieces and not given them . . . or her . . . another thought!

Eleanor closed her eyes, the comforting heat of the fire made her drowsy. It was all *such* a muddle, she thought, drifting . . . why did I ever try so hard to do something so impossible? Once Matty had told her approvingly, "You're your father's daughter, girl, never forget it!" She had been proud to hear that, proud to think that somewhere James Campion saw and understood what she did and thought it well done.

But it is so difficult, Papa, and I'm so lonely! she thought now. It was not like her to give in to self-pity. Ordinarily she would not have put that thought into words. But now she was confused, her confidence shaken, and she did not know where to turn. How very differently she had envisioned everything, even after she'd realized what her family was really like. Even then she had thought to remain friends with them, to share freely what she had with them. She had not expected betrayal and treachery. She had not expected to be isolated even from them. She had tried hard to be a friend to Fancy, only to discover that Fancy despised her, thought her unnatural, mannish, a figure of scorn and suspicion. "Oh, Papa," she murmured into the fire's listening heart, "shall I give it up now? Shall I leave Carolina? And where would I go, I wonder?"

The memory of Michael Ives's tall figure stole into her mind unbidden. Once again she thought she saw that fair hair, those bright perceptive blue eyes, the straight, proud nose, the wide serious mouth, the aspect of shy boy and mature man so curiously mingled in his restless, seeking, somehow infinitely sorrowful spirit. She had imagined, that day, just for an instant, that here was a man she could so easily love! How romantic, how farfetched!

"Good evening, Mistress Campion."

Eleanor started, looking up in shocked disbelief. But there he stood, or was he only still the dream she had been dreaming a moment ago?

"Captain Ives?" she faltered. "Is it really—? Of course it is you! Forgive me, I am somewhat absentminded."

She could not move, but only continued to stare up at him, her heart hammering in her breast. "How did you come here? I mean, why? . . ."

Matty appeared from behind him, a knit shawl wrapped about her shoulders, a satisfied smile wreathing her face.

"I rescued him from Dogon," said Matty, and her voice, her very solid presence restored reality to the dreamlike atmosphere. "And once again it seems the Captain has arrived without a horse to take him away. Tea, Captain Ives?"

Michael merely nodded, unwilling to take his eyes from Eleanor's lovely face. Matty poured the tea very quickly, looking from one to the other of them with a soft light in her eyes. Then she said, "I'll be going back to my place now, Eleanor. You're in good hands. Evening to you both."

Eleanor jumped up, quite flustered, as Matty slipped out the door and was gone.

"Now why did she go and leave like that?" she whispered, too embarrassed to look at Michael. There was no one in the house now except the two of them.

Michael smiled and sat down in an old Russia leather armchair across from her little stool at the hearth and began sipping his hot tea.

"I pray your forgiveness, Mistress Campion," he said, and, although his voice and manner were calm, she thought she sensed something agitated in him, some inner tension that spoke in the taut lines between his eyes, the way he held his body stiff and alert.

She was about to murmur something polite, but he was not listening.

"I know 'tis an unseemly hour to appear at your door. But I must speak with you. It is a matter of the greatest urgency, believe me, or I would have waited until a proper time to call." As he talked, his eyes were entranced watching the ruddy glow of the fire glinting through the tawny waves of her hair.

Eleanor's winter sea green eyes were radiant when she replied.

"I thought you were already at sea, Captain Ives. I had hardly dared to hope I might see you again before you left. I take it then, since you've troubled yourself to come all the way out here again, that you've accepted my apology. I am so very glad! When the days passed and you sent no word, I thought you had decided to ignore my note—"

Michael's face was blank. "Your note, ma'am? What note was that?"

"Why, my *note*," stammered Eleanor. "The note I sent you along with my letter to Ellen Fletcher. You do remember? You promised to get my answer to her safely. . . ." He was staring at her, uncomprehending. Eleanor began to feel icy cold with dread. "You did not receive either my note of apology or Ellen's letter, did you?"

"I've heard nothing from Belleterre since that first night," replied Michael, shaking his head emphatically. "Who took the letters for you? Did he tell you he'd given them into my own hands? If he did, he's a damned liar!"

Eleanor's voice rose a trifle. "The man I sent is no liar, sir! I would trust him with anything. But, no, he was told that you were not aboard ship. Your first mate, a Mister Rainey, took the letters and promised faithfully he would put them into your cabin himself."

Michael ransacked his memory quickly. Rainey had never mentioned any letters. If he had, how different things would have been! But, what had become of them? If Rainey had put them in the cabin, then they must have been somewhere on the writing table, along with a dozen charts and the logbook, bills of lading, supply lists, a half-finished report for Katherine and God knows what else in the midst of all that clutter. And suddenly he remembered Fancy Campion, Fancy all alone in that cabin for fifteen or twenty minutes, going through drawers, opening cabinets, reading things that were none of her business!

Michael groaned. Of course, he realized. Fancy had found the letters, and when she had left the *Sheila Deare*, the letters had gone with her, probably straight into Sydney Campion's hands. And now, thanks to his own carelessness and Mister Rainey's forgetfulness, Campion and his son knew that Eleanor had been warned of their

416

treachery. Now they knew about Ellen Fletcher and they understood at last what errand it was that had brought him to Belleterre seeking Eleanor!

"You look ill, Captain," said Eleanor, alarmed at his sudden paleness. "May I get you something? A glass of brandy?..."

"No, no, it's all right," Michael muttered, turning away from her anxious gaze. "I've been a damned fool... beg pardon, ma'am, but that's the plain truth. Your letters were delivered and then... they were stolen, unless I'm very much mistaken. Your man was quite right in trusting Mister Rainey, as far as that goes. But Rainey forgot to say something to me and... and..." he stopped, turning both hands straight out, palms up.

"Stolen? They were stolen from your cabin?" cried Eleanor. "But who? Who would care about anything I would write to you... except my family?"

Michael cleared his throat uncomfortably. "Your cousin, Miss Fancy, paid me a visit today. She hadn't forgotten about those dress goods I'd promised her. I'm afraid she was left alone in my cabin long enough to have found the letters and hidden them in her reticule. I don't like to say a thing like that about your kinswoman, but..."

Eleanor's head drooped despondently. She murmured, "I know Fancy, Captain Ives. Stealing is not beyond her. And now my uncle knows what Ellen told me. I expect he will make his move against me much sooner now. Of course I will rewrite my letter to Ellen, but by the time she gets it and is able to send further information to me—if she has been able to discover anything more—it will be too late."

"But you must fight," cried Michael urgently. "That's what I came here to tell you. I had hoped what happened here the other night would not turn you against me. After that, I meant to sail at once, but..."

"Yes," Eleanor said shyly. "Why did you linger?" She stood straight and tall, one outstretched arm touching the mantel, and she looked at him with strangely misty eyes.

"Because there was unfinished business between you and me, even after your cousin and I quarreled," Michael said bluntly.

"Please, please forgive me for what I was forced to do to you that night!" she interrupted quickly, distress evident in every tense line of her body.

"We'll not speak of it again. I understand. Or, at least, I understand it better now."

"You do?" she asked, with a curious intensity that went straight to Michael's heart.

"Aye, I do," he smiled. "And I'm with you, if you'll let me be. I'll take your indigo and sell it up in Boston faster and for a better price than you'd get anywhere else."

"Why?" she asked him very simply, her face coloring. "Why should you care? You are a stranger—"

His sudden brusque laugh startled her. " 'Stranger,' is it?" he exclaimed. "No, ma'am, not any more, not from this day on! In this one short day, Mistress Campion, I've been stolen from, insulted, threatened, warned—I don't take kindly to being warned, mind you!—and, on top of all that, shot at!"

" 'Shot at'?" she echoed faintly, her hand flying to her mouth.

Michael nodded. "Aye, mistress, shot at, twice. And, again forgive me if this offends your sensibilities, but I have every reason to believe your insufferable cousin, William, was behind it, William or one of his damned pirate friends."

Eleanor attempted to speak but could not utter a sound. Her eyes silently beseeched him to explain.

"I'll tell you what happened," he said gently, "but if I'm to be of any help to you, you must tell me everything *you* know. As you said, I've been a stranger to all this, but I want to help you, I think I can help you, and I hope you'll believe you can trust me."

Eleanor's mouth twisted. " 'Trust,' " she whispered. "Yes, I must trust someone, someone from outside." She lifted her head proudly. "I'll tell you whatever you want to know, Captain, and I'll appreciate whatever you choose to do for us here. But first, tell me what happened tonight."

Michael took a deep breath. "Very well, then. I took my supper at Hatheway's Tavern in town. There was a group of men playing cards. One of them, I'm sure you know him, was your uncle's friend, Maurice Matthews. A bit of unpleasantness arose, and Matthews began to talk very hotly about you and your uncle. He seems to know something that will endanger any chance you have of keeping your father's properties. He said your uncle's attorney has some sort of evidence or proof against you. It was all blurted out in the heat of anger and I think Matthews would have told the rest of it, but he was stopped before he could say another word."

" 'Stopped'? By you?"

"No, mistress. By then so much had already been said I would have been glad to hear the rest. But Matthews was cut short by a coxcomb buccaneer, name of Captain Keane. Keane sent Matthews and his friends scurrying out of the place quick enough . . . and then he had the damnable temerity to warn *me* to mind my own business!"

"But, William," she breathed. "You said this man was a friend of William's. How do you know? Who told you this?"

"Your cousin was in the place, mistress, hiding off in one of the private alcoves, listening to it all. When Keane left, he followed after him. William was careful to keep himself concealed the whole time, but just as he got to the door he took a long look at me and I saw him clearly. Not twenty minutes later someone took two shots at me as I was going back to my ship. Now that's all *I* know," he finished, folding his arms. "The rest is up to you."

Eleanor shrugged helplessly, shaking her head. "It's more than I ever knew," she assured him. "Captain Keane—who has not heard of that devil? And William! It's incredible to me, Captain Ives."

"What did your friend Ellen Fletcher say to you in the letter she gave me?" he demanded a bit loudly to startle her out of the confused torpor that had taken her over.

"Much the same as Maurice Matthews said," she replied slowly. "That my uncle had been writing to an attorney on Antigua, a man by the name of Richards. That Richards had been asking questions about me, even of Governor Able—about me . . . and about my mother. Ellen promised she would find out more if she could. You say I must fight my uncle," she turned bitter eyes upon him. "And I will fight, with all my strength, with all my heart . . . if only I knew what it was I'm to fight! My uncle feels that there is some way he can prove I am not my father's legitimate heir, that's obvious on the face of it. Yet I have had substantial support from attorneys in London that my father's will was in good order and my claims upon the property perfectly legal."

Michael tapped his cheek thoughtfully. "Tell me again what became of your indigo last year," he demanded abruptly.

"You know what happened to it," she replied. "Pirates sank the ship, sank her with her captain and crew still aboard. It was very strange," she mused. "You see, I had purposely arranged for the indigo to be carried on one of those old merchantmen that transport iron ore and lumber. Pirates don't usually bother with those ships:

their cargo is of little value in the ports where they do business and the ships themselves are too old and too slow to take as prizes."

"Wouldn't you say, then, that they seemed to know just what they were after?"

Eleanor looked at him very hard. "Why, yes, of course," she agreed. "When it happened I wondered why they'd gone after that old hulk. But what difference does it make now? Indigo is such an unusual cargo in these waters, it wouldn't have been difficult for word to get around about it...oh, my God!" She shuddered, staring at him, as the realization struck her. "William...and Captain Keane!"

"Aye, boon companions, I daresay," Michael nodded, a grim smile on his face. "William knew about the indigo, told Keane what he needed to know, and you lost the work and the income of a year's time."

"Yes, yes, I see it all now," she said dully, "and they are well aware that I am heavily in debt now. If anything were to happen to this cargo..." suddenly she began to tremble violently. "They know you've offered to take the indigo for me? You can't, now, you can't! I will not have you risking your ship, your life, helping me!"

"I'm taking the shipment," he told her forcefully. "You'll save months by selling it in Boston. Meanwhile, say nothing to anyone here. My ship is fast, we've outrun pirates before. The advantage is ours, because we know what to look for. You cannot lose heart now, I will not allow it!"

Despite the weary, defeated expression on her face, she looked at him with raised eyebrows, a touch of bright pink spotting her pale cheeks. Michael felt that he had gone too far.

"Forgive me, ma'am," he said quickly, "I do not mean to intrude or interfere with—"

"You misread me, Captain," Eleanor said, the sparkling green eyes very soft, very tender. "I am grateful for your consideration. And I am surprised. I have not been accustomed to such kindness. Our little world here at Belleterre is a very closed one, sir. We are surrounded by people who hate us and, as you see, conspire against us. When you came here a while ago, I was just sitting by this fire, wondering what would happen if my uncle succeeds...where I would go, what would become of my people?" She sighed deeply. "I am glad of your company this night," she added impulsively.

"As long as you like, ma'am," replied Michael very gently. She

420

cast him a grateful look and reseated herself upon the little stool, the full velvet skirt of her robe gathering about her feet in deep, leaf green folds. But Michael saw the tired, drawn lines about her mouth and eyes. He was about to speak, when she clasped her hands together in her lap and said, in a voice so low he could barely hear her,

"You have not said it, but I am sure you are aware of the insinuations made about me and . . . and some of the men I employ here at Belleterre. I know you are aware of them. William himself spoke of them when you were here to supper."

"Do you think it's that your uncle expects to use against you?" inquired Michael harshly. "I don't believe he could win a legal battle with such nonsense!"

Eleanor sighed. "Why not? If he could prove I had . . . I was intimate with a black man . . . or *men* . . . that's a criminal charge in Carolina, Captain. He could have me sent to prison."

Michael held his temper in check with great difficulty, a burning desire to go and find Sydney Campion and beat him to a pulp growing stronger by the minute.

"Even if you were in prison," he said calmly, "the properties would still legally belong to you. Your uncle might administer them in your absence, but not even a charge like that would give him title to this land. No, I think there's something else, something more. He's quite sure of himself, whatever his facts may be."

"I shall need my own attorneys," sighed Eleanor. "It's not only the land, it's the people, too. He doesn't *need* anything more. If I were in prison he would treat my people as slaves. Everything I've tried to accomplish here would be finished!"

"Attorneys take money," he said briskly. "And you shall have it. I'm going to give you a letter of credit, just tell me how much—"

"No!" she cried, eyes blazing. "I cannot accept it. Forgive me, you are very kind, too kind, but I will never take money from you, never!"

He shook his head over her and sighed. "All right, then. In the morning tell your men to bring the indigo to my ship. We'll sail on the evening tide and I'll be back here with all the money you'll need and myself to stand up for you against that bloody bastard uncle of yours. And you'll *not* say no to that!"

"You come, as you did once before, unexpected and most welcome," she replied quietly. "I can only thank you and bless you

421

for this." She smiled at him but Michael was quickly learning her beautiful face and its varied expressions and he knew at once that she was already anticipating the exhaustion of another defeat, wondering if the effort and the risk were really worth it.

They both fell quiet then. There seemed little more to be said. He would help her in every way she would allow, but it seemed he had no real comfort to offer her—nay, he had not even the right to comfort her!

"We were going to talk so long that night, do you remember?" she said at length. "I was going to ask you all about Ireland. I've never been there, you know, although it was my mother's home."

"I remember," he answered. "And I was going to tell you so many things about it, and about my home there and my people."

" 'Home,' " she repeated, an exquisite soft poignancy in her melodious voice. "Why did you leave it? Not for wanting to, was it?"

"No, not for wanting to," he replied. "Because it was lost to us."

"You cannot go back?"

"No. We cannot go back. None of us. The 'wild geese' they call us, isn't it? Like Ireland's heart's blood spilling over the wide world. I think sometimes it will go on flowing this way and that, here and there, until none of us will ever have a place to call 'home' again!"

He could not have said it to any other person in the world, not even Katherine, and even now, as he spoke, looking at the flames without really seeing them, she realized he had hardly been aware that he had said these things to her, that they had come out of him unbidden and quite naturally. The enormity of this did not escape her. It was as if some unseen, unspoken barrier between the two of them had crumbled and disappeared all in that one moment.

She leaned forward, her elbows on her knees, her chin resting in her hands, gazing into the ever-changing panorama of the golden fire.

"I don't know what to do, Captain," she said. "I've got to hold this land, that's all. It's the only thing I care about . . . or ever have cared about, since I knew it was to be mine someday. I hadn't even seen it, but I loved it anyway. My father is responsible for that. I was born on Antigua, but I never thought of it as my home. Father didn't, either. It's odd, too. You see, he hadn't cared much about it when he was younger, living here with my uncle and my grandfather. Father left Carolina without a backward glance, to follow my mother and marry her. He used to say it was because she was Irish that she taught him finally that the land is everything . . . and they both died so far away from what each of them called 'home'?''

She turned to him, her eyes glowing, her jaw set and firm. ''I cannot give it up! I cannot let them take it from us! It isn't just mine, you know. It belongs partly to everyone who lives here, who was born here and has worked here all their life. But I don't know what to do anymore! If only I were wiser, and stronger! If only . . .''

She buried her face in her hands, her shoulders shaking with emotion and she began to weep wildly, despairingly, rocking back and forth in anguish, back and forth on the little, low stool.

For a moment only he watched her frenzied sorrow and then he could bear it no longer. In one swift motion he was at her side. He pulled her gently to her feet and pressed her head against his chest, stroking her head and her quivering back with his strong, sure hands, whispering long-forgotten old words of tenderness with his lips touching her flushed, tear-stained cheeks. And she made no effort to pull away from him or to push him from her. Instead, she leaned against him for strength, sobbing incoherently.

''No, no, *mavourneen,* no, now, hush, girl, hush your weeping before you break my heart forever!'' he said, but he could not tell if she'd even heard him. Her arms, which had been hanging limply at her sides, crept up around his body and he felt the frantic pressure of her slim fingers kneading into his back as she cried. She had been strong so long, he thought, too long and all alone . . . his heart cried out to her. He stood there with his head thrown back a little and he held her hot face in his two hands, forcing her to look up at him and to listen to him.

'*Acushla,* be still! Be still, you'll make yourself sick with it! Eleanor, Eleanor, hold on to me! Do you think I'd let you go now? Do you think I'll *ever* let you go?''

Not thinking, not caring for anything save the lovely woman in his arms, Michael drew her small, grieving face to his and kissed her so gently, so very gently on the lips . . . afraid of the forces welling up within him, stronger every moment, afraid if he were to caress her according to his feelings he might crush her delicate, pink lips.

He kissed her again and then again and he placed her face against his own that she might feel a cooling relief, not realizing that his face was hotter than her own, that a fever of blood and spirit had seized him in its grasp and now he was as helpless to resist as she.

When she felt the heat of him against her, Eleanor trembled from head to foot. How had this happened, she wondered dimly, how? It is my fault, she told herself sadly. I must move away from him, I must take my arms away—oh, God, I am so ashamed of this!

She stirred in his arms, murmuring apologetic little sounds, unable to look him in the eye.

"No!" he cried harshly. "I will not let you go! Rest, Eleanor, rest here in my arms!"

She leaned back slackly, shaking her head. Her eyes were dry now, except for a few last gleaming teardrops on the long auburn lashes. And she looked so utterly sorrowful it wounded him to the very soul.

"I did not intend this," she breathed. "You are too kind, Captain, too kind."

"Michael," he said. "Michael. Stop pretending, for the love of God! It's too late for that now. I'm offering you much more than comfort, my dearest!"

She shook her head rapidly. "No, no, you musn't say that. Please let me go now. Please . . . Michael!"

But he would not release her. "I don't think so," he said.

Her eyes searched his face, seeking truth and reasons and someone to believe in. Then she exhaled, a searing sigh almost like a sob in its intensity. "What are we to do, then?" she asked him.

"I don't know," he told her honestly. "We've come far away from where we were. We've turned a bend in the road somewhere. I do not think we can go back. Do you?"

"No," she whispered, so close now he could feel her delicate warm breath stirring his lips.

"Tell me, Eleanor, what do you want me to do?" He would not seduce this woman. He cared too deeply to overwhelm her senses, to press the advantage he possessed knowing the strength of their combined desire. No, she would always have to decide for herself what she wanted and he would abide by her decision. He asked her to decide now, for his honor, for her own.

She looked at him, her gaze clear and sweet and steady.

"Come with me," she said. "Hold me close to you again. Hold me through this night. If you want me."

"If I want you!" he cried, thrilling at her words. "You are the only woman I've ever really wanted. I didn't think you existed. I used to dream of you, but I gave up that dream years ago. Yet, here you are. At last!''

"You dreamed of me?'' She smiled a little, but then she saw how serious he was, how grave and earnest were his words. His whole being was opened to her in that moment, his whole unguarded, wary, wandering being came home in the time it took him to tell her what she was to him and for her to hear it and understand that it was true.

"Come, then,'' she whispered, a strange tightness in her throat. She moved away from him through the leaping shadows cast by the firelight and, for an instant, he was almost frightened to see her disappear into the dark recesses of the large room. He called after her, following her quickly out into the hallway. Her slender hand slipped into his and she drew him behind her up the stairs.

At the top flickered the light of a single candle set in a sconce by the landing. When they reached it, she turned to him as though she would make sure he was real. She touched his lips with her fingertips, smoothing back the fair curls from his forehead and she laughed as he had never heard her laugh before. She laughed gladly, joyfully, with new hope in her eyes at the sight of him. Something tight, something painful and constrained in his chest seemed to burst asunder at the sound of her laughing voice and the look of gladness as she looked at *him*. He caught her to him again and knew he could not, must not, lose her, ever.

"You are not angry with me now, are you?'' Michael asked her, not really thinking what he was saying, conscious only that she was in his arms.

Eleanor looked up at him in surprise. " 'Angry'?'' she repeated. "But I have never been angry with you, my dear one!''

Michael stared at her, confused for a moment. "No, no, of course not!'' He smiled and kissed her. Why had he said such a thing? This woman loved him and he was at peace at last. There was a world of forgiveness in loving, forgiveness for a thousand forgotten things that might have been better done. Eleanor led him swiftly down the hall and into her room. They walked side by side and hand in hand; like two children they were, like children.

4 An Owl Across The Treetops

For hours Matty watched the stars turn slowly about in the black arch of the heavens, sitting wrapped in her shawl by a window that overlooked Eleanor's house. No one came out of that house. The light that moved in the front window died away and the small light upstairs was snuffed out. Matty smiled to herself and found that she was crying at the same time. They loved each other now. She had known it.

But, let him not ask too much of her, Matty prayed fervently, her eyes fixed upon the steady, sturdy moon above. Let him understand how she is, how she must be. Impatiently she turned away from her window. It was in the hands of God, she told herself. Be glad for the child. Be glad, too, for the Captain. He seemed a lonely man. Let them have joy of this night and each other. Tomorrow would, somehow, take care of itself.

And finally Matty slipped off her shawl and got into her bed. How empty it felt, tonight of all nights! Ah, well. She closed her eyes and thought of James Campion, whom she would always love. She thought, too, of her gallant French officer with love. So long ago, but she would never forget. A woman does not forget being loved, Matty thought, comfortably sleepy. As the years pass, everything else fades into unimportance except the remembrance of having been loved. Love him well, Eleanor, he is the first! He may well be the last, too, the only one . . . And Matty slept.

Outside, an owl swooped soundlessly across the treetops and Dogon watched the road and kept it well against the intruding world.

5 You Are The Dream

Burning brightly, the morning star hung alone above Belleterre in a sky as grey white as a pigeon's breast. There was no sound yet of the day, but night's creatures were already gone to their sleep.

Michael was awake, as was his custom, long before true dawn. He lay beside Eleanor in her soft, white canopied bed and gazed contentedly through the window at the sky and at the dark lean branches of the oak tree that the early wind swept brushing against the glass panes. His hand rested on her red bronze hair spread out about her on the pillow. He judged by the sky that it was nearly two hours until dawn. A lonely time in which to be awake, a time between real times, like the onset of the always solitary-seeming dusk.

But today he was not lonely! For the first time in his life he awakened into greyness and did not feel a part of it—a part of the torpor of the waiting earth longing to come alive with the first hot rays of the approaching sun, which would clear away uncertainty and define another day's business.

He looked down at the girl sleeping by his side. I won't leave her, he told himself. I've come home at last, he thought, I belong with her and in this place.

"Michael?" She spoke his name without opening her eyes and her hand searched around for him, closed on his bare shoulder. She smiled dreamily.

"I'm here," he whispered. "I'm here."

The green grey eyes, placid as the southern seas, slowly opened.

"'Tis nearly morning," she said.

"Is it, then?" he murmured reluctantly, wishing that the windows would fill up again with night's rich blackness and the safe, never-ending embrace of its love hours.

"You will be sailing soon."

"Not I!" he said it half in jest, but the undercurrents in his voice reached her consciousness quickly.

"Did you not tell me you would go today?"

"Oh, you want me to go away?" he smiled quickly and kissed her lips so that she would not notice that the morning-fear was strong within him.

"No, no, I never want you to leave me!" she cried. "But you will come back again."

"Are you so sure of me?" It was talk without meaning or substance, love talk such as he had spoken to a hundred women of a morning. He trembled now in his heart to think how easily, how glibly, it came to his lips again, when he did not want to be saying it to *her*.

"Should I not be sure?" Eleanor sounded troubled; the very sound of her voice struck him to the heart.

"Yes! Yes, yes, always!" He pulled her to him, curving his strong body protectively around hers, whispering the fervent words against her ear. "I'll be back very soon, I swear it, my dearest love, my only love!"

"How long?" She turned around, burying her face against his warm chest. He could feel that she was holding her breath against his answer; she was trying very hard to think of the things that were at stake and the reasons...spoken of during the night sometime...why he must go away, at once, the sooner the better, so he might be free to come back and help her. He thought very fast, as though his impatient thought might blow the ship's sails on their way more swiftly.

"A week to Boston . . . with fair winds. Ten days at most. It's the unloading and reprovisioning that takes the time."

"How long?" she repeated faintly.

"Six weeks, no longer. And then I'll take on all the uncles and cousins and lawyers and anybody else who offers you trouble!"

" 'Six weeks,' " she breathed, shivering a little. "It seems so long!"

Michael, to whom six weeks—or six months, for that matter—had always seemed as nothing weighed in the balance against the inexorable, slow, grinding out of the endless years, now found that six weeks seemed well-nigh intolerable a length of time to put between himself and Eleanor.

"It must be this way," he reminded himself as well as her. But would she be all right for six more weeks?

"Come with me," he said suddenly, burying his face in her thick, sweet-smelling hair, feeling the silk of it alive and vibrant on his skin. "Sail with me to Boston and meet my sister. Then we can come back and fight this thing through together."

"I'd like that," she said in such a way that he knew at once she would not go with him.

"I'll worry about you the whole time, here by yourself, not knowing what he's going to do next."

She silenced his words with a soft kiss on the lips. "No, now, don't worry. 'Tis really a very short time; we're making much of it but it's not so much after all. I can't leave here. I don't dare leave my people, Michael. The minute he knew I was gone I've no doubt in the world he'd send in men to take them away, put chains on them . . ."

"Now, how could he do that when they belong to you?"

"But they don't belong to me, you know that, Michael. I have no ownership papers for any of them. And my uncle simply sees them as valuable property waiting to be claimed. . . ."

"My God, like horses or dogs!" he exclaimed.

"Just so," she nodded. "You see why I cannot go."

He could see it but he did not want to. He left the warmth of the bed, wandering over to the windows to gaze out. He stood looking down at the far-stretching green and gold and the darker green of the meadows and trees that surrounded Belleterre and seemed to reach so far that they touched the bottom of the blue mountains in the distance. *Belle terre*, indeed. What a world is here, he thought. It reminded him of Ireland now as it emerged slowly in the morning mists. In some ways it was very different . . . the sky higher, more out of reach, the mountains taller. Nonetheless this was a fair, gentle land and he felt he could love it as he had loved no place since he was a boy. No wonder she would not let it go from her! No wonder she was willing to fight so hard to hold it! He understood her well and that was also something different for him.

"You know, it strikes me that William is right about one thing," he said suddenly as he looked about the land.

"Is he?" She could not keep the loathing from creeping into her voice.

"Just one, my love. If you were able somehow to diversify . . . if you did have some other crop, something you could market quickly the year round, something you could depend upon from year to year no matter what happened with the indigo, you would not be so dependent on just the one harvest. Tell me, do you grow any rice here? Or tobacco? They say Virginia Colony is growing rich on her tobacco."

She shook her head. "No, no rice yet. Nothing else but some vegetables, enough to feed ourselves."

Michael was thinking very hard. Surely there must be something. He backed away instinctively as he heard the sharp, windblown creak of a tree branch as it whipped against the window pane. And it came to him suddenly.

"Trees!" he said. "You've got trees all over the place! What kinds?"

She looked puzzled. "Many kinds. Cypress, tulip, hickory, gum, oak . . . most of the oak is just plain scrub, not much good for anything. Oh, and yellow pine, of course."

"Longleaf pine?" There was excitement in his voice, an eager smile on his face.

"Yes, that's what they call it here. Belleterre has more pine trees than anything else. They say my grandfather was not overly fond of them. He claimed he aged a year for every wild pine he cut and cleared for farmland. Michael, what are you getting at?"

"Don't you see? There's the answer. Yellow pine!" He said it almost reverently and she listened, still puzzled, somewhat amused.

"Eleanor, you've heard of naval stores, haven't you? Pitch, tar, turpentine . . . all of it gotten from pine trees, all desperately needed by shipyards up and down the coast of America. To say nothing of the *wood* itself, my love! The wood! We use only certain kinds of pine for constructing our masts and spars, resinous wood. We have to soak it down for months in a mast pond and then—oh, never mind all that! The point is, dear Eleanor, you've probably got a fortune in those woods and hills out there, yours just for the cutting!"

Eleanor looked incredulous, afraid to believe what he was telling her.

"We could cut the wood ourselves," she said, thinking rapidly.

"Surely someone could show us how to go about making the . . . the . . . what did you call them? Naval stores, that's it. Oh, Michael, Michael, do you really think it would work?" Her warm, jewel green eyes began to dance as her quick mind considered the possibilities.

"Of course it will work," he answered, watching with joy in his heart the happy look on her face, the disappearance of the weary, worried lines he had noticed before. "When I come back I'll contract with you for whatever you've got ready to ship out, and order more. Our company will buy everything you can sell us. And what we can't use ourselves, we'll put on the market and make a handsome profit for you and for us."

She looked grave. "But can you make an arrangement like that yourself?" she asked hesitantly. "You said your sister owns half of the shipyards. What will she say? And who owns the other half?"

Michael chuckled delightedly. "I do, my dear! And Rob Sturbridge, my sister's husband, would have been overjoyed, believe me, if he knew we'd found a way to build up the business without so much as looking back over our shoulders at Europe. When Rob was alive he spent much time and effort trying to locate enough of the right kinds of wood for us. Eleanor, I assure you, you'd be doing us a great favor."

She looked at him silently for a long time, until he became uneasy and wondered what was going on in her mind.

Then she said, "Is all of this really happening to me? I wonder, shall I wake up here in this room tomorrow and find that I have only dreamed it?"

"You've dreamed nothing, heart-of-my-own," he said softly. "*You* are the dream, have you forgotten?"

"No, I promise you, Michael, I'll never, never forget that."

He walked back and stood beside her, looking at her as the faint, delicate light filtered in across the room. Then he pushed aside the draped mosquito netting of Russian gauze and sat down on the edge of the bed. He picked up her hand to kiss it and his boy's heart pounded when he felt her long slender fingers curl tightly about his own, this first small innocent gesture of loving possessiveness striking him to the heart with the newfound power of love.

"What a morning to be discussing business!" he murmured with a remorseful little smile. "Forgive me." His mouth pressed hard upon her wrist and he could feel the tiny, steady throbbing of her pulse against his lips. "I would have had our night go on and forget this one dawn only. Surely Providence might have spared one sunrise among the millions since time began."

Eleanor, smiling at his earnestness, reached up and thrust both of her hands gently into the tangle of golden curls falling across his brow.

"I don't see the sun," she whispered. "I see only you. Maybe that is the reason we have just this bit of light, so we may remember the night, looking at each other." She hesitated just for a moment, for she was not yet used to the imperious demands love allows lovers, then the memories she herself had spoken of rose up within her mind and overwhelmed her body and she pulled him down to her with a sudden, surprising strength. And now it was she who first kissed him, no longer merely receptive to his parted lips but actively seeking him out, claiming her own possession of what they had made and shared together. Her kiss was like no other he had ever known; her mouth, active and trembling, evoked no feeling of self-satisfying lust he had known in other women who had used him as he had used them: not caring, not remembering.

Her kiss was as she was, honest and joyful, sensuous by instinct not experience, wanting to ask for more, much more, not quite sure how to ask. Michael's lean, darkly tanned body hovered over her creamy, flawless form. His hands framed her face on either side, his fingers pressing against her head and neck and he answered the unspoken question, the undeclared appeal for all, all there was, all there could be between them. He gathered her to him feeling her arms clinging about his shoulders. Then, at last, he understood the old words "and the two shall become one flesh." But it was so much more than one flesh, for flesh was much too soon parted again. No, it was union, a blending, an exchanging of souls one for the other. And that would not end. The exquisite realization of it at that one brief moment might end, but the memory of it, never.

Eleanor's once imprisoned passion, now let free and loose to seek its match in him, quite overcame her senses. She knew that she was crying out, wild, incoherent words, sounds, sobs, and still she was not able to express the searing flamelike delight her entire being was experiencing. She clutched him all the more, a remote part of her consciousness dimly aware that her fingernails were raking the warm skin of his back and shoulders and arms, but she could not stop herself . . . and there was a sudden profound silence in the whirling new universe upon which they had entered . . . it was like listening for a sound one knows will be there, listening together at the last few rapturous seconds of the struggle, hoarse and breathless, silent and waiting, listening, listening . . . and the universe roared out its cry of life dominant again and joy rediscovered from primeval times . . . and for one infinitesimal particle of eternity, the fusion of two beings *happens . . . and at once becomes a memory.*

6 Hostages To Fortune

Now, in the morning, their first morning in each other's arms, Eleanor opened her eyes and gazed down at the two strong masculine hands that gently clasped her. Not for the first time she noticed the old, silver-colored ring upon his finger. Curiously she looked closer and her forefinger carefully traced out the plain carved letters and the numbers on the side of the ring. "Ives," she thought at once, just as Matty had done. His father's ring, or perhaps an older brother. And, just as Matty had noticed, she noticed the coincidence of the initials and the French word they spelled.

"Tell me about your father," she said, still touching the ring. "It was his, was it not?"

"Yes," Michael said, pulling his hand away as though it had suddenly been burned. She said nothing, but turned around in his arms and looked at him with the silent, hurting eyes of the beloved one inexplicably shut out.

Michael cursed himself for a fool. Taking her small hand, he placed it back on top of his own, winding her fingers once more around the ring. And he told her the story of the ring as he had been told the story long ago. She listened in rapt silence, often kissing his fingers as he spoke and he saw that she was crying.

"You meant it for the boy," she said when he had fallen silent at last. "Your sister's boy. But it belongs to you."

"I never wanted it," Michael replied. "I never thought I—no matter," he amended abruptly. He turned his face away against the pillow, not realizing that she felt him slipping from her, that she sensed he was very far away, in just those few seconds. Here, somehow, in some way connected with this ring, Eleanor knew, lay the essential sorrow in him and the enigma of his being. She lay very still and watched his face in profile, and wondered what he was thinking.

He was thinking that he had, indeed, been saving the ring to give it back to Katherine for young Elliot. But now, ah, now, might there not be another child someday, a child of his own, to whom this ring of his father's would rightfully belong? And how strange, he reflected, glancing out through the rapidly lighting windows, how strange that he had told himself last night he had come home at last. "Here . . . in this place" . . . that was the very essence of the ring. *Here,* in this most lovely place, Belleterre, this would be where he would find his happiness and contentment, those dreams that had eluded him for so long. Here, if need be, he might make his own fight, as Rob and Sir Tom and his own father, Ian, had made their fight for the things and people that meant everything to them.

But, the old wretched thought nagged at him, what had *he* ever done in all of his forty-four wasted years, that entitled him to claim this ring . . . or the beautiful woman at his side?

He had been silent too long. Eleanor stirred uneasily in his arms. "Will you give it to Katherine's child?" she asked him again.

"What do you think I should do?" he asked.

"Could you not . . . could you not keep it awhile?" She faltered with the words. He kissed her again, his eyes fixed on the old ring.

Yes, for a while. He would keep it for a while and for once in his life, he would see something through to the end. Then it would be time to think about the ring again.

"Yes," was all he said and she did not ask him any more. After another moment or so, Eleanor sighed.

"I'd best write my letter to Ellen, my love, so you can take it with you when you go. But, Michael, are you sure? Antigua is a long long way off, through dangerous waters."

"The danger lies between here and Boston. Once the indigo is

433

safely sold, Antigua is but a quick fortnight's journey. Have faith, Eleanor. I do not tell you to hope. Hope is such a hopeless sort of word. Have faith in me, my dearest one, as God is my witness I shall not fail you!''

He kissed her full on the mouth and held her to him for an instant. Then, because the moment was too poignant and too painful, he pulled away and, kissing her lightly on the tip of the nose, he jumped from the bed.

"The sooner gone, the sooner back again!" he smiled and began dressing quickly. Eleanor lay back against the pillows, watching him with languorous wonder in her eyes. "My love, if you continue to look at me that way I won't be able to leave it all!" She smiled and yawned, stretching deliciously and watched him still. "Go along with you, girl!" he teased. "Have you never seen a man get himself dressed before?''

She shook her head. "Not . . . not . . . er . . . from the beginning,'' she laughed, blushing slightly. He picked up a little boudoir pillow and tossed it at her. Still laughing, she ducked and slipped out of the far side of the bed.

"I'll make some breakfast. I haven't any coffee but there's chickory if you like," she said, donning the green velvet robe again.

"Tea's fine. I've never acquired the habit of drinking coffee on an empty stomach," he answered, and he heard her call back something from the hallway on her way downstairs.

And now that she was gone from the room, he dropped his easy, bantering pose very quickly. They would both try hard to make this parting as painless as possible. They would joke and act very matter-of-factly and talk about sending the indigo into town. And that was just as well. He felt as though he would be tearing himself literally in half when he should leave her, but his feelings were so much more complex than even those of a lover. He was leaving her virtually alone and completely unprotected, in the midst of some vile unknown conspiracy that threatened her every moment. Yet, leave he must, and quickly, not merely because of the indigo or the money. The key to it all was to be found on Antigua and thither he must go and come back to her with all speed, so together they could fight this evil thing that Sydney Campion and his son were doing.

Surely in six weeks Sydney would not have managed to spring his trap, not in a short six weeks. Sydney was just as dependent upon fair winds and swift currents as he was himself, and whatever more was needed for Sydney's plan to work would be coming from Antigua. Michael realized he was rationalizing, hoping, basing his hopes and calculations on nothing. Sydney might strike today, or tomorrow . . .

Michael, finished dressing now, took another moment to look out the window again, across the fields and trees of Belleterre. I'll be back, he vowed, I'll be back soon! Yes, he saw it so clearly now, he must make a stand at last. Somewhere, sometime in his life, every man must draw the line and, finally and for all time, say "no more." He glanced a bit curiously at the steel ring again and his heart lifted. Whistling an old tune he'd not thought of since boyhood, he went downstairs to find Eleanor.

They sat at the table in the kitchen and drank their tea together. By noon, no later, her wagons would be dockside in Charles Town and the loading of the indigo would begin. The *Sheila Deare* would set sail on the evening tide and be halfway to Boston before Keane would have a chance to move. Yes, yes, he promised her half a dozen times, once that precious cargo was safe in his hold, he would fly before the wind all the way to Boston. Nothing was going to happen to this shipment from Belleterre!

"I am foolish," she said softly, covering his hand with hers. "I'm wishing you did not need to go today, and yet all the wonderful things we have spoken about cannot begin coming true until you do go!"

Michael smiled. "I think, until today, I have always been going somewhere, leaving one place to get to another place, not feeling it made much difference if I stayed, if I went."

"Will you always follow the sea, do you think?" she wanted to know, fully expecting that he would say yes, of course.

But he shook his head. "No. Not now. I am not like my sister, who loves the sea. I do not love it. It's only that for a long time I've needed to keep moving, to keep going *on* . . ." he laughed self-consciously. "The sea is the only place I've ever known where a man can keep moving, always moving."

"You have not been happy, I think," she said, a tiny catch in her voice.

He turned his hand over, catching her fingers, folding them tenderly inside of his as he pulled her to him and kissed her.

"I am happy now. It's enough," he said.

A bit later she gave him the letter for Ellen. He was tucking it into an inside pocket in his coat when there was a light, tentative rap at the kitchen door. Eleanor opened it without hesitation, which bothered Michael until he saw it was Dogon standing there, smiling. In his hands he held Michael's two Spanish pistols.

"Saw the smoke from the chimney, Mistress Eleanor. I guessed you was most likely stirrin' around. Here are those fine pistols of yours, sir. I didn't leave them lyin' in the dampness all night, don't you worry about that. They're just fine, sir."

Michael was suddenly, acutely, aware of the emptiness of the big house all around him, the size and dimensions of the vast property upon which Eleanor lived alone save for the watchful protection of this black man and others like him.

"Dogon," he said, "do you know how to use these arms?"

Dogon glanced at Eleanor, his face guarded. And she smiled.

"Well, now you come to ask, seems like I did learn a thing or two about guns somewheres," Dogon admitted reluctantly. He stared at Michael. "What you fixin' to do, sir?"

Michael removed the copper powder flask and the leather pouch with the lead shot from across his shoulder, and handed them to the astonished black man.

"Take good care of her, Dogon," he said soberly.

"You can't give *us* guns, sir!" cried Dogon, his expression plainly indicating an agony of indecision between delight in having the beautifully worked silver and rosewood weapons and fear for what would happen to him, to any black man in Carolina, should he be found with arms in his possession.

"Who need know, Dogon, besides Mistress Eleanor and myself? If you need to use them it won't make any difference then, anyway. Keep the pistols out of sight, especially don't let her uncle and her cousins know about them—*both* cousins," he added emphatically.

Dogon drew himself up very tall, a look of contempt and loathing on his dark face. "Never fear, sir. And, thank you. They'll be here waitin' for you when you come back." Then he fell silent, looking at Eleanor again, this time with some embarrassment. "*If* you'll be comin' back, naturally, sir," he murmured uncertainly.

Michael clapped him heartily on the shoulder. "I'll be back, Dogon. In a few weeks. But the pistols are yours to keep now."

"Dogon, will you tell someone at the stables to saddle a horse for Captain Ives? He's got to get back to Charles Town at once. Then see that the wagons are brought out and the mules hitched up. We're sending that indigo out today!''

"Yes, ma'am, I'll do that!" Dogon beamed. "And I'll fetch the Captain a horse myself." He headed out the door and down the path toward the stables.

"I will come and see you ride off," said Eleanor. Together she and Michael walked from the house. The sky was just beginning to turn faintly pink and a few birds flew about the silver birch trees along the pathway. Eleanor clung to his arm and he wanted to feel the touch of her there against him forever. He knew that he could not go away now, not unless he said the final thing that was in his heart, the most important thing of all. He felt so many, many words rushing and tumbling about in his mind. He was half afraid he would somehow say it all wrong.

"How quiet you are!" she remarked. They had reached the small garden across from the arched stone entryway to the coach house and stopped to wait for Dogon to bring out the horse. She sat down beneath a tree and he saw that her feet were bare and glistening from the dew on the grass. He must speak now, quickly, he told himself. Find the right words, man, it has been done millions of times before!

He turned his back and idly began plucking flowers in clusters from the garden shrubbery, his heart pounding crazily.

"My mother had a garden," he said. "She loved flowers. Field flowers, wild flowers, things nobody else paid any heed. They told me she used to raise roses, too. I don't remember that. But I do remember watching her tend the little ones she'd bring in from the fields and plant in her garden. This garden is a little like hers . . .''

He stopped talking, unaware for the moment that this was the first time he had spoken of Sheila Ives since the day she had died.

He turned back to Eleanor, his arms full of yellow Carolina jessamine blooms and purple chickory and wild fire pinks. She sat looking up at him with the dawning sun behind her adding golden flames to the living fire of her hair. To his mind she was the most perfect woman he had ever known, but one.

He held out his arms and the flowers dropped into her lap all in a heap of bright colours and scents.

"I love you, Eleanor. You know that, do you not?" he asked.

"I am happy that you do," she replied softly, gathering the blossoms tenderly to her bosom. "I have never said this to any

437

man . . . I never expect to say it again except to you: I love you with all my heart, Michael Ives!''

His throat constricted. It was done now, as good as any oath between them.

"Aye," he said proudly. "And when I come back, we'll marry, my love!"

Her reaction astounded him. The bright emerald glow in her eyes dimmed. Her face turned ashen, then flushed painfully red.

"Nay, Michael, do not speak of marrying, I pray you!" she cried.

He attempted a shaky smile. "I'd *best* be speaking of it, after last night!" He leaned down, fingering the open collar of her robe, trying to make light of the words he did not understand.

Eleanor jumped to her feet, the flowers forgotten and fallen around her. "Don't jest about it!" she exclaimed heatedly.

" 'Jest'?'' He stared at her in consternation. "I meant no jest, I assure you!" And suddenly he was very angry with her, suddenly he began to feel apprehensive. "I am asking you to be my *wife*. I have told you I love you. Why are you behaving like this? Why, for God's sake?"

Even as he spoke, the apprehension spread and grew inside of him. He watched her sweet face become set and determined, her mouth tighten firmly. It seemed to him that her eyes, so recently softly aglow with love, were now the eyes of a stranger.

"And I love you, Michael," she said. "I shall always love you. Time can be the only proof of that, of course, but I know it to be true. I love you and no other. I will be your mistress; I will sleep with you . . . but I will not marry you. I will not marry anyone. It cannot be, don't ask it!"

He was stunned, incredulous. "Why?" he demanded harshly. "Tell me *why*, damn it!"

"Please!" She spoke hastily, sharply, regretting it at once. "Michael, it's so difficult to explain. Can you not simply take me as I am and forget the rest?"

"I see," he countered furiously. "Of course! You love me but not enough to marry me. I suppose it would be a bit of a comedown, you, the daughter of a governor of Antigua and I—"

"You cannot think that! You cannot!" she gasped.

"What am I to think, then? My God, Eleanor, what kind of a woman are you?"

Her lips moved but no sound came out. Then at last, stiffly, she answered him, "I don't have to explain anything to you. Or to anyone. I am what I am."

"And what is that?" His words flailed her like a lash, but she looked at him without flinching. "You mean this, don't you? You really mean it!" He remembered her warm in his arms but a few hours ago, trusting him, loving him. There had been no mistake about that, she had given herself to him with a whole heart. But now . . .

"You said you loved me. You *do* love me! I believe that. Eleanor, you belong to me now!"

"NO!" She almost screamed the word, flinging her hands violently upward as if she would thrust away his very words. "No, I do not belong to you! Much as I love you . . . and God, at least, knows I *do* love you! But I belong to no one. *No one.* I . . . I belong to myself. Only myself." She paused, then added piteously, "I told you it would be difficult to explain. I should not have tried."

"You should not have *tried?* You haven't explained anything! All that you make clear in this is that you're trying to be something you're not. You don't belong to anyone, you'll not marry——" his voice parodied her tone mercilessly. "Nonsense! Those are all the things men say as we go rattling through life, before we meet the right woman, before we know where we belong, to whom we belong!"

"I know where I belong, Michael. Here, at Belleterre, doing exactly what I am doing."

His head jerked up proudly. "Did you think I would ask you to give it up?"

"No, no! Oh, I don't know! I haven't thought ahead like that!" she cried, her eyes pleading for an understanding and acceptance he could not give. "I thought you, of all people, understood how I felt about this land of mine. Last night——"

"You're not making any sense, girl!" he snapped. "Love of the land is understood by us both. But you cannot marry the land, and what becomes of it after you're gone if you've not raised up sons . . . and daughters . . . to care for it the same way?"

She shook her head desperately. "I only know I must be free if I'm to do it the way I've dreamed it! Oh, if only you could see! Sometimes I'm so full of hope, I know it will work out. Other times it seems impossible. But, it is not impossible. It . . . it's like the *indigo*, Michael!"

" 'Like the indigo'?" he shook his head.

"Yes, yes, just like!" she cried. "Indigo is hard to grow. It's strange, wild, unpredictable . . . except when it's cared for just right. I've proved that now. I've proved that indigo can be grown here, after they all laughed their heads off and swore it would never work. But it *does* work!

"And it's grown by free people, not slaves. That's the real dream, Michael. To prove what can be done by free men and women working together. They laugh at that, too. You know it. They laugh . . . and they hate it, they hate me. And they're trying to destroy it all. Well, I won't *let* them destroy it. I'll prove them wrong about that, too. Some of them even think I'm crazy. But, I spent almost all of my life seeing how it is when some are slaves and some are free. How very little difference there was between them and me, and yet their lives were *hell!* And the whole place, the whole island, everywhere I found slaves and masters . . . there was something so . . . so *deadly* there, so lacking in energy and spirit. . . ."

She shuddered convulsively and was silent, not having the words to convey completely either the vision that drove her or the memories that sustained that vision.

"What has this to do with marrying me or not marrying me?" he asked coldly.

She sighed. "It's very simple. I dare not put myself in a position where, because of a marriage contract, I would no longer really own or control my own property. You know the law. The moment I marry, my husband would assume title and authority. And even if my husband were to die, it would never be mine again. It would pass on to my oldest son or even to my husband's family . . . or his creditors. Forgive me, my love, but I cannot ask anyone else to take on the burden of what I am trying to do. And I cannot let this dream pass unnoticed, unheeded, into the hands of unborn generations!"

"It's as I thought, then. It's me you don't trust, isn't that it?" His voice was steel hard, hiding the hurt.

"Oh, Michael, Michael, my darling, it isn't that I don't trust you! I don't trust *myself*. You think I talk like a man, that I'm trying to be something I'm not, you said—but you're wrong! It is the woman in me that will not abandon one purpose for another. I've not time for myself yet. I've not time for turning inward to a husband and children, for giving all that's best of me to them. And that is the way it should be and must be when a woman marries. But I cannot give hostages to fortune, not yet. Perhaps not ever. I must be free until this thing is done and secured against the future!''

"It will take longer than your lifetime, Eleanor," he told her. "Believe me, I have seen such dreams before and I have seen how they destroy people's lives. Can you not allow yourself a little happiness?''

"Yes. A little.'' She tried to smile. "That's what I'm saying.''

Dogon appeared, leading a saddled horse behind him. Eleanor and Michael looked at him blankly. Then Michael thanked him and swung himself up into the saddle.

"You underestimate me, Eleanor," he said, gathering the reins into his hands. "But I'll come back as I said I would. And one day, perhaps when you know me better, you'll change your mind. Believe this: there is no way on God's earth I shall ever give you up.''

She touched the horse's face gently, then looked up at Michael with fresh tears in her eyes.

"Yes, do come back to me, Michael. But, *you* must believe *this:* I shall not change my mind. If you cannot live with that knowledge, my darling, then I beg you, find someone else and love her well. I will understand.''

"There *is* no one else," he said simply. He nudged the horse with his foot. "I will expect the wagons by noon." The animal turned obediently into the dirt road and sped off at full gallop.

Eleanor and Dogon watched him go toward the sun rising lazily in the eastern sky. They watched him out of sight and still stood there until they could no longer hear the horse's hoofbeats. And then she turned to go back into the house. As she did so, her eye fell on the flowers, all the brilliant golds and pinks, rose and purple and green, now trampled and scattered about in the grass. She reached out a hand to pick up one of the crushed jessamines, but resolutely passed it by. Squaring her shoulders, she continued walking, then broke into a run, a terrible cry of pain tearing itself from her throat.

Dogon looked after her with pity on his face. Then he gathered up all the discarded blooms and meticulously took them off to put with the trash.

That one was a good man, Dogon thought, not like the others around this place. Matty says he is the man for Mistress Eleanor.

Women are strange, he said to himself. There surely was no figurin'
women. And he went off to rouse the other men and begin loading
the indigo into the wagons.

Four

"Where God's Breath Blows"

1 Bound For Boston

Five big wagons came rumbling into Charles Town from Belleterre
at precisely noon that day. The lead wagon was driven by Dogon
himself. The indigo, wrapped in little squares of muslin, was packed
into crates and barrels left deliberately unmarked. Later, when the y
were well out at sea, Michael would mark them himself and only he
would know which they were.

Michael paced the decks anxiously as the loading went on,
watching the busy crowds moving around the wharfs and warehouses. He saw no one who seemed to be particularly interested in
activity aboard the *Sheila Deare*, yet it could hardly have escaped
anyone in Charles Town that it was the blacks from Belleterre who
were working there. And what else would they possibly be transferring
to the ship but Eleanor Campion's new indigo?

The muscular blacks moved quickly, nervous and jumpy here in
town. They were the butt of many caustic remarks and the laughter
and crude obscenities of town slaves and loafers idling the day away
along the riverfront. Michael kept his own men moving closely
among them, alert for any possible trouble that might arise. He was
as anxious to have them gone as they were to be finished and safely
home again.

Eleanor had not come with them, of course. He hadn't thought
she would. He had just hoped, and yet perhaps it was as well after
all. He was still angry and hurt from the morning. If they met so
soon again perhaps they would only pick up their quarrel where it
had left off. When he saw that Mister Rainey and the rest of his crew
had the loading well in hand, he went below and busied himself for
over an hour.

He came back up on deck carrying an enormous paper-wrapped parcel and sent Bailey down to fetch up several other similar parcels. These were placed on Dogon's wagon and an old, battered piece of canvas was thrown over them to keep them out of sight. He told Dogon the parcels contained a few odds and ends of things that would please a lady and enjoyed the absolute pleasure in the man's face at the thought of something special being done for Eleanor.

Late in the afternoon, the wagons were ready to leave for the fourteen-mile journey back upriver. Dogon came to bid Michael good-bye.

"Matty says I must tell you, Hurry yourself and come back soon," Dogon said as they shook hands atop the gangway. "Matty says you do not understand Mistress Eleanor so well yet. She cried very much after you went away," he added gravely.

"Did she?" muttered Michael. "Matty's right, I don't understand. All I did was ask her to marry me. That usually makes women happy, doesn't it?"

Dogon smiled expansively. "*I* don't know, sir. I have never asked such a question of any woman. I am a happy man as I am now. No questions, no tears. But Mistress Eleanor is not so much like other women. She is like the father. Her head moves in one straight direction at a time and does not turn aside. Matty says you must give her time to think. Matty says the Mistress loves you and you must not worry . . ."

"Hm," said Michael wryly. "Matty says a good deal, doesn't she?"

Dogon nodded, laughing. And then the wagons were driven away. Preparations began at once to take advantage of the high tide and a whipping strong northward wind that had sprung up. The big ship creaked and rocked, tugging against the mooring lines that kept her prisoner of the land.

"Hoist the bower anchors port and starboard!" shouted Michael. "Topmen aloft, loose the topgallants. Larboard watch below, starboard watch on deck, look lively there!"

He watched with satisfaction the swift movements of the barefoot crew as they raced silently to their tasks. In a few moments the yards were alive with nimble seamen working high in the rigging, untying the buntlines to lower the big sails one by one. Immediately the lithe bark felt the boom of the wind filling her canvas and she seemed to leap gladly from the murky, brackish harbor waters almost as if she could sense the fair, fresh sea running just outside the curve of the bay. The topmen yelled lustily, grappling with the whipping shrouds, pulling them taut and straight about the lanyards to the crosstree deadeyes.

Mister Rainey came to stand with Michael as they watched the muck-covered anchors slowly being hauled in and the anchor rings secured to the catheads with heavy chains, then raised to the channels and made fast as the fish tackle, secured aloft to the fore-topsail yard, was neatly hooked to the arm of each anchor.

" 'Tis a fair day to be going home, Captain Ives," remarked Mister Rainey, a beaming smile on his spare New England features.

Michael had been about to order the gangway secured, but he glanced sidewise at the mate, a look that Mister Rainey felt boded ill for someone.

"Something troubling you, sir?" mumbled Rainey uneasily.

"Some letters were delivered for me, were they not?" asked Michael mildly enough. But Michael's milder moments were sometimes deceptive. "Brought aboard by a black man from a place called Belleterre?"

"Aye, sir, that's right, That's right! I remember now." Mister Rainey looked aghast. "He said they were from a lady. He acted damned strange about the whole business, made me swear an oath I'd give the letters to no one but yourself. And then Dick Looney came running up and wanted me to go below and see was that peach brandy leaking from some of those kegs—so I put the letters right on your table where you'd be sure to find them. And so you did—did you not?"

"I did not, Mister Rainey," said Michael still more quietly. "But someone else did. It was only by accident that I discovered there were any letters."

"I—I trust no one's been inconvenienced through my fault, sir," said Mister Rainey, much abashed. Michael turned a steely blue eye upon him.

"Mister Rainey, once we've cleared port, muster the gun crews and have them begin close-order firing drill twice a day."

"*Guns*, sir? Guns?" choked Mister Rainey in amazement. "You think we shall have need of guns?"

"Yes, *guns*, Mister Rainey. You're repeating yourself," snapped Michael. "There's liable to be a bit of trouble before we see Boston. I want those two old six-pounders we inherited from Captain Jim

444

cleaned and hauled up to the forecastle deck and lashed to a train tackle. We're carrying a dozen swivel guns, are we not? I want them mounted along the bulwarks on the quarterdeck. And get as many wall pieces as you can find secured about the poop deck. When that's done, start those waisters of yours filling grenades with black powder and fuses. Wait, best get three or four of the swivel guns secured on the tops, too. Then lay on some canvas and netting around the tops, just in case."

Mister Rainey gulped audibly. "In case of what, Captain?"

"Attack," replied Michael shortly. "Best to rig boarding nettings around the rails while we're at it. See to it, Mister Rainey. And I want buckets of water beside every gun, and lanterns hung from the yards. Then you get those anchor-men drilling. And until we sail into Boston Bay, all watches stand four on and four off, do you understand?"

"N-no, sir!" sputtered Rainey. "Are we at war again? Are the French?..."

"Pirates, Mister Rainey," said Michael.

"Pirates. I see. But we've never gone to such—"

"Ship the gangway!" shouted Michael, leaping up upon the foremast shrouds. "Cast off!" He glanced back down at his be-mused first mate. "We've never carried Belleterre cargo before, Mister Rainey. Indigo. And it's known. *Now* d'you see, Mister Rainey?"

Rainey only nodded, a trifle pale about the lips, a trifle pinched at the nostrils. And he hurried off.

With eager haste the seamen hauled the broad wooden planks of the gangway aboard and in another few moments the *Sheila Deare*, with every foot of canvas unfurled, headed out into the open Atlantic, moving grandly through the narrow channels of Charles Town's outer islands and then northward, at last. The men sang as they worked, knowing that they were going home. Only Michael gazed back and knew that every gust of wind was taking him farther and farther away from home.

2 I Was Right . . . Wasn't I, Matty?

Some hours after Michael sailed, Eleanor was sitting on the parlor floor next to the hearth, with Matty nearby on the sofa. All around the room were heaped the presents Michael had sent back in the wagon with Dogon. Colorful wrapping paper and boxes, fine tissue paper, ribbons in every bright hue lent a holiday air to the somber room.

Eleanor was holding a heavy pile of ivy green-striped shalloon, twelve yards of it. Beside her, spilling across the floor like a wayward dawn cloud lay soft folds of palest pink damask picked out with gold and silver threads. Near that was placed a thick roll of Scottish weave green-and-blue plaid wool for winter wear. Nor was that all by any means.

Matty was busy examining and exclaiming over some exquisite maroon velvet while she still held the silver gray silk and the cerise satin spread across her knees. There was not a spare inch of space on the sofa, covered as it was with lengths of white sheer lawn and narrow-banded laces interwoven with ribbons of blue and pink, yellow and light green, and enough hand-fluted linen to make up a dozen new nightrobes and petticoats. And Michael had recklessly plundered the orders sent back to the ladies of Boston to include gloves and gauze neck scarves and shoes. So many pretty new shoes and sturdy, soft leather riding boots, evening slippers with red-lacquered heels and cunning silver buckles and little house shoes in half a dozen rainbow hues!

". . . and it's not only the material," Matty was saying, "but did you see that box with the coffee? Ten pounds of real coffee! And pins! And those fine embroidery needles we haven't been able to buy. He sent China tea and lemons, too—lemons, imagine it! And I haven't yet counted how many different kinds of wine. What a good, kind man your Captain is, Eleanor, truly!"

Eleanor, looking somewhat stunned, merely nodded.

"But, girl," prodded Matty, "haven't you opened that very big box with the blue bow on it? Do open it now, please. Oh, this reminds me of long ago when you were just a little girl and your father would go shopping in St. John's and then come home with beautiful surprises for us both! Do you remember, child?"

Eleanor sighed heavily. "I remember, Matty," she said. "I've already opened the big box."

Matty's smile faded. She cast Eleanor a puzzled glance. "What's makin' you so sorrowful, girl?"

Wordlessly Eleanor pulled the largest of the boxes to her and removed the top, tilting it upward so Matty could see inside.

"Ah!" The black woman uttered a long appreciative cry. "White satin! Looks to be miles of it! And just see all that lace . . . why, it's six inches deep!'' She fingered the lace lovingly with hands that had known the touch of the finest cloth in the world and the most precious jewels.

"Look under the satin, Matty. Something in there for you, too," said Eleanor.

Chuckling in surprise, Matty lifted the heavy slipper satin and found yet another length of it, this in rich yellow with yellow ribbons and lace to match.

"For me!" Matty tried to remember how long it had been since such satin had been part of her wardrobe. Many, many years, not since James Campion's death. "But the man's already packed in dress linens and broadcloth and that pretty calamanco stuff all for me. Why this gorgeous satin, too? Does your Captain Ives think we shall be going to balls and parties?"

The ghost of a smile flitted across Eleanor's lips at the sight of Matty's work-worn hands patting the lovely dress goods. But then she handed Matty a small card that had been affixed to the inside of the box cover. "Read that," she said with some effort, "and you'll see what's in his mind."

Matty took the card from her and read aloud the message Michael had scrawled on it:

> " 'This is for your wedding dress, my dearest Eleanor. If you and Matty begin on it right away, you will have it finished long before I am back. Then must you both make up the yellow for Matty's gown, for she shall be your bridal attendant. Until October, then, all my love, Michael.' "

But even before she had heard the last words, Eleanor was weeping. She picked up the first cool folds of the snowy satin and crushed them against her breast, her head bent over them. Tears ran down her cheeks, spilling onto the rich cloth.

Matty gently took the box and the cloth from her and put them away out of sight. Eleanor had told her everything except that Michael had asked her to marry him and she had refused him. Now, sobbing, Eleanor told her the rest of the story.

"You see I cannot marry now, don't you, Matty?" she cried. "I could not lie to him! I could not ask him to wait, keep him coming back to me with false promises and false hopes I cannot fulfill! I was right, I know I was right! Wasn't I, Matty? Wasn't I?"

Matty did not reply but sat quietly stroking Eleanor's hair. Come

447

back soon, Captain Ives, Matty prayed very hard. Please come back to her . . . for she is wrong. The strength of the girl is all in her spirit; if she lets you go she will not be breaking her heart, 'tis that great spirit of hers that will be broken. And she cannot see that now, there's the danger. Come back quickly, Captain Michael Ives!

3   A Stowaway

If it had been the usual kind of voyage, Mister Rainey might not have found Fancy until they were all the way to Boston. As it was, with every spare hand racing smartly around, carrying out Michael's stern orders, not above two hours had passed—and the *Sheila Deare* making wonderful time with a wide wake like whipped cream lashing out behind her—when a great deal of screaming and screeching was heard from bow to stern and in between.

Michael, his hands and arms covered with black grease, his shirt sleeves rolled up, was on his knees swearing grievous Irish oaths as he attempted for the fourth or fifth time to manipulate one of the old six-pounders on to a jury-rigged train track while three of his crew stood by holding the heavy cannon by rope braces to keep it from being flung straight across the deck and out crashing through a hole in the opposite railing. Then a woman's angry voice reached their ears. Michael groaned and jumped to his feet.

"What in God's name is that?" he barely had time to bellow, when one of the youngest men aboard made a dramatic appearance on deck.

The fourteen-year-old seaman looked dazed and terrified. His neat white shirt was torn half off his skinny body and he partly jumped, partly dragged his feet as he pulled a wild-eyed, scratching, raging Fancy Campion behind him. Fancy kept kicking out at the boy's bony legs with vicious little digs of her hard leather riding boots and, of the two of them, the boy was by far the more shaken.

"Let me go, you snake!" cried Fancy wrathfully, aiming still another kick his way. Fortunately Dick Lonney came rushing to his shipmate's assistance. Though only a year older than the boy, Dick outweighed him by thirty pounds and stood a head taller. Between the two of them they managed to drag Fancy before Michael and a fascinated ship's crew.

"Miss Campion, can it be you?" drawled Michael, standing with his greasy hands on his hips, looking at the girl in disgust.

Fancy snarled and struggled to pull her arms free. The two young

448

men looked beseechingly at Michael, who nodded, and they let her go gladly.

"What kind of ship you runnin' here, Captain Ives?" she demanded, tossing her waist-length, tumbled blond curls. Despite her struggles she looked quite fetching in an amber velvet riding gown cut daringly low across the breast, a matching amber ribbon pinned with a small black and gold enamel-work brooch about her slender throat. "Captain Ives, are you aware that I was retired for the evenin' and sound asleep when that . . . that ruffian barged in and laid his hands on me?" She glared at the poor boy and the other men snickered.

Michael folded his arms with a sigh and stared at her hard. "You had retired, Miss Campion? May I ask just *where* you had retired aboard my ship?"

"Oh, down in the . . . the . . . well, *I* don't know all the silly names you call things," she sputtered. "It was sure small enough, though!"

"Well, Washburn?" Michael turned to the disheveled young sailor.

"I came on her down in the cockpit, sir," answered young Washburn, unconsciously moving away from Fancy. "Mister Rainey sent me down to check them water casks in the hold and I thought I heard some funny kind of sound over my head . . . she's lyin' to you, sir, I swear it, she weren't sleepin' at all. I run up to the cockpit not knowin' what I'd find, and I found this . . . lady. She was pokin' her nose into Mister Blair's medicine boxes. I asked 'er to come with me very polite, I did, and all of a sudden she starts 'er yellin' and 'er screamin' and she like to tore my shirt to pieces!"

The snickering grew louder. Michael shook his head, smothering the impulse to strike Fancy's impudent face.

"Fancy, what the hell am I going to do with you?" he bellowed. "Where did you think you were going?"

"To Boston with you, Michael Edward Ives," she declared, smiling up at him saucily. "I thought I'd surprise you, sugar. Remember, I told you I'd see you again real soon?"

Michael swore swiftly. "What's our position, Mister Rainey?"

"No place we could drop her off, sir," replied Rainey a bit stiffly.

Fancy's great violet blue eyes widened and her red mouth puckered into a pout. "Well, you're not going to turn around and take me back again if that's what you're thinkin'!" she cried, stamping her foot in pique. "I won't go. And if you take me back to my father and William, I'll tell them you kidnapped me and . . . and you ravaged me!'' She smiled, very pleased with herself. ''You . . . and your whole crew, too!''

''My dear young lady,'' said Michael through clenched teeth, ''there are one hundred and nine of us aboard this ship. I doubt even you would survive it!''

Fancy's air of assurance disappeared and, looking about her at the grinning seamen, she bit her lip nervously and kept her eyes fixed on Michael.

''No, Mister Rainey, we're not turning back, not this voyage,'' said Michael, ignoring her. ''We'll not stop or pause for any reason until we drop anchor in Boston Harbor, please God!''

''Aye, sir,'' said Mister Rainey patiently. ''But what are we to do with this girl?''

Michael waved him away, turning back to the obstinate gun.

''Put her into your cabin and you move in with Mister Blair for the rest of the voyage. She's to stay there, do you understand? She can have her meals there, too. I don't want to see her above decks until we're home.''

Mister Rainey restrained a sigh. ''Aye, sir. And what will you do with her then?''

''God in Heaven, don't bother me about it now!'' Michael swore furiously. ''I'll haul her all the way to Boston and all the way back again if I must. Just get her out of my sight!''

''Michael! *Sugar!*'' protested Fancy. ''How can you be so cold to me, after everything that's happened between us?''

The men looked at one another and murmured, not quite daring to laugh openly.

''Take that wench below, Rainey, at once!'' bawled Michael in a terrible voice. ''And the rest of you, back to work! Get those guns into position before we lose the light. And from now on, we sail dark, only a stern lantern shaded three-quarters, understood?''

They understood his temper well enough, and jumped to with alacrity. Mister Rainey led Fancy away almost unnoticed.

None of the men had stopped working for supper and there'd be no food served this night until the *Sheila Deare* was as ready to meet trouble as Michael would have her. Thus it was nearly ten o'clock when the starboard watch wearily climbed into their hammocks and the next watch reported on deck. They were full-rigged and running dark and silent up along the North Carolina coast before Michael was able to return to his cabin. There was nothing else to do now but wait.

He had quite forgotten about Fancy. He was exhausted and filthy, his hands and clothing grimy from his climb up the tarred rigging to the tops to inspect the swivel guns. Now all he wanted was a good wash and a few hours' sleep.

But the moment he opened the door to his cabin he saw Fancy there, waiting for him. She was sitting curled up in his chair, staring entranced at the bright, swaying lantern she had taken the liberty of lighting herself. With a smothered oath, Michael rushed past her to pull the short, heavy canvas curtains closed over the portholes.

"You damned little fool, Fancy!" he growled at her. "You heard me give the order for sailing dark. Are you deliberately looking for trouble?"

Fancy blinked innocently. " 'Trouble,' sugar?"

"Do you have any idea of the danger you've put yourself in? We're expecting an encounter with *pirates* . . . the whole damned ship is rigged like a bloody man-o'-war, or hadn't you noticed?"

Fancy's ladylike veneer had had time to wear considerably thin while she'd been waiting for him.

"Don't you talk to *me* about trouble! You're the troublemaker, you are!" she hissed. "It would serve you right if pirates did get you. What call did you have insultin' poor Mister Matthews in front of those other gentlemen last night? And what you said about my papa! Everybody in Charles Town knows you went out to Belleterre and stayed the whole night alone with Cousin Eleanor! Papa says he doesn't care *who* your folks used to be back in England, *you're* no gentleman!"

"Ireland, not England!" snapped Michael scornfully. "And, of course, if there's one thing your papa would recognize it's a gentleman! Well, Mistress, *you're* no lady. And your father—"

"You shut your mouth about Papa!" cried Fancy furiously. "You've been makin' a fool of yourself, *Captain*. It's too bad, too, because I really liked you!"

Michael was bored with her little games, her vanity, her whole array of shallow tricks. He turned his back on her, poured fresh water from a pitcher into his washbasin and began to splash it over his face and arms.

"But you don't like me anymore, is that it?" he drawled.

"No, sir, I do not!" she asserted.

"Then tell me, just why the hell are you stowing away on my ship?"

Fancy shivered as his voice exploded at her. He glanced back in time to see the small quiver run through her body while at the same instant a look of incredible sensuality came into her eyes.

"Well, I was real put out with you, sugar," she whispered, greedily studying the heavy, hard muscles of his arms and back as he stripped off the filthy shirt. "I mean, a girl doesn't much like it when she offers her love to a man and he just ups and throws her out . . . and then rushes right off and takes her own—another woman to bed with him! You hurt me, sugar. You hurt my feelings. I have very deep feelings, you know." Her voice took on a soft, insinuating tone.

"Have you, now?" muttered Michael, scrubbing his arms and neck.

"Mmm," Fancy purred. "I'm a forgivin' person, Captain. I could even forgive you, if you acted real nice and friendly. I know why you went all the way out to Eleanor. There she was with all that indigo and there you were with this big old ship of yours . . . you see, I do understand business, Michael, even if Papa and William don't think so. And I understand that a man has to do lots of things he doesn't care for . . . in business."

Once again Michael was tempted to slap her impudent face. But Fancy wasn't finished yet.

"I've always wanted to see Boston and New York and London and Paris!" she trilled lyrically. "You could take me with you next time you cross over. Wouldn't that be *fun?* I've never been anywhere in all my life but Charles Town. And the men there are all so stupid and boring!"

Michael looked at her warily. A false note had been struck somewhere, not *what* she'd been saying, but the way she'd said it. He reached for a towel.

"So, this is all some kind of adventure, is it?" he demanded, watching her narrowly as he dried himself off. "You just woke up this morning and decided you were bored. Then you heard something that made you angry . . . and you decided today was the day you'd run away from home. With me. And that's all there is to it?"

Her big violet blue eyes flickered, her glance darting away, and he knew without a doubt she had been lying again.

"What else, Fancy?"

" 'What else?' " she repeated, her voice too innocent.

"Come, come, there's more to this than I've heard so far. Tell me and hurry up about it!"

And her eyes dropped demurely. He was not fooled by the façade but he listened.

"Well, sugar, now you bring it up. There's somebody . . . there's a man I don't want to see. I . . . I don't care for his attentions. He's much too forward and still my Papa keeps encouragin' him . . . Lord knows *why!*"

She sounded as though she were parroting words she'd heard in some maudlin theatrical production, reciting carefully the melodramatic nonsense she hoped he'd believe. But why?

" 'A man,' " he repeated, pulling a fresh linen shirt on. "What man could possible be too forward for your tastes, Fancy?"

"A friend of William's. A most detestable man," she said emphatically, relishing the words. And there it was again, that false note, again the little shudder of distaste—for effect, he had no doubt—again the sultry look of sensuality in her eyes and around her full red mouth. "His name is Jack Keane."

Michael's head whipped around. *"Captain* Jack Keane?"

Fancy nodded. "I like to pick my own men, if you please, and Jack Keane is . . . well, he's nothin' but a low, thievin' pirate! I'll be *damned* if Papa's goin' to push me around like he does William and everyone else in Charles Town. Papa—why, Papa's throwin' me into that man's arms . . . and I . . . oh, I just hate the sight of him!"

Michael's mind was suddenly terribly alert. Somehow all of this fitted together, if he only had all the pieces.

"Why is it you're not convincing me, Fancy?"

Her eyes flashed. "I don't care if you're convinced or not!" she declared with great hauteur. "But that's why I left Charles Town, to get away from Jack Keane. And I'm not goin' back for . . . for all the tea in China!" she finished lamely. Her chin rose at a defiant angle and suddenly she looked terribly young and foolish, terribly vulnerable. Michael felt a bit ashamed of himself. He'd seen Sydney Campion and wouldn't put it past the man to force his own daughter to wed . . . or bed . . . any man who might be of the slightest use or profit to him.

"Fancy," he said a little more gently. "It's Keane we're expecting to meet. Don't be afraid, we'll look after you. Just do as you're told and stay away from my men."

Her cheeks were suddenly quite flushed and there was a peculiar little thrill in her voice as she said, "Do you really believe Jack Keane will come after the indigo on the *Tiger Eye?*"

"The 'Tiger Eye'? What's that?"

"Why, the *Tiger Eye* is Jack Keane's ship," replied Fancy, strangely breathless. "Haven't you heard of her? She's a beauty. I've seen her. Keane's got lots of guns, too . . . more than you do, and his ship can sail much faster than this old bark of yours!"

Glancing at her out of the corner of his eye he did not miss the expression of open admiration that belied her protests about Keane. His uneasiness returned.

"Just where did you see Keane's ship?"

Fancy jumped, then attempted a nonchalant shrug. It did not succeed. She was aware of his eyes, implacable, the blue like cold forged steel, watching her.

"Oh, you know how things are in Charles Town, sugar!" she said airily. "And Norfolk and New York and all up and down the coast. Why, those pirates come and go as they please. They just drop anchor somewhere and nobody says a word. Nobody dares! It just so happens I saw the *Tiger Eye* in Charles Town harbor. I don't recall when, maybe last year or the year before. You know, sugar, Captain Keane and some of his friends used to be gentlemen before they . . . before they uh . . . went to sea. They are still welcome guests at lots of fine Carolina homes—"

"Including Rogue's Fall?" he asked shrewdly. But this time she was ready for him.

"*No*, not Rogue's Fall!" she declared. "I've never seen Keane or any of them there, only in town. But don't ask me any more questions about that odious man. Heavens, why do we have to keep on talkin' about him? I told you, I despise him!"

The abrupt break in her rhythm of speech, the extraordinary change in her tone and manner was startling, as if she had suddenly had to remind herself that she was fleeing a man she really loathed and feared. And something very careful in Michael warned him not to press her now. But he was sure she was not telling him the full truth.

"We don't have to talk about Keane, Fancy, not if it upsets you," he said, matching her earlier airy tone of voice. Now it was her turn to eye him with suspicion. "Let's talk about some letters, instead. Some letters you stole from this cabin, letters written by your cousin.

454

You did take them, didn't you, Fancy, and you gave them to your father?''

Fancy glared at him. "Yes, I did take them. And, do you know what? Papa just laughed when he read them! He said they wouldn't have been any use to Eleanor anyway. The way things are goin', why there's just no hope for her. You can count on it. Papa's got Eleanor almost exactly where he wants her!" She laughed unpleasantly and the fast-fading illusion of vulnerability vanished completely. "Time you get back to Charles Town—if you do—you won't find your precious Eleanor at Belleterre, sugar. Then you'll see what a dreadful mistake you've been makin'!"

Michael forced himself to remain quiet, to think coolly. She *knows,* he thought. He could see it in her eyes, in the smirking, almost ugly curve of her lips . . . she knows what Maurice Matthews knows and came so close to revealing at the tavern: she knows what Sydney Campion plans to use against Eleanor!

"A 'mistake'?" He spoke unsurely, with a deliberate air of wounded pride. "Yes, you said that before. What mistake have I been making, Fancy?"

She exhaled sharply and when she answered him there was triumph in her voice. "I can't say as I blame you, sugar. I mean, it did look as if Cousin Eleanor was the one worth goin' after. How she loves to play Lady of the Manor! What else could you have done but be impressed with her? You're a stranger to Charles Town . . . how could you have known what Papa's been able to find out about her? All the rest of us *thought* there was somethin' mighty peculiar about her; it's just we couldn't put our finger on what it was . . ."

"But your father was clever enough to discover the 'truth' about her?" prodded Michael very, very carefully.

Fancy smiled with malicious delight. "He sure did, sugar! And once he did, everything else made perfect sense. Oh, all the old town gossips have whispered just dreadful things goin' on between Eleanor and those black bucks of hers . . . now, now, don't you get fussed with me! You know it, you heard my brother speak of it. But, you see, the most amusin' thing *is* . . . we don't hold it against her. We wouldn't dream of condemnin' her for layin' with them, not now. Goodness knows, not *now!*"

Michael swallowed hard and reminded himself that she was a woman. His mouth very dry, lips tight, he said, "Why not *now,* Fancy?"

Her gay little laugh, rich with malice, rang out loudly in the small cabin. "Why, sugar, it's just too delicious! Especially when I think of you . . . you and her!"

"Tell me, Fancy," he whispered, his voice rasping and harsh.

She batted her eyelashes at him, mocking him. "Well, sugar, if you really want to know, you've been cozyin' up to a nigger woman! Eleanor is my Uncle James's daughter all right, but her mama wasn't his precious little Irish governess, no sir! Eleanor's mama is black as soot, sugar, straight out of Africa. She used to be Uncle James's mistress on Antigua—but she was his mistress a long time before that wife of his died of the yellow jack. When Eleanor first came to Charles Town, she left her mama behind in St. John's Town. And a little bit later she sent for her. And there they are today, the two of them, that nigger bitch she calls Matty and herself—and she's no more my uncle's legitimate heir than the man in the moon! See what a jackass you've been makin' of yourself, *Captain Ives?*"

Michael stared at her wild-eyed, hardly hearing the jeering laughter. Pictures flashed at random through his mind, suddenly making a new kind of sense: Eleanor's gentle trust in the black woman, Eleanor's trembling hand being tenderly steadied unobtrusively by Matty as she gave her the teacup, Eleanor showing the letter from Ellen Fletcher to Matty . . .

There was an urgent knocking at his door and Mister Rainey's voice called to him. Dazed, Michael opened the door.

"Captain, the watch has spotted a ship off our port beam, trailing us by an hour, no more!"

"A . . . a ship?" Michael managed to form the word, but in that instant it had no meaning for him. Mister Rainey glanced past him, saw Fancy.

"I'm sorry to disturb you, Captain, but you did say you wanted to be called the minute anybody saw anything. . . ."

Michael picked up his coat at once, his face taut and grim.

"Thank you, Mister Rainey," he said. "I'll go straight up. And will you please put this woman back where she belongs and keep her there if you have to tie her hand and foot!"

"Aye, sir," Mister Rainey nodded. "Come along now, Mistress."

Fancy moved past Michael slowly, provocatively, her vivid eyes full of amusement.

"Go on, get out, Fancy," he said, despising everything about her. At the doorway she looked back for a moment and he saw a trace of

456

disappointment on her face. Of course, he thought sickly, she wants time to gloat.

Then Fancy merely shrugged delicately and went away with Rainey. Despite everything, somewhere inside his reeling brain some instinct, *something* coldly noted how unlike Fancy this sudden, silent, meek obedience was. There was something else on her mind, a thing left still unsaid, something *more*. But now he didn't care. She had said enough.

He hurried on deck and found the men there anxiously squinting into the darkness off the ship's stern. Clouds covered the face of the moon. Someone pointed off to the west: that was where the other ship had been sighted. Michael searched the vast expanse of empty sea. Where was she? The night was clear enough; was the *Sheila Deare* the only ship in these waters running without lights?

"There, sir, d'ye see her? Ye can just make out her topgallants, wait till them clouds have moved off, then ye'll see her." It was Bailey at his elbow. Michael stared and thought he did see a spectral shape of sails far in the distance, a paler grey upon the face of the grey night sea. He nodded.

"There's something out there," he said. "Too far to make out what she is. But, where are her running lights? We ought to see them from our position."

"Well, sir," remarked Bailey after a moment's thought, "we're not the only ones might be worrying' about pirates, don't ye see?"

"It's possible," murmured Michael dubiously. And then the clouds fell back from the moon's arched stride and the sea around was brilliantly illuminated. A gasp went through the assembled crew.

"She's gone!" Bailey said, much troubled. "But ye did see her same as we did, eh, Captain?"

Michael sent the men back to their posts. The ship, if there was a ship, had disappeared. If it was Keane, how he must be cursing the bright moonlight! Damn the rogue, why didn't he just make his attack now and be done with it?

Restless, greatly agitated, Michael paced the quarterdeck until the moon found its way into another nest of clouds. And once again the watch cried alarm; once again they rushed to the railing to see the phantomlike vessel still trailing them, hovering back there in the dark. This time they watched it in silence.

Twice more their shadow-companion on the water appeared cloaked in clouds, springing forward when the moon was hidden, falling behind when that light reemerged. Michael told himself it might simply be that the other ship could move no faster, or that her captain was wary of the *Sheila Deare*, wondering as he was himself, why she was running dark.

Hours passed. He could not bring himself to go below until the moon was far down on the horizon. Whatever . . . whoever . . . was out there had not been seen again. Michael left orders to be awakened at dawn and stumbled into his cabin dizzy with lack of sleep and food.

He slammed the door shut and bolted it, then carelessly splashed his face and neck with cold water. His skin felt feverish, his head pounded. To his immense disgust he saw his hands tremble before his eyes. He threw himself on the bunk without undressing. The old ship creaked familiarly, rising and dipping in its normal rhythms. He closed his eyes, no longer able to fend off the flood of desperate thoughts that had tormented him for hours. He could still hear Fancy's voice, he could still see the amused contempt on that self-consciously pretty face of hers.

He jumped up and roamed about the small room, torn by the conflicting feelings that raged in him. He turned down the lantern and the cabin was suddenly dark. He pulled back the heavy porthole curtains and gazed moodily out upon the sea. With the moon gone, the water surrounded him, black and glistening phosphorescently under a skyful of crystal stars.

"I am black, but comely," said the *Song of Songs*. . . . black, but comely . . .

It was all madness, he told himself, remembering the pale creamy beauty of Eleanor's body, the wondrous green eyes, the silky auburn hair, remembering her in his arms.

"My God!" he shouted. "My God!" Matty's face had entered his thoughts. Matty's face, as beautiful in its way as Eleanor's, but not like Eleanor's, he insisted, not like it at all! It was a lie, a damnable lie, a scheme composed of wickedness worthy of a devil like Sydney Campion, who would go to any lengths to get what he was after.

But what about the *proof*? There was proof; an attorney named Richards, he had furnished proof; he could back up Sydney's accusations. Bah, Michael scoffed, when had there ever been an attorney anywhere who wouldn't falsify any kind of evidence if he were paid enough?

...I will be your mistress; I will sleep with you, but I will not marry you. I will not marry anyone. It cannot be, don't ask it!

She had said this, loving him, knowing that he loved her with his whole heart! Michael moaned, tried to shut the voices out. But they would not be shut out. They went on hammering away at him.

Maurice Matthews was saying: *The attorney's got all the evidence, Campion told me so himself. Daughter or no daughter, that woman will never inherit from James, nay, not so much as a farthing! A lady! Not so, not when 'tis proved against her ... not when Sydney proves she's naught but a—"*

And Eleanor's sweet smile when she had told him: *My mother's people were Irish. ...*

What was he to believe? Where could she have gotten her unusual notions about running the plantation, a plantation in the heart of slave country, with free black labor? Was it from a black mother and a white father who had loved wife and daughter both whatever their color, whatever the blood that flowed in their veins?

Love. Michael ran his fingers distractedly through the disheveled blond curls. *Love.* He loved Eleanor. She was the same today as she had been yesterday, was she not? And wasn't their love all that really mattered? Had he wandered the earth in bitter loneliness for almost forty years and found, at last, what he had been searching for ... only to throw it away now, because men were blind except to colour and justice was only a pretty, abstract theory that speeches were made about and books written about and nobody really wanted?

... and if it is not a lie? If it is the truth, What will you do? He faced the question over and over again ... *Do you not love her? Is she not the same woman ... the same? ...*

He fell back upon the bunk, exhausted, drained. And even as he drifted into sleep he remembered that if Campion's story were true, then Eleanor had lied to him, hidden it from him, lied about her reasons for not marrying him ... her, to his mind, *flimsy* reasons.

Did she love him? If she was afraid to trust him how could she claim to love him? Or was it possible that she really did not know, herself? But how could a secret like that be kept from her?

There was neither comfort nor peace in sleep that night. Even when he was able to sleep, moments at a time, he dreamed of a child's hand, small and plump, wearing his father's steel ring . . . a small hand, chubby, and the gleam of the metal softly silver against the dusky fingers. . . .

There was no way of knowing reality; there was only nightmare. Nothing more was needed to complete the anguish. Love had become a rack upon which the measure of two people must be tried, however painfully.

4 The Attack of *The Tiger Eye*

Just after dawn Michael went up on deck again, moving about restlessly, silent, his face pale and haggard, his eyes fixed obsessively upon the horizon. A score of times he shouted up to the weary men on watch, demanding they keep a sharp eye out, questioning familiar things: the distant play of a school of porpoises, the faraway lightning of a rainstorm to the east, the closer appearance of a jagged line of shoals on the ship's port side.

The ship, if it had been there at all, was nowhere to be seen. The *Sheila Deare* slipped smoothly through an empty sea-lane, one of those most frequented by merchantmen, not too far out from settlements and towns along the shoreline. They had not sighted a Royal Navy vessel, neither sloop nor frigate nor man-of-war since leaving Charles Town. But that was not unusual. Most of the British ships in American waters were concentrated in the north, on the lookout for French privateers out of Port Royal, and throughout the Caribbean, looking—without much success—for pirates.

Michael's extreme agitation conveyed itself to the already apprehensive crew, although for their sakes he tried very hard to appear calm. He found it pained him equally when he thought about Eleanor and when he did not. Three or four times he had determined to go back to Fancy, question her more closely, shake her story, force her to admit that she was lying. But he could not bring himself to approach the devious little trollop.

Mister Rainey said nothing, but he was shocked at Michael's manner and appearance, disturbed that the normal, unvarying routines aboard ship had been so profoundly disrupted. In all the years he had sailed at Michael's side, there had never been so upsetting a voyage as this one. He went on his rounds of the ship greatly distressed. When this was over at last, he might speak a few words in private to Mistress Katherine Sturbridge. Perhaps it was time to think about opening that little grog shop he'd been saving for, perhaps it was time to quit the sea.

At eleven in the morning they were heading for Virginia waters, passing near Albemarle Sound, a favorite hunting ground of the southern pirate Brotherhood. Michael stared moodily at the clear skies. Where the devil was Keane? Had that specter in the night been the *Tiger Eye?*

"Sail off the port bow!" the topmast watch suddenly shouted. "Movin' fast, just come off Albemarle!"

In front of us? thought Michael incredulously. "What ship?" he cried. "Can you make her out?"

"Not yet, sir, she's too far away!" bellowed the topman.

Mister Rainey appeared, a perplexed frown on his face.

"She can't be the same vessel we saw last night, sir."

Michael grimaced. "Can't she, though? We lost her in the dark, Mister Rainey, but she could have moved east, then north and maneuvered to meet us head on. She may just have wanted to get a good look at us, make sure who we were."

Mister Rainey glanced up at the topman. "She'll be about five miles off yet, no way to see her make or colors now. Orders, Captain?"

"I'm not taking any chances, Mister Rainey," said Michael tersely. "Beat to arms, Washburn!"

Young Wash ran for his drum and began pounding out the rapid signal that sent every man in the crew rushing quickly to his assigned place.

"What is it? What's happening?"

It was Fancy, come on deck from a cabin that was supposed to be locked and guarded. Michael swore swiftly, seizing her arm.

"Get below!" he barked angrily. "Go to your quarters and bolt the door behind you. Don't open it on any account unless someone here tells you to!"

"Is it Jack Keane?" she demanded, her eyes glittering with excitement. She pulled away from his grasp and leaned precariously out over the quarterdeck railing. "I can't see anything. Is it the *Tiger Eye?"*

"Bailey!"

Hastily Bailey detached himself from the gun crew in the bow and presented himself before Michael.

"Take this woman below and keep her there!"

"Yes, sir!" Bailey caught Fancy by the waist and dragged her from the deck. And Michael put her from his mind for the time being. He knew, much as he despised her, that if it came to it, he would never let her fall into Keane's hands. But now he had other things to worry about.

Minutes passed with hideous slowness. The *Sheila Deare* was very quiet, every eye focused on the tiny, barely visible vessel creeping steadily ever closer.

"I see her now, sir!" called the topman. "She's a snow. Flying British colors!"

"Thank God!" murmured Mister Rainey fervently.

"Maybe, Mister Rainey," remarked Michael. He shouted up, "When she's in hailing distance, signal for a parley with her Captain!"

"May I ask why, sir?" Mister Rainey was clearly surprised.

"Perhaps he's got some information on pirate activity in these waters. It won't do any harm to ask."

The swift little snow moved closer now, close enough so that they could all see the colorful British banner fluttering gaily from her topmast and the row of cannon arrayed along her decks. The topman of the *Sheila Deare* held his horn to his mouth and called, "What ship are you?"

There was no answer. The topman called again but the speedy snow merely maneuvered her way silently larboard of the *Sheila Deare* and the two ships were almost alongside one another when the snow's British ensign was suddenly hauled down and a blood red banner with a golden hourglass in its center was hoisted up in its place.

"What flag is that?" puzzled Mister Rainey. "I've never seen the like of it before."

"Privateer!" retorted Michael with a foul oath under his breath. "More bloody English than all your *joli rouge* skull-and-crossbones put together, whatever those renegade Britishers among the Brotherhood have garbled that into. Just a 'pretty red' flag, eh? God, they're so damned subtle! That hourglass, Mister Rainey, is there to warn us that our time is running out. By God, the effrontery of those bastards! Look at the guns she's carrying. Do you see what her Captain's doing? Look there . . . she's moving into position to rake us good and proper with a broadside. We've got to get her athwart our bow and keep the hell out of the way of those guns! Bring her 'round, boys, steady on those topside braces!" he ended the furious harangue by shouting lustily.

Cannon fire suddenly ripped the warm air. "God damn them!" Michael swore as he saw some of the *Sheila Deare*'s braces shot away.

"We're carrying too much sail for this, sir," Mister Rainey cried. "We'll be swamped!"

Michael nodded. "Fighting sail, then. Trim that canvas. Clew up those courses there. Furl the topgallants, Lonney, step lively for Christ's sake, boy! Lower the caps . . . No, no, damn it, keep her jib clear! God's breath . . . here comes her bowsprit right over our poop! She'll crush the foremast in another minute! Is that madman trying to *ram* us?"

"Nay, Captain. I think he's trying to force us about for a clear shot at our starboard quarter," said Mister Rainey quietly.

"Ha! There's her bloody name now!" cried Michael. "It *is* the *Tiger Eye!* Aye, it was Keane all along, trailing us like a blasted hound last night. No, Mister Rainey, she's not trying for a broadside . . . look, look there up in her rigging: grappling hooks! Keane's going to try to board us. I didn't *think* he'd want us sunk, not with our cargo intact. You men at the guns, start firing! Don't wait till they're looking down your throats, fire!"

The two decrepit old six-pounders had already been unlashed for action. Now the portside gun was run out on its makeshift track. The swivel guns were fired in quick succession and, when the smoke drifted off a bit, Michael saw that some of the snow's timbers had been damaged amidships and her sails were taking a beating. But now the *Tiger Eye* fired over the *Sheila Deare*'s quarterdeck, the ball smashing into the water uncomfortably close on her starboard side. The deck was drenched in salt spray.

"By God, he's playing with us!" blazed Michael ferociously. "Fire that goddamned cannon!"

The gun was elevated into position and Dick Lonney brought the glowing end of a cotton-wick match down onto the vent. A quick puff of flames and smoke, followed by a roaring flash and the ball went flying well over the short distance separating the two ships, crashing down upon the snow's quarterdeck. A loud roar went up from the enraged crew of the pirate vessel.

"Well done!" cried Michael. But he knew the old cannon was not up to the job. One or two more shots like that one and it would overheat and explode. Still her crew worked confidently swabbing the hot gun down.

The *Tiger Eye* luffed about more into the wind and once again it seemed as though she were going to ram, but Keane was a brilliant seaman, Michael saw at once, and the distance of water between them lessened every second.

The first of the grappling hooks was tossed, finding a secure niche as it bit deeply into the railing of the *Sheila Deare*. One of Michael's men ran forward with his knife and hacked it loose but, even as the rope end swung free, the man fell screaming for a long, awful moment as one of the buccaneers' flintlock pistols put a close shot straight into his eye. More hooks were thrown and a heavy barrage of grapeshot riddled the protective netting, cutting it to shreds. Now nothing could prevent the pirates from boarding.

Michael had armed himself with two English walnut pistols and a short cutlass, perfect for fighting in close quarters. A dagger concealed in his boot completed his personal armaments. Most of his men had nothing more with which to defend themselves than knives and dirks of various kinds. They were, after all, merchantmen, not part of the Royal Navy.

Michael saw Bailey come on deck again and wondered fleetingly about Fancy. Bailey's crew managed to get off one more flaming, rumbling shot. This time the ball smashed into the *Tiger Eye*'s handsome spritsail forward of her long graceful bowsprit. With a horrendous cracking sound, the bowsprit shivered and the spritsail shrouds tore loose, only the braces and fairleads holding steady.

"Well, God bless!" cried Michael in amazement. His gun crew seemed stunned at their unexpected success but then they cheered more loudly than the rest of the crew. And in the midst of their cheering an enraged voice rang out above the noise.

"*Jesus Christ!* Will you have the sons-of-bitches shoot Jack Keane's ship out from under you? Jump to, you dogs! A gold *pistole* to the first man aboard that hulk!"

The speech had been delivered amid a volley of gunshots that swept across from the deck of one ship to the other, leaving several of Michael's crew dead. The pirates now roared approvingly in their turn, and suddenly the air was filled with them as they swarmed over free braces, grabbing onto ratlines and railings with swift and practiced agility.

464

Michael's topmen fired their swivel guns bravely enough but the oncoming buccaneers used their long boarding pikes like spears, impaling the topmen against their own stout masts, then swinging on to the crosstrees to take control of the swivel guns themselves.

With their own guns now trained against them, a hail of deadly fire raining down from above, the men of the *Sheila Deare* were hard put to fight off attackers leaping upon them with boarding axes and cutlasses. They were being mercilessly cut down on all sides.

Michael himself was quickly surrounded and fighting for his life. The firing of the wall guns, which had been fairly steady at first, soon grew sporadic as the shot began to give out and the inexperienced gunners retreated before the sweating, swearing, half-naked invaders.

There was no chance to reload the pistols. He had fired them both point-blank into the sneering face of a gigantic Tripolitan attired barbarically in orange-striped breeches and gold vest, his glistening chest weighted down with fine gold chains and huge pearl necklaces. The Tripolitan's flashing sabre nicked Michael's arm just above the elbow but a glance told him it was only a flesh wound.

That short glance almost cost him his life. He failed to see a small, crouching ape of a man creeping up behind him, well concealed by the crowded bulwarks, where men were fighting toe to toe, slipping and sliding on deck boards already slimy with blood.

The little man leaped, a strange string of foreign-sounding oaths issuing from his mouth, and bore Michael to the deck beneath him. Quickly he pulled Michael's head up and back, about to cut his throat, when Bailey pounced upon him, pulled him up and tossed him easily over the side of the ship.

Stunned for an instant, Michael staggered to his feet in time to see Bailey scrambling up the rigging, intending to try to retake the tops and put a stop to the overhead gunfire. Lonney and young Wash hove into view and followed Michael's gaze upward.

"He's done it!" yelled Wash gleefully.

Bailey had indeed gained the mainmast tops. But suddenly he cried out and clasped his hand to his throat, then toppled headfirst a hundred feet to the deck below.

Wash was shaking, tears of fear and anger coursing down his cheeks. Heedlessly he began to run across the deck, trying to reach Bailey's body and drag him aft. But Dick Lonney pulled his friend back. Sobs shook Wash's boyish frame. Bailey had been his friend, he choked incoherently, Bailey would never see his wife and children back in Boston again, Bailey had died all alone...

"We all die alone, lad," snapped Michael. "And the rest of us are as good as dead right now if we can't turn this fight around. Are you boys ready to try something that may turn the tide in our favor?"

The boys were eager to try anything. Wash's tears dried on his cheeks as he listened to Michael's hastily conceived plan. If they could manage to shatter the closely tangled yards of the pirate ship they might cripple her so she could not continue to hold her position steady. With the grappling hooks still in place, a sudden pull abaft the port side of the *Sheila Deare* could unbalance the smaller, lighter snow and send her lurching out of control eastward while the bark might pile on sail once more and hasten north and out of sight.

"We'll have to move quickly," cautioned Michael. "Everything depends on speed now."

The boys nodded. The three of them crept stealthily down the length of the deck, when that same furious voice they had heard earlier shouted out once again, this time directly above their heads.

"All right, you seadogs, boarders away!"

Michael looked up and over the railing just in time to see a second wave of pirate boarders swinging lightly across on lines from the snow. But this was no wild sally, every man for himself and pick the target he liked best. This time they were led by Jack Keane himself, followed in orderly fashion by a dozen more of his comrades. Keane looked quite different from the richly outfitted figure of elegance in the claret-colored velvet and gold-lined cloak Michael had encountered at Hatheway's Tavern, yet there was no mistaking the lean, dark face with its bird-of-prey expression, or the shoulder-length black hair so like that of the Cavaliers of the previous century, or the thin, well-formed lips beneath the handsome nose. It was Keane all right, now attired in blue breeches tight at the knee above high black leather boots, a ruffled white shirt open to the waist caught and held by a purple velvet sash edged with gaudy golden fringe. The long hair moved freely with the deft motions of his muscular body as he jumped clear of the boarding line and landed eye to eye with the captain of the *Sheila Deare*.

"Stop there, Keane!" cried Michael, raising the cutlass in his right hand.

"Ah, Captain Ives, is it not?" laughed Keane, his voice full of swagger and braggadocio, a look of sardonic amusement in his brown eyes. He glanced for an instant beyond Michael, then said, "Belay the cutlass, Ives. It's kindly advice I'm offering you . . . right now three of my lads are planning which way to cut up your Irish carcass."

Michael glanced over his shoulder. Keane had not lied. There were three buccaneers surrounding him and the two young boys. As he looked, the pirates moved in upon the boys, brandishing their boarding axes. They were standing amidships on the upper deck, not ten feet from the door which opened on to the narrow passageway leading down to the after cabins. And suddenly that door burst open and Fancy Campion came running out. There was a wide, ravishing smile on Fancy's flushed face and her arms were eagerly outstretched.

"Jack! Jack, my darlin'! Is it all over now? Aren't you surprised to see me? Papa doesn't know where I am . . . he'll be frothin' at the mouth when he finds out!"

Keane's dark eyes had gleamed with pleasure at the sight of her but as Fancy rushed toward him she inadvertently placed herself between Wash and Lonney and Keane's three cutthroats. Immediately the two boys broke and started running down the deck. Michael turned to shout after them but they disappeared down a hatchway. A few seconds later several shots were fired in the distance. It was impossible to tell, in the midst of the intermittent gunfire, whether or not the boys had been hit. Michael stiffened, turning back to Keane with a look of utter hatred. And Fancy had wound herself about Keane with a possessiveness that bespoke long intimacy between the two. Keane kissed her good-naturedly, but never once took his eyes from Michael.

"Fancy, my love, I thought we'd said good-bye for a time back in Carolina. And now I find you here with this handsome Boston man. Are you fickle or faithful, I wonder, sweetheart?" he jested lightly.

"So that was it, Fancy?" murmured Michael coldly. "You weren't running away from him; you were planning to meet him all along."

Keane threw back his dark head and roared with laughter.

"Running away, was she? Is that the story my little tart told you, Ives? Oh, she's a rare one, my Fancy, that's why I'm fond of her. Full of surprises, she is. Don't tell me you've not sampled her talents by now, Captain Ives? Knowing Fancy I find that hard to imagine!"

"Jack, honey!" Fancy protested but a ripple of laughter and a knowing shrug from Keane silenced her. Her smile disappeared and she pulled loose of Keane's encircling arm. "Oh, finish it, will you, Jack? I'm sick to death of him and this old tub. The indigo is aboard, I saw Eleanor's people loadin' it myself."

Keane nodded. "Aye, we'll put a prize crew on board and make for Stag Run Bay tonight. Well, Ives, have you decided to drop that cutlass or are you going to die like a hero? I've nothing against heroes, so . . ."

Even as he spoke, Michael had moved slowly about to Keane's right side, always aware of the three armed men just behind him. His only chance would be to take Keane by surprise, thrust him back against the three and try somehow to fight them all. There was still gunfire coming from the ship's stern and the sounds of battle were not much diminished. Surely some of his own crew might still appear in time!

He lunged suddenly, the cutlass slashing toward Keane's surprised face. Fancy screamed. Keane parried the unexpected thrust clumsily, taken off guard for the moment. Michael moved another few feet around, listening carefully for the movements of the men at his back. Out of the corner of his eye he glimpsed a flashing ax blade descending. Quickly he stepped aside, at the same time bringing his left elbow back with all his might. The sharp blow caught his assailant hard in the gut. The man grunted with pain, stumbled and fell clumsily to one side. Before he could recover, Michael kicked the dropped ax through the ship's railing into the sea.

But Keane leaped forward with a snarl, his sword blade easily a foot longer than the short wide cutlass Michael held. The sword grazed Michael's brow, missing his eye by a scant inch or two. He gripped the cutlass and circled, looking for an opening, a weakness in Keane's defensive tactics which might offer the slim chance of getting past the long reach of that sword. Keane thrust with a slight unconscious hook to the side, withdrew after each such thrust with an unguarded recoil to the opposite side. Michael watched warily, kept moving and tested his observations with two further deceptively awkward feints. And each time Keane countered swiftly, recovered swiftly . . . and off to the side that Michael had anticipated. Once more Michael bore in, waiting for the opening. Keane hooked to the left and, with an expression of irritation, withdrew his weapon slightly to the *right* . . . here was the instant Michael had been praying for. He lunged straight forward, plunging the cutlass toward Keane's heart, when Fancy, with a loud cry of alarm on her lips, moved to her lover's side. Keane shouted angrily, whipping his body around, and Michael's blade missed its target. Instead of Keane's broad chest before his eyes, he now saw Fancy's wide horrified gaze as the point of the cutlass thrust toward her breast.

Michael drew his arm back violently, the force of his attack dissipated in the fierce effort to avoid hitting Fancy. He heard her scream; he saw her hands fly to her throat in horror as she stepped back against the ship's railing. Keane closed with him, the steel sabre ringing against the edge of the cutlass, and the cutlass went flying from Michael's hand.

"Kill him!" cried Fancy, her blue eyes glittering with fear and hatred. "Kill him, Jack, kill him!"

Those were the last words Michael heard as one of the men behind him brought the broad end of a belaying pin down upon the back of his head. He pitched forward on the deck, a dark patch appearing amid the golden curls as the gaping wound began to spout blood.

"Blast you, Haiver, I was about to finish him myself!" roared Keane. He thrust his rapier into the purple sash at his middle, looking thoughtfully down at Michael's body. "Well, turn him over, man. Let's see if he's done for."

They got him turned about and he lay perfectly still upon the bloody boards, his arms twisted out at stiff, unnatural angles.

"Is he dead?" whispered Fancy.

Keane touched Michael's body with the toe of his boot and shrugged carelessly. "Just the way you wanted him, my dear. After today I'll have to call you my lucky charm. He'd have had me spitted on that little sword of his if he hadn't set eyes on you."

Fancy took a few steps forward and stood looking down at Michael. The feverish glitter in her eyes did not escape Keane, or the way she licked her lips, or the twin spots of color in her hot cheeks. He smiled to himself, knowing Fancy as he did, and he thought impatiently of the leisurely voyage back to Carolina with her in his cabin, her blood warmed by the sight of violence and death, two things that had never yet caused her to be bored.

"All right, Christ in Heaven I'm sick to death of the stink of blood here!" Keane shouted suddenly. "Round up whatever's left of these dolts and put them below. Throw the bodies over the side. Haiver, get below and find me a cargo manifest. Let's see what else we've commandeered besides that indigo."

"The indigo's unmarked," murmured Fancy, still staring down at Michael's still form. "He's put it in different places all over the hold."

Keane nodded, smiling. "I'll find it, love," he said. He glanced once more briefly at Michael and then went striding off to join his men. They were going through the pockets of the dead crewmen of the *Sheila Deare*, taking bits of money and an occasional cheap piece of jewelry from the bodies before throwing them overboard.

Fancy was momentarily left alone. She stood contemplating Michael's helpless body before her. She smiled to herself and bent over him, running her fingers sensuously along the side of his cheek and down his neck. His skin was still warm.

"What a shame, sugar," Fancy whispered. "You were really a fine, fair man. And you were such a fool!" There was a soft purr of pleasure in her voice. Her hand touched his throat, then moved again, trailing slowly across his collarbone, then very lightly down along his right arm, pinching the hard muscles with a cruel playfulness. Around her the shouts of the pirates sounded loud and raucous and full of victory, but Fancy seemed not to hear them.

She picked up Michael's limp, outstretched hand and placed it against her own half-naked breast, forcing the stiffening fingers to curl about the bared flesh. Her breath came in short overwrought gasps. She remembered that one all-too-brief moment a few days before when this man had succumbed to the power of her naked desire, those few seconds when he had returned kiss for kiss with her . . . only to spurn her after all. The memory still burned. Fancy pushed the limp hand from her body, cursing him. How proud he had been, how arrogant! She was about to turn away from him when she noticed that strange steel ring she had wondered about still on his finger. Her pretty mouth twisted. Had he worn that ring when he had run his hands so willingly, so anxiously over Eleanor's body? Had the hard steel of it left its imprint on Eleanor's white skin in the abandon of their embraces? Eleanor's white skin, thought Fancy, smiling again.

A movement nearby caused her to look up suddenly. Jack Keane stood there watching her, his dark eyes cold, unfathomable, his mouth tight. Fancy looked at him a long moment, then tossed her golden head. With a vicious twist she pulled the steel ring from Michael's finger and placed it on her own, letting the insentient hand fall to the deck once more. She jumped to her feet, her blue eyes blazing with the same triumph she could suddenly hear for the first time in the voices of Keane's men.

And still Keane said nothing, only looking at her with a question in his eyes.

Fancy held up her hand that he might see the ring. "I wanted it, I took it," she explained simply.

Keane seized her slim wrist, glancing without interest at the steel band. "Hardly a bauble fit for such a pretty hand," he said.

Fancy laughed. "I like it," she said. "I like this little ugly old ring. It's hard-lookin', like a man. It feels like a man's touchin' me," she added, looking up at Keane with bright challenge in her eyes.

"A man *is* touching you!" Keane snapped, swiftly pulling her to him. Ignoring the men around them, he leaned down and kissed her hard, bruising the soft red lips, his teeth biting into the flesh of her mouth. A thrill pierced Fancy's loins, a quiver of delight shook her as she felt the teeth cut her lip and she tasted the salt tang of her own hot blood. Without a second's hesitation, almost as if it were a continuation of the same gesture she had used with Michael minutes before, she took Keane's hand and boldly placed it on her breast, pressing his fingers fiercely against her, so firmly, indeed, that the steel ring on her own hand crushed cruelly hard into his skin. When Keane exclaimed and would have pulled loose, she held him all the harder, staring fixedly down at the old ring, thinking of the way Eleanor's face would look when she would see that ring, that particular ring, on Fancy's finger.

Keane watched with a cold, appraising eye as the grimy survivors of the *Sheila Deare*'s crew were herded along the deck toward the forward hatch. He was thinking there wasn't one of them who would fetch a decent price on the Jamaican auction block, not one who would last out a year working in the canefields. . . .

Suddenly one of the captives, an older man, saw Michael's body lying on the deck and broke free of his guards trying to reach the spot.

"Haiver!" shouted Keane, "look to your dogs!"

Haiver came running and dealt the fellow a murderous blow to the side of the head. "Get back there with the others," he snarled, feeling the displeasure of his Captain.

The old man stumbled but did not fall. "Have you killed him, then?" he demanded, undaunted.

"Aye, we have. And you'll be next, old man," sneered Keane. He glanced at Michael with sudden distaste. "Get this one over the side!" he roared. Next to him he felt Fancy's body quivering and he was overcome with desire to possess her now, now while she was still like this, still at a fever pitch of passion, now with her senses swayed by bloodlust.

Two of the pirates picked up Michael's body. The old man glared at Fancy, his face full of horror.

"What's that on your hand, girl?" he cried. "My God, his ring! Give it to me! Give it to me, it's of no value to you. It was his father's. It belongs to his sister now you've murdered him! Give it to me, I'm begging you, and I'll see that Mistress Sturbridge gets it. . . ."

Fancy clasped her hands together before her. "Oh, no, Mister Rainey," she cooed sweetly. "The ring is mine now. Spoils of war, isn't that what you men call it? And you'll never see his sister or anyone again, not where you're going!"

Keane signaled impatiently. The two pirates flung Michael's body overboard as Mister Rainey cried out in fury and despair. Ignoring them all, the first mate ran to the railing and watched his captain's body sink quickly down into the green lapping mouth of the sea.

"He's gone!" moaned Mister Rainey softly. "He's gone!"

Keane signaled Haiver to get rid of the troublesome old man. But before Haiver could move, a distant crackling rumble transfixed them all. And a moment later the quarterdeck of the *Sheila Deare* was shattered by a thunderous bombardment of cannon fire from some unknown quarter. The air was suddenly alive with screams and the splintered timber flew about in every direction.

Keane leaped to the ship's railing, straining his eyes to scan the horizon. "What is it? God in Heaven, where are the lookouts?"

"None were posted," shouted Haiver. Another ominous rumble was heard and a shell plummeted into the water dangerously close by. The pirates clamored fearfully, thoroughly unnerved by this unexpected turn of events. Those who had already gone below to look over the cargo now came running topside, dropping the boxes and bales they were carrying. They raced to gain the best vantage point so they might see what was coming. Someone, under Keane's glowering eye, climbed the rigging and stared westward into the sun . . .

"Ship approaching northwest by west, three points forward off the port beam!"

"*Ship?* What ship, you fool?" exclaimed Keane.

"Frigate!" came the fearful words, shouted down in a panic-stricken voice. "Royal Navy frigate! Thirty-eight-gun frigate bearing down fast!" Another shock of cannon fire and the two entangled ships rocked crazily, the decks awash with steaming foam.

Keane could barely make out the approaching warship at so great a distance, wrapped about as it was in the smoke of its own great guns. But there was no mistaking the three tall masts and the raised quarterdeck as it plowed heavily toward them, closer every minute.

Keane glanced about. There could be no question of standing and fighting. His only chance was to try to outrun the stoutly armored frigate. And, damaged as she was, the *Sheila Deare* could never keep up with his swift little snow. Even the *Tiger Eye* was shivered amidships and dragging her bowsprit forlornly in a tangle of shrouds and ripped canvas.

"Cut loose! Cut loose, for God's sake!" he shouted. "We can outrun a frigate! Cast off those boarding lines. Belay that damned bowsprit and get us free of this hulk! Mister Haiver, take the lady to my cabin at once. Back to the ship, men, back to the ship!"

Haiver obediently pushed his way through the mob of crewmen as they rushed to free their own ship from the already listing *Sheila Deare*. And, even as Keane had called out his orders, the frigate's heavy guns sounded again. They were close enough now to see the scarlet sparks leaping from the warship's gunports. The *Sheila Deare* was struck squarely on the mainmast. The mast cracked with a horrible groaning sound and fell aft amidst crashing yards and spars, its rigging and sails shredding as the enormous timber crushed the ship's railing and stove in the deck not six feet from where Keane was standing. Fancy shrieked as the resounding shock threw her to the deck. Haiver just managed to pull her away before the topgallant yard, swinging wildly in a great arc, broke loose of its shrouds and came smashing down in a heap of jagged fragments.

The men of the *Tiger Eye* scrambled madly back to their own vessel and began chopping away at the shrouds and spars that held them fast with the *Sheila Deare*. The grappling hooks and lines were a dead loss, cut free with all haste. Haiver took Fancy half-fainting to Keane's cabin and then joined his captain aloft in the rigging where he was superintending the frantic efforts of his men to break free of the bark.

A moment later, with a great creaking lurch the interlocked ships finally parted. A shell whizzed past the snow's own mainmast, hitting the water not ten feet away. With a great shout the crew of the snow watched the frigate fall behind, and the smaller, fleeter vessel slipped safely away to the southeast with the wind full at her back.

The frigate fired again and again, laying on all sails in a determined effort to sink the privateer, but the shots fell increasingly short. And finally the frigate *Royal Falcon* gave up the chase and hove about to aid the sorely distressed *Sheila Deare*.

The Boston men worked desperately to free their comrades trapped below decks and in the ruins above. They chopped away at the tangled shrouds and netting, cursing the stiff, black-tarred ropes that resisted the weary strokes of knife and ax wielded by men half dead from wounds and the shock of battle.

Through it all, Mister Rainey seemed entranced, paying no attention whatever to the chaos around him, paying no attention to the severe head wound he himself had received. He stood staring down into the churning green water into which the body of Michael Ives had disappeared.

At length the Captain of the *Royal Falcon*, assessing the damage done the Boston bark, announced that in his opinion the *Sheila Deare* was still seaworthy and might make for her home port. The Royal Navy, he added pompously, would be glad to offer escort to the damaged ship. At this Mister Rainey roused himself to the extent of remarking very loudly, his voice choked with bitterness, "Twas the Royal Navy nearly put us under, *sir!*" The Captain of the *Royal Falcon* sputtered darkly about "damned upstart colonial ingrates," but what really infuriated him was Mister Rainey's fanatical insistence that both ships must remain where they were while the *Sheila Deare* lowered her boats to begin a search for the bodies of her dead.

The Captain of the *Royal Falcon* tried reasoning with the first mate, tried arguing with him, finally threatened to sail off and leave the foundering bark as she was. But Mister Rainey ignored the blustering officer and kept his strange watch over the green waters where Michael's body had disappeared.

"But the man's *gone*, don't you understand that?" roared the irate Captain, very red in the face.

Mister Rainey shook his head. "I'll not believe that until they come and lay his cold corpse on the deck before my eyes," he asserted. "I know Michael Ives. He'll never give in to the sea, not him. Mark me, Captain, we'll find him and we'll find him alive."

So the longboats circled the spot and the exhausted men tossed their rope-knotted hooks and dragged them in again and again, while the copper sun drifted across the North Carolina shore, its late lingering afternoon reflections lighting the green grey sea . . . so like a woman's eyes . . . into a soft bronze haze . . . so like a woman's hair.

Five

"Someone To Share The Dream"

1 William's Plans

Fancy Campion's disappearance caused a stir of sorts in Charles Town, once people realized that she had, in fact, disappeared. Sydney waited a little while before giving serious thought to her continued absence. He was used to Fancy's whims. This was not the first time she had chosen to remain away from Rogue's Fall. Fancy left home whenever she was taken with what she termed the *fidgets*, or when she became interested in some new man or rediscovered an old beau. She always returned home again when she was no longer amused.

But eventually Sydney ordered Viola, Fancy's maid to search through his daughter's things. The maid reported that one of Miss Fancy's small portmanteaus was missing, along with her amber riding habit, some undergarments and a few trifles of jewelry. Discreet inquiries, which caused much hilarity among Charles Town's better families, revealed no clue to her whereabouts.

Her loving brother, William, refused to become concerned.

"It's Keane, I expect," he remarked laconically over an afterdinner cordial with his fuming father.

" 'Keane'!" repeated Sydney, biting off the word as though he might choke on it. His son shrugged, a twisted smile on the thick lips.

"Yes, Keane," said William placidly. "I warned you Fancy was wild for him."

"Nonsense! She's only met the fellow once," scoffed Sydney indignantly. "She barely spoke to him at that. They weren't together an hour!"

William laughed. "Our little Fancy doesn't *need* more than an hour!"

"Enough, William!" returned Sydney sharply. "The idea is unthinkable. And, too, she has no idea where he is."

"I wonder," said William coolly. "Not much escapes Fancy, not when it involves a man. You saw her yourself that night at Eleanor's, doing her best to impress that fellow Ives."

"'Ives'!" exploded his father, momentarily forgetting all about Fancy. "You fool, William! You're as undependable as your slut of a sister. You might have ruined everything for us. Couldn't you at least have killed him properly and have done with it?"

William's sallow faced flushed with anger but when he spoke his tone was light and careless. "My apologies, Father. But perhaps it's just as well I didn't. There might have been an official investigation. The Governor himself would have been forced to—"

"Never mind the Governor! *I* could have managed the governor. But to have let Ives see you with Keane! You blunder, William, you blunder dangerously. Of course Ives will have told dear Eleanor what happened at Hatheway's. . . ."

"No need for alarm, Father," yawned William. "We won't be worrying about Ives any more, not after Jack Keane finishes with him."

Sydney shook his head impatiently. "No, no, don't you see? The very moment word reaches Charles Town that Ives's ship was taken by pirates, Eleanor will bring the whole story to the authorities!"

William's bushy brow, identical to his father's, rose perceptibly. "You did say you could manage the Governor?"

Sydney's fist smashed down hard on the table. "Damn you for an imbecile, I don't mean that flunky! I mean the King, the Council, I mean, William, the companies in London with their heavy investments in American ventures! If that girl is allowed to tell her story. . . ."

"'That girl will not be listened to, will she, Father?" said William

476

softly. "I remind you, we haven't much longer to wait before a 'lady' name of Eleanor Campion doesn't even exist. Once that lawyer, Richards, gets here from Antigua, our little cousin's going to have changed by magic into some nameless high-yaller wench. Now, maybe the King might like to strip her down of a night, but he sure as hell isn't goin' to want to hear a lot of damn gibberish spoutin' out of that little red mouth of hers!"

In spite of his testy mood, Sydney could not resist a smile. He filled his own brandy glass again, was about to set the bottle down, glanced at his son and, still smiling, emptied the bottle into William's glass.

"Well, for a man who's had a hankering for Eleanor all these years, you surely sent that Ives fellow straight into her lily-white arms that evenin'! But why in hell risk your own neck takin' a shot at him in the dark like that?" Now Sydney's smile was wide, toothy, charming, a wolfish grin his son understood well.

"I wanted to kill the bastard," replied William simply. "Why not? I owed him, didn't I? He insulted me in front of my own family!"

"Hell, boy, *I* insult you every chance I get!" laughed Sydney harshly. "You haven't come stalkin' around me wavin' a flintlock in your hand. Of course, I got you damned good and scared of me, I've seen to that. Builds character, that's my opinion. Makes a man mean. But you've been a disappointment to me, William. You're not mean enough, not by half. Why, your sister, Fancy . . ." Sydney's eyes narrowed as he remembered once more that Fancy was missing. "Listen here to me," he said suddenly, "you take yourself a little hunting trip, hear? It's been a time now since you were over to Stag Run. You take some of the men and ride up there in the morning. And if your sister's there you damn well bring her back, Jack Keane or no Jack Keane. I will not have that girl mixin' into our business. If she's got an itch that bad, she can find some imbecile around here to scratch it for her! We should have heard from Keane by now, anyway. I want our share of the cargo from Ives's ship. He's had ample time to sell it off and you and I are goin' to have some heavy expenses as soon as Richards gets here."

William nodded. No doubt he'd find Fancy exactly as he expected. "How long will it be?" he asked Sydney, a sudden impatience flaring within him as it had so often lately. "Richards. How long before he'll arrive in Charles Town?"

"I've already told you that. Anytime within the next two weeks, three at the outset. That was his last communication to me."

"Two weeks," mused William, licking his thick, rubbery lips. "Then maybe another week or so for the hearing and all that. And it will all belong to us, finally. Too bad for Eleanor, eh, Father? She only had to marry me and things would have worked out so differently for her!"

Sydney leered at his son. "I guess she just didn't take to your winnin' ways, son. But you'll do just fine once that property and all those niggers are ours. You can have your pick of any girl in the county. Oh, by the way, have you given any thought to what we'll do with Eleanor when this is all over? By God, I'd like to see that proud baggage humbled right and proper!"

William saw the old, searing resentment rise red in his father's eyes, a resentment born of the galling memory of an older brother, James, who had so lightly abandoned his property . . . his empire in the making . . . to follow his heart's desire and who had, nevertheless, managed to gain for himself considerable honors, influential friends, even a royal governorship before he'd died. That memory had rankled in Sydney's breast for many years, then flared into vivid focus all over again when Eleanor had suddenly appeared, Eleanor Campion, the *heiress* from Antigua, Eleanor with her crazy notions and her devoted army of black bedmates.

"What are we going to do with Eleanor? Is that what you're asking me, Father?" repeated William, an eerie quality in his voice. "Why, I thought you knew what I had in mind. I'm going to put her up on the slave block at Graham's Wharf, just like any other nigger wench you'd use for stock breeding. Not to sell her, just to shame her. And afterward when I'm finished with her, I'll put her to work in the fields. Unless you've got some objection to seeing a relative of yours brought so low? I mean, since she *is* your own brother's child? . . ."

The obsessive glitter in Sydney's eyes reassured William. Now he knew without a doubt, Eleanor Campion would be his to do with as he pleased. He tossed off the last of his drink, feeling his father's gaze hard upon him, knowing that for once in his life Sydney Campion was not thinking him a fool.

"And, Father," he added briskly, "we are going to have to buy a husband for Fancy one of these days soon. It'll cost a bit of money, persuading someone of our own class to marry her. Best you keep that in mind.''

"You just bring that little trollop back here, William," grunted Sydney. "I'm going to whip the hide off her before I'm done. Then we'll arrange a suitable weddin' with all the fancy trimmings!''

"What if Keane doesn't want to let her go?''

"Bah! Keane's a businessman. He'd hate to lose his Carolina markets—and a hiding place no British warship has ever heard of. He'll send her packin', William, don't you worry none!''

"Oh, I'm not worrying," replied William, in something of a reverie. His mind had wandered far afield from what they'd been discussing. It was an image of Eleanor Campion . . . no, not Campion, though, just Eleanor, or perhaps some softer, more fanciful *slave* name they might give her . . . that was what filled his thoughts at the moment.

That image differed little from the one he had secretly nurtured for years: Eleanor as his wife, subject by law to any whim or desire of his. And the image now, as always, was Eleanor naked, her head bowed submissively, her hands chained before her while the beautiful red hair tumbled unbound down her exquisite white back . . . and something powerful and hard, something long and dark, snakelike, whiplike, lashing again and again that perfect, milky white skin until the strands of hair and the coursing blood blended one into the other, scarlet and auburn, crimson and flame.

Eleanor would pay for Captain Ives, William was thinking; she would pay for Ives and for all the others, those ugly black brutes from Africa and the islands, those beasts always in rut like bulls, like stallions, always ready to take their pleasure at the mere sight of a pair of woman's breasts, or the curve of her buttocks, the swell of round, hot thighs. How William hated them all, they who did not need the refinements of pain and torture imaginatively inflicted before desire spent itself upon blood and lacerated tissue. William smiled faintly. Father doesn't really know me, he thought, Father doesn't know me at all!

2 Dreams of Belleterre

Eleanor awoke to the cheerful sound of Matty's lusty singing downstairs in the kitchen, pots and pans rattling and clanking as she moved about the big room. The back door slammed and the singing broke off abruptly as Matty shouted something, then the door slammed again and a child's smothered giggle trailed away as small footsteps raced across the rear veranda. Matty was talking to herself now, rather loudly, while she wrenched open the big woodburning stove and began slamming firewood into it as fast as she could. The tantalizing odor of frying ham and fresh-baked bread, and a wonderful hint of coffee pervading it all, wafted upstairs.

Eleanor jumped out of bed, realizing that the sun was already high. It was close to ten o'clock in the morning! Why had Matty let her sleep on and on when there was so much work to be done?

She stretched luxuriously, enjoying the feeling of the new lawn nightrobe against her skin. She and Matty had made it together, sewing quickly, talking a great deal about everything in the world except Michael Ives.

She looked out over the fields, empty now, the indigo gone on its way to Boston. The rich, black brown earth freshly turned over the buried stubble of the beautiful plants seemed to Eleanor now full of promise for the future. Throughout the winter rain would fall, washing into that soil a new richness for the spring planting of another crop.

She looked beyond the fields close to the house, noting neat gardens, fruit trees, autumnal flowers in full rainbow blooms of purple and gold and orange. And beyond all that, the varied greens and browns of that newly realized wealth of Belleterre, the trees that Dogon and Daniel and the other men were already hard at work cutting down as Michael had suggested.

For just this moment, sadness deserted her and the bitter memory of her parting with Michael faded a bit. Surely on such a morning, so gloriously full of promise, crowned as if in blessing by the radiant sunshine . . . surely on such a morning she might feel her heart lift at the thought of the good things that had come tumbling so unexpectedly into her hard life! The trees . . . a new harvest, its possibilities almost limitless, a newer, surer, perhaps even steadier source of income for all of them at Belleterre. Bills would be paid at last, wages long, long overdue distributed into the patient hands of those who had worked and hoped and waited without a murmur of complaint, food could be laid by for the future, clothing and a few toys for the children, more precious books smuggled in somehow, for Matty's little classes.

"New tools, plows, mules!" she cried with childlike delight.

Soon they could begin to clear and plant up along the Santee River at Stag Run. Why, they could build their own wharves, ship directly from their own property. Her dreams spun on and on in golden circles, thin and fragile as spider webs sparkling in the rain, and as lovely.

God bless you, Michael Ives! She interrupted her dreams, allowing herself to think of him and wonder where he might be right at that moment. Somewhere out upon the sea, perhaps even thinking about her as he sped homeward to Boston . . . and then to Antigua, he had promised, and finally south again to Charles Town, to Belleterre, to *you*, a mocking little voice inside of her pointed out. To marry you, what do you think of that, Eleanor Campion? But of course you'll send him away again, will you not? You'll refuse to marry him just as you did before and a man like that wants a wife, children, a home. . . .

But it's all right here, protested the voice of love she was trying so very hard to ignore. Everything Michael Ives wants in this world is here, he said it himself!

Quickly she turned away from the sun-crystaled window and began to dress for the day . . . what was left of the day, she reminded herself guiltily. Renewed vigorous singing, together with more rattling of pots, told her that Matty was getting ready to come and wake her up, anyway.

With flying fingers she did up the laces of an old blue homespun gown, slipped a much-mended pair of heavy stockings over her feet and then, with a sigh, looked away from the rows of bright new shoes in her armoire, choosing instead her usual, everyday sturdy boots. When would she wear such dainty shoes and slippers? She almost laughed but the laugh turned into a sharp, painful sigh as the obvious answer leaped into her mind. A *honeymoon* would be a fine time to wear all those pretty things. She did not quite realize how very hard she slammed the bedroom door behind her as she went downstairs.

Matty, dressed becomingly in a new frock of white with alternating ribbon stripes of dark and light blue, greeted Eleanor with a frown of severe disapproval. She stood, hands resting on her slim hips, next to the behemoth of a stove and shook her head slowly from side to side.

"You bound and determined to go about lookin' ugly?"

Eleanor flushed. "What are you doing down here? You've got

every pot and pan in the house all over," she said, ignoring Matty's pointed question.

Matty flung her arms out passionately. "This house needs a good scrubbing down, that's all! Needs a coat of paint, too. Sit down and eat something and we'll talk."

Eleanor laughed in spite of her melancholy feelings. Matty's musically inflected English, with something of the original tongue of her own people and something of the fluent French she had learned, was never so pronounced as when she was playfully bullying someone, whether it be Eleanor herself, or one of the children.

"Why did you let me sleep so late?" Eleanor asked reproachfully as she sat down before a huge plate covered with steaming ham slices, fried eggs and hot, fresh bread. A polished pewter mug of black coffee stood beside the plate.

"There was plenty to do," said Matty, filling a plate for herself, sitting down across from Eleanor. "And I wanted to think."

"Think about what?"

"What will happen now. When Captain Ives brings the indigo money. You've got to start thinking about how things are going to be soon, when we are rich again."

"Matty!"

Eleanor stared at her in astonishment. Never once since she had known the vibrant woman her father had loved had Matty so much as mentioned the subject of money, not when they had been well off back on Antigua, not when they'd been . . . as they were still . . . dirt poor in Carolina. And then she saw Matty's mischievous grin.

"Well, girl, no harm in enjoying things once in awhile, is there?"

"No, there certainly is not," said Eleanor firmly. They ate then as they had not eaten in a long time and drank several steaming cups of the wonderful fresh coffee.

"Six weeks," mused Matty a bit later. "We'll have plenty of wood ready for your Captain Ives by then. Dogon says there doesn't seem any end to that pine the Captain sets such store by."

Eleanor nodded thoughtfully. "Matty, have you ever thought about Stag Run?"

Matty blinked, then wrinkled her nose distastefully. "That swampy old place? Why should I? I don't know what your grandpapa was thinking about when he laid claim to that land. There's nothing up there but Indians and wild animals all through those woods. Why, it'd take two years just to clear ten good acres for plowing that place!''

Eleanor smiled. ''That's just the point, Matty. It's going to be cleared, my mind's made up about that. I mean to have Stag Run cleared and planted and running just like Belleterre, with *miles* of indigo all the way down to the harbor. But right now it's mostly woods, acres and acres of woods by the river and along the shore. Well, all those trees are just so much more timber we can ship out and make a good profit on, do you see?''

''I see you're set on having your own way, as usual,'' replied Matty dryly. ''But why don't you forget about Stag Run for now? You've got a good piece of land a lot closer to home, already cleared with a fine house standing on it already. Rogue's Fall belongs to you, too. When are you going to send that uncle of yours packin' and take what's yours?''

Eleanor's eager smile faded. ''I thought I'd give them some time to find a place of their own. Oh, Matty, it's all so stupid, so unnecessary! You know I planned to give them Rogue's Fall free and clear. I don't know what my uncle did with his own inheritance but he can't have much left. He must have sold his land off piece by piece to keep going. When I first got here there was never any question in my mind about letting him keep Rogue's Fall . . . until I saw what he'd made of it. Slave land. If my uncle had his way it would all be nothing but slave land. So I can't give it to him. I *won't*, even if he is blood kin. I don't care what the rest of Carolina does but as long as I have anything to say about it there won't be any land anywhere with *Campion* slaves on it!''

''What will you do, then?'' Matty pressed her.

''I'll fight,'' said Eleanor, her eyes gleaming. ''Michael showed me there isn't any other way. When he comes back he will be bringing the money we'll need to fight my uncle through the courts, since he must have it so. He thinks to take Belleterre and Stag's Run from us, but he will be the loser, Matty. I swear it! And he'll lose Rogue's Fall as well. In the meantime, we'll keep on working here as we always do until we have the means to make a fight of it. My uncle seems to think he can prove I'm not my father's lawful heir. But I am and there's nothing he can do about it!''

''It is hard, the waiting,'' murmured Matty vaguely. ''Charles Town to Boston, Boston to Antigua . . . and each night I think about your uncle and I wonder, *when?* When will he strike? Will we be ready for him? So much depends upon your Captain."

"He knows that," replied Eleanor. "He will come swiftly."

"Pray God he does!" exclaimed Matty with a sudden shiver. Eleanor looked at her strangely and she forced a little artificial laugh. "The air is full of autumn, is it not so? A new breeze blows and I am not so young anymore. Don't look at me like that! Do you think I am never weak, never afraid? Do you think I am so very different from other people?"

Eleanor said, "Yes, oh, yes, I do think you are different, most of the time. But now you seem like the rest: you feel one thing and you say another. Don't do that to me, Matty, please don't! I know you're afraid. I'm afraid, too. We share that. Too much depends on the sailing of one little ship. It's only wooden beams and planks, canvas and rope, in the middle of all that powerful ocean! That's frightening me, that we are so vulnerable, waiting for that little ship to save us."

"The ship is nothing, girl!" snapped Matty unexpectedly. "The man's *love* will bring him back. To love is dangerous enough, and powerful, too, like the sea itself."

"Then why did you shiver so when I said he would come swiftly?"

Eleanor's voice was cold, her eyes questioning. Matty sighed.

"I told you, child. The autumn wind blows. . . ."

"No! It wasn't that," asserted Eleanor. "What's wrong? What do you know that you're not telling me?"

Matty simply shook her head. "Nothing. I know nothing. I am afraid and so are you. Our fears speak, no more."

Then she stood up and silently began to clear away the dishes.

Eleanor seemed about to say something more but she turned on her heel and left the kitchen. She walked quickly to the little chest in the hallway where she kept her riding bonnet and gloves, and her father's ancient fowling piece, a beautiful early flintlock rifle with intricate inlays of tiny carved deer and flowers in ivory and silver wire along the stock. James Campion had seen to it that his daughter knew how to fire such a weapon. Now Eleanor tucked it under her arm, picked up the horn and ivory matching powder flask and shot box and retraced her steps to the kitchen. Matty glanced at her, noticed the weapon she carried.

"Where are you going?"

484

"I'll ride up to Stag Run and look around. I won't be back till late, I expect," said Eleanor coolly.

Matty's voice rose in alarm. "You're not goin' to that place all by yourself!"

"Of course I am. It's not so far," answered Eleanor, tossing her head a bit defiantly.

"Take Dogon with you, or Daniel, please!" begged Matty. "You can't ride through those woods alone. No telling who's hiding out there. Wait, let me go out and get Dogon—"

"No one!" said Eleanor sharply. "It's broad daylight and I can take care of myself. It's high time I had a good look at that land."

"'That land'!" spat Matty. "It's nothin'! Snakes and bears, panthers, Indians, those wild crazy *woodsies* camped along the river, they're no better than animals themselves. You can't go!"

"You can't prevent me," said Eleanor. She tied the ribbons of her old-fashioned bonnet beneath the firm, set chin, pulled on the worn leather gloves and walked out the back door, heading straight for the stables. Matty started after her but she knew there was no stopping Eleanor when her mind was made up. A few minutes later, as Matty stood in the doorway watching, Eleanor rode away north, mounted on the fastest horse at Belleterre, a skittish two-year-old white stallion even Dogon had had trouble controlling.

Matty folded her arms, feeling once again that slight chill that had come over her before. She glanced up at the high, rushing clouds, wind-driven across the deep, pure blue of the autumn sky. The chill was in that air, Matty told herself. The trees knew it, too. How their topmost boughs shuddered and tossed uneasily as the wind beleaguered them, hag-ridden by the changing of the seasons.

She watched the clouds and the trembling trees and the swift ripple of the silky, bluish grass in waves across the back lawns, and she told herself more than once that such a wind disturbed even a sun-comforted day like this day. She told herself that the fear that was growing stronger inside of her every moment was nothing but what she'd said to Eleanor: like a little early whispered warning in Death's cold voice, reminding people now and again that youth, like the summer, was fast-going and age, like the autumn, was a time for shivering.

At last she slammed the door shut against the relentless wind and refused to think about Eleanor out there alone somewhere, riding a foolish white stallion who raced the wind for pleasure. Of course there was no surer way of fixing her mind entirely upon Eleanor than this, so all the time she spent washing the dishes and tidying up the kitchen she thought of a hundred things she might have said and ought to have said to keep the girl from going off as she had. How was it that they had come so close to quarreling after all the years of such a special kind of peace between them? Matty reminded herself that Eleanor was afraid, afraid and anxious and angry, almost angrier with herself because she had entrusted her future to a stranger than she had been even over the danger that threatened everyone at Belleterre from Sydney Campion.

And I didn't help, Matty berated herself as she arranged the damp dishtowels to dry near the kitchen window; *I didn't help because I've never found a way in all this time to make her see that she can trust someone else to understand the dream she dreams, that she must allow someone else to share that dream with her or it will die when she dies. Why did I have to let her see I was troubled when we talked of Captain Ives? And . . . why was I troubled?*

Quite abruptly, Matty sat down before the hot stove and clasped her hands tightly in her lap. It was not the chilling wind that had made her shiver, no. That had been a lie and Eleanor had guessed it. Something *was* wrong, something was terribly wrong. It had no face yet, no name to it, but it seemed to rush in upon her with all the force of the rising wind outside. She was no superstitious African girl, not anymore. The lore she had learned early from her desert nomad people was long forgotten and she believed in the Christian God. Yet at this moment, she could have wished for one of the tribal shamans or even for the muttered incoherencies of the voodoo women on Antigua. She herself did not have the seeing gift and she needed to know why she heard inside her head the crashing of stormy waves in a distant sea and why she suddenly was unable to remember what Michael Ives looked like, the precise cut of his features, the varied expressions of his face, or even the sound of his voice.

Matty sat for hours, thinking, not thinking, watching the sky's amazing changes through the window. Clouds moved along ever faster, no longer white but a whirling grey black, ominous, seeming to take over the whole world. The trees bent low to the ground and the old house creaked, hollow whistlings haunting the chimneys, stirring up the dust of ashes on the hearths.

The sudden sharp banging of an upstairs shutter startled her. She

486

ran up and refastened the heavy wooden shutter with difficulty, fighting the wind to keep it shut. Mechanically she walked from room to room, fastening all the shutters closed. Above her head she heard the crack and ripping of old worn shingles being torn loose from the roof. And suddenly she began to run, panic-stricken, down the steps, out of the house, battling the wind with her body now as she struggled to reach the row of small houses beyond the stables.

She saw the men hurrying back from their work in the timber stands, leading their frightened mules step by step. They had unhitched the flat wagons and left them half loaded with cut wood back among the trees. By now the wind was pulling up bushes and flower beds and vegetable gardens and the sky was almost as dark as nighttime. Matty hastened on until she caught sight of Dogon, who took her into his house and lit a candle while he waited till she got her breath.

"We should never have gone out this morning," he said. "Daniel, he knew a hurricane was coming, said he could tell it by the way that old broken leg of his kept aching and drawing all night long. Good thing we got the indigo shipped. Daniel says this one's going to be worse than one he remembers when he was a boy. That one tore this countryside to pieces and flooded clear up the hills."

"Dogon!" Matty gasped impatiently. "She's gone up to Stag Run!"

Dogon put the candle down very carefully. "By herself? Alone?"

"Oh, yes, all alone, she wouldn't listen to me, wouldn't listen to anything! Just took that crazy horse and James's old gun and off she went!"

"How long ago?"

Matty frowned. "Hours. Three, four hours, maybe more, I can't remember. The sky was still clear when she rode off."

"She might have turned back when she saw it blowin' up so bad."

"I don't know," whispered Matty. "She was precious angry. With me. The way she was riding. I don't think she'd have noticed if it started pouring rain on her."

"I'm going after her," Dogon said. He felt around carefully under the mattress of his narrow bed. "Why was she angry?"

"Oh, what difference does it make? We were talking about her uncle and the trouble he's starting, and then we got to talking about Captain Ives . . . it's all mixed up. Man what *are* you doing there?"

She broke off, leaning forward curiously as Dogon removed a tightly wrapped parcel from beneath the mattress. He did not answer her, but carefully unwound several thicknesses of oiled paper and then she saw the two pistols gleaming in the candlelight.

"No need for her bein' angry about Mister Sydney Campion," murmured Dogon softly. "I'm going to kill that man before he ever gets a chance to start anything here." He stuck the pistols into the broad leather belt at his middle and hurriedly donned a heavy black drugget long coat, over which he tied on a formless oilcloth cape.

"You know what they'll do to you if you're stopped and they find those pistols?" whispered Matty.

Dogon shrugged. "I'll fetch her back. And then I'm going to pay a visit at Rogue's Fall."

"You can't!" Matty's voice implored for the second time that day. "We have to wait, we have to be ready for when Captain Ives...when he comes...." She fell silent, listening with a strange glaze in her eyes to that persistent crashing sea sound inside her head. Dogon shook his head, snuffing the candle.

"No more waiting, Matty," he said firmly. "And we can't depend on anyone but us."

"They'll kill you," she said faintly. But he did not reply. And in another moment he threw open the door and strode out into the gathering storm without looking back. The wooden door swung violently back and forth on its hinges. Matty felt entranced, as though she were reliving a nightmare step by step the way it had been before. She rose and closed the door behind her and went back to the big house to light the fires and wait for Eleanor. Just as she reached the back door and pulled in the mops and brooms that had scattered over the veranda, the first drops of rain began to fall.

3 Ride To Stag Run

It had been closer to six hours earlier when Eleanor left Belleterre and the only storm raging then was the one in her own heart. Under a deceptively tranquil sky she rode north and east toward the coast, giving the stallion his head more often than not. She had been to Stag Run only once, not long after arriving in Carolina, but the way was simple enough. There were no settlements once she left the southern tidewater country. She passed tiny plank-and-sod houses two or three times but saw no one about, and then the great coastal woods surrounded her, swallowed her alive, cut off the view of her lone figure from even the sun's gaze, so close and tall grew those giants of trees.

The forestland was strange; sometimes eerie and dark, sometimes pierced through from verdant treetops to unfamiliar rose and yellow tiny flowering bushes with great shafts of sunlight finding room to light up the way where some dead tree had fallen. Dappled sundrops occasionally dotted the black forest floor and she was aware of the fleeing footsteps of deer very close by, running from the crashing hoofs of the stallion who disliked where he found himself very much and had slowed his headlong pace considerably.

For a long time Eleanor had been breathing in a subtly different taste in the air, a taste of salt and marshland added to the scents of the forest. She watched for the first of three broad salt meadows interspersed with low wooded hills. At the first of those flat swampy bogs Stag Run began, running westward to the mountains, eastward to the sea, north to a far point she had never seen and would, she knew, soon have to have properly surveyed against the old charts her grandfather had left.

As she rode along alone, the myriad busy harmonious sounds of the forest gradually filtered into her consciousness and her quarrel with Matty seemed ridiculous. Of course they were both jumpy and on edge these days. The only wonder was that they hadn't quarreled much worse, much sooner. She remembered Matty's dire warnings about the land she rode through now and smiled to herself. She had seen snakes several times . . . and each time they had fled from her approach, as much terrified as the deer. Once she had heard the peculiar coughing snarl of a panther quite far off and even that had not disturbed her overmuch. Birds ignored her, for the most part, or swooped down to scold the noisy beast she rode, flitting daringly past his twitching ears. The stallion reared once or twice and then learned that Eleanor would not always let him have his way. He seemed resigned, then, and moved as she guided him.

And then she found the first of the salt flats, to the right of it a glimpse of the sea. She was on Campion land now. Despite the long hard ride she pulled herself erect in the saddle and spurred the stallion on. She made note of the heavily timbered land about her and knew that she could never bring herself to fell all of those wondrous giants, not even for the sake of the indigo. Here and there, she promised herself, the best stands of trees would be saved. As for the salt meadows, she could bring in cattle that fattened well on salt hay. Nothing must be wasted; everything must be turned to account. Carolina, north and south, was such a vast land, she knew. Might it not some day count for a country, a nation by itself? It was all she knew of America, save for the little Michael had told her about New England. But New England seemed as remote and far away, as utterly unreal to her as that old England that laid claim to all the riches, all the future of this place she loved. Old England was Antigua, was Europe, which she had never seen and never cared to see. Here, *here*, she thought, her eyes sparkling with delight, here is something new and unspoiled where new things can be tried and new ideas must be made to work, and even the dreams of women can have the power and the strength and purpose that men's dreams had always inspired in the world. Almost in a state of ecstasy, Eleanor urged the stallion forward. A still-gentle breeze flapped the stiff brim of her hat annoyingly on her brow and the veil to which it was attached became undone. Impatiently she pulled the hat off and tossed it away without a thought. Now she rode with her eyes fixed upon the ground beneath her, watching for the sight of that rich dark loam the indigo required.

She was so absorbed in her strange mystical state of exhilaration and very practical considerations that she had passed beyond the third and last of the salt flats and turned a gentle curve leading down toward the shore before she realized it. There were higher hills on three sides leading down to the beach, cutting off her clear view of it. It was only when she caught sight of a distant, opposing jut of land across a great spread of water that she recognized at last the fine natural harbor drawn so clearly on the old maps at home. She slowed the stallion to a walk, the better to enjoy that lovely sight when she would round the final curve and find the waters of the bay lapping mildly blue green against the pale, sparkling sand.

The bay indeed spread brightly turquoise in the sun, but the sight that met her eyes so startled Eleanor that her firm hand on the reins trembled and the stallion looked back anxiously over his shoulder. She found herself clinging to his neck, the reins gone slack, the reins forgotten altogether, as she looked out upon the dozen or so ships at anchor in the sheltered harbor! Ships of every type and condition were there, from a small French frigate to a battle-scarred British ship of the line. Small boats moved busily among the ships and back and forth to the beach.

Then she heard the sound of human voices, even the shrill

laughter and shouting of children playing nearby. She looked back toward the trees closest to the beach. A haphazard arrangement of makeshift huts and cabins, some mere lean-tos roofed over with dirty bits of discarded canvas, had been strung out among the trees. Cooking fires tended by women dressed in every bizarre fashion imaginable were blazing warmly before almost every shack and shelter. The steady, rhythmic sound of an ax splitting kindling wood mingled with the furious shouting of several of the men down by the water arguing violently over some article just brought ashore in one of the boats. Blows were struck, the angry words grew louder. Eleanor saw several of the busy women leave their cooking fires and draw nearer the men, forming a circle near them, watching them quietly. Suddenly one man, the first to have been struck and knocked to the ground, leaped with a knife in his hand and pulled his opponent down into the sand. The two rolled over and over, grunting and panting, their companions shouting, the silent women moving in closer yet.

And, as quickly as it had begun, the quarrel ended. The man with the knife pulled himself to his feet and the knife was dripping blood, which ran down his arm. He laughed and bent to wash the blade clean in the surf; the blood was not his own. His enemy lay where he had fallen and did not move again. The other men laughed, too, and they all went off together cheerfully, their women following behind them. Only one woman remained to look at the body and even she did not weep. Nobody had bothered to pick up the box of goods that had caused the incident.

Very, very slowly, Eleanor slid off the stallion's back. She seized the reins tightly, winding them about her arm, and turned the horse around, walking back the way she had come as quietly as she could, around the curve of the hill and into a thick stand of trees until she could no longer see the ships in the bay or hear the people along the beach.

Now she slid the old gun from its saddle strap and forced her hands to move with their practiced, steady sureness as they measured black powder and rammed shot and primed the ornate frizzen pan, then set the cock at half. And all the while she was doing this, her mind was reeling from what she had just witnessed.

Who were these people? What were they? The questions hammered fearfully in her brain. Matty had talked about "woodsies," those wandering stragglers who camped here and there for a year or two while the hunting was good and always moved again. Eleanor thought of the ships she had seen and shook her head. These people were no ordinary squatters settling on land they neither knew nor cared was already owned.

My God! she realized in a flash, they are pirates! *Pirates.* Now she understood why she had come across no Indians, not so much as a small village anywhere about. The pirates had probably killed them, sent the survivors scattering, and simply took over Stag's Run. They'd moved in here, taken the land, the harbor, everything, made this place as much their own as they'd done on New Providence Island in the Bahamas, on Barbados and Tortuga and a dozen other freebooter strongholds.

Yet it was hard to believe they would have taken such a risk. This was the mainland, after all. Usually their kind avoided encampments on the mainland, this was not their way. Her mind kept repeating irritating, irrelevant facts that no longer applied . . . whatever the way of the Brotherhood had been in the past, here they were now, obviously well entrenched, obviously feeling safe and secure. From the looks of the place they'd been living at Stag's Run a fair amount of time.

But, this is Campion land, this is *my* land, she thought with sudden icy anger. The initial shock had evaporated, the first fear was gone now. This is my land and they will be driven off!

She must ride quickly straight back to Charles Town, inform the Governor, summon a Royal Navy fleet while the pirates were still ashore, their ships still at anchor, crowded together in the bay. A naval bombardment, one or two fireboats would wreak havoc among that crowded little fleet. And it must be done at once, tonight, tomorrow morning. If the stronghold were attacked after the ships had put out to sea the Navy would only scatter and lose them and end by capturing a few women and children . . . and the vengeance those devils would exact up and down the coast, looting and burning villages and towns, would be unspeakable.

She patted the stallion's head and spoke to him in soft tones. He was a nervous beast at best and now everything depended upon her ability to force him back through the thick forest behind them, moving at top speed, in perfect control. She was about to climb into the saddle again and return the way she had come when she heard the hoofbeats of several approaching horses, moving along at a leisurely pace, heading straight down toward the beach encampment.

She crouched very low against the hillside, pressing her body close between the trees, peering out warily to catch sight of who it was riding so openly, so fearlessly in this wilderness. Was it only a few more of the pirates returning from a morning's hunt, laden down with fresh meat? If that was so they would be tired and hungry, likely to ride right by and never notice her, if the horse stayed quiet. She raised the fowling piece and steadied it against her shoulder. One shot was all she would have if they did see her. And, afterward? . . . She thought fleetingly of the two fine pistols Michael had left with Dogon. Matty had been right, of course. She should never have come up here alone like this. But, characteristically, she gave only a little offhand shrug and gripped her father's weapon all the tighter.

The oncoming horses slowed perceptibly, now merely ambling along. From the sound of them there seemed likely to be no more than five or six riders. Beside her the stallion stamped his feet and tossed his great head. She prayed he would remain silent. It seemed to take forever for them to reach her. She could feel the cold sweat of fear trickling down her back, between her breasts. The heavy blue homespun felt hot and itchy, the sturdy boots unbearably heavy when she longed for barefoot freedom to run and run and never look back. . . .

She heard low voices talking, the bass rumble of a stout man's chuckle. Once again, cautiously, her head quite low, she peered out. And this time they were near enough for her to make out their elegant attire, the fine colorful velvet hats and matching cloaks, the well-wrought hunting weapons at the sides of their saddles. These men were certainly not pirates! They were obviously a party of gentlemen out on a hunting expedition and they were in grave danger. Eleanor knew she must stop them before they attracted the pirates' attention.

Quickly she leaped atop the stallion and rode straight out into the open track toward them. As she rode, digging her heels into the horse's sides, she waved frantically, trying to warn them. She did not dare shout for fear of being heard below. As it was, the horse's heavy feet sounded as loud as thunder to her ears, but she urged him on all the faster.

The little knot of horsemen came to a standstill, watching in some amazement the sight of the galloping white stallion heading straight into their midst, ridden by a wild-faced young woman with

493

long, flaming hair streaming down her back, a weapon from the previous century held under one arm.

Eleanor reined in sharply as she came up to them, dust from the horse's hoofs whirling about her.

"Go back! Go back!" she cried breathlessly. "There are pirates below! Hurry, for the love of God, hurry up! We've got to reach Charles Town!"

She did not pause a second longer but lifted her reins to go on, thinking they would surely turn and follow her. But suddenly a hand reached out, a hand gloved in the finest, softest deerskin, and took the reins from her so quickly she did not have a chance to resist.

"Dear, dear Eleanor!" said a familiar voice, faintly chiding her as one might chide a naughty child. "So, you've finally discovered our little secret here at Stag's Run!"

She shook her head, confused, pushed the windblown hair from her face and eyes and looked up, not really having seen any of them clearly before.

"William!" she gasped.

"Eleanor," her cousin responded with mock civility, touching the curved brim of his tall green beaver. "Gentlemen, you all know my cousin, Mistress Campion of Belleterre?"

Eleanor looked around at their faces—amused, smug, flat peasant faces, with small close-set eyes . . . gentlemen! They were her cousin's cronies, who worked, *when* they worked, at Rogue's Fall in the daytime and prowled the taverns and brothels of Charles Town with William at night. She drew herself up very tall in the saddle, ignoring William's hand grasping her reins. "Our little secret," he had said, "our little secret." She smiled an ironic little smile. How absurd not to have guessed at once who was behind this secret pirate bastion! Captain Jack Keane . . . and William, of course. She nodded to herself. William . . . and undoubtedly her uncle, too; what kind of arrangement had they made with Keane and his friends long ago? long ago when Stag's Run was just a forgotten tract of forest and shore, an unknown, sheltered harbor safe from patroling British warships! That's where they'd been getting their money from, their share of every captured cargo, every ravaged settlement, every sale of captured white women so highly prized by plantation owners on the remote and isolated out islands all over the Caribbean.

"You have such an expressive face, Eleanor," drawled William, quite enjoying the moment. "I see you are beginning to understand a

494

little bit. So kind of you, my dear cousin, to warn us of the danger we were gettin' into!" William laughed and so did his friends.

"Take your hand from the reins," Eleanor said sharply. William, still laughing, shook his head. He reached across and took the gun from beneath her arm, throwing it deep into the woods. Then he turned the stallion in the direction he and his men were facing and led it along beside them.

"Eleanor, well, well," he said pleasantly, hideously pleasant, "this is a bit awkward, you know, my dear. You weren't supposed to find out about our friends up here just yet. I wonder what Father will say. No," he shook his heavy head playfully. "No, that's not true. I *know* what Father will say: 'Handle it yourself, you fool, I've told you how a hundred times!' " William chuckled. "Now, Eleanor, don't that sound just like Father, eh? Eh, Eleanor? Oh, you'd best hold on to your pommel for a bit, m'dear, these next few yards are always a little rough when the horse isn't accustomed to riding on sand."

His innocuous courtesies made her flesh crawl. "William, stop it!" she cried. "Have you lost your mind entirely? Are you really the fool Uncle Sydney thinks you? They will hang you for this! They will take you back to England in chains and hang you on Executioner's Dock along with Keane and the rest of them. Did you ever once stop and think about that?"

William glanced at her owlishly from beneath a shaggy, raised eyebrow. "That rogue, Ives! He *did* tell you about seeing me with Jack, didn't he? Oh, well, it doesn't make the slightest difference now. You see . . ." he added, then seemed to change his mind about saying any more. "Edward," he spoke to one of the men behind him, "do you see the *Tiger Eye* out there in the bay? I can't make her out. I don't think Keane's returned yet. Father's not going to like that."

They had passed several of the shanties along the beach, gathering quite a crowd of boisterous followers trailing along after them, calling familiarly to William, shouting crude obscenities at Eleanor. More than one grinning fellow had put his hands on her legs and thighs as she rode by trying to ignore them. Then one, more daring than all the others, had tried to lift her bodily off the stallion. William stared down at him coldly and struck him a hard blow across the cheek with his bone-handled riding whip. The man howled like a jackal, but did not attempt to defend himself. Instead

495

he clutched his torn cheek and slunk away muttering. And Eleanor noted with icy dread in her heart how much importance William had among these outcast scum.

"Where's Jack Keane?" William demanded as they pulled up before a small but snug-looking shack. A girl in the crowd pushed her way forward and leered up at Campion's heavy-jowled face, swaying her full hips as she spoke.

"Oh, 'e wants ter see Jack Keane, do 'e, now, luv? 'E're worrit about that whorin' little sister, ain't 'e? Tell us true, naow, Miaster Campion, 'e's cum to fetch 'er back 'ome, right out of poor owld Jack's arms, eh? That fancy lydy with 'er fancy name," she snickered, looking around among her friends for approval of her daring to speak thus to William. "''es, Miss Fancy, that's a good 'un! Miss Fancy is Jack Keane's fancy woman! Be 'e wantin' to know where she's gone, eh?"

William had listened patiently to her mincing words, spiked through with unmistakable venom. Eleanor assumed at once that this girl had been Keane's woman before Fancy . . . Fancy! she thought suddenly, sickly. Oh, God, Fancy, too?

"Never mind my sister, slut. Where's Keane?" demanded William, getting off his horse.

"'Ere, inside, sleepin' . . . or was till 'e cum 'ere," the girl replied sulkily. "Jack sent Miss Fancy 'ome to 'er pa. 'ent none on yer cum acrosst 'er?"

William was about to reply when a very loud voice from inside the shack roared out, "Moira, shut your damned mouth and go away. If that's William out there, send him in to me!"

"Yes, Jack, darlin'!" replied the girl immediately. As William took Eleanor in his arms and lifted her from the stallion's back, Moira jerked her head toward her and whispered, "'E sellin' this one, too?"

He was surprisingly good-humored, for William, Eleanor thought, knowing how he loathed this kind of girl. But he merely laughed, vastly amused, and answered, "Not at any price, Moira. Keane's offered for her a dozen times himself, but Mistress Eleanor belongs to me, you see." He pushed his cousin roughly toward the doorway of the shack.

Eleanor flushed, and pushed him back as hard as she could, momentarily catching him off balance so that he nearly stumbled. Moira threw her head back and screeched with laughter, and the

496

crowd gathered about them laughed, too, with derision. William was feared here, feared, but despised by them all.

As the raw laughter rang out about the beach, the door of the shack suddenly was thrown wide open and Keane stood there, glowering. He glanced very briefly at Eleanor, some question in his dark eyes, then snapped at William, "Get her in here, Campion. Have you nothing better to do than stand about for the amusement of these dogs?" And before William could make another move, Keane took Eleanor's arm and pulled her quickly inside. William followed, leaving his own men outside, and closed the door again.

"Sit over there, girl, and keep your mouth shut," said Keane, pointing to a small wooden bed in the corner of the room. "Campion, devil take you, man, what are you doing out here? If you're after your sister you're too late. I sent her back home with a proper escort at dawn today and your father's bloody welcome to her, for she's all the profit he'll see from this last venture of ours!" He glanced at Eleanor, who had not moved an inch, and his thin mouth tightened with anger.

"Damn you, woman, do as you're told in Jack Keane's company! Why is she here, William? What new madness is this?"

Eleanor moved back, out of Keane's range of vision, but she remained on her feet, listening. William's face was a study in anger and disappointment; she saw that around Keane he cringed as he did with Sydney and when he spoke his voice, although choking with supressed rage, was servile.

"She came of her own accord; we know nothing about it. But she's seen too much and learned too much to leave just yet. She must stay here a few weeks, I'll let you know when we want her back again. What do you mean, that what you said about profit? Now, listen to me, Jack, we were depending on—"

"Blast it, man, weren't we all?" thundered Keane, pale with a thin man's consuming rage. "No use, Campion. It was almost all over when the damned Union Jack came at us with thirty-eight cannon firing down our throats. We were lucky to get away at all!"

"Then . . . the cargo? . . ." breathed William.

"Cargo? *Cargo!* Don't prattle to me about cargo when I've just finished telling you my ship's half wrecked and only the devil knows when we'll have her repaired. Why, we had to put in for shoring up for the time being at Cape Lookout, never made Cuba, never even made the Bahamas! The whole enterprise was a dead loss, sirrah, or

497

would have been without your sister's diverting company.'' Keane's smile appeared as suddenly as his rage vanished. Eleanor, momentarily forgotten by both men, shuddered.

William's shoulders slumped. He sighed, shaking his bulldog head. "Father's in a state as it is. I don't know what he'll do when he finds out about this. We have . . . we have heavy financial obligations facing us.''

Keane snorted, turning on Eleanor with an outflung hand. Finding her still standing, he studied her angry eyes and composed features for an instant, then laughed and pushed her so that she fell back upon the low bed. "Why fret, Campion? Here's your answer. Sell her to me—I'll give you a good price, you know that—and all your troubles will be at an end. I'll keep her a while . . .'' his narrowed, appraising eyes roved over her appreciatively . . .''and then I'll sell her again, somewhere in the islands, no one will ever hear of her, I promise you that! Come, what do you say, Willie-boy, eh? Two hundred pounds in gold and you can have it now. Bring that back to your father and tell him he's rid of her for good.''

William shook his head again, unable or unwilling to hide his anger now. "I've told you before, Jack, you can't have her. We need her in Charles Town all proper and legal, with the papers signed and sealed and everything done out in the open. And afterward,'' he licked his thick lips that were perpetually dry, "afterward I'll be keeping her myself a very long time.''

"I'm a patient man, Campion,'' snapped Jack Keane. "A year, two years—she's young enough to last it out and keep her looks. I'll wait that much—''

William uttered a short, grunting laugh. "Two years! Done, then, Jack, you may have her . . . for two hundred pounds gold . . . in two years. If you want her!''

"And in the meantime,'' pressed Keane, turning his back on Eleanor, apparently having lost interest, "what are we to do with the wench? Do you really trust me to keep her hidden out here with us—and not lay a hand on her?''

William stared at Keane very hard. And finally he said, "If you touch her, Captain, you'll find yourself without a place to come running back to, and you'll not be welcome in Charles Town again. The governor will have a Royal Fleet clean out Stag Run and you'll have to make your peace with Stede Bennet and the others. The Brotherhood might even decide you're no use to them anymore. No, no, you'd lose a great deal, Jack. Keep my cousin locked up here and just make sure she doesn't get loose."

Keane rubbed his chin speculatively. "How long?"

"Two or three weeks. Father will let you know."

Keane looked at Eleanor again and smiled ruefully. "Well, my girl, you've heard your cousin."

"I have," said Eleanor acidly. "You're a grand pair of animals, the two of you! So, you'll bring me back to Charles Town, will you, cousin? You'd better kill me before you do, or I'll have an interesting story to tell the Governor!"

"The Governor!" laughed William, echoed by Keane. "If you do see him, give him my best, won't you? And Father's best? He's already got the best Jack Keane has to offer and oh, how he takes it, my dear! You don't really think this arrangement of ours would have been possible without the Governor's blessing, do you?"

Eleanor stared at him aghast, her green eyes wide with horror. And she saw in his face that he told her the truth. Suddenly she felt extraordinarily tired, drained alike of energy and hope. To call herself a fool would have been a waste of what little strength she had left in her. She lowered her eyes, sickened by the triumph in William Campion's face.

There was a momentary silence in the little room, then Keane spoke up brusquely. "Done, then. We'll keep her for you. Send word when you want her back. I'll put Moira to watch her. When are you going back?"

"Right away," replied William. "As soon as we've had a meal. There's a lot to be done at home."

Still talking, the two men left the shack and Eleanor was alone. She jumped to her feet as soon as the door was closed and ran to it only to hear a heavy wooden bolt being drawn across it from the outside. She turned to the solitary window in the place, a tiny opening near the low ceiling. Too small to climb through even if it had not been cross-barred. And now, at last, alone and far from home, she realized the enormity of the disaster that had befallen her.

"Oh, God! Oh, my God!" she whispered, and pressed her fingers against her trembling lips. Whatever it was that her uncle and William planned for her in two or three weeks, could it truly be any worse than the fate she had heard her cousin and Keane discuss so casually? She would *belong* to William and then, in two years, Keane might have her, Keane could buy and sell her like a brood mare, like a slave—*if he still wanted her,* that's what William had said. And once more, barely mouthing the words, she moaned, "Oh, my God!"

"But I'll not live and let it happen!" she thought suddenly. A frenzied passion seized upon her, causing her to rush like a madwoman about the shack, tearing clothes from nails in the walls, opening and tossing out the contents of a battered sea chest, even pushing the small bed from its corner and searching beneath it. There had to be some kind of weapon in here somewhere! A man like Keane was bound to have pistols, knives, something.

But there was nothing. Eleanor did not know Jack Keane, did not realize that he would never have left her to her own devices without so much as a backward glance if there had been the most minuscule chance that she might escape or do herself harm.

When she did, at last, come to this realization, Eleanor stood very quietly leaning against the door for a long time, numbed, too long terrified to feel it now. She watched the sun's rays slanting in through the tiny window, she saw the rapid movements of insects through those rays, and through those bars, in and out, in and out so freely while she . . .

After awhile she sat upon the edge of the bed, still watching with fascination the changing light through the window as the day wore on. And it seemed to her that a much cooler breeze had begun to blow than she remembered on her ride to this cursed place. Eventually the breeze became a stiff wind that made a strange uncanny rushing sound as it broke against the bars and, divided, swooped into the room in all directions at once. And the light was going, too, much sooner than she would have thought. She laughed hollowly, shivering in the dress that earlier had seemed so warm. She had no idea how long she had been in this prison. How many hours had passed since she had ridden out to warn William and his friends of the danger awaiting them? Hard to tell how long: it might have been an hour or two, it might be almost evening by now. Even as she watched the faint light seemed to disappear altogether and a broken blackness filled the window. Then a wild dart of lightning broke the blackness, a moment later followed a tremendous thunderclap and the wind rose to a howl.

Outside she heard voices, people shouting to each other, running this way and that, panicked. More than once she heard someone say the word "hurricane." What were they doing at home right now, she tried to think. Leaving the fields, taking the animals to shelter, bolting windows and doors, looking about anxiously for missing children. Thank God the indigo is safe, she thought faintly, and then the irony of that thought struck her. What matter the indigo now? She would never live to see the good of that money, nay, she reminded herself, feeling the sorrow well up within her till she could not stand it . . . there would be no good come of that indigo money, not for her, not for Belleterre, not for anyone there. It would all belong to her family soon, the money, the land, the people. Even me, she thought grimly; even I have been evaluated, appraised, a price set on me, a bargain struck over me. So it had all been for nothing . . . and when Michael Ives came back to Carolina he would never find her, never see her again . . . never.

It was that, finally, that brought the tears and the hideous tearing pain in her chest and throat as she sobbed and screamed, not caring who heard, not realizing that the hurricane wind drowned out even the storm force of her anguish. And when she had worn herself out empty for a while of terror or regret, of sorrow or disgust, she fell asleep there, curled up at the end of the bed, with her eyes still turned in the direction of the window from which came only the maniacal voice of the storm.

4 The Search

The hurricane had approached northwest, up along the Florida coast, and thus made itself felt in Charles Town first, before continuing its whirling, slashing way farther north to the Santee River, to Stag Run and its peaceful, sheltered harbor.

So it was that Dogon had set off to find Eleanor with the onslaught of the storm at his back and lashing around him. He rode a black horse, small and thin for such a journey, a mare, but tough and hardy and intelligent. The mare would endure, like Dogon, who had endured very much and still thrived. He rode the mare wisely, forcing himself to pace her properly, neither too fast nor too slow, although caution would have prompted a more deliberate rate since it would be easy enough for the horse to slip and fall in the muddy mire the rain was rapidly making of the ground, and every instinct in the man told him that something evil, something immensely evil, had happened to Eleanor Campion, so that it was all he could do, in the beginning, to keep himself from urging the mare to go her fastest.

He knew the way to Stag Run. He had been one of those Eleanor had taken with her on that trip five years before, when she had wanted to inspect the property. There was only one way she could go, and one way she could ride back . . . if she had, indeed, turned about and come back. Through three salt flats and down to the harbor. Dogon's eyes stung from the fierce assault of the rain. Half the time he kept them closed and wondered that the mare never faltered, never seemed uncertain despite the ever-increasing darkness around them and the rain that seemed more like waves of some churning ocean than any rush of separate drops.

When they entered the forestland, it was like a place of the dead, without light or sign of life anywhere. Dogon rode on through the mud, begrudging and yet pitying each heavy, much slower step the mare had to take now and the extra time, always the time slipping away, no sight of Eleanor or the white stallion. If he had not met her by now, Dogon knew, then he would not find her on her way home.

He left the funereal depths of the forest and rode out upon the first salt marsh. Forcing his eyelids to remain open despite the driving rain, he saw with much misgiving that the marshes were filling in very quickly and soon each would be a lake of water separating the land connecting them into little islands cut off one from the other. Now he did urge the mare forward faster and faster. They passed the second marsh with water sloshing up over his feet in the stirrups. Quickly onward again and then, with a cry, Dogon pulled the mare up sharply. He squinted down into the mud and the gloom . . . he had seen something, wasn't quite sure what it was, but something with color and form not natural to this place. . . .

He walked the horse onward, a step at a time, until he saw the object again. Once a pretty, brave sight: a woman's riding hat of deep blue velvet with three pert curling feathers of green, blue and turquoise at the crown and a long winding veil of blue to match the velvet. Now it was almost covered with mud, lying forlornly, abandoned, blown several yards from where Eleanor had carelessly thrown it down, just enough color showing to be seen by the sharp eyes of a man who was looking carefully, very carefully.

Dogon spurred the mare forward once again. The third salt meadow, closest to the sea, was like a swift-moving river, yet somehow they got across it and made for the hill leading down to the harbor. Then, just as Eleanor had done hours earlier, Dogon, too, saw the many ships at anchor, saw the shanties and cabins among the trees at the beach-line, saw men and women scrambling about, shouting, pointing uselessly up at the angry sky, and Dogon turned the mare about and made for the shelter of the hill, to stop, to think, to figure out what he had just seen.

A few moments later he left the mare tethered to a sturdy tree trunk below and climbed stealthily on his hands and knees to the crest of the rounded hill. From here, wrapped about in his oilskin cape, he could lie flat on his stomach and watch what went on below him.

Thus it was that he did not hear or see William Campion and the men with him as they rode back to Charles Town against the advice of Jack Keane, who had invited them all to stay out the storm with his friends and a congenial keg of rum from Barbados. But William was hell-bent to get back to his father and tell him the bad news he had to relate. No doubt Fancy would have given Sydney all the details of the fiasco at sea, but that Eleanor was being held prisoner by Keane Fancy did not know. William knew that both she and Sydney might relish the thought. Still, they must be concerned about it. An alarm would surely be raised when she didn't return to Belleterre in a reasonable amount of time. William's usually slow mind had even arrived at a solution to that: the storm. Eleanor must simply be thought to have perished in the storm. When the time came that they would produce her for their own purposes, she would not have the chance to tell the truth, and no one would care anyway, that was the beauty of it!

So William rode on, largely ignoring the storm, while Dogon lay on his stomach on the hill above the harbor at Stag Run and kept watch for Eleanor. He was there quite a long time before his patience was rewarded. He saw someone leading the white stallion, bucking and rearing and striking out furiously with his front legs, leading the stallion into a makeshift stable of sorts where a few horses were kept for hunting.

Eleanor was down there, in one of those shacks, reasoned Dogon. He did not know who those people were or that they were pirates, but rather took it for granted that they were simply poor squatters of some sort who had given Eleanor shelter in the hurricane. He could not explain satisfactorily the ships in the harbor, but they were of no concern to him just then. Only Eleanor concerned him.

He knew better than to go riding openly into any settlement of squatters, however, so he left the mare behind and made his way on foot down the other side of the hill and, more slowly, along the line of trees that framed and concealed the peculiar houses. He managed to look in at several windows without being seen himself. In each place he saw people huddled about cold hearths, complaining about the storm, worrying about the state of the ships. Children cried; dogs wandered about, uneasy at being indoors, scratching at the closed doors. In one hut several men were drinking rum and playing cards, ignoring the foul weather altogether. Bit by bit, from little snatches of conversation he overheard, Dogon realized into whose hands Eleanor had fallen.

Hidden by the sodden darkness, he crept on from house to house, his heart hammering in his chest, wondering where she was, what they had done with her, if she was already dead. He knew better than to expect any kind of mercy from such people, who would have killed her just for the horse, or for any small piece of jewelry she might have been wearing. Dogon touched the hard bulge at his waist beneath the drugget coat and the oilskin cape. He still had the two pistols. There had never been the slightest doubt in his mind that a shot from one was meant for Sydney Campion, a shot from the other for his degenerate son. But for the time being, the Campions, *père et fils*, as Matty sometimes scornfully referred to them, would have to wait. Eleanor was here; there wasn't any place else she could be, and he was going to find her and get her safely away. And if she *were* dead... Dogon grimaced. Then someone else would have to kill the father and the son, then the two pistols would exact justice right here, as long as he might live to go on firing them.

And back behind the curve of the low-lying hill, the black mare stood patiently in the rain, waiting, enduring.

5 Captain Jack Keane

With a mighty slam the wooden door burst open and Jack Keane, much the worse for his share of the keg of rum and a bad run of luck at cards, stood drenched, in the open doorway. His black, shoulder-length hair, glistening from the rain, hung in waves on either side of his saturnine face. There was no candle or lantern lit in the shack and it was not until another bar of lightning jolted an instant of brightness into the small room that he saw Eleanor asleep at the end of his bed.

Keane had come back with the express purpose of falling asleep at once and thus passing the remaining dreary hours of the storm till it be over and work might resume upon the bowsprit of the *Tiger Eye*. Keane was tired. He had been sound asleep much earlier when William Campion had arrived, bringing with him his problems and his spirited and haughty cousin. Worrying about the ship's repairs, drinking the worry away, eventually Keane had forgotten the Campions for now.

He swayed on his feet as the wind moved him. With a curse for it and the rain and the rest of the world thrown in for good measure, he lurched unsteadily into the shack and shut the door carelessly, not bothering to bolt it from the inside as was his custom. Eleanor, inured to loud noises by the continual, monotonous pounding of the thunder, slept on, exhausted, unaware of his presence.

Keane was not so drunk, however, that he was insensible to her beauty. He had developed an obsessive lust for her, quite as strong as William's although of a somewhat different character. Upon several occasions Keane had seen her in and about Charles Town, always from a distance. Now, at long last, he had the opportunity to observe her close up. He moved with surprising stealth to where she lay and looked down at her, and a light glistened slickly in his predatory eyes.

If there had been any pity in the man, and there was not, he would have been moved now at the sight of Eleanor's wan, tearstained cheeks, the long, auburn eyelashes sweeping her white skin, the pale, slightly parted lips, the wonderful red hair dried at last into long strands of loose curls that framed her face and neck and shoulders. She lay there like a child, curled closely against herself, knees drawn up, her slender, shapely arms flung out toward the tiny, barred window through which the wind-driven rain poured into a dismal pool upon the far side of the room.

But Keane saw none of these things, or, if he did see them, they were not in the least significant to him. His eyes were fixed upon the softly stirring breast, upon the long graceful curving line effected by the turn of her back and thighs. He looked at her for several minutes and she did not stir and he grew impatient to see that admirable body assume a new position.

And then, rather suddenly Jack Keane was cold sober again, clearheaded, exhilarated, no longer bored or fretted by the storm without.

He thought about that fool, William Campion. He thought about the thousand pounds sterling he knew he could get, no questions asked, for delivering Eleanor Campion to a certain Spanish gentleman on an obscure island in the Canaries. He thought how absurd had been his own promise to leave the girl untouched and he reasoned with ease that William must have known such a ridiculous promise would never be kept. A matter of form, Keane thought, only a matter of form between two gentlemen. Campion wanted her left *unharmed, unmarked*, for the bit of nasty business yet to come in Charles Town. Injury was not Jack Keane's style with a woman, never had been, and he could not possibly conceive of the necessity of brutalizing any wench he possessed, not when, since the tender age of seven or eight, he had been the darling of every woman he wanted, beginning with his own nurse. Oh, he might *slap* a wench, once in awhile, to teach her her place, but Keane's way was the way of honey and flame and since he had, by birth at least, once been a gentleman, he well knew that ladies, like street trollops, shed their reluctance with their petticoats and ended exactly the same, on their backs.

Even William, Keane told himself now, with his usual sardonic smile, even William Campion was not so stupid as to really believe that Jack Keane could keep his hands off such a piece of goods as Eleanor for three weeks.

He watched her, smiling to himself, as he walked round the bed to his sea chest, and almost laughed aloud when he saw that she had ransacked it and left his clothing scattered about on the floor. He picked up a clean shirt, another pair of breeches . . . these for later, and kicked the rest aside, out of his way. He watched her still as he stripped off the wet vest and cambric shirt he wore, flinging them into the corner for Moira to find and launder for him.

He found he was chilled through and cursed the lack of fire, and then he did laugh aloud, thinking that in a few more minutes he would find warmth aplenty. Wearing only the tall black boots and breeches, his wide-shouldered, spare body naked to the waist, he approached Eleanor. She had moved a little and her sleep was troubled, she moaned deep in her throat and moved her hand, no more. Keane crouched beside the low bed and fixed his hands upon her shoulders, slowly turning her body about so that she was lying flat. Unconsciously she protested this intrusion and struggled faintly to regain the position she had occupied, but Keane tightened his grip upon her and pressed his bold lips against her throat. She stirred, half waking, tried to move and found she was pinned by a great weight. For half a moment she was confused and lost, then her eyes flew open, she saw the grinning face so close to her own, and she drew in a great gasp of air to scream. But Keane never gave her the opportunity to make a sound. He covered her mouth with his lips, and at the same time, in a smooth, sliding motion, his right hand moved from her shoulder to the neck of her modest gown. He pulled the cloth from her body, lifting her, holding her closely against him, and struggle as she might, she could not push him away or stop him from wrenching the tough homespun material down below her bosom. Underneath the dress she wore a plain linen camisole, sleeveless, cut low. Keane made short work of this, too, simply tearing the cloth apart. Wildly she slapped at his face, a sharp stinging blow which ended, briefly, the long well-nigh unendurable kiss. Keane caught her to him, holding her against his chest in an iron grasp, feeling the fire take hold of him as the incredible heat of her naked bosom was transmitted to his own cold skin. She twisted her head from side to side, seeking to avoid his eager mouth. Keane freed one hand and grabbed the back of her head, holding her immobile. He bent his face against her cheek and whispered something into her ear.

"No!" cried Eleanor, finding her voice at last. She pretended to weaken, to slump against Keane, her head resting for a moment on his shoulder. At once he loosened his painful grasp and laughing at the difference between her passionately uttered refusal and her sudden surrender, he laid her back upon the bed, whispering honeyed words and sensual promises such as women liked to hear. Eleanor lay there and stared at him, unflinching, apparently won over to his desires. But Keane was not surprised. He had heard many things about Eleanor Campion.

"That's better, my girl," he said at length. "Virginal modesty really doesn't become you. Your cousins have told me so much about you and those blacks of yours, oh, and that fellow, what's his name? *Ives*. How was it, having a white man after them? You'll have to tell me what you like, my love, tell me all the pretty things those Africans do for you. And what you do for them, too." While he spoke he had pulled her boots and stockings from her feet and now he said, "You do the rest, my love, I want to watch you undress. Come now, up with you, and let's have that bedraggled old gown and all those petticoats off! Tomorrow we'll find you something more becoming to wear while you're here."

He drew her to her feet before him and sat on the bed, his eyes fixed upon her body. She stood on her bare feet, trembling, trying to pull the torn pieces of her camisole back around her. Keane frowned. He reached out and slapped her hand away, then began to tear the skirt of the blue gown slowly straight down the front. His head was bent as he did so. Eleanor's eyes darted wildly about the room, looking in desperation for some means of escape, and with a final rending tear, the gown was in ruins on the floor and Keane's practiced fingers were already at work on the only petticoat she was wearing. She shuddered as he was suddenly overcome with desire and pulled her tight against him. . . .

"Don't do this!" she begged him. "Please, don't!"

Keane's dark eyes looked up at her, the smile gone. " 'Don't do this'?" he barked. "Be careful, my girl, or *this* will be the least of it!" He crushed her flesh with one hand, clawing angrily at her with his fingernails until she screamed with pain. At once he stopped. "Don't do *this*, Mistress Campion . . . why not, pray? Ives did it; only the devil knows how many others have had you, well, be fair, why not Jack Keane?" As suddenly as he had hurt her a moment before, now he gently rubbed the raw and bleeding skin . . . she had little time to recover herself, however, for he had cleverly worked his other hand up beneath her petticoat.

Maddened by this new invasion, Eleanor struck him again across the face. Driven by a fury she did not know she was capable of, she slapped him, pounded him with her fists, scratched at his eyes until with a roar of fury he pushed her away. She glanced toward the door, not knowing whether or not it was bolted or unbolted. Even as she took a few swift steps toward it, the door opened noiselessly and Dogon was standing there. Keane, rubbing his eyes, swearing he would kill her as soon as he got his hands on her again, had not yet realized anyone else was with them. Dogon held the pistols carefully beneath a fold of the oilskin cape which he had drawn up across his chest. Eleanor nearly screamed with relief at the sight of him, thinking surely he must be but one of a party of rescuers from Belleterre, but the black man swiftly put his fingers to his lips to beseech her silence, then beckoned her to come to him. Slowly, heart pounding, breath coming in unequal gasps, she moved to the doorway. Quickly Dogon pushed her behind him, out into the rain.

"Run!" he told her. "Go by the hill. My horse is there—run!"

"Who the devil is that?" shouted Keane, jumping to his feet. He stared, red-eyed, at a tall, heavyset black man who was pointing a gun at him not six feet away.

"What's this? Where's the girl?" demanded Keane, starting forward. And Dogon fired one of Michael Ives' pistols. But he was not a practiced shot, the ball went wild and struck the wall behind Keane. The Captain laughed and kept moving toward this apparently harmless madman. Outside, along the beach, caught up in the raging storm and almost lost to view, Eleanor ran with the last bit of strength remaining to her. She had heard the pistol shot; she paused, looked around, expecting to see Dogon running to join her. But the rain was torrential now, the spiral tail of the storm lashing its last few ferocious hours out upon the helpless earth beneath it, and she could not even make out the shack or any of the other huts or shanties. Even the trees were indistinct. The wind almost knocked her down. She turned again, suddenly afraid she would become so confused she would forget which way to go, and she ran on toward the hill as Dogon had told her, battling the wind with every movement of her weary body, naked and vulnerable to the sharp pelting of rain and stirred-up sand alike as each seemed to cut into her delicate skin.

Dogon prayed his second shot would not miss. As Keane came for him, mouthing raw oaths in his anger and disappointment, the black man held the other pistol steady and squeezed the trigger. There was a second bright pink flash, a smell of hell in the smothering air, smoke filling the small area, and Jack Keane staggered backward, shouting all the while, and fell to his knees, a great gaping hole in his left shoulder pouring out blood profligately.

Neighbors on either side of the shack had thought they'd heard gunfire, then dismissed it as fancy, or just more thunder. But with the second shot their doors opened and they ran outside in alarm. A tall figure in a long coat and cape over it was backing out of Jack Keane's shack, still holding the just-fired pistol. Someone spied Jack himself on his knees, clutching at his shoulder, yelling, and like mad dogs of a pack, they closed in about Dogon.

6 Through The Hurricane

Eleanor did not hear the second shot fired. She managed to reach the hill and work her way around it. She saw no horse at first, but the mare neighed loudly and close by, sensing a familiar human. Eleanor found her tethered there, soaked and trembling with cold, her big eyes rolling with terror from the night, the storm, and having been left alone so long. Eleanor patted the mare's side awkwardly, having no strength to talk above the roaring wind, and nestled as close as she could against the horse, to wait for Dogon to return. By now, dimly, she had realized he must have come for her alone. There was no army of rescuers from Belleterre or anywhere else, only faithful Dogon.

Again a measure of time elapsed, how much, how little, she never knew, while she waited, shivering, for him to come. She did not think the two of them could make it home together on the mare's back, but they would manage somehow, even if they had to walk every step of the way. Then she wondered why he was not coming and it occurred to her at last that he had not gotten away. Every instinct in her screamed that she must jump upon the horse's back and ride while she could. If Keane still lived they would pursue her. She wondered even now why they had not appeared sooner. She forced herself to creep, like an animal, on her hands and knees, around the curve of the hill again. She saw nothing, heard nothing but the wind and the rain. There were no lights visible, either aboard the ships or in the houses on the beach. There was nothing, no one.

She stood up, buffeted unmercifully by the insatiable wind, and, cupping her hands to her mouth she shouted hoarsely.

"Dogon! *Do-gon!* Where are you? Dogon!"

But there was no answer. She called his name again and then again, heedless now of who else might hear, frantic to find him and get away. A dozen times or more she cried out for Dogon until she had no voice left to make a sound. She sank down upon the soaked scrub grass, shuddering, her arms folded about her knees, her head bent in despair.

Then she heard the impatient neighing of the mare below. And she thought she must go home to Belleterre and get help. There was no other way.

She fought her way back to the mare, slipping, sliding, falling more than once in the mud. But she made it, loosened the reins and somehow pulled herself upon the animal's back. With a toss of her head, the black mare started forward, then realized her mistake and turned of her own accord and began to gallop straight back toward the salt flats, with Eleanor barely conscious, clinging to the reins.

They were dead out into the first of the newly made lakes before Eleanor realized what had happened. Suddenly the little mare was foundering frightfully, half walking, half swimming across the flooded flatland. Eleanor felt herself slipping down, slipping away into the cold wet alien darkness.

Renewed terror revived her briefly. She wound the leather reins around and around her naked body and knotted them with stiff, numb fingers. Then she collapsed across the horse's neck, her feet dangling loosely in the over-long stirrups. She dug her hands into the mare's sparse mane, trying to remember to hold on, and they rode the wild night together, how many hours, how many miles Eleanor never knew. She lost consciousness somewhere inside the vast expanse of hickory and oak forest and thus she was not aware that the hurricane had already done its worst and had left Charles Town and the river plantations far behind many hours earlier.

By three-thirty or four o'clock in the morning, the black mare was limping unsteadily along a now tranquil road leading to Belleterre. What had been a whipping nightmare of a sky tossed in the capricious claws of the hurricane was quite back to normal once more and looked down quietly scintillating with calm silken stars that never seemed to have known there had been nightmare and terror and death there at all.

Six

Trial

1 Fancy Goes Calling

Fancy had a difficult time persuading Papa that her little "adventure," as she called it, with Jack Keane, really amounted to nothing at all. In the end, however, as usual in disagreements with Fancy, Papa was convinced. Whatever Sydney Campion said about his daughter, whatever he thought privately about her escapades, Fancy was his favourite child. Sydney warned her very strictly about Keane and lectured her at length about not "mixing business with pleasure," and Fancy nodded her pretty, honey-colored head and fluttered her lashes over the huge, violet blue eyes, agreeing with every word he said until Sydney found he had nowhere else to go.

Fancy *was* contrite, that was obvious to Sydney, although he rather misread her reasons for contrition. Actually, several weeks at sea in the confines of Keane's cramped cabin on the sorely damaged *Tiger Eye* had somewhat taken the edge off her appetite for love. In the end, Keane had bored her fully as much as she had bored him. Neither of them had been particularly depressed by this fact, both being old hands at the love game and aware that this was the way things usually went. They had parted more or less friends.

Sydney was deeply relieved to hear that, until William arrived home soggy and chilled to the bone, in a thoroughly foul temper, during the middle of the hurricane. To Fancy's enormous satisfaction, when Papa heard what *William's* various pieces of news were, Papa at once exploded almost apoplectically and turned his entire attention to her brother. No money, no indigo, no telling how long before the *Tiger Eye* would be ready to return to sea . . . and Cousin Eleanor every inch the reluctant heroine straight out of a novel, being held prisoner at Stag Run!

While William coughed and sneezed and explained and explained again, while Sydney raged and roared at him for a bungling ass, Fancy once again found herself growing uncommonly bored and slipped away from the domestic hearth. She slept out the rest of the storm, spent the following day going over her considerable wardrobe with an eye to much refurbishing in the near future, and sat up half of the next night rereading an old French novel with a highly critical eye, wondering what on earth she had ever thought she might learn from it in the first place!

Thus the second morning after the hurricane, as Charles Town and the surrounding countryside laboured wearily to set things to rights again, Fancy found herself unutterably bored, bored to distraction, and dying to find something interesting to do. William and Sydney were barely speaking to each other; neither of them was speaking to her and they left quite early to go into town on business.

As the sun was high and bright and the autumn day not too cool, Fancy began to think about the only thing in the world that had not bored her: Belleterre. She hated Rogue's Fall, hated the very name of it, for it was not genteel, and it was small and mean and poorly furnished, according to her high standards. For that matter, the same could be said on the subject of furnishings about Belleterre—Fancy had said it many times, and for years and years she had dreamed lofty dreams of redecorating Eleanor's house (once Eleanor had vacated it, of course). Fancy had even extracted a promise from Sydney, given in a weak moment, that when all of this "unpleasantness" was at an end, the house at Belleterre would be hers and she would have enough money to make it over to suit herself.

Suddenly the bright thought struck Fancy that, to all intents and purposes, Cousin Eleanor could be said to have already vacated the premises. What, then, could be more delightful on such a cheery day than to ride over to Belleterre and go through the house room by room, taking all the time in the world she wanted? There were whole sections of that house Fancy had never seen, an attic reportedly filled with antique treasures, and, of course, Eleanor's estate books and accounting records. What an awful pity they had lost the indigo money, Fancy thought, to say nothing of their share of the rest of the *Sheila Deare*'s lost cargo, but Fancy believed faithfully . . . believing was the *only* thing that Fancy ever did faithfully . . . that one must look on the bright side. Soon there would be a great sale of slaves from Belleterre; Stag Run would be properly developed, planted in tobacco and rice, and that would be income they did not have to share with Jack Keane or anyone else.

Fancy dressed eagerly for her excursion in a light wool town frock of blue and yellow, topped her shining blond curls with a fetching blue bonnet and set out for Belleterre in her own little two-wheeled chaise driven by one of the Rogue's Fall stablemen. She sat upright and somewhat excited on the short ride, for she expected to find the place desolate and in chaos, all work stopped, while Eleanor's blacks sat about grieving and wondering fearfully what was to become of them. That notion pleased Fancy, entertained her all the way to Belleterre.

For once, she'd like to *see* Matty try to stop her doing as she pleased when she got there!

Fancy's chaise turned in the broad driveway. She noted with surprise that work was going on as usual. In the distance she could see work gangs of black men riding wagons pulled by mule teams back and forth from the timber stands. Children played unconcernedly. Several gardeners were picking up fallen tree limbs and other debris left in the wake of the storm. They were working on either side of the driveway. And now Fancy began to feel dreadfully uneasy, for, as she approached the house, she noticed that these men stopped what they were doing, straightened up to look at her gravely as she passed by. Her driver, quicker to pick up the unspoken feelings of these blacks, began muttering nervously to himself.

"Speak up, Joshua! What are you sayin'?" snapped Fancy, turning her head to look back. They were still standing there, watching her, not moving!

Joshua shook his head. "Somethin' wrong, miss," he blurted out under his breath. "They's somethin' real bad 'bout this place today!"

"Oh, don't be stupid, Joshua!" He said no more until they pulled up at the front entrance.

"You goin' to be long, miss?" His tone of voice clearly implied that he hoped she would *not* be long at all. Fancy informed him pertly that she would be as long as she wished. Another glance across the grounds showed her that the gardeners had gone back to their work. Bother Joshua, anyway! She ran up the front steps and opened the door without bothering to knock, then walked in blithely humming a little tune Jack Keane was fond of.

Straight down the hall she went to the closed doors of the parlor. On the other side of that room was Eleanor's little study and the account records. Without hesitation, Fancy threw open the double doors and was about to barge in when she stopped suddenly, a horrified little gasp escaping her lips.

"Eleanor!" she managed to squeak out at last, as her cousin looked at her steadfastly, neither smiling nor frowning, without expression of any kind.

A low, cozy fire crackled on the hearth. Eleanor was lying on the sofa, covered with a light quilt, a multitude of soft pillows propped behind her back. She was wearing a house robe of white and her hair was tied back simply at the neck with a length of aquamarine ribbon. She was terribly pale, Fancy saw at once, with deep shadows beneath her grave eyes and several long, raw-looking scratches on her cheeks and neck. And Matty was there, too, of course. She had been sitting on the little stool by the fire, pouring spice tea . . . the room was filled with its delicious odor . . . until Fancy's entrance. Then Matty had jumped to her feet and now stood glowering, her arms folded, protectively at Eleanor's side.

"Eleanor!" Fancy cleared her throat with difficulty and began again. "How . . . how are you, dear? My, isn't this wonderful? Isn't this a miracle from Heaven! I . . . we all thought you'd . . . you know, the storm and everything . . . we thought . . ."

"I know what you thought, Fancy!" said Eleanor at last. "Why did you come here?"

"Why? I—I—I came to find out if anyone had word of you, or if they'd found your . . . found you yet. I've been worried out of my mind, Eleanor, precious, just worried out of my mind!"

"So worried you came in humming!" This time it was Matty who spoke, her voice thick with sarcasm and hatred she did not bother to conceal.

"Eleanor, dear, forgive me. I am quite flustered, you know!" Fancy went on, deciding her best course was to try to ignore Matty. Her mind was staggered by the implications of Eleanor's reappearance. Eleanor knew all about Papa and William, of course. Fancy shuddered. But at the moment what was most important was to discover whether Eleanor realized that Fancy was a party to all their schemes and conspiracies. She was acutely aware of Eleanor's clear eyes upon her, of Eleanor waiting for her to speak. Good God, thought Fancy, never mind all that! She was desperately conscious now of Eleanor's being free and home again and quite capable of ruining the rest of the Campions beyond hope!

This thought helped rally Fancy's failing nerve and restored some of her usual audacity. She must be very careful now how she handled Eleanor if she was ever to get out of this house and back to warn her father and brother! If she could only make Eleanor believe that she had had nothing to do with any of it, knew nothing of it, was not considered smart enough or important enough to have been taken into her family's confidence. Having thus decided upon a strategy of sorts, Fancy moved a step or two farther into the room.

"Stop!" breathed Eleanor, her voice very low, throbbing with emotion. "Not another foot, Fancy, not another inch, I warn you!"

Fancy was shaking badly. Nevertheless she must try to brazen it out to the end. "Eleanor, dear, what is the matter with you? Were you hurt? Are you ill? Why are you acting so . . . so unlike yourself? Of course, you and I have had our little differences in the past, but darlin' now that you've been spared after all of us thought you were dead, surely the two of us, at least, might put our differences behind us and rejoice together at this . . ."

Eleanor was shaking her head very slowly, very deliberately and Fancy floundered and fell silent.

"It's no use, Fancy," Eleanor said coldly. "Your little pretense is unnecessary. I know all about you and Keane." She barely voiced the name. "I know about Stag Run, everything. I, too, have always been sorry for the differences between you and me, but until the other day, Fancy, I never knew that you hated me so much!"

"Hated you, Eleanor? Hated you? *Me?*" cried Fancy.

Eleanor shrugged. "You were always a part of it, weren't you? Right from the beginning. Somehow or other I'm to be gotten out of the way, legally, too, that was a nice touch! And then everything that was—is—mine would be yours. Yes, I said 'hated,' Fancy. What else could it be but hatred and jealousy that could make you consent that I be sold, sold a *slave*, I and all my friends here? Did you know that William intends to keep me about for a while, just to amuse him, and then he will sell me to Jack Keane . . . who will keep me for a while and sell me again to someone somewhere who will ask no questions, not even my name! Oh, God," Eleanor trembled uncontrollably, reached out and clasped Matty's hand. "Not even my name!" she repeated, all the strength suddenly leaving her. She fell back among the pillows, her lips white, her eyes shut. Matty put her hand most gently on her side and came toward Fancy with a light in her dark eyes that filled Fancy with horror.

"There's a man dead," said Matty. "A Belleterre man!"

"Th-there is?" whispered Fancy, backing away.

"Dogon," said Matty, "he saved her. And your friends killed him. There is blood upon your soul, girl. How you going to wash it clean again?" And then she was standing right before Fancy.

"Eleanor! Tell her to stay away from me! Eleanor, speak, hurry, before she kills me!" screamed Fancy, waving her hands ineffectually.

Eleanor's eyes opened slowly. She seemed confused for a moment. But Matty did not see this. Matty laughed, an icy, terrible laugh utterly without mirth, then raised her hand and struck Fancy hard across the face. The blow staggered Fancy and she fell back against the doorframe, still screaming, close to hysteria.

Matty was about to strike her again when Eleanor called out in a ghastly weak voice. "No, for the love of God, no, Matty! I can't bear it. Leave her alone!"

Matty lowered her hand reluctantly and stationed herself once more beside the mantel to watch Fancy with intense concentration.

"No one at Belleterre will harm you, Fancy, not today, I promise.

516

But don't come back again. And you'd better go now. You have a great deal to tell Uncle Sydney and William.''

"Yes. Yes, Eleanor, I am just leavin'!" fluttered Fancy very quickly. She turned to run down the hallway but before she could take a step, Eleanor called to her.

"Wait, Fancy. I meant to say . . . you have a great deal to tell them from *me*.''

Fancy turned back with a doomed expression. Despite what Eleanor had said, she still half believed she would not get out of the house at all. "Yes, Eleanor?" she whispered tremulously.

"Go back to Rogue's Fall, Fancy, and tell my uncle and my cousin that I am prepared to fight them, to fight all of you and whatever filthy scheme you have concocted together to destroy Belleterre!'' Eleanor, resisting Matty's strenuous attempts to keep her on the sofa, threw aside the quilt that covered her and stood up. Now she took a few faltering steps forward, seeming to gain strength as she moved.

"If they try to come here we'll fight them and whoever comes with them, tell them that, cousin! Tell them that they will never, never take what belongs to me by law from my own father. Very soon now Captain Ives will be returning to us and he will have the money and the means to expose your treachery so that even the governor must—''

"Captain *Ives?*'' Fancy broke in suddenly, the entire intimidated expression on her flushed face changing incredibly. "You did say Captain Ives, did you not, Eleanor? The same Captain Michael Ives I had the pleasure of meetin' here at Belleterre?''

Eleanor stopped, looking puzzled and impatient. But now it was Fancy's turn to move toward *her*. Fancy chose to saunter across the room and there was now a malicious smile hovering about the corners of her dainty mouth.

"Of course the same," snapped Eleanor. "And when he comes—''

"But, Eleanor, my dearest," cooed Fancy triumphantly, "poor Captain Ives will not be comin' back to Belleterre. I thought all this time you knew that!''

"What nonsense is this, Fancy?" Eleanor's eyes were dark with a gathering rage she had been surpressing the entire time Fancy had been there.

"Not nonsense, Eleanor, God's truth, that's all," answered Fancy righteously. "Why, honey, the last time I saw the Captain's ship, she was sinkin' fast off Albemarle Sound."

"*What?*" Eleanor's voice was so low Fancy saw her lips form the single word more easily than she could hear it spoken.

"And the last time I saw the *Captain*, he was quite dead, my dear. Dead and thrown overboard along with several of his crew. No, Eleanor, Michael Ives will not be comin' back to rescue you. Michael Ives is dead!"

"How do you know this?" demanded Eleanor, her eyes glazed.

"Well, it won't do any harm to have you know, I suppose," murmured Fancy, enjoying herself mightily. "I hope it won't hurt your feelin's too much to learn that when Michael sailed out of Charles Town, I was aboard the *Sheila Deare* with him. He was going to take me to Boston and then to England and even to Paris! It was such a lovely lark, just me and Michael in that little cabin of his!"

"You're lying!" cried Eleanor.

"Am I, dear?" Fancy went on. "We'll see. Well, we weren't even two days out when Jack Keane came after us. Oh, Jack was so angry with me when he found me there! Jack's a very jealous man, insanely jealous, as a matter of fact. His ship attacked Michael's ship, like two little boys playing paper boats in a bucket! They were so serious! Jack wanted the indigo, of course. He took your indigo last year, did you know that, too? Oh, Jack's a scandal! But anyway, the two of them got to fighting, you see, over me? And, well, it was terribly sad and all that, but Jack won. And poor Michael is—gone. That's all there is to it. Except . . . I saw him killed with my own eyes and I saw them throw him overboard and that is the truth, I swear it!"

Fancy's blue violet eyes were positively shining with veracity; Eleanor saw at once that Fancy spoke truly, or what she believed to be truly. And she recalled the bit of conversation between Keane and William about the ship Keane had not succeeded in taking, and the cargo that had eluded him. Little had she suspected they were talking about the *Sheila Deare*!

But she could not accept what Fancy was saying, not ever. Somehow, some way, there had to be a mistake, a lie, an accident.

"Michael never took you away with him!" Eleanor cried, seizing upon that one part of the incredible story, refusing to face the rest.

518

"Oh, but he did!" retorted Fancy.

"You lying little hypocrite! You've never told anyone the truth about anything in your whole life! What makes you think I'll believe a thing like that?"

"This." And Fancy pulled off her soft leather riding glove and held her hand up in front of Eleanor's face. She had almost forgotten about the useless little trinket! Fancy thanked her lucky stars now that she had kept it on her finger all this time, over a plain little ring that held it in place.

Eleanor stared at the dully gleaming steel of the large ring on Fancy's hand. She saw the engraved initials, worn thin, "I.C.I." very clearly. There were not two rings like that in all the world.

"Michael gave me this ring in his cabin," lied Fancy with all of the malevolence in her being. "In his bed, cousin dear. I remember I was complaining about it pressing so hard against my—"

With a shattering scream, Eleanor threw herself bodily at the younger woman, seizing Fancy by the throat in a grasp so terrible in its intensity that Fancy at once felt her air cut off. She fought back, almost strangled, taking hold of Eleanor's hair, slapping out blindly at her face, trying to reach her eyes. The world was turning black very fast, however, and a wave of nausea overcame Fancy. Her eyes went wild, her head fell back. Then, as if in a dream, she sensed other, stronger hands forcing Eleanor's fingers loose of her throat, one by one, with horrible slowness. And then Fancy was free again. She opened her eyes, rubbed her tender neck, and saw that Matty had led Eleanor away from her, Matty was whispering broken words of comfort and of warning. Fancy began to slip out of the room and suddenly Eleanor turned again and screamed at her,

"Give me that ring! Give me the ring or I'll let them kill you, I'll tell them to kill you!"

Nodding fearfully, Fancy drew the ring off, but she would not go near Eleanor again. Instead, she threw the ring with all her might across the room, heard it clink as it struck the marble mantel, and saw it drop straight down into the fire. With a smothered cry, Fancy turned on her heel and raced out of the house.

She threw herself into the chaise, screaming at Joshua to get her home, get her home fast! As the scared driver whipped the horse all the way down the drive and back on to the road, Fancy collapsed into hysterical weeping, pressing her hands to her eyes so she could not see the hostile, accusing faces of the black men of Belleterre watching her go. But even with her eyes hidden she could not shut out the immutable look of hatred she had seen in Matty's dark eyes. Oh, it would be a long time before Fancy stopped dreaming about Matty! A black woman had struck her! Never in all her life had any black dared to raise a hand to her! William was right, she sobbed, and Papa was right; she cowered in the velvet-lined chaise seat and thought, sell them all, sell them and send them far away!

2 A Waking Dream

Eleanor had not noticed Fancy's going. She seemed mesmerized as she saw the ring fall among the flames. Matty instantly pulled away the fire screen and seized the poker.

"We'll get it out, we'll find it!" she promised. But her heart sank when she could not even see the small object in there among the blackened wood and glowing embers beneath the grate. It must have gotten stuck in the middle, she saw, right where the fire was hottest and the flames highest. But Matty kept on poking and pushing the hickory logs furiously, scattering the burning particles all over the tiled hearth. The fire spat and roared back resentfully, sending up a rocket display of brilliant sparks shooting through the chimney.

Then suddenly Eleanor was on her knees before the fire, pushing Matty away. With her bare hands she pulled apart the charred, flaking kindling twigs that remained, turning over each burning log and inspecting them all minutely while the fire flickered uncertainly, broke itself into a dozen separate blazes and flared up again and again.

"Eleanor, no! Stop it, stop! Eleanor, are you mad?" screamed Matty as she tried to drag Eleanor away. But Eleanor didn't hear her voice. She did not even feel the hellish flames licking at her fingers with deadly hot tongues. She searched and searched, caring for nothing else, and all the while she kept saying, "It's mine! She lies, she lies, he never gave it to her! He loves me. I know he loves me!"

Then Matty, too, fell to her knees, tears spilling down her thin cheeks, still making ineffectual attempts to pull Eleanor away. The heat that suffused her skin was frightful. She buried her face in her hands, crying aloud to Heaven for the only help they might hope for now. And Eleanor, too, cried aloud. Matty looked at her fearfully. She was holding the steel ring in her burned hand. The ring was covered with ashes and soot. Eleanor wiped it clean with a corner of her robe, looked at it tenderly and turned it over and over, kissing it, pressing it against her cheek.

"I've found it!" she whispered in a ghastly voice Matty did not recognize. "It's all right. I've found the ring and I'll save it for Michael when he comes again!"

Only then would she allow herself to be led back to the sofa. Only then, still clutching the ring tightly in her scorched fingers, would she permit her burns to be tended. Matty opened the teapot, still half filled with cool liquid, and poured the strong tea directly over those poor burned hands.

Eleanor seemed not to notice, seemed not to feel the pain Matty knew she must be feeling. But Matty hurried about her task, pushing other, more terrifying thoughts to the back of her mind until she had applied an ointment she made herself and then bandaged the hands in gauze. The burns, luckily, were not serious and would heal in several days. She told this to Eleanor, but Eleanor did not hear her.

Eleanor lay back among her pillows, cradling the steel ring clumsily in her bandaged hands, talking ceaselessly of Michael's return.

At last Matty settled down again on the little, low stool and watched Eleanor's blank face and shocked, staring eyes. So this was what the cold autumn wind had been trying to tell her, Matty thought bleakly. And this was why she had heard the sound of the waves crashing ceaselessly, why she had not been able to remember his face or features clearly. He was dead. Michael Ives was dead, down at the bottom of the sea, lost to them all.

And we're here alone, with nothing to defend ourselves from the Campions! Matty wiped her wet eyes and shook her head as she looked at Eleanor. Better you had died in the storm, girl, she thought, oh, much, much better than to see you here like this and know what lies ahead of us now, one way or another!

The tears flowed afresh down Matty's tired, hopeless face as the fire slowly ate itself up and died away and beautiful Eleanor Campion lay in a waking dream that was not true, and the steel ring that had been from Sturbridge to Ives and back, and back again, rested against her breast far from the hand of its owner . . . yet not quite so far from the root stock of the Ives as Matty imagined or Eleanor herself yet realized.

3 Master Richards Awaited

There was no ship from Antigua that day, or even a letter from Master Richards concerning particulars of his arrival in Charles Town. Sydney and William returned to Rogue's Fall irritated and impatient but hardly disconcerted, until they encountered Fancy. Still highly agitated from her visit to Belleterre, Fancy blurted out the harsh facts about Eleanor in a voice full of woe and self-pity. As usual her personal feelings were totally disregarded once Sydney had made sure of the facts. His wrath was awesome and so all-consuming that it did not admit of fear, but William experienced a terrible jolt of panic when he heard that his cousin had gotten away from Jack Keane and especially when he heard her brave words as transmitted by Fancy. Even as Sydney cursed him for the fool he was and reminded him that Eleanor's threats were empty and useless, William could not get over a feeling of foreboding and a growing doubt that their involved plot could succeed.

Over and over again he made Fancy recall every detail of her conversation with Eleanor and then every detail of what she believed had been the fate of Michael Ives and his ship. This antagonized his father considerably. Sydney dashed off a message to the governor, asking whether there had been any news of the *Sheila Deare* since she had set sail for Boston. The message was delivered late in the evening and the messenger given strict instructions to wait for the answer.

The Governor's answer, when it came, was not entirely reassuring. It merely stated that nothing further was officially known about the bark. This was not at all unusual. News of the sinking would not ordinarily begin to circulate until the ship had been missed in her home port and other New England vessels would then spread the word from place to place. The Governor also added, in a terse little postscript, that he believed it unwise for the present to make any kind of formal inquiry about the *Sheila Deare*. Such an inquiry might draw unwelcome attention to the Governor's high office and arouse yet another public outcry against the increasing numbers of pirates and incidents of their activities in Carolina waters. . . .

"Bah!" snorted Sydney, throwing the Governor's reply to the floor. "Cowardly knave! Cur! He's glad enough to take his piece of the pie when it's sliced up!" But Sydney was satisfied with things, for the moment. William was not. Despite their hitherto comfortable arrangement with the Governor, what would they do if Eleanor should now decide to demand a meeting with him and tell him everything? What if she should be crafty enough to make sure there were officers of the General Court and Councilmen present at such a meeting? The Governor might be forced to take some adverse stand . . . at the very least the Campions would be devilishly hard put to keep it all quiet and go ahead with their plans.

William was badly shaken, what with one thing and another and being a fool to boot. Sydney was simply angry. Sydney loathed incompetence and now had had occasion to see this human frailty amply demonstrated by his own son, and by Jack Keane (he was sorely disappointed with Keane on more than one score) and even by Master Richards, who ought to have arrived when he was needed, whatever their original agreement had been.

Thus, even though he was not in the least alarmed by the turn of events, early next morning Sydney left William to wait once more at the docks in case Richards arrived that day. He himself went to the offices of his friend, the Governor, and obtained several documents signed and sealed by his friend's own hand. To be sure, these documents could not lawfully be used until the formality of the hearing at which Master Richards's testimony and evidence was to be so very essential. Still, Sydney preferred to leave nothing to chance.

He also took the opportunity to talk over certain happenings of the past several days. The Governor, like William, did not care for the way things were going. He shook his periwigged and powdered head considerably over Keane's carelessness in allowing both Eleanor's indigo cargo and then Eleanor herself to elude him.

However, reported the Governor, there was one possibly bright spot in the midst of the gloom: it had come to his attention that someone from Belleterre had come riding into town at dawn, reportedly seeking the services of a physician. One of the field hands, it was, and he had been heard to remark that Mistress Eleanor was "poorly."

Sydney could hardly have hoped for better news just then. If the girl were ill, then she would not be able to start any trouble just yet. *Time*, Sydney declared emphatically to his friend the Governor, *time* was the key to the whole thing. The Governor showed him to the door, promising to be available at short notice once Sydney was ready.

"Ah! Ready, indeed!" nodded Sydney, and went off mumbling to himself, " 'the readiness is all'!" Sydney was very fond of quoting Shakespeare and quite content to leave quoting the Scriptures to the dark master he so well emulated every day of his life.

And it would seem that Sydney Campion's unflagging trust in his rising fortunes was justified, for when he found his son a bit later on, William was in the company of a gentleman with the innocent, smooth face of a rosebud, looking to be hardly twenty, with damp, skimpy brown locks brushing across his bland brow and large, round eyes of an indeterminate, watery hue. This gentleman, carrying a locked leather case in one hand, fanning himself excessively with his hat in his other hand, was followed close behind by a black boy of perhaps eight or nine years, who stalwartly dragged along the remainder of his master's baggage.

This, then, was the long-awaited Master Richards, Christian name Robin, given him long ago by a once proud, once hopeful doting mother and never referred to anymore by anybody anywhere. Sydney, like William earlier, was momentarily taken aback by Master Richards's boyish appearance. But within moments he, too, discovered that the rosy face and round eyes were deceptive: the expression in the eyes was guarded and sly, the entire character of the features was interestingly off-balance and the manner and voice of the attorney were like nothing so much as those of a large and predatory insect. Quick and jumpy, sibilants drawn out almost unbearably, to be followed at once by long, snorelike gaping intakes of breath . . . such was what there was to be seen of Master Richards. His conversation on the pleasant journey out to Rogue's Fall demonstrated much more than passing-well his earnest preparedness for the case on hand and his entire willingness to lie, give false testimony under oath, forge records and generally make himself useful and agreeable to Sydney Campion. For once, Sydney was not disappointed in his estimation of another human being.

"Ugh! He's horrid, simply horrid, Papa!" was Fancy's private confidence to her father that same night. And Sydney smiled.

4 On Matty's Shoulders

"Has Mistress Campion suffered some great shock recently?"

The physician, a rumpled-looking tall young man named Dr. Gordon, had asked Matty this question after spending many careful moments examining Eleanor. He had noted the bruises and scratches on her skin . . . Matty told him only that Eleanor had been out in the hurricane and almost lost her life as a result.

And then, hesitating a bit, Matty added, "She has had word of a death. Someone very close, very dear."

"Ah," nodded Dr. Gordon, the sympathy in his voice matching the look of tender pity in his bright, alert grey eyes. "And she heard of this death?"

"Yesterday," replied Matty. "Doctor, how long will she be like this?"

Dr. Gordon sighed. "She is in a state of extreme shock as you can see," he explained. "I have no way of knowing whether it will be a few days or—" he noticed the fleeting expression of fear on the black woman's amazingly lovely face and wondered about it. He had been about to tell her the truth of the situation, that it was most likely hopeless and Eleanor Campion would never recover her senses. But now he only said, "It might even take a bit longer. But there is something else, something that makes the problem more complicated."

Matty hardly heard his last few words. She felt frozen, numb, positive that he was trying to be kind and therefore was not telling her the whole story. Eleanor's condition had not changed since yesterday afternoon. Matty and Ada had gotten her upstairs to bed and taken turns caring for her. But it was plain that her mind was deranged. And Matty was convinced that she would never recover. She would not want to come out of her dream-state and be forced to remember once more that Michael Ives was dead. . . .

"Yes? You said, something *else*? What else?" Matty started, realizing that the doctor had fallen silent and was looking at her peculiarly.

"She will need extraordinarily careful nursing if she's not to lose the child," he said, setting several bottles and vials of various medicines and drugs on the table near Eleanor's big bed.

Matty blinked, staring at him. "The child?"

"She's but six or seven weeks gone yet," he said very briskly. "This is always the most difficult time and now, with the additional burden of—"

"Excuse me, sir," Matty broke in, her voice shaking, "you did say she's carrying a child? But she's never said a word about it! You must be mistaken, Doctor. She would have told me."

"The signs are unmistakable to a trained eye," Dr. Gordon said a bit stiffly, instantly regretting his tone of voice. He was a rather young man and new in his profession. He was an excellent doctor but was rather unsure of that yet and anyone appearing to question what he said made him terribly nervous. "And, of course, this being a *prima partum*—a first pregnancy—she might not have realized it yet herself."

"A woman knows such things!" It was Matty's turn to speak stiffly. She, too, regretted it at once. "I'm sorry, sir," she murmured. "I am greatly concerned for her."

"Ah, of course," he said more gently. "Er, Mistress Campion is . . . when was she . . ." he struggled to be delicate but could not find the way. "Her, er, husband? Surely he was not the one who died?"

Matty's head went up proudly, her eye flashing dangerously.

"The girl's not married, Doctor, and you know that! You've been in Charles Town long enough to know about Mistress Campion. So don't you go poking your nose into things that aren't any of your business!"

Young Dr. Gordon flushed painfully and stammered, "I know. I just thought, perhaps, she had married very recently, very quietly. All I wanted to know was precisely what had caused the shock to her system. If she cannot be brought out of this, she's liable to grow weaker and weaker and slip away altogether. I had hoped her . . . the baby's father might be of some comfort to her."

Matty felt the tears start. "He was coming back to marry her," she whispered. "Killed at sea by pirates."

"God!" sighed the doctor, looking sorrowfully at his patient. Then he went away after leaving instructions for Eleanor's care with Matty. But he was sure that the next time he would be summoned to Belleterre it would be to the bedside of a dying woman. It was one of those days, growing increasingly more frequent, when Dr. Gordon wished he had chosen another field of endeavor.

Matty had no intention of calling him back again whatever the situation turned out to be. She did not trust him to keep his mouth shut and in that respect she did him a great injustice. But at the moment Matty had far more important things to worry about than a young doctor's sensibilities.

She stood for a moment by Eleanor's side in the darkened bedroom. Then she went to the windows and pulled aside the heavy drapes, letting the September afternoon sunshine fill and brighten the room. For a short while she busied herself straightening the covers, putting away clothing, inspecting the array of medicines the doctor had left. And then she sat down next to the bed and stared unflinchingly at the stark white face and lost, troubled eyes before her.

"You've got to listen to me now, girl," Matty said very firmly and a good deal more loudly than she usually spoke. "You know what that doctor said. You're going to have a baby. You're carryin' Michael Ives's child, you hear that? I *know* you hear me; something inside of you hears me, Eleanor, and I'm goin' to keep right on talking to you until you come back to us. You've got yourself something to take care of, honey, something that Captain Ives would want you to take care of. Eleanor, think about the baby! Just try to fix your mind on that baby that's coming. Please, child, we all need you; your baby needs you!"

Anxiously she scanned the girl's face for the merest sign of understanding but there was none. Eleanor murmured incoherently under her breath, tossing her head back and forth feverishly, but she did not seem to know Matty and she did not appear to have heard a word. She still clutched Michael's ring in her hand and the only time she changed at all was when anyone attempted to take the ring away from her. Matty spoke again, this time taking her cue from the ring.

"That ring, that's an Ives ring, isn't it? It doesn't really belong to you, honey. It belongs to an Ives child, the child you're carrying. You go right on taking care of that ring just like you're doing, but you've got to take care of that child, too, all the time till he's born and raised so you can give him his daddy's ring. Listen to me, now, Eleanor, listen to me, girl! You can't just go away from us like this. Oh, I know you'd like to right now; I know it hurts to come back and remember everything but you've got to do it! You've always been strong, honey, ever since you were little you've been strong and braver than anyone in this world. Well don't you see? You have got to be strong now, be brave *now,* for that baby's sake. Eleanor, are you listening to me? You've got a *reason* for goin' on now, no matter how badly you're feeling. You've got to come back to us, *now,* you've got to help watch out for Michael's little baby. Do you hear me, Eleanor? *Do* you?"

For an instant the tossing head was still and the vacant eyes seemed to focus on Matty's face. Matty held her breath and prayed very hard. And then Eleanor looked away, moaning, and resumed her senseless rambling.

Matty swallowed, forcing back sobs. She would try again later and tomorrow and the next day, however long it took. She would not give up. This was James Campion's daughter, this was James Campion's grandchild. Not to be allowed to slip away, not ever!

She closed the bedroom door behind her and went downstairs to think quietly. If only Dogon were here to talk it over with. She turned her thoughts from Dogon at once. There was no time to grieve for the dead now, not while the living—and the yet-to-be-born—required her energy and her wits. There was no one she could talk to, and she must decide quickly what would be done.

She had not for one moment forgotten the threat that Sydney Campion posed. Every instinct in her cried out that Eleanor must be gotten away from here, quickly, safely. But there was no place for her to go, no money to go with. And, Matty knew very well, if Eleanor were herself she would never agree to leave Belleterre under any circumstances.

But Eleanor was not herself now, might never be well again, and there was the child to consider. The longer Eleanor remained at Belleterre the greater the danger from Sydney loomed. And finally Matty decided the only safety lay in flight. One light carriage, traveling swiftly, could carry Eleanor north, out of Carolina, perhaps even as far as Boston and the sister of Michael Ives. Matty had heard that the sister was a rich woman. Surely she would not refuse to help the woman who was carrying her dead brother's child!

But Eleanor obviously could not travel alone. Someone would have to go with her. Matty knew she must be the one. She shook her head, trying to clear it and order her whirling thoughts. She crossed over to the window and looked out across the fields. The men were leaving work for the day, driving in the mule teams, wagons loaded down with timber. Smoke from the supper fires curled lazily out of the chimneys of the little houses. Children ran out to greet their fathers, women stood in doorways, watching the men coming, waiting with grave, worried faces. What would she tell them? The moment Eleanor left this land, all of their lives were forfeit; without Eleanor, they would be slaves again and this time it would be always. Could she go out there now, as a golden sunset swept across the evening sky, and face them all and tell them their days of freedom were over?

528

Matty shuddered and turned her back against the pretty scene framed by the window. She folded her arms against her body. How tired she was, how tired . . . already . . . and the suffering, she knew, was only beginning!

When she left the study moments later, she was dry-eyed, her jaw set and hard, her mind made up. Tomorrow morning she was taking Eleanor Campion away. Like her own child, Eleanor was, she could not love her more if she were Eleanor's mother. They had all lived in a fool's paradise the past five years; none of them was really free, not for a moment! In the north, penniless, friendless, what would *she* be, she herself, but an unwanted black animal, called free, called trash? Eleanor would never know; at least she would be spared *that*. But *she* would know, oh yes, for the rest of her life *she* would remember that she had turned her back on her own people and on all of their hopes and dreams and fled away to save one woman and one unborn child.

Matty climbed the stairs with feet that dragged on the worn carpeting, clinging to the banister as she went. For a little while she would sit with Eleanor. Later she would pack a few things. She would harness extra horses to lead behind the carriage and sell those horses one by one as they traveled. That would buy food and lodging, feed for the horses they must keep. Beyond that, and that would be early tomorrow morning, Matty had not thought, did not dare let herself think. But when she sat by Eleanor's bed once more and the golden sunset sank away into the lavender grey of cool evening, she did think at last, of Dogon. Almost, she imagined, almost she could hear his soft, firm tread on the stairs, in the hallway, even outside on the veranda, under the trees, on guard as always against an intruding, cruel, and senseless world.

Tomorrow morning, Matty thought. Tomorrow.

5 Flight Into The Nightmare

But tomorrow was today and much too late already. Matty had confided the secret to Ada. Beyond one single glance of anguished understanding, one quick clasp of hands in farewell, Ada had made no reference to the truth she had been told. She and Matty packed, dressed Eleanor, succeeded in getting her downstairs again and into the parlor. Then Ada slipped away to the coach house to get the boys to help her harness the light carriage. Two horses, Belleterre's best, would pull the carriage and its two passengers. Four other horses were harnessed on long leads behind. Ada herself drove the team up to the front door, then ran inside the house to get Eleanor, leaving her own sleepy-eyed young son in charge of the carriage.

In the dim parlor Eleanor sat unseeing, unknowing, dressed in a stylish new traveling suit Matty had made of the bright green and blue wool plaid cloth, a small matching hat with a long heavy veil upon her neatly arranged hair. Matty had wound the veil about Eleanor's face and throat . . . the fewer eyes that saw the expressionless features, the continually moving lips, the better they would be on their long journey.

Matty herself wore black, a white cotton turban covering her own head. She was Eleanor's maid and as such must look the part as much as possible. Ada looked at her with a tearful little smile, then embraced her warmly.

"Here, take this. You'll need it on the way," she said, pressing a worn shilling into Matty's palm.

"No. No, I can't," cried Matty, kissing her on the soft, plump brown cheek. "Where'd you ever get this much money?" She tried to smile.

Ada refused to take the shilling back. "Been savin' up," she said softly. "It's to help her—and the baby. If she ever wakes herself up again and knows things, Matty, tell her we all loved her, will you tell her that?"

Matty could do no more than nod, pressing her lips very tightly together to keep from crying out. Ada leaned over and placed one of Eleanor's arms abour her shoulder. Matty took the other arm to do the same, that they might lift her to her feet and outside into the waiting carriage, when suddenly the horses whinnied violently and at the same instant a loud banging was heard at the front door. Ada looked wordlessly at Matty. Carefully they positioned Eleanor as she had been. The banging became louder. Matty touched Ada's shoulder briefly and started down the hallway.

"Maybe . . . maybe it's only that doctor again," called Ada hopefully.

Matty paused and looked around. "It's not the doctor, Ada. God help us all, it's not the doctor!"

She took a very deep breath and threw open the door. A very irate gentleman was standing there, pounding the plain walnut stock of his flintlock pistol on the much-dented wood. Matty's eyes moved swiftly beyond him, to the carriage and the horses. No use, she saw at once, no use, no hope. Six mounted guards surrounded the team and the vehicle. Two guards on foot stood just behind the irate gentleman.

"Bit too quick for you, eh, Bessie?" said he with a smirk as he shouldered his way past Matty, followed closely by the two guards.

"Where's the lady of the house?" he demanded, standing uncertainly in the middle of the hallway. "Fetch her out, Bessie, fetch her out at once!"

"Beggin' your pardon, sir," stammered Matty carefully, "whom shall I say is calling?"

" 'Calling'? Listen here, Bessie, or whatever they call you, you tell Eleanor Campion that Edwin Smith, Deputy to the General Court, Colony of Carolina, is here to serve her with a warrant. Now you go and do like you're told!"

"A . . . a warrant, sir?" faltered Matty, her mind racing. "What that be? Mistress Eleanor, she'll want to know, sir!"

Smith tucked his pistol into his boot and laughed. "Never you mind, girl," he said. "Where is she? Not gone yet, I'll wager! Good thing the Governor's on his toes or we'd have had to chase after you and bring you back. Wouldn't be much left on that skinny black hide of yours time we got through with you!"

"Um, Mistress Eleanor's right here in the parlor, sir. We was just fixin' to go into Charles Town, to the doctor's house. Doctor Gordon, y'know? He's Mistress Eleanor's doctor. Mistress Eleanor, she's feelin' poorly. . . ."

Matty led the way as slowly as she could, trying to figure out what kind of a warrant the man had, how much power he actually possessed. And then they came upon Eleanor, sitting in stately fashion upon her sofa, the traveling veil gracefully draped about her, the end of it fluttering delicately in the rush of air from the open doorway.

"This be Mistress Eleanor, sir. But she's real sick, she's got to get to the doctor fast," mumbled Matty as Ada, a stricken look on her face, hovered anxiously about Eleanor.

"Mistress Campion?" shouted Smith, pulling some large white folded papers from a pocket in his greatcoat. "Mistress Campion, I am Edwin Smith, Deputy to the General Court of Carolina. I'm here to serve you with two warrants requiring your presence in Charles Town at a hearing before the Governor, the Judge of Probate, the Assessor, and the Council. The first warrant is a civil matter, concerning the illegal claim you have made regarding certain properties in the colony of Carolina. This is in the name of the complainant, Sydney Campion."

He handed Eleanor one of the folded documents. Matty was able to catch it before it fell to the floor. Smith paid no attention, nor did he seem to find it odd that Eleanor neither moved nor spoke. Matty pretended to open the paper to make it easier for Eleanor to peruse it. In reality she glanced at it quickly herself, trying to make out the legal gibberish that covered the page in a large and florid handwriting. At the bottom was the Governor's signature and seal. Smith opened the second and larger of the two documents and seemed content to hand it, too, to Matty.

"This second is a criminal matter. I have here a warrant for the immediate arrest of the woman calling herself Eleanor Campion...that is yourself, madam, and also of one black female slave known as Matty, formerly calling herself Madame de Trevois, transported from the island of Antigua. Where's that one?" he turned to Matty.

"I'm Matty, sir," she replied. Smith frowned at her, one eyebrow raised skeptically as he saw her seeming to read the writing on the two documents.

"You? Your name is Bessie, isn't it?"

"No, sir, sorry sir. I'm Matty," she answered him very, very carefully.

"Hmph! You and your lady here do like to go changing names about, don't you? Well then, why doesn't she say something? What's the matter with her, anyway?"

He approached closer to Eleanor. Quickly Matty interposed herself between them.

"Please, sir, I told you Mistress Eleanor is very sick. She probably doesn't even hear what you've been sayin' all this time. Just leave her to me, sir, I nurse her real good!"

"Get the devil out of my way, nigger!" snapped Smith impatiently. He struck Matty a quick backhanded blow across the face, and pushed her away, going straight to Eleanor. "You," he shouted, "you're to come with us at once, do you understand me?"

Eleanor made no reply. Smith pulled the long veil from her face, cursing soundly as the fragile cloth tangled in his fingers. And then he stepped back very suddenly, going quite pale.

"Here, what's this?" he demanded, turning to Matty again. "Why she's...the woman's mad! So that's what you've been

532

hiding, eh? Sick? I'll say she's sick! Sick out of her mind! Wait until Master Campion sees her! And the governor!''

He jerked his hand at the two guards, who pulled an unprotesting Eleanor to her feet and half dragged her down the hallway and out of the house. Matty wrung her hands and ground her teeth in rage. But she must keep her head, she must!

"This property is confiscated to the Crown and all Negro slaves upon this property are likewise confiscated until the matter be settled in court before the Probate Judge and His Excellency, the Governor. Come along, woman, you're to go with the other one.'' Smith shoved Matty ahead of him with a hard hand.

"If you please, sir, could I ask you one question, sir, 'cause I don't rightly understand this business no way!'' Matty whined. She saw Ada weeping and thought of pride and that this was not the time to show pride. That time would come later. Matty understood about later. She had been taken as a slave once before.

Smith snorted as if he'd never heard such an absurd thing, then he said, speaking very quickly and through his nose, "They'll tell you all you need to know at the inquiry. But you can stop right now pretending that woman is anything but what she is to you!''

"What she is?'' breathed Matty, forgetting herself enough so that she looked him straight in the eye. "What *is* she to me? What do they say she is?''

"Black bitch!'' sniffed Smith, quite put out. "Move along! It would take one of you devils to deny your own! Your daughter, Bessie or Matty or whatever you call yourself today . . . the red-haired wench is your own daughter! A fine little game the two of you have been playing all this time, dishonoring an old founding family like the Campions, coming and going as you please, telling the whole world you're all free, as good as any white man!''

Matty stood stock still in the doorway, saw them lifting Eleanor up onto one of the soldier's horses.

The man already mounted grinned, catching her and pulling her back against him, holding her to him with one big hand about her waist and the other spread across her breast. Matty saw this and screamed, forgetting everything but Eleanor in the instant. She ran from Smith and, seizing a riding whip from the seat of the forgotten carriage, she began to slash the astonished soldier with it.

"You take your dirty hands off that girl!'' Matty cried, her rage lending her a strength she had never possessed before. "Leave her alone! Don't touch her again!" She was in a condition to kill if she weren't interfered with and, at the same time, she was weeping so hard she couldn't see what she was doing.

A blow to the head knocked her reeling and the whip was snatched away from her. Smith held it and wound it about in a coil, looking at her very thoughtfully.

"You got a taste for the whip, eh, blackbird? Well, I daresay you'll get plenty of it before long." He had them take her behind one of the horses and a long leather lead was fastened securely about her wrists, then attached to the pommel of the saddle being ridden by another soldier, this one of sallow complexion and dour, down-in-the-mouth expression. He looked back at Matty and spat.

Smith remounted his own horse. "You two follow me. The rest of you close up this house, lock and bar the doors. I'm leaving men on guard at the end of the drive and I'll send the others up here to help you round up every one of those slaves. Put them into one of the barns and keep them there until the Court decides what to do with them. They give you any trouble, you quiet them down . . . but try not to kill them, will you? They're part of this property dispute and right now the Crown is responsible for them."

He raised his hand and they rode down the handsome drive, Smith, Eleanor still tightly clutched by a soldier only partly subdued by two or three misdirected whipmarks about his arms and shoulders, and finally the third horse and rider, leading Matty like an animal to market. Matty stumbled along, choking and coughing as the blood from her wounded head flowed unstaunched along her brow and down her cheek and mouth. The soldier rode just slowly enough that she was able to remain on her feet, half running, half walking. Already she could feel the sharp bits of gravel digging into her soft house shoes and there were fourteen miles yet to go.

They passed a larger mounted troop heading up toward the house, some galloping as they spread out quickly into the woodlands and pastures. Before they were out of sight of the house Matty heard shouts and gunfire and raucous laughter and shrill, terrified screams.

But none of it meant anything to her just now. The only thought that stood out distinctly in her mind was what Edwin Smith had said to her: Smith had said that Eleanor was her *daughter*! She lifted her head for a moment and looked up ahead at him. Eleanor was *her* daughter? Was that what Sydney Campion was trying to prove? Was that the terrible threat he had been holding over Eleanor's head all this time? Matty tried to follow Sydney's reasoning: Eleanor was her daughter; she had been James Campion's mistress, never his wife, and therefore Eleanor was not his legitimate heir. Was that the way it went? But, the *will*, thought Matty desperately, what about James's will? Even that firm of solicitors in England said the will was in good order. How was Sydney going to get around that? There was no way he could, no way in this world!

For a second or two she laughed at the insanity of it all, remembering James Campion and his careful, thoughtful ways, his well-thought-out will, his precisely kept records and accounts.

But then she saw in James's place the younger brother, Sydney Campion, also a careful man, also a precise man, a patient man who thought everything out, too. And she understood at last: all that was happening today, to her, to Eleanor, to all of them, had been carefully planned for long ago and none of it would have been set in motion now if Sydney was not sure, quite sure down to the finest detail, that he would win. If only Dogon had lived to kill the man and kill the son, thought Matty fiercely! She raised her arm, trying to wipe away the blood from her face. The soldier looked back again and deliberately jerked the lead line taut. Matty threw her head up and stared at him with burning eyes. He warned her not to try anything or she would be dragged all the way into Charles Town. Matty bit her lips to keep from cursing him. And then she concentrated on putting one foot ahead of the other, step after weary step in the bright hot sunlight.

Eleanor sat leaning heavily against the soldier's body, heedless of his groping fingers and his hot, foul breath in her ear. She stared ahead of her and saw, as if in a dream, the gentle slopes along the Ashley River, the brown and green reeds, the fragile ferns, the patches of dogwood and honeysuckle, poke and black gum plants ripe with autumn berries. The sky was a smooth satin blue, the early morning sun sailed bouncing along with the Ashley's current. In her hand, well concealed beneath a riding glove, she carried Michael's ring. In her body, well concealed beneath her uncomprehending, insulted flesh, she carried Michael's child. She had no thought for Belleterre. She did not look back as they left it behind them. Somewhere, just up ahead she knew, there would be Michael. She waited, knowing only that he would come. There was no need to look back, was there?

6   Justice

The hearing was held promptly the following day, not quietly and discreetly in the Governor's private offices as His Excellency himself most earnestly desired, but, at Sydney Campion's insistence, most publicly and ostentatiously in the Charles Town courthouse, which then served as the chamber in which both civil and criminal justice were administered in Carolina. Sydney wanted everyone in Charles Town to know his cause and applaud his victory when it would, in due course, be announced. He had seen to it that word reached his neighbors and old friends among the plantation owners, the tidewater wealthy, as well as the businessmen, merchants, bankers and slave dealers in town. This would be their victory as well as his own, the end of Eleanor's defiance and duplicity.

The courthouse held upward of two hundred people. Three times that many crowded about the imported marble steps before the impressive carved doors were finally thrown open at eleven. Those who could not manage to push and shove and edge their way to a seat inside did not go home as the bailiff several times instructed them, but waited instead beneath the open windows and hovered noisily about the entrance, hoping to hear the proceedings they could not watch with their own eyes.

Fancy Campion, attired in modest, clinging grey silk edged about with violet and silver lace, found herself the object of many an interested eye, the subject of more than one loudly stage-whispered conversation as she followed her brother into the courtroom and took her seat down in front beside her father at Master Richards's table.

Sydney had warned her that she might be called upon to testify. Now Fancy's emotions were at a fever pitch of anxiety as she worried about saying exactly what they wanted her to say and nothing, positively nothing, else. But, to see Fancy smiling all about her, to look at her charming little head with its chic little bonnet of violet velvet perched bravely upon the seductive honey-colored curls, to watch that little head bobbing and that dainty, silk-gloved hand waving occasionally to her friends as though she were in a box at the theater, no one in the world would have imagined that poor Fancy was quite a nervous wreck.

She dreaded courtrooms and judges and the mysterious things having to do with such dismal places and such somber people; she dreaded Papa's temper, in this matter especially, for about Eleanor, Sydney was increasingly a Tartar; she dreaded rosy-faced, bland

Master Richards to whom William had taken such an immediate liking, for whom her father had such profound respect. But Fancy had heard them going over the case after supper the night before and she had been treated to a small sample of Master Richards's courtroom talents. Remembering that, she glanced at him and, quailing, looked quickly away. More than anything else, Fancy dreaded the terrible moment when they would bring in Cousin Eleanor. She knew she must stop saying "cousin" at once, but it was such an old habit, silly old habit... would she slip up and still say "Cousin Eleanor" when she was in the witness-box? Would Papa sit there and glower at her? And Master Richards! What a melting-down she was liable to get from that buzzing, snorting, flame-tongued master of words if she did make the slightest mistake!

Fancy had heard the story going around that her cousin—that Eleanor—was mad, didn't know who she was anymore, couldn't or wouldn't speak or mind anyone, but Fancy had asserted at once that she did not believe it and would never believe it. It was just some new devious trick of Eleanor's, she had told her family several times; wait and see, Fancy predicted, Eleanor would never give up so easily... Fancy gulped hard, unable to get around the fear she had of that first moment when Eleanor should be brought before them all, and Eleanor must look out upon the unfriendly faces of her neighbors, the determined faces of her relatives, when Eleanor would look at Fancy, straight into Fancy's eyes. *I never, never knew you hated me so much!* Eleanor had looked at her then, just the other day, remembered Fancy, and oh, what a fearful look that had been! *I shall faint,* thought Fancy, *I'll never bear it, I shall faint dead away!*

The Governor and his entourage entered through the judge's doorway and His Excellency sat up on the high bench facing the assembled audience. Although he was a short, rotund man, always a bit red in the face, a bit bloodshot in the eye—due to a lifelong beef and whiskey diet—nevertheless the Governor looked rather resplendent this morning in an artfully curled white wig and flowing red court robes, his wrist and neck linen positively glittering with diamond studs, his small, dainty hands quite elegant with many jeweled rings. Fancy could not take her eyes off those jewels and, when the Governor, thirty-five years married, looked down at her from his lofty seat and solemnly winked one deeply sunken eye at her, she felt immensely cheered and resolved to look to him for comfort during the trying time ahead and perhaps even after it.

Sydney bowed slightly in His Excellency's direction and sat back confidently in his chair. Master Richards, dressed in black appropriate to the occasion, seemed even more rosy-cheeked and round-eyed in his white powdered wig, but the wig also seemed to bring out a previously unnoticeable twist of his pale lips and a consequent hoisting of his small nose and a flaring of his unsubstantial nostrils that quite complemented the always sly and shifty look in his eyes and rendered him, altogether, an apparition to be taken quite seriously, to be, in fact, feared.

Master Richards patted a huge bundle of papers on the table before him and ran over in his mind the opening remarks he intended to address to the Judge. He was the sort of fellow who never missed anything, who could never afford to miss anything and he was well pleased now that in the case at hand he had not missed anything whatever. His work was prepared, his evidence unassailable, his triumph assured. Large audiences never made him nervous, nor did the presence of important personages like the Governor. And, too, he was secure in the knowledge that it would be entirely a one-sided affair. There was no opposing attorney, no argument to be attacked and overthrown; there were no other witnesses than himself; there was no evidence in the matter other than that which he had brought with him from Antigua. And the beauty of it all was that Mistress Campion, soon to be stripped of that name forever, could not ask the court for legal assistance. Once proved the offspring of a black parent, the court had no choice but to consider her black, too, and under the law a Negro was not a person but a piece of property and, as such, obviously could not retain the services of an attorney. All in all, estimated Master Richards coolly, it shouldn't take very long.

The Judge of Probate entered at last, also magnificently arrayed in crimson and white though no match for the Governor in the way of jewels and snowy neck linen. He took his place hastily and signaled for the prisoners to be brought into court. At once every conversation ceased, every hurried whisper faded, every eye strained to look. It would have been hard to find one sympathetic soul in the entire hall or outside in the crowd. Eleanor's neighbors told themselves and each other that this is exactly where it was all leading to in the first place. Fly in the face of tradition, challenge the existing order of society and this was where it got you . . . those were the general sentiments of the onlookers. There was a great amount of self-righteous nodding of heads as the door was opened to admit the woman they could openly refer to as "that wench" and feel satisfied they had come to see it proved just so.

And yet... when Eleanor entered and they all saw her, an involuntary sigh of shocked sympathy went through the crowd. One elderly lady cried out and, shaking her head, hurried from the room with her lace-mittened hand pressed to her lips. Someone with more friends outside than inside, ran to the window and shouted: "She's in chains, Bert! You never seen the like of it!"

A general commotion arose from the people outside and the Judge demanded order instantly or the court would be cleared. So Eleanor took her place in an atmosphere of comparative silence and Matty was quickly sent in beside her. No show of sympathy touched the onlookers now, and when the black woman sat down beside Eleanor, knowing the rumor that was about to be confirmed, their hearts hardened immediately against both women.

Eleanor and Matty had spent the previous day and night locked inside a small, inadequate cell behind the courthouse. Neither of them had been given food or water. Matty's neat white turban was gone, her black dress was torn and covered with dried mud. The deep cut on her head had stopped bleeding at last, but the makeshift bandage she had tried to cover it with, a small ragged piece of her hem, was dirty and too tight and pressed painfully upon the wounded place. Matty's feet were bare. The house shoes she had been wearing had been torn to shreds long before the terrible journey into Charles Town ended. Her feet were cut and scraped, her wrists welted red, and swollen from the leather line they had bound around them. And, of course, there were the chains, two sets of chains for greater security: one about the ankles, the other a complicated affair that bound the arms behind the prisoner's back and was attached to an iron ring about the prisoner's neck. Nobody paid a great deal of attention to Matty. They were quite accustomed to seeing runaway Negroes chained this way. Fancy had no difficulty at all in meeting Matty's tired eyes. Fancy sat up straight in her chair and stared with malicious enjoyment at Matty's face and form. Never again would that woman spy on her and insult her at Belleterre! Never again would that woman be able to lift a hand to her! Matty saw the light in Fancy's eye and the tiny smile playing about her lips and looked away. No one was very interested in her.

But, to see a white woman—a woman who *looked* white, at any rate—to see a gloriously beautiful, auburn-haired, sea green-eyed, milk-skinned female chained hand and foot, that was something else entirely! They looked and looked as though they would never be done looking, and the whispers sprang up again.

At first they were so intrigued with Eleanor's chained ankles and the iron collar identical to Matty's tight about her slender neck that they did not realize Eleanor did not know where she was, or who they were, or that they were there at all. They were fascinated by the ruined bodice of the pretty green and blue plaid gown, torn by the clumsy fingers of the smith as he had put the collar on her neck. The torn cloth hung loosely over her bosom, displaying a generous portion of that lovely, full breast to the common view.

They were enthralled by her tawny hair, hanging unbound below her waist, half covering her face whenever she bent her head in discomfort as the iron ring chafed her skin and made breathing very difficult. But mainly they were confounded to look at her sitting there beside the black woman, to think that those two were mother and daughter, the same flesh, the same blood! And that was what they had come to see proved, and, of course, to watch the bringing down of the haughty, to ensure the shaming and the punishing of the proud and arrogant liar who had almost succeeded in hoodwinking them all.

William Campion, too, was enthralled at the sight of his cousin and throughout the hearing he was observed by a few to look at no one else there but Eleanor. And whatever the testimony being given, whoever happened to be speaking, William reacted to nothing but only sat hunched over in his chair at Sydney's side, watching Eleanor, once in a while rubbing his thick lips with the back of one restless hand.

It did not take very long before the audience noticed that Eleanor stared about her without blinking; her mouth was slightly parted and she appeared to be talking. At first they assumed she was talking to Matty, but they saw that, although the black woman, her *mother*, kept watching her anxiously, *she* was unaware of it; she was carrying on a conversation with some invisible being! They murmured about this, some of them, and surreptitiously made a sign against the evil eye. A few wondered why her hands were bandaged but no one questioned it seriously.

"M'lud," began Master Richards, respectfully addressing the Bench, "we have before us both civil and criminal charges which have been brought against this female, Christian name of Eleanor, and also upon the other female, we *presume* Christian name Matty. Since these two females have at times used other names which might be confusing to the issue, may I beg Your L'udship's indulgence and ask that they be addressed and spoken of under these two names, that is, Eleanor and Matty and no other?''

The Probate Judge, after glancing timidly at the Governor, replied that this would be agreeable to the Court.

"Proceed, Master Richards," he added unnecessarily, since the attorney was already picking up the first of many documents at hand.

"M'lud, if the late James Campion were here today, it is very likely that he would be charged upon this cause as well as these two women. We have proof positive that the late James Campion did willfully commit fraud against the Crown when he wrote out his last will and testament. This document, by the way, is a copy of James Campion's death certificate." Richards passed the document through several minor clerks of the court up to the Bench. "M'lud, we respect the memory of the late Royal Governor of Antigua sufficiently well to remind the Court that he wrote his will under the influence of his Negro mistress, this same Matty, for the benefit of herself and of their illegitimate daughter, this same Eleanor, who has unlawfully called herself and let herself be known as Eleanor Campion."

Richards paused and everyone looked at Eleanor, expecting her to protest. She remained oblivious to the entire hearing. But Matty had heard him well enough and understood him. It was Matty who stood up and cried out so loudly that everyone out in the street heard her,

"That's a lie! It's all lies, every word he says is a lie! She is not my daughter, although I have always loved her as dearly as if she were, but she is *not*! I have never had a child . . .''

But Master Richards was ready for her. He waved still another of his assortment of documents.

"Certificate of birth registration of a girl child, Christian name of Eleanor; mother's name: Matty; mother's condition: slave in the household of James Campion; father's name: James Campion; child's family name: *none*. Father never made lawful provision as is done in such situations to give the girl his family name, Father probably didn't know it was necessary, probably believed his will would take care of it all. But, as Your L'udship knows well, it does not, never

has, and cannot. A bastard she was born and a bastard she remains."
Master Richards smiled at the Judge and then at the Governor and
then paused once again, glancing at Matty.

"I was never James Campion's slave, never!" she cried with
parched lips, her throat dry and hoarse.

"What were you if not his slave?" demanded Master Richards.

Matty's head rose proudly. "I was his mistress, that is all."

"You were part of his household, were you not?"

"I was," said Matty.

"Were you paid wages?"

"No! It wasn't like that at all! You don't—"

"Ah!" Richards allowed a moment for his point to sink in. "Now,
as part of his household, aside from *personal* services rendered the
late Governor of Antigua, did you have any other duties?" he
inquired slyly.

"Of course I did," snapped Matty. "I looked after his daughter.
His daughter. I was in charge of the entire household. I prepared the
menus and looked after the sla—the servants, and—"

"You were about to say 'the slaves,' were you not?" pounced
Richards. "So. You looked after the slaves. What slaves? James
Campion's slaves? The father of a woman who does not believe in
slavery, who refuses to own or hold slaves on property she claims as
hers . . . do you mean to say that James Campion owned slaves?"

"Yes, yes, but you don't understand! On Antigua all blacks are
slaves!" exclaimed Matty. "James had no choice, but once he took
men and women into his home, they were never treated as slaves or
thought of as slaves. They were kindly treated and paid wages
and—"

"Just one moment," said Master Richards, drawing out the *s* in
his first word until he sounded like a snake about to strike, "one
moment, if you please! Did we, did this *court* just hear you say with
your own mouth, 'on Antigua, all blacks are slaves!' You did say
that, did you not? 'On Antigua, all blacks are slaves!' But you have
denied that *you* were a slave! You don't deny that you're black, I
suppose," he winked at the onlookers. "No, I don't rightly suppose
you could deny that. Not as some others we know have denied
it . . . and shall be proven false in this courtroom today!" And now
he glared, wide-eyed and *horribly* rosy, straight at Eleanor.

"I was not a slave on Antigua," said Matty coldly. "I was a free

542

woman. I was married to Major Eugene de Trevois, I was his widow when I met James Campion—''

"And became his mistress," inserted Richards, hissing the word until someone in the room tittered.

"Yes," replied Matty. "And when I did, James already had a daughter. Eleanor Campion, this lady here with me; Eleanor was already six years old before I ever saw James Campion. I had not even arrived on Antigua with my husband when Eleanor was born. Your certificate is false!''

"Ah! 'False'!" hissed Richards lightly. At once he placed the birth certificate upon the other side of his little table from the rest of the papers. In quick succession he picked up and waved about several other papers." We shall see what is false here. Now then, I have here, together with a sealed letter from the present Governor of Antigua attesting to their perfect reliability, *bona fide* copies of the landing papers of one Major Eugene de Trevois and wife on Antigua, noted down in the books of the customs office at St. John, also a copy of the Major's death certificate noted in the records of his Parish Church on Antigua . . . please pass these up to His L'udship . . . all of which serve to demonstrate but one point: namely that the Negro woman is lying, that she and her French husband went to Antigua several years *before* she claims, that the Major died in battle in Spain after she had left him to reside in a separate domicile and became James Campion's mistress, and that—''

"No! No, no, no! Not one word is true!" asserted Matty.

"M'lud, I have myself spoken with several prominent gentlemen of Antigua," went on Master Richards swiftly. "And they were kind enough to give me their sworn affidavits stating that they had known Governor Campion's wife, Rose Campion, that they had, in point of fact, attended her funeral. They had ample opportunity to observe the Governor and his wife prior to her death and they each told a sadly similar story with regards to that unhappy, unfruitful union. . . .''

At this point, Sydney shifted noisily in his seat and uttered a deep sigh. Master Richards paused delicately and gazed upon his client with an expression of gentlemanly sympathy.

"Much as it pains my client to reveal so publicly the intimate facts of his family history, Sydney Campion has given me permission to tell this court the truth, sparing no one living or dead, so that in the end, the ultimate truth may best be served. This is, if I may make so bold, a courageous and forthright move on the part of Master Campion and I am sure that this community, which has known and loved him and his family all these years, will appreciate the spirit with which this sacrifice of private feeling for public good has been made!''

Nothing could possibly have titillated the senses of the people in the courtroom more than this delicious hint of scandal Master Richards now trailed before their noses much as the carrot is dangled before the donkey or the rabbit before the racing hound, for exactly the same purposes, with exactly the same result.

''Madame Campion, sad to say, was not acceptable to the father of James, she having been employed in the service of a wealthy British family as Governess to their two young children. This family, of the Hereford branch of the Burlinghams, spent some little time here in Charles Town, during which stay James Campion met and lost his heart to the Governess . . . a common enough error on the part of impressionable young men, we would say, but unhappily, when James's father refused to allow such an improper union, the simple error was compounded. James Campion abandoned his father and brother, left behind his estates and responsibilities, and followed the Governess back to Antigua, where the Burlinghams were then living. And there James married the unknown girl, having no knowledge of her origins except that she was born in Ireland somewhere, having never met or communicated with anyone in her family.

''Not two years together had passed before James Campion began to bitterly regret allying his name and fortunes with a poor Irish peasant girl, to whom service with a good family had been an immeasurable step *up* in the world. Rose Campion, moreover, suffered from poor health. The climate of the islands did not agree with her. She was too delicate for childbearing. The Governor's wife, in point of fact, was unable or unwilling to render her husband proper wifely obligations and within two years of the marriage, as I have already said, James Campion was seduced by the habits of the tropics and the loose ways of the islands. He turned for his pleasures to diversions outside of his home: gaming, drinking, women . . . *black* women. . . .'' Master Richards bowed his head regretfully. Not a sound could be heard in the room. Presently he lifted his sorrowful countenance once more and continued.

''Thus it was, M'lud, that not long after their marriage, while

Madame Campion was still very much alive, Campion sought out this Negro woman you see before you and made her his mistress. Their illegitimate child was born less than a year afterward and it was only out of respect for his dying wife's wishes that James Campion did not then take his black mistress and her child into his household, did not do so, in point of fact, until several months . . . the usual decent interval . . . after his wife's funeral. This is the sad tale as it was told me by gentlemen who were there and saw what was going on. So," he summed up with a great gaping gasp of air, "every single piece of evidence, and there is evidence aplenty, points to the unmistakable conclusion that this woman, Eleanor, is this Negro's natural child and is, therefore, of mixed blood and cannot inherit under the law!"

"My God, sir!" cried Matty, thoroughly aroused to fury, "have you no shame? If you really did speak with any of James's friends on Antigua you assuredly did *not* hear such a story from them! Who are these gentlemen you say told you these lies? What are their names?"

The Judge was profoundly disturbed by Matty's continual interruptions. He began to address her very sternly, but Master Richards begged him to desist, saying that although he was under no obligation to answer the slave, he was more than glad to do so.

"I shall give you one name," he announced grandly. "You are familiar with a certain Reginald Little, gentleman of Antigua?"

Matty's face clouded over,. "Master Little?" she said uncertainly. "Yes. He was James's friend, a solicitor, retired from practice. It was Master Little who . . ." she glanced helplessly at Eleanor— "he is the man who sent me here to Eleanor."

"Ye—ss, just so!" said Master Richards. "He is the old friend who found you upon the slave block in St. John and purchased you from the slave dealer for fifty pounds! You were a slave then, bought and paid for, shipped to Carolina as a gift, the sentimental gift of an old friend honoring the memory of the dead. Would it surprise you to know that Master Little was the solicitor who helped James Campion draw up his will, who assiduously entreated James Campion *not* to enter into deliberately fraudulent statements and claims . . . entreaties which, as we know, were ignored? Master Little, though quite elderly now, has a remarkably clear mind. He is only one of the gentlemen who told me the true facts of the situation."

"Never!" muttered Matty faintly. "If he is still alive he could never have said such things, never signed his name to such statements!"

Master Richrads raised an extraordinarily thin eyebrow and began passing documents upward toward the Bench with both hands.

"The statements, M'lud, if Your L'udship would be so kind as to examine them?"

It required several minutes of careful examination of this whirlwind of documents by the Judge and the Governor himself before Master Richards could go on. The large hall was stirring with animated and sprightly conversation, which the Judge did nothing to quell. He knew very well that once Master Richards began to speak again every sound would disappear.

Matty sank down upon the hard wooden bench next to Eleanor and, trying to smother down a sob, turned to her with imploring eyes.

"Eleanor," Matty whispered as softly as she could, "child, please, you've got to answer them! I don't know what else to say. I don't know what to do! They've got all those lies written down and sealed just like they were right, but they're wrong! Eleanor, listen to me!

"Look at me, child. We're coming to the end of a long bad road and I don't know where to turn now. There's no one to speak out for you but me and to them I'm no one, I'm nothing! Honey, please, talk to them yourself, make them understand how it really was. You were always so strong, like your daddy. Oh, Eleanor, poor, poor child!"

As she spoke and received no response whatever, Matty wept and moved closer to Eleanor. Unable to reach out her hand to touch that fair, insensible face, she had to be contented with laying her head alongside Eleanor's head, resting lightly against the girl's shoulder while the tears coursed down her cheeks.

But Matty's fear and agony, the tenderness with which she touched and spoke to Eleanor, had an adverse effect upon the audience and now people pointed and spoke aloud and swore that anyone could see by just looking that they were really mother and daughter; it went beyond any kind of friendship anyone there had ever heard of, it would have been evil and unnatural if it had not been so very natural . . . to a mother, to her daughter.

Finally all of the documents were handed back to Master Richards and he was commanded to go on.

546

"Thank you, M'lud," he nodded pleasantly. Turning a look of calculated scorn full upon the two chained women, letting the onlookers see that look and ponder on it, he touched yet another set of papers, yet such was the power of his expressively passionless face that everyone in the assembly knew at once that the document at hand was of no importance, was somehow a mere bit of trivia and insignificance.

"This is, of course, James Campion's will," Master Richards tapped the pages, refused to look at them, would not put His L'udship to the trouble of looking at them. "Now, this *will,* as I have said, is nothing more or less than a fraud. James Campion was aware that he had living blood relations, close relations, here in the Carolinas when he made this will. Yet these relations, present in court today, are not mentioned in this will. No provision is made for any of them, such was the dark and baleful influence upon James's life of this Negro mistress of his.

"Somehow she prevailed upon James Campion—and in what manner I am sure the gentleman here will understand (I will not detail it before the ladies of Charles Town)—this black slave seduced James Campion to her will absolutely, without reserve, weaning him away from all consideration of his brother and that brother's children . . . to the benefit of *her* half-breed child, for the good of *her* illegitimate daughter, until she succeeded in having James make a will leaving everything he possessed to that daughter. Everything he possessed, M'lud, was *considerable.*" Master Richards lingered possessively himself over the last word, imparting to it worlds of meanings and insinuations it never had before.

"Three enormous estates in Carolina, dozens of black slaves upon those estates, buildings, furnishings, tools and supplies—a handsome fortune indeed. And for twenty years James Campion's younger brother, widowed, left with two small children to raise alone . . . without benefit of a beautiful black mistress! . . . for all those years, Sydney Campion worked diligently and devoted himself to the preservation and upkeep of those estates belonging to his missing brother. During those years, Sydney Campion's own poor resources were laid out generously in the upkeep of his brother's lands—"

" 'The upkeep'?" demanded Matty, struggling to her feet again. "When Eleanor got here those lands were falling to swamp and forest, and the only house still standing at Belleterre was in ruins.

Eleanor had to start out with nothing! He did nothing to help her, everything to hinder and discourage her!''

Matty was ignored, but the Judge did, after all, wish to inspect the infamous will, just as a matter of record. Master Richards was an officer of the court, like himself, wherever the King's Court was held and thus his word was unimpeachable.

A short time later the will, too, was handed down again and the Judge nodded gravely. The Governor exchanged approving smiles with Sydney at his choice of attorneys and William sat watching Eleanor. Master Richards gathered up his great heap of documents and put them all very neatly aside.

Sydney was then called upon to testify. He told the same story Master Richards had told, but Sydney was speaking to people who knew him and supported him. When he reached the point in his highly emotional narrative at which he confessed himself thoroughly heartbroken at the conniving and deceit of one who was, let us not forget, related to him by blood if not by affection or by law . . .

"If I had known of the girl's existence I would certainly have sent for her when James died. And despite her—background—I would have done something for her, found her a proper home, a good husband of her own kind. But that was not to be. Instead, this woman arrived here in Charles Town claiming everything, everything! She told me she was my brother's legitimate child and the sole heir to his property. I bowed out, M'lud, I simply bowed out. I offered my advice, my assistance, anything to help my brother's child, but yes, I did bow out, not wishing to let her see how deeply I felt the injustice her father had done to me and mine when he made what I *believed* to be a lawful will. Why, she even showed me a letter from a firm of attorneys in London to prove that the will was proper. What reason had I to doubt her?''

"Um,'' remarked His L'udship, leaning down with a curious gaze, "what reason *did* eventually make you doubt her?''

"I . . . I beg your pardon, M'lud?'' stammered Sydney, losing just a touch of his amazing composure.

Master Richards hissed in the general direction of the Bench and hastily came to his client's assistance.

"What His L'udship means, Master Campion, is, when did you first begin to have some concern that the woman you thought your brother's lawful child was, in point of fact, *not*?''

Sydney frowned. "She was most unlike my brother in every

548

respect. Her stubborn, fanatical insistence that the use of slave labor was evil . . . my brother never, to my certain knowledge, had the slightest objection to the use of blacks . . . and Indians, too, when you could get them . . . to do work beneath the dignity of a gentleman. But most of all I saw the deep affection between the girl and the Negro woman. I wondered at it then, and still I said nothing. But when I became aware of Eleanor's plans for the other two properties . . . one of them my own home! . . . the question presented itself to me—''

"The, uh, 'question'?" inquired the Judge, like an echo.

Sydney frowned even more. "Yes, M'lud. The question being: What kind of a woman was this? Even allowing for her peculiar upbringing in the islands, where civilization does not penetrate to the same degree as it does upon the mainland and certainly in Carolina, even allowing for a touch of the strange and exotic in her origins, I was forced to ask myself, what are we dealing with here? If this is my brother's child, what can its mother have been? Nay, but what can its mother *be*? for then I began to pay much closer attention to the relationship between those two. I watched them together, I confess it. I set my children to watch them, and all of us concluded the same thing: this was a mother, this was her child!''

"No!" Matty was heard to moan, but no one cared. It was Fancy's turn to speak at last. She was not in the least nervous anymore. She knew what she was expected to say and her silly inclination to refer to Eleanor as "cousin," though it was still technically the truth, had taken flight forever an hour or so before. Fancy's little head had been turned by Master Richards's talents and she thought, although she had once known better, that what he was saying made such great sense it *could* be true, couldn't it?

Fancy took her seat in the witness-box with a pretty show of ankle as she ascended the three small steps. She faced Master Richards with superb confidence and answered every question he put to her without one mistake.

"Oh, yes, sir," Fancy said at the end of her testimony, "I heard Eleanor say that any number of times! She told me that Matty was like a mother to her. That's what she said, 'like a mother' to her 'and more than a mother'!''

"*Like a mother. More than a mother,*" Master Richards repeated, staring ominously at Matty and Eleanor until everyone in the room had quite forgotten how many times they, too, had said such kind words about some dear family friend, some beloved aunt or relative . . . "like a mother, more than a mother" became directly an indictment and a confession of guilt.

Matty wept no more and tried no more to plead for truth. She leaned her head as far back against the wooden bench as the iron ring would allow her neck to bend, and she closed her eyes against them all; she shut out the sight of them and longed to be as Eleanor was, oblivious of them.

The end was very near. Master Richards had several points to make that required the Judge to render a decision. The remainder of the business was brought off with dispatch. In his sonorous voice Master Richards called out his various points in turn and, in turn, His L'udship responded. There was a certain sort of rhythm achieved in the interchange between attorney and Bench, a singsong tempo like the prayers and responses of minister and choir, a pulsating cadence like the tolling back and forth of some great doleful bell . . .

"She is illegitimate . . ."

"Granted."

"She is of mixed blood . . ."

"Granted."

"She cannot and has not inherited . . ."

"Granted."

"As a person of mixed blood she is considered to be Negro . . ."

"Granted."

" . . . and as a Negro, becomes, together with all other Negroes belonging to the properties now rightfully owned by Sydney Campion, part of that property to do with as Master Campion pleases . . ."

"Granted."

Now it was over. Without even knowing it, without having had the smallest chance of fighting this monstrous injustice, Eleanor was now publicly stripped of name, family, property, honor, stripped of humanity and made—a thing!

As Master Richards had known from the outset, the only point he really had to win was that Eleanor was Matty's child and illegitimate. Once the Bench had accepted that, the rest followed as a matter of course. It ended very quietly. Matty had kept still at last. People rose to their feet when the Judge left and when the Governor left, but they milled around feeling vaguely dissatisfied. They did hurry over to congratulate Sydney and his family, of course, and they managed to work up a respectable air of victory befitting the day, for a short time at least. But Eleanor had been a great disappointment to them. They all knew of her fiery temper and outspoken manner. They had looked forward to a furious tirade from her. Now she was disposed of. She and Matty were led away out of their sight. From now on the two of them no longer really existed. One might always speculate about what would become of them. What would Sydney do now? And did you *see* the way the Governor kept ogling Fancy Campion through it all? . . . with such questions left for discussion over dinner and for days to come, the crowd eventually broke up and went their separate ways.

7 Orders

"I want them all brought into town tomorrow," William was saying to the Captain of Foot. William had left his father's side and slipped quickly away to the fort over Charles Town harbor to make his arrangements.

"Shouldn't your own people be transporting them slaves, Mister Campion?" drawled the Captain as he combed his sparse mustache with his fingernails.

"Don't be impertinent, sir!" snapped William peevishly. "It is your place to turn our property over to us when we stipulate, at the place and at the time we stipulate. That's the responsibility of the Crown, Captain."

"Oh, Lord!" sighed the Captain and removed his feet from the table at which he had been eating a bite of cold supper.

William's eyes bulged unpleasantly.

"Oh, all right, Master Campion. In town, you say? Where in town?"

"Graham's, the holding pens behind the wharf. Graham will be expecting you in the morning. Don't lose any of them, Captain, I wouldn't want to have to bring suit for damages against the Crown."

The Captain squinted up at William's burly form and merely jerked his chin once. It was not worth arguing over. Campion would find that a bit of damage had already been done by a few overzealous soldiers on guard at Belleterre.

"Oh, by the way, sir, them two females. Do you want them taken to Graham's, too?"

William, on his way to the door, glanced back. "Oh, yes," he said. "Absolutely, Captain. They must go to Graham's like the rest."

"Very well. Say, you wouldn't happen to know, would you, what kind of price you'll be asking for the red-haired one? Wouldn't mind havin' a taste of that myself, eh?''

"She is not for sale, Captain," replied William frigidly.

The Captain blinked and scratched his mustache out of order again. "Well, I say, if you're not goin' to sell her, why the devil do you want her at Graham's, eh?"

But William Campion was gone and it was none of the Captain's bloody business anyway, as he reminded himself, settling back to his supper.

8 Under The Protection Of The Crown

Supper of a sort was served to Eleanor and Matty, too, that evening. Tasteless hard corn bread and precious little of it, a cup each of soggy, saltless rice, a pint each of lukewarm water. Slave fare. Matty fought down the impulse to throw these slops into the face of the soldier who had brought it to their cell. She had not eaten in nearly three days. She'd better eat something now.

She knew enough not to gulp the food down quickly; on an empty stomach it would only sicken her and leave her emptier than before. She took her ration and sat down on the floor, which was covered with ancient, moldy straw, forcing herself to chew slowly. They had unchained her arms for the night, but the iron ring remained on her neck. She was utterly exhausted, her strength nearly gone. She looked over at Eleanor, who sat very still in the corner, her food untouched.

"You've got to eat," said Matty. Eleanor did not move. Matty looked away, sighing. If only there was someone she could talk to! Someone who would listen and understand her need to think aloud now. What was to become of them? Last night they'd been kept in a smaller cell adjacent to the courthouse. Now they had been brought to the fortress. What of tomorrow? Would they be separated from each other? Matty thought it likely, but they must not take her away from Eleanor, not now, not yet! She would have to find an opportunity to tell them about Eleanor's condition. Perhaps they would allow her to care for the girl, at least until her child was delivered.

Matty put down her empty tin plate and looked wearily around the dusky cell. The last light of evening, golden and red and violet, sped past their tiny barred window set high up in the wall. She could hear the surf beating against the concrete and shell foundations of the

552

fortress, like a gigantic, mindless drum forever beating time that had no meaning for someone chained in a cell.

Eleanor was silent now. Her lips moved no longer; not the faintest whisper of a sound escaped her. Matty crept over to her, dipped a torn piece of her dress into the water and gently sponged the girl's face. She got her to swallow a bit of water, but she could not eat. She was oblivious to Matty's frantic cajoling. There was no need to worry about her or about the child, thought Matty grimly. They would both be dead long before the time came for the birth.

Matty gently pushed Eleanor back upon the foul straw and told her to go to sleep. Did she really sleep? Matty wondered. She saw Eleanor's eyes close, heard her breathing gradually grow slower and more shallow, but did she sleep in the state she was in? Did she dream?

Matty lay down nearby, thinking about the day that had gone and the day yet to come. No one disturbed them. They were under the protection of the Crown. They were safe, for the time being. Matty smiled a bitter smile and refused to think about James Campion this once. But her resolve was a trap. She dreamed about James instead.

Eleanor's eyes opened. Faint light flickered down to her from a high, barred window. Something fearful in that made her tremble for a moment. But, whatever the memory was it went away without revealing itself, like a shadow passing into darkness and disappearing.

A sea breeze was blowing steadily, its fresh tart scent reaching down even into this squalid cell. Something else stirred within her, something to do with the sea, vague and formless but not shadowy this, oh no, this was all light and loveliness. What was it? Her cramped fingers moved a little. Beneath the bandages she felt the ring, safe and hidden, under her protection. She brought her hand to her mouth and kissed the ring, unconscious of what she did. The name "Michael" passed into her mind. All was well, Michael. She closed her eyes again and soon she was asleep, holding the old ring close to her heart. So many dreams had been dreamed upon that ring one might have lingered about it to whisper comfort to her troubled mind. But even in sleep her wary being guarded her well from remembrance. She did not dream or even hear the murmured memory of a dream.

Seven

"The Iron Collar"

1 Aboard The *Deidre*

More than two thousand miles away to the southeast, a sleek three-masted sloop raised anchor and slipped away with the night tide, her sails full atilt from bow to stern to catch the strong, easterly-blowing trade winds off the Atlantic. A sullen smoke grey fog rushed along the surface of the sea, surrounding the sloop like a cloud between it and the clear black sky above and the transparent blue black water below.

The sloop *Deirdre* hastened north from the Leeward island of Antigua, bound for Charles Town, two weeks more if the wind held true and there was no new hurricane in this, the heart of the hurricane season.

The *Deirde's* masts and yards were outlined red, green, white and amber in the mist with winking, swaying oil lamps. The entire ship was boldly lit up for safe running through jagged rocks and reefs and treacherous whirlpools that made this nightmare passage more dangerous than the Atlantic crossing. The crew was standing double watches, would go on doing so until they reached port. They were a taciturn lot, most of them, with little enough to say to those among them who had not sailed with them before. They did not complain about the extra duty or the lack of sleep or the immoderate haste with which they had sailed south to Antigua and now were heading back again with even greater urgency. They did not keep their careful watch for pirates, although these were pirate waters. For the sloop, only two years old and Boston-built, was faster than most ships afloat and could easily outrun any privateer. The *Deirdre's* crew kept their watch for the narrow channel passages of deep, clean water that would get them safely through or around all obstacles in their path. The Captain of the *Deirdre* remained on deck with his men twenty hours out of the twenty-four, marking out the safe passages on his charts, staring impatiently through the persistent fog, or watching, tight-lipped, the slightest slackening of the sails.

The Captain, too, had not much to say except to issue necessary orders. Men who had been to sea with him before understood his moody silences as well as they sympathized with the icy anger in his bright blue eyes. Captain Ives bore upon his pale brow a raw new scar where murdering pirates had struck and almost killed him, but otherwise he was well and strong, filled with a nervous energy that showed itself in his restless quick pacing about the deck and the unconscious habit he had recently acquired of striking his clenched fist hard against his thigh as he paced.

Mister Rainey, his old mate, who had saved his life off Albemarle, was with him for this one last voyage. When they had finally come limping into Boston Harbor on the *Sheila Deare,* weeks late and given up for lost, Mister Rainey delivered Michael Ives to his sister's house and, next day, had paid the money down for the little grog shop he had always wanted. Life had handed up one great miracle in all of Mr. Rainey's long experience with the sea. There would be no other. Mister Rainey was through with the sea now. He had defied a Royal Navy Commander to force the sea to give back Michael Ives. He had carried Michael home again and sat by his side praying every mile of the way up the coast.

For days Michael was unconscious, close to death, unable to speak coherently or tell them how he had managed to cling to life until they had found him. And then the story came, bit by bit, slowly, painfully.

He had been unconscious as his inert body entered the sea. Of what occurred after he had been struck on the head he had no memory, not until the shock of the cold water had revived him and he found himself dazed, groggy, in fearful pain, fighting instinctively to stay afloat. For a long time, as he choked the sea water from his lungs and struggled against the pounding of the waves, he had no clear notion as to where he was or what was going on around him. He swam weakly, seizing hold of the tangled wreckage of fallen shrouds and spars and lines, continually dashed and pounded by the heavy swell. He tried unsuccessfully to pull himself up but he had not the strength. He kept lapsing back into unconsciousness, only to be revived again and again and find himself in the same desperate situation, each time a bit weaker and more despairing. He saw the approach of the Royal Navy ship of the line. It seemed like no time at all until Keane pulled away and fled for his life. Once again Michael had attempted to climb back aboard the *Sheila Deare*. He had tried to shout and get the attention of his crew. But those who were still able crowded about the opposite side of the deck, intent upon watching the pursuit of the pirate ship. Nobody heard his ever-more feeble cries for help.

At last, feeling that he was near the end, Michael had managed to enmesh himself in some of the tangled rigging that floated out from the ship. He lost consciousness again and thus did not know of Mr. Rainey's fanatical insistence upon instituting a search for the *Sheila Deare*'s lost captain. Boats were sent out to row about the immediate vicinity and it was one of these boats which came upon him at last. Men on deck, working at hauling in what rigging could be salvaged, cutting away what could not, had spotted something caught in the ruined shrouds. A shout went up, Mr. Rainey heard it and urged the boat crews on . . . and they found Michael, senseless, close to death.

When he awoke fully at last, when he remembered everything he became like a raving madman. In and out of his nightmare world of pain and weakness, asleep or awake from then on, memory tormented him. A thousand times he asked what day it was, what time it was, and when he was answered he would groan and struggle to get up on his feet. He had some wild idea of turning the *Sheila Deare* about and making for Antigua (Mister Rainey did not understand about Antigua until much later).

As for turning the ship about, her mainmast was gone, her quarterdeck a gaping hole, half of her crew was dead or badly wounded. It was a wonder of the world she had not gone down at Albemarle. Mister Rainey guided the poor old *Sheila Deare* into her home port and cursed the malice of the sea as fervently as he prayed to keep the ship afloat and to restore Michael Ives to himself again. And Mister Rainey had been persuaded to make one final voyage only after Michael had told him the whole story about Eleanor Campion. He would give much, would Mister Rainey, to see Michael Ives happy and at home somewhere away from the mindless sea.

At eleven this night, with Antigua's high volcanic cones and perilous coral reefs well behind, Michael Ives stood on deck intently watching for the lights of tiny Anguilla to appear port side in the fog. Here the *Deirdre* would turn west, then due north into an empty corridor of ocean, swinging wide about to avoid the Bahamas altogether. It was a harder way to go, straight out into the unpredictable Atlantic, much harder than simply huddling close inshore about Hispaniola and Cuba, sheltered from the cutting winds and raging swells that claimed so many ships each year. But Michael's mind was fixed on what might even now be happening at Charles Town; he had no time now for another encounter with the Brotherhood who ruled those warm, safe waters. One day he would catch up with Jack Keane again, of this he had no doubt, but he had not chosen the company's swiftest ship and risked his own life and the lives of his men on this desperate journey to throw it all away for a battle that would wait. Not when he had searched deeply in his own heart for the truth and found it was there all the time: He loved Eleanor Campion with every particle of his being and nothing in Heaven or on Earth could ever change him. . . .

2 The Ring Is Gone

"Once I knew that, Kate," he had told his sister, "I knew everything I needed. The whole time we were coming home I thought I must go mad with wondering and doubting. Mister Rainey says they had to tie me into my bunk when the fever took hold and then I would shout at him and curse him and curse Fancy Campion . . . all of them, all of them!"

And Katherine had listened to him speak on and on about Eleanor, about nothing else save Eleanor and a wondrous bit of land called Belleterre.

Then Katherine, smiling, only a hint of a tear in her steady grey eyes, had said, "Twas worth every bit of the pain, Michael mine, and all of the suffering, if you learned that you loved her at last, truly and completely. Ah, what a girl she must be, this Eleanor of yours, that she has had the power to put such a look into those sorrowful eyes of yours! God bless her and keep her safe from harm till you return to her, my dear. I didn't know you when you were a very small boy, but Willy and Aunt Helene told me many and many a time what a happy little fellow you once were, always laughing and playing and with such a light, I believe, as I'm seeing in your eyes this minute. I've only known the old, unhappy look of you, for so long now that I thought it would last forever and I'd die without ever seeing you at peace with yourself."

Michael had taken her hand between his two and bent his bandaged head to kiss her fingers.

"It was never you," he said quietly. "You know that, don't you, Kate? It was always myself I blamed . . . and still do blame . . . for our mother's death. . . ."

Katherine gasped, wondering that he could speak of Sheila now so simply, so easily, after all the many years of silent anger and grief.

"Forget, Michael," she said firmly. "Forget that now. And forgive. You must learn to forgive that little, frightened child that you were that day. Forgive him and let him go in peace, Michael. For if you don't forgive that child that lives on in you, how shall you ever learn to love and forgive a child of your own? But I think Eleanor will teach you about that," she added tenderly.

During the time he was recuperating and gaining back his strength she never once mentioned the old steel ring, but the day did come when he caught her looking at his hand with a peculiar, strained expression on her face and he knew she longed to ask him about the ring.

"I'm afraid it's gone, my dear," he told her ruefully. "Mister Rainey tells me that Fancy took it from me before they threw me over the side. I think it's gone for good. I'd give anything in the world not to have lost it, Kate, believe me. Strange, you know, I'd come to feel quite good about wearing it. I told Eleanor about it, what it's come to mean to all of us . . ."

Katherine stifled a sob and shook her head impatiently to drive away the tears that had sprung involuntarily to her eyes.

"I had hoped you'd left it with Eleanor," she said. "You'll be wanting it one day for your own child. Maybe somehow you could get it back from her cousin, buy it with gold if you must."

"You don't know Fancy, my dear!" he replied bitterly. "She took it for spite and she'll keep it—or throw it away—for the same reason. No, I think I must find another ring for *my* son . . . if we ever do have a child," he concluded, his face clouding over as he remembered how he had left Eleanor with her love for him shining in her green eyes and her refusal to marry him fresh on her lips.

But Katherine did not know that part, of course. "*If* you have a child," she repeated slowly, looking troubled. "Michael, the . . . the things Fancy Campion said to you . . . about Eleanor . . . you would never let *that* keep you from having children?"

"What? That Eleanor may be of mixed parentage? That we might have a black child someday?'' His voice was sharp with anger and pain, his tone caustic, his glance dark. "I've thought of it a hundred times. I don't know whether Fancy's story is true or false and I don't give a damn, Katherine! It's Eleanor I love and if God ever blessed us with a child, it would be *her* child—how could I not love it?''

Then Katherine had looked at him a long while and kissed him.

"You *have* found what you were looking for at last," she said rapturously. "Thank God! It's all right now; everything will be all right now!''

All right now . . . all right now . . . Katherine's words still whispered hope to him even in this most dismal of nights with the fog obscuring the face of heaven itself and the sloop feeling her way warily among the narrow channels north. *All right now.* But it was not all right, nothing was all right, not knowing as he did that Master Richards, Sydney Campion's attorney, had already left for Charles Town two weeks before . . .

"Two weeks yesterday, Captain Ives," he heard once more the light, agitated voice of Ellen Fletcher, Eleanor's friend on Antigua. "I wrote Eleanor again, of course, as soon as I found that my fears of him were unhappily true. But I don't know that she's had time to receive my last letter, so she had no way of knowing what that dreadful man will do. And it's all made up out of whole-cloth, every bit of it! Friends of mine have taken the trouble of making inquiries and now they've finished, why, it's appalling what they've discovered!''

Michael had sat on the edge of a pretty cream-colored sofa in Ellen Fletcher's morning room, sipping tea from a fragile china cup and trying desperately to restrain himself from running out of the house and back to the Antigua docks where the *Deirdre* had just dropped anchor two hours earlier. He had promised Eleanor he'd be back in six weeks or less. It was over two months now and he was still two thousand miles from Charles Town . . . and Ellen Fletcher had just told him the one thing he dreaded most to hear. By now Richards would have reached his destination and Sydney would have begun his action against Eleanor. He could not delay a moment more than absolutely necessary on Antigua and yet he had to hear Ellen out; he had to go back to Charles Town armed with the truth, whatever that truth was.

"Why no one in St. John had the least idea of what that young man was," Ellen was saying. "A scoundrel from the start, that's what we discovered. He's not even a qualified attorney. He was only a law student at Cambridge. He was caught stealing books from the school library and selling them in London, then gambling away the money he'd got in the book shops! He was *transported*, Captain, transported and no return! Nothing but a common criminal. He played at dice and cards as though he were still a gentleman on the voyage over and won enough money from the ship's officers and some of the passengers to pay for good lodgings and clothing and eventually to set himself up in a little law office. You've no idea, Captain Ives, just how difficult it was to find all of this out! The man's ingratiated himself everywhere, made himself invaluable in the right places. It's shocking, positively shocking!''

Michael put down his teacup and urged Mistress Fletcher to tell him everything as quickly as she could. And when she had finished her incredible tale, he asked her to write it out and sign it and have her friends sign it, too. He would be back to pick it up before he left Antigua.

Then he went away and began a painstaking search that took him from the town of St. John to several sugar and banana plantations on the other side of the island, and then back to town again with a set of written statements from James Campion's old friends, statements telling a vastly different story from the one Master Richards was telling in Charles Town. He also had a long list of places and people to visit in St. John and he began to accumulate as many signed and sealed documents as Master Richards was even then using to impress the court and the Governor in Carolina. Nor was Michael done yet.

He stopped at the customs office and looked into the parish church where Matty's French husband had attended Mass every Sunday. He found the old gentleman, Reginald Little, who had helped James Campion draw up his will. He stopped at the vestry of the church where Eleanor had been christened and had a long talk with the sexton who kept the records. He looked in at private homes and public offices, at taverns and gaming rooms and brothels.

He found himself standing atop a little green hillside overlooking the sea and he knelt by the grave of Eleanor's mother and read aloud the inscription her heartbroken husband, James, had put upon her marble tombstone, surmounted by a wise and smiling guardian angel with outstretched, compassionate arms:

Here lies Rose McKenna Campion of County Kerry, Ireland Born June 11, 1673. Died April 4, 1697, Age 24, of Yellow Fever.

Beloved Wife of James Campion, Governor of Antigua
Angelic Mother of Eleanor Campion, Age 2 years.
Beauty, be thou remembered,
Love and wisdom learned we of thee
Gone to join the hosts of Heaven
Wait a while in Paradise for me.

" 'Beauty, be thou remembered!' " Michael repeated under his breath, copying down the words and dates to take with him. He said a prayer for the woman buried there and, plucking a small wild flower from the side of the grave, he charged her immortal soul to be mindful now of the daughter she had left behind. He placed the flower carefully wrapped in a piece of paper inside his breast pocket and went down once more into St. John.

This time he ignored the fine big homes and stately streets of the town and hurried off into the small, crowded, dirty winding ways where the poor lived and where freed men and women stayed who had nowhere else to go, where newly arrived transported prisoners who had bought their freedom had lodgings at sixpence a night.

Here he found a man who knew Master Richards, who had come over from England on the same ship with him and who, yes, once in a great while, did a bit of business with the attorney. What kind of business, Michael demanded, having already been told what kind of business from somebody else—*legal* business, claimed the man, not looking Michael in the eye.

"And *you?* Why were *you* transported? What was *your* crime?" persisted Michael, shifting suddenly to another tack. And the answer from the surly fellow's lips, the answer that sent Michael at last to the office of the Governor of Antigua with the whole terrible story . . .

"Forgery," mumbled the man who knew Master Richards. "They sent me over for forgin' passports and the like. See 'ere, lookit wha' they done t'me. Ain't tha' ruddy gorgeous?"

He held up his right hand and Michael stared, then turned his head away. The thumb and forefinger had been cut off and in the center of the dirt-encrusted palm had been branded the letter *F* with an iron large enough to burn it in from the bottom of the fingers down to the beginning of the wrist.

"But surely you could not continue your usual . . . business . . . not with your hand like that?" Michael put it to him.

The forger laughed, greatly amused. He had been promised

immunity from punishment if he repeated his story to the Governor and if he told only the strictest truth. And he liked to brag of himself.

"Wha? Cap'n, that 'ere? Tha' don't stop *me*, it don't! I'm just as good wi' me left 'and as me right, summat better mayhap! Master Richards, 'e knowed tha'. Wait, I'll show yer. Gov'ner Able, lookit this—naow, ain't tha' your own signature just like you signs all them fine proclamations and sich?"

He seized a pen from the Governor's desk, dipped it into the ink, and scribbled hurriedly on a piece of paper, then handed the paper over with another laugh. Governor Able looked down and saw his own name written there, just as he himself wrote it every day of his life. He put the paper aside and exchanged a look with Michael.

"Pray God we are not too late, sir!" he exclaimed, and, taking up a fresh pen and clean paper, he began to write a long letter.

It was that same night that Michael Ives set sail from Antigua, hurrying north to save Eleanor as fast as his sister's fastest ship, and his love, could take him. And the same sea that upheld his ship and drove it skimming and plunging over its surface, was the sea which pounded ceaselessly upon the fortress walls in Charles Town where Eleanor lay lost in her strange double-sleep, around her slender neck the heavy iron collar of a slave.

3 Find A Way!

Graham's Wharf was a lively, bustling place at the very center of the shipping trade buildings in Charles Town. It belonged to old Arthur Graham's eldest son, Nathanial, now, but the old man had built it himself; he had built a whole complex of structures to accommodate his flourishing business. Behind the wharf—the largest wharf in the city in those days—Arthur's first little office still stood, a modest one-room headquarters for the vast enterprise that had made the Graham family one of the foremost families in the colony. Nathanial kept the small structure for sentimental reasons and it was quite an attraction to visitors. But immediately behind it, and stretching quite a distance on either side, were the impressive buildings in which Arthur's four sons labored to be worthy of their eminent deceased parent and to enlarge and oversee the still-growing and even more abundantly thriving slave business.

The offices were to the left of the wharf as one sailed into the harbor, and the various attendant facilities for receiving, holding and selling the slaves were visible to the right. Upon the wharf itself stood the auction block, a fairly large rectangle of wood construction, raised up several feet for the purpose of giving buyers and dealers and onlookers a clear, unobstructed view of the merchandise. Several upright stakes with ancient, rusted chains and cuffs attached to them were built into the block; these were used mainly for exhibiting male slaves not quite broken to the whip or to the idea of slavery who might attempt to break free through the crowd gathered about. Occasionally the stakes were also available for public punishment of recalcitrant slaves, the disobedient, the unwilling or rebellious, and the habitual runaways. Sometimes, in very serious cases, the public punishment became public execution in the form of hanging, burning to death, or whipping. A slave who killed another slave was usually hanged and quartered; a slave who killed his master or any white person was liable to be mutilated in a number of ways and then burned alive.

But such spectacles were not usually a part of the scene at Graham's Establishment; generally punishments were meted out at the fortress or at Charles Town square. Graham's imported nearly a thousand black slaves from the coast of Guinea each year and even with the number imported by other merchants there were never enough Negroes available to satisfy the needs of the colony. Many buyers came seventy miles or more to purchase labor for their houses and plantations and so keen was the competition for the best of the blacks that gentlemen were known to leap down from their carriages and come to blows when they were outbid by another. Prices were as high as the merchants wished them to be and it was not unusual that a full-grown young black man sold for three hundred pounds. The money paid out for the rare beautiful female had several times gone above five hundred.

On the morning following the court hearing, soldiers of the Crown marched Eleanor and Matty from the fortress through the streets of Charles Town to Graham's Wharf as they had been instructed by William Campion. The two women were chained as the day before and, for an additional precaution, an extremely heavy iron chain full three times the thickness of the other chains, was now fastened to their collars so that they were linked together and forced to walk very close, one behind the other, with a soldier before them and one behind, and one at either side. The Captain of Foot had left hours before to gather up the rest of the Belleterre Negroes and bring them into town.

It had turned October and although the sun was brightly shining, there was a crisp, chilling wind blowing in off the water. Matty shivered continually and tried to hurry along, but they were surrounded by jostling, jeering crowds who blocked the way very often and had to be warned over and over again by the soldiers. Eleanor seemed not to notice the cold air or the crowds. Her face very white, a slight perspiration upon her forehead, she hobbled along with the shackles on her ankles, her eyes fixed upon the harbor they were finally approaching.

Matty had not, of course, known where they were being taken; now, when she saw the streets they turned into and the harbor in front of them she realized at last what the Campions meant to do about Eleanor. They were quite in earnest, she thought, they were really going to sell their own flesh and blood for a slave! She was annoyed with herself then, that any small part of her should have been surprised at the limitless cruelty of those people . . . didn't she know them well enough to know they would do their utmost to hurt and destroy Eleanor?

Two ships were in from Guinea, nearly one hundred and fifty slaves left alive from the torturous voyage in one, slightly over a hundred from the other. Graham's had posted notice of a large sale for several weeks in advance. Nathanial Graham was beside himself with pleasure that Sydney Campion's Negroes, from Belleterre, would be part of the great sale as well. It would crowd his pens, he advised William this morning, but it was only another few days and Graham's would, as Graham's always had, manage very well.

William and Fancy had driven back into Charles Town early in the morning, William to speak to Nathanial privately, Fancy to indulge herself in little thrills of horror: with a few friends from town she wandered about the slave pens holding a scented handkerchief under her dainty nose—the stench was simply dreadful!—and vied with her companions in pointing out the best-developed black men. To Fancy and the others, as they strolled about from one tightly packed pen to the next, the weeping, groaning inmates of those pens seemed more or less like crude exotic animals in a collection, kept to amuse the rich as the King of France kept his pet lions and monkeys. That they were people never entered Fancy's spoiled little head and the mere suggestion of such a thing would have sent her into gales of laughter. Oh, Fancy knew the blacks well, though, she told her friends; they all knew about these dark sullen creatures, not a one of them had grown up without a house full of similar creatures to wait upon them, to work their fields and keep their animals. And Fancy knew, they all knew, what vicious vindictive beasts these blacks could be, could they not? Her favorite example was always Matty...

"I'm goin' to be here on sale day and watch that black bitch stripped down and set a price to," Fancy announced, her voice a trifle hard as she remembered how Matty had struck her... but she didn't tell her friends about that. "Her and her proud face and her airs! Thinks she's a real princess, she does... and why?" Fancy's heart-shaped face crinkled into little laugh lines... "Because she's slept with two important white men, that's her pedigree: Mistress Roundheels, doin' heaven knows what-all terrible things that men like!"

"You ought to know, Fancy dear!" replied a girl she had known from her childhood, looking at Fancy with wide eyes and a slight sneer.

Fancy made a little joke of it and they walked on while she searched for Matty. But Fancy made a mental note to drop her old friend for that remark. "Now where is that black slut?" she wondered aloud in her most delightful voice, but inwardly she managed to blame Matty for this latest insult on top of everything else.

It never occurred to Fancy that she would find Eleanor in one of those pens. It was her understanding that Eleanor, too, was now a slave like all the others, but surely Mister Graham could not put a white-looking woman in with those naked black bodies! She left the area where the men were kept and crossed a stone corridor to the female side, her heart beating much faster in anticipation.

She passed cage after cage, disappointed at each one. She saw twelve-year-old girls with glazed, stricken eyes staring about them in horror; she saw young mothers with nursing babies who watched her walk by and turned their backs upon her; she saw strong, ripe young women with raw stripes on their naked backs from floggings on board ship. She saw no old women, for they were of no value and she knew, although the new slaves did not, that when the mothers were sold, their children, for the most part, would not go with them.

She was almost at the end of the slave yards before she caught sight of Matty, in the last pen of all. Matty was still chained hand and foot and the fearful African girls were crowded around her, fingering her torn dress and her heavy chains, all talking at once in six or seven different tongues. Matty was black like them, but somehow she was not the same as they. She puzzled them, almost frightened them until they saw the pitying look in her eyes and heard the gentle tone of her voice. They could not understand what she said, neither in English nor in French nor in her own native Libyan speech but she was the only woman among them so much older than themselves and they turned to her instinctively as they would to the mothers and aunts and grandmothers they would never see again.

Matty had found herself a place near the very front of the pen they had brought her to and now, with the chattering, often weeping, young girls all about her, Eleanor was effectively hidden from view. And this was what Matty wanted, this was what she had quickly maneuvered to gain, because she had heard Fancy's light mocking voice echoing down to her long before she saw the girl walking toward her with quick, purposeful steps and an expression of triumph on her face.

"Why, Matty, here you are at last!" trilled Fancy, coming to a stop before the pen. She noticed how close Matty was and hastily moved several feet back, away from the reach of those angry black hands. "I just had to stop by and say 'Good morning,' Matty. My, my, it certainly is . . . *close* in here, don't you find it close, Matty? Whoever purchases those girls is sure goin' to have to give 'em a good bath!"

"Come to gloat, Miss Fancy?" called out Matty coolly. The black girls about her looked up timidly, most of them never having seen a white woman besides Eleanor in all their lives.

"Gloat, Matty? Gloat? Oh, Matty, you've always been so stupid!" cried Fancy, quite vexed. "You know, I wanted to bring you back to Belleterre to keep house for me when I move in . . . I would have, too, no matter what my brother said, if you'd ever shown me the least little courtesy or consideration! But you have always set yourself above me and my family, like none of us was good enough for you! And whatever happens to you now, it's your own fault!"

Matty got to her feet very slowly, the chains clanking faintly at each motion she made. "I would rather be dead than be your servant!" she said stonily. Fancy gasped and moved still farther away. In so doing, she was able to see the rear of the pen more clearly and she saw Eleanor sitting alone on the floor, her head leaning back against the steel bars, her eyes closed.

"Eleanor!" cried Fancy, forgetting herself for an instant. Her tone was one of genuine horror, for just that instant. But it was long enough for Matty to comprehend and try to make use of.

"Why are you surprised, Miss Fancy?" she questioned the girl quietly. "Your brother's going to sell her, too, you knew that."

Fancy winced. "Yes, yes, I know. But I didn't think they'd put her in here with all these . . . all you . . ." she trailed off, still staring in horrid fascination at Eleanor.

"Why not, Miss Fancy? She's the same as the rest of us, isn't she? She's my daughter, don't you remember? You said it in court yesterday, don't you still believe it today?"

"Yes, I still believe it!" snapped Fancy, biting her lip. "I was just surprised to see her, that's all."

"And you felt sorry about it, a little bit sorry, didn't you?" pressed Matty even more softly, utterly without guile.

Fancy moved a bit closer and lowered her voice. "No, I did not!" she protested. She heard her friends laughing, following behind her in leisurely fashion. "Is she still crazy, Matty? She looks so strange. She looks ill!"

Matty's hand snaked out suddenly, pulling the chain taut, but she managed to seize Fancy by the arm. "She is ill," she said harshly.

Fancy tried to pull away but could not move from the spot.

"I'm taking a chance on you, girl," said Matty swiftly. "We don't have any time to talk about it, but your cousin, yes, your cousin, is going to have a child in a few months. And the way she is now, she can't eat nor take care of herself. She'll be dead in a week unless someone does something to help her!"

"What do you expect me to do?" Fancy wrenched her arm free and jumped back quickly. "I can't do anything for her! I don't want to!"

"She's your blood kin, whatever else you believe," asserted Matty desperately. "Find a way to let me stay with her, take care of her till the baby is born. You can do that, can't you? You can do that much!"

Fancy was fanning herself violently with the scented handkerchief. She looked over at the black woman with confusion in her eyes.

"Whose child is she having?" she asked. "One of those black bucks at Belleterre? Or . . . or? . . ."

"You know as well as I do. It's Michael Ives's baby," replied Matty. "Do something, Fancy. Find a way or you'll be guilty of murdering Eleanor and her child, just as sure as if you'd shot them both! Find a way . . . ." Abruptly she fell silent as Fancy's friends, laughing and making playfully obscene remarks, finally joined her.

Fancy turned very quickly and hurried away, her friends protesting, almost running to catch up with her. As she neared the entrance she thought she still heard Matty's voice saying, "Find a way, find a way, Fancy!" but nobody else seemed to notice and she decided it was her nerves.

The group emerged into the sunny, chilly morning, talking and laughing and taking in a huge gulps of fresh air as they complained of the smell of the slaves and the pens that held them.

Fancy felt terribly weak in the knees and insisted on waiting for her brother inside the big carriage. The others kissed her and petted her and carried her off to the carriage and sat her down inside of it and gave her dozens of pieces of good advice about feeling faint. Only one of them had the good sense to tell her that if she had any brains after today, she wouldn't show her face at the sale or she would faint dead away in front of everyone and disgrace herself. Then they went their various ways, leaving Fancy with her teeth chattering and her hands clasped tightly together on the big plush seat, wondering what she ought to say to William.

William, meanwhile, had had his little confidential talk with Nathanial Graham and on the whole was quite satisfied with the way everything was being handled on his and his family's behalf. Graham predicted a great success with the sale and kept rubbing his hands together and then rubbing them flatly up and down on his coat front and apologizing to William for doing so . . .

"It's the chalk, you know, Master Campion," said Nathanial quite earnestly and mildly, for, aside from his damnable trade he was a pleasant enough fellow, a churchgoer from time to time, and had a wife and children who were fond of him. "We use chalk all day long in the office, or, rather, the clerks use it but it's all the same, for the stuff gets into the air and on a man's clothing and up his nose and there's no getting it out or off, the whole staff of wives has had a stab at it and it's no use, we're quite inundated with chalk—"

568

" 'Chalk'?" William uttered the monosyllable with extreme disinterest, looking away out the window.

"Yes, the clerks use it constantly to mark up prices on the board. People come in, you see, and want to know what's for sale and talk about money and prices and so forth, and we like to give 'em an idea of what's expected. And it keeps changing and we keep erasing and—"

"Yes, yes, Graham, that's all very well," snapped William curtly, "but I want to be sure you and I understand each other now. I see my sister has returned to the carriage and is waiting for me, so once more through it and I'll bid you good day and see you next in three days' time, at the start of the auction."

Nathanial blinked and rubbed his hands some more. "I am well aware of your situation, Master Campion," he said, his pride up just a bit. "We shall keep your . . . we shall keep the red-haired girl here with the others, let her wait through the . . . er . . . preliminaries and the entire auction. But then we are to withdraw her from the sale and say there has been, oh, a mistake, a change of some sort, and she is not for sale." Graham shook his head gloomily. "I don't like it, sir, not a bit of it. They'll be wild for her. Truly, they'll be quite mad for her once they get a look. You may start a riot here. Bad for business, Master Campion. Father would never have allowed it!"

"But *you* will, Graham," declared William harshly. "I want no riots, either. Just let her stand out there; let them see her, let them speculate. Let her watch . . . everything. It's entirely for my own amusement, and it will be the start of breaking that haughty tart to my will. Terror, Graham, fear and terror, marvelous things, fear and terror; work wonders, miracles, prodigies in the human spirit . . . even in Negroes," he added sharply, reminding Nathanial with his words and the look in his insolent, bulging eyes that the woman they spoke of was no more than a slave, albeit a beautiful one. This timely prompting had its effect upon Nathanial Graham. He was, after all, a man of business, a man of reputation and much inclined to self-esteem. Nathanial did not like William Campion—indeed, *nobody* liked William Campion, but there was business to be done, business of a very profitable nature. If William had his eccentricities . . . and the entire city of Charles Town whispered about William's eccentricities . . . what wealthy man did not? It was none of Nathanial's concern, so long as the auction was carried off with its customary success and Graham's emerged to the good.

He and William shook hands very cordially, therefore, Nathanial once again apologizing for the invisible cloud of chalk dust he insisted permeated every pore of his body, and William strolled back to his carriage to find his sister immensely agitated, tearing her handkerchief to shreds.

He managed to avoid any reference to her state of mind and feeling by ordering the driver to turn round and go home at once, then he sat back in his seat and stared up at the tufted velvet-lined ceiling of the vehicle. He heard Fancy moving about, he heard her little sighs and murmurs and he decided to ignore her.

"Oh, William," she said at last, as they had left town and were on the road to Rogue's Fall, "Oh, William, I am distressed, brother! I do believe I am so distressed I could weep!"

"Really, m'dear?" William opened his eyes very wide and turned them downward in their sockets until they bulged in her general direction. "What troubles you?" His tone clearly implied that he didn't care what it was, didn't want to know what it was and wished she wouldn't tell him what it was.

"William, I do not know what to do," she went on all atremble. "'Find a way', that's what she said, 'find a way.' Well, there's no way and if there is I can't find it, I'm sure!"

William's langour began to dissipate. "'She'? Fancy, for the love of Heaven, *will* you once in your life tell something straight out?"

"William, I have just found out that Eleanor is in that place, in those pens with all the nigger girls. And Matty's there, too, tryin' to look after her precious Eleanor as usual!" Fancy sniffed. William looked at her coldly.

"I know that," he said. "What more?"

"How do you know there is more?" She scrutinized his face carefully.

"I know *you*, sister dear," he replied very shortly and leaned forward. "What is it?"

Fancy hesitated and then a strange little smile possessed her full mouth and an ugly little line extended itself between her arched eyebrows.

"Eleanor is carryin' Michael Ives's child!" she told him scornfully. Her brother's face paled into an unpleasant yellow white hue and his eyes started nearly out of his head. He looks just like a frog, Fancy thought suddenly, almost giggling. Why didn't I ever notice that before? William looks just like a big, ugly frog!

"Who told you this? Matty? Of course it would be Matty. Why, though? Why would she tell *you*?" His normally soft, slurred tones were sharp and high, on the edge of hysteria.

"She wanted me to help Eleanor, can you imagine?" Fancy jeered. "She kept telling *me* to find a way—"

"A way? What way? What did she want you to do? Tell me!"

"La, la, brother dear, but you *are* upset, aren't you? Well, Matty wants me to find some way that she can stay with Eleanor and take care of her until the brat is born. Seems Eleanor can't rightly take care of herself anymore . . . she's right, too, William. I saw Eleanor myself and she's just as crazy as she was yesterday, clear out of her head! She just sits on the floor and doesn't do any—"

"Shut up, Fancy!" William fairly shouted it. "Let me think!"

" 'Think'?" sniffed Fancy. "What's there to think about? La, I never would have said a word if I'd known you were goin' to be so put out, William!"

She assumed a hurt, self-righteous air, tossing her head and making a great show of dabbing at her eyes with the ruined handkerchief. But she saw that he was staring at her in silence, untouched by her histrionics. Presently she sat still and looked back at him with the eyes of a fox. "You're not gettin' much for your trouble, brother," she said. "Not only isn't she a virgin, but she's quite mad *and* carryin' another man's child in her belly! What are you goin' to do about that, brother?"

"Much!" he replied thickly.

"Do it, then," his sister told him. He nodded once, then sat back, folded his arms and said no more all the way home.

Fancy was satisfied. She, too, relaxed and sat back against the cushions, looking at the pleasant autumn fields and trees as the carriage rolled along into the country. She had grown up with William. She knew him well. She could not have picked a way to tell him about Eleanor more surely calculated to infuriate him than the way she had. She glanced at him from time to time and saw that he was not sleeping, but the muscles of his jaw and brow were fearfully constricted and his thick short fingers continually clasped and unclasped, leaving red marks on his fat hands. Fancy smiled to herself.

That for you, Matty! she was thinking. I'll teach you to put your black hands on me! "Find a way," Matty had begged, "find a way" . . . well, sugar, I surely did find a way, didn't I?

4   An Event At The October Fair

A high, sweeping wind out of the east assaulted Charles Town's handsome brick houses, causing the roofs to strain and rumble strangely, driving flocks of scolding, chattering robins and sparrows out of the dainty cupolas, pulling crumbling mortar and old broken bits of stone from the high garden walls, whipping dry autumn branches against shuddering windowpanes. The town's stray dogs and cats, which had been enjoying a few warm, sunny days of this Indian summer time, fled the wind in open places, deserted the dust-blown streets and slunk home to hide. The sun, very far away indeed, clung stubbornly to a cluster of dark whirling clouds and shone feebly white and cold.

It was not a propitious day for an outdoor gathering of the magnitude and importance of Graham's slave auction. But the annual October fair had just begun; the colonists of Carolina were accustomed to the idiosyncracies of their adopted climate and turned out in very large numbers for the festivities. Many had arrived a day or two earlier and were staying with friends and relatives or at local inns. Many had been traveling two weeks and more from plantations far to the west. Theirs was a holiday air not to be spoiled by a bit of wind or a reluctant sun. The recent hurricane had slowed down the progress of journeying inland visitors but it had not stopped them. And, as local planters appeared from estates along the rivers and up the coast, the normal population of Charles Town swelled to vast proportions and the streets were filled with strange horses, wagons, chaises, curricles, chariots, carriages and slave-borne sedan chairs rented by the hour and very dear at fair time. Planters brought their ladies and, often, their children with them to shop and gossip and see the latest fashions over from England while the men traded horses, bought land, farm animals and slaves, paid debts, and enjoyed the sights.

There were great horse races at Butler's Race Ground on Charles Town Neck, and cock fights at which the most famous gamecocks and their handlers assembled. Prodigious amounts of money exchanged hands before ever the cattle auctions and slave sale got started. Picnic luncheons were planned for parties of gawking inlanders who paid a shilling a head to be rowed out to inspect the new lighthouse on Middle Bay Island. But when the peevish wind showed no sign of abating and, indeed, grew stronger and angrier every hour past dawn, many of the merrymakers were discouraged and decided to forgo their plans for the day.

However, nothing discouraged the eager buyers who began to assemble around Graham's Wharf early in the morning. Numbers of fine carriages maneuvered for the best vantage points while the crowds on foot wandered off from the puppet shows and ropewalkers and fortune-tellers to gather by the auction block. There was the usual frantic pushing and shoving and milling about; several nervous horses reared and sent masses of screaming spectators running in all directions for their own safety. Gentlemen cursed the commoners for upsetting their fine-blooded animals; ladies shook their heads over the crowding and complained to each other with testy little smiles. But, this early in the day, the jostling and pushing were all fairly good-natured.

Graham's had run off handbills describing their most promising merchandise. It was when these ran out that good manners seriously began to disappear. Nathanial Graham saw to it at once that a large slate board was brought out from his own office and a young clerk, with a vast supply of the indispensable chalk in his pockets, endeavored to write up the information provided on the handbills so that everyone might see it. For a while the general milling about focused upon this clerk, who had a bad time of it between the determined buyers who edged closer and closer to him demanding that he write larger and faster and the wind that shrilled about his red ears and threatened more than once to overturn the slate board down on the heads of the crowd.

The sale was scheduled to begin at ten in the morning. At nine-thirty the Campion carriage arrived. The family was greeted by many old friends anxious to purchase one or two of the now famous Belleterre Negroes. Maurice Matthews was there, along with his tall blond son, George. Sydney Campion had decided that there was a good match to be made between Fancy and the lanky, grinning George and he made a great point of inviting father and son to join him and his family. Fancy was quite irritated with her father about this. She had known George Matthews since childhood. He had been her first lover, when they were both thirteen and bored enough with the less hazardous pursuits of the age to explore the delicious mysteries of sexual pleasure.

What a sharp disappointment that had been for Fancy! How far removed from the transports and raptures her frivolous French novels had led her to expect! What an absolute ass George had been! She had hardly spoken a civil word to him ever since, but George was convinced he had made her love him passionately and whenever they were brought together by mutual connivance of both fathers, George's constant foolish grin seemed to recall worlds of delight and full faith in their future of married bliss together.

Fancy was dressed in her finest, knowing she would be in keen competition with every other lady at the sale. She was not quite sure what fashion dictated one wore upon the occasion of a slave sale, but she was sure it must be something splendidly conspicuous. Therefore she had bedecked herself in pearl-silk stockings and bright blue damask shoes with little blue-silk-covered wooden heels that made a marvelously dancing kind of sound when she walked. Her gown was of the same shade of intense blue, quilted about the full skirt and set off with numerous bows of paduasoy ribbon. The blue lutestring had been made up into a short, fetching coat that fitted close about Fancy's ripe little body. Her kid gloves were of palest cream color and her bonnet was a miracle of velvet, lace and feathers in the same eye-catching blue as her frock.

She looked about her, eyeing the other ladies, pleased to see there were none present half so decorative as she. But they were all got up in their glittering best and sat or stood about or leaned gracefully from their open carriages like a cluster of bright, extremely animated tropical fish, surrounded by gentlemen in suits and boots and cloaks hardly less splendid.

After a few moments, Fancy turned her back upon George and glanced at her brother. They had not had a chance to speak again since the carriage ride yesterday. Master Richards had been feasted and sent off back to Antigua the richer by three hundred pounds that Sydney had borrowed from Graham's against his profits from the forthcoming sale. Now Fancy studied William's face with great interest, noting how he sat hunched over with his hands clasped tightly about the handle of an elegant walking stick, his heavy face set in an expression of murky expectancy as he stared up at the block. She was about to speak to William when she saw Nathanial Graham out of the corner of her eye, dressed for the day in a suit of black velvet and an unfortunate, ill-fitting chestnut brown wig. Graham looked exceedingly anxious about something and seemed to be hovering uncertainly a few feet away, trying to catch William's eye.

"There's Master Graham," Fancy touched William's shoulder. "I believe he wants to talk to you, brother."

William started, blinking violently. His head jerked around and Nathanial took this as a sign of welcome. He hurried over and stood up on tiptoes to whisper something in William's ear. Fancy strained to hear what was being said but she could not make it out. William's sallow face grew very red as he listened and he began to shake his head vehemently. Graham persisted, speaking even more earnestly and this time Fancy heard the words "more than a thousand pounds, Master Campion! Surely. . . ."

And William cried, "No, never! It's no use, Graham. The money has nothing to do with it!"

Nathanial stood down, his expression betraying the keenest disappointment and not a little anger. He touched his hat to Fancy and left them quickly. William was breathing very hard and his bulging eyes, when he looked at his sister, seemed to be burning.

"*What* had money nothing to do with, brother dear?" Fancy demanded. "A thousand pounds? I never thought I should hear *you* turn your back on such a pretty sum!"

"Hold your tongue, Fancy!" was all her brother would say. She would have pressed him but just at that moment the tremendous crowd fell relatively silent as Nathanial Graham climbed up upon the auction block to address them. Just behind him she could see several groups of slaves, chained together four or five at a time, being moved into place by Graham's assistants armed with short, stout clubs.

"He wants you to sell Eleanor, doesn't he?" Fancy whispered. "Why don't you? There's never been such a price paid for one slave, never! Does Papa know what you're doing?" Her tone was querulous. Her brother did not reply, but climbed out of the carriage and pushed his way forward to the very edge of the block, where he stood stolidly leaning upon his stick, his eyes fixed upon the wretched group of blacks in the background.

They were already tired out. All night long they had been prepared for the sale by a small army of Graham workers who appeared in the pens after the meager evening ration of Indian corn and salt had been consumed. The blacks were washed down with bucketfuls of cold water, then inspected for bruises and sores that might keep down their asking price. Those with the marks of the lash on their backs were coated with a high-smelling mixture of ash and vegetable dyes which covered the raw skin temporarily. After this, they were given coarse white cotton trousers and shirts, or shapeless calico dresses without sleeves for the women. And then the carefully planned division of them into job lots had been begun. Hitherto they had been separated merely according to sex, but now a further, finer sifting-out was necessary and no one in the business understood this process as well as Nathanial Graham.

It was always to be hoped that slaves might be purchased in groups rather than singly. This speeded up the sale and enabled the company to get rid of less desirable blacks without much lowering of their profit margin. If a rich planter bought three or four strapping bucks for his fields and a fine, ripe girl for breeding, he usually was pleased enough not to mind taking along an adolescent boy or, on occasion, an infant belonging to the girl and sometimes even the rare middle-aged survivor of the middle passage.

Nathanial was well versed, too, in those Africans held most desirable by his clients. Men from the Gold Coast and the Windward Coast and Angola were preferred. Those from Gambia were considered generally inferior and there was no point in trying to sell anyone over the age of seventeen from Calabar, as these were greatly inclined to melancholy and suicide. Carolina planters were not fond of Negroes from the West Indies, who spoke a peculiar "Black English" difficult to understand and were usually lazy rogues and troublemakers.

All of his regular customers preferred American-born and American-trained blacks, accustomed to the climate, the work and the discipline, who spoke good English and "knew their place." So there was an immense amount of interest in this particular sale when the word got round that more than fifty prime American Negroes were being sold off at once.

Nathanial, who sometimes liked to refer to his carefully arranged slave groupings fancifully as his "bouquets" or "nosegays," divided the Belleterre blacks equally among the various lots, putting one of them together with five or six Africans. Since there were about three hundred slaves altogether, it just came out right, fifty lots with Belleterre's slaves distributed about like a dash of salt or a pinch of gunpowder, depending upon the point of view. Further, Nathanial was always careful to separate people of various tribes who might speak or understand the same languages. Thus Fulani was divided from Malinke, Susu from Ngere and Toma. By the time they learned English, it was to be hoped they would also have learned obedience and, while they were learning both, they would have no means to communicate or conspire with one another. This was Graham's great art, taught him by his father before him, and it, more than any other single factor, had been the making of the house.

Throughout that long, cruel night Matty had stood with her face pressed against the bars of the cage, watching and listening as her friends and their children were parted from each other. She knew it was only a matter of time before they took her away from Eleanor. She had thought over her desperate emotional appeal to Fancy Campion and was sick with shame for it. What had gotten into her? Fear for Eleanor? A still-lingering hope that Fancy could not, after all, see her own cousin destroyed? But Matty realized now that Fancy would do nothing to help. There was no hope from that quarter and, with Michael Ives dead at the bottom of the sea, there was no hope at all.

Finally Matty had gone to Eleanor and tried once again to talk to her. It was no use. Eleanor was beyond hearing her. Days of mistreatment and lack of food had already taken their toll. The milky skin was a dead white now, the huge green eyes shadowed by purple smudges that looked like bruises. The smooth cheeks were hollow, the skin tight about the delicate bones. Matty inspected Eleanor's burned hands, saw that they were almost fully healed. She was about to remove the bandages when she felt something hard and round beneath them. Michael's ring. Eleanor still clung to it. Matty tried to take the ring away for a moment, to make disposing of the bandage easier. But Eleanor's fingers closed about the ring and, for the first time in days she cried out and stood up by herself, backing away into a corner of the cell with haunted eyes and bared teeth, uttering ghastly sounds of fear and defiance. Matty started to reassure her, then turned away helplessly. There was nothing more she could do.

She was astonished that no attempt was made to remove her from Eleanor, even more amazed when buckets of water were brought to them and orders given that they wash themselves. They were not molested nor dragged out into the corridors and stripped naked like the other women. They were left entirely alone and separate from the rest.

So, keeping a wary eye out for Graham and his men, Matty had painstakingly bathed Eleanor and tried to comb the disheveled hair back from her face and neck. The cool water dissolved most of the accumulated dirt and dust from her skin and seemed to refresh her. Matty gave up in her attempts to mend the ruined traveling dress and tucked the torn pieces under as modestly as she could. She sighed at the sight of Eleanor's tall, well-formed body arrayed in rags. Now, upon closer observation, she could see the subtle changes that had already taken place in the girl: the jutting breasts just beginning to droop a little, the hips a bit rounder, the entire figure less girlish, more sensuous than ever.

And suddenly, from the shadows beyond the dim light of the wall torches, there came a loud, appreciative whistle. Matty whirled and screamed something in French. Nathanial Graham and one of his men emerged from the darkness, staring avidly at Eleanor.

"By God, she's a beauty!" said Nathanial, wetting his dry lips that tasted like chalk. Matty watched him with glittering eyes, tensed for the battle she knew she would put up before they succeeded in taking her from Eleanor. But Graham ignored her. He entered the cell and shook his head thoughtfully as he looked at the girl. The man with him blocked Matty from moving but did not attempt to hurt or even touch her.

"Campion doesn't know what he's doing, refusing to sell a piece of goods like this," Graham remarked at length. "I'll speak to him in the morning. I see you've cleaned her up, woman," he said to Matty, not bothering to look at her. "But this rag will never do."

He fastened his fingers into the woolen cloth of Eleanor's dress and tore the garment from her. Matty sprang, trying to move around to the side of the other man, but she was pushed back firmly and held still. Graham smiled and ran his hand slowly along Eleanor's neck and shoulder, then pulled the already low-cut camisole she wore further down over her breasts so that she was almost half naked, the lacy straps of the light linen garment falling loosely on her arms like small sleeves.

"There, that's better," said Nathanial, stepping back to admire the effect. Matty cursed him in French and then in English, but he only laughed and went away again, taking his silent assistant with him. Matty looked over at Eleanor standing there dressed only in the white ruffled petticoats and the camisole they had worked on together. And Matty groaned, seeing how beautiful she looked despite everything. Then she remembered that Graham had said something about *not* selling Eleanor after all. What was that all about? What else did William have in mind for his cousin?

Shortly before dawn Matty buried her face in her hands and wept for the morning ahead and for all the yesterdays gone. She remembered the rich white satin Captain Ives had sent for Eleanor's wedding gown. What a contrast, she thought in anguish: the thought of beautiful Eleanor arrayed in such a gown . . . and Eleanor as she was now, pale as the white linen she wore, with her long red hair cascading over shoulders and breast like a mantle of blood. . . .

5 Slave Auction

And now, just a few weary hours later, it was that final tomorrow, windy, pale and cold, a strangely bedraggled day from the outset. Matty and Eleanor were led out of the pens into the faltering sunlight, shackles only about their ankles. The iron collars remained on their necks but the additional chains had been left off for the sale. Matty was sick with apprehension. She had seen the arrival of the Campions and she had seen the short argument Graham had had with William. When Nathanial returned to issue final orders he was very angry and she had overheard him talking to one of his brothers.

"This is the last favor Graham's ever does for him!" Nathanial had blurted out furiously. "I told him we could bring in a thousand for the girl but he wouldn't hear of it. Now I wish to Heaven I had not agreed with the rest of it. 'A small diversion,' that's what he calls it, imagine! That crowd is here to buy, they're in the mood to buy—they won't like it, I tell you, not a bit! It's not customary at Graham's—I dread what the ladies will think!"

And his brother had replied in an offhand way, "Crowds always enjoy a bit of blood, so long as it doesn't take much time. Calm yourself, Nathanial, the ladies will be thrilled."

Matty's apprehension grew as she wondered what was meant by this. And then Nathanial went out to address the crowd and she and Eleanor were brought alongside the block. She saw the gaily dressed crowds as a blur of color, she heard the sounds they made as so much incomprehensible roaring in her ears. There was a tight, hard knot of dread in her chest and she found breathing difficult. She recognized the feeling in the atmosphere, for this was not the first slave market she had seen. She forced herself to look out, into the crowd, and saw William Campion straight across from her, staring at

Eleanor, his lips loose, his jaw slack. And she thanked God that Eleanor did not know where she was or what was about to happen.

Nathanial finished speaking and came to take Eleanor by the arm. "Come with us," he told Matty, leading Eleanor up the steps and on to the block. Matty hobbled along as quickly as she could with the short thick chain hampering every move she made.

The crowd became wild when they saw Eleanor before them. Those who already knew the story quickly told the others. Nathanial took Eleanor slowly about the edge of the block so all might have a good look at her. A few crude country fellows reached out and pulled at her feet and grasped the hem of her petticoats. Nathanial kicked their hands away and warned them severely to behave or they would be removed.

Then he led Eleanor toward one of the upright wooden stakes. Eleanor was turned toward the people watching in fascination as a short length of chain was attached to the iron collar and then made fast to a rusted bracket embedded in the splintering wood. Matty, struggling in vain against a procedure she did not recognize and greatly feared, was chained similarly next to Eleanor. And Nathanial raised his hand once more to ask for silence.

"My friends, before our auction begins, one of our clients, Master William Campion, has requested the use of Graham's facilities for the purpose of punishment. This is unusual but we are glad to oblige the gentleman, especially so since the case involves a most serious breach of law. And perhaps this example will make clear to the Negroes about to be sold here today exactly what they may expect should they ever take the notion into their heads to defy their masters.

"The slave we are about to bring before you has committed several crimes, including the possession and use of arms against free white persons, as well as running away from his home, attacking and wounding a white man, resisting efforts to restrain him, which resistance resulted in the injury of several other white men and women.

"The charge was also made against this slave that he had had intimate relations with a white woman of Carolina. However this charge has been withdrawn, as the woman involved was proved to be of mixed blood . . ."

Matty cried out and twisted her neck frantically in the hard restraining fetters.

"Dogon," she whispered to Eleanor urgently. "Did you hear him? It's Dogon he's talking about. He's not dead! The pirates didn't kill him! Eleanor, listen, Dogon is still alive!"

Eleanor raised her drooping head and looked at Matty with wide, innocent, unfocused eyes. And just as she moved, two soldiers dragged forward a pitiable figure and pulled it upon the block. The indignant crowd looked upon this figure and cried out against the crimes it had committed. Matty saw it was indeed Dogon, weighed down by the heaviest of chains, ankles and arms shackled together, and his entire body wrapped round and round in iron. His face was so beaten and crushed from blows it was hard to recognize him. But Matty knew him.

"*Dogon!*" she called to him, oblivious of the murmuring crowd so close by.

The chained and weighted figure stirred a little at the sound of her voice, but otherwise did not respond. Instead, Dogon searched the crowd with his eyes until he found what he was looking for: William Campion standing only a short distance away, looking on with an expression of contempt and anticipation. Only then did Dogon turn his head painfully, with enormous effort, to look over at Matty. He saw her and, next to her, Eleanor. His glazed, stricken glance took in their sad plight slowly and then with increasing awareness. His wrecked face came alive, his lips trembled, he began to struggle against the chains that bound him.

Nathanial Graham snapped his nervous fingers impatiently and his own men came up to assist the soldiers with their prisoner. They began to drag Dogon across the block, opposite where Matty and Eleanor were displayed, toward another, stouter, wooden stake. Dogon allowed them to pull him along, putting up no resistance whatever. Their path lay a few feet from where William Campion stood watching. When this spot was reached, Dogon suddenly shouted a few words in his native tongue and, summoning up the last remaining ferocious strength his dauntless spirit had been conserving, he straightened his wracked body and, straining every muscle against the weight of chains, he thrust his stunned captors from him. With a mighty cry, Dogon made straight for William, his large hands reaching out unerringly until he had grabbed hold of William's throat.

People shrieked and screamed. The agitated horses snorted, eyes rolling, lips pulled back over flashing yellow teeth, voices raised in terrified sound. William Campion struggled to free himself. Gentlemen around him leaped to his assistance, showering the chained black man with a rain of blows from their walking sticks and pistol butts and fists. Nathanial was shouting. The soldiers recovered their wits and darted over, beating Dogon about the head and neck with their walnut rifle stocks. But Dogon held on to that fat throat through it all, with William's thick pudgy hands tearing ineffectually at the black fingers that were slowly choking the life out of him. Fancy's shrill scream could be heard above all other noises. Sydney descended from his carriage and ran to help his son, shouting furiously for them to do their duty and tear the black devil loose.

Matty barely breathed as she watched the chaotic scene. She saw Dogon as savage as any African torn from his home in the bush and she remembered his quiet nature, his wisdom and dignity and gentleness as long as she had known him. Tears flowed unheeded down her cheeks at the magnificent effort he was making to keep at least part of his solemn vow here and at such a time. . . .

Eleanor, too, seemed to be watching. Perhaps the roaring of the maddened crowd disturbed her tranquil dream-state; perhaps something of the feeling of horror and death in the air had reached the small still-vital part of her that was keeping her alive. At any rate, she was watching the struggle and her hands began to move in tiny, helpless gestures.

The struggle was uneven at best. Nathanial had summoned his chief overseer; that gentleman now raced from the pens with his cudgel in his hands and pushed his way swiftly to Dogon, tossing soldiers and men from the crowd out of his way with huge, powerful hands. One quick knowing blow on the back of the head from the cudgel stunned Dogon, loosened his death grip on William's throat. With a sickening choked cry, William Campion fell back in a swoon, his hands touching his neck as if to make sure he was not still held and strangled half to death. His frightened sister ran to assist him. Full half a dozen little bottles of smelling salts were quickly passed from the ladies in the carriages to restore William to his senses.

In the meantime, Dogon was dragged the rest of the way to the stake. Nathanial had chosen a tall, heavy post that had a crosspiece nailed and supported at the top. A thick iron hook was embedded in the crosspiece and now a short hempen noose was suspended from this hook. A little wooden box used for such occasions was thrust

582

beneath the noose and upon this box they pushed Dogon. The noose was put about his neck and tightened. Five or six men, including the soldiers and the overseer, stood holding him where he was, but there was no need for that now: the last-minute, desperate summoning of strength Dogon had just displayed was quite gone from him. The blow to his head had not knocked him unconscious but had rendered him helpless. The great weight of the chains seemed to pull him down so that he seemed merely a small, helpless, shrunken old man. He was greatly weakened by his long ordeal . . . Keane had sent him to William, who had delivered him up to the soldiers days ago. They had been given orders only to see to it he remained alive. Other than that, they were free to do as they pleased with him. They had stopped just short of death.

It was frightful to behold the change in him. Gradually the shocked and outraged crowd subsided, losing interest in William, and fastening their attention on Dogon. If anything they hated him more now than they had a few moments earlier. They watched with keen anticipation as Nathanial briskly approached the little group on the block, spoke a few quiet words to the soldiers, who immediately moved several steps to either side of the black man, and nodded to his overseer. The overseer leaned down and one of his assistants took the cudgel from his hand and gave him in its place a black leather horsewhip. He turned to the crowd, over which a grim silence had fallen at last, and addressed them briefly.

"The punishment is death." The crowd knew that. They muttered and waited impatiently for it to begin. The overseer kicked aside the small wooden box upon which Dogon had been standing and at the same time commenced his beating, moving off some little distance to make the best possible use of the horsewhip.

Dogon's weighted feet were suspended but a short distance off the block. The noose was a strangling noose, its knot fixed at the back of his head, not under his ear where it would have broken his neck at once. The death devised for him, by no means the first of its kind in Carolina, was a slow and torturous one. At first he feebly kicked out despite the chains bearing him down, as he felt the slow, inexorable suffocation of the noose on his throat and each quick crack of the deadly whip laid bare the skin and flesh of his body. With every whiplash the engrossed crowd unconsciously counted aloud until the only sounds to be heard were the whip and the voice of the crowd, the cracking and the counting, the one sound sharp and loud, the other low and rumbling, and both together like the beat of some gigantic evil heart. . . .

The green eyes watched, blankly, without apparent interest or understanding. All around seemed misted over, blurred out of reality. And yet something stirred in the troubled mind, something began to speak like an inner voice, urgent, commanding, a throb of words, a message repeated over and over again. Eleanor Campion began to hear the words and, as they repeated themselves, besieging her sleeping consciousness, she heard as if from a great distance, another sound, sharp, like a gunshot, then low and ominous, like thunder in the mountains.

And, without quite understanding yet either the urgent words that called to her or the strange frightening sounds from without, she moved restlessly in her restraints and blinked her eyes rapidly.

And then she awoke of a sudden and with no slow dawning of new comprehension: she heard, and the mist cleared from her eyes and she saw, she moved her hands and felt the collar fastened about her neck and the hard, splintery shaft of the wooden stake pressing in against her spine. She looked about with wonder for only an instant, then she knew quite clearly where she was, although not *why*. She saw the absorbed crowd all about her. She moved her eyes to see what they were staring at . . . and she saw Dogon. Dogon, whom she believed dead, now slowly dying, hanging in chains that dripped still-living blood upon the wooden block. Fear and pity gripped her as never in her life before. She threw back her head and uttered a wild, unearthly cry that sent cold shivers through the spectators.

"Dogon! No, oh my God, *no!"*

Matty's head shot around, a little thrill running through her.

"Eleanor! Eleanor, look at me! Child, look at me, let me see you're all right again!"

Eleanor gasped tearfully and looked in the direction from which she heard Matty's voice. She blinked the tears from her newly awakened eyes.

"Matty?" she breathed brokenly. "Matty, what's happened?"

Across the block William Campion, back on his feet and watching with satisfaction the long-drawn-out death of Dogon, heard Eleanor's cry. He shifted his gaze quickly; before anyone else there, even before Matty, he recognized the fact that Eleanor had come to her senses at last. He saw her struggle, perplexed, against the harsh chains. He saw her turning to the black woman beside her and he saw Matty's pitiful, despairing little smile. He saw Matty talk to her and Eleanor shake her head several times. She looked back toward Dogon, whose body hung limp, eyes staring blindly, in chains while the overseer lashed on and on, neither knowing nor caring whether his prisoner still lived or not. Eleanor screamed again and again, weeping and writhing frantically as she tried to break free and run to the black man's side. William felt the aching bruises on his thick, sagging throat and he smiled as he saw full comprehension of her situation at last make itself clear to her. He waited impatiently for what she would do, must do next. . . .

Nathanial signaled his overseer to end the useless whipping. The black was dead, probably had been dead for several minutes. The crowd sighed as if with one throat, and immediately began calling for the sale to begin. The body was removed, the first group of slaves was quickly brought forward. And Nathanial began calling for the bidding.

Then it was that William saw his cousin's eyes searching him out. He elbowed those on either side to stand away a little, so she might more clearly see him. And she looked straight at him, knowing all that had happened to her at last. Matty had told her very briefly. William raised his elegant velvet hat and gravely bowed it to her in mock salute, keeping his eyes upon her so he would not miss the expression on her face. He did not know what he had expected to see on the pale, ravaged countenance and he did not particularly care. Sorrow, terror, hatred, it was all one with him and all suited his purposes exactly. Whatever it would be it must by the very nature of things replace her customary look of contempt that he knew so well and loathed with all his heart. She might show him a hundred different expressions in the days and weeks and months ahead, but he was sure contempt would never be one of them.

Fancy, standing next to and a little apart from her brother, was interrupted in her close appraisal of the group of slaves just then being sold by a low, incensed sound emerging from his throat so very much resembling the growling of a furious animal that she jumped and trembled as she looked at him. She saw William's usually sallow face turned a dull crimson, a wild light in his protruding eyes . . . she glanced off and saw that he was looking at Eleanor and Eleanor was staring down at him, the old haughty look

585

of contempt blazing on her face as her huge green eyes gazed coldly, uncompromisingly into his. William's hands worked convulsively, fingers twitching in agitation beneath the smooth folds of his cloak.

So Eleanor had come back to herself, had she, mused Fancy thoughtfully. Wasn't that what William wanted? She nudged her brother with some force until he noticed her.

"William, stop it," Fancy remonstrated. "People are beginnin' to take notice! You're embarrassin' me!"

William squinted at her for several seconds, as though he hardly knew her. And then he laughed. The sound of it chilled Fancy through. But after that her brother was more himself. He settled back to watch the remainder of the sale without further emotion, all the while keeping his eyes riveted upon Eleanor. For, putting him from her mind temporarily, she watched in anguish as, one by one, her friends from Belleterre were paraded in chains across Graham's block and sold away to anxious buyers who shouted out their bids and several times fell to blows among themselves in their determination to obtain what they were after. She saw Ada go, and Daniel, and the children who had worked in the fields and played and laughed about the place and knew nothing of such days, such places as this one. She called to them as they were taken away. They looked back at her and risked harsh words and hurried blows to shout their farewells and their prayers for her and for Matty. If William had purposely planned each separate moment of heartbreak in exquisite detail he could have devised no more hideous torture for his cousin than that which she suffered on the block. Nor was this all.

When the final lot of Negroes had been disposed of and sent off in the charge of various servants of their new masters, the crowd lingered about Graham's Wharf waiting to see who would buy the two women still remaining. More than one wealthy planter had forgone the purchase of an additional field hand or two, reserving his cash for an attempt to outbid all the others and take Eleanor home with him. There was some small delay after the final arrangements had been made about the blacks. Nathanial Graham was busily engaged in conversation with some of his customers. It was late in the afternoon by now and those who had plans to attend several evening festivities began to shout in annoyance at the further delay.

"Come, come, Graham, trot her out, start the bidding!"

Nathanial scowled, glanced at William for the last time and, receiving no encouragement, shrugged his thin shoulders and once again spoke to his customers.

Matty looked at Eleanor without speaking. It had come, finally. Eleanor sighed. "There's only you and me now, Matty," she said.

"They will not sell you," Matty told her. "Your cousin has refused all offers."

Eleanor started. She had all but forgotten William as the dreary hours had dragged on. "Why?" she whispered. Matty looked at her steadily. Eleanor's shoulders sagged and she sank back against the stake. No need for Matty to answer. It was all very clear.

The men came and removed the chains attaching Matty to the stake. Eleanor flung her arms out, managed to seize the black woman and caught her to her bosom.

"No, no, not you, Matty, not you!" the girl sobbed. Matty kissed her quickly. The men pulled Eleanor's arms from about her. Eleanor screamed and slapped out at them, clinging all the more to Matty.

"Come, enough of that!" snapped Nathanial, sick and tired of the whole affair. "Get the woman out here!"

"Leave her, leave her! I beg of you, oh please, leave her to me!" sobbed Eleanor.

The crowd thought it better than a play and pressed closely about the block not to miss a word or a look. See how the daughter holds on to her black wench of a mother, they murmured to each other. And William looked on, his enjoyment quite complete for the moment.

"Eleanor," whispered Matty even as they pulled her out of the girl's white arms, "listen to me! One thing . . . one thing I have not told you—"

"Move, nigger!" One of the men twisted Matty's arm behind her back. She groaned but would not leave Eleanor even then.

"Eleanor, hush! Hush, you must hear me now. You are carrying the Captain's child, did you know that? Eleanor, do you understand me? You are going to bear Michael Ives's son!"

Eleanor's eyes widened . . . forgetting the moment and her surroundings and the watching crowd, a glorious smile lit up her wasted face for just an instant. Then she felt Matty slip away from her . . . she grasped the older woman's small hand and pressed it to her lips.

"I wondered," she said, "I wasn't sure . . . I don't know much about such things . . . oh, Matty, Matty dearest . . ."

And then Matty was gone from her. With one final loving glance the black woman stood erect and cast off the hands that would have held her. She walked proudly to the center of the block where Nathanial Graham began to describe her many attributes in glowing terms:

"Not a breeder, perhaps, my friends, yet capable of keeping others in charge and training younger ones. This woman is an excellent cook, seamstress and general housekeeper, speaks several languages, has been taught both reading and writing, consider *that* if you will. She has spent the better part of her life in high company, continually exposed to the tastes and demands of the upper classes..."

The ladies prompted their husbands to bid, thinking the quiet black woman they were peering at might be the very thing needed to get their lazy black girls in hand; of course you could see from the haughty look on her face that she thought herself too good for any of them ... but a taste of the lash now and then would be the very thing to bring her down a peg or two.

But the gentlemen were not much interested and the bidding was sporadic and halfhearted. Nathanial had been determined to ask a starting bid of three hundred pounds; with dismay he saw his buyers turn away, engaging in conversation with one another, and a few ambled off altogether.

"*If* I might have your kind indulgence just a few moments more," Nathanial spoke up very loudly. "It might be of interest to you to learn a bit more of this wench's background. She was born a princess, my friends, daughter of a great desert chieftain in far-off Libya..." There was not much reaction to this ploy. Nathanial licked his lips and talked faster: "When she was still but a girl, a famous French nobleman and army gentleman fell in love with her, paid her father a fortune for her, and made her his mistress!"

The gentlemen broke off their conversations and looked back at the block with somewhat belated interest, and the ladies, so anxious to bid but a moment earlier, frowned and shook their heads at this new piece of information. Nathanial was encouraged and went on, pushing Matty closer to the front of the block that she might be seen to more advantage.

"When the unfortunate French gentleman was killed in battle, not many weeks passed before his beautiful mistress came to the attention of none other than the Royal Governor of Antigua ... and His Excellency lost no time in taking her into his household, His

588

Excellency knowing a good thing when he saw it . . ." The gentlemen in the crowd guffawed at this and moved closer, helping themselves generously to their snuffboxes as if to clear their heads for deeper thinking.

"This black wench bore a daughter to the Royal Governor, that same daughter you see before you on the block, too . . . as white-looking as you or me, as white-looking, if you'll forgive me, gentlemen, as any white lady here among us. Now, shall we get down to serious bidding, my friends? I have already described to you some of this spicy tart's skills. I leave it to your own imagination to fill in the rest, which I forbear to do in the presence of these ladies but keep in mind the exotic background, gentlemen, and the un-doubted talents, not to be mentioned, I repeat, which she has acquired along the way! Do I hear three hundred pounds, gentle-men? . . . and cheap at the price?"

"Wait a minute, Graham, let's have a good look at her!" called one of the leading lights of the community, looking about at his friends for approbation. Shouts broke out on the instant, pretended outrage at Graham's inflated prices, demands to inspect the goods more closely . . . Nathanial was no fool. A sharp, decisive nod to his clerk and with practiced hands Matty's black dress was torn open from top to bottom and pulled back down over her shoulders, exposing her full breasts and narrow waist and soft, flat belly. She did not flinch but merely raised her eyes above the crowd and stared disdainfully at the distant horizon. Now the gentlemen pressed very close about and a smattering of outright applause, accompanied by throaty chuckles, broke out among them. Matty was turned about and back again; the tattered remnants of her dress were flung aside and admiring whistles and even cheers greeted the sight of her slim, well-shaped hips and legs.

As Nathanial had shrewdly supposed, natural lust brought the bidding up at once and it soon became quite lively. The ladies were irritated with their menfolk and ignored the entire transaction, and the only woman present who participated in the sale was a colorfully attired, extraordinarily blond female of more than middle years who expressed a desire to acquire Matty for her business establishment. But she was soon outbid as the shouts grew louder, the price higher, the mood of the gentlemen increasingly raucous. At length, to the utter astonishment of Nathanial himself, an unprecedented bid of eight hundred fifty pounds sterling gave Matty into the hands of an elderly, bewhiskered sea captain who had missed most of the sale and wandered along at almost the last minute with more money to spend than anyone else had left.

"Now what in the world is *he* goin' to do with her?" giggled Fancy as she watched Matty taken down from the block, and the old sea captain carefully counted out his payment in cash.

"What difference, sister dear?" drawled William hoarsely, rubbing his injured throat with an aggrieved expression. "She's gone, that's all that matters to us. And good riddance to a bold, dangerous tart!"

Eleanor saw them lifting the beautiful black woman into the back of a little open cart. The elderly purchaser waved his driver away with an impatient hand. The horse stepped forward, weaving his way very gingerly through the throng. Matty clung to the sides of the cart to keep her balance.

"*Matty!*" Eleanor screamed. "Matty!"

Matty lifted one hand and reached out, as if to touch the girl over the quickly widening space dividing them. She was beyond weeping now. She merely looked back numbly as the cart picked up speed and the crowd and the auction block receded. The last sight she had, before the cart turned a corner, was the vision of two outstretched, imploring white arms and a glimpse of Eleanor's long, flaming hair whipped by the angry wind.

William climbed back into the family carriage, insisting that Fancy accompany him. Sydney was already there. William closed the carriage doors and signaled the driver to leave the wharf quickly.

Still on the block, Nathanial saw the Campions leave and cursed them roundly under his breath. Sharp of William to get himself away now, before the rest of the farce was played, before the crowd realized that they had been misled. Sharp of William to leave it all to Graham's!

Nathanial cleared his throat a few times and broke the news to his eagerly anticipating customers that Master Campion had, at the last moment, withdrawn Eleanor from the general sale, having received word of an outrageously large offer from some undisclosed but very important source. Nathanial spoke with great trepidation and he was quite correct in his estimate of the crowd's outraged disappointment.

Hoots and catcalls and furious shouting answered his tremulous announcement and the angry demonstration continued the whole time it took to remove Eleanor, half fainting, from their sight. They

590

threw things and threatened to burn Graham's down around Nathanial's head. A few windows were smashed and, even after the girl was gone, they continued to voice their frustration for a long time.

But the fine carriages drove off and bit by bit the crowd began to trail off under the alert gaze of Nathanial's men together with several hastily summoned soldiers from the fortress. When the wharf was finally cleared, Nathanial breathed a sigh of relief. Dusk was coming on and the furious wind seemed to have spent itself and was heading meekly inland toward the mountains.

He ordered his men to deliver Eleanor over to the men William would send to fetch her to Stag Run first thing in the morning. Then he pulled down his dark shades, lit a candle in his office and, with his brothers, began to tally up the profits from this day's business.

But, grand as the final figures proved to be, Nathanial privately persisted in adding on what would have been the commission on another thousand pounds to the total. When he added up twice more and his three brothers congratulated themselves and him with a helping of rum all round, he could not quite find the hearty smile the occasion clearly demanded. In his heart he still felt . . . and he knew old Arthur would concur . . . that Graham's was out of pocket by that missing commission, that Graham's had been cheated by William Campion. Decidedly cheated, thought Nathanial bitterly even as he clinked glasses and toasted the house of Graham. And no one would ever be able to change his mind on the subject.

Eight

"Descent Into Hell"

1 I Can Be Brave For Him

One faint, distant sputtering torch was alight, thrust into the wall at the other side of the slave pens. It cast no illumination into the cell where Eleanor Campion was, its dull ruddy glow served only to emphasize the gloom, the emptiness, the eerie, hollow silence. Last night three hundred human beings filled these pens and formed a sort of community of sorrow; now the three hundred were gone their

591

separate ways, taking their sorrow with them, but the pens, the cages, the narrow stone corridors connecting them, the very walls themselves, seemed steeped in cumulative horrors and lingering grief.

Eleanor had been close to fainting when they had brought her back in from the auction block. She was vaguely aware of the clanging slam of the cell door, the rusty, unwilling scraping of the lock as it was turned, the clatter of something metallic upon the floor nearby, and the fading footsteps of the men who had brought her to this.

She glanced to one side and saw that a battered tin plate filled with Indian corn had been placed there for her supper, and with it a cup of water. She felt ill at the thought of such fare, or of any food.

She sat down on the bare floor, her knees drawn up, her face buried on her folded arms. Figures danced before her eyes, open or closed: Dogon in chains, the noose about his neck, and Ada, who had screamed when little Ezra was sold away from her, and Daniel, who had taken four strong men to the ground with him in his struggle to be free, and, above all else, Matty. Eleanor did not yet know what they had said about her and Matty, there hadn't been time up there upon the auction block for Matty to tell her everything. She did not know they had accused her of being Matty's daughter. But now the loss and agony she was feeling could not have been more terrible if Matty really was her mother. And still, she found she could not weep, neither for any of them nor for herself. She could not think clearly about the day or what had happened.

Her mind picked out an image to dwell upon, perversely, the image of one person who did not yet exist as such: the child, the child Matty had told her was even now in her womb. The child! It had no reality for her, even saying the word did not bring home the fact. She could not imagine it; she half believed it was not true after all.

She looked about warily to see if she were being watched, but there was no one there. Only then did she slip Michael's ring from the small bandage remaining on one hand, wondering fleetingly why the bandage was there. She held the ring against her cheek for a moment, then put it on her finger, tracing slowly and carefully the three letters carved into it. And the thought came to her quite suddenly that this ring now belonged to the child she carried. For a moment, for only one moment, she shook her head and smothered a sob and wished to God the child did not exist.

For herself, she thought in an oddly detached way, there was one solution. Wherever they took her, into whatever grim situation she was to be thrust, sooner or later she would find a way to die.

Someone would grow careless: one day a door would be left unlocked, a window unlatched, a knife or pistol left lying about where she would get it. . . .

"Oh, Michael, Michael, my love!" she murmured brokenly, kissing the ring. How easy it would be, how much more courageously she might bear whatever would be done to her if she could look forward to the peace and tranquility of the grave!

But now there was the child, Michael's child, and she was no longer free even to choose the death for herself that would also mean death for the child.

She pressed her hand flat against her stomach. Too soon for any sign of life or movement, she knew that much of such things. But she could feel how her own flesh had already changed. It must be true. She figured quickly. It would be born sometime toward the end of next May. She tried very hard to imagine the child's small face and limbs, but all she could see in her mind's eye were Michael's blond curls and startling blue eyes, his wide slow smile, the broad set of his shoulders, his long legs and lean, hard body. And he was gone, after having found so brief a bit of peace and happiness, gone without ever knowing there would be an Ives son or daughter to wear the old steel ring and share its traditions of honor and courage.

Eleanor raised her head and drew a long, sharp breath. This child must live! And *she* must live, she must endure whatever came her way so that Michael's child might come into the world. A wretched cruel small voice inside her taunted her with thoughts of what she might be bringing upon that child: it would be born a nameless slave, even as she was now, heir to nothing but misery and privation; it might be taken from her and sold thousands of miles away and never even know of its parents; it might be killed in infancy . . . . she shuddered, folding her arms tight against her body, trying to control the involuntary convulsions that shook her. All of the terrors she had so long anticipated had become reality. She was alone, helpless, friendless, abandoned by Fate itself. What more could she have to fear? Pain, humiliation, the end of everything worth living for? This was evidently to be her lot now. She faced it without fear, even without caring very much.

But a new and far more potent fear began to grow in her from that moment, a fear more poignant and terrible than any she had ever known before: she knew at last what it was to fear for her child! Always, before this, she had considered life as it directly affected her and those to whom she felt responsibility. But now something infinitely unique and precious suddenly interposed itself between her and life, something she must forevermore hold first, above any other consideration.

Eleanor touched the ring with her fingertips tenderly, thinking of her child that was to be.

"I can be brave, too," she said, remembering the old message of this ring. " 'ICI,' here, in this place, here must I make my stand and fight my fight, come what may! Here," she whispered, "and wherever God takes me and my child. I can be brave for him!"

A few moments later she picked up the plate of Indian corn and forced herself to eat it. And then, incredibly, she fell into a deep, dreamless sleep of exhaustion, a sleep that mercifully obliterated everything for a little while.

2 Return To Stag Run

Jack Keane and the *Tiger Eye* were gone from Stag Run. The snug little shack he inhabited when ashore was empty. The strikingly handsome, soaring bowsprit of the privateer vessel was missing from among the motley collection of aging ships in that hidden bay, its very absence making what remained there at anchor even more dismal-looking. Keane had completed his repairs to the damaged *Tiger Eye* and found his crew somewhat surly for lack of useful occupation, to say nothing of dire lack of funds.

Thus, not three days after Eleanor had escaped him, Jack had himself ceremoniously carried aboard ship on a litter, and set sail immediately. He had sent Dogon back to William, tied hand and foot, together with a short, terse note about Eleanor—not an apology for his carelessness, Jack Keane never apologized to anyone for anything—merely a brief message of explanation. And, too, he deemed it prudent for a time to avoid William until his anger had a chance to cool. A leisurely cruise in southern waters was the very thing to restore his strength and vitality and have a look around for new opportunities in his line.

William was delighted to have Keane away just now. William's plans for the not-too-distant future included a complete clearing-out of his associates in the Brotherhood from Stag Run, so that the property might be built up. Fancy wanted Belleterre for herself and her father; William desired to be as far away as possible from them both. Rogue's Fall could easily be run by an overseer, like so many other Carolina plantations.

William had given the situation a good deal of thought since first his family had recovered from the shock of meeting Eleanor and had set about finding the right way of disposing of her. Now all of that was behind them. They had a goodly amount of money and firmly established credit and, even more important, they were in general agreement as to how they should invest.

The Campions spent that night in Charles Town with friends at a celebration banquet that many in the city privately thought to be in shockingly bad taste, all things considered. William could not have given less of a damn what anyone thought of him. During the festive evening he told his father that he was leaving the next day for a rest and holiday upon his new estate, Stag Run, and that he probably would not be back for a week or two. Sydney blandly agreed that the events of the past weeks had been very trying and his son most assuredly deserved a rest.

As it turned out, William stayed up past dawn, and drank himself into a sleep that lasted twelve hours, somewhat upsetting his plans. And while he was sleeping Eleanor was awakened at dawn, taken from the slave pens at Graham's and hurried into a closed carriage. There a mantle was carelessly thrown over her shoulders and she was driven off through the neat, precise streets of Charles Town.

She was seated with her hands bound, one man beside her, two across from her and a fourth driving. She thought she recognized the men as William's close companions and she shrank away from them into a dark corner of the vehicle. But William, still rankling over what had happened with Jack Keane, had so warned and threatened his men, so bullied and worried them with what he would do if they so much as placed a hand upon Eleanor that she could not have been safer just then had he sent her to a convent. The men talked to each other, never looking her way through the entire long, hard journey, which was made even longer and more torturous by the fact that a carriage could not get through forestland and swamp where a single horse and rider could go with comparative ease. The carriage was forced to hug the shoreline all the way, jolting and lurching and careening wildly in and out of every little inlet and cove.

Eleanor wondered where she was being taken and into whose hands William had delivered her. When the carriage rolled away from the hard streets of Charles Town and turned off on to a dirt track, she assumed their destination was one of the local plantations. But soon the dirt track gave way to a peculiar rocky and uneven trail; she began to hear the sound of the ocean to one side and realized they were very far from Charles Town. The curtains of the carriage had been carefully drawn shut so she could not see out. She had early given up her attempts to learn where they were going from the men around her. They would not answer her no matter what she said. So the carriage rumbled onward hour after hour in almost total silence. The men took turns napping as best they could in the swaying, springless vehicle and, later in the afternoon, ate sparingly of bread and cheese and wine, giving Eleanor a share of each.

It was nearly dark when the carriage reached Stag Run. As they slowed down, Eleanor found herself quickly seized and the mantle roughly cast over her head, muffling her face and body. The door was opened and she was carried out slung over one man's shoulder, gasping for air. Her captor carried her several yards and thrust her into some dark enclosed place. As she lay where he had thrown her, stunned and breathless, a woman she could not see spoke a few words to the man, then cut the ropes that tied her arms behind her. Eleanor struggled frantically to pull the confining mantle loose . . . and just as she did so and drew several deep cool drafts of fresh air, she heard a strangely familiar sound behind her. She jumped to her feet as the door was shut upon her and the heavy wooden bolt was drawn across it on the outside.

"I know this place!" she said aloud, tremblingly touching the dark door with her hands. She whirled about, looking up. Once more she beheld the little barred window opposite the door, set tantalizingly high in the wall.

"Keane!" she cried in despair, now realizing all too well where they had taken her. She was at Stag Run, back in the hands of the pirates . . . and fragments of William's conversation with their chief came back to her. William must have reconsidered his decision, he had sold her to Jack Keane! The memory of Keane's touch upon her body, the intrusive, unrelenting strength of the man, the dark, craggy face and hawkish nose, the black burning eyes, all of it returned in the instant. Her heart pounded as though it would break free of her flesh. So she was to belong to Keane! This time there was no Dogon to save her. She was Keane's slave, a thing to be used for a while and then passed on, to be used up utterly and cast away without a second thought.

Knowing it was of no avail to attempt to escape from the shack, she began to pace about the small space, wringing her hands, starting in alarm at every sound she heard outside. She expected to see Keane come swaggering in the doorway any minute.

But hours passed and he did not come. No one disturbed her. She had quite worn herself out with pacing and thinking and the once again futile search for some kind of weapon with which to defend herself. The darkness gradually softened into a misty moonlight dimness. Even this little bit of light helped calm her somewhat. She sat down cautiously on the very edge of the bed in the corner, wakeful and alert. This time at least she would not be taken unawares. She tried to bring order to her chaotic, rambling thoughts. Her mind dwelt upon Keane. It was he who had killed Michael, she remembered suddenly. Anger struck her like a physical blow. Because of him Michael was dead and would never see his child. Because of him Dogon had died a hideous slow death on the block. And now she was to serve his pleasure! The thought of it sickened her . . . until she reflected upon the alternative: William had wanted to keep her for himself. At least she was free of him now, whatever Keane was, demanding, lustful, arrogant, he was sane and she was sure that William was not. She had heard the whispered rumors about her cousin, incredible tales of cruelty and sadistic pleasures she had hardly understood at the time. If William had kept her, knowing that she would bear Michael Ives's child . . . Eleanor pushed the thought away hastily. Keane had said he would take her to some distant island and sell her there. It would be far from William Campion and his madness; there might be a way to keep herself and the child alive. Beyond that she could not think or plan. Whatever happened with Keane he was not William. Perhaps she could strike some bargain with him, force herself to be obedient to his whims, servile, anything, anything at all to stay alive and keep the child alive!

3   William Campion's Journey

And then William Campion came to Stag Run, alone, on horseback, as the moon rose silver gold over the wind-tossed trees.

William had awakened from his drunken sleep just before supper-time. At first he could not understand what had become of the day. When they explained it to him, he had shouted hysterically and gone stalking down to the stables, demanding a horse, refusing all efforts anyone made to get him to wait, to bathe and change his rumpled clothing and have a bite of supper, even to put off his journey until the next morning.

He had roared insults that could be heard up and down the quiet residential streets of Charles Town and, in a few minutes, he disappeared into the dusk, lashing his hapless horse with ferocious energy. The memory of Eleanor's half-naked bosom as she had stood chained and helpless on the block was a goad driving him on, that memory and the realization that she was now his prisoner, far away on the beach at Stag Run. He raced the horse through forest and marsh and swamp and salt flat, whipping the beast all the harder when it staggered and almost fell under him.

He reached Stag Run before midnight. There was a single fire blazing sporadically on the sand near the line of shanties. A few of the privateers were playing at cards and dice in a desultory fashion. One of their women, inspired by kicks and curses, now and then went over and added a few more armfuls of brush to the flames.

William appeared before them on a trembling, foam-covered horse. His braces were undone, he wore no coat or hat, his hair was wild and disheveled, his face red and streaked with sweat and dust. The pirates squinted up at him without much interest. The woman pointed silently toward Keane's shack. William left the horse to fend for itself and rushed past them. The pirates muttered to each other, watching him, laughing, and told the woman to fetch out more rum.

4 Let The Child Live!

She heard the bolt sliding back across the door. She jumped up and stood, breathless, as far from the bed as she could get and watched the door thrown open. The moon shone on the other side of the shack, leaving the doorway in deep shadow. For a moment all she could make out was a very tall presence in the darkness, moving a foot or so into the room, slamming the door closed again. She heard someone breathing unevenly, raggedly, as if he had just run some great distance. She did not, could not, move or speak now that the moment had come.

Where she was standing, the moonlight filtering down from the window fell directly upon her, bathing her pale face and form in a silvery glow. She looked in that instant like a spirit creature, disembodied, created of the light itself. The auburn hair was like a dark thick veil of silk. The great eyes, staring startled and afraid into the shadows, were all the more beautiful to him who watched them because they revealed her fear and from her fear he took his pleasure. She had forgotten the long mantle they'd given her; it still lay upon the floor at her feet and she wore only the soft undergarments she had worn upon the block.

"Who is it?" she whispered. "Is it you, Keane?"

William laughed at that and moved into the light so she could see him.

"No, no, dear cousin, Jack's at sea again. It's only I, William."

Eleanor fell back, her face twisted with shocked surprise. One hand flew to her mouth. "Oh, no!" she cried. "Oh, no!"

William smiled. "Oh, yes, my dear. I should think you'd be relieved . . . poor old Jack rather frightened you, I hear. If it weren't for that black madman of yours who knows what fearful delights Jack would have shown you by now. By the way, Eleanor, how far along *did* Jack get with you before your dramatic rescue?"

Eleanor shook her head vehemently. William raised an eyebrow.

"Really? I can't tell you how glad I am to hear that. I trusted Jack, you remember? I've been out of sorts with him on your account, but, no harm done, eh?"

She stared at him dully while he busied himself starting a fire in the small stone hearth. When the fire took he stood by it, rubbing his hands continually over his forehead and shoulders and arms. Now Eleanor saw that he was soaked with sweat and covered with dust and that he had apparently come all the way from home without bothering to dress properly. He never took his eyes from her; they stared bulging half out of his head, pressing her, pinning her down, devouring her. She said nothing but waited for him to speak.

"I doubt you'll ever see Jack again," he said at length. "Now that Stag Run is mine I shall build here and, useful as they have been to us, I'm afraid Jack and his friends shall have to go. But, not you, dear Eleanor," he said very softly, licking his thick lips. "Not you. I shall keep you here, *cousin*, while you amuse me, and then out into the fields with you. By that time we ought to have a substantial amount of acreage in tobacco and rice—perfect place for rice, don't you think?—and you can earn your keep side by side with your nigger friends."

Eleanor was not deceived by his mild, soft tone. She cleared her throat and forced herself to speak to him.

"You've . . . you've sold my friends away. You don't have enough hands to work all three places."

"We shall manage, never fear," laughed William. He approached her so suddenly she had not time to move away. He took her by the arm with one hand and with the other he touched her middle. "Perhaps we shall breed another crop to answer our needs, eh? Shall we breed and raise up a crop of slaves? I understand Ives dropped just such a one into that lovely body of yours, cousin. If you delight me as I think you must, perhaps we'll let the brat live and bring him up a pet for Fancy . . . if I don't covet him myself. What say you to that, Eleanor? Shall the child be allowed to live? Or shall I send in Moira with her sharp little knitting needles? Oh, she's very skillful, Moira, rid you of the brat in five minutes' time. Come, what do you say, cousin? Cut out the imp with no ado and you none the worse for it, after a day or so? Just say the word, my dear! And if you don't fancy Moira for a chirugeon, why, I'll do it myself and save the half-crown fee she charges."

All the while he spoke, William was slowly, inexorably bending the arm he held, twisting it, forcing it back. Waves of pain and nausea gripped Eleanor. He wound his thick fingers into her hair and pulled her to him until their mouths were inches apart and she was overwhelmed by the sick, stale stink of his breath.

"No, please," she whispered faintly, trying to turn her face away. The hand buried in her hair twisted suddenly, nearly snapping her neck.

"Fond of it, are you?" jeered William, his eyes like glittering coals in the firelight. "Want to keep the brat, is that it? Well, and so you shall, Eleanor, so you shall," he purred. He buried his swollen face in her neck, half kissing, half biting the delicate flesh of her throat. Eleanor writhed in his arms but could not move as much as an inch so tightly was he holding her.

He looked up at her face and saw her expression of loathing and disgust and was pleased with it. "Tell me what you would have me do," he prodded her. "Choose, Eleanor, I've waited too long for this night as it is. Let the brat live and obey me in all things. Or, it may be torn out now and the last of the Ives blood is gone forever." He eyed her cannily. "Either way, I shall have what I'm after. Decide."

"Let it live, for the love of God, William, let the child alone and I will . . . . I will do whatever you wish!"

"Ah!" he nodded, knowing all along what her answer would be, not really caring but curious. "Very well, then. We shall leave the Captain's son and heir in peace for now"—and Eleanor trembled at the knowledge that her child would always be the threat he would hold over her—"in . . . *relative* peace," he murmured, chuckling.

At once he was at her like an animal, snorting and biting her throat, her lips and ears, while his hands quickly tore the white camisole. Eleanor closed her eyes but he would have none of that. He wanted to be able to see every expression on her face. He jerked her chin viciously and warned her to remain still. Then he dragged her over to the little bed and, sitting down on the edge of it, he forced her to stand facing him. With practiced fingers he removed the petticoats and undergarments, muttering to himself all the while. When she was quite naked he tossed the discarded clothing in a heap in one corner and looked her up and down closely.

"Oh, yes, 'tis very true, you are with child," he spoke in a breathy, rasping voice she hardly recognized.

"Yes," she breathed, trembling violently.

"What was that you said? Don't whisper so, my dear, I might misunderstand you and that would be unfortunate, wouldn't it?"

"Yes, yes, I'm sure!" she cried out. Without thinking, Eleanor blindly struck out and hit him on the shoulder with her fist, trying to pull away. William roared with fury and deliberately clawed her viciously with his nails. She screamed in agony, feeling the sudden rush of her own blood cascading down her naked body.

William shuddered at the sound, his face transported with pleasure. He took his hands away and looked closely at the bloody marks his fingernails had left upon her creamy skin . . . and then he bent his head over her and, shaking with new horror, she felt the rasp of his dry, hot tongue. Now she forgot everything, struggling insanely, twisting, squirming, smashing him with her fists and screaming ever louder, but William evaded her ineffectual blows and laughed at her.

And suddenly he picked her up and threw her onto the bed. He stood looking down at her while he unbuckled his thick leather belt. Eleanor gazed up at him, her eyes barely focused, and saw that there were still traces of her blood upon his thick lips. She groaned, then scrambled wildly from the bed, trying to reach the door but in an instant he was there, blocking her way. He spun her around with ease, forcing her to her knees on the hard-packed dirt floor.

It was almost as he'd dreamed it, almost. Here was Eleanor naked, terrified, on her knees before him, her long red hair down her back and falling over her shoulders in damp tendrils like thin rivers of red blood . . . William lifted the belt, wrapped the end of it about his right hand and raised it high. . . .

Eleanor heard that first savage blow before she felt the awful racking spasm—the leather belt whipped through the air with a strange, whirring sound, then suddenly bit deeply into her back like a white-hot sword and the slow pulling away of it through her lacerated skin was even more excruciating. She twisted around and looked up at his bloodshot, staring eyes, her hands held up to ward off the next blow.

"William!" she gasped, "don't do this, for God's sake! What good am I to you like this? Take your pleasure of me if you must, but no more, no more!"

"My 'pleasure'?" he repeated, savoring the word. "But, my darling Eleanor, this *is* my pleasure, didn't you know?" He smiled down at her, raising the belt once more.

"Just a bit more, my pet," he crooned thickly. "A bit more and we'll be ready for other sport!"

Eleanor cringed as the belt came crashing down again and then again, raining blows upon her helpless body. She prayed she might faint, she implored Heaven for the oblivion of the past days, but she was to be spared nothing. Just when she felt the world grow black and dim and her senses swam in a blur of pain and despair, William tossed the belt from him and fell upon her. And it was as if the other had been nothing, nothing at all, compared to this new, most hideous torture of all. It went on for what seemed at first like hours and then into a timeless hell of torment in which she could no longer distinguish each separate different pain one from the other, but all blended together to transport her body and soul into one unendurable rape.

She no longer screamed or even moaned. She did not think of the child or of Michael or of herself as an entity separate from the animal who used her thus. She was only *aware*, horribly, intensely aware of *William* as though the whole world, the universe and all in it had shrunk to the limits of this small dark terrible room.

Some time a few hours before dawn, William pushed her away. She lay where he left her, discarded as the mantle she had dropped when she came there, and she looked at him with glazed eyes as he rummaged about and finally discovered an old, torn shirt Keane had left behind.

"Put that on," William commanded. And she did so, barely able to move. The rough cloth grated against every open wound on her body but she made no sound. William lay back on the bed, his arms folded behind his head, a patchwork coverlet thrown over his ugly nakedness.

"You're a spiritless thing," he said contemptuously, yet there was a sleepy, satiated look of pleasure on his sallow face. "Is that all I can expect of you? Tears and misery? You'll bore me to death very soon . . . and there are so many other things I've planned for the two of us, Eleanor. It won't always be like this . . . I've been very hungry for you, my dear, for a very long time—"

"Do you intend to kill me?" she broke in, her voice scratchy and raw, barely audible.

"Kill you?" He seemed astounded at the idea. "Kill you? Of course I don't mean to kill you!"

"You'll do it anyway," she sighed, looking significantly at the belt he had thrown on the floor. "You asked me for a bargain and I agreed to obey you. You said 'choose' and I did so. But I shall be dead and the child with me before ever it is born."

William looked annoyed. He yawned several times and rolled over on his pendulous stomach.

"You have much to learn, Eleanor. I shall spend the next week instructing you. If you die it will be because you do not learn quickly. Once this period of study is over, you will be my personal attendant. You will prepare my meals, see to my clothing and wigs, do everything, in short, that is required for my comfort and satisfaction. Once in awhile we shall enjoy such evenings as this. And once in awhile I shall lend you to a few of my dearest friends. Do you understand me, my dear?"

She nodded mutely, slowly, crouched like a whipped dog by the dying fire.

"Good," he nodded. "As for the child, try not to remind me of the child, Eleanor. Try very *hard* not to remind me of it. I am not always in such good spirits as I am tonight. I might become angry, you see, and then I will remember Captain Ives. I will envision you and him together, conceiving that intolerable brat. I leave it to your imagination to discover the results. Now rest, cousin, I will require you again in the morning.''

He fell asleep almost immediately. She watched him for a long time, thinking that she could not have imagined such a hatred as she felt for this man could exist in a human heart and not tear that heart to shreds for sheer savage force. There was no way of pretending to please or satisfy him as she had vaguely planned in the beginning.

Even the normal attractions a woman might make use of to divert a man would hold no interest for such a man as this. It was *fear* that aroused him; he could sniff it out in the very air around him like some predacious beast and, when he found it, every instinct in his twisted soul cried out for pain and terror to relieve him.

Eleanor sat, stunned and mute, upon the cold dirt floor and watched the pale waning away of the moonlight as it moved slowly across the bars of the window in the wall. Outside the small, tumbledown hovel all was very still. The occasional sound of voices she had heard earlier around the open fire was gone now. Only the insistent rush of the surf against the beach reached her ears. She thought how free, how free the ocean is, wild and rambunctious and willful, roaming where it will and no man powerful enough to hold or hamper it!

She wrapped her bruised, aching arms about her and leaned her head against the wall to await the coming day. William tossed and mumbled uneasily in his sleep. She thought with horror of the morning and of the ''lessons'' he would yet delight in teaching her. One more such ''lesson,'' she knew, and he would crush out the life of her unborn child, finding amusement in her pain, pleasure in her sorrow.

She must get away, she must escape! The words filled her mind, returning again and again, hammering at her, insisting, like the ceaseless voice of the surf so close by. Escape!

She glanced around with bitter eyes; all that had happened before this day was only a dream; now this small awful place and what it held had become the only remaining reality. There was no escape, not for her, not for her child.

She shivered repeatedly and crept stealthily closer to the crude stone hearth. How cold it was now that the fire had dwindled down into a small heap of white ash and dull red embers! Her teeth were chattering in the chill October air. Gingerly she reached out and touched the stones. They were still warm. She moved even closer, curling her half-naked body about the hearth, huddling over the dying embers, rubbing her hands together. The little remaining heat rose up and penetrated the newly healed burns on her palms and she remembered how she had sought Michael's ring amid the flames of another fire.

The ring, all but forgotten during this last ordeal, shone with a steady little glimmer in the wavering ruddy light. Eleanor looked at it and could not look away. Her whole being seemed to fasten upon that small object on her finger and the single word its worn letters spelled out leaped up as if to reproach her. *Ici,* she read, *here.* Here, here! She stifled a cry of anguish from the very soul. Rising painfully to her knees, she grasped the overhanging hearthstones with both hands to support her body. She leaned her full weight upon her hands and pressed her face to the roughhewn stone, weeping silent tears for the vow she had sworn to protect the tiny life entrusted to her, a vow she could not keep.

A sudden, grating sound shocked her motionless. The sound ceased. She drew her face back, hardly daring to breath. Slowly, cautiously, she pressed the stones upon which her hands still rested . . . and immediately she heard the sound again, and one of them moved a bit under her fingers. She gazed frantically over toward William's sleeping form. Had he heard? Had the sound awakened him?

Willliam slept on. She waited there in the stillness, counting the very breaths he took, making sure there was no change in him. If he were to wake now . . .

Not now but soon enough, she thought, much, much too soon! It came to her as she knelt there, frozen with apprehension, that from this night on, whatever remained of her life would be spent just so, waiting, watching, fearing.

An immense, ferocious anger suddenly leaped up in her. She felt the cold earthen floor beneath her knees, she felt anew the pain and humiliation of her position. Revulsion filled her soul, pride that William planned to kill in her now rose up as it never had before, pride and anger brought life back to her exhausted, tortured body. She lowered her hands from the hearth and looked again at Michael's ring.

No! No more! Never again! Oh, no, she thought, William would not use her so again; he would not use her love for her child and its dead father as the lever to force her obedience; he would not *live* to feed upon her fear a second time! *No*, the fierce internal cry came louder to her mind, no and no again! Escape, the surf called back to her, escape and live!

What had she been about, she wondered in that instant? What had she been thinking of, she, her father's daughter, to suffer the degradation inflicted upon her by a madman? She had been asleep, all the time asleep and dreaming while they had taken her land and scattered her friends and vilified her before the world! But the sleep was ended, the dream was over—"Awake, awake, Deborah: awake!" she suddenly remembered the ancient song. She was awake now, come what may it was time to act.

Again she looked over at William. A pang of fear, almost despair, stabbed her. Escape him? How? How escape, naked and alone, with no weapon to defend herself, surrounded by enemies, no place to go, no means to go anywhere?

Her glance fell upon the door, bolted on the inside. Hopeless; doubt bedeviled her conscious thoughts at every turn; hopeless even to think of escape. But while the conscious thought distracted her, the will she had already set in motion seconds earlier began to work. Her hands were already reaching about on the dark floor, seeking the discarded mantle she had flung aside hours before. Her fingers encountered the rough cloth, drew it to her, pulled it around her body and settled the hood low over her head and face.

Even while the thought came, mocking and cruel, what do you think you're going to do now?... she watched William with new eyes, eyes that saw his regular, steady breathing and signaled it was safe to go ahead.

She started to stand up. Where are you going, taunted the voice inside her head, and what will you do if he wakes up, now, or a moment from now, what will you do?

I will kill him, came the calm reply, so clear, so positive it shocked her. *If there is no other way, I will kill him*, it came again, and the internal dialogue continued: How will you kill him without a weapon? don't be a fool, wait, wait for a better time....

She hesitated, staring uncertainly around the room in which there was neither sword nor knife nor gun nor any object that might be used for a weapon.

And while she hesitated and once more despaired, her body turned as of its own accord, her hands felt about carefully for the loose hearthstone she had forgotten. She pushed the stone. It grated against the stone next to it but it moved more freely than it had before. Gritting her teeth, praying the sleeping man would not hear, she worked the stone back and forth. Each time it was looser, and a little soft shower of dust came down.

Time, you're wasting time, she thought fearfully. Go to the door, pull the bolt back, run, hurry while there's still time and he is still asleep! She forced the thought away and worked the stone with maddening slowness. One loud screech of that makeshift wooden bolt and, she knew, William would be upon her. She must be able to fight him, she must!

Then, as the stone came loose and she felt the cold weight of it in her hands, she hesitated once more. Another quick glance showed her that William had not moved. Why not make sure he could not stop her? Why not kill him now, as he slept? He could never follow her, never hurt her again. She might be miles away before the pirates would realize what had happened and go looking for her . . . if they would even bestir themselves on such a quest once William was dead!

Kill him, came the thought, *hurry! kill him!* Oh, sweet revenge for Michael's death, for Dogon and Matty, for all the horrors this man had brought upon them! *Kill him now!*

On bare, soundless feet she stole to William's side, the stone held ready in her hands. His face was concealed from her by shadow. Was he lying there watching every move she made, amusing himself, waiting to pounce?

And that would be murder. In a world where honor is a personal choice and every heart defines it differently, who would ever blame her? Who else would even call it murder? All the right was on her side, all the guilt on his.

Then once again pride spoke and Eleanor turned away. *I will not do murder,* she told herself sternly, and a little jeering voice inside of her whispered *Fool!* But she did not hesitate or turn back again.

The door was only a few feet away. Heart pounding with a new faint hope of hope, she moved toward it. She groped for the end of

607

the bolt, missed it in the darkness, searched for it again and at last seized the thick wood firmly. Inch by inch she pulled it back, stopping when it stuck, closing it again, beginning all over again, patiently, slowly, and all the while she held the stone in her left hand and did not think of it.

The awkward bolt moved reluctantly in wooden shafts much warped by wind, salt sea air and rain. But it was almost done: only another two or three inches remained and the door would be open. Eleanor exerted every bit of strength she had for the final effort. The bolt shot out of her fingers, squeaking and grating as it slid and slammed resoundingly against the last shaft.

In an instant William was out of bed and lurching across the floor at her, his hands reaching for her throat, his eyes glittering with rage. The noises that came from his mouth were those of a crazed animal.

"*No!*" Eleanor cried out, whirling about to meet him. Hardly realizing what she was doing, she pulled her arm back and brought the stone crashing straight into William Campion's face!

He staggered back a few feet, blood gushing from the wound, holding his hands up in front of him as if to ward off another blow. Eleanor stood, paralyzed with fright, still holding her improvised weapon.

William reeled past her blindly, slamming headfirst into the door, then, turning, he swayed on his feet and lunged for her with an inarticulate howl of fury. She felt his fingers touch her. If he succeeded in seizing her now he would surely kill her. She moved back, kicking out at him. But he rushed at her, caught her, and threw her to the floor. His fingers closed about her throat as she writhed and struggled to break free. She was choking, gasping for a breath, her strength going. With one final desperate surge, she lifted her hand and smashed the stone across his head. She heard him grunt, then he stiffened, his body jerked spasmodically, and he fell away from her, collapsing heavily on the dirt floor.

Eleanor struggled to her feet and ran to the door. Surely someone would have heard by this time! She opened it a few inches and peered outside. There was not a soul around, not even a single sentry to keep watch by the cold fire on the beach. Ahead of her, only yards away across the silver sand, was the bay with its tall silent ships rocking at anchor. Several small boats were pulled up on the beach.

She looked back at William. He must be dead, she thought, he had not moved, she could not hear him breathing. She was free to go. She stepped outside, pulling the mantle about her, and closed the door behind her. She was free ... or was she? Where in Carolina could she go now, a slave, wearing a slave's iron collar about her neck? Once before she had escaped this place, but then she had a home to go to, a safe refuge. Now, she realized numbly, there was no one to take her in, there was no safe place. She had thought fleetingly of taking one of the horses the pirates kept nearby, but no horse could carry her far enough fast enough even if she did manage to ride away without rousing the privateers.

She must go! Every second she hesitated meant greater danger of being discovered. She glanced up at the sky and saw with dismay that the moon was down, the morning star winked lazily down from the east. Two hours till dawn, she thought, not even two hours, go, go *now!*

Without thinking or looking back she sped swiftly across the beach, the mantle billowing out behind her. She ran for the small boats, praying they were not tied up or too high on the sand for her to be able to push one into the water. She found a group of five or six, dinghies, capable of holding ten men. Too large, too heavy. She ran on, out of breath, stumbling and tripping on the broken shells and sharp stones beneath her feet. There was one more boat, apart from the rest, to this she moved as a last resort. It was lying in wet sand, the early incoming tide bringing little eddies and currents of water splashing about the bottom of it.

Eleanor reached it and gave it an experimental push. It was smaller than the others, a ship's boat, used by sailors to put ashore for fresh drinking water, and would hold perhaps three men with their water casks. As she pushed, the boat moved a little. She ran around to the stern end and rocked the small vessel back and forth to free it from the clinging sand. This done, she pushed with all her might. The boat inched forward reluctantly, then stopped, caught against a rock.

She ran to the bow end and pulled frantically. Again the boat moved. And again it stopped, the stern settled upon a thick clump of weeds. Back and forth she worked, always drawing the boat nearer the shallow water where she might wade in and push it for a distance, then climb aboard.

It took a very long time to accomplish this. She forgot about the pirates and about William, she forgot about everything in the world except the need to launch the boat and be gone out of the bay before dawn. Meanwhile, the tide picked up and worked against her, pushing the boat back again and again. Tears of vexation streamed down her sweating face as she forced herself to go on. And, at last, she felt the boat float lightly upon the water, thrust back by the tide, drawn out and almost out of her grasp by the strong undertow. She pulled her weary body into it and inserted the two short oars into the oarlocks. She sat and pulled hard upon the oars and felt the boat fly forward. She cursed the rumbling squeak of the locks each time she lifted the oars. She had to pass close to several of the big ships. She huddled, hunched over on the hard seat, guiding the boat steadily along, clinging to the black shadows the ships cast on the water. The pirates did not keep a watch aboard these ships at night, not so much as a lantern cast a light upon her as she slipped past them and moved on out into the central channel. Now she could feel the full strength of the morning tide, growing as the hazy dawn moved in gray and ghostlike from the Atlantic. Waves lashed the small boat about. In a few moments she was drenched with icy salt spray. She looked back to see how far she had come, and the beach loomed in the distance a dark, harsh yellow with a thin fringe of black trees behind. The boat dipped beneath a wave, threatened to overturn. She clung to the oars, wrapped her feet tightly about the narrow wooden boards beneath her, and waited it out.

When next the boat rose upon the crest of the waves, she was out of the bay, in open water, and the beach was all but invisible to her. Now she righted the boat carefully, and began to row a course parallel to the land, straining all the while to fight the tide and keep from being swept in against the hidden shoals and reefs. She fought off pain and terror and the need to sleep; she must not drift, she must not let the boat beach itself on a sandbar. There were islands somewhere about, that much she knew. North of Stag Run there were small islands dotted about the mouth of the Santee River, carefully marked on the charts made by her father long ago. Indians lived on some of the larger islands. Could she seek refuge with them? She pulled upon the oars, feeling that her back must surely break with each stroke. She had heard of runaway black slaves being taken in by sympathetic Indians . . . and she had also heard of the terrible massacre at Albemarle by ravaging Tuscarora Indians not twenty years past.

Resolutely, her lips tightened over clenched teeth, she rowed on as the sun moved overhead and turned the pounding waters burnished gold and purple rose. Would Indians be any worse than the tender mercy of William, if he still lived, or of his friends? . . . or, indeed, of any white man's hand in all of Carolina, now?

Escape, the voice of the roaming water had called to her hours ago. *Escape!* she looked into the glassy water now as she felt the sun's gathering heat burning down upon her head and aching shoulders and back. Escape. And if this was all, if this was the last refuge, and the water had only called her to itself . . . why then, she would die, she and the child, and share that great deep grave with Michael forever. So be it, she nodded to herself. And then she took another breath and pulled another stroke upon the oars.

Nine

Payment

1 It Will Be All Right

"Where is Eleanor Campion?"

His Excellency, the Royal Governor of Carolina, looked up at the tall angry man leaning over his desk. The Governor blinked several times, trying desperately to collect his thoughts. He felt a chill, he felt the beginning of a severe attack of the megrims coming on. He shrugged helplessly and his gaze swept once more across the overwhelming mountain of papers and official documents his most unexpected and unwelcome caller had placed before him.

"Your Excellency, I demand an answer! You've already inspected all of this evidence a dozen times over. You've read and reread the letter from Governor Able and you've admitted the proof of forgeries. I've been as patient with you as I'm ever likely to be! Now, for the last time, tell me where Mistress Campion has been taken!"

The Governor sighed. His voice quavered when he replied, very slowly, very reluctantly.

"My dear Captain Ives, the truth of the matter is, I simply do not *know* where she is. She was legally declared a slave—legally, you understand? And she was sold at auction—young man, please! Try to calm yourself!" he cried in sudden renewed alarm as Michael ground his teeth in rage, his fists curled at his sides. "Now, this may be difficult for you to comprehend, since you do not know our ways here in Carolina, but the evidence against her was undeniable. We had no choice but to proceed as we did. It is indeed a pity that you could not have appeared sooner and presented your proofs. What reason did we have to suspect Master Richards of treachery . . . of . . . of forgery?" The governor felt about desperately in his coat pockets for his snuffbox. He was ill, really he was quite ill!

"You might have questioned Sydney Campion's motives," snapped Michael. "As for my whereabouts, I think you have a pretty clear idea what happened to me and my ship!"

The Governor swallowed hard. "We had heard . . . rumors . . . that you were attacked by pirates . . ." he murmured faintly

Michael sneered. "Your Excellency, more than one royal governor has been sent back to England to stand trial for crimes and gross misconduct in administering the Crown's colonies. I am prepared to bring charges against you—"

"'Charges'? Charges? Against *me*?" sputtered the Governor, looking at Michael as if he were mad.

"Yes, against you, sir!" replied Michael heatedly. He leaned over the desk, his face inches away from that of the panic-stricken little man before him. "Conspiracy to defraud, complicity in the activities of pirates in this colony, accepting bribes from those same freebooters, corruption in office . . . need I go on, sir? You have allied yourself with thieves and scoundrels, overturned the will of the late Honorable Governor of the Crown colony of Antigua in order to profit yourself and to ensure the profit of your friends, and you have robbed and wrongfully imprisoned his daughter! I ask you again, sir, where is Eleanor Campion?"

The Governor shook his head feebly. "I knew nothing of what Campion was up to," he breathed. "Nothing! I was not present at the slave auction. The young woman was taken away after her Negroes were sold. The estates were assigned to her relatives and I considered the matter closed, closed, do you understand me? If anyone knows where Mistress Campion is, then it must be her cousins or her uncle. The auction was ten days ago; from that day to this there has been no word of her, I beg you to believe me!"

Michael straightened up, reached about and picked up the hat and cloak he had thrown aside an hour earlier when he had forced his way past the guards and confronted the astounded Governor.

"Where was the auction held?" he demanded.

"I believe it was at Graham's Wharf," replied His Excellency, "Graham's is our largest slave dealer."

"I shall go there," said Michael. He gestured toward the pile of documents on the desk. "In the meantime, you have some work to do, sir. Rectify the mistake that has been made. Correct the records. See to it that a public notice is issued . . . and have Sydney Campion and his son arrested immediately."

"A-arrested?" whispered the Governor, mopping his perspiring brow.

"For their own safety, if you like," Michael called out as he strode from the large room. "For assuredly if I find either one of those gentlemen I will kill them without hesitation! I'll be back, Your Excellency!"

The heavy door slammed shut behind him, but to the trembling governor it seemed that Michael's furious presence still filled the chamber. He passed a shaky hand over the documents and shuddered.

"I warned Campion!" he murmured. "I warned him again and again, I told him this was too risky! And now, what shall I do? What?" He sat very still for several minutes and then, apparently calmed, he summoned his clerk to him.

"Send a message at once, to Sydney Campion . . ."

"At Rogue's Fall, Your Excellency?"

"No, no, Campion's in town today. God's blood, if Ives finds him! . . No," he recollected himself with great effort, "there's a meeting of bankers and merchants he was planning to attend. At Hammond's place. He'll be there, I expect."

"Very good, sir. And the message?"

The Governor looked at his clerk with bloodshot eyes. "Tell Campion to get out. Tell him to leave Charles Town, leave Carolina at once. His life is in danger. Did you see that man who just left here? His name is Ives. Tell Master Campion that Captain Ives is alive and here in Charles Town and looking for him. If Campion does not do as I say, he will be arrested and sent to England for trial. Now hurry, you fool, and see no one follows you!"

The clerk betrayed no surprise but merely nodded and sped on his way. Once he was gone, the Governor slumped back in his satin-upholstered chair of state and began to move all of Michael's papers into one high stack on the side of his desk. Even as he reached for his quill pen and several sheets of fresh paper, he was thinking aloud,

"We'll come out of this all right," he assured himself firmly. "Yes, yes, with Sydney and his damnable brood gone, who's to say a word against me in the docket? Ives can't make his charges against me stick; he's only guessing, he'd have no way of proving I've been involved with Keane and the rest! The thing to do now is assist Ives in every way, with the girl . . . wherever William's taken her . . . with the property, everything! A public apology, amends, confiscate Campion's money, give it to her, give her the run of Charles Town for all of me! Yes, yes, that's the way of it . . . all a terrible mistake, frightful miscarriage of justice, that kind of thing . . . court's been insulted, Crown's been insulted, *I've* been insulted, lied to, given forged evidence, placed in untenable position! Yes, it will be all right, it must be all right!"

2   The Client's Privacy Must Be Protected

Nathanial Graham faced the icy eyes and stern face of Michael Ives with cool indifference.

"No, Captain Ives, you cannot inspect the books, you cannot look at our records and if you attempt to do so I shall send for the militia. You have no right to make such impertinent demands upon an honest business establishment—"

"By God, I'll bring this 'honest establishment' down around your ears, Graham!" thundered Michael. He picked the diminutive Nathanial up easily and held him off the floor, shaking him like a rag doll. "I want a list of every man, woman and child you sold from Belleterre, who you sold them to and how much was paid for them! And I want Eleanor Campion, have you got that through your *honest business skull?*"

He threw Nathanial down with one final bone-cracking shake and glowered at him impatiently.

"On whose authority have you come barging in here, threatening me, disturbing me at my place of business, Captain?" demanded Nathanial, brushing off his neat suit of clothes with a steady hand.

Michael stared at him as if he had not heard the question right.

"'By whose authority'? I'll tell you, little man! The Governor knows I'm here and will not interfere with what I do here. Now, before I tear this place apart with my bare hands, where was Eleanor Campion taken and who took her away?"

Reluctantly, arms folded, chin jutting out to show that he would not be intimidated, Nathanial replied briefly, "She was not sold, I'll tell you that much. It was never intended that she be sold."

Michael looked puzzled. "I was told half a dozen times over what happened to her at that trumpery hearing her uncle arranged. They said she was a slave. She was brought here, put on the block, and—"

"*And,* as I have told you, Captain, she was not sold!" asserted Nathanial. "I have no idea what's become of her. She was removed from our establishment the next morning..."

"Who was it? Who took her?" shouted Michael.

"I don't know who they were. Men employed by her cousin. They arrived before dawn and put her into a closed carriage. No one has seen her since."

Michael paled, his hand flying to the hilt of the sword he wore. "'Her cousin'?" he faltered. "Her cousin... William?"

"Just so," nodded Nathanial curtly. "Now, will you leave before I am forced to—"

"You little toad!" barked Michael contemptuously. "Where did they take her? Rogue's Fall? Is that it? Out to William's place?"

"I hardly think so. Rogue's Fall is not the family home any longer, not since the properties were reassigned," said Nathanial with a slight sneer.

"Belleterre, is it? What, have they moved themselves right into her house, too? And they brought her back there, a slave? Those bloody bastards!" Michael turned on his heel and headed for the door.

"Excuse me, Captain," Nathanial called after him, "are you going out to Belleterre now?"

"I am!" roared Michael.

Nathanial sat down at his desk once more and dipped his pen into the inkwell, pulling open a thick, heavy ledger book.

"You will find it much changed," he remarked, and began to write.

With a snort of rage, Michael stalked out. Nathanial looked over at the open doorway for a thoughtful moment or two, then went to bolt the door against any similarly precipitous return of the captain.

Well now, he thought primly, the Campions can never say Ives learned anything from *me!* He could have mentioned Stag's Run, but at all times Nathanial considered the reputation of his firm. Much as he might dislike William Campion, the man was a client, after all, and Graham's respected the privacy of all their clients. And by this time, Nathanial was positive, Eleanor Campion had undoubtedly been sold off to Jack Keane (there were few financial transactions in Carolina of which Nathanial was not aware) and was far, far away.

3 I Hate This House!

Fancy was exhausted. The family had been in process of moving to Belleterre for days and days. Heavily laden wooden wagons rumbled and creaked in and out of the driveway and courtyard of the house at Belleterre, for although the house was fully furnished Fancy did not intend to leave behind a single possession at Rogue's Fall. She left William's rooms as they were. William had not returned from Stag Run and Fancy declined to wait for him before the great move was accomplished. But the rest of the house she had so long despised and could not wait to abandon was stripped bare by a severely overworked, complaining staff of Negroes who more than once threatened to speak to the master of the house if Miss Fancy did not show a little pity. At this, Fancy sniffed and drove them all the harder. Pity was not Fancy's forte . . . and besides, Sydney Campion had given her a free hand with the new arrangements. Fancy had seen very little of her papa since the fortuitous day of the slave auction; Sydney was spending more and more time at business meetings in Charles Town.

At first it was a thrill to find herself sole, undisputed mistress of the lovely old house, no Matty to watch her disapprovingly out of the corner of her eye, no Eleanor to patronize her. Fancy threw open the doors and windows of dusty rooms that had been closed for years and set her servants to washing and polishing, airing and dusting and rearranging with a vengeance.

But within a very short time she began to feel strangely nervous at Belleterre. The sight of those vast, empty fields, the silent stands of forest around them, the quiet, deserted cottages and neglected vegetable gardens all made her feel like the unwelcome intruder she was. The last of the summer flowers had faded and the beds were tangled with quick-growing weeds. Each morning as she glanced out of the window in what had been Eleanor's old room, she imagined that the meadows had shrunk just a bit more overnight and that the waiting, watchful forest of brush and crowded sapling trees and thorny vines had moved in closer, had reclaimed another piece of the land her cousin had cleared with patient devotion.

Fancy was not sure what her father intended to do with the place. All along she had envisioned Belleterre as the beautiful focal attraction of the area, alive with music and balls, great dinners and famous folk arriving and departing in elegant carriages. But, as the days went by with no one to talk to except the weary blacks, Fancy's old dreams lost their power to excite her. She had told all friends very bluntly to stay away until the house was quite perfect, and they had taken the hint. No one visited, not even for tea. No one, that is, save grinning, stammering, blushing, winking, blinking George Matthews, who had taken a cup of tea in the parlor and stared at her with his heart in his eyes and the same old proposal on his lips until Fancy could bear him no longer and ordered him off the place with a most unladylike oath to speed him on his way.

Even her discovery of the veritable treasure trove of lovely dress goods Michael had sent Eleanor did not cheer her for very long. She found the big white box with the white satin and lace in it; she had read Michael's little note . . . and all at once her plans, formed in an instant, for making the satin into a gorgeous ball gown, dissolved in a sudden fit of horrendous bad temper. She had torn the note to shreds and flung the rich cloth back into Eleanor's armoire, then stamped out of the house for a good long walk. But no matter where she went she seemed to feel Eleanor's eyes watching her. A dozen times she turned to look back at the house and fancied someone had just pulled back from an open window so they would not catch Fancy looking at them.

Resolutely, her temper far from cooled, she turned past the stables and coach house and found herself faced with a pack of snarling, half-starved dogs, pets and hunting dogs that had belonged to the Belleterre workers, now gone vicious from loneliness and hunger. With a terrified shriek, Fancy turned and ran, the dogs yelping behind her and snapping at her heels.

She reached the house out of breath, perspiring, frantic with fear, and slammed the door behind her just as the dogs came leaping up the stairs onto the broad veranda.

She could still hear them growling and scratching at the door as she leaned weakly against it, her knees shaking. The downstairs hall was dark, only a bit of light filtering down in faint haziness from the second-floor landing. As usual, she noted angrily, none of the servants was about to see to her. One of the dogs outside began to howl . . . the sound of it made Fancy's flesh crawl. She wanted to run upstairs and hide in her room, although she could not have said exactly what it was she wanted to hide *from*. But the shadows in the hall and slanting across the staircase frightened her even more than the hungry dogs outside. Something seemed to be lurking in those shadows, watching her, waiting to swallow her up if she came toward it!

Fancy quivered, pressing her back against the door. This house was not hers, the thought came with astonishing clarity; this was Eleanor Campion's house, every inch of it, every board and nail and stone of it belonged to Eleanor . . . and it always would!

She closed her eyes, trembling, and seemed to see and hear half a hundred scenes she had lived in other days when Eleanor was still there and Matty, always Matty, grim and silent at her side. She remembered the last time she had been here with the two of them . . . how she had taunted Eleanor with Michael Ives's death, how she had flung that stupid ring into the fireplace and run away from Eleanor's grief and anger . . . and then from the silent hatred of the people of Belleterre.

Her lips parted. She opened her eyes and peered fearfully into the shadows of the quiet house.

"I hate this place!" she murmured, and the shadows seemed to listen. "I hate this house, I hate it!" she screamed, pounding her small fist uselessly against the door behind her.

And, as if in response to her pounding, there came a louder, heavier, more insistent and purposeful pounding just outside. Fancy backed away from the door, realizing that the dogs had quieted down; she backed away into the shadows and screamed: "Go away! Go away!"

The pounding ceased. For an instant the only sound was her own quick, panting breath and then the door was flung open wide and a sudden burst of sunlight silhouetted the tall, angular form of a strangely familiar man.

"Who . . . ? Who's there?" whispered Fancy, unable to see his face. There was a touch more confidence in her voice at the presence of a flesh and blood human being . . . until the intruder took a few steps into the hall and she realized who it was.

"No! Not you!" she shrieked, wringing her hands. "Go 'way! Get out, you're dead!"

Michael quietly closed the door behind him. "Not so, Fancy. You and your paramour left a bit too soon. I'm not a ghost, no thanks to you."

"Wh-what do you want?" Fancy stared at him in horror.

"I want Eleanor," he replied simply, and his tone of voice was terrible with cold, deadly rage. "Is she here?"

"Eleanor?" stammered Fancy, her mind awhirl. "N-no, she's not here. Of course she's not here. This is my house now."

Michael was at her side in a few quick steps. He seized her wrist and held it tightly. "Where has William taken her? Don't try to lie to me, Fancy. I know when you're lying, remember? Just tell me where they are and nothing will happen to you."

"Happen to me? Happen to *me*?" she cried. "You're crazy, Michael Ives! Everything has changed since you left . . . you've got some catching up to do, sugar! And if you don't get off of my property in one minute, I'll call for help and have my niggers throw you off!"

Michael dragged her back across the hall and threw the door open again. "Look out there," he ordered her. "Look, Fancy. I've not come alone to Belleterre this time. Your servants know we're here and we'll not leave the spot until the truth is told."

Fancy glanced outside and saw full two dozen stern-faced men on horseback, waiting, more than one of them looked at her with hatred in his eyes and when she recognized several as crewmen from the *Sheila Deare*, she cringed and tried to break loose from Michael's grasp.

"You plannin' to kill me?" she tried to brazen it out.

"Not I," he said. "You're not worth the trouble. But I'll do this much for you . . . I'll give you a word of warning. You will tell me *now* where she is and I will go and find her. After that I'm bringing her home to Belleterre . . . don't be here when I come back, Fancy. Get out, get as far away from here as you can go and don't ever show your face around here again."

"You *are* crazy!" she cried. "Don't you understand what's

619

happened? I told you about Eleanor, I told you that night on your ship. And they proved it all in court, too. She's nothin' but a nigger; she's been foolin' everybody all this time! She had you fooled, too. And you were goin' to marry her! Marry her!'' she laughed shrilly. ''Wouldn't you have looked the gawk, though, when she whelped that bastard she's carryin' and gave you a black nigger child!''

She had the satisfaction of seeing Michael Ives stunned, staring at her incredulously. She pulled her hand away from his unheeding grasp and began to rub her wrist sullenly.

'''Child'?'' he repeated. ''Eleanor is carrying my child?''

''*Your* child?'' Fancy sneered. ''Who's to say? She's been carryin' on with all those black bucks of hers out here . . . could be anyone's child. No need you takin' the blame!''

As he had longed to do more than once and yet refrained, Michael now raised his hand and dealt her impudent face a hard, resounding slap that left her head ringing. Fancy cowered away from him, knowing she had driven him too far this time.

''Where is she?'' He stood over her, immense, wild-eyed, threatening.

''Stag Run,'' Fancy whimpered quickly. ''William's got her out there at Stag Run, in Jack's cabin.''

''' 'Jack'? Jack *Keane*?'' he bellowed. Fancy nodded tremulously.

''My God, there's a pair the Devil's marked out for himself! How long has Eleanor been there?''

''Ever since the sale. Almost two weeks, I think,'' she replied, fervently wishing that he would take his grim-faced men and go away.

''Who else is there besides Keane?''

''I—I don't know. Lots of them. You'd never get in alive.''

''How many ships?'' he persisted.

Fancy looked baffled. ''A dozen, two dozen; they come and go.''

''And the *Tiger Eye*?''

Fancy's information was behind the times. ''I suppose it's there, too,'' she said.

''Then she would be aboard,'' Michael reflected, talking to himself rather than to her.

''No, they don't stay on the ships there. They've built little shacks along the beach. They've got women with them, and children.''

''How cozy!'' he remarked ironically, then jumped upon his horse and signaled the men to follow him. "Remember what I said, Fancy: get out, leave Belleterre while you can!"

She watched them ride swiftly away and breathed a great sigh of relief to be alone again. And then, nearby, she heard the snarls of the returning dogs. She slammed the door closed hastily and, turning, found her servants clustered together in the hallway, staring at her with frightened eyes.

Fancy ignored them all, drew herself up with what little dignity remained to her, and began to climb the stairs. But as she reached the second-floor landing she called down in a very loud voice,

"Viola, you come up here and pack my things this minute! And have Joshua ready to ride downriver with a message for me. Hurry up, hurry up, you stupid girl, or I won't take you with me!"

Viola came quickly enough and timidly ventured to ask where they were going. Fancy, already throwing open bureau drawers and tossing clothes and jewels and fans and gloves all over the bed, left the rest to her maid and sank down upon her favorite gold velvet chair to pen a short note.

"Where are we goin'? *I'll* tell you where we're goin', missy!" she declared. "We are elopin', that's what we're doin'! I have decided to take George Matthews up on his everlastin' proposal of marriage and, just as soon as you get everythin' packed up, we're goin' straight to the Matthews place and get George and then the three of us are goin' away for a nice, long honeymoon!"

Viola's plain, pleasant face creased into puzzled folds.

"But, Miss Fancy, I thought you didn't like Master George! Seems to me you just about *hate* that young man, way you laugh and carry on 'bout him every time you see him . . ."

Fancy glanced over airily. "Why, Viola, you stupid thing! How did you *ever* get such a notion? George Matthews and I have been sweethearts since we were babies, almost!"

And then, in a lower voice that hardly trembled at all, she added, "You shut your damn fool mouth about George and me, hear? Or I'm goin' to have to sell you for sure, you black slut!"

4 The Dishonour Was His

Sydney Campion, whatever else might be said about him, had never run from anything or anyone in his life. And he was not about to start running now.

He received the Governor's verbal message without the slightest change of expression, sent the Governor's clerk back to his master with no reply, and continued with his meeting as if there had been no interruption whatever. It lasted another two or three hours and was followed by a light luncheon, which Sydney consumed with apparent relish. He thought a good deal about the implications of His Excellency's warning and decided that his position, on the whole, was one of strength. He was surrounded by staunch friends and business associates, men who were loyal to him and his family for one reason or another, more devoted to him, in fact, than to the Governor. If His Excellency chose to panic now, after all that had happened, then it was because His Excellency was always inclined to panic rather than think or act rationally.

Sydney declined even to stop off and call at the Governor's house on his way home. He invited several of his cronies to join him for further refreshment after the luncheon. These gentlemen retired to a tavern in the center of town and Sydney told them that Eleanor Campion's lover was back in Charles Town, stirring up trouble, making threats, even trying to intimidate the *Crown,* for, as *Royal* Governor (a situation relatively new to the hitherto proprietary colony of Carolina) . . . His excellency most certainly could be said to represent the person and the power of the British Monarch!

Sydney's masterful summation of the Governor's plight, to say nothing of his own, commanded a powerful reaction from his friends. Someone suggested calling out the militia at once. Sydney hastily squelched this notion, knowing as he did that an order of arrest might even now be issued for himself and his son. He would have to attend to *that* later on. But now he reminded the gentlemen that this was a personal matter between his own family and the ruthless Captain from Massachusetts Bay. Therefore a plan was enthusiastically adopted for seeking out Captain Ives directly, a move he would not be expecting, judging from the nature of his remarks to the Governor. Find the man and face him down, settle the entire matter before the day was over.

Thus it was that a goodly number of armed Charles Town gentlemen, followed by a crowd of curious citizens, headed straight for the docks where the sloop *Deirdre* was at anchor. The sloop was manned by a skeleton crew at this time, the majority of the men having accompanied Michael out to Belleterre.

Mister Rainey was still aboard, "holding down the fort," as he put it, and had taken the wise precaution of arming himself and the twelve men with him. Mister Rainey had returned to Carolina as to an enemy country and expected trouble from the moment the *Deirdre* sailed into Charles Town harbor. He was not disappointed in this expectation. Sydney and his friends approached the ship and demanded that the Captain be called out at once.

Mister Rainey appeared on deck with an old blunderbuss on his arm and invited Sydney and the others to leave. They declined to do so. One or two random shots were fired. Mister Rainey's men showed themselves at various strategic points about the sloop and a shouting match ensued, which drew an even larger crowd.

Into the midst of them, just riding back from their fruitless journey to Belleterre, came Michael and the remainder of his crew, all heavily armed. The crowd hastily parted to let them through and, in a moment more, Sydney found himself surrounded by two dozen mounted horsemen, with the sloop and her angry crew and the brackish waters of the harbor at his back.

Michael dismounted and stepped alone onto the narrow plank dock, appearing not to notice Sydney. He called up to his first mate in a voice ragged and cracked with weariness and thirst, but his tone was half jesting, almost playful.

"What's the trouble here, Mister Rainey? Not insulting the locals, I should hope?"

Mister Rainey shifted his blunderbuss from one arm to the other and answered in his dry, laconic voice, "*Gentlemen* to see you, Captain." An uncertain laugh broke out here and there in the crowd.

Michael turned around slowly, allowing his gaze to wander from face to face, looking deliberately past Sydney and his friends.

"*I* see no gentlemen here, mister!" he shouted back to the sloop. "Only a pack of dogs at their master's heels!" The crowd gasped. Michael whipped about quite suddenly, looking directly at Sydney, dropping all pretense of raillery. "What? Still here, Master Campion? Didn't your close friend, the Governor, take the trouble to give you my message?"

Sydney stepped out in front of the men he had brought with him, who were muttering angrily among themselves.

"Perhaps you would care to deliver it in person, Ives. My friends might enjoy your dreary little melodrama more if they heard your ridiculous threats from your own lips!"

Michael nodded brusquely. "I said I would kill you, Campion, and that I will do. You and I know the reasons. You were unwise to ignore the warning I sent, but that is your affair."

"Kill me?" repeated Sydney scornfully. "For what? For a woman? A slave! You've missed the point entirely, Captain. It's all over. Justice has been rendered at last, my brother's property restored to me, and the woman is gone."

" 'Justice' !" shouted Michael. Turning away from Sydney he addressed the gentlemen hovering behind him, brandishing their weapons with a defiant air. "Gentlemen, before blood is shed here unnecessarily, I must inform you that the Governor has been presented with substantial evidence proving beyond the shadow of a doubt that what occurred at the hearing Master Campion arranged was a pack of lies from beginning to end; the evidence was forged, the attorney Master Campion brought here from Antigua is a transported criminal whom the Campions paid to help them defraud their relative, the legitimate daughter of the late Governor of Antigua, Eleanor Campion!"

"May we ask, who brought this latest set of evidence, Captain?" asked one of Sydney's friends sarcastically. "Was it not you, yourself? And you are the woman's lover, are you not?"

Michael shrugged. "I have not the time for debate, sir. Pray consult His Excellency on the matter and discover the truth for yourselves. But, you would be well advised to make that discovery before you commit yourselves to a dangerous course of action here and now!"

"Dangerous to whom, sir?" drawled another of the gentlemen, casually touching the hilt of his sword.

"To you, sir, if you insist upon supporting this man whom you seem to regard as a pillar of the community. Go your own ways, gentlemen, my quarrel is not with you but with Master Campion and his son."

Three or four of Sydney's friends looked at each other nervously and put up their weapons. One cautioned that it might be best to wait and see what the Governor had to say. Sydney glanced at them with contempt.

"I take it, then," he said loudly, "that you propose to murder me here in cold blood?"

Michael's face seemed carved of stone, but the light of the rage he had carried with him so long seemed to burn from his eyes.

624

"Here or wherever suits you, Campion. But assuredly not in cold blood. And assuredly not murder. We do not do such things in Boston, though it may be your custom here. I have something to do now and cannot tarry longer, but name the place and the time and I will be there."

A long drawn-out sigh ran through the crowd and more than one observer remarked to his neighbor that, all in all, it spoke well for the Captain that he wished to settle things on the field of honor.

Sydney flushed darkly. Delay was something he had not expected and could not afford. He did not answer right away and, seeing this, his friends pressed around him, urging him to accept Michael's terms, vying with one another to offer their services as seconds. Not one had a single doubt but that Sydney would finish the younger man quickly. He was an excellent shot and, as the challenged party, he would, of course, choose to fight with pistols rather than swords.

"Come, come, sir, I've told you I am in a hurry!" snapped Michael.

Sullenly, because there was nothing else to be said now, Sydney replied, "Tomorrow morning, then, at dawn, on Button's Common."

"I will be there," said Michael coldly. "See that I am not alone!"

"For shame, sir!" cried one of Sydney's supporters. "The remark was uncalled for. We will answer for Master Campion's appearance."

Michael nodded and turned away, heading toward the sloop's gangway without another word. Sydney watched him go and suddenly was gripped by panic. He must finish the wretched affair at once, before anyone else saw the Governor! He called out, something inarticulate, even those around him did not quite hear the words. Michael, thinking he was being addressed again. turned impatiently.

"No more today, Campion, I told you—" he was saying when Sydney thrust aside the friends about him and wildly fired his pistol at Michael. Michael leaped aside with a startled oath on his lips and instantly drew his own weapon and returned the shot.

Sydney faltered; the pistol dropped from his hand. He clutched his chest convulsively.

"He turned to fire! You all saw him! He meant to murder me . . . he only pretended . . . !" Sydney gasped out the words with a final desperate energy, then fell back, dead, into the waiting arms of his horrified friends.

Michael stood without moving, the pistol forgotten in his hand. They laid Sydney down upon the dock and covered his body with a cloak. Then they looked at Michael again, but no one spoke.

"Is there any man among you who says he spoke truly?" demanded Michael. They looked at each other and whispered.

"Twenty men, nay, fifty, a hundred of you saw what happened," Michael persisted. "He fired without warning and before I had touched my own weapon. Speak up! Who will deny what they saw with their own eyes?"

Finally, reluctantly, one man called out, "You are correct, sir. The dishonor was his, not yours."

One by one, in low troubled voices, the others assented. Then they picked up Sydney Campion's body and took him away. Michael watched them go, sick at heart that it had been so badly done, sicker yet that it had had to be done at all.

Mister Rainey came and stood by his side as the last of the crowd dispersed, most of them heading straight for the governor's house.

"His ball only missed you by a few inches, Captain," Mister Rainey remarked quietly.

"Aye," murmured Michael bleakly. "He died as he lived."

"He deserved it, and I'll swear to that though I be a God-fearing, church-going man! What was all that bilge about the 'field of honor'? I thought you came back to this pesthole to put an end to him and his! Too much talk, all that, and you were a damned fool for turning your back on him!"

"Well, it's over now, his part, I mean. Mister Rainey, I've found out where she is!" Michael clapped the mate across the shoulders. "Stag Run, that's where they took her. And she's with the son. Have them take these horses back to the stable and prepare to lift anchor as soon as I return."

"Where are you going now, sir? Shouldn't we be off to that place and find the lady right away?"

Michael's grave face lit up with the ghost of an ironic smile.

"We shall have to have some assistance, Mister Rainey," he said dryly. "It seems Jack Keane and his friends have made a neat little nest for themselves at Stag Run. Now I remember, I heard Keane speak of Stag Run the day he boarded us. There are a dozen, maybe two dozen ships there in the bay, and the Royal Navy none the wiser all this time!''

"A nest, is it, Captain? A viper's nest,'' declared Mister Rainey darkly. "Oh, I'd like to meet that bloody-handed devil again!''

Michael nodded. "You will, you will, Mister Rainey. For I'm going back to the Governor now and, with his kind endorsement we shall set sail on the morning tide for Stag Run and we'll take the Royal Navy along with us.''

5 North With The Grey Geese

Eleanor awoke to glorious golden warmth, the mid-October sun brilliant in a sky of pure and cloudless blue. For the first time in days . . . how many had it been? She was not sure, nine, perhaps ten . . . she was glad to throw off the old mantle that was her cloak by day, her only blanket at night. She sat up, stretching luxuriously in the unaccustomed heat, and glanced quickly, warily, about the little hidden glade in which she slept. There was no sign that anyone had been there, yet she knew the Indians would have been by much earlier to look at her and quietly shake their heads and go away again. They came each day, sometimes bringing food or strings of tiny blue shells or small gourds filled with redroot tea and a bitter-tasting, pungent medicine she recognized as horehound juice. The tea restored her strength and the juice helped heal her many cuts and bruises.

She was not entirely sure where she was; still somewhere on the mainland, a bit farther north than Stag Run. The islands she had tried so desperately to reach were beyond her powers of endurance. Hours of futile rowing, trying to make some headway against the oncoming thrust of the tide had proved her goal impossible. Pain, hunger, thirst, exhaustion, all had overcome her valiant efforts and by noon of the day she had escaped William Campion she was asleep in the bottom of the little boat, asleep and adrift.

She awoke in the late afternoon as the boat bobbed and thumped against the smooth, round stones of a small shallow inlet. At first she thought she had reached one of the islands; one dismayed glance at the sea to the east and the sun fading fast in the west and she realized the ocean currents had pushed her back again to the mainland. It was not until some time later that she thought to be grateful she had not been swept out into the open sea as she had slept.

The Indians, of a tribe she did not know, had been watching her for a long time. When she climbed stiffly from the boat, wincing at each painful movement of her sore limbs, they came to have a closer look. They touched her skin, murmuring to themselves about the angry red welts and raw, inflamed lacerations where William's belt had struck her. Some few, mostly women, gently took hold of her long hair and, holding it up against the sunset sky, let it fall loosely from their fingers.

Eleanor stood very still, trying not to show she was afraid, enduring the curious touches bravely. But she was very close to collapsing and when one very old woman suddenly pulled away the cloak she wore, revealing her naked legs and blood-soaked shirt, she began to tremble violently and the crowd of thoughtful, quiet dark faces about her seemed to whirl around and run together strangely. The same old woman looked over her shoulder and issued an imperious command of some kind and instantly a gourd of fresh, sweet, cool water was handed over and held to Eleanor's mouth for her to drink. She choked and coughed in the effort to swallow, her throat dry and swollen, but the water revived her. She threw her head back to catch every drop.

With this motion the hair fell away from her neck and breast and the iron slave collar became visible. The old Indian woman touched the alien thing, her brown eyes narrowed. Then she spoke sharply and at some length to the others and they seemed surprised and angry, too. Eleanor wondered if they had ever seen such a thing before, but if they had not, still they understood very well its meaning, and its meaning troubled them. They tried to remove it but their well-intentioned efforts cost her much pain and were to no avail. They looked at her in silent speculation for a while and then disappeared into the woods without another word.

But an hour later, after she had wandered a little way along the shore and found a sheltered place to rest, and a little stream which would provide drinking water, the Indians returned, bringing with them a warm fish broth and a loose-fitting shift of dressed deerskin such as their women wore. They also gave her the first of the small gourds of horehound medicine. When she would have thanked them they faded away once again into the thick woodlands.

She had bathed in the stream, too tired to care whether or not they were watching her, then poured the noxious black liquid over her bruises, drank the delicious broth and fell asleep on a soft carpet of leaves and pine needles with the old mantle wrapped about her.

From that day, she had never once seen the Indians. She mystified them and they kept their distance. Yet there was nothing she did that they did not see, from fishing in the little stream to climbing atop a great pile of rocks that jutted out into the water so she might discover what lay on either side of the inlet, to gathering nuts and berries, small crabs and turtles along the beach. She spent her days this way, and she slept a great deal and her strength slowly returned. For a time she did not think about anything except food and sleep and healing. Only after she had recovered sufficiently to remember that winter was coming on and she must make some plan for the future, did she gather the courage to climb those rocks and see what was on the other side.

It was a clear day, her sixth in this place, and she saw the islands she had been trying to find, low, green black and faintly misty-looking out across the water, too many miles to get to even if she still wanted to go. And then she looked south along the shore and saw how small a distance she had come after all: the cunningly inward curved hook of land that curled deceptively like solid earth about the hidden bay at Stag Run lay before her eyes not three miles away! She scrambled down from the rocks hastily, and fancied she had almost seen the cooking fires in the pirate shanties, perhaps even the tallest mast tops of the ships at anchor there. Why had they not come looking for her by now, she wondered? How easily they might have found her, brought her back triumphantly to William!

Even her little boat lay exactly where she had left it, quite easy enough to see from the water. On that day she had hurried to pull the boat up on shore and struggled to drag and push it under a concealing pile of shrubbery and palmetto leaves. And then she had sat down to think.

Her plan, when it was formed, had but one aim and that was to travel north, always north, hiding, moving at night, following the line of the coast until she should somehow reach Boston. There was no other place she could think of where she might find refuge . . . not *welcome*, she did not expect a welcome anywhere this side of the grave . . . but she thought of Michael's sister, Katherine Sturbridge, who might give shelter to her dead brother's child.

Eleanor realized that this scheme was more dream than plan. She forced herself to think of the obstacles in her way. It was already approaching November; the farther north she went, the colder and more dangerous the weather would become. A large part of her journey was through the south and as long as she remained in the south, penniless, alone, wearing an iron collar, she might be captured, sold, imprisoned, even killed. A thousand hazards awaited her . . . but all she had to do was look once again at what she knew lay three miles from the inlet and she remembered all too well what fate lay in store for her *there*. Had she killed William? She thought so but she could not be sure. To the people she knew back there—she had almost said *back home*—in Charles Town . . . save that she had no home anymore, least of all in Charles Town—to those people what was she now but a runaway slave who had killed her master?

She turned her back upon the pile of stones and looked to the north. Soon; she must start soon. If only she could reach Virginia, might she not find passage on some vessel bound for Boston? She had no idea yet how she would pay for such passage. She imagined a story of shipwreck and time spent among friendly Indians to explain her situation . . . until she felt the galling weight of the iron collar on her neck. There was only one explanation for that band and, with it, no story she might possibly conceive would be plausible to any white man in America!

Still she must go, find a way somehow to have the collar removed, push on in the meantime in spite of it, in spite of all the other considerations that might so easily stop her. She put from her mind the thought of what dangers lay ahead and planned to leave on the morning of the seventh day. But it had poured that morning and the next as well and she lingered till the sun would return to dry her clothing and guide her footsteps north.

Now, this morning, with the wild cry of a lone marsh hawk wheeling high above the glades, she had awakened to feel the heat of the awaited sun and she knew with a certainty that this was the day she would leave this place.

She washed herself in the stream, plaited her hair back in a long, bright braid, and ate a bit of the meat her Indian benefactors had brought the night before. She packed the rest of it, along with the blue shell strings, in several of the gourds tied together with stripped thorn vines. She thought of leaving something of her own behind as a token for all the unobtrusive kindness she had been shown, but she had nothing except Michael's ring and the ring was not hers to give away. She doubted that the Indians would make use of the boat, yet she uncovered it and placed a branch of woodbine and a handful of wild flowers in it and hoped they would understand what she would have liked to say.

She had just picked up her mantle and a short piece of hickory limb she used for a walking stick in tangled and uneven places and was about to set out along the trees fringing the shore, when a peculiar sound reached her ears, a dull, repeated booming noise like thunder over the sea, and yet too short and thudding and occurring much too close together to be thunder.

She gazed about in some confusion, hearing the booming noises growing sharper and louder every moment. And how close they sounded, how fearfully close by! She glanced furtively in the direction in which she had been about to set out, but the sea was empty of all save soaring gulls, and the beach was deserted. And even as she turned to look south, toward Stag Run, where the noise was loudest, the Indians passed her, rushing toward the shore in great agitation, shouting and gesturing frantically. They were plainly terrified of the strange sounds, yet they were angry, too, and the young men clustered about the old ones, pointing and arguing urgently. They looked at Eleanor and her heart sank. Did they blame her in some way for this new intrusion on their quiet lives? When several came hurrying to her she dropped her slight burden and clutched the piece of hickory resolutely to defend herself.

But they offered her no threat, merely drawing her along with them down to the same high pile of rocks she had once climbed and then, always careful of her, they pulled her to the top with them and all talked at once, to her and to each other, still pointing to the source of the frightening sounds.

By this time Eleanor had no need to look where they pointed; she knew cannon fire when she heard it and she fully expected to see a battle taking place among the pirate ships in the hidden bay. From what little she knew of the Brotherhood she suspected that this was one of their many personal squabbles. Nevertheless she strained to see what was happening, terrified that this new invasion of privateer vessels might mean the arrival of a larger and even more dangerous force of pirates, who would surely investigate farther along the beach than Keane's men evidently had done.

What met her startled eyes was not an attacking force of pirate ships, however, but a fleet of six British frigates lying broadside the Stag Run harbor in a close semicircle, all firing their big guns in turn, their targets none other than the assorted ill-prepared vessels lying helplessly at anchor, unmanned and unprotected. Looking closer, as the thick smoke from the cannonfire puffed and drifted away on the wind, she was then able to make out the presence of another, smaller ship, a sloop in full sail, moving boldly along one side of the bay, hugging the far southern hook so as to stay out of the frigates' line of fire, but moving closer and closer to shore nonetheless, and tiny white bursts of smoke issued from smaller guns being fired from the sloop.

The frigates' main targets were the pirate ships. Eleanor could not help but notice that no shot was fired at the shanties and cabins along the beach. She could even see the outraged pirates running out of their houses and milling about helplessly as their only means of defense or escape, the ships, were ruthlessly bombarded, and the water of the harbor so churned up and agitated by cannon balls and grenades and crashing pieces of masts, timber, spars and flailing ropes and crashing, spinning hulls that it appeared as though a newer and more terrible kind of hurricane had just come piling in from off the Atlantic.

And still the daring little sloop continued to slip in closer to shore. The pirates had armed themselves with flintlock pistols and various other weapons and returned from their mean hovels to do battle where and with whom they could. They spotted the sloop heading into shore and ran for it. A volley of shots rang out from every yard and railing of the trim vessel and half a dozen pirates fell. The rest ran back, some firing uselessly over their shoulders as they went. A few moments later, boats were put over the side of the sloop and her crew hurried into them. Several of them, too impatient to await the careful turn of the winch as the boats descended, jumped into the fairly shallow water and swam for shore ahead of their shipmates. As the small boats were swiftly rowed toward the beach, a few stray cannonballs from the frigates nearly struck them. The frigates were also angling in closer, encouraged by the complete lack of return fire from the pirate ships. Several more broadsides strafed even closer to the houses on the beach. A crowd of women, many carrying small children, emerged from the little houses, screaming and running off into the woods. Meanwhile the boats from the sloop and the men who had jumped into the water arrived on the beach, gathered themselves together and set off like a small, compact army directly for the shanties. The pirates, still firing, fell back again and then again while this small determined group advanced without pause. And finally the pirates held their ground and stood together to fight hand to hand with the audacious landing party. Eleanor saw the glint of the sun on their swords and knives, and the pink puffs of flintlock black powder rifles being discharged at close range. The Indians with her watched with grim expressions on their quiet faces and she could tell that they had a horrible familiarity with such weapons and what could be done with them. Suddenly she remembered how there had been no Indians anywhere about the pirate encampment, how several small villages had been deserted, and she understood now why her friends of the past several days were so secretive and kept so much to themselves. They had experience of Keane's men, no doubt of it, and she longed to be able to explain to them that they would be safe again because of the new warships in the bay. But she saw that they could see no difference between the pirates and the naval forces and that they greatly feared a renewed persecution once the strange white men had succeeded in killing the other white men.

Feigning a calm assurance she was far from feeling, for her own lot was no better than before, she ventured to touch the Indians gently on the arms and, almost patting them like children, told them over and over again in a happy, positive tone of voice that they would be safe very soon, pointing and smiling at the frigates, pointing and frowning at the pirates. And after quite a long while of this, they seemed to understand what she meant. They conversed at great length with each other and, although Eleanor could not know what they were saying, they had quite well grasped the idea that she knew both warring parties, that the new ones were good and would destroy the old ones but would not hurt *them*. And, since the Indians had always realized it was from the same common enemy they both shared, the pirates, that she had been running away, they were delighted now to see her so happily and expectantly watching the victory of people who were her friends!

All of the Indians strong enough to scramble up on top of the rocks now did so and sat there enjoying the spectacle, even commenting sagely on the various turnings of the battle and cheering every time one of the pirate vessels sank beneath the water. This alarmed Eleanor greatly. Although they were too far away to be heard, even if the great guns were silent, she was afraid they would want to move closer still to the fray, that they would attract the attention of the landing party, which had now scattered the remaining pirates, and were, for some reason she could not fathom, dashing in and out from one wretched house to the next.

She decided the time had come for her to leave. Indeed, she was half afraid she had waited too long. Soon the crews from those frigates would be coming ashore. They must not find her. She felt vaguely glad that the pirates' nest had been cleaned out at last and their hiding place no longer was a secret, but to have dwelt upon that thought would mean she would have to think about Stag Run, Stag Run, which had once been hers, and all that had once been hers, and this was a dangerous self-indulgence she would not allow. She slipped down from the rocks quietly, hoping no one would notice her absence, picked up her gourds and her hickory walking stick, drew back her shoulders squarely and marched off swiftly beneath the trees, out of sight of the shore but with the guiding sound of the surf always to her right side. In a short time she was deep in a long, sunny tract of fragrant pine forest, the sounds of battle gone, and only the cries of a spirited lance head of grey, flecked geese flying far overhead in the opposite direction to tell her she was heading north.

6 Warriors From The Sea

Michael cursed and swore foully as he ran to the next miserable hut and kicked in the door. He stood peering inside for just an instant, tall, bare-chested, his white linen shirt torn in a dozen places, his sword uplifted and ready. But the place was empty, like all the others. He turned, shouting to his men, who needed no incentive to pursue the fleeing pirates into the forestland behind the houses. Four or five remained always just behind him, ready to take on the stray buccaneer who had lingered to defend his scant possessions.

"God damn the Royal Navy to hell!" Michael muttered between his teeth now as he emerged into the bright sunlight in time to see a cannonball from one of the warships crash straight into a particularly small and wretched-looking lean-to not ten feet away. "They'll kill her with their bloody marksmanship! I told that fool Admiral or whatever he calls himself not to shell the beach! Christ, there goes another!" He leaped aside and the men with him jumped violently as another shell splintered the house they had just left. Michael waved them on down the beach, but he was heartsick with the failure of this, his last hope of finding Eleanor. Only two or three more shacks to search, and then what? Impatiently he pushed the thought away, ran his fingers through his sweat-soaked hair, and ran on ahead. Behind him he suddenly heard a woman's scream . . . his heart froze in his breast, he wheeled about, the word "Eleanor!" on his glad lips . . . and saw only that one of his men had taken in charge a dark-haired buccaneer wench who was trying to claw his eyes out.

Michael turned back to his task, raced into another shack, found a two-year-old child wailing in terror, trying to hide itself beneath a pile of moldy-looking blankets in the corner. He picked up the screaming baby and handed it to Mister Rainey, calling back as he ran on, "Take care of him, mister!"

This was the last building of them all, a bit larger than the rest, a bit more solid-looking. He noticed absently that there was a wooden bolt on the door, but the bolt was not drawn and the door was a jar. Michael swallowed hard, hesitated only a second, then pushed it wide open.

There was a low, sagging bed in the corner, a small, high, barred window in the opposite wall, a makeshift stone fireplace, odds and ends of filthy rags lying about. Nothing else. No one, no one at all.

He walked into the dirty little room and looked about him. She was not here. And this was the end of it, he told himself bitterly, this was all. Whether Keane had killed her or carried her away . . . Keane or *William*, he reminded himself and a flame of hatred scorched his heart on the instant . . . whichever it was, Eleanor was gone and he had nowhere else to look for her. He sank down upon the little bed, his sword at his side, staring dully at the dirt floor. He looked over at the fireplace, once, twice, thrice his disheartened gaze swept over the rough stones . . . and once more. There was a stone missing in the very center of the upper arch.

Odd, he thought idly, not caring, but . . . odd. He glanced, not caring, over the space of the floor until he caught sight of the missing stone lying against a wall. Grey stones, rough, undressed stones, unusual in Carolina, where any kind of natural stone was rare. Grey stones, his mind kept coming back to it, grey stones, common as dirt anywhere else. But, the stone on the floor was not grey.

Not caring, he looked away. Then he looked down again as the sun poured through the tiny window and illuminated the odd missing stone in an ugly, rusty, reddish brown color. Michael got up and took the stone in his hand, holding it up to the light, turning it over. He shuddered. The rust color was a stain, a large stain of blood, thicker in some places than others, where the stone had struck its mark, where the living blood had flowed. The blood was many days' old. He dropped the hideous thing with sudden revulsion. Someone had used that stone to kill with . . .

He glanced back at his sword, lying on the low bed, and he saw the fresh, bright red stain of blood upon its keen blade, blood he had spilled not ten minutes ago. He heaved a great sigh and shook his head. What difference, after all, old blood, new blood, stone or sword? Death was death, always ugly.

And suddenly he conceived the peculiar notion that he must wipe off the bright red stain upon his sword. He cast a closer look about and found the pile of rags he had noticed earlier. He picked one up and was about to wipe the sword blade upon it when he chanced to look down again. He had noticed something white among the dingy rags, something that was also cloth, like them, but cleaner, newer . . .

He dropped the first cloth and picked up the other. It was a woman's petticoat, or, rather, the edging of such a garment, fine lawn cloth and handmade Brussels lace, sewn delicately with narrow blue satin ribbon. A lady's garment, he thought, plundered where and where was its luckless owner now?

He held the lacy bit against the blade and then he cried out in horror. He recognized the bit of lace, rare lace, expensive lace, plundered by himself, no other, plundered on his own ship by his own hand from the rich store of goods on their way back to the ladies of Boston!

"She has been here!" he said aloud, dropping his sword, heedless that his naked back was to the open door.

"Captain, what do you expect me to do with this—? God, man, are you mad? You lads, over here!"

All this from Mister Rainey uttered in utmost consternation and alarm as he had followed Michael with the screaming child in his arms, paused for a few moments outside and then come in to find his captain alone and defenseless. Dick Lonney and the others came on the run and filled up the small close room with their hurrying, sweating, panting presences . . . to stand and gape at the captain, who held a scrap of white cloth before him and seemed not to know they were there.

"Here, Dick, do you take this squalling infant and find his dam, take him from me this instant!" commanded Mister Rainey. Dick removed the child reluctantly and Mister Rainey touched Michael very gently on the arm.

"We have not found her, sir, not her nor the *Tiger Eye*. My guess is that Keane's taken her away to sea with him. As for the cousin . . ." he shrugged.

"She was here," Michael said. He picked up his sword and sheathed it. "Are there any captives? I want to talk to them."

"Only that woman, sir. She's spittin' mad and like enough to say anything," another of the men spoke up. "She was Jack Keane's doxy, or so she claims."

"Bring her to me," said Michael. "She'll know where he's gone, and where he's gone, we'll follow!"

A moment later the girl known as Moira was ushered into the shack. She seemed unwilling to enter the place and, when she was pushed from behind, she quickly moved as far away from the hearth as possible and stared with an awful expression of dread at the floor before it.

"They tell me you're Keane's tart. Is that true?" began Michael.

"True enough," came her insolent reply, but still she did not look at him, only at the hearth and then at the floor.

"Where is Keane?"

"Jack? Long gone, guv'," she sneered. "You brung the 'ole damn Naevy for nothin' much!"

Michael paused, watching her eyes. "Why do you keep looking at the floor over there?"

She jumped, looked away deliberately. "Not me! *I* ent lookin' at nothin'!"

Her manner was so agitated that Michael pressed her, sure now that she knew much more than she was letting on.

"Where is the red-haired girl who was brought here ten days ago?" he demanded. "Did Keane take her with him?"

Her eyes widened. " 'ere, now, Jack didn't 'ave nothin' to do with all 'at, nothin', I swear it! Why, 'e were gone days and days afore she come!"

Michael glanced across the room, met Mister Rainey's silent gaze. "All right, then, if Keane didn't take her, it was William Campion, wasn't it?"

Moira's mouth twisted. "Naow, 'e didn't take 'er nowheres, either!"

Michael was fast losing what little patience he had. "Someone took that girl from this camp," he snapped. "You tell me it wasn't Keane and it wasn't William Campion. It had to be one or the other. You're lying to me. I have no time for your lies. Perhaps a touch of the *cat* will bring out the truth . . ."

Moira shrank back from him, wringing her hands. "Naow, don't 'urt me none, oh, don't! I'll tell 'e what 'e wants ter know, I will!"

"Do so," murmured Michael softly.

"Jack *were* gone, that be true, so 'elp me. And '*is* men, 'er cousin's men, they brung 'er 'ere and they left 'er 'ere. And then *he* come, William, near to midnight it were, and 'im drunk and 'arf crazy. Next mornin' this 'ere door were swingin' open on the wind and we found 'im . . . lyin' on the floor right over there . . ." she pointed to the spot with a shaking hand . . . "and 'is 'ead were all broke-up-like, where she'd 'it 'im with the 'earthstone. There, 'e see that stone what's all red and 'orrible? That's the one she did it with, and she run off!"

"Run off? You mean, she escaped?" cried Michael, a strange thrill in his voice.

Moira shook her head. "Not much," she said flatly. "She took a boat from the beach—we seen the marks where she dragged it into the water—and she took it clear out of the bay."

"How do you mean, she took it *out* of the bay? Why do you say that? Mightn't she have simply rowed around the south hook and gone ashore again?"

"Naow. She got caught in that 'ere mid-channel current and she got took out to sea, else we would've found the pieces of the boat sooner nor later, don't you see? She be drowned-dead, drowned-dead, I'm tellin' yer, these ten days gone!"

Michael stood staring at her with cold blue eyes, saying nothing for such a long time that she began to sniffle and wring her hands again, casting beseeching looks over at Mister Rainey.

"Sir," said Mister Rainey very quietly, "is that all you want the girl for? Shall I take her out now?"

Michael started, his thoughts very far away indeed. Then he sighed and said to Moira tonelessly, "She killed William Campion, is that what you said?"

Moira nodded vociferously. "Oh, she killt 'im, all right. I told you, we found 'is body right 'ere in the mornin' and we buried 'im out in the marsh. Jack wouldn't like all that, not in 'is place, and 'e ent goin' to take very kindly to wot you chaps 'ave done 'ere today, neither! 'E'll be back to Carolina, you'll see, so soon as 'e 'ears wot's 'appened 'ere, and then 'e's likely to set fire from one end of this bloody colony to t'other, mark my words! Jack Keane don't let no one slip *'im* the sharp edge, not my Jack!''

"Mister Rainey, take her away and put her with the other prisoners. The Navy can have the lot of them!"

Mister Rainey signaled the men to take her away. The naval bombardment had ceased and already several boats had landed on the beach and the Royal Marines were routing out the pirates who had stampeded into the forests on the heels of their women and children.

Mister Rainey, about to follow the men outside, paused in the open doorway and looked at Michael gravely.

"Are you coming, sir? They'll be setting the torch to these shacks in a little while."

Michael waved him away, shaking his head. "In a moment, Mister Rainey, in a moment."

Mister Rainey seemed about to say something else but evidently thought better of it and left Michael alone, softly shutting the door as he went out. Michael never noticed his going at all.

Drowned-dead, drowned-dead—the girl's words spun around and around in his brain. And so this was the end of it. Eleanor was dead. The three words seemed unreal. He glanced down at the scrap of cloth in his hand, then over at the stone she had used to defend herself... but his mind refused to let him picture the dreadful struggle that had taken place here, nor the desperation of her futile attempt at flight. She was dead... and, he suddenly remembered, his child with her. There would never be another love for him, not should he live to be old. So it was finished, no other woman, no other child to carry on the Ives name—how little that mattered now!—and no other place on the face of the earth but Belleterre—gone from him, too—that he would ever call "home."

The enormity of his loss began to lick like a tongue of hellfire around the edges of his consciousness. He sat down on the little bed in the corner. Outside he heard the shouts and pounding footsteps of the Navy men and the marines rounding up the buccaneers. Already they had begun to set fire to the shacks at the far end of the beach.

He would have to leave here in a minute or two. He shook his head and forgot them all. And the thought came to him, with a crushing jab of agony that quite took his breath away, We only had the one night together. Just that, but it summed up the full aggregation of his grief and every precious moment of that singular lost night of love came back upon the instant to torment him. One lovely night out of a lifetime of sadness, one white rose among the thorny years gone by and those yet to come. How vivid her sweet face seemed to him in memory, how vivid each varied sound of her melodious voice, each graceful movement of her exquisite body. He thought with a sudden piercing fear that time would dull the vividness of his memories of her, that time would soften and dilute and ultimately diminish the sharp, bitter realization of all he had lost. Men considered time, in this aspect, merciful and kind, but not he, no, never! He would not bear to live so long that one bright image in his heart would dim. "Beauty, be thou remembered!" He recalled the poignant words engraved on her mother's tombstone and his heart reached out over the miles and years in perfect understanding of James Campion's tribute. And then, he bowed his tired head and wept for her and for himself and for that little lost life that he would never know.

Out on the beach a large and surly band of prisoners was being distributed into the longboats to be taken out into the ships and back to Charles Town and the fortress cells awaiting them. The single small fires set in each separate shack had spread and joined together to make a rustling, cracking, spitting line of flames and smoke stretched out for a hundred yards or more and still moving. Several armed parties of marines were still searching through the surrounding woods and bringing out of their hiding places other fleeing pirates, who surrendered willingly enough when they saw how the Marines went about stabbing willy-nilly deep into the concealing brush with their bayonets affixed to the long rifle barrels.

The officers and commanders of various of the frigates had assembled to confer upon their next immediate actions and were standing or sitting about on the sand in a little knot close to the water. They largely ignored the final operations of their men as they sped up and down the beach, in and out of the woods, firing an occasional warning shot now and again. The screams of the women had died down and even the dazed children were very quiet as they looked with shocked fascination at the flaming, crashing, blackening timbers of what had been their dwelling places.

Suddenly the officers looked up as a new alarm was sounded by the men on the very far perimeter of the encampment. At first it was hard to make out what they were shouting about. The officers assumed that another, perhaps larger and better armed group of pirates had appeared from yet another encampment farther up the coast . . . and, indeed, this assumption seemed the only correct one to be made as they saw their men running quickly together and forming the traditional three-line cluster ready for firing upon an advancing enemy force. The officers, all save the Admiral and his aide, hurried to join their men.

But no shots were fired and the British force looked at each other and then at their officers quite puzzled, still wary, still prepared for trouble. They watched as a very large group of Indians emerged from the trees along the north bend. The Indians were armed, to the extent that they carried bows and quivers of arrows and tomahawks in their belts, but their women were with them and they were smiling and waving and talking in a very friendly fashion as they came.

"Hold your fire," was the order quickly spread along the firing line. The Indians continued their approach, passed through or around the cautious British, and stopped to survey the fire with broad smiles. One or two little shacks remained standing, where the flames had not yet carried. One of the Indians, uttering a piercing cry that was echoed by his fellows, ran forward, seized a burning bit of fallen timber and tossed it with great accuracy atop the roof of the larger of the two shacks.

Mister Rainey, who had seen the Indians come in, at once broke away from the men of the *Deirdre* and ran as fast as he could toward the shack, Jack Keane's shack, knowing he had not seen Michael leave it yet.

But at that moment Michael threw open the door and stepped outside just as the quickly burning thatched roof crashed down in flames behind him.

"Whose bloody damned idea was that?" Michael bellowed above the voice of the fire, and he glared at the Navy until he saw the cheering Indians. Mister Rainey reached his side and pulled him clear of the blaze.

"Not fond of our pirate friends, what?" laughed one of the frigate Captains, indicating the Indians. "I daresay these poor devils have had a bad time of it since Keane set up camp here. No wonder they couldn't resist coming in for a closer look!"

"Does any man here know what Indians these are?" wondered a young lieutenant. "Anyone who can talk to them?"

Now the Admiral came forth and addressed himself to the Indians with becoming dignity, speaking the Queen's English very slowly, very articulately, very loudly and to no avail. The Indians clearly did not understand a word he said, but they listened politely and the Admiral was encouraged when every so often they would nod and appear to recognize some of his words. And they did recognize them, or rather the sound of them, as being of similar origin to words their recent visitor had spoken. When the Admiral finished and the Indians waited silently for another few seconds to make sure he *had* finished, they broke out into swift and voluble speech themselves, interrupting one another constantly and growing very excited as they spoke.

Michael watched this interchange for a few minutes, then drew Mister Rainey away down the beach. It was time to get back to the sloop and leave the Royal Navy in command of the situation. The boats from the *Deirdre* had been hastily pulled up on the sand and now Michael issued orders in a flat, cold voice. His men were very quiet and downhearted. They knew the search was at an end and that the Captain's lady had not been found. Word had spread of what Moira had told Michael and, to a man, they believed that Eleanor Campion was dead. They pushed the boats into the water without a word and began rowing back to the *Deirdre*. As so many had swum ashore rather than wait for the boats earlier, there were not enough seats for them all. The boats must come back and pick up the rest. Michael chose to wait, unconsciously clinging till the last moment to this place where Eleanor had died . . .

He spoke quietly to Mister Rainey, his blue eyes fixed upon the boats riding atop the blue waves. He talked of ordinary things, of giving out a double measure of rum to the men, of his desire not to return to Charles Town now, but to sail north to Boston. The boats let off their passengers on board the sloop and headed back to get the rest. A few moments more and they would leave Stag Run behind and Michael vowed to himself that he would never look upon this place again. . . .

"Captain," said Mister Rainey, grasping Michael's wrist in a sudden grip of amazing strength.

"What is it, Mister Rainey?" Michael broke off his discourse and looked at the mate in astonishment. Mister Rainey opened his mouth, moved his lips, but could not seem to utter another sound.

"My God, man, what's the matter?" cried Michael. He turned to look where his enraptured officer was staring so intently. At first he saw only that the Indians had been joined by another, smaller number of their tribe, and that the Naval officers and men were shouting and pointing in his direction, and a general air of tremendous excitement had broken out all along the beach.

But then he saw what Mister Rainey had seen. He gasped, rubbed his eyes with the back of his hand, looked again.

"Oh, sweet Jesus Christ, can it be?" he whispered. Beside him Mister Rainey released his hand only to clutch him in a fervent embrace, tears coursing down his thin, matter-of-fact New England face.

The Indians moved down the beach, talking, laughing, pulling along with them, in their very midst, a woman draped in a dark mantle and a hood much too large for her. She seemed confused, frightened, most reluctant to be where she was. The Naval officers had, with some difficulty, pushed their way through to her and seemed all to be talking at once. She looked up at them, making an effort to understand their eager, animated words.

And then, as they pointed to where Michael stood and could not seem to move, she stared and, at last, she realized what they were all trying to tell her. She lifted her head and the hood fell back, the glorious Titian-hair gleaming in the sunlight. She cried out, raising her hand timidly, uncertainly, in a mute gesture of greeting . . . and, with a scream of joy no man there ever forgot all his life long, she thrust herself free of the seamen and the marines and the officers and the Indians. She broke away from them all and began to run with outstretched arms toward Michael.

"Eleanor!" Michael breathed the word. Mister Rainey gave him a little push.

"Go to her, Michael Ives, and give thanks to God Almighty for His infinite mercies!" cried the first mate, heartily.

Michael moved as if in a dream, slowly, afraid to look away from her for even an instant lest the sight of her would prove only a cruel illusion. But she was real, she was true, she was alive! She was laughing and weeping together and his name was on her lips as he came to her and caught her into his arms.

"Michael! Oh, Michael, my love, my love!" she exclaimed, clinging to him, feeling the marvelous strength of his tall, sinewy body as he pressed her to him, raining kisses on her hair and her brow and her cheeks. He could not speak; he had no word just yet for Eleanor *alive;* his mind was still filled with the sorrowful words of mourning that had flooded through him a short while before. He could only hold her and weep, mingling his tears with hers as their faces touched and their lips met.

He moved his right hand from about her to touch her hair, her cheeks, her soft throat . . . and his fingers encountered the iron band around her neck. *That* made it real, at last. *That* melted away the dreamlike quality of this meeting and restored to him his thoughts, the hundred raging emotions that had etched away like acid in his heart for so long; *that* cold hard iron collar of slavery gave him back his voice.

"It's all over," he told her. "Everything's been set to rights. I found the evidence and the truth is known now. You can go home, Eleanor, home to Belleterre. Oh, Eleanor, my only love!" he cried brokenly, "I'll never leave you again, never!"

Her great sea green eyes were shining. "Nor shall I ever leave you, Michael Ives," she vowed solemnly. He took her two slim hands between his own and kissed them . . . and he saw, incredulously, the soft silver gleam of the old steel ring on her finger.

"I've kept it safe, my darling," she murmured, "but I never dreamt twas for you I'd been keeping it. I thought to give it to our son, love, but you shall do that yourself!" She slipped the ring off and placed it in his palm, folding his fingers about it. "This ring, and our child, they were all that was left me in this world."

Michael put the ring on and cupped her chin gently in his hand.

"I know," he said, smiling for the first time. "Fancy told me of the child. And when I thought you dead, my dearest, know you that I grieved for it as well as for you . . . that I had never known my own child nor ever would, that I had known you so little . . . oh, God, Eleanor, so little, so short a time!"

He pulled her against him once more and kissed her fiercely, yet tenderly mindful of the small life nestling close between their two bodies. All around them cheers and shouts rang out. The Indians

644

watched her happy face carefully, watched the tall, yellow-haired man embrace her protectively and were satisfied. They slipped away, back into the woodlands, unnoticed as they wished to be. They would go home and make a new song to sing around the cooking fires, a song of how a white woman with hair like the setting sun had come to live among them, how, because of her, a mighty fighting force had destroyed the evil men who drove away the game and harmed their people. Strange and mysterious this woman had been, the song would tell, and not always wise, for when they had missed her at the very moment of the victory and had tracked her down in the pine forest so they might bear her back to the good white men who would take care of her, she had not wanted to go with them. She had resisted them and tried to run away until their strongest, fleetest brave had simply picked her up and borne her off in his arms. She had pointed to the iron band around her neck and she had been afraid, but the Indians knew better. They had not known about the one special man, that was true enough, but they had known she was wrong to fear the mighty warriors from the sea.

Oh, what a song this song would be! Already, as they walked through the sweet-scented forest, with the undisturbed towhees and song sparrows chattering above them, some began to pick and choose the words they would use for the telling of the story and the women hummed many melodies to find the best.

Ten

"Unseen, Loving Presences"

1 Eleanor and Katherine

She stood alone, tall and graceful in a moss green silk robe, looking into her floor-length mirror with wide, almost surprised eyes. One hand strayed up to touch the masses of flame-colored hair so elegantly arranged in long, slender curls against the creamy skin of her neck. She stepped back from the mirror and, childlike, made a swift little pirouette on the high wooden heels of her white damask shoes. The layers and layers of silk, lawn and gauze petticoats swirled out around her legs and she laughed at the cool, luxurious feeling.

They had left her for only a few minutes and then she must finish dressing. A while ago the small room had been filled with talk and laughter, busy women rushing back and forth. Now it was very still and peaceful. Downstairs she heard the music of violins and viola and cello, more talk, snatches of singing and a great deal of laughter. She glanced once more, quickly, at the pale, composed face looking back at her so calmly from the mirror and then she moved across the room to look out the window.

She saw with delight the delicate snow that had been falling so softly on the lawns and fields of Belleterre since early morning. The sky was dove grey, the earth below already frosty white, the only touch of color the rich green of the sweeping branches of pine trees in the distance. Even the little cottages seemed visible only as dark smudges against the snowdrifts, their curls of black smoke like banners flying from the chimneys.

Her heart lifted to see that smoke. So many of those cottages were no longer empty. One by one, Michael had traced the people of Belleterre, by letter, by messenger, often going himself, even as far away as the most remote of the fall line plantations. He used the records so meticulously kept, so reluctantly opened by Nathanial Graham and he paid without question whatever price was demanded to bring her scattered people home again. Only a few of the cottages remained deserted now and two of them would never be filled.

Dogon's house. Matty's house. She shook her head and brushed away the tears that sprang to her eyes. She told herself this was not a day for tears but for rejoicing, for remembering and loving all the more those two dear absent friends. Because of them she was alive, because of them and because of Michael she and Belleterre were beginning life all over again.

She watched the sky intently, thinking of Matty. *"You were right, Matty darling, she whispered to herself, you were right. I was afraid of all the wrong things. If only I could see you now and tell you that! If only you could have been with me today. How beautiful you would have been in your yellow gown, dear, dear Matty!"*

She thought of Dogon. In a way it was much easier to think of him, to pray for him, to open her heart to him now, for she knew that he still lived on in spirit and could hear and understand her, beyond pain, beyond all suffering. In the spring, she knew, she would miss Dogon most: when the fields were harrowed and tilled and the men went out to work, in the spring she would miss him at every turn. But he was at peace . . . and she did not even know whether Matty was alive or dead. Michael had discovered the name of the old sea captain who had bought her and spread the word of his search on every outgoing ship, but they had not been able to trace him yet.

"But we'll not give up, Matty, I swear it!" she said aloud. "Michael and I will search until we find you and bring you home again. But, oh, Matty, I wish you were here today! It's Christmas Day, my dear, and it's my wedding day!"

There was a light tap at the door and Ada came in, all smiles, carrying the white satin wedding gown high in her arms, its lace train carefully held up off the floor by two solemn-eyed little girls who had been born at Belleterre five years earlier. One was dressed in pink and one in blue, with matching ruffles and bows enough to delight any girl's heart. Ada herself was already attired for the ceremony in a frock of beige moiré, a great apron tied about her waist until it was time to go downstairs.

Eleanor removed the green robe and held up her arms while Ada settled the white satin in place and gently smoothed it down over her bosom and shoulders. She and Eleanor had made the gown together and Ada had had secret misgivings about her abilities as a seamstress. Now she began buttoning up the back, twenty-two tiny pearl buttons that slipped out of her fingers or found their way into the wrong hooks or persisted in turning under and losing themselves beneath the narrow binding until Ada's face was grim and perspiring.

"Don't hurry so, Ada," said Eleanor mildly, smiling at the two little children who had seated themselves primly on the edge of her bed and were staring at her as though they'd never seen her before. Ada shook her head ruefully.

"We're *almost* there," she said. "Good thing we had all that fine cloth, honey. You're a mite bigger round the middle than you used to be; you're startin' to show, I do believe! High time you and your man got married. What'd you want to wait so long for anyway? You're near to four months gone now, aren't you? If it'd been *me*, I would've grabbed that Captain by the hand and marched him into Church the day after he found me, that's what *I* would've done.

Hold still, honey, we've got just two more of these little devils comin' up . . ."

"Are you scolding me, Ada?"

Ada looked shocked and then she sighed. "I guess I was. Twasn't you that's botherin' me, just this dress. It's got to look just so in front of all them folks, and I keep thinkin' how Matty would've done it. Why, Matty would've had these buttons closed up in a minute . . . and there's the veil to pin, too. Matty would've—"

Eleanor put her arms about the frowning black woman and kissed her warmly. "Matty would be proud of the way you've done everything, Ada. I'm proud and I'm grateful to you. Don't spoil this day worrying and fretting . . . *that's* what Matty would have said if she were here. Just think how much is behind us, how much we have to look forward to! And we're going to find her, you know. We'll never stop looking!"

Ada dabbed a handkerchief about her eyes, nodding fiercely, trying to smile. "Come on, buttons!" she said firmly. "Ain't got all day!" The last two little pearl buttons slipped neatly into place at once. "Hmph!" remarked Ada cryptically. She stepped away and crooked her head to one side. "Well, it fits," she said. "I'll be damned!"

The two little girls burst into giggles until Ada's glare silenced them. "Now the veil and then I'll go down and tell them we're ready."

The veil was handmade Limerick lace, capped with white satin roses at the crown of the head, falling in a cascade of transparent folds to the floor. And when it was arranged and pinned, in spite of all her resolutions to be steadfast, Ada looked at Eleanor and wept without restraint.

"You're like an angel, honey, just like an angel!" She squeezed Eleanor's hand, then headed for the door, shooing the little girls out ahead of her. "Mistress Sturbridge will be back in a minute, I expect. Now don't you sit down on that satin and don't lay a finger on that veil. It's all pinned just right now, so don't you go fooling around with it. . . ." Her voice trailed off as she half closed the door behind her and hurried away down the hall.

Eleanor was practicing the management of train and veil together when Katherine Sturbridge entered the room with a bouquet of white hothouse violets in one hand and a small, velvet-covered box in the other.

"How beautiful you are, Eleanor!" she exclaimed. "I'd hug you but I think Ada would have fits if anyone touched her masterpiece!" She looked closely at Eleanor's face for an instant. "Tell me, now, how is the bride?"

Eleanor smiled, kissing Katherine on the cheek.

"The bride is very happy," she said softly. "Especially so because you and your little boy came down to be with us today. You are very beautiful yourself, you know."

And it was true. Katherine's white gold hair was gathered high on her small, proud head in soft waves and puffs, bedecked with ribbons of grey velvet and silver lace. Her gown was of the same grey velvet, edged about with corded silver satin trim. Helene's diamonds and rubies twinkled at her ears and throat and at both slender wrists. Her serene grey eyes held a new glow of happiness. Any lingering grief Katherine suffered because of Rob's untimely death was locked away forever in her heart. Now, with Michael's wedding and the new child that would be born to him and Eleanor in May, she felt that the family had arrived full circle at last, the past a memory, already a fair claim on the future.

She held out the velvet-covered box to Eleanor. "Michael sends this, dear, his wedding present. He was quite ready to bring it up himself, imagine! But I persuaded him he mustn't see you yet. This comes, as you know, with his love. And with my own, Eleanor."

Eleanor opened the box. There, lying upon a bed of black velvet, was a string of purest white pearls. "How lovely!" she whispered. "How perfect!"

Katherine fastened the pearls about her neck. "They belonged to our mother," she said. Standing next to Eleanor she looked over at their reflected images in the mirror. "I never knew her. She died when I was born. But you are very like her picture, the same color hair and skin. Only the eyes are different . . . I have her eyes, they used to tell me."

Eleanor fingered the pearls gently. "Sheila Carey Ives," she murmured. "How Michael loved her!"

"Then he has spoken of her! I'm very glad, my dear," said Katherine. "My brother never spoke a word of her in all his life since she died . . . until he fell in love with you. I don't know why, I've never understood it, but Michael has always blamed himself for her death. Not me, never me, although that would have been natural enough. But since she died he's been unhappy, as though some

shadow lay across his whole life and kept him from his dreams."
Katherine put her arms about Eleanor. "I thank God for you, my
dear new sister, whatever happens now, I've seen the shadow pass
from Michael's life. I've seen him happy and at peace. God bless
you, dear Eleanor, and the little child you carry!"

The tears glistening in Eleanor's sea green eyes were brighter than
any diamond. Katherine dried them with her own handkerchief,
shaking her head in vexation.

"There, now, see what I've done! We must go downstairs and we
can't have you weeping like a baby!" Her own eyes were suspiciously
bright but Eleanor said nothing. Just as she picked up the violets,
Ada came back, out of breath and smiling broadly.

"They're waiting, honey. Time to go!"

2 Christmas Wedding

The small wedding was being held in the parlor at Belleterre,
attended by all the people of Belleterre and the crew of Michael's
ship. Elliot Landon had brought Katherine and young Elliot from
Boston. Willy was there, of course, grizzled and red-faced and
misty-eyed, hardly believing that Michael was really to wed at long
last. Mister Rainey, attired in a suit of blue serge with dazzling white
Holland linen at the throat and cuffs, had early stationed himself
next to the punch bowl to make sure none of the young fellows from
the ship started their merrymaking too early.

The dim old parlor was gleaming with bright candles and shining
pewter candlesticks and plates; red holly berries and green leaves,
intertwined with ivy and tied with red and white ribbons, were
arrayed throughout the hall and parlor and the dining room and
wound about the banister of the staircase. A huge pine tree stood in
one corner of the room, its dozens of tiny candle flames lending a
rainbow glitter to the silver-painted cones. In another corner, surrounded
by winter greenery, a little string orchestra alternated playing Christmas carols and wedding songs while they waited for the bride to
appear.

Michael was alone in Eleanor's tidy little study, gazing out the
window at the snow just as she had done upstairs. He saw how the
snow softened the winter landscape, and he remembered how Belleterre
had looked to him that day in mid-October when he had brought
Eleanor home.

Fancy had been gone, her few servants hovering about fearfully, not knowing what was to happen to them. The house itself was not much changed except for the addition of a great deal of strange furniture that Michael had set the servants to work removing at once.

But the grounds were another story. Eleanor had insisted upon wandering about through the brown, stubbly fields, staring at the abandoned wagons and tools left lying to rust. She walked in and out of all the deserted, desolate little cottages, speaking familiar names into the silence and, finally, she had wept brokenhearted at the sight of Matty's little house with its cozy schoolroom and books.

That had been a bad time, a time when Eleanor was lost and afraid, frantically happy to have him with her again, but still too caught up in the suffering of the past weeks to think of or believe in the future. It was then that Michael swore they would find all the lost people and bring them back. They would start all over again. He made her look ahead to the spring when Belleterre's fields would be green again and filled with the men and women and children who belonged there, to the spring when a new crop of indigo would be started, to the spring when their child would be born.

Eleanor had clung to him, the sound of his voice, the sight of him. She had believed what he said simply because it was he who said it. And he did it all, exactly as he promised. He found Ada and her boy, Ezra, first and brought them back. Little by little Eleanor began to take heart. Little by little he was able to leave her for a few days at a time, with Mister Rainey and the lads always close by for company, while he made his investigations and found the others whom Graham's had sold away.

In all those weeks he had never touched her, except to kiss her and hold her in his arms as they sat and talked in front of the big fireplace in the parlor. Sometimes he saw a haunted, wordless fear in Eleanor's eyes, he held her and felt a sudden unconscious stiffening of her limbs and he knew she was remembering William Campion. He became increasingly afraid for her, and for himself. Would she ever be able to let the frightful memories go? Yet when he asked her to marry him, reminding her that he had said he would come back and make her his bride, he was surprised that she had nodded her head at once and agreed.

"And what about all those reasons you had for never marrying?" he asked her, wanting to be very sure. "We don't have to marry,

651

Eleanor. I'll stay with you all my life if you'll have me, but I'll not stand you marrying me out of fear or because you're going to have my child. The child will have my name, married or no. But I've not forgotten that Belleterre has been the whole world to you, Belleterre and all the things you've worked for here. If you still believe that marrying me would destroy that dream of yours, then never marry me at all, just love me and I'll be happy.''

She shook her head and held him very close. "I was wrong," she told him. "Matty knew it. She tried to make me see...and then there wasn't any time left. But without you—Belleterre, everything, was lost from me. You gave it back to me and when you did that, you made it your own, too, don't you understand? It's your home now as much as ever it was mine. I don't want it without you. Without you it has no meaning now. And, Michael, I do trust you, that you really do understand what I've dreamed of accomplishing here. I really believe now that no matter what may happen you will carry on and teach our child to keep the dream alive. I love you, Michael, and I *will* marry you. I want to be your wife and share my life with you, always!''

Michael hesitated, hating himself for what he was about to say. But it must be said. "You will marry me. You love me," he stressed, "and, still, you are afraid." He looked away, unable to bear the pain in her large eyes.

She had waited silently for so long that he thought she was not going to reply. His heart turned over, for he would marry her, aye, and stay with her forever, whether she shared his bed or not, but he wanted her, wanted her as he had never wanted any woman in all his life. And he wanted most of all to show her what fear had made her forget: how tender, how gentle, how infinitely patient love could be.

When she did answer him at last, her voice was so low he barely heard her. She put her hand against his and locked her fingers through his fingers, so that she touched the ring he wore. And she had said,

"I will not be afraid of you, Michael.''

3 The Steel Ring and The Gold

Now it was the day of their wedding and her words echoed in his mind. He felt in the pocket of his coat for the gold wedding band he would soon slip on her finger. It was there, waiting, with its inscription she would understand, for he had told her about his visit to her mother's grave. "Beauty, be thou remembered!" Eleanor had taken the little faded flower he had plucked and the page on which he had written the entire inscription. Now it would be hers, too.

By now, he thought, Katherine would have given her the pearls, the pearls his sister had brought away with her from England and never worn. She had always insisted that they must go to her brother's bride. He had scoffed at her notions, so positive had he been that he would never wed . . . and now . . .

He heard a hush come over the company gathered just outside in the parlor and the orchestra stopped playing in the midst of an old country carol. It was time. He patted the pocket with the ring in it and started for the door just as Mister Rainey tapped and then opened it.

"Ready, Captain?"

"Aye, ready, Mister Rainey."

They went into the parlor and made their way to where the priest was waiting. Michael caught Willy's eye as he passed and Willy grinned and winked at him. Michael returned the grin and the wink and Willy, suddenly recollecting the solemnity of the occasion, instantly assumed an appropriate expression of severest gravity.

A small black face, surrounded by bouncing pink ribbons, peered down through the top railing of the staircase and a piping high voice issued forth importantly: "Everybody hush now. We're comin' down!"

Immediately an invisible hand snatched the small person backward and out of sight and the orchestra began to play the wedding march. Michael looked up and saw his sister coming down the stairs slowly, smiling, holding a little nosegay of holly with long, trailing red and silver ribbons. Behind her, solemn and careful, stepped young Elliot, handsomely attired in a suit of blue plush. He carried a white satin pillow, held in both small hands, and on the pillow was Eleanor's prayer book. Elliot kept his eyes fixed on his mother's back and followed her without faltering. There was a little pause then and, a moment later, there appeared on the stairs two little girls with gleaming brown eyes, carrying baskets of wheat and mistletoe.

And then Michael's heart pounded as though it must surely burst with pride and love as he saw Eleanor, walking down head high, in an aura of white, as brightly beautiful as the falling snow outside.

Her hair was like a burnished crown, her eyes warm emerald green and glowing with love. Her gaze swept over the assembled, upturned faces and she smiled mistily at them all, but then her eyes sought Michael and, finding him, she nodded quickly and moved to his side with Ada behind her holding the lace train.

Katherine's eyes were fixed steadily on her brother's face as she listened to him make his marriage vows. She saw him smile down at Eleanor, taking her hand in his. Katherine thought of Rob Sturbridge and her own wedding day long ago. She thought, too, of Sir Tom and of beautiful Helene, of little Elizabeth, who had been cruelly cheated of her wedding; she thought of Ian, her father, and of Sheila, her mother, and that she had never seen either of them. . . .

"With this ring, I thee wed," Michael was saying as he slipped a golden wedding band on Eleanor's slender finger. For a moment the gold ring and the old steel ring hovered together, glinting, one bright, one soft, in the candlelight. Katherine's vision blurred. The flames flickered and seemed to cast a luminous haze about the bridal couple, separating them from all else around. For an instant she heard only their two voices, each in turn, and then murmurs of other voices, whispers, like echoes, and in the dazzling haze she thought that there were others watching and listening and that the room, already suffused with a feeling of joy, grew radiant as though it had been blessed by unseen, loving presences.

4 Make A New Way

Moonlight on the silent snow, the scent of violets in the air, a crackling, hissing fire on the hearth . . . a clock somewhere chimed two and was still again. There were no blazing candles now, or music, or laughing, singing, dancing guests. Save for Katherine and those who had come with her from Boston, all quartered comfortably in another wing, the old house was empty and at peace.

Michael sat in an armchair beside the fire, watching Eleanor's sleeping face. She was very pale. She had been tired when they brought her upstairs after the long, hectic day. It was Michael who had seen the last of the merry company to the door at eleven. Katherine had slipped away a bit earlier to make sure little Elliot was sound asleep and then, tired out by the long journey and the excitement of the day, had decided to go right to sleep herself.

Michael and Willy had a final toast together and Willy tried to say the things that were welling up in his heart, but when he began to speak of the old days, even of the day he had found Michael hiding in the ruined tower, Willy had only choked up and cried a bit and mumbled his good wishes, embracing Michael in a great bear hug and then stumbling away to his bed. Michael watched him go fondly, and wondered how it could be that suddenly Willy, *his* Willy, had grown so old?

But his thoughts were not at all melancholy or nostalgic as he went upstairs a few minutes later. He knocked lightly at the door of Eleanor's bedroom and, when there was no answer, he went in quietly. Someone had built a fire and left a single candle burning on the nightstand by the bed. The bridal gown and veil were hanging in Eleanor's open armoire; her little bouquet had been thrust into a bowl of water and set on a small table near the hearth.

And Eleanor was asleep. The bedcovers had been turned down and she lay very still, one hand thrown out across the pillow beside her. She was wearing a thin white lace night robe with satin ribbons at the wrists and sewn high under the bosom.

He stood looking down at her, overwhelmed by feelings of love and desire. Then, careful not to wake her, he pulled the coverlet over her and pinched out the candle. Moving soundlessly, he undressed himself, slipping on a loose, comfortable blue robe. Only a few feet beyond the fireplace the room felt quite chilly. He added two or three large, fragrant cypress logs to the fire and sat down, suddenly realizing how tired he was himself. He would have wished the company gone away much earlier but that they had all been so very happy, so pleased for him and for Eleanor.

He leaned back in the soft, comfortable chair and remembered that he had come home. Dim memories of the last terrible weeks in England, dimmer and therefore even more terrible memories of Kilbree House floated disjointedly through his mind but now they brought no pain with them, nor even sorrow, for all that had been suffered by himself and those he loved was finished. Now he could let the memories go and be done with them once and for all. It was a new time, a new life, a life nevermore to be lonely.

He thought of the last night, the only other night, he had spent in this little room. Caught up in such thoughts and quite tired out, he almost dozed off in the chair, until he heard Eleanor sigh and toss about in her sleep and then cry out softly again and again, "Michael? Michael!" Her tone was frightened and her voice small, like that of a lost child.

He was at her side in a moment. "I'm here, my love," he said. "Open your eyes, Eleanor, see, I am here with you." He lay down next to her and took her into his arms.

"Michael!" she looked at him dazedly. "I dreamed I had lost you again! Oh..." she blinked and gazed around the room in some confusion. "I didn't mean to fall asleep. But after they went away, you were long in coming. I only thought to rest a moment—"

"Hush," he whispered, his lips against her hair. "I know, I know. It has been a very long day for you. Go back to sleep now and I'll hold you and keep you warm." He kissed her ear softly, smoothing back the silky red tresses that spread darkly on the pillow.

" 'Go back to sleep'?" she murmured very low, turning and resting her head on his chest. "Is that what you wish?" She raised herself up on one elbow and looked closely at his face. "You're tired, my dearest, it must be very late."

"Just past two," he replied. "Look: see where the moon rides over the hills? Going down soon; I'd say your clock is wrong by nearly an hour."

Eleanor laughed a little, moving around so that her body curled close against him. "Thank you for the navigation lesson, Captain! Can you really tell time like that, by the moon and stars?"

"On clear nights like this one. The snow makes it easy. Look at the shadows growing longer and longer on the fields. When I came up those fields were very bright."

"When you came up? Have you been here very long, then? Why didn't you wake me, Michael?" Her voice was troubled and low.

"Because you look so beautiful asleep," he answered easily, lightly. "I watched you. I thought it was a happy sleep until I heard you call out."

She shook her head. "I hate to sleep now. Everything comes back again in my dreams, oh, such terrible dreams they are, Michael! I wake up very often and find that I've been crying. Then I'm afraid to sleep again. It's foolish; I've told myself it's foolish and will pass." She drew a long, deep quivering breath. "I'm so glad you were here!"

"Don't be afraid, Eleanor," he said firmly. "Don't ever be afraid again. I'll always be here. Tell yourself that before you go to sleep. Some little part of you will stay on guard and remember it, and the dreams will stop. Will you do that from now on?"

"Yes," she promised. "Michael, you are very wise, do you know that?"

He laughed softly. "No, not I. Not wise, never wise. One learns a good many things going through life, but knowing a good many things and being wise are not the same. *You*, on the other hand, are the wise one in the family."

" 'In the family,' oh, that sounds lovely!" Impulsively she kissed him lightly on the lips. "But, in what way am *I* wise?"

The touch of her mouth on his made his heart pound wildly. It was all he could do not to pull her to him and possess her lovely body at once. His senses urged him forward, but he checked himself sharply. Not yet, he thought, slowly, carefully, with love . . .

"You are wise, my love, because you learned what you wanted in life very young and once you were sure of it, you took hold with both hands and refused to let go. *That* is wisdom, if I understand wisdom at all."

"Wisdom? Or just stubbornness?" she chuckled a little. He said nothing. No matter, she thought, it hadn't really been a question anyway. She lay still, contentedly close to him, quiet. The room was silent save for the murmuring voice of the fire, the sudden crack and splitting of a log falling into the red embers. Minutes passed. He was so still she thought he must have fallen asleep. She looked over at him. His eyes were open, his breathing labored.

"Michael?" She felt a sharp, cold pang of dread.

"Yes, I am here." His tone was calm, reassuring as before, he did not realize she was watching him. "Don't be afraid. The dreams will go away. . . ."

Her heart ached at the lonely sound in his voice. "I'm not sleeping, Michael," she said distinctly. "Michael, shall I always be like this?"

With effort he replied. "Like what, Eleanor?"

With an inarticulate cry she pulled away from him and sat up on the other edge of the bed. "*This*, like *this*! We talk and we talk . . . I love you, you know I love you, but it's as though I'd died and my spirit was here, and I keep trying to reach out to you, trying to touch you, but my hand passes through *air*, touching nothing, feeling nothing! I remember, Michael, oh, I do, I remember the feelings that were between us that night! But I can't forget the other things, I can't. I'm numb. I . . . I can't *feel* anything now." His hand touched

657

her, but she pulled away. "I shouldn't have married you, Michael! I'm not the same. I'll never be the same again, never!"

His first instinct was to comfort her, to cradle her in his arms and soothe her to sleep. Time, he thought, time will heal her, as it healed my sister. But some other, deeper, surer insight told him differently.

He drew her back against him, burying his hot face in the soft flesh of her throat. He felt her stiffen, her entire body began to tremble violently. Pity flooded through him. He forced the feeling away. If he stopped now, if he allowed her fear to turn him aside it would be that way forever. He did not even trust himself to speak lest words of sympathy should help keep her frightened and hurt as she was now. He must make her feel again, remember again, not with her mind but with her senses, with her heart.

Gently he untied the ribbons at her breast, pulled the lace gown from her body with hands he willed to be firm. She did not protest. He placed her back upon the pillows, brushing her hair to the side, and he kissed her, softly, tenderly at first but more and more insistently. She tried to return his kiss, he felt her lips moving, she pulled her head away and began to say something—

"No!" he said, his voice husky. "No more words, Eleanor, no more! Put your arms around me, touch me, you'll not be touching empty air!"

He leaned over her, eyes bright with desire, hungrily drinking in the faint, sweet aroma of her skin. He bent his head and kissed her again, and kissed her cool, full breasts. He felt her arms creep loosely about his neck and then she sighed and shook her head.

He caressed her with the warm, ceaseless pressure of hands that fondled and wooed as he had never in his life sought so to awaken a response in any woman. Her legs, perhaps unconsciously, were pressed tightly together; when he touched her the muscles trembled and she moved away involuntarily.

His own mounting desire gripped him painfully. His need for her was becoming an unbearable torment he could not ignore much longer. Yet, for her sake, for both their sakes, he must wait, he must!

Then, at last, he saw that her body was remembering the feel of love, whatever fears still blocked her mind and held her back. He raised his head and looked at her face, saw the mixed emotions fight for possession. Her lips were parted, her eyes glowing, her breath coming in quick panting spasms. Now, he thought, yes, now . . .

"Eleanor, kiss me," he said, suddenly taking his hand away.

Almost dutifully, she touched her lips to his . . . something seemed to explode in his head at that touch. He pulled her into his arms, half raising her up from the bed.

"Kiss me properly, damn it!" he cried, amazed at the vehemence in his voice. He felt like crushing her; for an instant he almost hated the love he felt for her, wanting only to possess her, not knowing, not caring whether she wanted him or not.

Her kiss, open-mouthed, warm, somehow desperate, only drove him to a deeper frenzy. In dizzy dismay he realized he, too, was afraid, had been afraid all along. He doubted himself, doubted his ability to reach her after what had been done to her. The realization froze him.

"My God!" he groaned aloud. His arms went slack, he let her go and his head fell upon her breast. He felt defeated, bewildered, helpless and utterly, shatteringly *alone*. . . .

"Michael?" she whispered into the shadows.

He shook his head, unable to answer, his eyes filling with scalding tears of rage and hatred for the man who had left her this way. He felt her hand groping uncertainly, touching his face, her fingers discovering the tears.

He weeps for me! She suddenly remembered the very instant she had fallen in love with him, not half an hour after he had first come into her life. His taut, tanned features beneath the tangle of blond curls had been disciplined, guarded; his piercing blue eyes polite but remote . . . and then she had caught a glimpse of the person within, the man so alone, so vulnerable . . . and she remembered that he had trusted her enough to allow her that brief glance as deep inside as his very soul.

The remembrance was a shock. It all came back so quickly it almost took her breath away. The other memories, good and bad, all of them, were too mixed up to try to sort out now.

Begin again, she thought with amazement, *how simple it is, only go back to the very beginning of love and make a new way.* . . .

She took his face in her hands and lifted his head to gaze into his eyes. "I love you with all my heart, Michael Ives," she told him and this seemed more the real marriage vow. "Never weep for me again, never!"

She put her mouth to his, opening her lips eagerly. For a few seconds he lay there unmoving, and then his entire body was wracked with one great shuddering sigh. He kissed her fiercely and exulted in the passionate response he felt from her. There was no more doubt now, no more fear between them. Michael knelt over her and felt her arms pulling him down. The night spent itself profligately, stars speeding their way madly through the rich black sky heedless of the dawn pursuing them, as the two lovers spent themselves upon each other, recklessly, triumphantly learning the passion of each other's bodies again and again. They learned the touch that leaped into a demanding flame; they learned the taste of each other's tears; they learned the little death of flesh even briefly parted from its newfound other self.

And when dawn spilled into the lonely, starless sky, extending its golden warm fingers even as far as their two bodies lying, a curve within a curve, Michael marveled at the widely unsuspected passions of women. He held her with her back against his body, his arms about her, and she stirred drowsily.

He laughed, his voice husky from the night, and felt a faint fluttering under the fingers with which he stroked her belly.

"By God, my darling," he chuckled, "I thought you almost fast asleep!" But she was smiling radiantly, and she laughed, too, a deep throaty laugh of happiness.

"You felt it, too," she said tenderly, pressing her hand down on his where the faint fluttering had stopped and then begun again.

"I felt it," he nodded, somewhat confused. "I thought—"

"I know," she whispered. "See, there it is again!"

"But," he faltered. "What is it?"

She threw herself into his arms and covered his face with kisses.

"It's *life*, my darling!" she cried. "Yours and mine, moving in me. It's our child, Michael, for the first time he stirs and turns and lets us know he's here!"

He held her to him, and thought his world complete, all, all he loved, all he wanted was her in the compass of his two arms, she and this child so miraculously, it seemed to him, sprung to life in those few moments.

"So that's what it feels like," he murmured, more to himself than to Eleanor. And he was grinning like a boy.

"Only a few months more, my darling. Just think, only until spring and you may hold him in your arms! Oh, Michael, how I love you!"

5 The Winter's Wait

For the next months, throughout the short Carolina winter, they lived at Belleterre as on an island, wanting it no other way. They never talked about Charles Town, they never mentioned their neighbors on the surrounding plantations. Some day all that would have to change. Like it or not, Belleterre, Rogue's Fall, Stag Run all did exist, would continue to exist and would thrive despite the enmity of a shocked and bewildered gentry who would have preferred to forget the entire Campion family. If there were some who felt shame for the suffering and injustice inflicted upon Eleanor they never spoke up and their shame was quite insignificant when placed in the balance against their undying resentment. They resented Sydney and William Campion far less for having consorted with pirates and outlaws than they did Eleanor for continuing the same system of employing and protecting free black labor.

His Excellency the Royal Governor, came through the trying time fairly well, all things considered. He had had the fear of God rather rudely knocked into him by Michael Ives. It was with an enormous sigh of relief that he watched Michael's sloop *Deirdre* sail back to Boston under the command of Mister Rainey, carrying away Michael's relatives and friends. His relief would have been complete if Michael, too, were leaving Carolina.

Immediately after the Christmas and New Year holidays His Excellency decided it would be the politic thing to do if he paid a brief social visit at Belleterre, ostensibly to congratulate Eleanor upon her lawful repossession of the properties and upon the occasion of her wedding. But his real reason for making the uncomfortable, chilly, fourteen-mile carriage trip was to discover at first hand what Michael Ives had up his sleeve.

Michael expressed cool satisfaction at the way things had been settled, especially with the support of the hastily summoned Naval fleet that day at Stag Run and he did not refer to his earlier threats to bring charges against His Excellency . . . not that His Excellency had the slightest doubt but that Michael Ives would bring charges with a vengeance if he had a mind to do so. That positive assurance alone would have been enough to keep the Governor a fairly honest administrator for the time being. However, he had other problems on his mind, problems which daily loomed larger and more troublesome.

Privately he expressed his concern to Michael. He had wondered how long it would take Jack Keane to discover that his encampment at Stag Run had been put to the torch and his friends rounded up and sent to prison or hanged in Charles Town. He did not think that Keane would ignore such an affront.

"There will be reprisals, sir," confided His Excellency as Michael politely accompanied him back to his waiting carriage. "Reprisals such as we have never seen before, mark my words. Keane will come back to Charles Town before the year is out!"

"We'll say nothing about Keane to my wife, Your Excellency," retorted Michael, a note of warning in his voice. "If you hear anything about him, send me word. I look forward to another meeting with that bastard!"

The Governor settled himself back in his carriage, pulling a heavy fur robe over his shivering, silk-clad shanks. A brisk January wind was stirring and he was anxious to get away from Belleterre. The sight of so many silent, staring black faces full of contempt for him made him very nervous; he could not wait to leave. He leaned a bit from the door as he shut it and remarked, "I daresay you'll have nothing to worry about up here, fourteen miles from town. No, sir, it's we who'll have to bear the brunt of Keane's attack when it comes . . . we'll be lucky if he doesn't leave Charles Town in ashes!"

As the carriage pulled away, His Excellency would have sworn an oath on the Bible that there had been a slight smile on Michael Ives's severely polite face at the mere mention of Charles Town in ashes. His Excellency shuddered and took a very long drink from his silver traveling flask. He sincerely hoped he would never see Belleterre or anyone connected with the place again.

The lazy, comfortable weeks of winter passed happily. Remote from the rest of the world and hardly aware of it, Belleterre slowly greened into a soft, drizzly, misty springtime. A broad, curving wing of tall white lilies lined the edges of the drive. Honeysuckle and magnolia budded and bloomed. Roses and violets brought the first dazzling displays of color to the grounds, followed by the azaleas bursting into springtime glory in a show of pink, purple, orange and flame-colored blossoms. The grey brown fields were hoed and spaded deep, turning up the rich black loam to the face of the sun. Almost overnight, it seemed, there were green shoots springing to life in long, even rows as the new indigo crop began to grow.

Michael himself worked in Dogon's place, out at dawn every

morning in the fields or overseeing the work at the timber stands. Twenty years at sea passed as lightly from his wide shoulders as an afternoon shower and with as little regard. He had never loved the sea; he had been born loving the land and to it he now returned with the same daily joyous zest as that which brought him back each evening to Eleanor's waiting arms. With many eager tutors to assist him he soon learned the tricky ways of the indigo and he wondered more than once at the strength and determination Eleanor had had from the beginning, for the work was fearfully hard and hot and long. Sometimes he thought of her as he'd first seen her, come in straight from hours in the fields, her dress wrinkled and grass-stained, her long hair all undone and hanging down over her neck and shoulders.

When the evenings were clear and cool, after supper he would walk with her a little way from the house and they would talk about the indigo and the lumber and all the business of the day. She grew big-bellied but not awkward and she still walked with the same incredible, gliding grace.

She was not allowed to go out during the heat of the day. She accepted the doctor's orders with resignation, but she insisted upon working on the accounts in her little study. She sewed enough baby garments "for twins," as Michael put it, and she had everything ready to receive the child long before it was due.

She thought more and more about Matty. Orders had been left at every pier and wharf in the city. Word was spread among sailing men whom Michael knew and each new ship entering Charles Town was greeted with a written inquiry. Eleanor wrote lengthy letters to customs offices in America and in Europe. The results were always the same, Matty could not be found.

Without saying anything about it to Michael, Eleanor began to spend the afternoon hours at Matty's little house, teaching the children of Belleterre to read and write as Matty had done. Ada followed her here, as she followed her everywhere, fussing and fretting over every move she made. Ada was only truly happy with her when she could get Eleanor to sit and rest with her feet propped up in a shady spot on the big veranda.

The indigo grew taller and stronger and filled the fields with a cool verdancy. Now the plants needed only watchful cultivation and long days filled with sunshine. Many of the men who worked the indigo went out with the mules and wagons to help cut lumber and construct the sheds that would be used for making pitch and tar and turpentine that would be shipped to market in the autumn.

Michael was happy and at peace as never before in his life. Sometimes, half awake and sleepy in the morning, he felt that he had always lived in this place, had always worked it and loved it and never wanted anything else but Eleanor and the land.

He negotiated in secret to buy a small strip of marshland that lay between Belleterre and Rogue's Fall. When the sale was final, he set up a huge wall map he had drawn himself, showing the two estates now joined into one. The land at Stag Run was drawn in, too, and the names of those who already owned all the land that separated Stag Run from the rest of the property. Then he showed the map to Eleanor.

She stood before the map with his arms around her, and delicately touched the bold lettering he had done.

"Another empire, my love?" she teased him. "Like the one in the north?"

"Why not?" he answered boldly, smiling with pride. "And one day we will add the land from here to Stag Run, and give our child a whole world of his own. Let him stand where he will, let him look from horizon to horizon and it will all belong to him!"

Eleanor squeezed his hand. "'All the land from the mountains to the sea,'" she mused. "Isn't that the old Irish dream?"

He nodded. "Aye, it is. All the land, and all the people free...that's an Irish dream, too. And we'll do it. Together we'll do it!"

"'Together,'" she repeated softly. "The best of words!"

As the weeks wore on, Eleanor found herself thinking more and more of Matty. She wanted Matty with her when the baby would come, that was all she said to Michael. But she had difficulty sleeping and took to walking about the house at odd hours, restless, too quiet. She was afraid; she did not have to tell him, he saw the fear in her. He saw her conquer it and reconquer it every day and it troubled him that she should have to face such a struggle when she needed to conserve her strength. He mentioned his fears to Eleanor's doctor.

"It's the time, Captain Ives," said the doctor blandly. "All women are like that, whether it be their first or their sixth. Time stretches out longer for them, gives them more opportunity to worry about all manner of things. When Mistress Ives is delivered, she'll be herself again. But Captain Ives," he added, "do try to make her rest much more...."

664

6 The Child Must Be Born At Belleterre!

"I want you to come to Boston with me," Michael said to her shortly after he had spoken with the doctor.

Eleanor looked over at him in surprise. " 'Boston'? When?"

"The first week of May. We can get away by then. Daniel will take care of everything here and there won't be any trouble, the governor will see to that."

She put down her needlework and studied his face earnestly. "Why, Michael?"

"I want you to be with Katherine when the child is born, not down here in the country, miles away from everything...."

"Why?" she asked again, a tiny frown creasing her white brow.

He looked away uncomfortably. "I've told you why. Please, Eleanor, will you come?"

She swallowed very hard, her mouth suddenly dry. "There is reason for concern?"

"No, damn it, no, of course not!" he snapped, instantly wishing he had never brought it up. She would refuse. He had expected it.

"Our child must be born here, at Belleterre," she said quietly, just as he had known she would. "Don't fear for him, Michael..."

"I do not fear for him... or for you," he declared vehemently, looking at her with a steady gaze as though she might find the answer to her unasked question mirrored in his eyes. "I only thought it better," he murmured then.

They did not speak of Boston again. Michael wrote his sister and asked if she might be able to come south for a visit in May. Katherine's reply was swift: now that young Elliot was attending school full time, preparatory to entering Yale College, she saw no earthly reason, barring unforeseen illness, why she would not be at Belleterre in plenty of time to assist at the birth and afterward.

"I am glad Katherine is coming again," said Eleanor when he told her. She laughed a little, her eyes very bright. "And now I hope you will stop worrying about me!"

But he could not stop worrying, of course. He was not even quite sure when it had begun. Perhaps the first time he had seen her become very dizzy and breathless after climbing the stairs, or when he had noticed how thin her arms and face were growing. When he had made mention of that, Eleanor had only laughed at him and told him that he was lucky she was not getting fat instead...

But now that she had seen how much concerned he really was, she became very careful. She stopped talking about Matty. She took great pains to rest during the daytime, to conserve her energy for the evenings when she and Michael were together. The last weeks before her time, her cheeks were pale but her eyes were full of laughter and light. Little jokes and stories about her childhood were much on her lips. She forced herself to eat more than she cared for and she dwelt at length upon the time after the baby's birth when they would take a long trip north . . . "to show him off!" she said gaily.

Michael laughed and kissed her. But he could not fail to see that she was all spirit and willpower, that her strength was draining away into the child as May approached. He saw the pale, almost transparent skin grow tight across her cheekbones, he saw the dark shadows under her eyes, and her eyes themselves, so warmly tender, so full of confidence whenever she looked at him, seemed to have become the very focus of her entire being. They had taken on a strangely luminous quality and shone brightly out of a face now sharply etched and hollowed thin. Whenever she looked at something now, she looked at it a long, long time as if she must penetrate the nature of it even to its innermost atoms, and then she would turn away from it, satisfied, and those huge grey green eyes would gaze thoughtfully into empty air. She seemed unaware of any of these things, unaware that any kind of change had befallen her. At the beginning of May she wrote to Katherine that she was very well and looking forward to her visit.

Eleven

"From Living Hand To Living Hand"

1 Keane Comes Back to Carolina

Jack Keane returned to Carolina sometime in the spring, bringing with him a number of the Brotherhood and a strange, shifting sort of pirate fleet that was always changing in kind and number of ships as the captains gained or lost interest in the venture and came or went away at their own pleasure. But there were never fewer than eighteen or twenty vessels, nor fewer than four or five hundred men who sailed them.

Keane descended upon the Carolina coast in a fit of savage violence unusual for him, although not unusual for his comrades. His aim, as the Governor had feared from the first, was to leave Charles Town in flames, after first seizing the place, looting and stealing, humiliating the arrogant citizens whom he blamed for his misfortunes. His ideas, always grandiose, did not seem so impossible now that he had the backing of so large a force. Even the strong fortifications of Charles Town did not give him pause. Besides, he was in no particular hurry to get there. He began his reprisals for Stag Run farther north, attacking and destroying small coastal settlements in a leisurely route south.

Charles Town had no notion exactly when Keane had begun his raids.

Word came in slowly from the distant towns. Stories of murderous attacks were told by a few survivors who had fled to take refuge with friends and relatives in Charles Town.

The army was sent out in scattered bands and found . . . nothing. The navy always seemed to arrive where Keane had just been and gone, finding settlements abandoned, picked clean, still smoldering in ruins from the fiery torch Keane was lighting all along the Atlantic.

Grimly Charles Town prepared for siege. But Keane had no intention of sailing directly past the fortified outer islands of the harbor, or of bringing his vessels in under the long-range cannon upon the fortress walls. While Charles Town looked to the sea, scanning the shifting blue horizon night and day for the first sign of pirates, Keane audaciously brought his ships straight back to the deserted bay at Stag Run. He left the ships with small crews sufficient to bring them south when called for, then he set out with three hundred men, moving overland through swamp and salt marsh and forest, to the very edges of the upriver plantations. The great, stately country homes were still empty this early in the year; the wealthy families who owned them had remained in Charles Town, leaving the management of the estates and the slaves to their overseers.

This suited Jack Keane admirably. It pleased him to think that he was going to destroy the houses and plantations that supplied the wealth of the haughty Carolina gentlemen who had done business with him for years and now were bent on exterminating him and his kind. The small details of what had happened when the Royal Navy bombarded Stag Run did not much matter to Keane; Eleanor Campion and her family were insignificant to him . . . and he did not even know that Michael Ives had not died. Keane saw only that the Governor, who had profited handsomely for looking the other way and let the Brotherhood go about its business in peace, had decided for reasons of his own to end the amicable arrangement. It was he who had the authority to send the Royal Navy to Stag Run; now it was the Governor and those who supported him who commanded Keane's hatred.

Thus, Keane cared nothing for looting on this venture. He was hell-bent on revenge and a show of power such as had never before been demonstrated by the Brotherhood. He wished to burn the grand mansions to the ground, kill the slaves or scatter them, destroy stables and horses, tools, wagons, barns and domestic animals, even trample down the crops growing in the fields and devastate the fields themselves so they could not soon be used again.

But Keane's men were losing patience. They had grumbled and complained almost from the beginning about the poor pickings at the other places they had raided with him, simple villages and settlements inhabited by poor farmers and planters who possessed very little beyond the clothes on their backs and the little wooden cabins sparsely furnished with the meanest of handmade tables, chairs and beds. The pirates had expected to come away with treasures of jewelry and money, small art objects and other valuables they could sell for a fortune elsewhere. They had spent weeks pillaging and burning and had little to show for their efforts. Now he had marched them inland away from their ships with promises of rich goods and plenty of women, large stores of food and meat sorely needed aboard ship . . . and he demanded that they burn everything, move quickly, not even stopping to rest, not even taking the time to search through the houses of the wealthy.

Keane found himself with a near mutiny on his hands. Camped out in the heavily forested area lying well east of Belleterre, the pirates held an impromptu meeting and considerably revised Keane's original plans, offering their leader the dubious choice of going along with the new plan or losing his head on the spot. Keane had no choice but to agree to their terms. They, in turn, were quite willing to burn down whatever was left after they had finished with it. They were not in the least concerned about the army that was out searching for them that very minute. They had contempt for the army, and the navy hadn't the slightest idea where they were. They ceased grumbling and settled down under the spring trees for a good night's sleep, to get an early start on the next morning's business. It was the first day of the second week in May.

2 Smoke In the Trees

Eleanor was in Matty's house, finished with arithmetic, reading a story to the children. They had been very good and sat very still during the trying mathematics lesson; now they were relaxed and whispering among themselves, laughing here and there at something funny in the story. So when they became a little noisier than before, Eleanor only smiled to herself and turned a page. But suddenly they had left their seats and run to the window, pushing and crowding, all talking excitedly and pointing at something off in the distance.

Eleanor put the book aside and called them back to order. But they turned fearful eyes upon her and stayed at the window.

"Very well, show me what it is," she said calmly, although the fear in their small faces alarmed her. She moved to the window. At first she could not see what might be upsetting them. Her first instinctive glance toward the drive and the road beyond it showed there were no armed men invading Belleterre, no soldiers, nobody at all.

"No, see, see?" The children pointed in the opposite direction. "Over there, Miss Eleanor! See? Smoke! Something burnin'. There be a big fire in the woods, look at all that smoke risin' up!"

Then she did see it, the black funnel of smoke shooting skyward over the trees. Her first thought was of Michael. He had taken a large number of men out with him that morning to mark hickory stands for cutting. A forest fire, she thought, her heart jumping . . . they'll be trapped!

And then she realized that the smoke was coming from a source much farther away than Belleterre land, over toward the Moore plantation. She stared and the children fell quiet, clustering about her, some holding on to her hands or plucking at her skirts. One little boy began to cry. She picked him up with some effort, trying to concentrate on the smoke, to figure out what might be causing it. Even as she watched, it began to billow as the wind picked it up, and long trailing ropes of gray and white smoke rose up beneath the black.

And then it struck her. "That isn't trees burning," she murmured. "That's the house! The Moore house is on fire!"

Quickly she set the little boy back on his feet and opened the door. Several of the women were rushing out of the houses, shouting, pointing to the smoke. They came and took the children home. Eleanor hurried to the back lawn where Michael had set up a big ship's bell for an alarm. It could be heard in the most distant fields and even in some parts of the Belleterre woods. She knew the Moores were not at home, but she thought of the panic that would spread among their slaves if the fire spread. She must send help from Belleterre. . . .

Ada came racing out the back door when Eleanor continued to ring the bell. Men were coming in from the fields, wagons laden with heavy logs bounced and swayed as the mule teams pulling them were driven at top speed in response to the bell's call.

"What's the matter?" demanded Ada in a panicky voice. Eleanor pointed toward the smoke.

"Fire. At the Moore's."

Ada's eyes grew wide. She studied the direction of the smoke and then grasped Eleanor's arm to stop her from yanking at the bellpull.

"We're all right here," she declared. "Wind's blowin' the other way. It won't come here. Look at you, flushed and shakin' like a leaf! Let go now, ain't nobody missed hearin' that thing by this time!"

"We've got to get help over there, Ada," panted Eleanor, wiping her hand across her sweating brow.

Ada's face became quite severe. "Ain't nothing to do with us," she said coldly. "Let them take care of their own place. Wouldn't catch them come runnin' here if we were on fire!"

Eleanor shook her head. "Ada, they aren't even there now. I'm not thinking of the family, I'm worried about their slaves. The overseers will desert them, you know that. What if the cabins catch fire?"

Ada's head dropped, but then she looked up at Eleanor again with a peculiar expression, unreadable, somehow indecisively angry.

"Wait!" she cried. "Listen to me! Do you know what made that house go on fire? Nobody livin' there means no cookin' fire in the kitchen and no fires in any of the rooms. So, how did it happen?"

Eleanor became impatient with her. "What difference could it possibly make *how* it happened?"

"Difference is," stated Ada flatly, glancing around her at the people who gathered on the lawn, "some fires are *set* fires, set on purpose, you understand me, honey? And who's over yonder to set a fire except them slaves they keep there?"

Eleanor looked at her, aghast. "Ada, what are you saying?"

"I am saying," said Ada clearly, "there may be a risin' over at Moore's place . . . a slave risin'. And if it's that, you got no call to send anyone from Belleterre over there. Those people will be like crazy men by now. I ain't blamin' 'em, you understand me, Eleanor? I ain't blamin' but I *saw* what it's like with them and nobody's going to be safe around them while it's goin' on. You ask any of us, go on, talk to everybody, they'll tell you. You just wait, wait till later when they're tired out and don't know what to do next. Then we can help 'em all they need. But not now, honey, not now, believe me!"

Eleanor looked about helplessly. Everywhere she saw faces nodding in agreement with Ada. Then Daniel came forward and spoke to her very gently.

"You got to listen to Ada, Miss Eleanor," he said. "If the slaves are risin', it's best we get ready for 'em here."

"You mean get food ready and medicine? . . ."

Daniel shook his head, his face pained. "No, ma'am. I mean it's time we take out the guns Captain Ives gave us. Don't know what they're like to do. We got to look after this place."

Eleanor looked at him sadly, shaking her head. He was talking about his own people as if they were enemies. Daniel felt sorry for her but he knew he was right.

"You kick a horse long enough, day comes he's goin' to kick back," he said. "Don't much matter to him who he kicks just then. He's goin' to feel pretty bad after, if he kicks his friends, but he don't care when the kickin' fit hits him. You men," he turned from her and called out over the crowd around them, "you put these mules in the barn, then go home and get your weapons. Captain Ives will be back before long with the rest of us; we can take care of ourselves, whatever's comin'!"

The men dispersed quickly, quietly, to do what he said. The women waited in little groups, and then followed the men away.

Ada put her arm around Eleanor and pulled her out of the hot sun, into the house. Eleanor seemed dazed. She sat at the kitchen table, staring blankly at a glass of lemonade Ada put before her.

"They know us," she said slowly, "they know we're not like the others, we're not slave-holders . . ."

"You're white folks," said Ada firmly, drinking a glass of the cool lemonade herself. "That's all they're thinkin' of now. And us? God, girl, they don't know what to make of *us* over here. All they know is, we're free and they ain't. That's enough to make them hate us."

3 Keane's Men At The Moores'

The black slaves at the Moore plantation did indeed have reason to hate, if Ada had only realized how mistaken she was about the probable cause of the fire. Keane's men had descended upon the place just after daybreak. Moore's overseer and his four assistants, didn't have time to desert the slaves. The pirates took them and hanged them upside down over a large fire. This was done to discourage the terrified slaves from trying to run away; similar punishment was promised them if they disobeyed the buccaneers in any way whatsoever.

The Moores owned about one hundred slaves. Of these they kept twelve with them in town; the rest were all field hands, stablemen and semiskilled workers—a blacksmith, carpenters, and the like. They lived in wretched squalor in tiny mud-daubed log houses without windows. When Keane's men came they were rousted out of their houses and shut inside the largest of the stables. The stables had plenty of windows and the slaves witnessed their overseer's death quite clearly. A handful of pirates, chosen by straw lot and soon to be relieved at their posts, were stationed on guard around the stables. The remainder of the pirates broke into the main house and in no time at all discovered that there was precious little in the way of portable valuables for them to plunder. The Moore ladies took their jewelry with them wherever they went. A few pounds sterling and some odd bits of French and Spanish coin were found in a desk in the library, adjacent to a collection of Morocco-leather-bound books worth roughly twenty thousand pounds. The disappointed looters overturned the library shelves, tumbling the books all over the floor. They passed by oil paintings brought over from Europe at enormous cost as they swept upstairs to the bedrooms. They pulled down brocade and velvet draperies and handworked wall tapestries, intending to use these to cart away their treasures. Ignoring hand-made English highboys and French settees and Italian marble table-tops, they threw open drawers and ransacked wardrobes in their search. Silver candlesticks and ornaments, a rare gold frame about a mirror, Mistress Moore's second-best silver table service, these were the only riches taken and little enough they were, too; there would be fighting among the men later on, Jack Keane knew, when it came to dividing such poor spoils. Jack himself smashed windows and mirrors and crystal glassware with a sort of ferocious abandonment. When the men came down to the main floor once again, he set the first fire in the library, he alone of them all realizing the value of the books that blazed up so readily and he alone enjoyed the spectacle with an ironic nod to the portrait of some ancestor of the Moores who glared down gloomily from the library walls.

The house disposed of thus, the pirates returned outside and dragged out the young black women for their sport. Keane watched them with bored, impatient eyes. The day was half gone, the sky had been filled with smoke for hours. It was time for them to move on before that smoke brought inquisitive visitors on them. Finally, walking past the laughing, grunting groups of men and the struggling, weeping women, he set fire to the wretched quarters with his own hand. By the time this was finished and the locked stable, containing the rest of the slaves, was also afire, his men were ready to leave. They marched off in good spirit, the frightful screams of trapped men and women and horses and dogs ringing in their ears. They were a lazy lot and would have been content to wait until another day before they struck at the next plantation, but Keane urged them on. Direct in the westerly path lay Belleterre. Keane had never been there, had only heard the Campions speak of the place and did not now realize where he was heading, only that, from the top of a hill he saw the large house and well-tended lawns and fields, and he saw that there were few men about. A fine, valuable property he thought, and immediately he was filled with renewed vigor and purpose. He told his men they would take this next place and stay the night, not setting it afire until tomorrow. This novel idea pleased them and they, too, felt fresh and ready for the task Keane had set them. They fell in behind him readily enough and approached Belleterre.

4   A Battle Plan

Half an hour after Eleanor had summoned the people, Belleterre looked deserted. The children with their mothers were behind bolted doors. The stables and barns were shut and locked. Twenty men armed with pistols and knives and clubs were hidden in the trees and outbuildings all along the eastern perimeter of the living quarters, including the main house. The indigo, the vegetables, the shrubs and flowers all lay serenely in the midday sun and nothing, not so much as a stray barnyard cat moved in the fields, over the lawns and gardens, along the drive and pathways. The smoke they all watched had dissipated to a large degree, blown off toward the mountains. A strange quietness hung in the air, the quietness of waiting and of watching. After a wild flurry of birds had fled by overhead, there was not another sound from the trees or meadows.

Miles away, Michael and his men had also noticed the smoke coming from the Moore plantation. Since dawn they had moved much farther into the woods than planned and they could not hear the alarm bell ringing. It was Michael's first impulse, as it had been Eleanor's, to go straight to the Moore place with what men he had on hand and offer whatever assistance was needed. He led the men from Belleterre eastward along a narrow forest track that curved wide around the indigo fields and the houses, heading away toward the Moore's at the same time that Keane and his force reached the northern outskirts of the estate.

Eleanor had gone upstairs into the master bedroom when she heard the first shots fired, so far away yet that they seemed like nothing more than small twigs cracking underfoot. She ran to the bedroom window and saw a large force of men slowly, cautiously circling the fields. Two or three lay still upon the ground while the others kept moving. There were more shots. Several of the intruders stopped beneath an oak tree. A flintlock musket was pointed upward toward the branches. The musket was fired . . . a body fell crazily, crashing through the lower limbs of the tree, striking the ground. The body was kicked and mauled, then left behind as the attacking force advanced.

She pressed her fingers tightly against her lips as she watched this, forcing herself to make no useless outcry. She turned away from the window resolutely, and opened Michael's sea chest, which stood at the foot of their bed. In the chest lay an assortment of fine weapons, which he kept well cleaned and oiled. Near the guns were boxes of shot and flasks of powder. Quickly, efficiently, she picked up each of the guns in turn and loaded them. There were seven in all, five pistols and two fowling pieces from Spain. She placed them methodically in a row upon the bed, shut up the chest, and called Ada.

"We'll take these downstairs," she directed, "I hope you can shoot."

Ada shook her head. "Never been so close to one of those things."

"Yes, you have," said Eleanor briskly. "The soldiers had them. Come now, help me bring them down and I'll show you what to do. It's easy enough." The two women picked up the little arsenal of guns and headed toward the hall just as another volley of shots was fired, this one a good deal closer to the house. Ada winced at the sound, glanced at Eleanor. To her horror, Eleanor's face was distorted, her mouth twisted, her eyes rolled up beneath the eyelids. She leaned helplessly against the wall. Two of the pistols fell from her arms.

"Eleanor, what is it? What's the matter?" Ada fairly shouted the words. She put the guns she was carrying on the floor and went to put her arms about Eleanor.

"Wait . . . don't touch me! Wait a moment . . . please!" gasped Eleanor, looking up at Ada with a little apologetic smile that was frightening to behold. Ada stood where she was, her arms raised uncertainly, watching Eleanor's face twisted into a grimace once again, and she yelled something Ada could not make out and stamped her foot down on the hall floor with such vehemence that the windowpanes five feet away rattled. Then she straightened her body and lifted her head. Her cheeks were greyish white, her lips almost blue.

"It's all right now," she said. "Let's get these guns downstairs."

Ada groaned and shook her head from side to side. "It's comin'," she said, her voice full of woe. "The baby's comin', isn't it? Don't try to fool me, honey, I've been through it, I know all about it!"

Eleanor drew a deep breath and picked up the fallen pistols. "Well, if you know all about it, then you remember it takes practically forever before anything happens. Michael and the men will be back in a little while and then we'll be all right. Come on, Ada, we've got a lot to do!"

She went on downstairs, put the guns on the sofa in the parlor, and went about locking every door. Ada pulled the heavy oak table in the kitchen up against the back door and piled the chairs on top of it. They ended up in the parlor with its long row of windows on one sunny wall.

Eleanor insisted on showing Ada exactly how to load and fire the guns. Her lecture was interrupted by the almost continual bursts of gunfire outside and by another spasm of pain that took her breath away and left her unable to speak for minutes. Ada prayed as she had never prayed in all her life, not even on the auction block. Captain Ives, where was Captain Ives? She crept over to one of the end windows and peered out cautiously. The Captain was nowhere in sight. And the attackers were almost within reach of the stables. . . .

"Thank God!" Ada cried out joyfully. Eleanor looked up sharply, her heart in her eyes when she spoke.

"Is it Michael?" she whispered.

Ada's smile vanished. She turned to Eleanor. "No, honey, I don't see him yet. But whoever those men are, they're not slaves. They're not *my* people, that's all I meant. I can see them now. They're white."

Eleanor's understanding smile brought tears to Ada's eyes. But then they looked at each other, thoroughly perplexed.

"Who are they?" Eleanor asked. "Not soldiers, I know they're not soldiers—"

"No, no, they don't have uniforms or those hats," Ada agreed. "I dont know *what* they are, but I'll tell you one thing—"

A stray shot crashed through one of the windows not a foot from where she stood. She screamed and ran across the room to Eleanor.

"Give me one of those things," she said, grabbing a pistol out of Eleanor's hand. "I don't give a damn in hell who they are or who they think they are, if one of them shows his ugly face in that window I'm goin' to shoot him quiet or die tryin'!"

Eleanor laughed and hugged her . . . the hug turned into a grip of iron as another labor pain began. Ada held on to her, squeezing her hands, murmuring softly encouraging words, silently praying it was only a false labor. Maybe the pains would stop; it was too soon anyway . . . Ada told herself a lot of foolish things she didn't believe and had the good sense not to repeat to Eleanor.

After what seemed an eternity, the pain died away. And what there was to be of this initial skirmish in the battle for Belleterre commenced full-scale. The black men in hiding, those who were still alive, came out in the open, firing as they came. Fearlessly they charged the vastly outnumbering force of pirates with clubs and knives. A few scythes and several pitchforks glittered in the white-hot sunlight. The pirates lost a few more of their fellows, a fact that enraged them. They closed together in a mass and turned to face the black scum that dared to defy them. Jack Keane appeared suddenly, leading a couple of dozen men from his own ship. He was on the left flank of the main force and quickly, almost contemptuously, cut down the blacks as they ran forward.

"Who's that?" muttered Ada. "Somebody special, *he* thinks! Hmph, look at that . . . dresses like some fancy woman!"

Eleanor risked a quick look. "Oh my God!" she cried to Ada, "It's Keane! Now I know who these men are—pirates! They're pirates, Ada, and we haven't got a chance!"

"We got as much chance as a lot of people ever get," said Ada philosophically, as she looked down at the pistol in her hand. "Remember, Captain Ives will be here soon, we got to think of that."

Eleanor smiled. "You're right. We'll think of that and we'll hold them off till he comes!" Suddenly she whirled around, swinging her pistol up. "What was that sound?" she cried.

"Please don't shoot, Miss Eleanor," came a very small trembly voice.

Ada's son, Ezra, walked slowly into the parlor, staring wide-eyed at the sight of his mother and the Captain's lady with guns in their hands, guns by their sides, guns in their laps. "It's me, Mama," Ezra said.

Ada's eyes blazed with anger and worry. "I thought I told you to stay with Aunt Rose! What'd you come back here for, boy?"

Ezra ran to her and put his arms around her neck. "I come to look after you and Miss Eleanor, Mama. All the other men are outside fightin', I'm goin' to stay right here and help you."

Ada kissed him, shaking her head over him. "Well then, best you learn right off how this thing works. He can keep loadin' for us, can't he, honey?" she asked Eleanor.

But Eleanor was slumped over to one side, her eyes glazed from an agony she could not conceal. Small, inarticulate sounds issued from her throat. Ezra was terrified at the sight of her. Ada shushed him, went to Eleanor and wiped away the perspiration from her face and throat. There didn't seem to be anything else she could do now. She straightened up with a sigh, not thinking, and several shots ripped through the windows, sending shattered glass flying in every direction.

"Get down!" Ada shouted, cursing at the top of her voice as she flattened her body as much as possible against the floor. Ezra crawled over to her. Quickly she showed him how to load the pistols, there was no time to explain the two fowling pieces even if she remembered half the things Eleanor had told her. Then, gun in hand, she looked anxiously at Eleanor.

"Gone again," Eleanor managed to whisper and even smile. "I'm going to go over to that end window there and you stay at this side. They're coming at the house now!"

With wild hoarse shouts and cries, the main body of pirates ran toward them, Keane in the lead. They had no way of knowing that there was anyone waiting for them inside. Eleanor waited until they were only a dozen feet away, then she took careful aim and fired. One of the pirates screamed and fell back, clutching his eye. Ada fired and hit one in the shoulder, but he kept coming.

They split their force, some circling around to the back of the house, some pounding on the front door. Those near the parlor windows quickly moved back and to the side, regrouping and arguing violently among themselves. Ezra reloaded the guns. Eleanor bit her lips against the returning, mind-numbing pain and gripped her weapon desperately. If Michael did not come soon . . . if Michael did not come . . .

The pain held her in its fierce power. Ada called to her. She could not make out the words. A face appeared at the window . . . agony and hot anger contended for Eleanor's attention. She gripped the leg of a sturdy table for support, aimed with a wavering hand and shot again, then sank back limply from the effort. Dimly she was aware of a bloodcurdling shriek and little Ezra looked up and said proudly, "You got him, too, Miss Eleanor!"

The pounding on the front and back doors grew louder. She thought she heard windows being smashed in the kitchen. They would never get in that way, the kitchen windows were very small and set high in the walls. But the pounding never ceased and now she heard wood splintering out in front. The back door would hold a while longer; the front door was a different matter.

"Stay here," she told Ada. She took the fowling pieces, one under each arm and staggered dizzily out into the front hall. The door was already cracked in a dozen places; great jagged patches of sunlight broken by blurred movements showed her the men ranged about outside. She stood behind the door and fired each gun in turn, point-blank. The pounding stopped immediately. From the parlor she heard Ada firing once, twice, three times. She dragged the empty guns back inside with her, intending to pull the double doors shut upon the parlor. Between them, she and Ada and the boy could shove some of the heavy furniture against the doors.

She came in and found Ada and Ezra busily reloading the pistols, glancing at the windows every few seconds. But there didn't seem to be anyone out there at the moment. Eleanor loaded the fowling pieces again.

"We're going to close off this room, barricade ourselves behind the furniture," she said through clenched teeth. Ada nodded, set the primed guns aside and started to pull the doors across. In the midst of doing this, she stopped suddenly and stuck her head out into the hall. When she turned back to Eleanor her face was filled with despair.

"Eleanor, they've started burning the house," she said. "Can't you smell the smoke yet? That's why they broke those kitchen windows. They must have thrown torches inside. We can't stay here, honey! What'll we do now?"

Eleanor's shoulder slumped. She looked around, confused. Yes, there was the smoke. She saw it, already beginning to drift through the rooms. She couldn't seem to think . . . Ada and the little boy looked to her, waiting patiently for a decision. But she didn't know what to do now, she didn't know!

She looked outside. The pirates were grouped at a small distance from the front steps, watching. They knew she would have to come out now, they could afford to wait another few minutes. She saw them talking to each other, she heard some of them shouting to others behind the house, heard them shouting in reply. No matter which way, front or back, when she and Ada and the boy came out, they would be there.

She saw Jack Keane among them, so close to her that she could even make out the golden earring he wore, and the brazen chains glinting on his bare neck and chest. Only a few minutes, she thought, only a few more minutes. . . .

Then she saw flames coming from the row of little houses. Not all the pirates waited so patiently; several of them had decided to amuse themselves by starting to burn down the houses where Belleterre's women and children were waiting for their menfolk, trusting that they would return in time.

The sight of that fire spurred Eleanor into action once again.

"Ezra, can you run quickly?" She forced herself to smile calmly at the child.

"Yes, ma'am," he spoke up. "But I ain't runnin' away, Miss Eleanor!"

"No, no, of course you'd never run away. I wouldn't ask you to do that," she exchanged a glance of affection with Ada. "But we need help here, don't we? Now your Mama and I, we can hold them off, oh, a long time more. We've got all these guns, plenty of powder and shot. But maybe Captain Ives and the other men don't know we've got trouble here. So when I tell you it's all right, I want you to get out of this house very fast, understand? You get out and you run as fast as your legs take you, go and find Captain Ives, Ezra. He went into the woods where the hickory trees grow. You may have to look very hard for him, but you keep on going, Ezra, and don't stop and don't look back, don't come back until you've found the men. Can you do that?"

"Y—es, ma'am," Ezra replied doubtfully. "Don't seem right, leavin' two ladies all by themselves . . ."

"Boy, when Eleanor says so, you cut and run, you hear me?" cried Ada sharply. "By now Captain Ives will have seen the smoke here and he'll be hurryin' to us. You tell him what's happening, tell him it's pirates, a whole damn lot of 'em!"

"Yes, Mama," murmured Ezra, convinced finally that the two women were not merely trying to send him safely away. "But how'm I goin' to get out?"

Flames and thick smoke cut them off from the kitchen. The little study was on fire now, the parlor walls already scorched. Eleanor took Ezra to the parlor windows.

"Keep your head down," she told him. "But peek outside every so often. When you see those men run around to the front door again, you climb out there. Make sure none of them sees you, get into the indigo fields. You'll have to crawl through there, then run for the woods on the other side. Once you're in the woods you'll be all right."

Ezra looked up at her. "What're you and Mama goin' to do?"

Eleanor patted his head. "Don't you worry about us. We're going to keep those pirates so busy they won't even see you go . . . they won't even see Captain Ives and all of you coming back!"

Ezra grinned broadly. "That's good, that's like a battle plan, ain't it?"

Eleanor nodded. The next pain was coming on. She pushed the

boy's head down and turned away from him so he would not see her body contorted helplessly. Smoke filled her nose and throat. She struggled for breath, and drew the smoke deep into her lungs. She coughed and retched, slowly made her way back to Ada.

"Help me stand up," she said. Ada took her under the shoulders and pulled her to her feet. For only a second she allowed herself to cling to the comfortable bulk of Ada's body, then she straightened up and took the guns.

"You know what we've got to do?" Ada nodded, looked back for one long moment, at her son crouched silently waiting at the windows. Then she, too, seized the remaining guns, thrusting two of them into the tight sash of her apron.

"I know," she said. "Come on."

The two women walked from the smoke-filled parlor into the front hall, where fresh air from the ruined door enabled them to breathe more easily. Someone outside saw a glimpse of them. Eleanor raised one of the guns. "Stay behind me, Ada," she directed. "We'll have a better chance if they're not sure how many of us there are."

"We ain't got *no* chance, honey," Ada uttered a sorrowful little laugh. "You think that boy'll get away like you said?"

Eleanor turned away, wordless, just as the front door burst open before her and the brilliant sunshine temporarily blinded her. She thought the dark figure rushing in must be Keane himself . . . she fired straight ahead. The figure staggered and fell back, making no sound. She dropped the smoking gun and walked out, stepping over the body on the threshold.

Blinking in the strong light she stood on the topmost step, the second gun raised, ready to fire. All around her were the pirates. A great shout of triumph went up from them.

"You!"

A man walked toward her, naked sword in hand. She did not back away but stood her ground stolidly. And then she saw that it was not Jack Keane she had killed at the door, Jack Keane was standing before her now, holding up his hand to keep his men from making a move.

"Well, by the Devil himself, look at this!" Keane's voice amazed, amused, annoyed, all in the same instant. He stood looking at her, his dark eyes cold, belying the jaunty sound of his words.

"You do remember me, don't you, Mistress Campion? Ah . . ."

his insolent gaze touched upon her middle briefly. "I see someone else succeeded where I failed. What a disappointment that was, my lovely!"

The pain was closing in again; she fought against it with every ounce of strength she still possessed. "Ives," she mumbled, "not Campion, Ives."

"'Ives'? Ives? What's that?" demanded Keane.

Eleanor forced her head back, her eyes held his steadily as she looked at him with pride.

"Not *Campion* any longer. My husband's name is Ives."

Keane frowned, then a light dawned. "By God, not *Captain* Ives?" he blustered incredulously. "*Is* it Captain Ives, out of Boston?"

"It is," Eleanor replied quietly, fighting for breath.

"There's a gentleman hard to kill," laughed Keane, but his laugh was deadly. "And . . . er . . . where is your Captain now? Or like the proverbial sailor, has he done his best . . . and departed for other ports?"

As he was talking, mockery in his cruel broad smile, Eleanor saw out of the corner of her eye another pirate just approaching from behind the house. The man saw her, saw the gun in her hands and raised his pistol. But a deafening cracking sound rang out from behind her back. The would-be murderer fell clutching his stomach. Ada kept a sharp watch on them all.

Eleanor knew that in another moment she could not stand on her feet. She advanced a step, pointing the flintlock weapon directly at Keane.

"Get out!" she said. "Get off my land or I'll kill you right now!"

Keane's men crowded closer, but he only laughed and, reaching out with the tip of his sword, he whipped the gun barrel to one side and then seized it and flung it away. She screamed at him and threw herself bodily upon him, hitting and scratching like an animal full of pain and rage. If this was to be the end of Belleterre, then let it be the end of her, too!

"Shoot, Ada! Shoot!" she shrieked. She felt rough hands pulling at her. She heard shots, many shots, fired from different directions, then she couldn't seem to hear anymore. The hands that had pulled her off Jack Keane released her abruptly and she sank moaning, grinding her teeth, down on the floor of the veranda. It seemed to

682

her that Keane had turned his back on her swiftly, that he shouted words she could not make out. Then there were more shots . . . her nostrils filled with the stink of hot black powder in the air. She thought they would kill her then; she hoped they would kill her quickly so the pain would stop. But, as she raised her head a few inches, she saw that they were running back across the lawns, trampling through the flower beds and out across the fields . . . and men were running after them, firing and hitting some of them!

Ada dropped the guns from her hands and dragged Eleanor down the front steps and onto the cool, moist grass. Behind them the house was enveloped in a gigantic swirl of flames and smoke borne high on the wind. When Ada let go of her arms and sank down beside her, gasping for fresh air, there was a great, sickening crash and the blazing roof fell in upon itself. Eleanor sobbed.

"Never mind the house, honey," cried Ada, squeezing her hand hard. "Never mind anything. Captain Ives is here! Captain Ives is back. We're all right now, Eleanor. Praise God, we're saved!"

5 Full Circle

Michael's men had reached the Moore plantation. There were half a dozen dazed survivors, young girls covered with blood and bruises, sitting naked and staring silently at the remains of the locked stable. Michael sent the girls to the next nearest estate along with a man who had orders to ride downriver and fetch back the army. Then he hurried back to Belleterre, spotting the smoke half a mile away. He and his men moved in unnoticed, unchallenged, finding the house besieged and the pirates too concerned with getting inside to realize until it was too late that they had been surrounded and were cut off.

Michael saw Eleanor face Jack Keane. At that sight, a fire hotter than the one ravaging the house burst into flame inside of him. He ran on, leading the Belleterre men, firing as they went. Keane turned around, came down the stairs, shouted something . . . and Michael shot him once, through the heart. He pitched forward, dead, on the edge of the indigo fields. Leaderless now and confused, the rest of the pirates ran for their lives, each man for himself, with the hideous specter of cold eyes staring out of remorseless black faces following closely behind. The Belleterre men picked off as many as they could and gave chase to the rest, driving them into the forest.

And it was over. The army would round them up, find out where their ships were hidden. That would be the end of them.

The women and children opened their doors and came running to meet him. Michael led them back to the main house. At first they could not find Eleanor in the dense smoke and hot, simmering air. Michael groped about the burning steps, along the veranda, frantically calling her name. Someone seized his arm. He wheeled about, ready to strike, and saw that it was Ada.

"I got her over there on the grass, Captain, but I can't move her any farther. You'd best get that doctor here. Your baby's comin' ahead of his time!" She drew him over to the place where Eleanor was lying, coughing and choking, her fingers spasmodically tearing at the grass.

"How long has she been like this?" he asked, lifting Eleanor in his arms.

"I don't know, maybe an hour, maybe more. The pains came on her real bad right at the start. It's not supposed to be that way. It's supposed to start off small and easy. And they're coming closer together all the time. Here, Captain, you'd better take her to Matty's place."

Michael carried her swiftly away from the burning house, down past the stables and coach house, with Ada going before him and many of the other women following them. Ada turned down the bedcovers and drew the shades against the sun. She had forgotten all about the pistol stuck into her apron. Now, nearly half an hour after the pirates had been driven off, a tiny, stealthy sound of bare feet on the wooden floorboards of the small house caused her to jump . . . her hand went automatically for the gun.

"Don't shoot, Mama! It's me, Ezra!"

Ada dropped the gun and hugged the boy, allowing herself at last the luxury of tears. Michael came out of Matty's bedroom, where he had undressed Eleanor and bathed her feverish face and throat. Ezra ran over to him and took his hand.

"Been lookin' for you, sir! Miss Eleanor, she and Mama fought those pirates brave as men, and they sent me out to bring you quick! But I been hiding down in the indigo when I saw you here already! Where's Miss Eleanor?"

Michael couldn't seem to speak. Ada said quickly, "Miss Eleanor is just fine, child. She's all tucked up in Matty's bed there and her little baby's gettin' ready to be born. You be quiet now and don't bother the Captain.''

"No, no, Ada, he's no bother,'' said Michael, finding his voice at last. He picked Ezra up and held him close for a moment. "You're a brave chap, laddie. I won't forget. Do you think you could do something else to help now?''

Ezra was delighted to be sent off again, this time to find Daniel and tell him to take a horse and ride for the doctor.

Ada busied herself making a pot of tea. Several of the other women had come in, greeted Michael, and went inside to sit with Eleanor.

"She saved that boy of mine,'' Ada remarked quietly, setting the tea things down. "You would have been so proud of her. She stood right up to that man Keane and she ordered him to get off her land! God, Captain, she's the bravest woman living!''

Michael was staring at her, the tears running down his cheeks. Ada took his hand as she had taken Eleanor's earlier, nodding quickly, crying herself. Then she produced a handkerchief and wiped her face briskly.

"Well now, we got ourselves a deal of work ahead, rebuildin' that old house,'' she said cheerfully. "You and those two in there are goin' to be mighty cramped here for a while. But you'll manage. Now, drink your tea, Captain. Doctor'll be here in no time at all and Belleterre will have a new baby tonight!''

He scrutinized her face so closely that she dropped her eyes, unable to bear his unconcealed fear. He said, "It will be hours before the doctor comes and you know it, Ada. What's wrong with her? She's in so much pain, such constant pain. There doesn't seem to be any time at all between one and the next. That isn't right. I know it isn't!''

Ada searched for the right words, but there weren't any. "Everyone is different, Captain Ives. First child's the worst. There's no rules set down about it, except it's long and it's hard. I don't want to lie to you, Captain. Seems like that child can't make up his mind if he wants to be born or not. But he will. You just say a prayer it's soon.''

"It can't go on this way much longer,'' he said. "She won't live through it.''

Ada had no answer for him. She knew it was the truth. A moment later, Eleanor called his name. He ran to throw open the door and knelt by the side of the bed.

"You are real," she whispered. "I wasn't sure." Her eyes clouded and she looked around fearfully. "Keane?" she cried weakly, struggling to sit up. Michael gently pushed her back upon the pillows.

"Keane is dead," he told her. "And the others are gone. The army will catch up with them. Don't worry, my darling. The doctor's on his way. Everything is all right now."

She smiled a vague, sweet smile, her eyes glossy with pain. "You're always telling me it's all right," she murmured. "But it wasn't just a terrible dream this time, was it?"

He longed to hold her close in his arms, to kiss her and soothe away the pain. He bent and kissed her lips and felt how cold they were. Tears filled his eyes. He thought she wouldn't notice but her hand crept up and her fingers touched his wet lashes.

"I told you, don't you remember, my dearest love? Never weep for me again, never. Please, Michael, promise me! Never, never weep... again..." Her voice trailed off. Then suddenly she writhed, thrashing about the small bed. *"Matty!"* she screamed. "Matty!"

One of the women led him away, looked at him with deep unspoken sympathy, then closed the door to the bedroom.

He sat alone in the small parlor of Matty's house, alone in the darkness. He had been there for hours. One of the men had come to tell him that the fire was burning itself out; the smaller fire had died away earlier. He remembered looking out the window and seeing the charred, smoking ruins of Eleanor's house. He was glad when the sun finally set and he could no longer see those gaunt, blackened timbers silhouetted against the sky.

The doctor had arrived back with Daniel just after sunset. That was a long time ago, he thought. It was close to midnight now. Through all the hours of the endless afternoon and evening he had sat there, not moving, not talking, only listening to Eleanor's screams in the next room. Women rushed about quietly, coming, going, looking in on him once in a while. Ada tried to give him soup. He left it untouched. Later someone brought him a supper tray. Someone else spoke to him very strongly... he waved them away impatiently and bade them leave him alone. He must stay where he was. Why did they want him to leave? He could not, *must not* leave this house. There was no reason to it, none that he could name, but he knew for a certainty that if he went from there, if he ran as far and as fast as it would take him to escape the awful sound of her screaming, then he could never, never come back again, he could never face her again.

More hours passed. The parlor remained in darkness. Someone offered to light the candles, make a fire. He shouted and they went away from him.

He sat bolt upright, his whole body stiff and tense, his hands clenched into tight fists in his lap. It seemed to his weary mind that he had at one point begged the doctor to let him go in to her, speak to her for only a minute. He wanted to ask her to forgive him, although he was not quite sure what wrong he had done. The doctor had said he would see about it. Sometime later the doctor returned and told him it would be best if he did not go in just yet. Something in the doctor's voice had sounded faintly hopeful to Michael and so he had allowed himself, briefly, to hope. He had sat where he was obediently, quietly, and waited.

After a little bit, the screams stopped. Another long time passed and he heard a thin little cry, more like a mournful wailing, and then nothing more.

Still, it was only when he heard footsteps entering the pitch-black room that he became afraid again. The little scrap of hope he had clung to left him in a sudden forlorn rush.

Ada sat down beside him, putting a lit candle on the table before them.

"You've got yourself a son, Captain Ives," she said, her voice thick with weariness and emotion. "A fine big boy, Captain."

He nodded, saying nothing, leaving time for her to say the rest, but she said nothing else.

"Eleanor?"

Ada did not reply. He seized her by her shoulders and pulled her close to him, his eyes staring wildly in the flickering candlelight. He would ask again, he would demand that she answer, that she say something!

Then he saw the tears of pity and of sorrow in her eyes. With a cry he thrust her away and raced to the bedroom door. Something there was in him at that moment that remembered doing all this before! A wild something in the back of his mind screamed a warning at him even before he threw open that door . . .

A fire blazed on the hearth . . . there they were, just as he remembered them! There they were, the doctor, the women, the newborn infant being wrapped in a blanket.

Michael ran into the room and stopped, paralyzed, unable to look around at the bed, at what he knew must be lying upon the bed.

"Captain Ives!" The doctor started toward him, his face sad, kindly.

"No! Leave me alone!" Michael shouted. The women looked at one another with frightened, secret faces. The infant awoke at the sound of his father's anguished voice and began to cry.

Michael was trembling, icy with dread, but he would not fail this time! He turned to the bed . . . memories of a beautiful red-haired woman lying sprawled in a pool of blood flashed behind his eyes . . . he grasped the bedpost and willed himself to look down.

Eleanor lay as though in sleep, a faint, tired smile curving the corners of her delicate, firm mouth. Her shining red hair was neatly brushed and tied back at the neck. She wore a plain white bedgown and her hands were folded upon her breast. The firelight glinted and flickered against the wide golden band on her finger.

"I did everything I could, Captain Ives," the doctor was saying, hovering, concerned, at his back. "She simply was not strong enough—"

Michael choked. "She was not strong enough?" he demanded hoarsely. "She? Mother of God, sir, she was stronger than the lot of us, stronger than you or I . . . " He stopped. He had nothing to say to this man. He had nothing to say to anyone. It was finished. He kissed her cold lips and her brow, let his fingers rest for a moment on her hair, and then he turned away. He walked unsteadily to the door.

"Captain Ives, here's your son, sir!"

The black woman stepped in front of him, holding out the tiny bundle in her arms. Michael stared down at the child blindly, almost without comprehension, then shook his head and rushed from the room, an anguished cry on his lips.

The women looked after him, whispering.

"Poor baby," sighed the nurse, snuggling the bundle against her breast. "Poor, poor little child!"

6 Beauty, Be Thou Remembered!

Katherine Sturbridge's trunk was packed and locked and waiting down at the foot of the stairs. In two days she would sail on the refurbished *Sheila Deare* and reach Charles Town in time to welcome her brother's first child into the world.

Katherine had worked feverishly preparing for the journey, driving everyone in the house, at the shipyards, and at the mills quite mad with her arrangements and rearrangements. Elliot Landon understood her very well and fortunately was not at all perturbed with all the rush and bustle. Things would run smoothly when she was away and she knew it.

She had given serious thought to taking her son south with her but Elliot was doing beautifully at school and seemed happier than he had in a long time. She would do nothing to disturb that tranquility. Secretly she wondered if Elliot might feel jealous if he saw his mother with a baby in her arms, even someone else's baby. He was, in some ways, a strange little boy. She rarely could guess what he might be thinking or feeling. No, it was best to leave Elliot where he belonged—where, she hoped, he was content.

Everyone had gone to bed quite late that night, Katherine last of all. Despite the noisy sounds of coaches and carriages rumbling through the street outside, she fell asleep as soon as her head touched the pillows.

It seemed to her that she had only closed her eyes when she heard a tremendous knocking and pounding downstairs at the front door. She sat up at once, wide awake. Perhaps it was only some drunkard. She waited for the sounds to stop or for the housekeeper to investigate. But Katherine's housekeeper was deaf as a post and did not even hear the commotion. With a great yawn and a deep sigh of resignation, Katherine slipped into her robe and house slippers and went out into the hall, calling the maids, calling Willy.

But Willy was ahead of her, as usual. He opened the door and peered out suspiciously, and then he said something to someone Katherine could not yet see.

"Willy, for heaven's sakes, who is it?" she demanded crankily, hurrying down the hallway. Before he had a chance to reply, she had pushed past him and looked out herself. There was a carriage drawn up before the house and a gentleman with his back to her stood holding the carriage door open. A young black woman emerged, carrying an infant wrapped in blankets. The gentleman took her elbow and assisted her in climbing up the few narrow stone steps to the door.

"Michael! Michael, my God, it *is* you!" Katherine threw her arms around her brother and kissed him heartily. Then she drew back, shouting for someone to fetch more light . . . and she caught sight of Michael's face, gray with fatigue, his lips tight and grim, eyes guarded, expressionless.

"This is my son," he said to her, indicating the sleeping infant in his nurse's arms. "I would have written you, Kate, but I thought a letter might be delayed or lost and you would have started south already. This way is better."

"Your son! Oh, my dear!" She smiled with delight . . . and then, abruptly, the smile vanished. "Michael, what of Eleanor? Where is she?"

Michael avoided her anxious gaze. "Dead," he said in an odd, flat tone.

"It's a very long story, Kate. Could you send the girl upstairs, give her a quiet room somewhere? She's dead tired. We've been traveling night and day for nearly two weeks. Mary," he turned to the young woman, "go along with this man. He'll look after you and the boy. And, Willy, have them fix her something hot to eat, can you do that?"

Willy was staring bemused at the sleeping baby. "I can, Michael, and I will, only tell me—tell us—what happened?"

Michael spoke mechanically, carefully controlled, as if he had said the same words so many times they had ceased to mean anything to him.

"The house was burned down by pirates. Keane's men. She fought them off. The boy was born later that night. And . . . she died."

" 'Died? Ah, now, Michael, lad . . .'' began Willy softly, his old voice shaking. A fierce glance from Michael's cold blue eyes silenced him.

Katherine took charge of the situation at once. "Willy, upstairs, Aunt Helene's old room will be perfect. Have the maids make up the bed with fresh linen and get someone to take Elliot's cradle down from the nursery. Then tell Cook to prepare supper for two."

"Nothing for me. I'm not hungry," said Michael swiftly.

"Nonsense!" snapped his sister. She helped him off with his hat and cloak and led him into the drawing room. Only when he was sitting back in a soft easy chair, his feet warming by a freshly lit fire, a glass of brandy in his hand, would Katherine allow herself to settle down across from him.

Then he told her the entire story from beginning to end. Sometime during the telling Willy entered and put food in front of him. Katherine insisted that he eat. He picked at the delicious meal in silence, tasting nothing, barely swallowing. His sister drank cups of strong black coffee and watched him thoughtfully. And finally she said,

"Why are you here, Michael?"

He looked up in surprise. "Isn't it only natural I'd come to you?"

She tilted her head to one side. "Mmm. Natural enough," she murmured. "But that's not why you came, is it?"

He hesitated before replying and then he said bluntly, "I'm leaving the child, if you'll have him, Katherine. I cannot look after him. I . . . I have decided to go away."

"'Away'?" she said sharply. "When? You just arrived."

"Tomorrow," he answered. "I only came to Boston to bring the boy and to see you again before I go."

"The *boy*, the *boy*!" she exclaimed with distaste. "That's what you call him? What is his name, Michael? What is your son's name?"

He shifted uneasily in the big chair. "He . . . he hasn't a name. Not yet. I never thought of it. I told you we'd been traveling day and night—"

"Yes, yes, so you said. Traveling day and night to come to me and to leave your son, this *boy* of yours, with me. I see. For how long, Michael?"

He seemed puzzled. "You misunderstand me. I am giving him to you. Keep him. Adopt him, look after him. I'm signing over my share in the business to him—and there's Belleterre, too, of course. He won't be a burden to you."

"As he is to you, do you mean?" Her voice was tinged with irony and not a little anger.

Michael swallowed down the rest of his brandy at once, then sighed, shaking his head. "Katherine, please, leave me alone. If you will not take the—if you will not take him, say as much. I'll make other arrangements."

"Is that what Eleanor wanted?" Her voice was quite crisp.

"Eleanor? Eleanor has nothing to do with it! Eleanor is dead!" The words were wrung from him in agony and he stared hollow-eyed at his sister.

Katherine calmly poured herself another steaming cup of coffee.

"And what about Belleterre?"

"What about it?"

"Who is managing things now? What will happen to all of those people while you are gone? Have you also made 'arrangements' about them? And who will safeguard their freedom without you and Eleanor?"

Michael flung his arm over his eyes and cried, "I don't know, damn it! I haven't thought about any of that! The people will be all right. Maybe Elliot could send someone down there to look after things—some sort of overseer or manager, someone like that. I don't know. I don't want to think about it. What does it matter now? What does *anything* matter now?"

Katherine rose to her feet and stood looking down at him, her gray eyes dark with anger.

"I thought you told yourself you had finally found a place you could call *home!*" she lashed out at him. "What about that, Michael? You're going to run away? Just . . . run away? Forget everything and everyone? Forget your own son? Forget *Eleanor?* Is this how it will end after all?"

When he lowered his arm she saw the suffering like a kind of restrained madness in his eyes. Her heart broke for him but she knew it was not yet the time to offer consolation or soft, comfortable, meaningless words.

"Well?" she demanded stalwartly. "I think you'd better explain yourself!"

He stared at her, a touch of anger putting color back into his chalky face. "I shouldn't have come here," he mumbled.

"You shouldn't have come here like *this,*" she agreed with marvelous composure. Deeper anger nettled him. He stood up and began to pace around the room, quickly, impatiently, as he had once paced the decks of his ship at night.

"It's all of a piece: her death, Mother's death. I knew she was going to die, Kate. I knew it for weeks before it happened. And when it did, when she . . . was gone, I believe something in me, some last thing left in me, died with her. *Home!* Home is a word!

692

Home is where someone you love is waiting for you, that's all it is. Not land or a house. Just *someone*. Belleterre was home as long as she was there. Now she's gone . . . what's Belleterre to me? I've lost houses and lands before, twice before, remember, sister? Remember?" He shouted the word, willing away the peaceful, healing years, forcing her thoughts back and back to one frightful night, one night and one place.

"Don't make me hate you, Michael," she said coldly. "I remember. I remember everything!"

"You had Rob. All those years, you had Rob!" It was almost an accusation, irrational, frenzied. And when he had blurted it out, Katherine suddenly realized exactly what was wrong. Eleanor had died two weeks ago but he had not even begun to accept it yet. He had forced it from his mind, made himself concentrate on the complicated journey north with the maid and the baby. He said that Eleanor was dead, but he did not really believe it. He had not really felt it completely and he had not yet mourned for her. The pain, Katherine knew, must be gotten through before there could be healing. Her anger melted away at once. Somehow, some way, she had to help him, she had to reach him.

"Yes, my dear," she said, drawing a deep breath. "I had Rob, thank God. I was lucky. I was lucky, too, long before that. When *my* mother died I had Sir Tom and Aunt Helene. I'll take your son, Michael. Don't worry about that. But, if you're really going away in the morning, won't you talk to me a bit now? Talk to me as you used to do long ago. Come, Michael, who knows when the two of us will ever talk again?" Her voice was tender, full of love, soft and utterly without guile.

He looked at her very hard, wretchedly ashamed of what he had said, but he could see that there was no reproach on her beautiful face. He sat down again.

"I haven't been able to think, I mean, really think about anything, not since that night," he said much more quietly. He seemed to relax somewhat, his guard momentarily lowered. Katherine patted his arm, saying nothing for the moment.

"I left the house . . . it was Matty's house . . . and I walked around the woods for hours and hours, until dawn. I got to remembering all the times Willy and I used to go hunting and fishing years ago, never worrying ahead of time where we'd find ourselves the next night, where we'd camp, just wandering where we wanted, stopping when we felt like stopping. And it came to me that I'd like to do that again, just go, no thinking, no more worrying . . . just pick up and go and never look back again. I made up my mind I'd do it, head out into the mountains west, you know?"

"Just . . . disappear, you mean?" Katherine prompted him quietly.

"Yes," he nodded. "Disappear. But first there was the baby to think of . . . and I didn't want to think of him. Oh, I'm not damn fool enough to blame his mother's death on him. That would be insane. But, don't you see, if I kept him with me, brought him up, the day would come when he'd look at me and I'd see it in his eyes!" He stopped talking abruptly.

"Yes? You'd see what in his eyes, Michael?" she asked quickly.

He sighed raggedly. "That he knew it was my fault she'd died, that I wasn't good enough to save her, to protect her. I wasn't strong enough or wise enough. I should never have let her stay down there! I should have insisted she come here to Boston, to you, but I let it go. I knew Keane was on the rampage. The governor himself warned me, but I felt so safe, so secure far away from the coast, far from Charles Town. And . . . I don't know, Kate . . . maybe I even *wanted* Keane to attack them . . . all those coldhearted aristocratic bastards there . . . they let her suffer, they saw her lose everything, they saw the slave collar put on her neck and they didn't lift a finger to stop it! Maybe I wanted them to be punished for it!"

"How could you have stopped Keane, Michael?"

He shook his head. "I don't know. I could have done . . . something."

"And you would see all that in your son's eyes one day, is that what you believe?"

He nodded. "Yes. I would see it. But more than that. Every time I look at him, I think of her. I don't want that. I don't want to see him or to know him . . . I don't want him to know *me*. Tell him anything you like. Tell him I died, too, if that's easier."

"Yes, I agree with you," his sister said slowly. "It would be much better for him to believe his father was dead than to know that his father had abandoned him." She held her breath, praying desperately . . . dear God, please, give me the right words! I can't get through to him, nothing I say makes any difference . . . please help me, please help him!

Michael recoiled at her hard words. " 'Abandoned him'? I'm not abandoning him! I've brought him to you, his aunt."

She was silent for so long then that he knew what she was thinking, what she was feeling.

"Yes, all right, you're right. I am abandoning him, if that's the way you want to put it!" he cried.

"That is exactly the way I put it. You are abandoning your son, your home . . . yes, your home . . . you chose it, didn't you? You're turning your back on everything you believe in, everything that Eleanor lived for . . . and died for! I see it all very clearly, Michael. I only wish that you did, too. One thing more and then I'll say good night to you. I'm very tired, Michael. I'm going back to bed and I'm going to sleep very late in the morning, so I won't be seeing you again." She stood up, feeling as though a part of her were dying. One last effort, one last hope, she thought, and if that did not reach him . . . she swallowed, her throat dry and tight and aching.

" 'One thing more'?" he asked, looking as though she had struck him.

"Yes," she said, holding out her hand. "The ring. Give me back the ring. It doesn't belong to you anymore. You've given up the right to wear it. I'll save it for your son. I'll tell him its history. I'll try to bring him up to be worthy of it, the way we were brought up. Give it to me, Michael."

Bewildered, he brought his eyes to focus upon the old steel ring on his finger. He had not consciously looked at it or thought of it since Eleanor had given it back to him. He looked and looked, as though he had never looked at it before in his life. The worn initials and dates sparkled a little in the firelight . . . and he remembered the flash of the firelight gleaming on Eleanor's gold wedding ring as she lay in his arms so many times . . . and as she lay, peaceful in death, in Matty's cottage.

He blinked rapidly. The steel seemed to dissolve into gold, the gold image in his mind shimmered and hardened into steel. The three initials, I.C.I., ran together with the letters he'd had engraved inside the wedding band . . . *Beauty, be thou remembered* . . .

"Give me the ring, Michael," Katherine was saying somewhere far away, somewhere almost beyond his consciousness. His hand moved to slip the band from his finger, but . . . he could not do it! He looked up at his sister, shaking his head in wonder. He felt that he would choke from the pressure of the unshed tears inside of him, yet he was dry-eyed. She had said, "Never weep for me again, Michael," and he had obeyed . . .

But suddenly, here was Katherine on her knees before him, crying, grasping his hand, nor would she suffer him to pull away. Here was his sister weeping and saying,

"Oh, Michael, let yourself feel again! Weep for her, weep for that lovely, brave girl! You had such little time together . . . so much trouble . . . so much pain! Weep for that, dearest brother, and then weep for the little child upstairs who will never know his mother, as I have never known mine . . . and weep for my son, too, Michael, weep for Elliot, who will never see his father again! Must you make it worse than it has to be? Must you leave us all so entirely alone, so terribly, terribly alone?"

He drew a long, shuddering breath and allowed all the pain to go through him at once. He was amazed at the frightful power of it, the sheer physical shock of it. He *did* weep then, for a long, awful time, with Katherine's hand tightly clasped in his. He wept and talked about Eleanor and about Sheila, about all of them, and while he spoke the fire burned low and it seemed that the room was very still and listening to him. Katherine Ives Sturbridge, most pragmatic of women, felt those unseen, loving presences all around them. She prayed for Michael as she smoothed back the tangled blond curls and noticed that his hair had started to turn grey about the temples.

Sometime later, when he was quiet and composed again, he looked down at the old ring very thoughtfully.

"No," he said. "I'll not take it off just yet."

"Tomorrow, then?" breathed Katherine warily, watching him. "Before you leave?"

"Before I leave," he nodded. "Yes, I will leave tomorrow."

Her heart sank, sick with failure and hopelessness.

Then, suddenly, he stood up, pulled her to her feet. "Come with me."

He took her by the hand and together they climbed the curving staircase to the second floor, then quickly walked down the well-remembered hall. He tapped at the door to the room that had once been Helene's. Katherine did not trust herself to speak, not even to wonder . . .

The door opened a few cautious inches. Mary, now dressed in a warm woolen robe, saw that it was Michael and opened it fully. Just across the room, beside the hearth, a cradle was still rocking gently. She had been singing the baby to sleep.

Michael walked over and looked down at the cradle for several minutes. Then, very carefully, he picked up the sleeping baby and held the soft cheek against his face. He looked at Katherine.

"Keep him for me," he said, but in a very different way. "Just for a little while. I'm going back to Belleterre tomorrow. There's work to be done there, years of work. There isn't a house left for him to live in, but I'll build him another. You keep him safe for me until I can bring him home again. I won't let his mother's dream die with her. My God, how much she feared that! I'd almost forgotten. I'm going back, Katherine. We've been driven out and driven out and I nearly let it happen to us again. But this time, I swear before God, no power on earth will drive me or mine from the land! And when this boy is a man grown, he will have his home and his own lands and he will understand that we do not run away, eh, Kate? Never, never again!"

"Here, in this place . . ." He glanced at the ring that rested lightly against the fine golden hair on his son's small head. He put the child back into the cradle with a kiss and then straightened up, looking very tall and suddenly much, much older.

"Thank you for making me remember, Kate," he said. "Tomorrow I go back to begin again. Keep this boy of mine until I can send for him. Let Willy tell him all the old tales, everything about us Iveses and Sturbridges. What a family we are! Will you do that, Kate?"

"With all my heart, Michael," she pledged, her heart overflowing with gratitude. "And now, tell me, what name will you give him?"

"Thomas," he answered without hesitation. "For Sir Tom, the father I remember best. And James, for Eleanor's father. He taught her about freedom and courage and about honor. Thomas James Ives. That is this boy's name."

"It's a good name, a proud name, Michael. Now let him sleep, and you must sleep, too. You've a long way to go . . . back home."

An hour later, the handsome Boston house was dark again. Michael slept peacefully at last. Katherine finally let go of the extraordinary day and closed her eyes with a prayer of thanks. Mary was tucked up in Helene's big bed, sound asleep after the long, exhausting journey.

The baby, wrapped warmly in wool and satin covers, opened his eyes and stirred about.

The door to the bedroom opened a few inches at a time. A grey head peered in cautiously and then an old man, rather red in the face, still tall and lanky as ever although a bit bent in the back, made his way stealthily across the room to the cradle. And there he saw the baby's blue eyes winking up at him, the tiny fists waving around, a bit of a crooked smile on the little pink mouth.

"Well, well, yer awake, are yer now?" chuckled the old man softly.

He rocked the cradle with a practiced hand and touched the baby's fist with the other. At once the little fist uncurled and the fingers closed firmly around his gnarled, old fingers.

"Aye, it's me, same as ever, Tom-O, my lad!" whispered Willy, for he believed babies were born knowing everything and only forgot as they grew up. "You knows me, don't yer? Oh, yes, and you knows that you and me is a'goin' to be friends, just like me and all yer folks, eh, Tom-O?"

He laughed to himself at the name he'd just invented; they had told him the proper name of course and he approved, but it would be years before the boy need bother with all those fancy, proper things. Willy sat and watched the child and told him the best way to bait his fishing hook and where the first mountain flowers showed above the snow in early March. . . .

The baby's eyes closed, but Willy didn't mind. He went right on talking, and if sometimes he said Kilbree when he meant to say Spring Mount and sometimes Boston and even now and again Belleterre, it didn't really matter at all. He was an old man and he had known them all, Iveses and Sturbridges and Eleanor Campion. He was an old, old man holding the hand of an infant and they understood each other perfectly.

THE BEST OF JACKIE COLLINS

LOVERS & GAMBLERS
by Jackie Collins   (A30-306, $3.50)
LOVERS & GAMBLERS is the bestseller whose foray into the world of the beautiful people has left its scorch marks on night tables across two continents. In Al King, Jackie Collins has created a rock-and-roll superstud who is everything any sex-crazed groupie ever imagined her hero to be. In Dallas, she designed "Miss Coast-to-Coast" whose sky-high ambitions stem from a secret sordid past—the type that tabloids tingle to tell. Jackie Collins "writes bestsellers like a female Harold Robbins."   —*Penthouse*

THE WORLD IS FULL OF DIVORCED WOMEN
by Jackie Collins   (A30-307, $3.50)
The world is their bedroom...Cleo James, British journalist who joined the thrill seekers when she found her husband coupling with her best friend, Muffin, a centerfold with a little girl charm and a big girl body. Mike James, the record promoter who adores Cleo but whose addiction to women is insatiable. Jon Clapton who took a little English girl from Wimbledon and made her into Britain's top model. Daniel Ornel, an actor grown older, wiser and hungrier for Cleo. And Butch Kaufman, all-American, all-man who loves to live and lives to love.

THE LOVE KILLERS
by Jackie Collins   (A30-305, $3.50)
Margaret Lawrence Brown has the voice of the liberated woman who called to the prostitutes to give up selling their bodies. She offered them hope for a new future, and they began to listen, but was silenced with a bullet. It was a killing that would not go unavenged. In Los Angeles, New York, and London, three women schemed to use their beauty and their sex to destroy the man who ordered the hit, Enzio Bassolino, and he has three sons who were all he valued in life. They were to be the victims of sexual destruction.

THE BEST OF BESTSELLERS FROM WARNER BOOKS

OUTSTANDING READING FROM WARNER BOOKS

PALOVERDE
by Jacqueline Briskin   *(83-845, $2.95)*
The love story of Amelie—the sensitive, ardent, young girl
whose uncompromising code of honor leads her to choices
that will reverberate for generations, plus the chronicle of a
unique city, Los Angeles, wrestling with the power of rail-
roads, discovery of oil, and growing into the fabulous capi-
tal of filmdom, makes this one of the most talked about
novels of the year.

HANTA YO
by Ruth Beebe Hill   *(36-160, $4.95)*
You become a member of the Mahto band in their seasonal
migrations at the turn of the eighteenth century. You gallop
with the warriors triumphantly journeying home with
scalps, horses and captive women. You join in ceremonies
of grief and joy where women trill, men dance, and the kill-
tales are told. "Reading *Hanto Yo* is like entering a
trance."—*New York Times*

RAKEHELL DYNASTY
by Michael William Scott   *(95-201, $2.75)*
From the first time he saw the ship in full sail like a winged
bird against the sky, Jonathan Rakehell knew the clipper
held his destiny. This is his story of conquering the seas,
challenging the world and discovering love in his dream—
the clipper. His is the bold, sweeping, passionate story of a
great New England shipping family caught up in the winds
of change and of the one man who would dare sail his ship
to the frightening, beautiful land of China.

THE BEST OF BESTSELLERS
FROM WARNER BOOKS

A STRANGER IN THE MIRROR
by Sidney Sheldon

(A36-492, $3.95)

Toby Temple—super star and super bastard, adored by his vast TV and movie public yet isolated from real, human contact by his own suspicion and distrust. Jill Castle—she came to Hollywood to be a star and discovered she had to buy her way with her body. In a world of predators, they are bound to each other by a love so ruthless and strong, that is more than human—and less.

BLOODLINE
by Sidney Sheldon

(A36-491, $3.95)

When the daughter of one of the world's richest men inherits his multi-billion-dollar business, she inherits his position at the top of the company and at the top of the victim's list of his murderer! "An intriguing and entertaining tale."

—*Publishers Weekly*

RAGE OF ANGELS
by Sidney Sheldon

(A36-214, $3.95)

A breath-taking novel that takes you behind the doors of the law and inside the heart and mind of Jennifer Parker. She rises from the ashes of her own courtroom disaster to become one of America's most brilliant attorneys. Her story is interwoven with that of two very different men of enormous power. As Jennifer inspires both men to passion, each is determined to destroy the other—and Jennifer, caught in the crossfire, becomes the ultimate victim.

BEST OF BESTSELLERS
FROM WARNER BOOKS

THE CARDINAL SINS
by Andrew M. Greeley   (A90-913, $3.95)
From the humblest parish to the inner councils of the Vatican, Father
Greeley reveals the hierarchy of the Catholic Church as it really is, and its
priests as the men they really are. This book follows the lives of two Irish
boys who grow up on the West Side of Chicago and enter the priesthood.
We share their triumphs as well as their tragedies and temptations.

THE OFFICERS' WIVES
by Thomas Fleming   (A90-920, $3.95)
This is a book you will never forget. It is about the U.S. Army, the huge
unwieldy organism on which much of the nation's survival depends. It is
about Americans trying to live personal lives, to cling to touchstones of
faith and hope in the grip of the blind, blunderous history of the last 25
years. It is about marriage, the illusions and hopes that people bring to it,
the struggle to maintain and renew commitment.

To order, use the coupon below. If you prefer to use your
own stationery, please include complete title as well as
book number and price. Allow 4 weeks for delivery.